Night Heat

HEATHER GRAHAM

Night Heat

MIRA®

ISBN 1-55166-787-8

NIGHT HEAT

Copyright © 2001 by MIRA Books.

The publisher acknowledges the copyright holder
of the individual works as follows:

BRIDE OF THE TIGER
Copyright © 1987 by Heather Graham Pozzessere.

ANGEL OF MERCY
Copyright © 1988 by Heather Graham Pozzessere.

BORROWED ANGEL
Copyright © 1989 by Heather Graham Pozzessere.

Visit us at www.mirabooks.com

Printed in U.S.A.

CONTENTS

BRIDE OF THE TIGER

CHAPTER 1

The sculpture was magnificent.

It was in the Roman section of the museum, with a plaque beneath it: Anonymous, A.D. 100, Black Marble.

Tara was entranced by it.

It was a life-size tiger, standing—watching. The ancient artist had caught all the tension, passion and cunning vitality of the creature. The beauty was there, the danger. One paw was raised as it stalked its prey, its grace casual, its quest unmistakable. Though the sculpture was carved in sleek black marble, Tara could almost see the true color in the eyes; they would be a tawny gold, like candle flames, like the endless sun, with a heat that was just as piercing. The tiger was all power, all grace.

Tara realized suddenly that she was alone with the beast, and smiled whimsically. She wanted to be alone to marvel at this creature.

There were lions and boars in the room, salukis and mystical cats, maidens and warriors. But nothing compared with the tiger, a fact that was made clear by its position of prominence, dead center, encircled by velvet ropes.

Still fascinated, Tara began to circle the creature. She glanced at her watch, aware that she couldn't linger much longer, or she would be late for lunch. But she did have a few minutes.

The tiger was lean and sleek, yet each muscle and sinew was well-honed and clearly delineated—again she got that sense of sheer power. It didn't need to move or growl to display that power. Primal, subdued, awesome, it touched her senses beyond all logic.

Her back was to the doorway when she became aware that someone had joined her in the room. Watching the tiger? Or watching her?

She looked up. In the glass case around a majestic granite centurion, she could see the reflection of a man. He appeared to be as tall as the centurion, seemed to tower there, blocking her way. He stood in the doorway, as striking and as haunting as the ancient works of art on display.

He was silent, not moving. As powerful as the tiger.

A chill played along her spine in a peculiar dance. Whimsy took hold of her in the most disturbing fashion. Like the tiger, he was a hunter. Subtle, entrancing, deadly. He would tread silently, watch, then encircle his prey. He would play with it, perhaps. When he grew bored of his game, he would pounce with complete arrogance and confidence and lethal precision.

You're mad! she accused herself. He wasn't a tiger, and this was a public museum. Crowds were everywhere; guards lingered just yards away.

Tara took a breath, mentally ridiculing herself. Still, she moved carefully. She didn't want him at her back. She wanted to circle the tiger again and face him, then laugh at herself, because he would just be an ordinary man.

She came around the tiger, casually.

But her ridiculous feelings of hypnotism and tension did not leave her. He was not just an ordinary man.

She stared at the tiger but looked beyond it, to the tall, compelling stranger in the doorway. Silent, hands on hips, he, too, watched the tiger.

Her heartbeat began to quicken.

His short, well-cut hair was dark, nearly jet. He wore black corduroy jeans, a cavalry-style leather jacket. Both hugged his trim form nicely.

A form like the tiger's. Slim, but with strong, smooth muscles at the shoulders, at the thighs, encased in that midnight corduroy. He radiated a sleek and subtle power. Beautiful, dangerous. Taut, tense and vital, apparently casual, never really so.

And she still felt that, like the tiger, he was on the hunt.

She inhaled sharply as her scrutiny reached his face. It was weathered and bronzed, rugged, though still young. Firm jaw, high smooth cheekbones, full mouth, dark, arched brows and—

Golden eyes. Tawny eyes. Alive with their color, like a candle's glow, like the sun...

She was openly staring at him, Tara realized.

He was returning her gaze, aware of it.

Slowly, his sensual mouth twisted into a small, subtle smile.

Tara felt her face flame; she quickly averted her eyes.

She had to go, she reminded herself; she would be late for lunch. But she couldn't possibly go through the doorway where he was standing. The tiger man. All subtle, graceful power...stalking. Stalking—her?

She told herself that she was being ridiculous. Millions of visitors came to the museum, and they did not come to stalk Tara Hill. The notion was absurd.

It wasn't a notion. It was a feeling.

Walk past him, fool! she ordered herself.

And then her breath caught again, because he moved, just slightly, into the room.

His hands remained on his hips. His gaze was fixed on the work of art to which she was mentally comparing him.

He was closer, she realized. She felt hot and flushed, and totally irritated with herself. But there was just something about him, something that was both base and noble, that lured and enticed. She wanted to read the message in his eyes. She was painfully tempted to touch him and discover whether he, too, was of marble or true flesh and blood. Sleek and agile, alive and breathing...

He captivated one. He touched something beneath the cool exteriors of civility. He lured; he repelled. He fascinated....

And he terrified.

Absurd, Tara thought once again. But she felt frozen, willed to stillness, by the mere presence of a stranger. Her palms were damp; her throat was dry, and the ripples of heat and fear and excitement still played havoc all the way down her spine.

Run past him! she commanded herself.

Walk normally; don't be an idiot!

She moved the silver fox fur of her collar closer to her face, squared her shoulders, and started to walk.

So did he.

They passed each other. He nodded to her. She lowered her eyes, hurrying, breathing deeply.

His scent was subtle, clean and pleasant, elementally male. It was filled, too, with a sense of primal power.

The tiger was stalking. He would strike at any moment.

He walked right on by her.

When Tara reached the doorway, she couldn't help but turn back.

He was staring at the tiger. Tall and lean and as dark as the beast, in his black cords and leather.

She turned, smiling ruefully at her foolishness, and hurried out of the Roman section to the stairs. He'd had no interest in her whatever—just in the treasures of the museum.

Too long in the country, girl! she chastised herself. Well, that was all changing now. She had run, and she had hidden, but it was time to face the daylight.

She had started off rather well. Only a few days in the city and her apartment felt like home again, she was ready to start work on a fascinating assignment, she had come to the museum, and she was meeting Ashley for lunch.

Her smile broadened as she thought about telling Ashley all about her encounter with the tiger-man. Ashley would love it. Paranoid, Ashley would call her.

And, of course, she had been. To have thought of the man as being as ruggedly beautiful, powerful and dangerous as the tiger.

And to have thought that he might actually be stalking her. As if she were prey.

Ashley would definitely be amused.

Tara ran down the steps of the museum to the street, still grinning as she hailed a taxi.

She didn't see the tiger-man tread lightly down those same steps behind her, following her every movement with his eyes, carefully noting the direction of her cab.

Then advancing to the car that awaited him at the corner.

CHAPTER 2

Rafe Tyler had no need to hurry. A shift in the wind had brought the soft sound of her voice to him; he had heard her instruct the cabdriver to take her to the Plaza.

As soon as the taxi pulled away from the curb, he raised his hand to the hovering limousine. He hopped in beside the driver.

"Where to?" the snowy-haired chauffeur inquired.

"Follow her cab," Rafe said. He leaned back to rest his head against the seat and closed his eyes. He was tired from a month of constant travel, but this lead on the girl had been too good to ignore. She was the last avenue of discovery he had left.

"Damn traffic!" the chauffeur grumbled impatiently.

Rafe opened his eyes again, grinning. "Don't let it worry you, Sam. I want a few minutes to pass anyway."

"What if we lose her?"

"We won't. She's obviously got a luncheon appointment."

"How do you know?"

"Sixth sense?" he teased, then admitted, "I overheard her. She's heading for the Plaza, probably the Oak Room. She'll be easy to find." He frowned suddenly, turned to push aside the glass barrier behind him, and leaned halfway over the seat to rummage in a storage cabinet.

Warily, Sam glanced in the rearview mirror to watch his employer's movements. "Rafe? What are you up to there, boy? Now I'm not going into that place with you—"

"Sure you are, Uncle Sam!" Rafe laughed, returning to his seat, a dignified suede jacket in his hand to replace Sam's uniform coat.

"I'm not—"

"Hey, I can't walk in alone! I have to have a lunch appointment myself, right?"

Sam started to grumble under his breath. Already the collar that hadn't bothered him all morning had begun to bother him. "I swear, if I hadn't been working for the Tylers since they first set foot in the States—"

Rafe's smile faded. He interrupted his old employee and friend with a flat reminder. "This is all about Jimmy, Sam. I wouldn't be asking you, otherwise."

They fell silent until the limousine pulled up in front of the Plaza. Sam was doffing his cap and changing jackets even as the doorman opened the back door. A little confused at finding no passengers in the rear of the elegant vehicle, he scratched his chin.

In the meantime Rafe had left the car, smiling pleasantly as he approached the doorman with a generous tip. By the time Sam was out—now clad as nondescriptly as any businessman, Rafe had been assured that the limo could sit just where it was until he and Sam were ready to retrieve it.

Rafe rested a hand against Sam's shoulder to steer him through the lobby. Sam always felt uncomfortable at the Plaza. "Too much opulence!" he muttered, shaking his head at the display windows full of gems.

"Sam! We're just going to have lunch. We're not moving in!" Rafe chastised him.

"Ostentatious!" Sam said under his breath.

"Ah, come on! It has warmth and character!"

"It's better than some," Sam admitted. Then he sniffed. "The waiters always look at me as if they think I don't know which fork to use!"

"They don't care if you use a fork at all—as long as you leave them a decent tip," Rafe assured him dryly, stopping Sam at the entrance to the Oak Room. Before the maître d' approached them, Rafe had already found Tara Hill. She was sitting with a redhead who was as svelte and fashionable as she was. Luckily, the table behind Tara, which angled to her right, was empty. He could study her easily, but she would have to twist to see him. He should even be able to hear her conversation fairly easily.

"Mr. Tyler," the maître d' began.

"Afternoon, John. My uncle is here on holiday. He'd enjoy a view."

"A view?"

Rafe grinned. "The blonde and the redhead. Think you could arrange to get us behind them—the table right over there?"

"Certainly, Mr. Tyler. Certainly. Gentlemen, right this way."

"The man reminds me of a penguin," Sam murmured.

"Sam," Rafe groaned, "anyone in a tux looks like a penguin."

He helped his aging "uncle" into a chair, then drew up his own for a nice view of Tara Hill. Engrossed in conversation with the redhead, she hadn't noticed their arrival.

He was glad to see that her silver fox fur was gone—obviously left in the cloakroom. He could study her more thoroughly without the fluffy garment, which concealed her throat and chin. She wore a simple gown, a teal silk with a scoop neckline, her only ornament a gold chain belt about her waist. He was certain, though, that she would look just as appealing in rags. Her beauty was in her height and grace. She was, he knew from experience in sizing people up, about five foot eight and one hundred and twenty well-arranged pounds. Her legs were long, lightly muscled, very sleek. Her hips and breasts were pleasantly rounded; her waist was very small. Her throat was slender, and her cheekbones were exquisitely high. Her eyes, silver like the fur she had worn, were large, expressive, and framed with rich dark lashes that contrasted arrestingly with the golden beauty of her hair, which she wore in fashionable layers at a length just below her shoulders.

Rafe absently picked up his menu. His assessment of her was totally objective. She was a very beautiful woman, but, more importantly, she was—he hoped—the means to an end. She was his last chance to pick up the trail where it had disappeared into South American bureaucracy. She *should* be beautiful—she was Tara Hill. Until two years ago, there hadn't been an American male alive who didn't recognize her.

"Drink!" Sam said suddenly.

"What?" Rafe queried, frowning.

"Am I supposed to order a drink?" Sam asked.

"Do you want a drink?" Rafe asked. He glanced up to see their young waiter standing patiently.

"Hell, I'd like a whole bottle of Jack Black!"

"Then you should have a drink!" Rafe laughed. He gazed at the waiter, amusement deep in his tawny-gold eyes. "Two Jack Blacks on the rocks, please."

"Thank you, sir," the waiter said. "And may I suggest the veal? It's excellent today." He walked away.

"Haven't they got hamburgers?" Sam asked.

"We'll get you a hamburger," Rafe promised.

Sam fell silent, sitting very straight in his chair. Rafe chuckled again.

"For heaven's sake, Sam! Loosen up! You'll have everyone staring at us. And talk. Act natural."

"What should I talk about?" Sam ran his finger beneath his collar again.

"Anything," Rafe replied. The waiter returned with their drinks. Rafe ordered two hamburgers and was assured that he could get them. Their menus were taken away, and Rafe tried to hear the conversation between Tara Hill and the pretty redhead. For several seconds he could barely make out their words. He concentrated harder, then started slightly, aware that they were talking about him.

"I don't know, Ashley," Tara Hill was saying ruefully. "It was just the oddest sensation. He stared right at the tiger—oh, it's really a wonderful, wonderful piece!—but I still had the feeling that he was looking at me." She shivered slightly, delicately, then laughed. "Too much country living, I suppose. He reminded me so much of that damned tiger."

"Primitive, eh?" Ashley queried.

"I guess. But then, of course, I finally got up the nerve to walk by him, and he wasn't after me at all."

Ashley laughed delightedly, picking up her wineglass. "I love it. Maybe he was after you. Men might well be, you know. Are you forgetting that you've been called one of the ten most beautiful women in the world?"

Tara looked annoyed. "Years ago—and any woman can look great with an entourage of dressers and makeup experts. Ashley, he wasn't staring at me for my looks."

"I thought you said he wasn't staring at you at all?"

"I did, didn't I? I—I don't know."

"Well, I'm glad about one thing."

"What?"

"You noticed him. You never notice men. You talk to them, you're polite, but you gaze right past them."

"I don't—"

"There's hope! And I'm ever so glad that it's come now! This trip will be marvelous. I'm convinced we'll have a wonderful trip! Twelve hours of work, and the rest of our time free! And maybe you'll actually be willing to dance with someone." Ashley sobered. "I just—"

"What?"

"Oh, Tara! What happened affected you so drastically that you've hidden away from the world for two years! I just wish we weren't going to Caracas. It's our main port of call. Are you sure you want to go back?"

Tara smiled a little unhappily. "No. But after what happened, George Galliard might be the only one who'd give me work."

"Don't be ridiculous—"

"Oh, come on, Ashley! Admit it—I was involved in a horrible scandal. Guilty or innocent doesn't mean a damn thing once your name hits the media! And maybe it will be the best thing in the world for me. Once we're aboard the—"

"Rafe!" Sam suddenly cleared his throat loudly. "I say, Rafe, I think I'd like another one of those Jack Blacks on the rocks!"

Rafe stared at Sam, ready to throttle his old friend. "Damn it, Sam!" he exploded, quietly but vehemently. "I just missed something important."

"You told me to talk!"

"But softly, Sam, softly!"

"Damn kids these days. Can't make them happy, one way or the other!"

Rafe ignored him. He was a thirty-seven-year-old "kid" but maybe to Sam's seventy-eight that was young.

"Sam," Rafe sighed, "if you want another drink, just motion to the waiter."

Sam started to rise.

"Subtly, Sam, subtly!" Rafe moaned, tugging Sam by the jacket to bring him back to his seat. He caught sight of their waiter and signaled; the waiter nodded and brought two more drinks.

It was then that Tara noticed the men at the next table. The very uncomfortable, older man—and him. The tiger-man. The man from the museum with the cat-gold eyes and midnight hair. And the lithe, tightly muscled build. Unconsciously, she picked up her wineglass—and drained it.

Rafe caught her eyes on him; he saw her stunned—and slightly panicked—expression. Damn! Groaning inwardly, he gave her a smile, raising his glass slightly.

"Well, the best part of this deal," Ashley was saying blithely between mouthfuls of fruit salad, "is that we get to keep everything we model!

Can you imagine? Some of those designs are priceless!" Ashley paused, staring at Tara. "What on earth is it? You look as if you've seen a ghost."

"It's him," Tara said.

"Who him?" Ashley frowned.

"Don't look now. It's him, the man I was telling you about. Who reminded me so much of the tiger."

Ashley turned immediately.

"Ashley! I said don't look now!"

"Well, how will I know what you're talking about if I don't look?" Ashley stared straight at him. Tara had to do the same thing. He appeared quite amused. He returned their gaze with a buccaneer's secret smile, then returned his attention to the older man at his side.

"Whew!" Ashley whistled softly.

"What do you think?" Tara asked.

Ashley laughed. "If I had been alone in the same room with him, Tara, I sure as hell wouldn't have run! Or maybe I would have. Ooh! Dangerous type. Hypnotic. You'd have to crawl through half a million singles bars to find something like him. No, you never would. He just wouldn't be there. He's—he's incredible. Snag him, Tara!"

Tara shook her head in annoyance. "Ashley," she whispered urgently. "I told you—I felt that he was watching me, homing in for a kill! And here he is again. Doesn't that seem odd?"

"He's eating lunch, Tara. The same thing we're doing."

"This is a huge city!"

"And coincidences do occur! I once had the same cabdriver twice in the same day. Now *that's* odd!"

"Ladies, excuse me."

Tara quickly looked up. She hadn't seen their waiter approaching, and now he was setting down a silver tray that held fresh wineglasses, an ice bucket, and a bottle whose label made her certain that it was much more expensive than what they had been drinking.

"From the gentleman at the next table," the waiter informed them.

"Oh, we can't accept it!" Tara protested.

"But we will anyway!" Ashley exclaimed, laughing delightedly.

The wine was poured, and short of creating an embarrassing scene in the middle of the dining room, there was very little that Tara could do about it.

"Please thank the gentleman very much for us," Ashley was saying quite cheerfully.

"Oh, hell!" Tara muttered as the waiter bowed and moved away. "Ashley, do you know what you've done?"

Ashley just laughed, her green eyes glittering like emeralds. "Tara, you've been in hiding too long. He's got his eye on you, but if you're not interested, I am!"

"Be my guest, then," Tara murmured.

"Tara Hill, what do you want to do, shrivel up and die because of one unpleasant episode?"

"Unpleasant!" Tara exclaimed.

"All right, that's an understatement. But you can't give up on men just because of Tine Elliott! Oh, Tara, I was right all along. You're taking this job because you can get to Caracas! You think you're going to find him—"

"I don't want to find him!" Tara cried.

"Tara, he made you too...aloof. Too hard, too cynical. Maybe if you did come across him again—"

Tara interrupted her with a soft groan. "Ashley, I'm not aloof. I just learned a lot about the male of the species from Tine."

"Mmm-hmm. They amuse you these days. You don't take a single introduction seriously. You meet charmers, rich men, handsome men. You smile at them over drinks and then politely slam the door in their faces. You've got to let one through that door."

"Ashley, I don't want to let anyone through—"

She paused suddenly with horror, aware that her tiger-man had come to their table, that he was, in fact, standing right behind her.

She looked up slowly, and saw his legs first, the way the black cords wrapped around his muscled thighs and lean hips.

Beneath his jacket, his shirt was a soft kelly silk. It clung nicely to his chest, delineating its sinews and muscular structure. The open jacket enhanced the breadth of his shoulders.

And then there was his face.

Handsome, bronzed features. Too dark, too rugged for New York City on a misty, overcast day. His manner was perfectly civilized; his presence was anything but.

Like a great cat, he belonged in the jungle....

"Excuse me, ladies. May I join you for a moment?"

Tara picked up her newly filled wineglass and drained it, eyeing him warily—and discouragingly, she hoped. The wine went down like velvet, and it did help. She quickly composed a courteous turndown.

"I'm sorry; this is a personal—"

"Please, sit down!" Ashley interrupted, awed.

"Thank you." His eyes, topaz, sunny gold, fell upon Tara again.

He offered his hand first to Ashley.

"Rafe Tyler."

"How do you do, Mr. Tyler," Ashley murmured, adding a slight and very feminine Southern slur to her words. "I'm Ashley Kane, and this is Tara Hill."

His pleasantly assessing gaze fell guilelessly on Tara. Yet for a second, she was convinced that he had seen or known of her before. Before the restaurant, before the museum.

"I hope you'll forgive the self-introduction, but I couldn't see another way." He looked at Ashley. "I saw Miss Hill at the museum. And when she appeared again, just a table away, I was rather hoping that it might be fate."

"Fate can be absolutely wonderful!" Ashley gushed. Tara kicked her under the table. Ashley, it seemed, was in no mood for finesse. "Ouch!" she complained loudly.

"Should you be leaving your companion to...flatter us?" Tara asked bluntly.

He just smiled and indicated the table behind them. "My uncle had some business to attend to. He's finished his lunch and gone on to his appointment."

Tara glanced at the other table and saw that the older man was indeed gone. She turned back just in time to see a busboy clearing away her untouched salad, as Ashley assured him that they were quite through with their meal.

The waiter poured more wine.

Tara felt her heart begin to beat too quickly, and she tried to quell her irrational fears, as well as the budding sense of excitement his presence brought—despite all her indignation and the inner knowledge that he was nothing more than a tiger on the prowl.

Yet he didn't seem at all obnoxious, or even really interested in her. While she tried to unravel the web of emotions within her, he chatted easily with Ashley. He traveled frequently on business, it seemed, and they were discussing various countries and cities.

The Tylers were into a number of concerns, he said. Jewelry was their main interest, requiring most of his travel.

Ashley laughed, her eyes still bright while she sipped her wine. "Did you grow up in the family business, Mr. Tyler?"

"Rafe," he corrected her softly.

"Okay, Rafe. The question still stands."

"No," he replied. "I've only been back with it about two years."

He turned abruptly to Tara. "You're not drinking your wine," he said. "Isn't it good?"

"Oh, no, it's lovely," she said, picking up her glass, then wondering with annoyance why she had done so. He smiled; she sipped her wine, wondering again at the sensation that rippled through her at the sun-gold touch of his eyes.

He turned his attention to Ashley once more. They were discussing the merits of ocean cruises. Tara thought that he had an accent, though it was slight. Something British, but not English.

She leaned back, wishing once more, very fervently, that she could tell him to go away. But there was really no reason to do that—he seemed to be most interested in Ashley, and Ashley seemed very pleased to be with him.

She should just leave, and she would, as soon as she finished her wine.

Four glasses on a nearly empty stomach, she reminded herself dolefully. And she really couldn't drink wine. Tine had told her that often enough, hadn't he?

Was Tine really the reason she couldn't trust anyone? One affair in her life, and that one affair had led to hurt, then betrayal—and tragedy. Tine...handsome, charming, masterful Tine. She'd been no match for him when she had met him. Too innocent to mistrust him.

But this man, this tiger-man—not even Tine would have been a match for him. Rafe Tyler. What was he after? What was it that he stalked? For a moment it seemed that her blood ran cold. Was he a reporter?

No, no, she assured herself. Reporters didn't order such expensive wine. They didn't dress with the negligent flair that was a part of Rafe Tyler.

He was just a man, albeit an experienced one, an affluent one. Handsome, charming, and alluringly male. If she wasn't so...wary, she might enjoy him. He was flattering and pleasant. Really, she had no right to be rude.

Another glass of wine, she realized ruefully, and she'd be overly charming herself. Why hadn't she eaten? It was something about him. He was talking to Ashley, yet she was the one who was mesmerized. She hadn't even been able to pick up her fork. She didn't seem capable of rising, excusing herself and leaving. The only physical feat she seemed able to manage was that of bringing the wineglass to her lips.

She just hadn't been back very long. Back in the world, in the company of others. In her upstate farmhouse, there had been little in life that was difficult. She'd seen her neighbors, chatted with Mr. Morton at the store. No worries, no cares. She had never used her real name, nor had she encountered the slightest problem. There had just been the garden, her sketches, an occasional ride in the forest or swim in the lake. It had all been perfect, until her savings had begun to dwindle, and she had realized that she had reached the now-or-never point. She had had to return to work—and to the real world. She couldn't run forever.

Time and events had given her a certain hardness. She could smile through any line, lower her lashes to any flattery, converse, sip drinks, dine—and never be touched. She had met some nice people, too; that was true. And they had become friends. But after Tine, she had discovered that she just couldn't be affected by a man. There had been good times with Tine, but the end had been so horrible that she couldn't remember any of them. Just the betrayal. His use of her; his total disregard for her.

She smiled slightly, off in her own little world. She would never be innocent again. She wasn't cold; she just couldn't be swayed, flattered—or seduced. It was like a numbness inside her, not something she did purposely.

She gritted her teeth, fighting a wave of dizziness.

That had all changed suddenly, hadn't it? Because Rafe Tyler had a massive affect on her. She'd only just seen him for the first time; she'd barely met him. Yet the disturbing impact he had on her was as frightening as the promise of his power.

No, she thought. She was just so startled by it that she had been shaken from her customary poise. She resolved to behave normally.

"Do you live in the city, Mr. Tyler?" she asked with a forced smile, determined to join in the conversation.

Ashley and Rafe stared at her as Rafe hiked a rakishly amused brow. "She's with us again," he said.

"It's the wine," Ashley told him conspiratorially. "And don't you dare kick me again, Tara Hill," she warned as she caught the silver sizzle in her friend's eyes.

"Can't drink wine, eh?" Rafe inquired lightly.

"Not worth beans," Ashley replied bluntly.

"Ashley, are you sure you wouldn't like to give him a rundown on my life from start to finish?" Tara murmured with a warning frown.

But though Ashley was having a good time, she loved Tara dearly. She was convinced that the only way Tara would ever salvage any happiness was to hop right in.

"She's a transplanted farm girl, right out of the dust bowl," Ashley said seriously. "Just seventeen when the George Galliard rep found her at high school graduation. And from there, of course," she teased lightly, "Tara was transformed into the totally sleek and perfect beauty you see before you now. Of course, she does have this penchant for changing into blue jeans. And she looks great with hay in her hair."

"I'll bet," Rafe murmured quietly.

Tara watched as his disturbing gaze subtly roamed her face, so much like a caress that the entire room suddenly seemed to sway and grow hot. Maybe it was the wine....

She smiled, and even managed to do so pleasantly. "Mr. Tyler, it has been a pleasure to meet you. But if you'll both excuse me..."

She attempted to stand, but to her total embarrassment she slid back into her chair.

Rafe and Ashley chuckled openly. He leaned across the table and the expression on his face offered a gentle empathy that touched her despite all her resolve.

"I have to admit," he told her softly, "I have a hell of a time with wine myself. You never ate anything, did you?"

"I..."

Why was she answering him? She owed him no explanations. He was a stranger who had rudely interrupted their lunch.

He was up then, coming around the table, bending his dark head to whisper against her ear, "Try standing again. I'll steady you. We'll go somewhere else and get some food into you."

She moved her lips to form the word No. Sound didn't come, only the gasp of her breath. Because he was touching her. Hand gently on her shoulders, he was offering his support. She could sense him, feel him, and it was causing that horrible rush and confusion of emotions all over again.

He was strong, secure. He was sexually fascinating in a way that defied all reason and description.

She wanted to fall into his arms; she wanted to disappear, to run, to find some safe place where she might never see him again and therefore never feel the lure of his tiger power....

Too late. She was standing, and his arm was about her waist, long fingers played masterfully over her ribs.

Possessively.

As if the tiger had made the first swipe at its prey.

And the prey...the prey was stunned into submission. The tiger could play a while longer before pouncing for the kill.

She leaned against him too easily. Heedless of the wisdom and intelligence of her mental warnings, she felt as if she had been created just to be held by him.

What in heaven's name was wrong with her! She was worldly; she was wise. He was a tiger-man, full of vigor and shocking vitality, exuding energy. Tall, remote, carelessly charming—when he so chose.

Blatantly masculine. So unrelentingly sexual that any fool would fall for him at the slightest invitation.

Tara stiffened and straightened. She wasn't a fool. She had learned a great deal about life, the hard way. She didn't need any lessons from a man like Rafe Tyler.

And, damn it, the man *was* after her!

CHAPTER 3

Moments later she was standing, albeit a little weakly, far away from him. Ashley was beside her as Rafe went to the cloakroom with their stubs.

She was amazed to discover that they had been sitting at the table for nearly three hours—it was time for an early dinner, and it might even be logical for them to move to another restaurant with the coming of the evening.

Tara shook her head uneasily. "I don't think we should be doing this. Oh! We didn't even pay the bill!"

"Rafe had it put on his tab," Ashley said blithely.

"Ashley! How could you let him?"

"Tara, it was lunch. Not a night at the Bonsoir Hotel!"

"Still..." Tara paused, not at all sure why she was arguing so strenuously. "Ashley! We don't know anything about him. He could be a murderer or a rapist. A criminal—"

"How many criminals do you know who keep open tabs at the Oak Room?" Ashley demanded dryly. "And who look and dress like that?"

"Jack the Ripper was supposedly quite distinguished!" Tara snapped back.

"Oh, come on!" Ashley exclaimed, laughing. "You don't really believe he's a criminal."

"No," Tara murmured uneasily, and dropped the subject because Rafe Tyler was coming toward them.

He was back, their coats in his hands. Tara found herself watching the way his fingers moved over her silver fox, and unbidden thoughts came to her mind. Thoughts of his fingers, his hands, moving with that same careless ease over naked flesh. She flushed, mumbling a thank-you as he helped her into her coat.

Ashley was smiling sweetly. "You're not a cutthroat or a wild rake, are you, Mr. Tyler?"

He hiked a brow, casting his gaze toward Tara. "Nor any other type of dangerous knave." He chuckled softly. "I've yet to cut a throat, I assure you."

"Pity!" Ashley laughed. "Tara could use a bit of seduction in her life right now. Work on that one, will you, Mr. Tyler?"

"Ashley!" Tara gasped. She was accustomed to the fact that Ashley said whatever came into her head, but she couldn't believe that her friend was going this far—with no discretion at all!

"Well, it's true!" Ashley blandly tossed her short red curls. "She's just come back to the city from years away."

"Years?" Rafe Tyler lightly mocked Ashley's Deep South accent.

"Just two, Mr. Tyler," Tara said flatly, staring at Ashley with a look that promised murder if she didn't cease and desist. She stared back at Rafe. "I believe I'm a bit of a loner. I like life that way."

"Ah, a woman with a mysterious past!" Now he was teasing *her*.

"Not at all," Tara lied as casually as she could. "I'm really quite dull." She had always meant to be dull, at any rate. It was true; as a child she had dreamed of escaping the poverty that had eventually claimed the lives of her parents and that of her baby brother before he'd learned to walk. But her dream had included a house in the country, a husband who loved her, and a whole passel of children. Dreams had taken her from poverty— they had also slashed her heart.

"I know a great Chinese place on Columbus, very casual and busy and lots of people—if you find safety in numbers, Miss Hill," Rafe said, barely concealing a crooked grin.

"Chinese sounds lovely," Ashley purred.

His eyes were on Tara. She saw the laughter in them and was suddenly, perversely annoyed. He was doing this to subdue any wariness on her part, she thought. Sure, lots of people, a totally innocent proposition! It doesn't matter, she wanted to scream. I know you're after something!

But what was it?

He could have any woman, she realized uneasily. He was just that type of man. Striking and assured, fluid and graceful, every movement hinting at a dynamic excitement that women found irresistible. Nor was she immune, and she had thought herself so savvy and smart....

"Shall we?" he queried. Light sparked, yellow and gold, from the depths of his eyes.

A challenge? A dare? She returned his gaze, a silent answer in steadfast silver.

I know what you are! Lean and hard, as cunning as that tiger, and every bit as charismatic. But I've been that route before....

His hand fell on her arm again. In seconds they were outside. Tara was amazed to see that darkness had fallen.

But the fact that Rafe Tyler didn't hail a cab did not particularly surprise Tara. He led them to a waiting limo. It was everything she might have expected—roomy and luxurious, with a bar, phone and a television. There was also a miniature desk, as if someone carried on business from the rear of the vehicle during traffic jams.

Tara was not even seated beside him. She was on the far right; Ashley sat in the middle, next to Rafe Tyler.

There was little traffic. In a matter of minutes, they were pulling up to a curb again. The restaurant was exactly as he had described it. Neat and clean, but very crowded, with tables almost on top of one another. Tea and noodles were served instantly. Rafe poured tea for Tara, smiling while she sipped at it, saying nothing, understanding that the hot liquid was the thing she needed most.

Curiously, dinner went just as lunch had. Ashley and Rafe talked. She told him about modeling; he listened intently.

And still Tara felt his eyes on her. Felt as if he were weighing her, assessing her, thinking deeply about her. Why? She wanted to scream. But then, in between bursts of panic, she felt wonderful little ripples of excitement cascade along her spine. She wanted to touch him, to feel the texture of his hair, to run her fingers along the muscled flesh beneath his shirt....

Dinner ended, and he offered to drive them both home. Tara became uneasy, realizing he would know where she lived.

Where—but not which apartment.

"Lovely!" Ashley answered.

Tara was struck with the sudden urge to run down the street—run anywhere from this sense of danger. But that would be absurd. And it would be a kind of surrender, too. Yes, I am afraid, she thought. Afraid that I can't withstand him.

They drew up before Ashley's apartment building. Ashley blew Tara a kiss. "See you tomorrow at one! Don't forget—fittings!"

Rafe excused himself to see Ashley to her door.

Alone in the rear of the limo, Tara leaned back, her heart pounding. There was a chauffeur in the front, she knew. A chauffeur who worked for Rafe Tyler. Long accustomed to the man's nocturnal habits?

Nocturnal habits! Her teeth started chattering slightly, and she twisted her fingers in her lap, wondering what she was doing, waiting alone in the back of a luxurious limousine for a man to return. Ashley was the one who had baited him all night. Why the hell hadn't Tara insisted on being brought home first?

Because he hadn't intended to let her go first! And she hadn't even fought, because she had known that she would lose....

No, it wasn't that at all. There'd been no battle. Surely he was a respectable man, albeit a devastating one, assured and adult, and definitely male.

Very male. Very attractive—because of that potent masculinity.

Tara released her hands and nervously stretched her fingers. She envisioned him coming back to the car, sitting beside her, staring into her eyes with that subtle, rueful smile. There would be no need for words. He would reach for her, and she would utter a small sound of protest, but it would be no more than a whimper caught in her throat. His arms would engulf her, and she would be swallowed in heat; his mouth would be firm and persuasive, but brook no resistance, should she find the strength to offer it. His kiss would be like fire. She would feel his fingers moving over her flesh with the same tender expertise with which they had touched the silver fox, but unlike the fox, she would feel that caress, and, knowing that she was a fool, she would still delight in it, gasping when his lips left hers to trail down the bare flesh of her throat.

No! In panic at her own vision, Tara almost gasped the word aloud. Furious with herself for being such a guileless coward—after all she had been through!—she nevertheless began to grope for the door handle. Let him think that she had run. That was exactly what she intended to do.

Blindly, Tara leaned forward. The door handle refused to budge, then quite suddenly gave way. Ready to leap for the pavement, she looked up.

Into his golden eyes.

"Was I gone so long? I'm sorry," he said smoothly.

Tara couldn't think of a thing to say. His foot was already inside; she had no choice but to back away.

Still smiling, he moved in beside her and tapped on the window. He looked back questioningly at Tara.

"Where to, Miss Hill?" he asked softly.

She stuttered out her address, furious at the sound of her voice, more annoyed still with the amusement on his features.

He repeated her address to the driver, and the limousine pulled out into the traffic. Rafe sat back, idly folding his hands before him, watching her with his slight, devilish grin.

The city lights flickered around them, giving occasional glints of substance and bursts of shadow. For a moment she tensed, remembering her fantasy. His arms around her, the potent kiss. The sleek feel of the rugged planes of his face beneath her fingers...

He didn't touch her. He didn't lean toward her.

"You've just come back to the city?" he asked casually.

"Yes."

"Long vacation?"

"Yes."

They passed beneath a streetlight. Tara noted that his eyes were really green, with brilliant pinpoints of topaz around the pupil that gave them their compelling quality of yellow gold.

Shadow came between them again. In that shadow he seemed to move slightly. His gaze appeared to change slightly, to become as gentle as the darkness.

He was going to touch her....

She could feel the air grow tense between them. Little shocks seemed to leap through her, seemed to flame and warm her blood, heat her skin. She wanted to cry out, to leap away....

Or into his arms.

"This is it," he said suddenly, and she started violently.

His lip twitched, but he said nothing, and merely opened the door. He stepped to the curb and turned, offering his hand. She took it, swallowing sharply, keeping her eyes lowered as she gained her footing. His hand was so warm. Hot and alive with power.

He released her, and his fingers lightly touched the small of her back as he led her to the door.

The doorman was on duty, but Rafe Tyler walked her to her apartment anyway.

The grand elevator, carpeted and mirrored, suddenly seemed ridiculously small. He filled it. They didn't speak, and as the cubicle took them higher, Tara felt her blood race like lava. Her fingers began to tremble. Her breath came too quickly, and, God help her, surely he could hear the beat of her heart.

She wasn't alone yet. Not yet. His arms could still come around her; his kiss could still sear her....

The door opened. She walked down the hall and stopped nervously in front of her apartment, fumbling for her keys.

He took them from her fingers and deftly opened both locks.

This was it, she thought. He would lead her in and follow, close the door and lean against it. And she didn't know if she would long to scream or slide heedlessly into his embrace.

He stepped back. The caress of his eyes was his only touch.

"Good night, Tara," he said, his tone low and husky.

It was a promise in itself, something that touched her as surely as fingers might, with the same effect.

"Good night." She managed to form the words, trembling as she spoke.

And then his hand did move. He raised it slowly. His knuckles came to her cheek and brushed the soft flesh there.

He smiled and stepped away. She watched him move down the hall.

And then he turned back. His eyes fell on her curiously, disturbingly. It was a slow, total assessment. Her blood chilled, then heated. At first she felt his scrutiny touching her, like a breeze, lightly, then intimately. Velvety, vibrant and warm, knowing all of her, from head to toe.

His eyes met hers. She could tell that he had found all he saw appealing. He looked as if he could, like the great beast he so resembled, forget all convention, step back to her side and sweep her into his arms, into his very being. A savage conquest: desired—taken.

She quivered inwardly, wondering what her reaction would be. Outrage, surely.

But maybe not. The urge was almost painful. The urge to go to him, to curl into his arms...

Except that there was more to his look, something very disturbing. As if he hadn't *wanted* to find her appealing, though he had stalked her. But it was as if now that he had caught her, he wouldn't deny what he felt.

But it was only a physical appeal.

Then his eyes softened, if only for a minute. There was the slightest flame of tenderness within them.

"Tara, get inside."

She stepped back.

He smiled. "And lock your door!"

She nodded, not realizing that she was blindly obeying his command.

She leaned against her door once she was inside, having lost the strength to stand on her own.

Tara listened to the light fall of his footsteps as he moved down the hallway, back to the elevator. She gave herself a shake, moved into her apartment, showered, made herself a cup of tea and turned on the television set to watch the late movie from bed.

Rational, normal things to do...

But they didn't make her feel rational or normal. She was keyed up, wide-awake and very nervous.

She knew that Rafe Tyler had stepped into her life to stay for a while. What she didn't know was what he wanted.

Rafe walked into his study and headed straight for his desk, then sat and parked his legs on the gleaming wooden surface. Lacing his fingers behind his head, he stared up at the ceiling for a moment, then leaned forward and rummaged in his bottom drawer for the bourbon and the shot glass he kept there.

He splashed out a portion of whiskey and leaned back again, this time surveying the oil paintings on the paneled walls. There were five of them, all of ships at sea. Proud ships, rising high against the horizon.

He downed his drink, shuddering slightly as the liquor burned his throat. Then he opened the top drawer and pulled out a manila folder. He laid it flat on the desk and opened it.

Tara Hill, the woman who had occupied his day and night, stared at him once again from an eight-by-ten glossy.

It was a younger Tara Hill who looked up at him. She couldn't have been more than seventeen or eighteen in this picture. Her hair was longer and very straight; she wore little makeup, and her eyes carried a glint of dreams and fantasy and eager fascination that they lacked today.

Rafe turned sheets of paper, passing more and more photos, until he came to the most recent one he had, one that was two years old. She had changed. Her hair was far more sophisticated, feathered and sensual. She was slimmer. And her eyes carried a look of weariness that was more haunting and alluring than even the bright innocence of the earlier picture.

Rafe slapped the folder shut and readjusted his long legs over the corner of the desk as he leaned back, wincing. The photos had never touched him before. But then, *he* had never touched *her* before. She had been an object to be studied, and now she was real. He had assumed that she would be hard-bitten and cool, careless of her impact on the lives of others.

He didn't—couldn't—believe that anymore. Not when he had been touched by the shimmering silver in her eyes, had felt the soft and fluttering pulse of her life beneath skin as smooth and evocative as translucent silk....

He grimaced. He had touched her hand, no more. Gazed at the perfect ethereal beauty of her face. Rested his fingers against the delightful small of her back, and yet even then he had imagined he felt her heat, warm and subtle and promising a blaze of love and passion, an inferno....

Rafe slammed his feet to the floor, uttering an exclamation of self-disgust. Was this what Jimmy had felt? This overriding, uncanny desire? This lure that had to be followed, this hunger that had to be appeased?

He groaned aloud. Jimmy had been younger. Easily led, easily tricked. And by God, Rafe determined, *he* wasn't Jimmy. He'd seen the world in all its facets; he knew the harlots and the whores, the ladies and the thieves. The world had molded him, touched him with its many cultures, given him a wisdom about human nature that defied country and custom.

But tonight he might as well have been as raw and naive as Jimmy. He had ached, yearned to reach for her, touch her, hold her, caress her— and forget everything. And if he had touched her, she would have surrendered to his hold. Or would it have been he who surrendered, to practiced wiles, to a known beauty?

Rafe raised his hands to his temples. What was she, then, a lady or an elegant tramp? And in that moment he knew the truth. He had touched her but done no more because though she might have gone to him for the moment, she would have run in time. And he still had enough of his wits about him to know that he had to treat her carefully, building her trust, until she decided to talk.

Rafe started suddenly, aware that there was a hesitant tapping at his door. He stood, crossed the room and threw it open. Before him stood a slight woman with silver-dusted chestnut hair and enormous blue eyes. She appeared to be no more than a very attractive forty, but Rafe knew her to be a year or two over fifty.

"Myrna!" he exclaimed, startled at her presence. He moved, inviting her in. "I didn't know you were here."

Myrna smiled wanly and moved restlessly into the room, wandering to the window to stare blankly out at the darkness before turning back to Rafe.

"I'm sorry. I shouldn't be disturbing you. I hope you don't mind—I planned on spending the night. I came around eight. You were out."

"I just got back and—"

"Yes, yes, Maggie went up to her room hours ago—I told her to."

Maggie was his housekeeper.

"Myrna, you know you're always welcome," Rafe told his step-mother gently.

Her smile became a little less hesitant. "You mean that, don't you, Rafe?" she said a little wonderingly. "I've—I've been very blessed to have you."

Touched, and slightly embarrassed, Rafe grinned ruefully. "I don't know about that, Myrna." He continued quickly, "But what's wrong? You seem upset."

"Upset" was an understatement, but Rafe was at a loss for a better word. Myrna had been upset for the past two years, and Rafe sure as hell couldn't blame her. She'd lost her husband to heart failure and her son to mysterious circumstances within a month.

"I, uh, I am upset, Rafe," Myrna murmured. Then she smiled and crossed the room, staring up at the oil painting of the *Highland Queen*. She turned back to him suddenly and chuckled girlishly.

"I was awfully afraid that I'd...interrupt you. I take it you were out with some exquisitely beautiful woman?"

Everything in his body tensed, but Rafe was careful not to let emotion show in his face. He leaned against his desk, crossing his arms over his chest, and grinned in return.

"Yep," he answered, and she nodded, pleased.

"Well, I'm glad you're alone now."

Rafe walked around his desk, indicating that she should sit on the soft white leather sofa across the room. "I think you need a drink, Myrna. Bourbon okay? I can call Maggie and have her make us some tea if you'd rather—"

"Oh, heavens no! Maggie played nursemaid to me long enough tonight!" Myrna protested. "I'd love a good shot of bourbon. A manly drink, isn't it?"

Rafe grimaced. "I don't know about that. It does seem to go down smoothly."

He poured them each a shot, then took a seat beside her. She gulped down hers with a toss of the glass, shuddered, then faced him squarely.

"I saw her picture, Rafe. That model who disappeared. She's back with Galliard Fashions."

Rafe drained his glass quickly, dismayed that Myrna already knew that Tara Hill had emerged from obscurity.

He set his glass on the coffee table and faced his stepmother squarely. "I know," he told her honestly.

"Oh, Rafe!" She clutched his hand, and her fingers were shaking. "I know that you did everything you could, that you searched and searched, that you left your profession behind you, that you did everything already. But I have to know! I just have to know what really happened. If Jimmy is—"

"Myrna, Myrna," Rafe said softly, clasping her fingers tightly, wrenched anew by the bright tears he saw hovering in her eyes. "I'm going to find out," he promised.

She nodded, looking down to her lap. "You're not even my blood, and I've asked you to give up everything—"

Rafe shook his head impatiently. "I gave up working because Dad died and someone had to run his empire. I might have been a wanderer, but he always knew I'd come back when I was needed. And Jimmy was my brother, Myrna. My little brother. I promise you—I'd never be able to rest if I didn't follow every damn possibility."

She was still looking at her hands, and nodded miserably.

Rafe stood. He'd been fifteen years old when his father had married Myrna; her son, Jimmy, had been only seven at the time. But a tie had formed between them instantly, and in the years that followed, the stepbrothers had become closer than those bonded by blood.

"One more shot of bourbon, Myrna," Rafe said. "Then off to bed with you. You could use some sleep." He brought her a second drink and watched while she swallowed it. Then he helped her to rise and led her to the door. He kissed her forehead. "Get to bed."

She lifted her huge blue eyes to him, eyes that still brimmed with tears. "You've been the very best son, Rafe. The very best."

"Hey, you're a damn good stepmom, too."

Her smile warmed; her tears seemed to dry a little. "Good night, Rafe. I'm in control, I promise. And I'll—I'll trust you."

"Thanks, Myrna. This will take a little time, and you can't make yourself crazy, right?"

She nodded, stronger now. With a smile and a little wave, she moved down the darkened hall to the suite she still maintained in the Tyler mansion on Long Island.

Rafe closed his study door, turned out the lights and went through the connecting door to his bedroom.

He didn't turn on the light. Wearily, he stripped and headed for bed, then paused and turned to the mullioned floor-to-ceiling windows that looked out on the gardens. There was a full moon tonight. There was a breeze, too. The moon's glow fell on the water splashing in the main fountain and made fantasy diamonds of it against the velvet of the night.

A perfect setting for a Galliard girl, Rafe found himself thinking. Not just any Galliard girl. Tara Hill.

Dressed in something flowing, something almost translucent—chiffon silk. A gown that was soft yet would mold to her hips and breasts with each fluid movement of her long legs. Its color would be somewhere between blue and silver, like her eyes. Good God, he could almost see her walking the path, almost smell the fragrance of her perfume and her flesh....

He turned away from the window and angrily padded over to the bed, ripping the covers away with a vengeance. Damned bloody moon! It had been proved centuries ago that the moon gave rise to fantasies.

Rafe slammed a fist into his pillow and curled onto his side. Still she remained with him, her scent seeming to linger on his flesh. He closed his eyes tightly but could not dispel the vision of her in his room, walking toward him. He could discern her figure beneath the diaphanous gown, the lush round rise of her breasts, the shadow between, the dark, entrancingly peaked circles where her nipples rose in anticipation of his touch. The sway of her walk, the length of her thighs, the moon-touched silver of her eyes as she looked at him, the feel of her fingers as they rested first against his cheek and then on his chest. He could even hear her whisper to him....

He sat up, grunting between clenched teeth, holding his head between his hands. Had he been awake or asleep? That touch of her fingers had been nothing but a layer of sweat beading onto his naked flesh as he dreamed.

He closed his eyes tightly and vehemently shook his head. He finally banished her presence and brought to mind his stepmother's glistening tears, recalling the agony in her voice. He thought of his brother Jimmy. Young, good-looking, happy-go-lucky. Sensitive and courteous, and such an easy mark when it came to a beautiful woman. One who might have cried, clung to him, used him.

Tara Hill—pretty poison. Or was she?

It didn't matter. He lay down again, very aware that he could not fall in love with a fantasy. But he smiled grimly in the night. He intended to have that fantasy. She would be dealing with Rafe Tyler this time.

Not Jimmy.

And by God, he meant to have the truth. The whole story. It mattered not one whit how he went about procuring it.

He closed his eyes once more, finally exhausted by his determination. But his dreams wouldn't quit. It seemed that he was plagued by whispers moaning in the wind, clarified by the moon.

Whispers hinting again and again that, despite the odds, despite the facts, she might be innocent. As real and innocent and beautiful as the shimmering silver of her eyes....

CHAPTER 4

Tara arrived fifteen minutes late for her fitting, and George wasn't about to let her get away with it.

"Tara, back to work means back to work! Either you're with us or you're not. You don't want a job? Fine—I've got dozens of girls who would die for the opportunity. Girls not yet a quarter of a century old, if you get my meaning, *ma petite!*"

Tara winced slightly behind her sunglasses and gritted her teeth. George had been really angry at first; he hadn't even bothered feigning his French accent through the first two sentences. And George liked to "be French." He might have been born in Brooklyn, but he was convinced that American women wanted French fashions. Maybe he had a point. He had managed to make his name synonymous with fashion the world over.

But he didn't fool her. Not anymore. She had known him too long now. They had been friends; they had endured their squabbles. They had undergone an investigation together—he'd been dragged into it, all because of her! But still, he had tried to shield her, had tried to talk her out of running away. And he had taken her back without blinking when she had squared her shoulders and determined to work again.

"I'm sorry," Tara murmured, lowering her head and trying not to show her grin. His toupee was slightly awry—and he was a man who did not admit to baldness. He was of medium height, with a wiry build, and his manners were perfect—when he wanted them to be.

He was also cruel at times. He liked to remind Tara that he had taken her on as a dirt-poor ragamuffin and changed her into a priestess of high fashion.

Tine had been worse! she reminded herself abruptly, and felt suddenly frozen. In her two years of solitude she thought she had matured. She thought she had faced all the facts and learned to live with them. But just as she had done through all the previous night, she was reliving the past. Yes, Tine had enjoyed his moments of mastery. Reminding her that even with her scholarships, she would never have been able to leave her parents to go to college. That if it hadn't been for him, she wouldn't have been able to give them relief in their last days. That they would have died in pain and dirt and filth, and she would have wound up just like her mother—except healthier. She would have raised a passel of lice-ridden brats, scrounging in the welfare lines.

Tears pricked her eyes behind her glasses; it hurt even now. She wanted to fight, just as she had always fought Tine. She wanted to rage out that her mother had been one of the kindest women on earth, that she had always been poor because she had taken in any stray, any child, and that her father's only crimes had been his lack of education and tireless efforts to make other men rich by his labor and sweat....

"Mon Dieu! Take those glasses off and get over to see Madame Clouseau! Schedules, schedules! *Ma chérie,* we leave in ten days!"

His tone had grown gentle, and Tara sighed, aware that George really did care for her; it was just that he had become accustomed to treating his models either like little children or slaves. He had a remarkable ego—and perhaps it was justly deserved, for it was his fashions that had given them all their tenuous claims to fame.

"I'm going, George," she began. "And I really am sorry—"

"Tara!" he exclaimed, looking at her closely for the first time and frowning. "What have you done to yourself? You look like—like absolute hell!"

She grimaced dryly—she didn't look great, but she didn't look all that bad, either! She hadn't slept more than an hour the night before and had a few shadows under her eyes. All because of that damned Rafe Tyler! He had triggered something in her, and all she had done, hour after hour, was toss and relive her life and...

Dream. Dream of something different from anything she had ever known. A man with the grace and power and fluidity of a tiger—who loved her with the gentle, tender manner of a kitten.

"I, uh, I slept badly last night, George, that's all. I've only been back about a week now; my apartment still seems a little alien and—"

"Alien!" George snorted in disgust. "It has been yours for eight years! Tonight you will take the pills I give you—they will ease you into sleep."

Tara sighed wearily. "I don't take sleeping pills, George."

"You will not work, Tara, unless you learn to sleep. Now, I am serious—I cannot have you looking like a refugee! Like an emaciated pauper. Like—"

"All right!" Tara snapped. "I'll sleep, I promise! But no pills!" She continued to mutter her opinion of sleeping pills as she stepped past him to the rear of the showroom, then to the fitting rooms beyond. He chuckled softly behind her. If nothing else, she was at least off the hook for her tardiness, she thought.

Madame Clouseau was there amid a tangle of measuring tape and sporting a mouthful of pins as she worked over Cassandra Law, a stunning young woman with a headful of nearly blue-black hair. Perhaps, Tara mused, George had taken her back as an employee only because she was a blonde. George, as well as having a flair for color in clothing, loved to play the artist with his models' hair. There would be only four of them on the trip, and they were entirely different in their natural coloring. There was Cassandra, with her raven locks and indigo eyes; Ashley, with her brilliant red curls and green eyes; Mary Hurt, a brunette with deep mahogany eyes; and Tara, with light-blond hair and silver-tinted eyes. Colorful, different—just the way George liked things.

Cassandra was standing on a stool, a white satin strapless gown molding itself around her luscious form and ending elegantly in a froth of rhinestoned tulle around her ankles. She grimaced at Tara in pain as Madame stuck her with one of her countless pins.

"It sounded loud out there," Cassandra murmured, looking anxiously at Tara. "You okay?"

Tara nodded. "Fine, thanks. I've learned to weather the storms around here quite well."

"You're late!" Madame Clouseau snapped, pushing a straying tendril of steel-gray hair behind her ear.

"I'm sorry."

"Start with the black velvet evening gown, please," Madame said. "Cassandra, get this off. Now where is Ashley?"

"I'm here, I'm here! And I'm not wearing this!"

Ashley appeared in a burnt-orange concoction that clashed horribly with her hair. She didn't wait for a reply—Ashley was marvelous at ignoring Madame's imperious manner—but smiled at Tara. "You're late! Does that mean that something erotic happened last night?"

"No, it means I overslept."

"You will wear the dress! George has said so!" Madame exclaimed angrily.

"Damn!" Ashley swore to Tara. "I certainly will not!" she told Madame. "I shall go see George right away and handle the situation myself!" She started for the front, then turned back. "Tara, I want to hear all about it later!"

"I'm dying to hear about it, too!" Cassandra laughed.

"Will you please get to work!" Madame called out, clapping her hands sharply.

"What a wonderful kindergarten teacher you would have made!" Tara told her sweetly, then, secretively smiling and giggling to one another, Tara and Cassandra hurried to the back. They passed Mary on the way; she was mumbling under her breath as she tripped over the hem of the elegantly seductive peignoir she was wearing.

It was a long day. Tara went through outfit after outfit and appeared before George—pinned to perfection by Madame—with a multitude of purses, evening bags, shoes, coats, hats and stockings. He picked everything apart and redesigned each complete ensemble until he was satisfied. He did the same with the others. Ashley and Cassandra complained, while Tara and Mary remained silently amused. In between, Ashley described the tiger-man to Cassandra, and the two of them plagued Tara to death with questions regarding her few minutes alone with the man. Cassandra swore that Tara led the most exciting life, and Tara silently reflected that excitement had brought her nothing but misery before. Mary seemed to be on her side, though.

"Don't ever trust a man like that! If he's that devastating to you, he's that devastating to all women. And he probably keeps a scorecard of his conquests!"

Ashley shook her head vehemently. "Not this guy. He would only be interested in the *crème de la crème*!"

"Ah, but he needs his *crème* all the time!"

"It doesn't matter, anyway!" Tara said at last. "I'll never see the man again. Let's drop it, shall we? Please?"

She counted herself grateful that they did. Mary was taking classes at Columbia, determined to be an architect when her days as a model came to an end. She began to talk enthusiastically about a certain professor, and Tara found herself swept into the mood, laughing with the others. She longed to agree to Ashley's suggestion that they all go out to dinner at the end of the day. But she remembered what George had said. She would have to get some sleep.

"I've got to go home," she said with a sigh. "Sorry—I've just got to get some rest."

Ashley instantly looked contrite and worried. "Are you all right, Tara? Want me to come with you? I can make you something to eat. You can shower and go straight to bed."

Tara shook her head. "No, thanks, Ashley. I'm capable of making my own dinner—honest! Go, have a good time!"

They parted on the street. Tara let the others get the first cab, and, to her frustration, it took her almost half an hour to get another. It was nearly seven when she reached her apartment.

She kicked off her shoes by the door, sighed softly and went into the kitchen to put on a kettle for tea. While she waited for the water to boil, she drew a hot bubble bath. When her tea was made, she took it and a paperback thriller into the bathroom, where she relaxed in the tub, while a frozen dinner cooked in the oven.

She couldn't seem to get into the book. It was wonderful—but her mind was a mess. She didn't want to think about the past, but she couldn't seem to help herself. She kept remembering that she was going to Caracas again. And she kept seeing that city, and then Tine, herself—and Jimmy.

Tara sighed, sipped her tea and set it down on the tile floor, gave up on the book—and settled back into the bubble bath, closing her eyes.

Caracas...

It had been all over by then. All over between her and Tine. She had met him at seventeen, fallen in love with him before she was twenty.

By the time they had reached Caracas, she had almost hated him.

She wasn't quite sure when the beginning of the end had come. She had adored Tine at first. He had been like a benevolent magician, come to turn her world around, to offer her money to ease her family's distress, to give her fame and glamour. He had asked nothing of her—not at first.

He had been tall and slim and capable of the slowest, sexiest smile in the universe.

Tine had known how to bide his time. She had been raised rigidly and morally. But on her twentieth birthday she had gone to him, and before her twenty-first birthday they were living together.

The trouble had started in small ways. Her family had embarrassed him; she had been fiercely loyal. He wanted to control her contracts. He didn't want her sending money home; he didn't want her creating scholarships for the local high school students who were caught in the same economic prison in which she herself had been confined. He didn't want her to have lunch with her friends—not even to make phone calls!

When he had begun to insist that she marry him, she had backed away, already disillusioned. When she had begun to fight—he'd eased off, and reminded her that he had made her. Very subtly, he'd reminded her that he could also break her. And, of course, he had still been Tine. So good-looking, so male, so capable of overpowering the staunchest convictions that she could muster.

But in Caracas she'd escaped him. And, wandering through the city streets, joining a tour of the old cathedral, she'd realized that she really was coming to hate him, and that she couldn't stay with him a minute longer. He meant to rule her—and she wasn't about to be ruled or imprisoned by anyone.

On that same afternoon, walking past the shops, she had suddenly paused, caught by the reflection in a window of a young man's eyes.

She had turned quickly to meet him face-to-face. He didn't turn away. He had been young and handsome and more. She was accustomed to men's looks, accustomed to sighing with the realization that they were usually interested in just one thing.

It wasn't that he didn't display that same hunger. But it was tempered somehow with laughter and humor. His eyes had held a wistful appreciation, and he'd smiled so nicely that she discovered herself smiling back.

They talked as they walked along, and they wound up having dinner. He told Tara that he was a tourist. She told him her business. He said that he knew her business—any man with life and breath in him knew who she was.

And somehow she had poured out her story to him. And in speaking to him, she'd realized uneasily that she was afraid of Tine.

"If you need help, if you're ever afraid, just call me. I'll be there, understand?"

She knew his offer was honest. He really didn't want anything; he wasn't making any demands. He was actually offering to be her friend.

That night she'd told Tine that she was leaving him. First he'd reminded her harshly that they were both working. Then he'd tried his subtle magic on her.

And she had known that it was truly over, because she felt nothing for him. When she had told him that, he'd called her a liar, but it had been true.

Sitting in the tub now, she clenched her fingers tightly. Tine had been convinced of his sexual mastery. She didn't think she would forget, no matter how long she lived, how he had forced her that night. And how incredulous and furious he had been when he realized at the end that she had meant it—he could not move her, and she hated him.

He had started to laugh. "You should learn to enjoy it again, baby. When we get home, you're going to marry me. If you try to leave me, Tara, I'll kill you. Do you understand?" He had flexed his fingers, then wrapped them around her neck. "Don't doubt it—I'll kill you. I saw you today with that kid. I'm always watching you, Tara. I'll kill him, too." He'd chuckled again. "Maybe I'll just kill him anyway. I may need to."

"You fool!" Tara had retorted. "You'll never keep me this way. I hate you—and I'm not afraid of you!" But she was; she was near tears because he had just proved to her that he could toss her around easily enough—if he had her alone. She was so humiliated she nearly wanted to die, so miserable that she didn't think that she could ever really trust or love anyone again.

"Sweetie, remember—you're mine. I'll do whatever I want, whenever I want. And if you don't want to leave a trail of blood in your wake, you'll leave the boys alone."

He'd walked out on her then—cocky, cruel, assured.

Tara had hesitated in absolute misery—then called Jimmy.

If she'd been able to think clearly, she might have wondered at his rapid questions, about his lack of surprise that Tine knew about him. He'd told her to meet him at the glass factory, and at that point she certainly should have wondered what was going on.

The glass factory was out of town, up in the mountains. But Tara had gone, determined that she would never see Tine again.

The factory was closed. The taxi driver hadn't wanted to take her there, but she had feverishly convinced him in her broken Spanish that she was meeting a friend there. The kindly cabdriver had stayed with her in the darkness until she had seen Jimmy coming out of the trees.

He'd taken her gently in his arms and told her that he had the use of a friend's little house nearby. There was no road leading to it, so they walked through the trees, up the mountain. She told him something of what had happened—not all, since it was so horribly humiliating—and then regretted quite suddenly that she had come to him, because she was afraid for his life.

That was when the first shot had rung out. They were in a small clearing, the moon overhead, the night beautiful and cool. She could still remember the fresh scent of the trees, damp from a recent rain. She'd screamed, and Jimmy had instantly and protectively pulled her to the ground. Wary, ready. Or so it seemed.

Tine had appeared in the clearing, carrying a gun. She could remember his silhouette so clearly. She could remember the flash of his teeth when he smiled. She had lain there in terror as he casually glanced her way, then stared at Jimmy.

She could remember the sophisticated and beautiful brunette at his side—a woman who seemed to know him quite well, to be quite comfortable with this gun-toting activity of his.

And, despite her terror, she realized what an idiot she had been. He'd wanted to marry her—her income potential had far surpassed even his original imaginings—but there had been other women all along.

Then, to her complete amazement, he had told Jimmy that he wanted the mask back. And he had laughed and told the other woman that Tara really was an extraordinary prize—she'd lured Jimmy easily when no one and nothing else in the world would have been able to do so.

"The mask!" Tine had cried, firing a warning shot into the trees.

Tara had been incredulous when Jimmy fired back—and then she didn't know what happened at all, because she had ducked her face into the ground and shuddered as volley after volley of shots rang out. Leaves rustled, and Jimmy was gone.

Sirens had suddenly screeched through the quiet of the forest as the police had climbed their way up the mountain. Tara had dared to look up—just in time to see Tine clutching a bloody shoulder, leaning against a tree. He had stared at her and smiled slowly.

"Sweetheart, someday, somewhere, I'll find you again. Once more, my love, for old times' sake! And then, as I promised—bye-bye, darling!"

Tine had disappeared. The sirens had come closer and closer. She had screamed for Jimmy—but Jimmy, too, was gone.

She had been alone with the brunette—dead from a gunshot wound—when the police had arrived. She'd been arrested instantly, dragged into interrogation. She had sworn her innocence, trying to explain that Tine had been shooting at Jimmy. When George Galliard arrived to stand at her side in the confusion, they had threatened to arrest him, too. After all, he had employed both Tine Elliott and Tara.

George had sworn her innocence too and threatened to sue for libel and legal retribution. Heads would roll if he and Tara weren't released immediately, he'd insisted.

No one ever did discover who Jimmy was. Nor had Tine been found. After three miserable weeks, the charges against Tara had been dismissed. She and George had come home, and she had decided to disappear after the media blitz. The police had told her that Tine had been suspected of being in on the artifacts smuggling racket for a long time. The papers had picked it up, and she had found herself labeled the lover and accomplice of a notorious criminal.

Tara opened her eyes and took a deep breath. The water was getting cold. Her dinner was probably burning. She didn't want to think anymore—she just wanted to sleep.

She hurried into the kitchen, turned off the stove, and poured herself a glass of wine, which she quickly downed. Feeling a bit better—as if she would at least get some release from her own thoughts!—she dressed in a silk floor-length hostess-type nightgown, brushed out her hair and meandered back into the kitchen.

She bent over the oven door, intending to remove her dinner, then frowned, feeling a little dizzy. Too much wine after a sleepless night, she thought. The doorbell rang. She hesitated. If she didn't answer, whoever it was would go away.

But someone was insistent. The bell kept ringing. "All right, all right!" she muttered, pressing her palms to her forehead.

She should never have just opened the door. She didn't usually do anything so foolish—she always checked through the little peephole to see who was there. Perhaps she had been so annoyed and so dizzy that she had thrown the door open to stop the horrible sound of the bell as quickly as possible.

It was a mistake. A horrible mistake.

Because he stood there. Her tiger-man. Arching a brow with stern displeasure at her carelessness.

He was in black again: black trousers; black vest; black jacket. But a white shirt and a red tie. Elegant, casual. He might have graced the pages of an elite magazine. Sophisticated.

And the farthest thing in the world from civilized! In spite of the suit, in spite of his totally businesslike appearance, he still resembled a tiger. Taut and vital, exuding a leashed energy, yet cool and knowledgeable, on the prowl.

"Rafe!" she said, standing there.

"Yes, and you should be glad that it is. You might have just thrown your door open to a mugger."

The smile she gave him nearly caused his heart to stop, his blood to boil. Superior, aloof, a sensual curve of her lips.

"Perhaps that would be less dangerous. You can't come in, you know."

But he was already in, closing and locking the door behind him, frowning as he surveyed her eyes.

"Are you all right?"

"Of course I'm all right. But you can't stay."

"I have to stay. My dinner is coming here."

"Here?"

"Yes, I've ordered us two steaks, medium rare, linguine with clam sauce, and antipasto. It will arrive any minute now."

"Well, I'm so sorry, but you didn't ask me, and you can't stay!"

Did tigers smile, or did they simply grin? He leaned against the door, watching her, as comfortable in her home as a lover of many years' standing might be.

"You wouldn't really have me eat in the hallway, would you? And besides, your own dinner is burning."

"What?" she demanded, and then she smelled it—her frozen dinner, burning in the oven. "Oh," she murmured, and hurried out to remove the charred remains before the whole place smelled of smoke.

Tara grabbed an oven mitt, quickly threw the tray into the sink and flooded it with water.

Rafe was right behind her. "That was what you were going to eat? For a meal?"

"It was a fine meal!" she retorted. "Models are supposed to be slim, remember?"

She wanted to sail regally on by him and show him the door, but the dizziness overwhelmed her, and right before him, in the narrow space of the doorway, she found herself having to stop and grasp the frame to keep herself upright. She looked from the sleek material of his suit to his eyes and shivered, because it was there, that magnetism so unique, so dangerous, so appealing and sexual that her heart fluttered in a way it hadn't for years. No, never—she had never felt this absolute attraction before in her life.

"Slim?" he inquired softly as he took her cheeks between his palms, then threaded his fingers slowly through her hair. "You're perfect. More beautiful without makeup. Soft, like this, fragrant and natural in every way."

"I—" Tara gripped the door desperately for help. "You—you have to go."

The doorbell started to ring again. He smiled and went to answer it.

It was dinner. Two men in white coats brought it in on a table covered with a snowy-white cloth. They set it up in her living room. Tara couldn't seem to speak as she watched the whole thing taking place. The men tipped their caps to Rafe, then said they hoped she enjoyed her dinner.

And then they were gone. Rafe had taken two chairs from her dining-room table. He held one out for her.

"I told you—" she began.

"It's here. And your own meal is a soggy mess in the kitchen sink. Come on—you have to eat."

She paused, watching him warily. "Who are you, what do you want, and why have you been following me?"

He returned her stare. "I am Rafe Tyler," he replied. "And what I want is you. Can that be so difficult to understand? No subterfuge. I'm being as honest as I can. And civilized! I realize that what I want may not be something you...desire, so I want to get to know you. Dinner and walks and flowers. I'll worship from afar—for a while!" he said softly. He smiled, and she thought there was an amazing tenderness in his eyes. A tenderness as great as the primal heat and hypnotic energy that drove him.

She couldn't fight him. Wine and exhaustion were making her too drowsy, costing her too much.

"You're rather sure of yourself, aren't you?" she asked him.

"I'm a determined type of person."

"If I sit down and eat, will you leave?"

"If that's what you want, yes."

"I have to sleep," she told him primly.

He arched a brow. "Did you have trouble sleeping last night? Might it have been because of me?"

"Of course not!" she snapped.

He just smiled and seated her politely then sat down across from her. He served her, talking about the wonders of the restaurant from which the food had come. She ate, asking him questions. She learned that he really lived on Long Island but kept an apartment in the city. He told her that he had sailed quite a bit, traveling the world on steamers right after college. She was barely aware that he had poured wine for her—and that she had kept drinking—until her elbow fell off the table and she nearly lost her balance.

"What's the matter?" he demanded, sweeping around to help her.

She stared at him, shaking her head in confusion. She had heard him; she hadn't heard him. She felt delightfully light, and terribly sleepy. Very soft, very feminine. He didn't seem to be so much of a threat anymore. He was a man. An attractive and attentive one, and it was impossible not to like him.

"Tara!"

He seemed annoyed, though, annoyed and a little too macho.

"What have you done to yourself?"

She smiled, loving the feel of the fabric of his jacket against her cheek, fascinated by the gold and silver color of her hair where it fell across his shoulders.

"I told you—I have to sleep."

"What did you take?"

"Don't yell at me!"

"Then tell me!"

"It's all your fault. George told me to go home and sleep so I had a glass of wine. And then you gave me more."

His face was tense, and his arms were tight as he lifted her and carried her down the hallway, past the bath and the den to her bedroom. It seemed all right. Everything seemed to be all right.

More than all right. She felt ridiculously secure, comfortable. So relaxed, so ready to smile.

"You should be in bed," he said as he stopped in the doorway.

"I would have been. You appeared at the door."

Thick lashes hid the tawny gold of his eyes. She thought that he smiled a little secretively.

"I'm going to put you to bed."

"Wasn't that your plan?"

"No. Eventually, I plan to *take* you to bed. There is a massive difference, of which you will one day be completely aware."

"Ah! No ego problems there!"

He smiled, turned down her brocade coverlet and the sheet below, then laid her down with her head on the pillow. He sat at her side, studying her intently.

"They're quite unusual," she murmured, reaching up to touch his face, smoothing a finger over his brows.

"My eyebrows?"

"Your eyes. They actually have brown in them, and green—and a ring of blue at the very edge. Like crystal. And when you combine all the colors, they seem gold. Like a tiger's eyes, reflecting in the darkness."

"They're hazel," he said dryly.

He caught her hand and pressed a kiss against her palm. She inhaled sharply at the river of sensation that swept through her. She was tired and off guard, yet she couldn't seem to care.

When their eyes met, it seemed as if eons passed. Eons in which they strained to know each other, to absorb each other's soul, and thoughts, and heart.

He leaned toward her. And kissed her.

Never had she felt such magic. Lips that knew hers, commanded, yielded and coerced. Warmth and fever, magnetism, engulfing her.

Never had a kiss coursed through every nerve and fiber of her being, awakening a fever, a heat. His lips were forceful, his tongue demanding. Sweeping all the crevices of her mouth, hungry and restraining, hungry and setting free...

She felt his hands cupping her face, caressing her shoulders.

Moving intimately. More intimately than they should have been. She trembled as his fingers curved around her breast, his fingers playing over her nipples. He groaned, deep and hoarse, against her, and sudden truth and panic seized her.

She wanted him. Everything within her quivered for him, like a strung bow, taut and ready to let fly. She was fascinated by him. Where he touched her, she felt alive. Where he did not touch her, she longed to be touched. She wanted to see his shoulders bared to her touch. She wanted to explore his chest and muscular legs. She wanted...

All of him. It was like a drumbeat, frantic, insistent.

And it was so wrong! She didn't trust him; she barely knew him, and she couldn't believe she was letting things go so far. She was suddenly very frightened, whimpering slightly in her throat.

Perhaps he heard. Or perhaps some alarm had sounded within him, a warning that the time wasn't right.

He pulled away. Not with an apology. Pensively, painfully. She could see the tension in his features, the pulse throbbing in his throat.

He took her hands, planted a light kiss on each one, then let them go and rose stiffly.

"Go to sleep. I'll see you soon."

"Oh...no! Really, we can't."

He shook his head, smiling crookedly. "No, Tara. We not only can. We have to."

He turned and left her.

She struggled to think, to find logic. She didn't trust him. She didn't know why, exactly, but she didn't trust him. He wasn't following her because she was a "beautiful" woman. He would attract women without seeking them, all of them beautiful, all of them sensual.

He knew her, she was certain. He had watched her in the museum; he had followed her to the Plaza.

She shouldn't see him again.

She shivered, knowing that she would. He was right. She would have to.

Seeing him could become as necessary as...breathing.

"No," she protested aloud.

But no one heard her, and she gave up all attempts to be rational when sleep overcame her.

CHAPTER 5

He was there when Tara finished with her fittings the next day, in the showroom, idly talking to George—waiting for her.

Tara saw him as soon as she emerged from the back, and she held herself still, stunned and, to her annoyance, slightly panicky.

Morning had brought reason back to her. Humiliation, too. The night now seemed part of a dream, a very disturbing dream. She could remember him carrying her, could remember the feel of his arms. She could remember his smile and his laughter, and the way his hair had felt beneath her fingers.

She could remember his kiss, his touch on her breast. And she could remember the absolute feel of fire. Sensations that ripped through her. A wanting unlike anything she had ever known.

And she remembered him pulling away. Kissing her fingers, leaving her be when he could have...

Continued. With her so content, yet at the same time so explosive that she would have never thought to stop him. To seek restraint. To realize that they were virtual strangers and to remember that the one previous affair of her life had ended in absolute disaster.

Easy, she had told herself in the morning. It was a matter of will, and her will would control her actions. She didn't trust him—he was a tiger. Fierce, exciting, wonderful, beautiful—and dangerous. She couldn't quite fathom why, but she knew instinctively that she was being stalked. Therefore, she told herself, don't see the man. The next time he appears, keep the door shut. Don't answer the summons. Simply don't see him. The decision was made, so it would be easy.

He wasn't in black today. He wore a loose off-white jacket, tan slacks and a navy silk shirt casually open at the neck. His hands were in his pockets as he leaned casually against the golden oak bar at the rear of the store, nearly parallel to the models' dressing rooms.

He seemed to be listening politely to whatever George was saying.

"Is that him?" Mary whispered suddenly.

Tara discovered herself nodding reluctantly. Ashley had dragged it out of her that he had stopped by the night before, and the group of them had been teasing her all day.

Tara heard a soft whistle. She twisted and saw that Cassandra had come up behind her, too.

"That's spectacular," she murmured.

"Cassandra!" Ashley joined the group. "Get your tongue back into your mouth before you trip on it!"

"He might be worth the risk," Mary said philosophically. "Don't get too involved, of course. But his type is...rare."

"What type? Two arms, two legs?" Tara asked nervously. And then she laughed. "We must look like a group of high school girls standing here."

"Right you are!" Ashley proclaimed. "And since I do have the privilege of knowing the man..."

She smiled sweetly at Tara.

"Wait! I've got to get out of here first—" Tara began.

Too late—she made a grab for Ashley's arm, but Ashley was already on her way out, smiling graciously.

Cassandra and even the world-weary Mary followed behind her.

Rafe was charming. Tara still had not budged from the doorway, but she watched him. He met Cassandra and Mary, shaking their hands, making polite inquiries. George must have decided that he was a man of wealth and influence and, therefore, should be entertained and impressed. He himself was charming, solicitously telling his models what a long day they had endured, asking if they wouldn't like a drink—a question usually reserved for clientele at showings—whether they shouldn't all sit, and where Tara was? Obviously George knew that Rafe had come specifically for Tara, because he went on about how much Galliard Fashions had once done for Tara—and what Tara Hill had come to mean for Galliard Fashions.

"Ashley, where is she?"

"In the doorway," Ashley replied blandly, winking mischievously at Tara from her relaxed perch on one of the well-padded Greco-Roman settees—also customarily reserved for their affluent clientele.

The tiger eyes were instantly upon her. Warm and glowing, golden, and burning with a certain devilry. Damn him! He'd known she would never have opened her door to him again, and so he was here.

"Hi." He lifted his glass to her.

She really had no option. She left the security of the doorway and wandered out. It seemed that a silence fell. He watched her; she watched him. And her little audience of friends watched them both.

"Tara?" Only George seemed oblivious to the sparks. "Ah, *ma chérie!* What will you have? Hmm. We have an excellent Bordeaux."

"Fine. Thank you."

George poured her a glass of wine. She avoided Rafe, nearly sitting on Ashley's foot in the process. Ashley emitted a little yowl of protest, but Tara ignored her.

If Ashley didn't move her damned foot, she *would* sit on it! Ashley had gotten her into this predicament to begin with.

Or maybe she hadn't. Maybe he would have found her and followed her no matter what.

"So tell me again, Mr. Tyler, about this lady friend of yours who is so interested in a showing. We won't be taking any more appointments after Friday—for two weeks, that is—but I'd certainly squeeze her in before, if you wish. Or after, of course."

"Oh? Why are you closing the shop?" Rafe sounded totally engrossed in George's words, but he didn't take his eyes off Tara. There was something totally unsettling about the way he swirled the ice in his glass while he surveyed her with his half smile. She felt herself flushing uncomfortably, wondering what he was thinking.

Whether he was mulling over their last moments together, laughing because the sophisticated and aloof image had proved to be nothing more than a pawn to be taken in the easiest of moves.

"We're having a showing in Caracas," Ashley answered for George, but George went on with enthusiasm.

"Yes, South American buyers. It should be very exciting. Oh, I know, there's a great deal of poverty down there, but I'll tell you, there's no woman better dressed, more feminine, more enchanting than a true Colombian lady. And the aristocracy of Venezuela! Some of the Mexican señoras—the Brazilians! And Argentina! None know so keenly the allure of a truly wonderful fashion!"

"Is that so?" Rafe said.

Cassandra laughed. "Actually, we're all looking forward to it. We'll be aboard a wonderful cruise ship for seven glorious days, all in all. And only three sessions aboard the ship! George's—" she hesitated, smiling sweetly at George "—*grande* showing is in Caracas, and we're free as birds the rest of the time."

"Are you really? Fascinating," Rafe murmured.

George cleared his throat. "Well, Mr. Tyler, shall I make an appointment for this lady?"

What lady? Tara wondered. And she hated herself because she was sick with the thought that he might be married. But if she intended to stay away from him, what difference did it make?

"Certainly. This Friday, if at all possible."

"Certainly, certainly. The lady's name?"

Rafe arched his brows. "Mrs. Tyler, of course. Mrs. Myrna Tyler."

"Your wife, sir?"

"My stepmother, Monsieur Galliard."

"Oh, of course, of course, of course!" George said. "You do seem enraptured with Miss Hill. Should Tara model—?"

"No." He turned full face to George. "I would love to have Ashley model for her, if it's possible. Of course, I realize she is busy preparing for her trip—"

"I won't mind at all," Ashley murmured.

Tara kicked her.

"Well, then. Friday—say at three? Would that suit Mrs. Tyler, do you think?"

"Perfectly," Rafe murmured.

George chuckled softly, clearing his throat. "Strange, Mr. Tyler—wasn't it Miss Hill you asked for when you came in?"

"Oh, it was," Rafe said smoothly, and at his look, Tara felt blood rush to her face. He turned back to George. "Ashley and I are...old friends. I came to ask Miss Hill to dinner."

Tara jumped to her feet. "Miss Hill can't possibly go to dinner."

"Tara—how rude!" George protested uneasily. At that moment, she hated him. She was a model—not his damned upstairs maid! She made fabulous money, but she worked for it!

She turned on George. "George! You're the one who's insisting that I need sleep these days." He looked so baffled and confused that she ended it with a smile as she swept over to the bar to deposit her glass.

He sounded curiously like Ashley had the day before as he lowered his mouth to her ear to whisper, "Tara! The man is inviting you to dinner—he's not asking to have you for dessert!"

"Oh, yes, he is!" Tara muttered.

She turned quickly to find him watching her again. To see the amused golden light in his eyes.

"Really, Mr. Tyler. I can't. I have an early fitting—"

"No, no you don't, Tara!" Cassandra interrupted breathlessly. She looked at Tara, her eyes wide and innocent, and Tara decided that Rafe Tyler had hypnotized them all. "Tomorrow is Madame's late day, remember? We're not due in until noon. That's right, isn't it, George?"

"What? Ah, yes."

"How wonderful," Rafe said smoothly. Then somehow George had moved, and Rafe was standing beside her, folding his long fingers over hers, smiling. Pleased with himself. Like the tiger that had just consumed the canary.

"I don't—" she began, but as she watched him, the words stuck in her throat. At his touch she felt an overwhelming curiosity, a desire to be with him. She wasn't a teenager; she would never be innocent again.

And she would never let things get out of hand again!

She lifted her chin slightly and smiled. "Dinner. Since you insist, Mr. Tyler."

"Good night, Monsieur Galliard," he told George, smiling with just a trace of irony at the title, which slipped so smoothly off his tongue. Then he turned, and in a friendly, charming fashion said goodbye to the others, and told them that it had been lovely to meet them. He was certain, he said, that no man had ever been so surrounded by beauty.

"Quite poetic," she muttered as soon as they were on the street.

He arched a dark brow to her. His reply came with a subtle grin. "Jealous?"

"No."

"My God, you do know how to dash a man's hopes."

"Ashley might love to go to dinner."

"We did go to dinner."

She sighed softly. "I'm sure that Ashley would love to go to dinner with you—alone."

"Ah. Because you and I have already had dinner together—alone?"

There was something about the way he said it that made her turn about and smack him on the arm. Not hard. Just hard enough.

He laughed. "I thought you were having a rather good time."

"I was having a wretched time."

Laughing, he caught her hands and whirled her before him.

She found herself standing there, staring into his eyes. Her hands were still held in his. People were walking by them; horns blared, automobiles snorted exhaust fumes, and everything seemed to fade slowly away.

"Why were you following me?" she asked him.

"How can you ask that?"

"Why?"

"I think I've been as blatant as I can."

"Oh. Have you?"

"You know what you look like. You're not a fool. You can't tell me you've never had a man see you and feel compelled to follow you before."

"No, Rafe. I haven't. Of course..."

"Of course what?"

She shook her head and lowered her eyes quickly, moving to his side and hurriedly walking once again. She had almost told him about Tine. That no one had ever dared smile at her or come close to her because Tine had been there—her determined guardian.

"Hey!" he said, striding quickly to keep up with her. "We need to turn at the next corner."

"I'm not so sure—"

"Oh, yes you are." He caught her elbow and spun her back around. "French tonight, Miss Hill. Right this way."

"I just said—"

"What? What is it?"

"All right! I feel like your chosen prey! As if you know exactly who I am. As if the past..." She didn't know why, but she hesitated, inhaling sharply.

"You're behaving ridiculously. All right—I know who you are. Tara, you've been in dozens of national advertisements. I was fascinated; I am fascinated. Tara, for God's sake, what is the matter with you? Haven't you ever dated? Gone to movies? To plays? For long walks in the park? Met someone for dinner after a long day?"

"I..." She started to make a retort, and then it occurred to her. "No."

She had never dated. Not really. Not gone out, done all the little things to get to know someone. She had been at home, and then there had been Tine. And she had wound up with him—just as he had intended. But they had never dated. Never gone to movies. Never laughed in the park.

Rafe squeezed her hand. "It's fun. Give it a try."

She lowered her head again, horribly confused. She couldn't let herself be taken in by someone, not again. She just couldn't. Any remnants of youth and innocence had died on that last awful night in Caracas.

"La Maison," Rafe murmured softly, and she realized that they were at the restaurant. He was opening the door, ushering her in, his hand supportive and light against the small of her back. Inside the foyer, he gave his name to the maître d'. Seconds later they were escorted along a deep-maroon velvet pathway to an intimate table of dark, heavy oak. The lighting was dim; the tables were situated so that each was private, a trellis of dark wood separating each one from the next.

They sat down; Rafe ordered wine. His interest was in the menu. He mentioned various dishes that he had tried. Tara just sat there, watching him and wondering what she was looking for. Might there be a break in his facade?

Tara realized that she didn't want anything to be wrong. There was more to her feelings than just the tremendous physical pull the man had on her senses. She liked him. She liked the way he smiled, the easy way in which he had swayed George, the charm that had brought her friends around him like moths drawn to the light.

He looked up from the menu, caught her tense scrutiny—and smiled. "Am I passing muster?"

Tara flushed, but she refused to be swayed. "If you know who I am, you obviously know something of my past."

"Oh, yes. The mysterious past."

"There was no mystery about it," Tara said bitterly. "The papers had a field day."

"And hence, Tara Hill disappeared."

She shrugged. "I wasn't so much afraid of the papers as..." She hesitated, then shrugged. "I needed to get away from everything for a while. I'd made some rather serious mistakes in judgment."

He set down the menu and leaned back against the booth, smiling as he watched her. He picked up his glass, clinked it against hers where it sat upon the table, and sipped his wine. Tara didn't pick up hers.

"What are you—twenty-five?" he asked her.

"Twenty-six."

"Excuse me." He laughed. "Still, rather young to give up on the world, don't you think?"

"I didn't give up on the world. I simply had a lot of experience shoved into very few years."

"Oh." Still smiling slightly, he looked back at the menu.

"Are you laughing at me?" she inquired sharply. "I don't intend to be patronized."

He didn't answer, because their very French waiter had appeared. Rafe asked her if he should order for her, and she shrugged, not caring what she ate.

Rafe ordered in French. Not the high school or college French so many people liked to practice in French restaurants—the kind that caused waiters to grin scornfully as soon as their backs were turned. It was obvious that he spoke the language fluently.

When the waiter was gone, Rafe stretched a hand across the table. "I'm not patronizing you, and I'm not laughing at you. I believe you had a rough time of it. But you're still very young, and to judge the entire world by one previous experience is a mistake. Is that why you're afraid of me— your relationship with Tine Elliott?"

Tara stiffened. Of course he knew about her; she imagined that he sat down with the *New York Times* and coffee every morning. He'd study the headlines and move on to the stock exchange and the sports pages—she wasn't sure in which order.

So, of course, he knew all about Tine Elliott. About the fact that she had been charged with murder, suspected of smuggling—and had her life recorded in boldface black on white.

It just hurt her somehow. It made her feel as if she had to defend herself.

As if she had to convince him that she wasn't the woman they had portrayed in those pages.

"I didn't do it," she blurted out.

He leaned back, grinning an amused devil's grin once again. "You didn't do what?"

"Any of it." She picked up her wineglass and sipped at it nervously.

He leaned closer to her, catching her eyes intently. "Tell me about it," he told her.

She inhaled, not meeting his eyes. "It was a mess. I wanted to get away from Tine. I'd met a...friend. I was supposed to meet him, and I did. Then suddenly Tine was there with the woman who died. He wanted some mask—shooting started. And that was it. Tine and Jimmy disappeared; the woman was dead—and I spent the night in the police station."

She didn't mean to, but she shivered with the memory of fear. Fear of Tine. Of his threat. He had said that he would find her somehow, someday, somewhere.

And she was going back to Caracas. Back to the very place where Tine had disappeared.

She gazed up at Rafe quickly, then frowned at the tense, penetrating quality of his stare. It was as if she had said something that had touched him personally. She sipped her wine again, her throat dry.

But he leaned back, easy once again, darkly handsome and charming. "You're still frightened," he commented.

She shrugged, determined to talk no further. "It was a long time ago. Never mind—I think George was the only one who ever believed I didn't know a damn thing about any mask. The police didn't even want to believe that Jimmy existed. Do you believe me?" she inquired coolly.

He lifted his hands. "You said you were innocent. You're innocent, then. Go on, tell me more."

She shook her head vehemently, alarmed at the way she was feeling. Warmth flooded her veins, something secure that seemed to ease her shudders. Her thoughts of Tine had filled her with a reverberating fear; Rafe, so close, so sure, made her feel as if she had a buffer against that fear.

She didn't like it. It was the physical thing. It was the fascination, the longing to touch, the fire that scorched her when he looked at her, when he touched her. Like something that would grow until the heat was too much—and had to be appeased. She couldn't trust him; she didn't dare. So she had to keep her distance.

And she was going to have to go to Caracas alone. No buffer zones. She didn't think that she was looking for an answer to the past, but maybe she was.

She determined to change the subject. Picking up her wineglass, she challenged Rafe. "Where did you learn to speak French so fluently?"

"Ah, Miss Hill! You weren't listening to Ashley and me the other day. I was in the navy for a while after college, then I worked aboard a French freighter."

She shook her head. "I thought you went into your family business."

"I only came back to it recently."

"And that is...?"

"Various things. Shipping, jewels, trade." He shrugged, as though it wasn't important.

Their salads arrived, but even as she thanked the waiter and bent her head over hers, she thought that he was being purposely evasive. Why?

Or was she imagining things?

"What other languages do you speak?" she asked.

He seemed to hesitate, then shrugged again. "Spanish. A little Italian. Some German."

"Quite accomplished."

He laughed. "No, just well traveled. I always liked to see distant places."

"The life of an adventurer."

"No, the life of a laborer. I worked my way around the world. It was good experience."

"But you're back on terra firma now."

"Basically. A lot of the wanderlust is out of my system. I still travel, though."

"Business?"

"And pleasure."

"You grew up with a silver spoon in your mouth and went off to labor anyway. Very commendable."

"And you grew up in coal dust and went on to enchant the world."

He always managed to turn the conversation back to her!

But the wine was good, and the veal *cordon-bleu* delicious. The service was impeccable, the atmosphere intimate and private. She slipped off her heels somewhere along the line and relaxed. She studied him again and again, and could find no flaw. Not in his manner, not in his looks. And the more the night waned, the more she wanted everything about him to be just as it seemed. She would find herself staring at his hands and remembering their touch. Watching his mouth and remember how it had commanded hers, fierce and gentle all in one, practiced—unique in her experience.

"Pennsylvania, right?"

"You do read the papers," she responded dryly.

"Tell me about it," he said.

And to her amazement, she did. She tried to make him see it. The weary struggle on the miners' faces, the wives who strove so hard to make better lives for their children. The children who did grow up to a better life—and came back to demand that safety measures be taken as far as they could go, that doctors be sent in early so that fewer men died of the black rot that formed in their lungs.

"It seems amazing for this day and age," Rafe commented.

"Well, it exists," Tara murmured. "My parents..."

"What?"

She shook her head. "They're—they're both dead. But they were wonderful people. The best. My mother..."

"What, Tara? Go on."

"I just—" Now it was her turn to shrug. "Tine Elliott always liked to pretend they didn't exist. They were on and off welfare all their lives. Perpetually broke. But whatever they had, they shared. My mother took in orphans and the elderly—anyone who was down knew they could come to our house. She never had a decent dress, a nice haircut—and I think my father was able to take her out to dinner twice in her life. She was still the greatest lady I ever knew."

His hand closed over hers. "I'm sure she was, Tara. Greatness is always in the heart."

She was suddenly embarrassed by the ferocity of her defense. Idly she moved her food around on her plate and sought desperately for a means to change the conversation. "You have a stepmother, you said. What about your family?"

"Myrna? She's a sweetheart. My mother died when I was about five. All I remember is a gentle smile and a beautiful scent. Myrna married my dad ten years later. We're very good friends."

"And your father?"

He paused and sipped his wine. "Gone now, too."

"I'm sorry. Recently?"

"Fairly."

"That's why you're back—taking over the business?"

"Something like that."

"Do you have any brothers or sisters?"

He seemed to hesitate a long time.

"Just one. A stepbrother. Younger. Have you looked at the dessert menu? How about a coffee liqueur?"

They had marvelous napoleons and brandied coffees. Somehow the conversation turned back to her early years in the small mining town in Pennsylvania, and she discovered herself answering questions she normally avoided.

"You've sent a lot of money back into that town," he said without her having told him. "Is that why you've decided to come back to work now?"

She hesitated a second. The warmth of the brandy filled her veins, and she really couldn't see any harm in telling him things. After all, he knew almost everything about her anyway.

"Yes."

"But you didn't run home two years ago."

"No, I, uh, bought a little house in northern Michigan."

"Why?"

She sipped her coffee again. "I don't know. Yes, I do. I moved to a very small farming town. No one knew me. It was quiet, and nice. I learned how to grow marvelous vegetables."

He smiled. "I guess I'd better get you home."

He paid the bill and led her from the restaurant. Once again, his hand was on the small of her back. She leaned against him, inhaling deeply.

And though warnings screamed within her mind, she thought that she was all right. It was fun to dine with him, fun to lean on his arm.

Fun to imagine that they might get involved. That she would feel his kiss again, his hands upon her—

Slow down!

And then, of course, she was nervous. She wondered if he would take her to her door and insist that she owed him a nightcap. If he would stare at her with those tiger eyes on fire. Then she would be in his arms, and before she was aware of what was happening, their clothing would be gone and...

He stepped into the street and hailed a cab.

On the way to her apartment he talked to the cabby about the traffic.

Once there, he walked her through the lobby and to the elevator. And when they left the elevator behind, he walked her to her door.

Fire brushed her fingers when he took her keys from her.

He didn't step inside. He took her cheeks between his palms and stared into her eyes, searing golden magic in his.

His lips brushed hers, barely touching them.

"You are beautiful," he murmured. "Stunning. I don't believe that even Webster would have the perfect word for you."

She felt that she couldn't breathe. She longed for him to release her, before she could sigh and throw herself against him.

But she was no one's fool, she insisted. "Why were you really following me?" she demanded.

"I told you."

"I think you're lying."

He started to laugh, and for just a second his arms swept fiercely around her, crushing her against him. Letting her feel all the vibrant and electric heat of his body, all the muscled tension.

All the desire.

"If you don't believe that I want you, Miss Hill," he whispered softly, "you are not in the least observant!"

Now, he would come in now....

"You are beautiful," he said simply, and added in a curious tone, "I think I'm falling in love with you. Do I have half a chance?"

"I—"

"Don't answer. Wait. See you tomorrow night."

He released her, stepping back. "Get in. Close and lock your door."

He wasn't going to budge until she did, but she wasn't certain that she could move.

Eventually she did. She smiled and stepped into her apartment, and obediently closed and locked the door, and only then did she hear his light footfall down the hallway.

See you tomorrow night.

She hadn't agreed. He hadn't said when or where.

But she knew it would happen.

CHAPTER 6

Rafe stood by his bedroom window, staring out at the fountain, not seeing it, yet seeing it completely. In a different way. In his mind's eye, she stood there. The perfect Galliard girl, soft and flowing, shimmering blond, subtly smiling, the silver light of the moon dazzling in her eyes.

He saw her everywhere he looked. At his dining-room table, in the foyer, before the fire. Seated at the piano, walking through the garden. In his kitchen, in his bedroom.

He had told her that she was beautiful. Any fool could see that; the harshest cynic would not deny it. He had said it; he had meant it.

He had told her that he was falling in love with her.

And that, too, had been the truth.

Fool! he raged against himself, and he turned from the window and padded naked back to his bed, throwing himself on it, twisting to stare up at the ceiling.

She had to be real. The real thing. He could not sweep her from his mind.

Well...she was supposed to be on his mind.

Ah, yes! He was supposed to be the great detective. Dispassionate, ruthless in this quest. God knows, such things happened. It had happened in Caracas. The day she had met Jimmy, Jimmy had disappeared. What had she done to him? What had she embroiled him in that he hadn't been prepared to handle?

Rafe remembered Jimmy's last communication—a postcard from Caracas. A postcard of the glass factory. Brief, in Jimmy's scrawl, telling him that "things" were under control, but he had just met the most beautiful woman in the world and would stay to see her clear.

See her clear. Of what?

Had she been smuggling? Part of some larger scheme? That was Jimmy's business. Locating lost and stolen treasures. Had Jimmy latched on to her because he knew something about her? Or had he been watching Tine Elliott—while Tine Elliott watched him?

Rafe sighed and gave up on sleep. He rose and slipped into a robe and walked out through his balcony window. He could see the fountain again from here, catching and reflecting the moonlight. He could see her there.

It was better than imagining her in his bed—beside him.

Fool! She was yours for the asking. Things could have been cemented in one night. An intimate relationship to bring you closer and closer, to win her confidence...

It hadn't mattered. He'd forgotten his stepbrother; he'd forgotten half of what he'd set out to do that night at her apartment. She had smiled so wistfully during dinner, had kept her eyes on him so warily. And she'd sat before him in that lovely flowing gown, devoid of makeup, silver eyes huge and innocent, angel trails of hair spun upon her shoulders. And when she had been in his arms, he had felt the most urgent need to protect her.

And the most urgent need.

He groaned out loud again and murmured incredulously, "It's as if I'd die if I thought I couldn't have her in the end...."

He'd been in the most exquisite pain when he'd left her, he thought dryly, remembering her arms around his neck, her laughter, like a melody that crept under the skin, like a siren's song that played throughout his entire body.

Jimmy! he reminded himself.

Had that same innocence captivated and swayed his brother? Young and idealistic, Jimmy might have touched her—and fallen for anything.

Just like I'm doing...

He stiffened, thoroughly aggravated with himself. The police had arrested her. The media had harpooned her. For God's sake, she had been Tine Elliott's protégée for seven years; she had lived with him for nearly four of those years. How could she be innocent?

Rafe leaned against the coolness of the wall. Jimmy had disappeared; Tine Elliott had disappeared. Had they died on the mountaintop? He couldn't believe that Jimmy could be dead.

But he had to be. Otherwise he would have contacted them by now. And if he was dead, that death rested upon her elegant blond head. And here he was, falling in love with her, too....

He pushed himself away from the wall and gripped the wrought iron railing, staring out into the night, his face ravaged. She could be innocent. When she spoke to him, he believed every word she said. He wanted to promise that he was no Tine Elliott....

After two years, she was going back. Maybe it had all been planned. Maybe the rest had all been a charade. Tine Elliott might well have been on to Jimmy. He had used Tara to beguile and entice him. He had found Jimmy and found the mask. He had disappeared—Tara had faced the police and the press—and then he'd gone into hiding.

And now, two years later, maybe she was going back to him.

But maybe she was innocent.

He gritted his teeth harshly. He knew that he wanted her to be innocent.

It didn't matter, he reminded himself. Nothing could change his actions at the moment. He had to stay with her; he had to earn her confidence.

Damn it! He slammed his fist against the railing in sudden fury. He was thirty-seven years old, he'd been around the world and back a dozen times—and he was no high school kid, falling in love.

He could have been with her.

Should have been with her. Finding her, wooing her, seducing her—winning her complete trust. The golden opportunity had been there. And he had been so in awe of her smile, of her laugh, of her silver eyes, that he had felt like any anxious lover, determined not to mar everything beautiful between them. And ego had been there, too. Total scorn for anything less than her totally conscious and eager anticipation of the night.

He sighed again and left the balcony. He showered and dressed and went downstairs at five. The newspaper had come. Thank God; he could read and escape his own thoughts.

And wait...for the night to come. He would meet her at the salon again. Dinner and then a show.

Dinner and the show and then...

Slowly! Take it slowly, fool! You're supposed to be the hard one; you've been given a warning that Jimmy never had.

He set the paper down suddenly, feeling slightly ill.

What if she *was* innocent? The thought brought a harsh, bitter laugh from him, because if she was, she would never forgive him once she discovered why he had been following her.

To hang her, if he could. To use her, if he couldn't. No, she would never forgive him.

But he couldn't stop. God, he couldn't stop. He had to know if Jimmy was alive and needed help....

Or if he was dead, beyond all help.

"I think he sounds marvelous," Mary said bluntly. "I don't know what you're worried about. You practically attack the man, and he leaves—he takes you to dinner and doesn't expect a thing. Most unusual, in this day and age."

"I didn't 'practically attack'!" Tara protested, changing from a sequined ball dress to her linen sheath. "And he barged in when I didn't intend to let him."

"Yes," Cassandra interjected, "but trust me! Half the oafs out there think that dinner at a French restaurant is a ticket straight into the bedroom—and they actually get hostile when you say no!"

"And you still think that he's after something?" Mary queried.

"Of course he's after something! Her body!" Ashley said cheerfully. "What on earth is so unusual about that?"

"Well, nothing, really," Mary replied. "Except that according to what Tara said, he could have had that already."

"Now, wait a minute—" Tara protested again.

"Well, you said that you were feeling perfectly comfortable. And you'd have to be an idiot not to appreciate the man's...his, uh—"

"Body," Ashley said bluntly. "God knows, the man definitely has one!"

"No, no, no, it's not just size and muscles," Cassandra said dreamily, flouncing about on the plain corduroy-covered sofa in the lounge area of their dressing room. "It's—it's—"

"Sex appeal?" Mary queried. "Some men have it and some men don't. And—" she glanced at Tara curiously "—he's a have."

"And he's definitely infatuated with you," Cassandra said. "So just what is your problem?"

Tara shook her head. "I don't know."

"I do," Mary told her. "Tine Elliott was a striking man. You knew it the minute he walked into a room. Are you afraid that you're becoming involved with another Tine?"

Tara shrugged. "I don't know. Maybe. He knows everything about me—"

"Your sordid past," Ashley said cheerfully.

"Ashley!"

"Well?" she asked innocently. "That's just my point. What are you worried about? If he thought you were an easy mark because of all that stuff about you and Tine and the mystery man—"

"Jimmy," Tara said stubbornly.

"Whoever." Ashley waved a hand in the air. "You're missing the point. Obviously he's a very well-behaved gentleman."

"He's more than that," Mary suggested seriously.

"What do you mean?"

Mary smiled and tossed her rich mass of hair over her shoulder. "Children, children, while you gibber and speculate, I take things into hand. I checked up on the man."

There was a stunned silence in the room. Mary, enjoying her moment, walked regally toward the sofa. Ashley was quick to sit up and give her room. Cassandra and Tara glanced at each other and hurried over to her.

Tara planted her hands on her hips and stared down at Mary squarely. "Well?"

"His name is Rafael Tyler—"

"Mary!" Ashley snapped. "We all know that!"

"Aha! But do you know what that means?"

"No, what?" Tara demanded.

"Well..." Leisurely, Mary stretched out, setting her long legs on the coffee table, studying her blood-red nail polish.

"Mary, get to it!" Tara persisted.

Mary drew her legs up and smiled excitedly. "He can't be after your money, Tara. He's incredibly wealthy. He inherited one of the largest fleets of privately owned ships in the world. He also owns at least a dozen fine jewelry stores—somebody in his family learned early that the Caribbean ports could legally supply wonderful gems that could be sold in the States. Oh, and of course, the stores are all over the Caribbean, and South America, too. They're called Tyler and Tyler. Not terribly original, perhaps, but I doubt that he named them. His father was a sailor out of Glasgow who found the American Dream."

Tara lifted her eyebrows. "Sounds all right so far," she murmured. Mary still looked excited.

Tara grimaced. "Go on. You're going to choke on your information if you don't get it all out soon."

Mary laughed. "Okay. The man has never been married. He's considered one of the most eligible bachelors in the world. He sails, races, plays polo and keeps his finger on the pulse of his varied interests. He could court heiresses—or princesses!—and be considered quite suitable."

"So why would he be interested in Tara?" Ashley queried, confused.

"Thanks a lot!" Tara told her.

"Well, you're not a princess. Or an heiress."

"He doesn't need money!" Cassandra exclaimed. "Just love! I think it's marvelous. Just like a fairy tale. He sees her once. Their eyes lock across a crowded room—"

"It was an empty museum," Tara said matter-of-factly.

"Oh, quiet! You're destroying my fantasy!" Mary said, annoyed. She cleared her throat dramatically. "Their eyes meet—and it's love at first sight. Passionate, desperate love. He trails her, he finds her, he sweeps her away to a life of luxury—"

"She already lives in a penthouse overlooking the park," Ashley interjected, laughing. "And she isn't exactly cleaning out chimneys at the moment, either."

"It's still just like a fairy tale," Cassandra persisted.

Tara shook her head, looking at Mary. "That's all? You didn't discover anything...strange about him?"

"Strange? No. He's done a great deal of traveling. Seems his father believed that a young man should follow his calling. He could have had a cushy job from the beginning, but he joined the navy instead, then worked his way through foreign shipyards. Oh! He's been in on a few smuggling busts."

Tara stiffened instantly. "So that's it! He thinks I'm a smuggler."

Cassandra giggled. "You arrest smugglers—you don't take them to French restaurants for dinner."

"Mary, where did you get your information?"

"I've got a friend at the bank where Tyler keeps lots and lots of his money."

"You still don't trust him?" Ashley asked Tara. She fastened her zipper and walked idly to the door. "Why?"

"I don't know," Tara murmured.

"Give him a chance!" Cassandra exclaimed. "Do you know what happens to old models, Tara?"

She smiled. "No, Cassie. What happens to old models?"

"They shrivel up and die—all alone—unless they fall in love and get married."

"Thanks. I'll keep that in mind."

"Well, you'd better decide quickly what you're feeling!" Ashley whispered, hurrying back over to the sofa. "He's out there again—with old George eating right out of his hand!"

"He's what?"

"He's out in the showroom again."

They all jumped up and hurried to the door. Ashley was right. He was talking to George, who was gesticulating in flushed pleasure.

Rafe was in black again. A stunning black tux with velvet lapels, a starched white, pleated-front shirt, black cummerbund and a deep maroon ascot.

Tara moved back into the room and leaned against the wall.

"I wonder where you're going, Cinderella!" Cassandra breathed.

Tara looked over at Mary, who always seemed to be so steady and poised.

"Good God! Don't be an idiot! Grab him!" said Mary, which Tara found no help at all.

"George is coming back here!" Ashley said. She was right again. George, wearing a wonderfully pleased expression, was hurrying toward them.

He came in and shut the door, staring at Tara. "The theater! Tyler has plans for the theater. It's quite possible the photographers will be there. You must wear a Galliard design. The black, Tara, with the sequined flounces. That will be perfect! Sexy and austere all at once!"

Tara wasn't sure whether to be indignant or amused. "What am I going to see, George?"

"See? What? Oh! The Albee play. What did he say the name of it was? Oh, what difference does it make? A Galliard girl on the arm of *the* Rafe

Tyler. What matters is what you *wear!*"

She yawned elaborately. "I think I'll have to give him an apology, George. I'm so tired these days. And you were commenting on how awful I looked—"

"Don't be absurd, *ma chérie!*" There was mild irritation in his voice—desperation, too. "Really, Tara, how can you be so ungrateful? You needn't worry about sleep. Your fittings are well along. You can sleep late tomorrow."

"A day off?" Tara queried sweetly.

"What?" George blustered.

"I'm down to where I believe Madame is sticking me with pins for the fun of it," Tara told him.

"Oh, for heaven's sake, then. Fine, fine. You've got the day off. Just get the black on and wear it with élan!"

"I'll do my very best, George," Tara promised.

He nodded, turned around in a daze and left them. They were all silent for a minute; then they burst into laughter.

"What more could you want from a man?" Mary asked, and they all laughed again.

Ashley pinched Tara's cheek. "Well, you get into that black dress, *ma chérie*. And take your time. I'm going to run out and cheerfully greet tiger-man and see if old George won't pull out that marvelous ancient Scotch of his again!"

"Sounds good to me!" Mary agreed.

Cassandra chuckled. "Now, now. We make a ridiculous amount of money. We can afford our own Scotch."

"But it's so much more fun to drink George's!" Ashley retorted, rolling her beautiful eyes. "Especially with Tara's tiger-man. If she blows this thing, I'll be around to console the poor fellow." She grinned at Tara. "Get out there and be beautiful, kid!"

Tara grinned as the others left her. She went to the rack and found George's grand creation. It *was* a stunning dress. And it suited her coloring well.

She paused, hoping there would be no photographers around. She didn't want the mud raked up by the press again; George should have thought of that.

She shook her head. His creations were all George ever thought about.

He was internationally known—a sleeveless cotton blouse by George Galliard cost well over a hundred dollars. But it was a two-way street. Galliard clothed the rich and the famous—and the rich and famous had made Galliard because they wore his clothing.

And, she thought, smiling smugly, she had earned a day off. Not a bad agreement. Maybe she had something to thank Rafe for after all.

Minutes later she entered a scene much like the one she had encountered the day before. Rafe, totally resplendent, her three color-coordinated and bewitching friends arrayed around the bar—George amid them, the supreme ruler.

They were chattering when she came out. All of them except Rafe.

He stared at her in a fashion that was bewitching in itself.

Stared at her as if she was a goddess suddenly descended to the earth. Silent, still, a golden message of enchantment in his eyes. He didn't move; he didn't come toward her.

For a moment she couldn't move either. She could only meet his eyes, feel their golden heat. Feel it move into her, enthrall and hypnotize her. Become liquid and mercurial as it swept through her, making her feel dizzy, as if the room were spinning, as if the world had faded away...as if there were only the two of them. Meant to come together, the earth itself screaming that it should be so.

Ashley broke the spell. "George! My God, that's a stunning creation."

"Woman," Rafe corrected her.

And he stepped forward, coming to her. Reaching out a hand. She raised her own slowly; he enfolded it in long, strong fingers.

"My God," he breathed, his eyes locking with hers, then moving slowly over her bare shoulders and the cleavage displayed by the silken bodice and velvet trim. Over the length of her body, hugged and draped by fabric. To the slit along her thigh, the froth at the ankles.

It must have been at that precise moment, she would think later, when magic entered the night. It was the way that he looked at her, the way that *he* looked. So tall, so elegant and so darkly masculine.

Suddenly she wasn't aware of anything around her. She knew only the light in his eyes. The subtle but persuasive scent of his after-shave. The shivery feel of heat and energy that surged around him, engulfing her. She felt his hand on hers; she felt that this was a fantasy, that this was magic. And maybe she did feel a little bit like Cinderella at the ball—

she'd danced that first dance with the prince of her dreams, and she was falling in love. There was something so right about him. Not in appearance, not in height or stature or any other tangible way. Just him. His touch. The message in his eyes.

Had he been dressed in rags, she would have felt it. The absolute need to put her hand in his, and with that, the trust she couldn't logically give him.

"Shall we?" he murmured, and she nodded, unsure of her voice.

George said something to her; the others all waved and called good-bye. Ashley came running out with Tara's silver fox fur, and she accepted it gratefully.

Then they were out on the street, where his limousine awaited them. He ushered her in.

"Are you cold?" He adjusted the fur more closely around her shoulders. She shook her head.

He sat back. Day was still with them, fading to twilight. She could see his features so clearly: all the hard and handsome planes; all that was rough and rugged; all that was keenly beautiful. All that created that most intricate animal—man.

And still the magic held her. Held her so firmly that she could not find words to speak.

He reached over and took her hand, brought it to his lips and kissed it with a bewitching reverence. His eyes had not left her.

He touched her cheek. "Do you really want to see a play?"

"I love plays."

"That's not what I asked. Do you really want to see a play right now?"

God help her. She shook her head. She knew what she was saying, what she was doing. She hadn't had a single drink; but she knew exactly what she was saying by not speaking.

He watched her for a moment. Something inside her cried that she should protest, that she should ignore all she felt and gaily say that she was just dying to go to the theater.

He wouldn't have protested. He would have gone ahead. And he would have been a charming companion for the whole evening. He would have taken her to dinner, and then he would have taken her home, and he would have left her at her door with a good-night kiss that would have left her aching for more.

But she didn't speak.

He tapped on the dividing window and murmured something to the chauffeur, then sat back.

They stopped in front of an apartment complex that was nearly as well known as Rockefeller Plaza. Dear Lord—she couldn't think of the name of the place. It wasn't far from hers.

The chauffeur didn't appear. Rafe himself helped her from the car.

The doorman greeted him deferentially. Tara felt her lips lift in a smile as he nodded to her.

The lobby was muted luxury. Marble and oak, ferns and pillars. The elevators were subtly etched in gold.

She still didn't speak as they entered and rose high above the world, high above any normal concerns.

The elevator door opened. Tara would have stood still, staring blankly at the door. But her hand was still in Rafe's, and he was walking, so she followed.

A few steps brought them to a set of double doors. Rafe opened them and released her, standing slightly behind her to turn on a light.

She blinked, seeing the place arise from the darkness.

They were up on the roof, on the corner, and both sides of the back wall were glass, looking out on a panoramic view of the city, of the park. The stars were reachable through those sparkling panes. Even the moon—she could stretch out a hand and touch it, and she reflected that perhaps she already had.

It was contemporary, completely so. Mexican tile flooring in the entry gave way to deep pile beige carpet, white leather sofas, and a redbrick and copper fireplace. To the far left of the windows was a door, so artfully planned by some architect that it blended with the open beauty of the room yet led out to the balcony, where the heavens would seem even closer.

A little breathlessly, Tara stepped into the room, down from the Mexican tile to the sunken carpeting beneath. The fur trailed from her shoulders.

Watching her, Rafe could barely breathe. As usual, she was part real, part fantasy, her hair a golden contrast against the black of her gown, the silver fur just dangling over her shoulder. Her other shoulder bare.

Long, lithe, slim, elegant. He swallowed. What was it that she had? Whatever it was, it went far beyond the obvious. Was it the silver mercury of her eyes, the timbre of her voice? Motionless, poised, she might have been Tara the model, the face and shape that had seduced and enticed from a million pages of print. And that alone could humble a man.

But it was in motion that she had enchanted him. In motion that she had gazed, spoken, whispered, touched. It was the essence of the woman that had been his downfall. Something inside her, something undiscernible.

He followed her, reaching for her coat. "Do you like it?"

"It's spectacular."

"I like the sky."

"Yes."

Rafe set her fur over a chair. He moved to the left, to the kitchen, which was done in white and chrome. His fingers were shaking when he opened the refrigerator.

"Wine?"

It seemed that she hesitated, that she trembled.

"Yes, please. May I—may I go out?"

"Of course. I'll be right with you."

Tara stepped across the room to the camouflaged door; it opened to her touch. The chill hit her as she stepped out. She shivered and wrapped her arms around herself but did not think to return for her coat.

Night had come in full. There were plants on the balcony, fragrant from a recent rain. The sky seemed a blanket of velvet, and she had the feeling that she was wandering in that velvet.

He came up behind her, offering her a fluted stem glass from behind. She clutched it and sipped from it too quickly. Almost like a drowning man reaching for straws...

He touched her then. His body, the length of it behind her. His hand upon her shoulder pulling her close against him. His fingers stroking her neck. His breath falling upon her with warmth.

Tingling, rippling sensations played havoc throughout her. He simply stood there, and she felt liquid. She wanted him.

She closed her eyes. It had been two years. Two years since that horrible last time with Tine. Two years since she had felt that everything inside her had died, that she could never want anyone again, that she could never feel again...

She was afraid. Eager, anxious, nervous—and afraid.

"I've ordered dinner," he murmured, and she nodded.

He pointed over her shoulder to the stars. "Ursa Major. Perseus. Cassandra."

"You know them all?"

"Most. You learn the stars when you sail a lot. On a ship, in the middle of the ocean, it's as if they're all that exists. You feel very small."

"I can't believe you would ever feel small."

"Any man can feel small."

He paused, lightly rubbing his cheek against her hair, inhaling its clean fragrance. The night, the sea, the stars. They should have been a perfect opening, he thought. He could have quizzed her about sailing, asked her about Caracas.

No. He couldn't. Something had touched them. Something unique. He could no more end it than he could cut his own throat. He felt her tension; he felt the need to walk on eggshells, to hold the magic.

She sipped her wine and said nothing. For the longest time they stood there, staring at the stars, silent. And through all that time it grew. The knowledge, the awareness. His hard body against hers. Her soft one leaning against his.

At last she heard a little buzzer. He excused himself. Through the glass panes Tara saw two men arrive with silver serving dishes.

She turned back to study the night and sip her wine. Seconds later, Rafe was back. The men were gone. He led her back in and seated her, filling her wineglass again, dexterously removing lids from chafing dishes and filling her plate—seafood tonight. A thick bisque of shrimp and scallops and *langoustines*. Delicate puffs of rolls. Asparagus salad.

"You serve food superbly," she told him, trying to joke.

"I've worked in food service. I cook superbly, too."

"How commendable—if it's true."

He laughed. "Someday you can judge for yourself."

He sat down, and they lifted their wineglasses to each other.

It was then that she began to tremble. Really tremble, so that her glass tilted precariously.

She didn't know that her face had turned pale, that her hair was sun gold, her lips rose red against it.

Quickly, anxiously, he was on his feet. More quickly still, he was at her side, on one knee, rescuing her glass, taking her hands in his.

Fire, electricity, all the tension of the evening leaped between them. He looked into her eyes.

"You're afraid of me," he murmured.

"I'm just...afraid."

"I'll take you home." He started to rise.

"No!" She caught his hand; she still quivered. She lowered her head and idly inspected his fingers. And then she looked at him with such whimsical, wistful appeal that it seemed his heart had stopped.

"Will you be tender? Patient?"

It was that softly voiced question, the haunted emotion that colored it, the melody of her voice, the quiver of it more than anything, that ensnared his heart completely. Not her beauty, not her form, not even the wonder of her scent.

It was all that she laid at his feet in that moment.

He brought her hand to his lips and kissed her palm, then met her eyes again.

"Always," he vowed.

CHAPTER 7

Stars were part of a dream, part of fantasy, part of illusion. A velvet-dark sky, rhinestoned with stars.

This wasn't illusion; it was reality.

Tara didn't know what else was in the apartment. Another bedroom, perhaps; a study. She only knew that there was a hallway that passed by the kitchen, that they came to a room where not only the window was of glass but also a pane of the ceiling above them.

She'd been only dimly aware of the hallway, vaguely, from some distant frame of consciousness. She was acutely aware of Rafe's eyes, for during the passage from living room to bedroom, she never lost contact with his golden gaze. It *was* something from a dream: a tall, dark, handsome stranger sweeping her into his arms, carrying her up a short flight of steps from one level to the next.

And then there were the stars.

She saw them instantly, of course, when he laid her on the bed and stretched out beside her.

Larger than life, vivid, eclipsing any other sensation she had ever known.

Something, some logical swell of reason, warned her that he was a stranger—a man she barely knew. But raw emotion cried out against logic and won. She had known this was coming; she had wanted it. From the first time she had seen him, she had felt fascination, excitement, even a touch of fear at the power he had. And she was drawn....

She felt his hand on her cheek, and she swallowed slightly, bringing her eyes from the stars to meet his.

I barely know him! she reminded herself in desperation.

But it did no good, for she felt at that moment that she knew all that she needed to, that she knew him very well. She knew that he was somehow aware of her fear, that he would handle that fear like fine crystal and ease it from her. She knew it all over again, meeting his gaze, feeling his absolute hunger....

And a fascination to match her own.

He leaned over her, slowly. Then touched her lips with his, gently, then searingly. His mouth over hers, his tongue a sensual promise of everything to come. The sudden change was strident, like the sweeping wind of a storm. She caught her breath; she knew no more fear, for the passion as he delved into her mouth with heat and fire was something that demanded to be met, and meet it she did.

The wanting that had begun in fantasy, that had been denied, now spilled out through her. She felt his kiss not with her mouth, but with her body. She responded instantly, fingers digging into the rich dark length of his hair. She was tense, but completely alive, a drumming sounding through her blood, through her limbs, like lava, running, playing....

Wanting.

He moved away from her. In the starlit darkness she watched him swiftly shed his clothing, fluidly, each movement innately graceful.

Like a smoothly muscled cat, so beautiful in form, graceful in any motion, vital, corded, unique.

She stared at him and didn't know that she did so; she recorded in memory all the little things she could catch with the stars as illumination. The breadth of his shoulders, his long torso and longer legs, sinewed, sleek. A thick forest of dark hair on his broad chest, which tapered downward to the point where his sexuality so brazenly, urgently appealed to her senses.

She closed her eyes, shivering, thinking that she should be frightened. That she should have inhibitions, natural reservations, since it had been so long, and the last time had been...

Her mind blocked out the thought. Blocked out everything but the wonder of him. The tiger, the hunter, the magnificent beast, as captivated as she, a vow that he swore with his eyes, that leaped silently into her heart.

He didn't think he'd ever trembled before a woman, yet he quivered now. Then again, he, who was not whimsical at all, wondered if she was really a mortal woman. No one had eyes like hers, silver like the glow of the stars. Hair that touched his pillow like spun gold. A face like the finest porcelain, heart-shaped, classic, innocent...

Trusting.

So exquisitely beautiful that it was haunting. As anxious as he was, he could have stood like a spellbound kid, fascinated because she lay on his bed.

He lowered his eyes from hers, stopped at the foot of the bed and unlaced her high-heeled sandals. That contact alone sent his heart thudding.

She made a slight sound. He kissed her again, savoring the kiss, savoring her scent. He knew the perfume, but on her it was unique.

He drew her up to him as he kissed her, finding the zipper of her gown and pulling it down, and with that rasping sound, he felt his excitement increase, rushing and roaring like a tide, sweeping from his loins to his limbs and back again. She was so light. Easy to maneuver, easy to divest of Galliard's magical gown. No, it wasn't the gown. It was the woman.

Beneath the gown was some other magical creation. A strapless teddy thing in sheer, midnight silk. A sound escaped him as he saw her breasts hugged, outlined, erotically draped by it, and he dipped his dark head, taking her nipple, material and all, into his mouth. He heard an answering moan escape her, vaguely, distantly, for the feel of her nipple tautening and swelling within his mouth was almost more than he could bear. Another sound escaped him, and he swept away the material, once again impatiently maneuvering her form, stripping off her clothes with quick resolve.

He burned to hold her, but he held back.

Never, in picture, in substance or in imagination, had there been so perfect a woman. Slender neck; firm, full breasts; slim waist; a provocative flare of hips; and shapely legs that knew no end. No artist's brush needed to touch her to soften flaws, for there were none. She was beautifully, passionately formed, golden and glowing. In wonderful, elegant color, cream and gold, silver and rose. And her eyes...

A rain of diamonds, shimmering silver. Beckoning, trusting, innocent, vulnerable. He could see the rise and fall of her breasts, the slightest sign of movement.

Was this what Jimmy had felt? Had his brother, once upon a time, fallen in love with those eyes, with the innocence, with the vulnerability, with the trust?

His hands knotted into fists at his sides. This was it; this was every-thing that he had planned. Coldly, meticulously. He'd needed to get close to her. This close. Now he needed to know her, to win her trust, to fol-low her, to find the truth.

His fingers loosened.

It was impossible to be cold. Impossible not to believe.

In her. In magic. In the waves that engulfed them, that radiated be-tween them.

He'd promised tenderness. He'd promised patience. He hadn't said a word tonight about love, but that was hers, too, because he was falling, falling. He despised himself for a fool, but it was the simple truth.

He returned to her and engulfed her in his arms. Took her lips again in fire, plied his tongue within her mouth as he would his body within hers.

And touched her. Oh, yes, he touched her. Her shoulders, her breasts, the elegant line of her back, the thrust of her hips. He felt her kiss, her tongue inside his mouth, her lips, against his. Breaking from his, nibbling his.

He stared at her again. Brought his palm against the line of her cheek.

Her lashes fell. "I shouldn't be here," she said softly, in a tone of awe, not of protest.

"It was inevitable," he murmured. He couldn't endure even those sec-onds away from her flesh. He kissed the upper swell of her breast, then the lower curve, and finally took the delightful pink crest of her nipple into his mouth.

Her fingers dug into his hair, holding him close. "Since the museum," she said, trembling.

"The museum." His words were throaty against her flesh. He moved against her softness. She could feel him, hard, hot, against her thigh.

"Since the museum," he agreed.

"You were stalking me."

"I was watching you."

"Stalking. Like the tiger."

He paused, and she was horrified that she had spoken, for she thought she might truly die if he left at that point.

He lay at her side once more and caught the wings of her hair in his hands, staring intently into her eyes.

"Stalking...as if I were prey," she whispered, and, again, wondered why she had spoken when her whole body burned for him, when all the terrors of the past had been forgotten, when she had put blind faith in instinct and intuition, knowing that she was hopelessly—if foolishly— falling in love.

A rueful smile curved his lips as he gazed at her, his body so hard against hers, his eyes so intense, muscles taut.

"No, Tara, I am your prey. The hunter is the hunted."

His lips touched her ear, his teeth teased the lobe, and he murmured as if in awe, "My God. I wonder how I've lived without you. Without this...feeling. This wonder."

She wound her arms tightly around him. Something vague reminded her that she hadn't trusted him.

She knew that she could trust his words now. That whatever mysteries there might be about him, this much was true. Here was reality. Here was magic. Between them.

And sensation.

"Ohh..." The gasp escaped her as his kisses, ragged, urgent now, roamed her breasts again, and then beyond.

He touched her, moved her. Gently, demandingly, softly—urgently. She arched to him; she could lie still no longer. She rose, flinging her arms around his neck, feverishly kissing his shoulders, his chest, nipping slightly, testing his reactions to her lips and tongue against his nipples, her hands exploring the length of his back. He groaned softly and let her play, until the groan began to come from somewhere deep in his chest and the heat seemed to spew and sizzle between them. She found herself once again on her back, her fingers entwined with his, her eyes locked with his.

His face taut, beautiful, above her. His body wedged between her thighs. He lowered himself, not entering her, teasing, testing, watching her expression, savoring the little sounds that escaped her, the wonder on her face, making it glow, making it ever more beautiful.

Then she cried out; her fingers eluded his, and she touched him, shivering slightly, a little unsure, brought back to a delirium of passion by his husky whispered words of pleasure, of encouragement.

"Yes, take me. Oh, yes...." He raised himself slightly, watching as they joined together. Holding his weight, holding himself, sinking into her fully, completely, then holding tight once more as her body absorbed him, and watching her face again.

"Yes. Take me. Hold me. Tara..."

She thought that she would burst, that she would scream, and yet her body absorbed him, adoring him. She marveled at the slow, painstaking way he held her and then plunged, withdrew, and stroked....

"Ohh..." She wrapped her arms around him, burying her face against his neck, almost ashamed of the terrible rush of pleasure that consumed her. He stroked her hair; he held her; he whispered.

And lost control.

Deliciously, for by then she was arching to him, reaching. She wanted to hold on forever; she was almost desperate for that intangible thing she craved.

It was the best thing in the world. The best feeling. Being a part of her. He wanted it to go on forever. He held and held, and then release swept through him in great, erratic waves, trembling, pulsing.

From him to her. Like the heat that had brought them together. He arched in his turn, strained, taut, muscles rippling, felt that great fall of unbearable sensation, so great that he nearly collapsed, yet did not. The shudder that came rippling from her, washing him with the flow of her ecstasy, was sweeter still.

Only then did he take her tightly in his arms and roll with her, still a part of her, and determined to be so as nature brought them both back slowly from her splendor.

They were sleek, damp, breathing heavily, and still one. Their hearts pounded. Their breathing eased first, and then the drumbeats of their hearts.

Neither spoke. He had to touch her hair, so golden in the starlight.

And still she didn't speak.

"It was inevitable," he told her very softly.

"I know."

"Are you sorry?"

She moved at last, rising above him. He saw the beauty in the classic lines of her face, the passion in her eyes.

"No, Rafe, never. Never sorry for tonight!"

He smiled and placed an elbow beneath his head, pulling her back to his chest.

"Never—for tonight. Does that mean that I'm supposed to get up and take you home now?"

"I can go by myself—"

"No way," he told her flatly, then spun with a fluid motion, bringing her beneath him, eyeing her with determined passion, and a bit of devilry, too.

"Don't tell me that you have to be anywhere. You have tomorrow off. And you're going nowhere, love. Magic may only come once in a life-time—I'm not letting mine slip away. I'm going to wake up beside you and know that you're real, and then I'm going to make love with you by daylight."

For a moment he thought that she was going to protest. That she was going to panic and insist on going home.

But she smiled. Slowly. A sensuous smile, a beautiful smile that played upon the senses and sent his pulse reeling once again. Lazily, lan-guidly, gracefully, she stretched out her arms, then wound them around him, arching her body slightly, wickedly taunting him with the thrust of her exquisite breasts.

"We're waiting for morning?" she inquired innocently.

"No. Oh, no!" he told her.

And as his arms tightened around her once again, he lowered his head, his mouth moving hungrily over one of those exquisite mounds that had tortured him with such pleasure.

She responded with a gasp and then a soft siren's moan, sending him spiraling into an endless sea of sensation....

There were no longer stars overhead when they awoke. The sky was a beautiful blue, just touched by soft white clouds.

Tara was staring at that sky, and Rafe watched her silently, not moving.

His first thought on waking was wonder—that she should be there. Blond and luxurious, awakening from sleep in his bed. Innocent again, for though their legs were entwined, the sheet was cast just below her shoulder, and despite the abandon of the night, she appeared as sweetly virginal as Venus rising from some magical seabed.

Innocent...

He closed his eyes fleetingly, wondering if his resolutions of the evening could stand up to daylight. There would always be that infini-tesimal difference between night and day. Darkness always brought a gentle velvet cloak to hide scars—and suspicions.

He shook his head slightly, a smile ruefully curving his lips. No. Nothing was gone. He was still in love. If he was a fool he was a fool, and the hell with it.

But then there was Jimmy.

He inhaled. There was only so far a fool could go. He couldn't tell her anything, not yet.

He exhaled. The great, momentous changes inside him couldn't really mean anything. He still had to follow her. To find out if she was a victim, or a catalyst, perhaps.

His heart pounded. Now he had more reason than ever to follow her. To be with her. If she was innocent, if she was returning to the scene of past tragedy, more than ever, so much more than ever, he had to be with her. To guard her against—

Whatever might come.

And then, of course, when he gazed at her again, he saw how she watched the sky above her.

What were her thoughts? Regret, as she mulled over the implications of the night? Strangers and lovers. Was she wondering how to escape? Wishing desperately that she had smiled and said, Oh, dear, no! I wouldn't miss the play for anything!

He touched her cheek. Her eyes, those silver eyes that might have launched a thousand ships, met his instantly. And to his vast relief she offered him a smile, soft and somehow shy, and touched with the same wonder he had known himself.

But there was something more. As if she denied nothing and gave him all—except some thought, some resolution, something that she was holding back.

"You're not sorry?" he murmured.

"No, never sorry," she replied.

He kissed the tip of her nose.

"George is going to be furious," she murmured. "No pictures of his elegant gown in the society pages."

"We'll see that he gets his pictures eventually."

"Oh!" she said suddenly, fumbling to pull her arms from the sheets to gaze at her watch. "It's nearly twelve—"

"You've got the day off," he reminded her.

She laughed easily, relaxing on the pillows. But then she bolted up again, driving him half mad, because the sheet slipped and he was reminded in full, glorious daylight that she had the most beautiful breasts he had ever seen.

"You've got an appointment! At twelve. Remember? You're supposed to be taking your stepmother in for a showing."

"Are you trying to destroy a magnificent day?" he asked her, only half teasing. "Myrna is a grown woman. She's quite accustomed to going into the city."

"Shouldn't you call her?"

"I never intended to accompany her."

"Oh." She paused a minute, studying him, arching a brow slightly. "Curious, isn't it? You wanted Ashley to model for her."

He chuckled softly, rising above her. "What's so curious? I wanted you with me."

"You planned the whole thing?"

"Not exactly. I really had planned on the theater."

"And after?"

"It's always been your choice," he told her softly.

Tara wondered if she believed him or not. His dark lashes had fallen over his eyes with his words, and she shivered slightly. Was she mad...falling in love so quickly, so completely, when it seemed that there were still mysteries here? Things unsaid that she couldn't begin to pinpoint? A sense that...

He caught her hands and brought her back to the bed. He kissed her vibrantly, passionately, impatiently kicking the covers aside and laying the urgent hardness of his body against hers, brazen, bold, so sensually demanding that she responded in kind. He called to her, aggressive and sure; she sighed quite naturally. Her breath caught as he touched her. Excitement surged through her, and feelings of love and need overwhelmed her again.

He was impossible to deny. He was a force of high, windswept excitement. She loved the excitement, the absolute intensity. The male power that called on everything female within her. The feeling of his tongue within her mouth, the warm, living power of his body pulsing against hers, joining them.

She did think—vaguely—before she was so swept up in his rhythm that nothing mattered except the culmination of the passion that raged between them.

Today was his. Today was fantasy. And then she would withdraw, from

him and—with much more effort—from herself. From the all-encom-
passing need he was creating.

She almost sobbed, for so many things combined. The feel of him.
The spiraling desire. The soaring emotion that told her there was more,
that she loved his touch, his smile, his voice, the way he held her hand,
walked with her, talked to her.

Looked at her. With a tiger's eyes. Golden. Possessive, wonderful, alluring, exciting.

Mercury filled her body with heat. After all this time, to know a touch
that thrilled...

She wanted to lie beside him forever. To share his life. To waken in
the morning with his head on a pillow beside her.

She wanted to marry him.

To hear his slightly wicked laugh and have him take her like this, anytime, and know that it was real....

He rose above her, watching her body. Moving. Murmuring.

"Oh, yes...Tara, you're beautiful. Take me in, take me in. Let me see
this...us..."

A cry escaped her. Tremors began to wrench her body...his. He
shuddered in his final climax, collapsing against her, slick, sated; holding her still; murmuring something that caused a milder tremor to
shake her.

She didn't dare look at him. She closed her eyes and pressed her face
against the dampness of his chest.

It had to wait, it had to wait, it had to wait. She needed to go away, to
avoid seeing him again. She'd been with him now. She knew that it was
like nothing on earth, and everything that love was intended to be.

It couldn't be an affair. It couldn't be casual. It couldn't be lost. It had
to be real and forever, or it could be nothing.

Then what was it that still worried her?

After all this, why did she feel the niggling suspicions, the remainder
of mistrust?

How could she have done this? She, who had been hurt so badly, taken
in so blindly. She, who knew that love could grow bitter.

He pulled her atop him, and she almost smiled, forgetting her fears,
because the look on his face was simply so male. So triumphant, his
golden eyes gleaming like topaz.

"My God, I love you!" he declared intensely, voice low but seeming to shake slightly.

And her smile deepened wistfully. "Do you really?"

"I do."

She lay against him, her heart beating, her thoughts a prayer.

Let it be true.

Please, God, let it be true.

He *was* a wonderful cook, she discovered. He made fabulous omelettes with tiny shrimp and a delicious creole sauce. They ate in bed, loosely clad in robes, beneath the extraordinary blue of the sky.

For a moment she felt as if her heart had stopped, because she realized suddenly that he was, by nature, a passionate and volatile man, and his bed had probably played host to any number of women.

Jealousy streaked through her, painful and cruel. She lowered her eyes to her plate, then realized that he was studying her intently, smiling slightly as he noticed her change of emotion.

He touched her chin, raising it. "What?"

She shrugged, then laughed—because it was so ridiculous, of course. She'd only known that he existed for a few days.

"I was wondering how many women you'd had with you in this bed."

He made no firm denials. He was silent, watching her for a minute. "We both have pasts."

It was her turn for silence.

Once again she took refuge in staring at her food. He wouldn't let her. He caught her chin again, forcing her to meet his eyes.

"Past. As in Tine Elliott. You're not still in love with the man, are you?"

The question was harsh. Too harsh, she thought.

"No," she said sharply, deciding that the one word was enough; he could take it or leave it.

He continued to stare into her eyes, as if seeking something. Tension seemed to leap around them, in the air, part of them. He released her chin, sighing.

"I think you should marry me," he said.

She looked up at him quickly, laughing.

"What's so funny?"

"We're—we're strangers!" she told him.

He smiled as seductively as any cat, grinning with pleasure.

"Strangers?" he said with such insinuation that she blushed.

"We don't know each other," she said loftily, straightening to what she hoped was dignity, her shoulders squared.

Dignity was lost. Her stretching had pulled the terry material of the robe taut against her form, and with no hesitation he tweaked the rise of her nipple, laughing. "I know you very well."

Tara clutched the robe, nearly dislodging her plate. "I'm being serious and rational."

"So am I."

She shook her head, not knowing whether to laugh, too, or to protest vehemently.

He took their plates and set them aside then scooped her into his arms.

"I really need to get home," she murmured a little nervously.

"No."

"But—"

"Not today."

"Not today!"

"All of today, all of tonight, you're mine. I'll get you home in the morning."

"But this is so sudden. So intense."

"You said that we're strangers. I'm trying to let you get to know me." He caught her hand and brought it to his chest. "Feel my heart, my love. That's all you really need to know, isn't it?" The teasing quality left his voice—she felt he was speaking in earnest.

Yet she wondered if he was querying her—or himself.

"Really. I should simply sweep you away and marry you, and keep you forever and forever."

"I have to leave on a business trip."

"That's all right. Your willing bridegroom will follow."

She smiled and wondered just what had been wrong about his words. She thought she almost had it, but then he was moving again, sweeping her into his arms as he rose from the bed.

"What—"

"A shower. We'll have eaten together, walked together, laughed together—and showered together. 'Getting to Know You.' I'd sing it for you, but I can't carry a tune worth a damn."

With her arms about his neck, her eyes imprisoned by the passion in his, she could do nothing but laugh. "Whistle, then," she commanded, and he obeyed, and she laughed all the while that he brought her into the elegantly modern and squeaky-clean bathroom. He set her down to start the water, then he turned, eyes growing dark as amber, and untied the belt of her robe and eased it from her shoulders.

The shower stall was of beige marble, with curving seats cut into each end. As he plucked her from her feet to set her beneath the stream of water Tara noted that his taste was wonderfully attuned to hers. She loved old things, but she also loved the contemporary flair of his apartment.

Then she wasn't thinking about the apartment at all, because his hands were full of soap and moving over her body. Over her breasts, along her hips, between her thighs.

Gasping for breath, laughing, she tried to elude him, tried to elude the evocative sensation. Finding soap, she returned the caress, catching his eyes as she slowly sudsed his chest, his abdomen, his tightly muscled buttocks, in swirling circles.

Steam whirled around her, and she was absolutely fascinated as she heard the sharp rasp of his breath and watched the sexual tension seize his features, sharpening them, darkening his eyes, straining his cheeks.

Then *she* was left to gasp, for he caught her beneath the arms and spun around, setting her on one of the marble seats, kneeling before her. Suddenly, passionately, aggressively. Laving her navel with his tongue, parting her thighs and moving lower.

She cried out at the excruciating sensation, at the intimacy. Never...never...

She grasped for something to hold. Her fingers raked against the water, then fell into his hair. She whispered incoherently. She begged him to stop, because it was...too good. The feelings, oh, the feelings... She would explode, burst; she would die.

He did not stop. Until she did burst...explode...die a little. Drained, drenched, nearly delirious. Clinging to him, amazed.

He smiled his triumphant tiger's smile, and swept her from the tub, dripping wet, back to the bed. She was still limp. He moved over her and entered her, and she wrapped her arms around him, flushed, holding him.

She was amazed that as he fulfilled himself, he could bring her spiraling along with him once again.

* * *

She felt that she still burned with his touch even as she began to doze off, held in his arms, as the afternoon sun rose above them.

She was in love. Infatuated, insane—in love.

And then she remembered suddenly what had bothered her about his teasing declaration that they should marry.

He had said that he would follow her on her trip.

An odd thing, she thought, for her tiger to say. There were things that she did not know about him.

He should merely have said that he would sweep her away. From all of it. From her work, from Galliard. That he would hold her and have her and keep her forever.

That was what he *should* have said.

She shivered, convincing herself more thoroughly that if what they shared was real, he would be here when she returned. That he would wait.

And then the burning sensation swept through her all over again, as she remembered the way she had felt when he had...

She closed her eyes tightly.

She had to get away from him so that she could think rationally!

But as if reading her mind, he touched her again, his palm light against her flesh, drawing circles.

She'd promised him today. And tonight.

And perhaps it was something that she owed herself.

Tomorrow—away from him—she would be strong and rational. She would simply decide not to see him again until she returned, and that was how it would be.

But for the moment...

She felt his kiss against her spine, and she knew that if she had been standing, she would have been weak-kneed, ready to fall.

Today. Tonight.

A soft, strangled sound escaped her. Whatever came, she couldn't deny herself this living fantasy.

CHAPTER 8

"**S**mile, ladies, smile!"

George, sweeping by them—his own smile completely plastic—voiced the command softly, then turned his charm on the next reporter to snare him. He spoke more glowingly of his "girls" than he did of the creations they wore, yet his inflections were so perfect that any woman hearing him would think that the man was entirely too modest and that it was his stunning genius with material that gave the young women their beauty.

Tara smiled obediently. Flashbulbs snapped, and, blinded, she kept smiling and moving along with the others. The ship was just leaving port; confetti was streaming over the sides, balloons were flying, and there was a tremendous bustle all about. The casinos weren't open yet, but waiters were rushing around with free "Island Coolers," and it seemed that everyone aboard had gathered on the aft of the lido deck to watch the first showing of either the Galliard fashions or the Galliard girls. Or perhaps the press and the critics—all gathered to pounce on Galliard.

They were all dressed in casual cocktail wear. Ashley was in flowing teal, Cassandra in a mist of soft yellow, Mary in black and white stripes, and Tara in an A-line silk of massive orchids against silver that belted at the waist. As George spoke about the gowns, he called each girl forward, describing the material, the casual air of the dress, the comfort, how easy it was to wear. Reporters questioned him; he answered them with ease.

And they just kept smiling away, pirouetting now and then on command when a new question was broached.

"It's amazing what that man can find to say about fabric," Ashley muttered as she passed Tara.

Tara laughed. "He's an expert with words."

She didn't care. It was just after four o'clock, nowhere near dark, yet the sun was filling the sky in a way that kept the day light and bright, the heat at a minimum. The morning in old San Juan had been fun; they had gambled and shopped. And now, aboard the ship, with the tug pulling them out, a sea breeze was arising that caressed the skin with a wonderful feel. She loved ships; the crew was already proving to be extraordinary, and everything should be absolutely perfect.

And it was perfect. It was. She was going to have a glorious time. Except that...

Except that her mind was being pulled in two directions, and she was too keyed up and nervous to enjoy a thing.

She was going back to Caracas. Back to the "scene of the crime."

Tara tossed her hair across her face, afraid that her professional smile might be slipping. What was she worried about? Tine had disappeared two years ago. He certainly hadn't spent that time waiting for her to reappear. He had never really loved her. He had been crazy about her potential for income. It was likely that he had disappeared into Brazil or Argentina by now. Perhaps he had even moved on to Europe.

She never had to be alone. Never be a target...

But Tine wasn't the only one who had disappeared. Jimmy had disappeared, too. Was that the real reason she had come back? Because she thought that she owed him something? He wouldn't have been involved with Tine if it hadn't been for her.

But that hadn't been the truth, either, because Jimmy, it seemed, had had something that Tine had wanted. The mask.

She shook her head slightly. She didn't want to think about it. But then, of course, it was better than thinking about Rafe, and wondering if she was a fool, if there was really something to fear, if...

This trip would have been beautiful if she could have leaned by the rail with his arms about her, felt the sea breeze while returning his kiss, laughed and talked and looked at the stars far out on the ocean.

She had avoided him. Carefully, completely. He'd come after her at work; she'd slipped out the back. He'd come to her door. She'd ignored him. She'd answered the phone only once, to tell him quietly and determinedly that she was frightened of what was growing between them and that if the feelings were real, they would last. He had laughed and promised to be on the trip, and she had been glad to inform him that the cruise had been sold out for months and months and months—ever since the press had broken the news about Galliard's showings aboard ship.

He had been strangely silent. She'd wished she could have seen his face, his eyes. Then he had spoken softly. "Tara."

"Yes?"

"It's important that you know this. The feelings—they are real. I love you."

"I love you, too. I'm just—afraid." She inhaled sharply, held her breath for a second, then rushed on. "And you know why. You told me yourself. You know who I am—you know about my past."

"Tara, take care."

"I will."

"I need to be with you."

"Rafe, even if there were a way for you to get on that ship, I wouldn't want you to come."

"Unfinished business?" he queried softly, and she didn't know if there was an ironic insinuation in the words or not.

"Because I'm afraid."

"Maybe you should be. All right, take care, Tara."

And he'd hung up. He hadn't said that he'd call her as soon as she got back. He'd simply hung up.

Then, in a frenzy, she'd called the cruise line, checking to see if he'd obtained a reservation. No, he was not listed as a passenger. And no, there wasn't a single booking left.

So she was alone. No, not alone—good heavens, not alone! George was with her, and Ashley and Madame and Cassandra and Mary, and five other employees who ran around and bowed down to George.

There was suddenly a smattering of applause. Ashley nudged Tara. "Move! This is it! We're free! Piña coladas on the foredeck. Sun, wind, sand—"

"There's not a grain of sand anywhere near us," Tara interrupted her.

"But there will be!"

Tara laughed and started to follow her friend through the lounge, but just then she heard one of the reporters call out a question to George, and it was a query that stopped her dead in her tracks.

"I see that Tara Hill is back with you, George!"

"Yes, yes, of course," George responded briefly.

"Going back to Caracas. Tell me—was Miss Hill ever cleared of all the charges?"

"Of course," George replied.

Bless him, Tara thought, but she decided that she was tired of praying that the media would forgive her the past. This was one interview she wanted to handle herself.

"Tara!"

Ashley tried to stop her, but Tara swung around and moved to George's side, linking an arm with him.

"You're Sandy Martin—L.A.? Yes, I thought I remembered you!" She gave the man a bewitching smile. "Mr. Martin, all the charges against me were dropped."

"What about the woman who was killed? You still claim that you didn't know her?"

"I had never seen her before that night."

"And what about the man? The man with no known identity—who you claim existed?"

She laughed, as if the reporter was missing something entirely.

"Mr. Martin, obviously *you* think that someone existed—you ran dozens of pictures of the back of his head!"

A ripple of laughter broke through the crowd. She felt a sway of warmth, as if she had brought this particular audience to her side. Martin had turned red—and for once he seemed to be out of words.

"Do excuse me," Tara murmured.

George gave her a wink. She hurried off after the other girls; they hadn't gone far. Linking arms, they hurried through the lounge, smiling at passengers who gave way for their group.

"Bravo," Mary murmured.

"You think I'm off the hook?"

Ashley laughed. "No. You'll never be off the hook. But you did real well back there, kid. Real well."

"Oh, let's forget that nasty man, shall we?" Cassandra pleaded. "There's an absolutely beautiful-looking, tall, dark officer out there in the most becoming uniform. Let's change and get back on deck, shall we?"

"Two hours and the casino opens," Mary said.

"You and your one-armed bandits." Ashley sighed. "We'll meet out in the hall in ten minutes—okay?"

It was agreed all around.

Galliard's party had a majority of the suites on the main deck—just perfect, in Ashley's opinion, since they wouldn't have to run up and down flights and flights of steps all the time. The two pools and two of the main lounges were forward and aft from their cabin; the casino was just below them, as were the two main dining rooms.

She and Tara were in one suite together; Mary and Cassandra were sharing another. They were wonderful cabins, Tara thought, with two real full-sized beds separated by a dresser, a massive closet—necessary for them!—and even what was an extraordinarily large bath for a cruise ship. Across from the beds was a full-length mirror—another must, Ashley declared, quite pleased with it all.

She spun around with pleasure before pouncing on her chosen bed. "I love it, I love it, I love it!" she declared ecstatically. "Why, Tara, anytime we want—anytime day or night!—we can pick up this wonderful little phone and a gracious room steward will come bearing a silver tray of anything we might want! Breakfast in bed, coffee brought right before my nose! I'm in love."

Tara smiled and dug through her luggage for a sunsuit in white knit. They didn't eat until the late sitting, and she was determined just to sit out in the breeze until dinner. Even her sunsuit, she reflected, was George's creation. They weren't to appear in anything but his designs for the duration of the trip.

She shed her heels, dress and stockings and slid into the little suit, then sank onto her own bed and smiled at Ashley.

"Ash?"

"What?"

"You employ a full-time housekeeper. And she's a love. She'd bring you breakfast in bed anytime you wanted."

"Oh, you're missing the whole spirit of the thing!" Ashley sat up suddenly, eyeing her friend speculatively. "I know what your problem is. You're upset—and you should be—because you left that man behind. You're sitting there with your Galliard Girl smile in place, but underneath..." Ashley rose dramatically, walking to their little draped porthole to look out. "Underneath you're dying. You're wishing that I was nowhere near this room, that you were seated on a sumptuous king-sized bed and that at any moment the door would burst open and there he would be, dark, mysterious, exciting—"

"Ashley, you're getting carried away," Tara said dryly.

"Tell me it isn't true."

"It isn't true." Tara lied, because it was—and it wasn't. She was absolutely determined to be rational and careful about the whole affair. And yet...

Ashley's mere words had set her heart pounding. No, it wasn't her heart. It was her blood. Pulsing, growing warm. It was her breath, catching as she remembered him.

Ashley's lips curled into a taunting smile. "You told us it was the best night you ever had in your entire life. That you'd never imagined people could be so intimate."

Tara flushed. "I should have kept my mouth shut."

Ashley laughed happily. "I'd never have let you! In fact, you did tell me dismally little. And you're a liar. I saw it in your eyes. You'd love to have him sweep right in and—"

"Ashley, I'm not denying a thing about the attraction. But I wanted some distance. That's the truth." She paused suddenly, looking curiously at Ashley. "Did you ever remember what it was that you thought seemed familiar about his stepmother?" Ashley had told her that Mrs. Tyler had been gracious and attractive and charming—and very quiet. And that there had been something familiar about her.

Ashley shook her head.

"I never did put my finger on it. Maybe she just reminded me of Donna Reed or Harriet Nelson or someone like that. I didn't really speak with her, you know. George did a lot of finger snapping. I waltzed in and I waltzed out and he talked. I changed while they sipped champagne and she ordered. She was gone by the time I came out."

Tara laced her fingers behind her head and stared up at the ceiling. "I just wish I knew..."

"Knew what?"

"What the catch was!"

"Oh, God!" Ashley exclaimed, tossing her glorious wealth of auburn hair over her shoulder. "When Prince Charming walks in, Tara, you're not supposed to ask him about the state of the kingdom!"

"Ashley, you're forgetting—I've been used once. By the best."

Ashley chuckled softly. "I imagine that you haven't seen anything yet.

Tine couldn't nearly compare."

"Thanks a lot! So I *am* being used."

"No, no! That's not what I meant. Oh, get up, will you? If I don't get one of those piña coladas soon, I'm going to expire."

"You won't."

"Right on top of you—and you'll be sorry as hell!"

Laughing, Tara rose, and she and Ashley slipped out into the hall, where they were joined a minute later by the others.

Mary's dreams of the slots and Tara's wish to relax in the sun turned out to be just that—dreams and wishes. They were accosted from all sides by people—charming people, for the most part. Ashley did get her piña colada. It seemed that they spent hours answering the same questions, questions about fashion, about George, about the glamour of their lives, about color, makeup, exercise, and on and on.

Tara discovered that she didn't mind a bit. People already seemed to be different—something she had discovered before about cruise ships. It seemed that when you left dry land you left behind the belief that anyone might be a mugger, that being friendly might make you seem like a pervert. It was nice; it kept her mind occupied, and it made her feel great about the whole thing.

Not one person asked her about her past. No one accused her of murder. No one...

Until her friendly reporter "enemy" suddenly appeared at her side again.

"Seems odd, Miss Hill, that you're following your own footsteps. Same trip and all, two years later. What do you think you'll find in Venezuela?"

He was sandy-haired and freckled, with a boy-next-door type of face. Innocuous, friendly.

Like hell.

She smiled. "I'm expecting to find Caracas right where I left it."

He laughed; he didn't redden this time. His smile tightened.

"Some people think, Miss Hill, that you might be going back to look for your lover."

Tara felt her own smile tighten. She strove to remain expressionless— thanks to George's training, it was possible.

"Sorry. Tine and I were through a long time before any of that happened."

"Were you? Or maybe his smuggling really was successful. So successful that he's hoping to find you and smuggle *you* away with him this time to some nice safe haven in South America. Are you sure you haven't been in contact with the man, Miss Hill?"

"No. I'm afraid I haven't."

He was about to say more—another digging, wounding query, she was certain. But suddenly there was a tap on his shoulder. It was one of the ship's officers.

The reporter's eyes widened at the whispered message. "Excuse me!" he muttered excitedly, and Tara was reprieved.

She stared blankly at Ashley. "Saved—by something."

"Another story," Mary supplied ironically.

"What could possibly best Tara?" Ashley demanded innocently. "Illicit love and murder."

"Ashley!"

"Never mind," Cassandra murmured nervously. "Let's escape while we've got the chance. Dinner is in an hour and a half, and we have to go to the captain's reception or cocktail party or whatever it is."

Tara agreed with Cassandra—it was time to escape.

She showered first. When she emerged, wrapped in her towel, she found Ashley studying a door next to the floor-length mirror.

"What are you doing?" she demanded, amused.

"I wonder where it goes."

Tara shook her head, still smiling. "Ashley, it goes into the next suite. I'm sure it's locked. See—there's the closet, and there's the bathroom. And that little door will go right into the next suite. Which will have a door to the closet and a door to the bathroom and another little—locked—door that goes into the *next* suite."

Ashley grinned secretively and shook her head vehemently. "Tara, it isn't locked."

"Well, it should be," Tara said, rubbing her wet hair with a second towel. "I'll speak to the cabin steward about it. Someone has been lax." She paused and shrugged. "Maybe it's someone in our party. Maybe that's why they left it open."

"No. We're the tail end of our group."

"Then I'll say something about it."

Ashley was still standing by the door.

"What are you doing now?"

"Well—it *is* open."

"You shouldn't have even tried it! That's—that's sneaking into someone else's privacy!"

"How do we know that they haven't snuck into ours?"

"Oh, Ashley!"

"Aren't you the least bit curious?"

"No!"

Tara watched her friend. Ashley's fingers were still on the knob. "Ashley."

"Oh, come on!"

"Ashley—all we would see is a bunch of luggage! Or worse—what if someone is in there? We could get nice jabs right in the nose, and we'd deserve it."

"You're right, of course," Ashley said.

"Go take your shower."

"Oh, I can't stand it!"

And Ashley threw the door open.

"No one is in there," she whispered. "We won't get our noses smashed in, which is probably good." She started to giggle. "Could you imagine having to model George's fashions with black eyes? He'd have to make shiners the rage of the season!"

"Get out of there!" Tara warned her.

"Whoa!"

Ashley moved on into the cabin. Tara followed her.

"I wonder who this is for!" Ashley exclaimed.

All the suites had offered a welcoming bottle of champagne and platter of fruit. All the suites were nice.

This one was...

Well, the champagne was Dom Perignon. Tara had never seen half the exotic fruits before. And there were cheeses and pâtés and caviar.

The carpeting was deeper, and there was a single large bed with a soft crimson comforter that matched the full-length drapes.

"We've just got little curtains!" Ashley murmured. "I wonder who is in here? Oh—look! Luggage. Let's read the tags!"

"No," Tara protested—but she was the one approaching the luggage.

Before she could reach it, though, they heard a key turning in the hall-way door. Ashley let out a little squeak; she grabbed Tara's arm and they started to race back to their own cabin.

Ashley grabbed at the connecting door. Panicky, she pushed it the wrong way.

"Damn you, Ashley! Open it!" Tara hissed.

"I'm trying!"

"Someone's coming in."

"I know!"

"We're going to get caught!"

"We'll talk our way out of it."

"Talk our way out of it! Ashley—you're dressed. I'm wearing a towel! I swear I'm going to kill you if whoever is in this cabin doesn't decide to shoot us both!"

"It's going to be all right—"

"Ashley! Don't you ever listen? I don't even have any clothes on!"

Someone—a male someone—cleared his throat behind them.

Guilty as sin, they spun around—just as Rafe Tyler spoke, leaning back comfortably against the wall, watching them with golden amusement.

"I rather like you that way myself. Ashley, what do you think? George Galliard would be horrified, of course, but Tara has such a wonderful way with a towel, she could probably pass one off as his latest in casual wear."

"Oh!" Ashley breathed, and she was so relieved that she started to laugh nervously.

Tara wasn't amused at all. She was horrified, confused—and frightened. The way that he was looking at her...

"What are you doing here?" she snapped.

"That should be my question. After all, ladies, this is my cabin."

"Oh, yes, of course, we're so sorry—" Ashley began.

"What are you doing on this cruise!" Tara interrupted. "I specifically told you not to come!"

He arched a brow. "You told me? This is a cruise ship—a public cruise ship. Not your private property."

"The door wasn't locked." Ashley began to offer excuses, smiling away. "And it just seemed so intriguing. Come on, Rafe, you understand. A woman's curiosity and all that—"

"I don't want to see you," Tara interrupted again.

He lifted a hand. "This is my cabin," he reminded her.

Ashley looked from one of them to the other. "Listen, I really think I should be going now—"

"Ashley, stay!" Tara commanded.

"Ashley, I would like to speak with Tara alone."

"Don't you dare leave me standing here alone with him in nothing but a towel!"

"Tara, come on!" Ashley pleaded. "Be serious! Let me out of this. I mean, after all, the man has seen you in much less than a towel—oops, I mean—oh, please! Let me out!"

She tugged furiously at the door, which still didn't give. Rafe started toward them. Tara clutched her towel and backed away. Ashley smiled nervously and stepped aside.

Rafe twisted the knob—and the door obediently opened without a sound.

"Thank God!" Ashley breathed a sigh of relief and whisked through.

Tara tried to follow her. The door closed before she could do so.

She backed away from him, staring, trying to remain calm. Trying to remain...unaffected.

It wasn't easy; she had fallen in love with him. She should have thought she was in seventh heaven, on a ship with him, sailing away into the horizon, alone, laughing, touching...

But love was a frightening emotion—just as he could be a frightening man. A tiger in the jungle, with golden eyes that seemed to see everything and betray nothing.

"Let me out of here, Rafe," she said flatly.

"Tara—"

"I don't want to discuss it. I told you why I needed to get away, but you're here anyway. You're right—if you managed to book on the cruise, I have no right to want you off. But I don't need to be near you, either. So if you'll excuse me..."

"Tara, damn you!" he said irritably. "I'm here because I love you."

"If you meant that, you'd have given me the time I asked for."

"Tara—"

"Let me out of here! Please!" Her voice rose in desperation. She didn't dare give in; if he touched her, she would be lost. She would be with him again, and she would forget that she had been burned badly once, that there were still several good reasons why she shouldn't trust him.

He moved, opening the door for her. She wanted to rush past him, but she stood still, because she would have to touch him, brush by his windbreaker, to reach the sanctuary of her own cabin.

Sanctuary! A fragile door separated them.

She stood still.

"Tara," he said very softly, "I'm here because I'm worried about you—I'm worried about this trip. I'm here for your safety and your well-being. You want time. I'll give you all the time in the world—once this trip is over."

He was here for her safety.

Then he must think that there was something that she should fear. Something from the past. She wanted to believe him—she also wanted desperately to know what secret it was that he held, why he, too, should feel that this trip might be dangerous.

"I'll see to it that the dividing door is locked," she told him stiffly.

"Don't bother. I'll take care of it."

"Thank you, but I'll feel better if I handle the situation myself."

She fled through the doorway at last. She did brush his jacket. And she felt his scent, with which she had become so achingly familiar, touch her, enwrap her...seep into her.

She almost turned around. She almost slipped her arms around his neck to tell him that she loved him, that she was grateful that he was near, that she would gladly pass through that dividing door every night and sleep in the comfort and excitement of his arms.

The door closed behind her. She heard the bolt slide home.

And then she felt like kicking the door. It seemed that it locked easily from his side—but what about from hers?

Hurriedly, feeling ridiculously naked now that she knew Rafe was less than thirty feet away, Tara swept through her gowns until she found the oriental silk she was to wear that evening. Ashley emerged from the shower just as her friend slipped into the dress and looked at her anxiously.

"My God—you look like a thundercloud."

"I specifically asked him not to come!"

"I wonder how he got the cabin."

"God knows. It seems he can get anywhere he wants to go."

"Well, he is frightfully rich."

Tara didn't say anything. She sat in a huff to pull on her nylons, eyeing the door now and then.

Ashley sat down beside her. "Tara, I don't understand you. He's fabulous. You told me so yourself! A man like him comes along once in a lifetime. If you're lucky, that is!"

"Ashley, that's just the point."

"Oh, God!" Ashley moaned. "He's perfect—so ditch him?"

Tara shook her head. "Ashley, come on! He's mysterious. He's not telling me the whole truth."

"All right. He's a modern-day Bluebeard. He has his last six wives locked up in his mansion out on Long Island."

"Ashley!" Tara sighed.

"Tara!"

"Oh, I give up on you!" Tara moaned. "I'm just trying to protect my heart and soul, okay?"

"Well, thank the Lord you haven't got your virginity to add to that!" Ashley laughed. "I'll take odds that somewhere along the line on this trip *I'm* going to be the one sleeping alone on this side of that door."

Tara clenched her teeth and shot Ashley an evil stare. Ashley didn't even notice.

"Tara!"

"What?"

"I'll lay you a bet."

"On what?"

"I'll bet anything that Rafe was the one who somehow managed to get our reporter friend—the old inquisitor—out of your hair."

A shiver rippled through Tara.

She was convinced that Ashley was right.

CHAPTER 9

The cocktail party was a fun affair that everyone enjoyed—everyone but Tara.

The captain was a charming, handsome Italian, the purser was a charming, handsome Dutchman, and the various other chief crew members were also pleasant. As Tara noticed before, people in general were simply happy to be aboard. They talked, laughed—they relaxed. She wasn't as besieged now by questions as with dance partners, and under normal circumstances she would have been happy just because it was so nice to see so many people so comfortable and at ease.

Except that Rafe walked in about fifteen minutes after they arrived.

She was determined to ignore him. A difficult feat, for as soon as he walked through the doorway, she experienced the whole gamut of emotions that he always elicited. Longing...no one could ever forget being held in those arms. It wasn't even something in the mind; it was miserably physical. A trembling in her limbs, the feeling that the place had grown warm, that she was flushed...

Which she was, she thought, lowering her eyes from those of her dance partner, one of the distinguished, middle-aged chefs. Rafe's very presence was a call to her senses so blatant that it was embarrassing. If she saw him, imagined his scent, heard his voice—she instantly felt a weak shivering inside her, a heat that came straight from her core.

She ached to lie down with him again.

Don't look at him! she commanded herself. But it didn't matter; she knew he was in the room.

Everyone knew he was in the room. She had seen eyes turn when he entered. He had that quality. A presence, strong, hypnotic, fascinating.

Beautifully powerful, like a tiger...

The chef said something to her; she stumbled, stepped on his foot and apologized profusely, and heard his assurance that she could tread on him any time she chose.

She kept dancing with the chef until the charming Dutch purser broke in. But even as she chatted with him about Curaçao, their first port of call, where his native tongue was spoken, she thought about Rafe and could not resist the temptation to glance at him again.

He was dancing with Ashley, whose head was cast back as she laughed delightedly at something he had said.

Jealousy—that evil demon—slipped into Tara's heart again. Ashley was exotic, beautiful, blazing with vitality, sweet and warm. Surely *she* was the better choice for any man.

Tara lowered her eyes again. She gave the purser a dazzling smile, then felt like a fool, because she realized that she was trying to make Rafe jealous while neither Rafe nor Ashley was attempting any such thing— they were just dancing and enjoying each other.

She stepped on the purser's foot, too, and imagined a little bleakly that if they all got together to discuss the Galliard girls, they might shake their heads sadly and agree that the blonde had been a terrible klutz.

At last the cocktail party came to an end. They moved down a deck for dinner. George discussed the first show with them; Tara sipped her wine idly until she noticed that Rafe was sitting at the captain's table. The delicious dinner became totally unpalatable.

When it was over, Cassandra, Mary and Ashley decided to try their hands in the casino—Tara begged off and hurried back to her cabin, then wished she hadn't, remembering that somewhere along the line, Rafe would go into his own.

Ashley didn't stay in the casino long; she returned to the room. Tara pretended to be asleep, but Ashley didn't fall for it; she perched on the foot of Tara's bed. "Dreaming, huh?"

"Trying to sleep."

"No, you're not. You're thinking about the fact that his cabin is just inches away."

"Not inches, Ashley. Feet."

"But still, he'll be right beyond that door."

"Did you have a nice time dancing, Ashley?"

"Lovely. He's not mad at me."

"Why should he be?"

"Well, I did trespass in his cabin. But then, I wonder if he even noticed I was around, what with you there. Especially dressed in that towel and all. He's not mad at you, either."

"Why should he be? I'm the aggrieved party."

"Because he's here? That's absurd."

"No, it's not. It's sensible."

"Sensible. Nice way to spend your life. Lying here, in the dark. In this skinny, single bunk. Imagining that massive bed—just *feet* away. With him in it. Strong arms to hold you. The beat of his heart. The heat of his chest. The pulse, the vitality, the—"

"Ashley, you've been watching the soaps again."

"Okay, Tara. Lie there. Suffer. I just hope you don't talk in your sleep, because it might get a little too erotic for my innocent ears."

"Ashley, haven't you got any more money to lose?"

She laughed. "It's much more fun to torture you."

Tara rolled over. "I'm going to sleep now, Ashley."

Ashley laughed wickedly once again. "Sweet dreams."

"Thanks."

They were docked in Curaçao when Tara awoke in the morning. Determined to get off the boat and onto the island as soon as possible, she rudely shook Ashley awake and called to have breakfast served in their cabin.

She dressed quickly, while Ashley was still attempting to prop her eyes open with her first cup of coffee. "Come on, Ash," Tara urged her.

"We'll stop for breakfast?"

"We'll stop for breakfast. At a lovely little café with a table beneath an umbrella."

"Did you call Mary and Cassandra?"

Tara did. Mary told her that they were going to sleep in—they had stayed up until two in the casino, then danced until almost four.

"What a way to work!" Ashley declared, laughing, and then she managed to crawl out of bed, apply some makeup, and shimmy into one of George's coolly casual cotton jumpsuits.

Tara was already at the door. "Ashley!"

"I'm coming!"

Tara was halfway down the hallway. Ashley puffed along behind her. "What's your hurry?"

"Nothing. The day is young and beautiful."

"It should be. It's seven-fifteen."

They smiled at the man standing guard at the runway, collected re-boarding passes and hurried down. Soon they were in the plaza, and then they were walking along past the storefronts. The buildings were all pastel and charmingly Dutch.

"See, isn't this wonderful?" Tara asked.

"Sure—it's just great. Nothing's open."

Tara made a face and turned a corner, leading them back toward the sea. There was a café at the corner, facing the water. Charmingly colorful umbrellas sat over white wrought iron tables.

"Breakfast, as you wished," Tara told Ashley. She pulled her sun hat low over her eyes, crossed her ankles over one of the extra chairs and leaned back. A young girl came for their order; they asked for coffee and rolls and an assortment of cheeses.

Boats were already moving on the little inlet. Fishermen were hawking their catches. A woman walked along, selling handmade dolls.

Ashley, too, pulled her hat low and sank back. "How did you sleep?" she asked Tara.

"Divinely."

"No dreams?"

"Not a one."

"You're such a liar."

"This coffee is delicious."

"Why did you run off the ship? Chicken?"

"Because I didn't want to run into Rafe."

Ashley chuckled. "He didn't come near you all night."

"I know."

"Poor baby."

"Ashley—stuff a roll in your face, will you, please?"

"Love to, darling."

She started to do just that, then paused, suddenly aware that they were being watched. She turned slightly. There was a lively group of five young sailors behind them.

"We've got company," Ashley said.

Tara gazed past her, then wished she hadn't. One of the sailors winked at her. She didn't want to be rude, but she also didn't want to encourage him. She smiled weakly, then pointedly turned back to Ashley.

"Dutch?"

"I think so."

"Beer for breakfast."

"They're probably on a beer leave."

"Wasn't that for American fighters in World War II?"

"I think it's for any soldier, in war or peace."

"They're just a bunch of kids."

"Drunk kids, I'm afraid."

That was proved true just seconds later, when one of the young men swirled his chair and plopped down beside Ashley. He was darling, Tara thought, blond, blue-eyed—and probably no more than eighteen. It was a shame, she reflected, that it seemed all countries selected their most promising youth to offer up to the possibility of war.

But this young sweetheart had overimbibed. He started talking to Ashley, using language learned straight from the movies. Ashley was polite but firm. It got her nowhere. The other sailors were suddenly around the table, and Tara found herself fighting off hands as if she were surrounded by a pair of giant octopuses.

"Your mother should wash your mouth out with soap!" Ashley threatened one of them.

Fear gripped Tara suddenly, a fear she had never really conquered since Tine. It was a feeling of being overpowered.

She jumped up, suddenly not so sympathetic, and grabbed her bag. She tossed money on the table and took hold of Ashley.

"Let's go!"

But they were followed. Panic started to seize her as they headed back toward the main street with all the pastel shops. She felt a hand on her shoulder and spun around. One of the young blondes was smiling away.

"We make beautiful music, baby."

"No! *Nyet!*"

"Tara—that's Russian, not Dutch!" Ashley exclaimed.

How much English did they understand?

"Please, I know they work you hard on your ship! I know you don't get much liberty. But I'm not interested. I'm not—"

From behind, another hand grasped her shoulder, sweeping her around against something very hard.

She knew the scent; she knew the touch. Rafe.

He said something in Dutch, low, easy, but it was something the sailor understood. He blushed and bowed slightly. "Sorry. Enjoy the island, miss."

He turned and walked away. His friends waved a little uncertainly and followed him.

"Rafe! Bless you!" Ashley declared.

He was still touching Tara, who remained silent.

"They were just a little overzealous with their freedom."

"What did you tell them?"

"Just that you were spoken for."

"You didn't threaten them?" Tara muttered.

His hand moved away from her shoulders. "No, I didn't."

Ashley laughed, completely comfortable once more. "Well, whatever you did, it worked. Thanks! Do you speak Dutch?"

"No, only a few words."

"Why not?" Tara whispered. He ignored her, and she knew that she was being ridiculously rude. Absurdly, she felt close to tears. Could it really be that easy? Could she just smile and admit that she had been a fool and then everything would just be fine? It was easy to wish when he was touching her.

What in God's name held her back?

"Where were you going?" Rafe asked Ashley.

"Window-shopping," Ashley replied. "Want to join us?"

"Well, I have to go *that* way." He pointed.

"That way is fine."

They moved along the street. The shops had opened now. Ashley paused to buy T-shirts for her niece, nephew, sister and brother-in-law, and a little wood carving of a Dutch house for her parents.

Tara didn't know if she wanted any souvenirs or not, and she continued to feel tongue-tied. It didn't matter—Ashley and Rafe kept up a conversation easily.

They were in front of a dazzling window when Ashley suddenly stopped dead still.

"Ooh! Oh, Tara! Look at those emeralds! Have you ever seen such a beautiful necklace!"

Tara gazed into the window. The necklace was all alone, displayed on black velvet. There was one large stone in the center of a delicate gold filigree; it was surrounded by an elegant spray of diamond chips. It was simple; it was elegant. It was one of the most beautiful pieces she had ever seen.

"Do you really think it's good?" Rafe asked her seriously.

"Wonderful," Ashley replied. "Why?"

He smiled and pointed at the sign overhead.

"Oh! This is one of your stores!" Ashley said.

He arched a brow. "You knew?"

"No, no. I mean, not that you had one here. We did know that your family was in jewelry." She blushed. Her words betrayed the fact that one of them had done some research on the Tylers.

"Come on in. Try it on."

He stepped ahead of Ashley and opened the door. Tara wanted to remain in the street. Ashley hesitated just a second, then pulled Tara in with her.

Rafe was in white shorts and a navy polo jacket; somehow, he still seemed to fit the old-world refinement of the shop. There was a young girl behind a glass counter in which other gems were artfully displayed. She saw Rafe, smiled with pleasure and came out to greet him. He took both her hands and pressed a little kiss on her cheek.

Tara hated herself for the familiar jealousy that washed through her. But she found herself wondering about his wide-ranging life. He had been so many places. Would she always wonder about his past? Always feel these little twinges?

Always? There could only be an always if she gave in.

He spoke to the girl for a moment; she answered him cheerfully. He turned back to them.

"Would you excuse me for just a second? I want to look in on our bookkeeper. Frieda will bring you whatever you would like."

He disappeared toward the back. Frieda gave them a sweet, earnest smile and asked if they would like coffee or tea or something stronger.

Tara asked for coffee, just for something to do with herself. Ashley did the same.

But when they were seated in cushioned oak chairs around a small oak table, Frieda returned to them, the emerald necklace in her hands.

"You wished to see this, madame?"

Ashley almost choked on her coffee. Their incomes meant that their lives were definitely comfortable, but the size and perfection of that emerald put the necklace's cost into more digits than either of them could easily handle.

Rafe suddenly reappeared. On the soft carpeting, his footsteps had made no sound. He watched Tara, and he watched Ashley, and he smiled a little secretively. The necklace might well have been made for Ashley—sweet Ashley who had been in his corner through blind faith all along. He realized two things; he wanted Ashley to have the necklace because he was so genuinely fond of her, and he wanted her to have it because it was perfect for her. She appreciated its beauty with evident pleasure.

"Here, let me, Ashley."

He stepped behind her, clasping the emerald with its beautiful filigree and diamonds around her neck. Tara felt a twinge as his fingers brushed her friend's neck.

Frieda brought a mirror. Rafe stood back, surveying the necklace.

"It's perfect. A redhead in emeralds."

"It's stunning," Tara agreed, her heart aching a bit. It was. The necklace fell just above Ashley's breasts in a subtle brilliance. And Rafe had put it there.

"You make beautiful things, Rafe," Ashley murmured.

He laughed. "I don't make them. My jewelers do. But I'm glad you like it. After all, I hire the jewelers. And I'm convinced that you have impeccable taste."

Frieda handed him a memo board with a paper on it. He signed it.

Ashley stared at him suddenly, mischievously. "If emeralds are for redheads, Rafe, what about blondes?"

He looked straight at Tara.

"Diamonds. Nothing less," he said softly.

Again he turned to Frieda, exchanged a few words, then turned back to them. "Shall we go?"

"Wait!" Ashley said desperately. "I've still got the necklace on."

"Oh, yes. Frieda, could you get the lady a box, please."

"Oh, Rafe," Ashley gasped, her jaw dropping as she realized his intention. "I couldn't. Really, I couldn't. It just wouldn't be—I can't. I—"

He smiled with mild amusement while she faltered. "Ashley, if I were a florist, you would think nothing of accepting a rose. Trust me—I have a multitude of stones. Please, keep that one. Just please be sure to tell any admirer that it was created by my company."

He touched her again, taking the necklace, brushing his fingers over her flesh. Once again Tara unhappily realized that it had not been a gesture made for her benefit. Ashley had loved the necklace, it had looked exquisite on her, and he had taken pleasure in giving it to her. Like a florist with a rose.

They left the shop. Ashley continued to protest, glancing guiltily at Tara now and then. But Tara wasn't upset. Not at her friend, anyway. Rafe had a talent for giving a gift. He and Ashley walked ahead, while he told her how to judge an emerald, how to seek out the flaws, how to search for good color.

They came to another café; Rafe suggested a cool drink.

Tara had several, sitting silent while the two of them talked.

At last he glanced at his watch and warned them that it was nearing time for the ship to sail. He paid for their drinks and they returned.

As they walked up the steps, the captain was there—almost as if he had been waiting for them.

He had been.

Rafe excused himself to speak with the man.

"Tara, I didn't know what to do!" Ashley pleaded. "I still don't. I know that a woman of any character shouldn't accept a gift like this, but he has no interest in me. I mean, no interest in that way. You're the one he's sleeping with. I—"

"Ashley, it's probably true. He probably has so many emeralds that he just doesn't know what to do with them. You have dozens of George's thousand-dollar-plus fashions, and you don't think twice about that."

"Yes, but that's my job. Oh, the emerald is beautiful, and I do love it—"

"And you wearing it is the same kind of advertisement. Ashley, he meant it in friendship. You benefit, and so does he. To worry about it is silly."

"I hope so," Ashley said dubiously. "I wish you would stop this foolishness and leap on him."

Tara sighed and leaned against the wall, frowning. "I just wish he didn't have so much money. I mean," she hesitated, "not quite so much. I don't think I realized until today just how much he really does have. That kind of money, it's not just money. It's power, too. That's frightening, Ashley."

Ashley smiled a little sadly. "Tara, love is nice in any form, but you told me yourself that your parents adored each other—yet life was miserable for them. Look at the money you've poured into that town. He would be perfect for you—you can't wipe out poverty by yourself, and you know that being destitute is a rough life. Don't hate him because he has money."

Tara shook her head. "I never said I hated him, Ashley. I—I think I am in love with him. It's just—suddenly frightening to see his power."

"I don't think that has anything to do with money," Ashley said.

"You could be right. Hmm," Tara murmured, gazing over Ashley's shoulder to watch Rafe, who was still with the captain.

"Ashley, do me a favor. Go play with your emerald. I think we're going to have a little showdown."

Ashley smiled happily. "You mean you're actually going to be nice to that poor man?"

"I'm going to ask him a few questions."

"Gotcha. No, on second thought, I haven't gotten any of this! But I'm leaving!"

She hurried away. Tara stretched her back against the paneling and waited patiently. Then she frowned suddenly, noting a man's back as he hurried down a narrow hallway, heading toward the aft lounge. She pushed herself away from the paneling, trying to recall what it was that had been familiar about the man.

"Are you waiting for me?"

She swung around quickly. Rafe was there, his eyes somewhat skeptical.

"Yes. I want to talk to you."

"Do you really. How nice," he said.

Tara set her jaw stubbornly at his caustic tone. "Well?"

"You're the one who wants to talk."

"Will you?"

"With pleasure, Miss Hill. I'm always at your disposal. Want a drink?"

She'd probably indulged in a few too many on the island, she thought. Oh, what the hell. One more couldn't hurt.

"Yes. Thank you."

She wondered herself how she could be so stiff with a man she had come to know so well. She didn't want to be stiff. She wanted to turn around and pretend that there couldn't possibly be anything wrong, that everything about him was exactly what it seemed.

He led her to the forward lounge. It was darker, more intimate, than the one toward the aft. There were little booths here, and decorative little anchors carved in the woodwork separating the niches. Beneath them, the sea was aquamarine, the breeze light. Someone made an announcement in several languages about the ship leaving port shortly.

He ordered them both a beer, then signed the tab. He sat back in the seat, sipping his idly when it arrived, saying nothing at all, but waiting for her to speak.

"I'm curious," Tara began. "Not only did you manage to book passage on a sold-out cruise, but you have a cabin directly next to ours."

"That's no great mystery."

"Well, if it's not, I'm afraid I'm terribly slow. Please illuminate the situation for me."

He smiled slightly. "One of your friends apparently knows something about me, Tara. I'm surprised that you don't know. I own the ship. Or rather, Tyler Enterprises owns the ship. We own several."

"Oh."

At last his hand reached across the table for hers. He was still smiling, but his next words seemed more wistful, more fraught with tension. "Does that make me guilty of something?"

She snatched her hand back. "No. Yes. You could have told me the truth when we talked on the phone."

He shrugged. "Tara, you were determined that I shouldn't come. I was equally determined that I should."

"Why?"

"I'm worried about you."

"Because of Caracas?"

"Obviously."

"I've got another question for you."

"Shoot."

"Yesterday I was being harassed by a reporter who suddenly and rather mysteriously disappeared. Did you have anything to do with that?"

"Yes," he answered flatly.

"I can take care of myself."

"Can you? Seems to me that things went rather badly for you two years ago."

She inhaled sharply. "What did you do, threaten him?"

"No, I didn't threaten him, Tara. What is this thing you've got about threats?"

"Then what did you do?"

"I offered him a better story, Miss Hill. That's all."

"And that was?"

He laughed. "I don't know yet. I just promised him that he could have an important exclusive in the near future if he would quit torturing you. So, do I get hanged for that, too?"

"I'm not trying to hang you."

"Aren't you?"

She shook her head.

"Then am I forgiven?"

She shook her head again. "I don't know. I just don't know."

Tara jumped up suddenly, afraid to be with him. He'd answered honestly; he hadn't hedged or lied. But she could have found out the truth herself, anyway.

But what was wrong with knowing the truth about him? She still wasn't sure. You couldn't hang a man for being affluent. Or for being so affluent that his promise of a story was "better" to a reporter than digging into her past.

It was just that she wanted to trust him so badly. She wanted to believe that this was really it, that their love could go on and on forever.

"Tara." He caught her wrist, and she could have sworn that the depth of emotion in his arresting golden eyes was real. "Tara, I'm here because I care. Because I have to be. Please, believe that."

She nodded distractedly.

"Can you have dinner with me?"

"I, um, not tonight. I promised George I'd stay with the group. He's having pictures taken."

"After?"

"I'll—I'll meet you in the casino, I guess."

She jerked her hand away, a blush suffusing her cheeks. She needed to run away at this moment; she had promised to meet him later because she couldn't have done anything else. The need to be with him was far stronger than any warning signals.

Ashley was anxiously awaiting her in the cabin. "Well?"

"He owns the ship."

"Oh? And?"

"I don't know. I just don't know. We'll see."

Ashley continued to quiz her; Tara remained stubbornly silent as they showered and dressed for dinner. Ashley told Tara that Mary had seemed to have the captain wrapped around her little finger; he was spending all his free time with her.

"Well, that poor man had better watch out!" Tara said, laughing, but she was still nervous; she felt a stream of energy running through her, and she didn't know when it would slow down.

Sometime during dinner, she did calm down. She had agreed to meet Rafe. She wanted with all her heart to meet him. She dreamed of spending the cruise with him. Being held in his arms while the breeze moved around them.

The photographers arrived, and the models posed with their wineglasses held high. They stood; they sat. They did their very best to look totally elegant in George's creations.

Then they were left alone, talking, laughing—just like the other passengers.

Dinner came to an end when Mary nibbled at her dessert, then yawned softly, stretching. "Anyone for casino? I've got my numbers all picked out for the roulette wheel."

"I'll put forty quarters into a slot machine and that will be that!" Cassandra said agreeably.

Ashley started to rise, and Tara, too. But George halted her.

"Tara, could you stay behind just a minute, please?"

She frowned slightly, then shrugged, sitting again.

George smiled and waved the others away. When they were gone, he took Tara's hands and stared worriedly into her eyes. "Are you okay, Tara?"

"I'm fine."

"How are things with Tyler? I didn't mean to feed you to any wolves, you know. It's just, well, naturally, he can do a great deal for my prestige. But secondly, well, it's time that you—that you saw other men again. I didn't make you unhappy, did I?"

She shook her head. "No, you didn't make me unhappy. I like Rafe very much."

He nodded.

"Did you know that he owned the ship?" Tara asked.

"Guilty as charged."

"You didn't tell me."

"If he'd wanted you to know, he would have said something. I guess he *has* told you, now."

She nodded.

"Oh, Tara." He shook his head. "I just hope that I've been doing right by you. I thought that you needed to work again. Maybe even face the past. But the closer we get to Caracas, the more nervous I get."

"You can't really believe that Tine has been waiting there for two years on the possibility that I might come back?"

He shrugged. "From what you said, Tine really wanted that mask."

"I never had the damn mask. Who knows, he may have it already. And most likely he's living somewhere deep in South America and he'll never make an appearance again. Why risk arrest?"

George nodded sagely, agreeing with her logic. "To think that I made a nest for that smuggling snake all those years! Ah, well, you'll be with all of us. You won't be out of our sight for a minute! You'll be fine!"

"I think so. Thanks, George."

He gave her a little wave. She smiled vaguely and hurried up to the casino.

Rafe wasn't there. She saw Mary at the roulette table and asked her if she had seen him.

Mary gave her one of her all-knowing stares, plunked down a pile of chips and nodded. "He was here looking for you a few minutes ago. I told him that you had been delayed. I'm afraid I don't know where he went."

"Oh. Thanks," Tara murmured, trying not to show her disappointment.

She walked around the ship, going from lounge to lounge, but she didn't see him. She shied away from a friendly, slightly inebriated group who wanted her to join them. She was so keenly disappointed that she felt like crying.

She went back to her cabin, scrubbed her face, touched up her nails and finally decided to go to bed.

She lay awake for about two hours. Ashley came in, tiptoeing once she saw that Tara was in bed. In a few minutes she stretched out in her own bed, and Tara thought that she had fallen asleep.

But then she spoke.

"He's in his cabin, Tara. And I'll bet that the connecting door is still open. I'll lay odds that he'd be about the happiest man in the universe if you dropped in to, ah, say hi or something. In fact, I'm turning around now. I'm falling asleep. I'd never notice if you slipped through that door."

Tara hesitated, remaining still.

"I'm going to sleep now!" Ashley repeated.

Tara felt her heart thump painfully. She hesitated, then threw off the covers and tiptoed across the room.

The connecting door was open.

She twisted the knob, hesitating again, then pulled the door open. There was no logic, no rhyme, no reason. She wanted, needed, to be with him.

The cabin was dark. For a moment she wondered if he was there, or if he wasn't, perhaps, still in a lounge somewhere, in the casino, out walking the decks, watching the stars.

Gingerly, she made her way to the bed, and the moonlight betrayed his form. A shadow. He sat up, and in the darkness, she blushed.

He was waiting for her. She could almost see his smile, see the glitter of his eyes.

She curled up on the bed. His arms came around her.

"I looked for you," she whispered.

"I looked for *you*."

He took her hand, turning the palm up. He played over it with the tip of his tongue.

"I—I couldn't find you."

"You've found me now."

His hand slipped beneath the hem of her sheer gown; he moved, swift, sleek, vital, like a tiger, and the gown was gone, swept over her head, tossed to the floor. His hands cupped her buttocks, bringing her beneath him, and his eyes glittered with a tender magic in the pale moonlight.

"You've found me now," he repeated.

And with a little sigh she wound her arms around his neck, eager to meet his kiss and the excitement of his body melding with her own.

CHAPTER 10

Tuesday morning brought them to Martinique.

There were clear skies, a brilliant sun and a soft sea breeze. Rafe and Tara took off alone in a rented car, since he knew the island well. They climbed mountain trails in the little Toyota, stopped by roadside merchants, watched the sea and the harbor from the heights, and stopped at the small museum to see the relics of a time when the volcano had spilled out its wrath. They visited an old cathedral, walked along wet tropical paths and came back into town, where they wandered through the shops. The company had a jewelry store here, too, on a fashionable street. The manager and his assistant, aware that Rafe was coming, had planned a meal complete with French wine and a few of the island specialties. Tara admired a number of the pieces, but when Rafe told her softly that she was welcome to anything she liked, she shook her head with a rueful smile.

"Ashley's morals seem to have remained undamaged by her necklace," he reminded her. "I believe you told her it was all right, or else she wouldn't have taken it."

"It was all right for Ashley."

"Ah. Because she and I aren't involved."

"Exactly."

"Women."

"It makes perfect sense," Tara assured him. He didn't press her. Outside the store, Tara found herself smiling, wondering if she hadn't won the battle a little too easily.

"You didn't insist," she said teasingly.

"Was I supposed to? Would you have changed your mind?"

"No."

He smiled and walked ahead. She caught up with him, laughing. It was amazing what the night had done—amazing how much of any situation was nothing more than a state of mind. Today, with the sun above them, with the wonderful, colorful people all around them, everything seemed right with the world. She knew him. She knew the emotion in his eyes, the timbre of his voice, and she felt that she must have been half mad to want anything other than to be with him.

Rafe took her arm. "Actually, Miss Hill, I did not insist because I have a very particular gem in mind for you."

"Do you really?"

"Emeralds for a redhead, a diamond for a blonde."

Tara had paused to smell a bunch of fresh flowers that were still a bit damp from the morning showers, radiantly fresh. She felt a little tremor sweep through her.

The shopkeeper said something in French; Rafe laughed and paid for the flowers.

"What did he say?" Tara asked.

"That nature seldom created anything more uniquely exquisite than a flower, but you put the most glorious rose to shame."

"Oh." Tara blushed and turned to the man. *"Merci,"* she said softly.

He bowed deeply, offering her a wide smile.

Rafe glanced at his watch. "We've still got time to stop for a quick drink. I have the perfect place in mind."

It *was* perfect. It had a classic little balcony that sat high above the valley, looking over the town and the ships. It was open, and there were flowers everywhere. The umbrellas were candy-striped in a peach that was as soft as the fragrant air.

They sat there for a moment, sipping drinks the same shade of peach as the stripes in the umbrella. Then Rafe reached into his pocket and produced one of the little velvet-covered boxes with the Tyler insignia embossed in gold on top.

"This is the gem," he said simply. He didn't open the box; he pushed it across the table to her.

Curiosity won out over good sense. She opened the box and was not surprised to see that it was a solitaire. A beautiful stone, not huge and ostentatious, but certainly not small. Perhaps a carat, perhaps a little less.

Size meant nothing with this diamond, though. It was splendid in the perfection of its cut, in the rainbow spectrum of bursting color created by the sun's slightest caress.

Thoughtful, Tara closed the box, lowered her lashes, then pushed it gently back toward him. "Rafe—"

"Tara, I know you're not sure. I know you feel that time is very important, that we don't know each other well enough. I wish you would wear it anyway."

She shook her head, confused. "Wear it anyway? Rafe, it—it's magnificent. But it's an *engagement* ring."

She loved it when his lips curled just slightly at the corners. It reflected his ability to laugh at himself, at the world.

"Yes, it *is* an engagement ring. But if you're not ready to make a commitment, I understand. I still wish that you'd wear it. For now."

"Rafe, I'm sorry. I'm confused. You're offering me an engagement ring...but you're *not* really offering it to me?"

He laughed. "I knew you wouldn't accept it."

Belying his words, he took her hand. He flipped open the box with his thumb, took out the ring and slid it upon her finger. The fit was just the slightest bit snug.

Still confused, she searched out his eyes. His fingers wrapped around hers as he met her eyes, seemingly about to speak, and studied the ring on her finger again.

"Tara, I've been around the world a half dozen times; I know a hundred ports. I'm in love with you. I'm old enough, experienced enough, to know that I have never felt anything like this before in my life. I doubt if I ever will again."

His expression was a little rueful when he looked at her again. "Really. Any man would know that you're beautiful. Any man would want to touch you. Beauty has its own fascination. I don't know where it changed. When it was exactly that I started to long just to hear your voice. When I thought about you from the time I awoke to the time I went to sleep, and then again in my dreams. I couldn't breathe without imagining your scent. I couldn't look anywhere without imagining you there. It wasn't just the wanting anymore. It was the knowing—albeit not without more than a bit of an internal battle—that I would never get you out of my soul. I love you. The ring is offered in all sincerity—I want you to marry me.

I'd marry you today, this very hour—this second. But I understand you, too, Tara. I think that you love me. I know that you're frightened, and I don't blame you. But I'm frightened, too. For you. I don't know if it can help or not, but my ring will mark you as a woman who isn't alone, and that may protect you, telling others that they can't harm you with impunity."

Tara stared at him, speechless, as his words fell over her like the softest, most enchanting velvet mist. He loved her; she believed it. No man could speak so tensely, so softly, so deeply from the heart—and be lying.

It was just so hard to believe in fantasy. In magic.

And they were coming closer and closer to Caracas.

He ran his thumb down her hand, then closed his fingers over it, encompassing. "Tara, say something. You're making me feel like a fool."

"I don't believe anyone could ever make you feel like a fool."

"You're doing a good job, Miss Hill."

She smiled, her throat constricting.

"Do you love me, Tara? Or are the things you whisper just lies in the dark?"

"I love you," she murmured.

"Excuse me. I didn't quite get that."

"I love you."

"Then?"

"I just wish...I don't know. I wish you weren't quite so rich. Or powerful. Or something."

He smiled. "You're not exactly poverty-stricken."

She laughed. "Oh, but I am! My bank accounts were so low that I *had* to come back to work."

"That's because you give away more than you earn. I'd love to be your tax man."

"You don't understand—"

"Oh, but I do. I wasn't born wealthy."

"You weren't?"

He grinned. "My father was actually a fireman in Glasgow. He had a penchant for the sea. He joined the navy, and he loved it. He found some backers and bought his first ship. He started in the Mediterranean. The first ship was successful, so he was able to fund another, and so on. Then he discovered that there was money to be made in gems and artifacts. By the time he died, well, he had gone from rags to riches. But I still remember the early days. He never forgot them, either. He left half a dozen trust funds to be used for scholarships and other incentive programs back in Glasgow."

"Did he really? I'd love to have known him!"

"He was an all right guy," Rafe murmured.

"That's your accent!" she said suddenly.

"I don't have an accent."

"Only a slight one."

"You're avoiding the issue."

"I know. I don't have an answer."

"Tara..." He took her hand again, as if he was going to speak. Then he shook his head. "We've got to get back. The ship is going to sail."

"Oh, yes! And we have a showing this afternoon!"

Tara jumped to her feet, making a move to take off the ring.

It wouldn't budge. It was just that shade too snug.

"Divine justice!" Rafe laughed, taking her arm. "You see, you're supposed to accept."

"Oh, Rafe, I really can't—"

"It seems you have to, for the moment."

"But—"

He pulled her close. She felt as if she sensed everything around her acutely: the birds flying against the sky; soft clouds against the mountains; the buildings below them; the hawkers in the streets; the ships out in the sea; the ground beneath her feet.

His arms around her. She was in love. As she'd never been in love before. Knowing bliss just because they were together, because she could rest her face against his chest. She was dizzy with the feeling of it. The ring was stuck on her finger, where it belonged.

"Let's go," he whispered.

Arm in arm, laughing over everything they saw, laughing just for the pleasure of it, they returned to the ship. He left her at her cabin door, since she had to go to work. The Galliard girls were skipping dinner that night; the fashion show was set to begin at ten.

Of course, Ashley instantly saw the ring, and of course, being Ashley, she broke into a spate of endless congratulations, gasping in an occasional breath of air. Tara was convinced that at least ten minutes passed before she could get a word in edgewise.

"Ashley, I don't think I'm keeping it."

"What do you mean, you don't think you're keeping it? It's an engagement ring! A man asks you to marry him. You say yes, or you say no. You don't say maybe, let me try the ring for a while!"

"I didn't, Ashley. He put the ring on my finger, and it's stuck."

"Serves you right! What kind of a fool would turn him down?"

"I didn't turn him down."

"Then you're engaged."

"No, I'm not."

"Yes, you are."

"Oh, God! I'm going to try Vaseline."

She did, but to her amazement, she still couldn't get the ring off.

"You *are* engaged!"

"My finger is swollen because I've been tearing at it so long," Tara sighed.

"You're engaged."

"We're both going to be unemployed if we don't go and dress!"

Ashley agreed. Moments later, they were climbing into their first outfits of the evening. They were in a crew lounge just off the main ballroom. Cassandra was going on about the romance of it all.

Strangely, Mary was silent.

Madame told Tara that she was an idiot if she didn't marry the man. "Beauty is a fleeting thing, young woman."

Tara laughed. "Madame, these are the eighties! Marriage is not a woman's only option."

"Being alone is no great picnic either!" Madame retorted. She sighed wistfully. "I was in love, once. I wanted my career, though. That was years ago. Men weren't terribly liberated then."

"What happened?" Cassandra asked.

"Well, I had a glorious career."

"And hasn't it been satisfying?"

"Not as satisfying as a handful of grandchildren would be right now. But then, you young things, you know how to do it all. More power to you. You only go around once, you know. When you see something out there, grab it! Take it all, everything you can see!"

"What about love?" Cassandra asked.

"But she is in love with him!" Ashley stated.

"Talk about having your cake and eating it, too!" Madame said, laughing. "Young lady, you've had some bad breaks. Looks like the good ones are coming your way now. He's a nice man, all right. All the way around. You marry him. Be happy. You haven't been really happy since I've known you."

"She was once—" Cassandra said, then broke off awkwardly.

Mary continued for her. "No, she wasn't," she said bitterly. "Not with Tine. She was always fighting him. Right from the very beginning. She was just so young that she had to learn how."

"We get to Caracas tomorrow," Ashley murmured.

"Would you all stop it!" Tara begged. "You're making it sound like a death knell. Madame, I think something is wrong with one of the hooks in the back. Could you check, please?"

She hopped up on a chair. The gold lamé she was wearing was nearly backless, and it didn't feel at all secure.

"Oh, dear! Someone caught this on something. The button is missing. I'll have to use pins."

"Breathe carefully!" Ashley laughed.

"Oh, hush!" Madame told her.

But it was the truth. Everyone knew that Madame was lethal with pins. Tara stood still while the back of her dress was fixed.

There was a knock at the door. Cassandra went off to answer it, then came back in with Rafe. He was greeted with a burst of congratulations.

He was in black. Tara would always love him in black. He wore a vested tux, white shirt, black tie. Smooth, elegant. The black accentuated his hair and eyes and the sleekness of his build. The white shirt made his features look all the more bronzed, all the more striking. All men, she thought, looked good in nicely tailored suits.

But no one looked as good as Rafe.

He listened to the chatter from Cassandra and Ashley, then glanced curiously at Tara. He thanked them and came over to her, then placed his hands around her waist, lifted her from the chair, and kissed her lightly.

She gasped, "Ohh...my God!"

He drew away. "The kiss was that good?"

"No—I've got pins sticking in my back."

He shook his head. "Tara, you'll certainly never overinflate my ego."

The others laughed. He leaned toward her and whispered in her ear. "Are we engaged?"

"I—"

"We'll talk about it later, huh? I just came by to tell you that I'd be in the audience. George caught me in the hallway. He wants to buy us all some champagne in celebration."

"George knows?"

"Tara, everyone knows."

"Oh," she said a little weakly.

"Love me?" he queried, and she felt all the gold and amber tenderness in the eyes that demanded an answer.

"Yes. But—"

"Then it seems that we *are* engaged. Since the ring is stuck and George is buying champagne, and since I love you and you love me..."

She paused, but could not control the radiant smile that illuminated her features.

The magic was real.

He kissed her quickly. "I'll be waiting for you, gnashing my teeth each time I hear some guy sigh when you waltz by him!"

He smiled and left.

Ashley plopped into a chair. "That you could even think about turning him down is a sin! He looks just like Gable tonight! I can just see him at the foot of a stairway! If he were going to carry *me* off, I'd probably expire at the thought before I even got to enjoy it!"

"Ashley, I've seen you turn your nose up at a dozen adoring hunks!"

"Never the right hunk!" Ashley complained.

Tara smiled, still wrapped up in her happiness. Just before they left she noticed that Mary was still silent, and she made a mental note to talk to her later to see if anything was wrong.

Rafe stood at the back of the ballroom to watch the show.

The place was packed—this was an experience few people were ever likely to witness again, unless they were with the press, or wealthy enough to visit Galliard's showroom.

And Galliard's shows were all good, Rafe knew. Galliard was not of the belief that a model should be wooden. His models moved fluidly; they smiled. He always addressed them by name, and in a tone of voice that would lead anyone to assume they were people to him, not objects. This added something special.

Along with the lights, the music, the flowing magic of the gowns...and the women themselves.

Not that Rafe really noticed the others. Once he had gazed at her and noted merely that she was beautiful. It had been with an objective, even cold, eye.

Had that ever really been so?

Each time she appeared now, his heart quickened. He couldn't seem to breathe; his collar tightened. Whenever he saw her smile, he melted inside. Her hair trailed behind her in skeins of silk and gold, and he remembered how it felt to his fingers, when it brushed against his chest. Each time she turned his way, he recalled the way her eyes had glinted silver in the moonlight, silver with innocence, silver with trust, with passion, laughter.

He had to tell her. He had to get the words out now, before it was too late. If he lost her...

He swallowed, amazed at the pain that wrenched him. He had been so certain of himself, of his experience, of his immunity. He had told himself that she was just another beautiful woman. But she wasn't. She was unique. She had held away from him; she had come to him. Slowly she had smiled, taken his hand, and still, to his once hardened amazement, he couldn't quite believe that she was now more important to him than air, than water.

He had to make her understand.

But not tonight, he cried inwardly. The ring was on her finger. They would be with others, but then they would be alone, and he just couldn't take the chance of giving up this night.

Rafe blinked suddenly; the lights had come up, the show was over. He stood there, feeling the heat that rushed through him.

No, he couldn't tell her tonight. Tomorrow they would reach Caracas, and once they were there, he would find a way to tell her that Jimmy had been—was—his stepbrother.

He moved through the crowd, ready to wait in the hallway for the girls to appear.

He was still standing there when Sandy Martin, the ruffled, tawny-haired reporter from L.A. came upon him.

"Mr. Tyler!"

Rafe didn't like the man—he was a sensationalist. Rafe quirked a brow, waiting for him to go on.

"You promised me an exclusive," the reporter complained. "The whole ship knows that you and Tara Hill are engaged."

"Sorry, Martin. I wasn't really thinking about the press when I asked the lady."

"Lady," Martin said softly. It sounded a little bit like a sneer. Rafe's fists tightened at his side, and he clenched his teeth, reminding himself to be civil.

"Excuse me, Martin. What was that?"

Martin backed away a little. "I didn't say anything, Mr. Tyler. Nothing at all. But tell me, are you aware that she was accused of murder two years ago in Caracas?"

"I am aware of everything about her, Mr. Martin. And I believe in her innocence of any wrongdoing."

Sandy Martin snickered. "Did you ever know Tine Elliott?"

"No, I did not. What's your point?"

"Oh, nothing. He was as smooth as silk. Some people speculated that she'd bide her time and go back to him. It was supposed to have been a real hot and heavy romance. Which is easy to understand. I mean, Tara Hill has a lot more than beauty. She's like a walking, uh—well, you know what I mean."

"No. I don't know what you mean."

"Nothing bad." He laughed a little awkwardly. "She just kind of makes a man think of the best time he ever had in his life, you know?"

If he clenched his teeth any tighter, they would crack. He reached deep within himself for every ounce of self-control.

"Martin, I can't exactly ask you to leave my ship. I promised you an exclusive—you'll get it. But until then, do us both a favor, huh? Keep out of my way. If I ever hear you so much as whisper her name in your leering little fashion, I don't think I can be held responsible for my reaction. Now, if you'll excuse me—there are a dozen other places where you could be on this ship."

Sandy Martin didn't hesitate. He paled enough so that his freckles stood out on his face, backed away a step or two and started stuttering. "I didn't, uh, I didn't mean anything. Just that you're a lucky man. You know what I mean. Never mind." He turned around and fled just as the doors opened and Tara came out.

Smiling. Her silver eyes were only for him. Rafe caught her against his chest for a second, breathing in the scent of her hair, feeling her warmth, her heartbeat.

I'd throttle him if he touched her! he thought savagely.

"What's wrong?" she asked, suddenly worried, and it touched him deeply that she could read all the subtle nuances of his body.

"Nothing. When I hold you, nothing in the world."

They went downstairs, where Galliard's party took up half of the smallest, most intimate lounge. A few of the ship's officers occupied the remainder of the room.

The captain and Mary were together, Rafe noted, and he grinned, thinking that the man certainly seemed to have a bad case of infatuation.

George bought the first bottles of champagne, then declared that it was Rafe's ship and Rafe's engagement, and Rafe laughed and ordered the next round.

They danced beneath spiraling lights, oblivious of everyone else.

When the wee hours came, Rafe suggested that Tara retire with Ashley, then slip through to him.

She didn't bother with any pretense; they said good-night to Ashley in the hallway.

And then they were alone, she in his arms.

"It's amazing," he told her. "George creates the most bewitching clothing. This gown is fabulous on you—and I can't wait to get it off you."

She laughed, a breathy, wonderful sound that mingled with the rest of her to arouse him to a fever pitch. Something on the gown ripped.

"I'll buy it," he groaned against her hair.

"You can't. I own it."

"Good."

She fumbled with his tie, brushing his throat with the engagement ring. He carefully stepped out of his trousers, yelping slightly as she caught him again across the belly with the ring.

"Damn! Maybe I shouldn't have insisted on that thing!"

"It doesn't come off."

"From now on, it had better not."

"Stop moaning, then."

"You wounded me."

"I'll kiss it and make it better."

"Wound me, then, wound me."

And, laughing, she began to kiss him, and he began to kiss her, and their laughter subsided into the sound of their heartbeats and the ragged whispers they exchanged.

The cabin phone let out a screech. Rafe sprang from the bed to catch it before it woke Tara, who was still sleeping with the most beautiful, soft smile on her lips.

"Yes," he said.

"Call from the States, sir. Mrs. Tyler. Shall I put it through?"

He closed his eyes. Myrna. "Yes, of course, please," he said softly.

"Rafe, can you hear me?" She was shouting.

He kept his voice low. "Yes, clearly."

"Oh, God, I'm so sorry to bother you. I wouldn't except that, oh, Rafe, I just read the papers!"

She was trying to sound calm. He knew that she had been crying.

"I'm sorry. What are you talking about?"

"It's front page news up here. 'Millionaire Playboy to Wed Galliard Girl.'"

"Oh." Damn! The press did move swiftly!

"Rafe, I don't mean to question you. But you haven't—you haven't forgotten Jimmy? I don't mean to question your judgment, but she's our only hope! You won't risk finding him, Rafe? I mean, I've never known you to be taken in or fooled, but she was there. She was with him...." Her voice trailed away. Pathetically.

"I haven't forgotten, Myrna. Please, trust me."

"I do," Myrna said.

He wasn't sure that the words had conviction. He sighed softly. "Please don't worry."

"You'll let me know as soon as you learn anything?"

"I promise."

"I'm sorry, Rafe—"

"Don't be. Please. Trust me."

"I will. I'll talk to you soon."

"Soon. Take care."

"You take care, too. I couldn't bear it if you, ah, if you were hurt in any way."

"I won't be. Goodbye, and don't worry."

He hung up, then pressed his temples with his fingers. He glanced over at the bed. Her hair spilled over his pillow; she was still wearing that smile that could have melted rock.

He closed his eyes. He loved her; he believed in her.

But he couldn't tell her anything. He couldn't afford to have her turn against him.

And no matter what he felt, he couldn't jeopardize his chances. Myrna's chances. Jimmy's chances. What if it were all a lie? What if she had smiled at Jimmy the same way she smiled at him?

No...

He walked over to the porthole and moved the draperies.

They were in Caracas. He saw the mountain, purple and green, shrouded in mist, rising in front of the ship as they approached land.

Caracas...

He closed his eyes tightly. They were here; he could feel it, feel the tension rising like the mist. He and Tara had been coming closer and closer to the past.

They were here.

She stirred, shading her eyes against the morning light, then smiled tentatively, only half awake. "Are we here?"

Her lashes shaded her cheeks; her hair was sun against the sheets. The exquisite lines of her body curved as she stretched.

He came back to the bed, lay down beside her and took her in his arms. "We're not quite there—we're here," he murmured. And he kissed her forehead, then her cheeks, and then her lips.

The day could wait. It seemed urgent that he make the dawn last.

CHAPTER 11

It should have taken most of the day to make the move from the ship to the hotel. Between everyone's personal belongings and the Galliard creations and accessories, there was quite a bit to be transported.

But there were no delays, no customs problems, no traffic. And at the hotel, there was absolutely no wait at the reception desk. The manager himself greeted them. Everything had worked out incredibly smoothly.

Ashley and Tara were together again, on the fourth floor.

The room was very similar to the one she had stayed in last time in Caracas—with Tine.

Ashley laughed when the bellhop left. "What do you want to bet that this room has a connecting door?"

Tara smiled. "It does. He called in before we left the ship."

Ashley arched a superbly shaped brow, then grinned. "Why didn't you just move in with him?"

Tara shrugged. "Well, I'm working."

Ashley frowned suddenly, stood and walked over to the window. "Where is he now?"

"Well, I expected this to take all day. His firm buys a lot of its gold here. And he has a store here, too. He had some business to attend to. I don't expect him back until late afternoon."

"We don't have to do anything tomorrow until the big showing for the South American aristocracy. We could stay here, of course, but why on earth would we want to? Tara, are you really all right?"

"Yes, I'm fine."

"I mean, being here hasn't made you queasy or anything?"

"Ashley, I've always loved Venezuela. The people are great. I can't blame the place for what happened."

"Are you afraid?"

"Of what?"

"Of Tine being here somewhere."

Tara shook her head. "I'm sure I'm not worth waiting two years for when he could get arrested here. No, I'm not afraid. Besides, I'm not going to run off anyplace by myself."

"Think we're safe enough in public?"

"Sure."

"I was just dying to go back to the glass factory. Last time I bought the most beautiful swans! I wanted to see what else they have that might complement—oh! I forgot! It was at the glass factory—"

"The glass factory wasn't guilty, either!" Tara exclaimed, laughing. "That's just where I met Jimmy. And it's all in the past, Ashley. If you want to buy some glass, we'll get a taxi and go right now."

"Maybe we shouldn't. What if Rafe comes back?"

"What if he does? I'll leave him a note."

"But—"

"Ashley." Tara interrupted a little harshly. "I'm in love with him. I want to spend my life with him. But I had a `keeper' once. If I thought that I had to ask permission to go places, I wouldn't be with Rafe. I'll never live like that again! If I'd been the least bit wiser, I would have understood that Tine had no trust in me and no sense of security in himself—besides the fact that he was a criminal! Let's go. I'll leave Rafe a message at the desk."

Ashley, a little stunned by the passion in Tara's voice, saluted sharply. "Yes, Ma'am! I'll call for a taxi."

She did. Seconds later, they were outside the elegant lobby, being helped into a taxi by a doorman.

"What a beautiful day!" Ashley murmured. She attempted some of her choppy Spanish on the taxi driver, who good-naturedly corrected her.

He was answering her, showing her something out the window, when she frowned and shook Tara's arm.

"We're being followed."

"Oh, come on, Ashley."

"I'm serious. That taxi left the hotel right when we did—and it's still behind us."

Tara felt as if her heart skipped a beat. She couldn't help it; she was suddenly frightened.

There definitely was a cab behind them. And Ashley could well be right—it might have been following them since they had left the hotel. She squinted; she couldn't see into the cab very well. Even though they were on a crowded street—Caracas was a big, modern city—and moving slowly, the windows of both cabs were tinted.

They came to a traffic light. Tara could see that there was one person in the rear of the cab. A man, who appeared to be elderly.

She looked at Ashley and shrugged. "Ash, one of the big tourist attractions here is the glass factory. I think every tour takes you there."

Ashley thought about it. "I suppose you're right. Maybe I should tell our driver to lose him."

"Not on your life!" Tara protested. Their driver was already moving incredibly fast for her. And they were leaving the city behind them, speeding toward the mountain.

Ashley sighed and leaned back. "Well, don't blame me if that cab catches us."

"Ashley, if we told our driver to lose that cab, it would probably catch up with us anyway. Like you said, the old guy is probably headed for the glass factory, too!"

Ten minutes later, they had climbed high along the mountain trail; through the trees, Tara could see the buildings of the glass factory.

Fear crept over her. Nothing had changed. The sand, the dirt, the stone paths, and the trees were just the same.

Even the sky was the same, just beginning to cloud, beautifully blue above the vegetation that hugged the mountain. Eventually night would come, and it would be completely dark, except for the light of the stars.

Tine had disappeared into the trees. Jimmy, too, had simply disappeared. No one had ever found either of them.

"We're here." Ashley prodded her. Tara made herself smile, because Ashley looked so worried.

Ashley paid the cabdriver, who assured her they would have no difficulty getting back. They crawled from the cab, and Tara was certain that he was right—there was an abundance of tour buses and taxis parked on the grounds.

The cab they had noticed on their way was pulling in behind them. It seemed to slow, then continue—parking behind one of the tour buses.

"What do you make of that? The cab that was following us slowed down, then speeded up," Tara said.

Ashley frowned. "Maybe we should just go back."

"No. It's broad daylight. Nothing can happen."

"Maybe we should get inside. Either the store or the workshop."

Tara shook her head. "I want to see who was in that cab."

"How will you be able to tell? There are a dozen people getting off the buses."

Tara shook her head. "Let's just pretend we're waiting for someone."

"Okay."

They stood there and waited. People came and went. Most of the visitors seemed to be from cruise ships; they were laughing, wearing ridiculous straw hats and gaily showing one another their purchases.

"How long should we wait?" Ashley asked.

Tara shook her head and shrugged with disgust. "This is stupid. Let's just go."

"All right. We'll go in quickly."

"No, we won't! I'm not going to be neurotic. Let's go watch them working, get a soda, and then we'll shop and leave."

"Tara, if you're uncomfortable—"

"I'm not!"

"Okay," Ashley said. "Let's go, then."

They went down a few steps to follow the path to the workshop. Tara loved to watch the glassblowers—it always seemed so amazing to her that the men could take such a mass of nothing, heat it, and then blow and mold it into a thing of beauty. They watched a young mustached man with wonderful showmanship craft an exquisite owl. They applauded with the others and moved around the outside of the protective railing to watch an older man, stout and grim, form an elegant fluted glass.

Tara stared across the room. The railing followed the outline of the building; the artisans could be viewed from either side.

She frowned, noticing an older man on the other side. He was tall and stately and white-haired, and she could have sworn that she had seen him somewhere else.

"Ashley—look casually across. Do you think that man could be the man in the cab? Does he look familiar to you?"

Ashley wasn't exactly casual. She stared. The gentleman moved back into the crowd.

"He saw us looking at him, and he moved," Tara said.

"Ooh, Tara! He did look familiar!"

"I saw him. And I saw his back on the ship the other day! He came in on our ship—that's it! Curaçao! When I was waiting for Rafe. I saw him walking away, down one of the hallways!"

"But Tara, I wasn't there, and I saw him before and—oh!"

"What?"

"The restaurant! That's the man who had lunch with Rafe the day that we met him!"

"His uncle—or so he said."

"Tara! Why would he lie?"

"Why would his uncle be on the ship—why wouldn't Rafe even bother to have him join us once?"

Ashley had no answer for that one. Tara pursed her lips grimly and started walking.

"What are you doing?" Ashley asked anxiously.

"I'm going to ask him!"

"Wait, Tara—"

"Just hurry! Or I'll lose him!"

"Coming, coming," Ashley muttered.

There suddenly seemed to be people everywhere. Tara determinedly moved through them, murmuring a dozen excuse-mes. She came out of the building, into the sunlight again, and saw him hurrying past the soda machines.

She was so busy watching him that she didn't notice the tall, broad Latino she suddenly crashed into full force. He was young. He caught her arms, then gave her a sexy smile. "Hello."

"Hello. Excuse me." Quickly she jerked her arms free and dashed after her prey, Ashley still on her heels.

He was starting to move toward the buses. She followed. "Wait! Sir! Wait!"

She was almost on top of him. Unable to ignore her anymore, he stopped, an unhappy expression on his face.

"Sir! You're related to Rafe Tyler!"

"Uh—"

"Please. You were with him in the Plaza. Having lunch. And you were on the boat. And you were just following us!"

He grimaced sheepishly. "Not doing a very discreet job of it, eh?" he said with a sigh.

Tara frowned. "I don't understand. Why weren't you with us on the ship? You are his uncle, aren't you?"

"In a way."

Ashley, panting, reached them. "Hi," she said, out of breath.

"Hi," the man said.

"I'm Ashley."

"I'm Sam."

"Sam! Good, that's a start!" Tara snapped. "Now, Sam, what is going on here?"

Sam didn't have a chance to answer. From behind Tara came an unknown voice, accented, deep.

"My love! There you are! I've been waiting. How good it is to see you!"

Confused, Tara began to turn. She barely saw the Latin man with whom she had just collided, and then she was gasping, because he swooped her into his arms, holding her in such a crush that she could barely breathe, much less speak.

"Tara!" she heard Ashley scream. She dimly saw that Ashley tried to come after her but that another young man stepped in her way and crudely knocked Ashley down.

The old man, Sam, was white. She was terrified to see him start running and then fall from a well-aimed and determined blow like the one that had sent Ashley to her knees.

Tara opened her mouth and screamed. Her captor's arms tightened more securely about her.

"Someone wants to see you, baby! And it's worth a lot of money!"

She screamed again. She could hear a murmur of voices. She struggled, managing to tear a nice gouge out of her assailant's face.

But all to little avail. Tourists were beginning to murmur, as if they were beginning to realize that this wasn't a lovers' tryst at all.

But could anyone help? She was being swiftly carried toward a waiting compact car, the engine running, a driver ready to hit the gas the minute she was tossed into the back seat.

Panic seized her. She was afraid that she would lose consciousness.

She should have never come back. It seemed that Tine had waited for her after all.

No! She wasn't a fatalist—and she wasn't going to be anyone's victim. Not while she could still scream, still breathe, still move. She started struggling again, and screaming, wriggling so wildly that her captor had to slow down. She could see that Ashley was up again, shrieking that someone needed to help them.

Just then another car drove into the gravel parking lot. She could hear the sudden screech of the tires.

"Let her go! Now!"

Rafe's voice...

The man holding her hugged her tighter against him. She was aware of his cologne, aware of the rough fabric of his shirt against her cheek.

And then she felt another set of arms, wrenching at her, attacking the man.

The accomplice who had tripped Ashley was suddenly at Rafe's back. Rafe turned, slammed a fist into the man's gut, and turned back to Tara. This time when Rafe wrenched at her, her assailant let her go.

Rafe and Tara fell to the ground together.

Both men leaped into the metallic blue car. The tires screeched, dust and rock blew into their faces, and the car careered away down the path.

Rafe's arms tightened around Tara. She could hear the frantic beating of his heart, the rasping of his breath. He tilted her dirt-smudged face upward. "Are you all right?"

She nodded.

He helped her to her feet. Ashley, dusty, too, from her fall, came racing over.

Sam followed more slowly, watching Rafe unhappily.

"I've got to call the police. Ashley, stay with her. No, never mind. We'll all go together."

He caught Tara's hand and dragged her along to the shop, where he explained in Spanish what he wanted. A concerned salesgirl hurriedly handed him the phone. He talked to the police for a moment, describing the car, then hung up.

He gazed at Tara, and she wanted more than anything on earth to believe all the ravaged emotion in the golden gleam of his eyes. But she still hadn't spoken; she was definitely shaken, still trembling.

And still concerned.

Rafe had certainly made a timely appearance. And he hadn't registered the least surprise at seeing Sam.

"The police are coming. Can you talk to them all right?" he asked her.

She had barely answered when they heard the sirens.

One of the officers who came spoke English. He seemed to know Rafe—and he also seemed to be somewhat suspicious of her.

She hadn't met him two years ago—but it was more than possible that he had heard of her.

He questioned her. She told him exactly what had happened. When he seemed a little skeptical, Ashley interrupted vigorously, telling him that everything was exactly the way Tara had told it. Sam spoke up, agreeing with them both and demanding indignantly that the officer treat the victim more tenderly.

"Is someone trying to trail that car?" Rafe asked tensely.

"*Sí.* They will search for the car. We will do our best. Now, Miss Hill, you are certain you have heard nothing from this man, Tine Elliott, in the two years since he disappeared."

She knew that she was trembling. With outrage, with remembrance—with fear. "I'm positive!"

The officer nodded. "We'll take you back to the hotel. Please, don't wander around in the future."

"She won't," Rafe said grimly.

They returned to the hotel in the police car. It was a silent party. Tara was grateful to Rafe for his appearance, but despite her fear, anger was coming to a boil within her. Perhaps it was even the fear that was fueling the anger. She didn't know.

In the lobby, she suddenly balked, staring at Rafe. "Maybe you don't care about your uncle's health, but I do!" She spun around to face Sam. "Are you all right? I don't know why he's ignoring your existence, but I appreciate very much what you tried to do, and I'm concerned that you could have been hurt."

Sam flushed—his face crimson against the white of his hair. "I'm fine. Just a little dusty. A shower will take care of everything."

Sam wasn't going to give her a chance for any more questions. He waved quickly and disappeared into an elevator with an already closing door.

"Someone should find George and tell him what happened," Ashley murmured, and whether she was in earnest or merely wanted to escape the two of them, Tara didn't know. But the redhead gave them a weak smile and disappeared into the lounge.

"Are you sure you're okay?" Rafe asked Tara, looking her over thoroughly. "Maybe I should have taken you to the hospital—"

"I'm fine. I haven't got a scratch on me!" Tara snapped.

"Oh." He gazed at her again, more intently and seemed to stiffen. "Shall we talk upstairs?"

"Definitely."

They went up in the elevator, standing apart, exchanging not a word. Rafe opened his door.

Tara stepped in first. Rafe followed, pulling his dusty polo shirt over his head and tossing it in the corner.

"Should I order drinks?" he asked.

"Yes, I think you probably should," Tara said coolly. She wasn't feeling cool at all. She didn't know if she was still terrified—Tine was here! Alive! After her!—or merely devastated.

She didn't think that she could take it if everything she thought she knew about Rafe was a lie.

He walked to the phone and requested room service, gazing at her questioningly. She didn't speak, so he just ordered a bottle of rum and some Cokes.

He set the phone down and stood there, watching her with his jaw set, but a little warily, too, she thought. He knew what was coming.

"All right. What?" he asked.

"You don't need to ask that."

"Apparently I do."

"Okay. Sam was on the ship. Sam was following me today. Sam was with you in the restaurant. If this man is your uncle, why was he hiding on the ship?"

"He wasn't hiding."

"You gave me an engagement ring. Most men would introduce a handy relative to the woman they claimed they intended to marry."

He didn't blink. He just stood there in his jeans, feet slightly apart, muscled chest bare, flesh a little dusty. She almost lowered her eyes from his. He had that tiger look again. A look of cunning, of sleek power.

"Is he or isn't he a relative?"

Rafe cocked his head slightly. "He is—and he isn't. He worked for my father, and he works for me. But he met me the day I was born, so he's definitely family."

There was a knock at the door. Room service had arrived. Rafe let the man in, signed the bill, then fixed two drinks.

Strong drinks, Tara noticed. Well, he wasn't going to make her veer from her purpose.

He intended to, though. He handed her a glass that held far more rum than Coke and demanded a little harshly, "I don't think that Sam is really the important question at the moment. Someone just attempted to abduct you."

"I'm very aware of that."

"Are you? Good. There's safety in awareness."

"Rafe, what's going on!"

Tara realized then that neither of them had sat down. Nor were they touching. They were very carefully circling each other. For a moment, she thought that she was going to burst into tears. She didn't want suspicions. She wanted to run into his arms and believe that he could protect her against the Tines of the world forever.

And—oh, God!—she wanted to believe that he wasn't another Tine himself!

"Tara, I made Sam come in and eat lunch with me because I knew that you were in there—I overheard you tell your taxi driver to take you to the Oak Room. And I asked him to come on the trip for the same reason that I asked him to follow you today—to keep an eye on you."

She swallowed, feeling a smothering sensation come over her. He couldn't be like Tine, watching her, following her, spying on her.

"And you arrived so opportunely today because Sam called you to tell you that I'd left the hotel?" she asked him incredulously.

"Yes."

"Where were you, really?"

He hesitated. "At the police station. I wanted to see if anything new had been discovered. If they thought that there was any possibility that Tine was still in the country. All right! Yes, damn it! Sam was watching you, with orders to tell me if you left the hotel."

"Why?"

"Why?" It seemed as if his temper suddenly snapped. "You little idiot, that's obvious!"

"Don't call me an idiot!"

"You went off, alone!"

She shook her head. "I went to the glass factory, to a place that's always full of tourists—"

"And you almost met your ex-lover again. I didn't interrupt something you were looking forward to, did I?"

She remained deathly still; the only sound in the room was her sharp and horrified gasp.

She didn't say anything to him; she merely set her drink down on the bedside table and turned around sharply, heading for the door to her room.

"Tara!" He caught her arm, bringing her back around, closing his arms around her. "I'm sorry, I'm sorry—"

"No! Let me go!"

"I can't, Tara! I'm sorry. I just get frightened now and then myself. My God. I love you so much—"

Something inside her snapped, too. It was the shattering truth of the day. She was in Caracas and Tine was in Caracas, and he was going to get her if he could. She was overwhelmed by a memory of the past that she couldn't bear. A memory of being held and forced, helpless beneath a greater strength.

She panicked. She gasped out inarticulate words and beat against his chest.

And Rafe didn't understand. He knew only that he loved her, that deep inside he was very afraid. He was afraid that she could be taken, that he wouldn't be there to help her.

Fear that he was a fool. That she didn't really want his help. That he had given his heart and soul to some beautiful temptress, the same one who had caused Jimmy's downfall....

"Tara, stop it, I love you!"

Savagely, he swept her into his arms, carrying them both down hard on the bed. He was half tenderness, half fury. He wanted to touch her; he wanted to assure her. He wanted to erase the past.

"Tara!"

She stopped hitting him. Her eyes were blank. She was as pale as a sheet.

He knew an even greater terror as he watched her.

He moved to the side of the bed, kneeling beside it. He stroked her face, his heart thundering madly. A doctor, he needed a doctor.

"Tara, it's all right. Tara! Come back to me! I won't touch you. My God, what's wrong?"

He drew a shaking finger down her cheek. "I love you. Talk to me. Talk to me. Tara, what's wrong?"

Tears came into her eyes and overflowed when she saw him there. "Oh, Rafe!"

"I'm here!"

Her arms curled around his neck. He held her there, smoothing back her hair while she cried. And somehow, in whispered words, in broken words, the whole story of that last awful day came out, and what she didn't say, he could piece together. He stiffened as she spoke, knowing that if he ever met Tine Elliott, he would want to kill the man, to tear him into fragments of spindrift to throw to the wind.

She was quiet after a while. He stretched out beside her and held her, her head against his chest, still moving his fingers through her hair with a trembling tenderness.

"I love you, Tara. I would never, never hurt you."

"I know. I'm sorry."

"My God, I'd like to kill him." He felt the little skip and beat of her heart.

"He wouldn't be worth it," she whispered. And then she buried her face against his chest in such aching trust that he could hardly bear it. "He is out there, though. I know he's out there."

Then where is Jimmy? He almost shouted the words, but he didn't. They'd gone too far today; she couldn't take any more shocks.

And no matter how he loved and trusted her, there was always that last little doubt that he couldn't ignore. If it were just him, he would. He would be a fool; he'd gladly give his life; he'd gamble on his love.

But it wasn't just him. Jimmy was still somewhere. Either dead or alive.

Her tears were damp on his chest. Mechanically, he continued to soothe her, his thoughts meeting a blank wall. He brought her tear-streaked face to his and kissed her, and that kiss led to another, and suddenly it kindled a fire. Dirt and dishevelment didn't mean a thing as they made love.

The room grew dark. Rafe mixed another drink; they were able to laugh at each other's appearance, and then move into the shower together.

Rafe emerged before she did. He stood by the window and looked out as darkness began to descend in earnest on the city.

He should make her go home. He should dress, drive her to the airport, make reservations for two, and go home with her.

But he couldn't do that. There was Jimmy to think about.

And there was Tine Elliott. Rafe had too many scores to settle with the man.

The only thing that he could do was stick with Tara. Stick tighter than glue.

And be ready.

CHAPTER 12

Tara awoke the next morning because the phone was ringing. She really didn't want to open her eyes, and she didn't have to at first—Rafe picked up the phone.

But when she heard him say a sleepy good-morning to George Galliard, she knew that she was going to have to take the call. Rafe handed the receiver to her expressionlessly, and she took it.

"Good morning, George."

He called her *"ma petite"* and went on and on, telling her that he hadn't called last night because he had been sure that she had been resting. Tara thought that he knew she hadn't actually been resting, but perhaps he was being polite.

He went on and on—she didn't really get a chance to say anything for what seemed like a full five minutes. He was terribly worried. Perhaps she should board the next plane back to the States. Was she all right? How did she feel? If she couldn't manage the show, they could manage.

"Ah, Tara, Tara, Tara! I thought it would be good to bring you back here. I thought that nothing would happen, that you would go back to living normally—relaxed, you know. And instead, this!"

"George, I wasn't hurt at all," Tara said. "I'm fine. I can do the show with absolutely no difficulty."

"But your safety, *ma chérie!*"

"George—what can happen to me in an entire roomful of people?"

"Perhaps it was not Tine at all. Perhaps it was a random happening."

"Perhaps it was," Tara agreed. She didn't believe it—not for a second. She wished that she could. Tine Elliott was out there. God alone knew why; he hadn't really loved her. Ever. He was probably incapable of really loving anyone.

"Still, maybe you should get on the next plane."

That was definitely another thing she had thought about herself. Rafe had suggested it last night, quietly, when room service had delivered their dinner.

And it had been a great temptation. But it would have been wrong. What she needed to do was plan a way to trap Tine. If he wanted her—for whatever reason—he could find her. Maybe he had just been lying in wait down here, but she would never doubt that with his resources he could obtain false papers, a false identity—and come after her, wherever she went.

"I'm fine, George. The police have been alerted. I don't want to go."

"Bravo! We should end this thing, don't you think?"

"Yes."

"Then I shall see you soon. I'm sure that you are as safe as you can possibly be, with Rafe Tyler at your side."

She didn't glance Rafe's way. "Yes," she told George softly.

George repeated that he would see her soon and rang off. Rafe silently took the receiver back from Tara and set it on its cradle.

He gazed at her with arched brows, and she drew the covers up around her chest, hugging herself a little nervously.

"He thinks I should leave."

His eyes moved from hers, and he spoke very quietly. "So do I. And then again, I don't. I don't like the idea of your being frightened for the rest of your life because Tine Elliott might reappear."

"It's not just Tine," Tara murmured. She lowered her eyes to her hands, nervously clutching the sheets. "I don't think anyone ever believed me about Jimmy Saunders. No, I shouldn't say that. George believed me, and the girls believed me. But—well, I wasn't really that close to any of them. Not the way I've become now. I could only have lunch, shop and do that type of thing when Tine was off on business—smuggling, as it turned out. The fact that I met Jimmy, that he had become such a friend so quickly, was something I hadn't told anyone about, and so of course it looked like I was making things up."

She looked up; Rafe had moved. His feet were on the floor; his naked back was to her.

He seemed so stiff, as if all the muscles in his back and shoulders had tensed.

"Rafe?"

"I'm going to hop in the shower," he told her.

He stood, heedless of his naked state, entirely graceful and natural, and started for the shower. He disappeared into the bathroom, then paused a minute and turned back to her.

There seemed to be a careful mask over his features. He smiled. "Are you going to join me?"

Something in her expression must have given away her concern at his appearance. He came back to her and kissed her nose, then her lips.

"Going to join me?" he asked more huskily.

"Rafe?"

"I love you," he told her suddenly. He said the words with a vehemence and passion that was startling, then caught her chin in his palm, tilting her face to his and repeated his words more softly.

"I love you, too," she whispered. They stared at each other. The phone started to ring. Rafe swore softly and answered it.

"Mary. Good morning. Yes, she's absolutely fine. Yes, she's coming down to work. Here, I'm sure you'll feel better talking to her yourself."

With a grimace, he handed the phone to Tara. "I'll start without you," he told Tara in a mockingly aggrieved tone, clamping a hand over the receiver as he gave it to her. She laughed softly and told him she'd be there in just a second, covering the receiver herself to hide her own whisper.

Tara watched him walk into the bathroom, her heart thudding harder with emotion. He was beautiful, she thought. A bit savage, a bit primitive, and completely sophisticated all in one. A very elite tiger, a totally unique and independent cat. She bit her lip softly, so glad that he existed, so glad that he had chosen to love her.

Especially now. Any other man would have turned from her with all of this hanging over her head, with an ex-lover who was a smuggler, possibly a murderer...

And seeking some form of revenge, or something, from her.

But Rafe loved her. And it was so easy to love him back. The attraction was as natural as breathing; the ecstasy that had been such a physical tie had become something so much more.

She remembered that Mary was on the phone, and she jerked her hand off the receiver. "Mary!"

"You okay?" Mary asked, although Tara was certain that Mary had already been informed that she was fine.

"Yes, completely. Thanks for asking, though. Thanks for caring."

"Well, I suppose a person always wants to hear it from the horse's mouth."

"I look like a horse, huh?"

"Sure. A Thoroughbred. Where's Rafe right now?"

"In the shower. Why?"

"Good. I didn't want your expression to change any. I have to talk to you, Tara."

"About what?"

"I don't want to talk over the phone. You are coming down for the show, right?"

"Yes."

"Don't run off as soon as it's over. I have something to tell you."

"About Rafe?"

"Yes."

"Mary..."

She fought it; she fought the horrible sensation sweeping over her. She had been so in love. She was still in love, terribly in love, ridiculously in love. The fear didn't change that. But it did make her skin damp and clammy, caused goose bumps to appear on her flesh.

There just couldn't be anything wrong about Rafe, about the depths of her feelings, the need, the desire.

"Mary." She forced herself to inhale smoothly. "Mary, should I be afraid of Rafe?"

"Afraid of him? Of him harming you physically? Oh, no! Sorry, Tara, I forgot how sensitive you must be. No, no. That's not what I meant at all. I just think there's something you ought to know if you don't already."

"Mary—"

"I don't want to talk on these phones. I'll see you downstairs."

The phone clicked and buzzed. Mary meant it—she wasn't going to talk on the phone.

"Great!" Tara muttered. "Get me all upset and hang up on me! Just what I need!"

Her heart suddenly took off too quickly as she gazed toward the bathroom, and she wondered painfully what Mary was talking about. Her breath came too quickly; her palms were damp.

"No," she murmured.

The shower was running, but suddenly he was looking around the door frame; his seductive eyes were on her.

"Are you coming in?"

Her mouth felt dry. Of course! she wanted to cry.

She shook her head and fought for speech. "I'm just going to grab your robe and slip next door. All my things are over there."

His expression didn't change; she couldn't tell what he was thinking. Was he worried, anxious, suspicious, disappointed—or did he simply accept that she was supposed to be downstairs soon, cool and collected and ready to work?

"Don't leave that room without me!" he warned her darkly.

She smiled. "No, I won't."

His head disappeared back into the bathroom. She tossed the covers off and bolted out of bed, shivering miserably. She drew in a deep breath, grabbed his robe and slipped into the next room, anxious to ask Ashley if she knew what Mary was talking about.

Ashley wasn't there. There was still steam coming out of the bathroom; she had probably showered and gone down to join Cassandra and Mary for breakfast.

Tara sighed. If Mary had something to tell her, she wouldn't have told it to anyone else anyway. Mary was completely capable of keeping a secret.

Tara hurried into her own shower. She was still shivering; still anxious, still a little bit in shock.

And feeling miserably ill. As she stood beneath the hot spray of the shower she reminded herself that Mary had been appalled when Tara had asked if she should be frightened of Rafe. So it couldn't be anything too bad, could it?

She prayed not. She thought that she'd rather be thrown over a cliff by Tine than discover that she had been a fool, that she had been used when she had given in to instinct and fallen head over heels in love.

Twenty minutes later, she was dressed and ready. She almost left the room alone, but then she remembered the events of the day before and slipped back into Rafe's room. He was standing in front of the mirror, grimacing as he adjusted his tie.

Instinct prevailed again. Tara moved over to him and took the tie in her hands, her eyes on her task, her fingers trembling only slightly. She felt the warmth of his breath and slowly looked up into his eyes.

"What's the matter?" he asked her.

She smiled. "Nothing. And everything, of course."

"Why did you leave?"

She shrugged, concentrating on his tie once again. "Because you're a little bit too tempting in the shower, and this is George's big day before the grandes dames of South America. And I need some coffee desperately."

She knew he didn't believe her. But he didn't challenge her. When he moved to open the door for her, his jacket was slightly drawn back, and she stopped, gasping, aware that he was wearing a shoulder holster—and carrying a gun.

The blood must have drained completely from her face.

"Tara," he said impatiently, "this is protection. For you. God knows what that man intends. I only know what *I* intend, and that is that he isn't going to have a chance to pull anything. Let's go."

She didn't have a chance to reply; he took her elbow and led her out into the hallway. He was subtle, but she realized uneasily that he was prepared to have something jump out at them from every nook and cranny.

Nothing did. They met the others down in the dining room. Everyone else had eaten; they were all on their second cups of coffee. Tara knew she couldn't eat a thing. She kept staring at Mary imploringly, but Mary carefully kept looking away. George and Rafe talked, everyone asked after Tara, Madame showing special concern. Tara wanted to scream. It felt as if the tension was mounting with no break. What had she expected?

Not for things to happen this fast! Not for the attempt against her to be made in the first few hours that she had been here.

George rose, calling over to the assistants that they had better get started; they were scheduled to begin in an hour. He told the girls that the dressing room was stage left in the grand ballroom, and then he softly asked Rafe, "You'll be around?"

"Right outside the doorway," Rafe assured him. "And we'll have police in the audience."

George nodded and signed the breakfast check, and the party began to move.

The tables in the grand ballroom were beautifully set in peach and cream, with single fluted candles and white and peach roses. A small orchestra was warming up. There was a podium for George, and a special table for the press. George had the girls walk the runway to accustom themselves to it, and reminded Madame of the order of the program. Madame listened, then muttered that she was no fool, George should realize by now that she knew exactly what she was doing—and his models weren't dummies, either!

Rafe stood, arms crossed, beside George while the models tested the runway. As soon as they were ready to start for the dressing room, he returned to Tara's side, and fell into step with her. Before she entered the dressing room, he squeezed her elbow and told her that he would be right outside.

She stared into his eyes, those fascinating amber orbs, which were studying her so intently.

So caringly, so passionately. She sensed that he would gladly die before he let anything happen to her, and felt herself melting inside, because she loved him so much.

What in God's name did Mary know?

He kissed her lips lightly. "I'll be here. Go dazzle South America."

She smiled and slipped into the dressing room. She looked instantly toward Mary, but Mary shook her head, indicating that the others were all around them, Madame and one of her seamstresses, Cassandra and Ashley. And of course Ashley, bless her, kept close to Tara like a second skin, still concerned about the events at the glass factory.

Tara mechanically put on her first outfit. Madame moved around her, brushed her hair, touched up her makeup. They all talked, and Tara made conversation, too, without the least idea of what she was saying. She didn't know if she was more distressed about the knowledge that Tine was out there somewhere...or that Mary knew something about Rafe that made her acutely uneasy. Tara wasn't sure she could go through the whole show without knowing. She was afraid she would stop somewhere on the runway and simply start to scream.

But she didn't, of course. She was well trained. She moved on time; she smiled; she spun. She opened jackets, pivoted, smiled some more. Silks and gauzes flowed behind her. She even saw the audience, or parts of it. There might be a tremendous amount of poverty in South America, but not at this elite showing. The audience glittered with gold, silver, diamonds. She didn't think she had ever seen such an array of beautiful, elegant and sophisticated women, dark-haired, demure, aristocratic. Beautiful young women, beautiful mature women.

Each model had ten changes. Every time Tara walked around the end of the runway back to the dressing room she saw Rafe in the shadows and knew that he waited.

The show seemed interminable. She began to pray that it would end. And, of course, like all things, it did. George finished his last speech in his French-tinged English, added a few words in faulty Spanish, and then there was a tremendous burst of applause.

Tara knew that her employer was in his element. People were rushing up to him, complimenting his genius. He was ecstatic.

She gave him little thought, though. They were all back in the dressing room, the Galliard creations all being carefully replaced in their garment bags.

Mary caught Tara as she pulled her cool cotton sarong back over her head. "Dress slowly! I'll talk to you as soon as the others are gone."

Tara nodded. That feat wasn't as easy as it should have been—Ashley, concerned, kept urging her to hurry.

"Darn! I ripped my stockings!" Tara lied guiltily. "Ashley, please go on out and wait with Rafe, would you? Keep him entertained for me for a minute?"

"Okay. Mary are you going to be in here?"

"Yes, I'll wait for her. I won't leave her alone for a minute, I promise."

Ashley went out. Madame was still fussing around. Mary pretended to have a bunch of snarls in her hair, but then at last Madame left, reminding Mary to lock the door. Though the gowns belonged to the girls, they were still to be kept under lock and key. Not just anyone could own a Galliard.

The door closed. Tara turned to her friend. "Mary, I'm about to go insane! Damn it, tell me!"

Mary did, quickly. "Maybe I shouldn't tell you this. Maybe I should just have left things alone. I can't help it, though. I feel you have a right to know."

Tara frowned. "Mary, you've suspected something for a while, haven't you? What is it?"

Mary sighed. "Remember the captain on the ship?"

"Of course. He was charming. Oh, you thought so, too."

Mary nodded unhappily. "He is a charming, charming man. And horrible at deceit of any kind."

"Please, Mary, go on."

"I tried to tell you yesterday, but you were with Rafe, and then you and Ashley were already gone when I called your room. And then, well, no one could have gotten to you last night."

"Mary, please!"

"The captain let something slip when we were together. I had been casually talking about Rafe, saying what a wonderful, approachable human being he was for all his wealth and power. He agreed with me—he admires him very much. I started saying how happy I was for you—you'd had such a raw deal before. And then he told me that the whole thing two years ago had been a tragedy for Rafe, as well as you. I tried not to pounce on him, and I must have been fairly casual, because I got him to tell me the whole story."

"What story?" Tara nearly screamed.

"Tara—remember Jimmy Saunders? The man the police wouldn't believe even existed?"

"Of course," Tara said dully. "I could never forget him."

"Well, he *did* exist. In fact, he was born James Saunders, but his legal name was—or is—*James Tyler.* Tara, he's Rafe's stepbrother. Apparently, from what I could discover from my captain, Jimmy used his natural father's name at certain times for business reasons, to keep his association with the Tyler company unknown—I don't know exactly why. But he *is* Rafe's stepbrother. His family."

The world began to spin, black and misty. Tara knew she had to sit down before she fell.

Mary was prepared. She shoved a chair beneath Tara, who sank into it numbly, praying that she might stay that way.

"He's looking for his brother," she said tonelessly. "He found me, followed me, seduced me—assuming I could lead him to his brother."

"He never told you, then," Mary said unhappily.

Tara shook her head. She buried her face in her open palms. "Oh, God."

"Tara, I'm sorry—"

"Don't be. Thank God you knew. Oh, Mary."

"Tara, it may not mean anything. He might have looked for you because of Jimmy, then fallen in love with you for yourself. Tara, he can't take his eyes off you when you're together. And beyond a doubt, if Tine is out there, it's a damn good thing that you have Rafe's protection."

"Yes," Tara breathed. It truly had been a good thing.

"What are you going to do?"

Tara took a sustaining breath. She straightened her shoulders. The numbness left her, and a horrible pain took its place, but she gritted her teeth against it. "I'm going to have a chat with Mr. Tyler," she said.

"Tara—"

"That son of a bitch."

"Tara, give him a chance—"

She shook her head. Tears clouded her eyes. "No. It took me too long to see the light with Tine. This is much worse."

"Of course," Mary murmured. "Tine was only lethal to your health. The problem here is that you love Rafe Tyler."

Tara shook her head vehemently. "Then I'll just have to stop loving him."

"Talk to him. Give him a chance. Oh, Tara! Maybe I should have kept my mouth shut."

"No. Thank you, Mary."

She stood up. "Help me get out of things gracefully if anyone insists that we all lunch together or something. I have to talk to him. Right now."

"And then?"

"And then I never intend to speak to him again."

"Tara, you're forgetting! It's dangerous for you here. And I don't think it's that simple. I don't think you can just go home. You know that Tine is alive. And he knows that you're alive, and he'll be able to trace you eventually, even if you leave right now. You can't believe anymore that he's just gone under cover, hoping to survive and escape arrest."

"I don't know what I'm going to do right now," Tara murmured miserably, adding in a whisper, "except confront Rafe. Help me."

Mary lowered her head and nodded miserably. "Tara, listen to him, though, if he defends himself."

Tara didn't argue with Mary; she was too wounded. She still didn't want to believe the obvious; she didn't want to feel the pain. She had to end it.

She tossed her hair over her shoulder. "Come on."

Outside the dressing room, George was indeed trying to talk everyone into staying together for lunch. He was still concerned about Tara.

She struggled to stay calm, a difficult task, for as soon as Rafe touched her she wanted to scream, to burst into tears, to beat her fists against him.

She smiled. "George, I'll have to pass on lunch. I'm exhausted."

Rafe looked at her curiously but didn't dispute her decision.

"You'll be with her?" George asked.

"I'll be with her."

Tara smiled. She kept smiling as they moved away. She kept her head high, her hand lightly on Rafe's arm.

They entered the elevator and went up to his room. He opened the door, then closed it, standing behind her.

"What's the matter?"

She turned around and smiled at him, then sat on the foot of the bed and patted the spot beside her. "Come here."

He raised one dark brow high. He came to her.

She gazed at him, and stroked his cheek. "I'm still amazed," she murmured softly.

He caught her hand and kissed her fingers.

She shivered. With love, with hate that he could have used her so well. "Amazed at what?"

She lifted her shoulders, still half smiling. "That you saw me in that museum. That you were so taken—with me!—that you followed me. That you fell in love with me. That you're with me now, when I have a cunning criminal after me."

He didn't reply.

She twisted slightly, aching. He leaned back, bringing her with him, half atop him on the bed. Ragged, jagged edges of agony scraped at her heart, stopped her breath.

"Love is amazing," he told her softly, his fingers moving into her hair in a soft caress.

"Yes, when it happens so quickly."

One last time. One last time, she had to stroke his face. Give him a wistful and alluring smile. Ease her fingers over the tautly muscled breadth of his chest. Hear the sharp intake of his breath. Know that he wanted her.

That had been real, at least. The passion. The physical thing that had sprung up between them.

In that he hadn't lied. He had wanted her. Still wanted her.

Just as she wanted him...

"Tara..."

His body tensed and tightened beneath her, his flesh heating. The touch of his fingers betrayed the urgency he felt. His lashes were low over the glimmering fire in his eyes, and by God, she wanted her revenge, something to still the anguish that twisted and burned inside her.

"You were just captivated by me, weren't you, Rafe?" she whispered softly.

"Yes. God, yes."

"And it really is...love."

"Yes. You know how I love you."

She pushed against his chest, wrenching his hands from her body, slamming them away from her.

"You filthy liar. You're looking for your brother."

Amazement lit his eyes; then they turned hard, as hard as flint.

But she knew. She knew from that one second that it was true, and it was all she could do to keep from crying out.

"Tara, you don't understand—"

"I understand perfectly well. And I never want to see your face again, as long as I live."

She tried to move. He caught her, shifting his weight with startling agility. She was pinned down, a powerful thigh thrust between hers, an arm around her waist.

"Damn you—"

"Well, Tara. That was charming. Tease the man to death, then deliver your blow. But it's not that simple."

"Stop it!" she cried out. She was trapped. The fear was rising again. The panic. This was force, and she was overwhelmed. "Rafe! You know how I feel about—"

"Any feminine ploy in the book, huh? It won't work, Tara, because you know I'd never hurt you. I'd never force you."

She closed her eyes in absolute misery—but not fear. It was true! True, and horrible. She wasn't afraid. Not of his strength, nor of the power that held her there. It was different. She hated him; she had to hate him. But she didn't. She wanted to cry. She wanted to reach up and touch his cheek and feel all his wonderful fire. It was still there, the tension, the wonderful, explosive tension between them. The absolute dizzying need to touch him when he was near, and then, after that touch, to explore the simmering fire...

"Rafe, it's all a lie! I want to go; I don't ever want to see you again. I don't want you touching me."

What a lie. But he had to believe her. Because if he didn't, she would burst into tears of fear and uncertainty and misery. She would throw her arms around his neck. She would want him to comfort her, to soothe her, to make love to her....

How she wished there had been no past.

But there had been. And that was the only reason for the present.

"Rafe, let me out of here," she managed to whisper coolly.

"Not until you've listened to me!"

"I don't want to hear anything you have to say."

"You're going to hear it! And with your eyes open. Look at me, Tara!"

She did. She felt the warmth of his hand just below her breast. The power of his thigh cast over hers. The tension in his face, the vibrance of his eyes.

"Tara! Yes! I looked for you because of Jimmy. He's my brother—"

"Stepbrother, I understand," she interrupted blandly.

"Brother—we were raised together. God, what difference does it make? I loved him. I had to find him, for myself, for his mother. Is that such a horrible thing?"

"You seduced me—used me—to find him. You lied. God alone knows what you're really thinking or feeling."

"I'm trying to tell you! I do love you, Tara. I think it happened the first night we were together. Before we were together, even. Tara, forgive me! Maybe I was wrong, horribly wrong, to begin with, but that changed, and I couldn't just tell you then, because—because there was someone else involved. His mother was desperate. I was at my wit's end. If you'd turned away from me, I'd have lost her last chance. I'd have let Myrna down. In love or not," he said very softly, "I owed it to Myrna, to my brother, to take no chances. Can't you see? Please, Tara! Damn it, how can you believe that I don't love you now?"

She kept staring at him. She *didn't* know how. Then she grew desperate, because she was going to burst into tears at any moment.

"I've listened to you. Now let me go."

He didn't respond. She shoved at him in a fury, with an incredible burst of strength.

Still, if he hadn't chosen to release her, she wouldn't have been free. "Tara—"

"Leave me alone. Just leave me alone." She rose, turning on him, commanding, begging.

"You've got to believe me!" He stood, then walked toward her. He couldn't come any closer. He just couldn't.

A strangled sob escaped her. She rushed to the connecting door, ran through it and slammed it shut.

"Tara!"

His voice thundered after her, and she burst into tears as she slid the bolt into place.

CHAPTER 13

"Tara!"

His voice, rough, urgent, came to her through the door.

"My God, Tara, I'm not going to try to touch you or see you, but please, listen to me! I had no choice. If I'd tried to meet you with the truth, you wouldn't have given me the time of day. Myrna—Jimmy's mother—tried to reach you right after it all happened. But you had disappeared yourself. Galliard wouldn't let anyone know where you were. Tara, I do love you. I've wanted to tell you, to explain. Can't you see, it wasn't just me involved! I believed in you, but no one knew anything about Tine Elliott. At first I couldn't be certain."

He lost control for a moment. Tara felt the door shudder as he slammed a fist against it. "Tara!"

She felt numb again. So miserable that she was numb. A dead thing, with no strength, no will.

"Don't do this! Tara, Tine is still out there somewhere. You need me now. You—"

His words broke off with a sharp expletive. Distantly she heard the phone ringing in his room.

She knew when he left the door to answer it. She knew before he spoke when he returned.

"Open the door and come with me. That was the police. They think they have the man who attacked you yesterday."

She clenched her teeth. She couldn't go. She didn't think she could even stay standing.

She didn't recognize her own voice when she spoke. It was cold and hoarse. "I'm sure you'll recognize him. And I'm sure anything that can be dragged out of the man can best be obtained by your dubious means."

"Tara! This has to be done."

"Go do it, then."

She imagined that she could hear him breathing. She could even imagine the tension in his handsome features, the pulse ticking in his throat.

She did hear it when he inhaled sharply in decision. "I'll leave Sam and a house detective outside your door. Don't open it to anyone."

She didn't reply. She leaned her head wearily against the door.

"Tara!"

"I have no intention of opening my door."

"When I get back, Tara, you're damn well going to open it!" he promised her.

She heard him walk away. She closed her eyes, furious with herself, because silent tears streamed down her cheeks.

She didn't know how much time passed before she went over to one of the beds and lay down, ridiculously tired. Facts kept passing through her mind, events, sights. Foolish. They only hurt worse.

She didn't know if she'd dozed or if she had just lain there partially asleep. She became slowly aware of a tapping at her door, slow and hesitant at first, then growing louder and more urgent.

Keyed up and suddenly aware that she had every right to be frightened, she leaped from the bed and stared at the door. Silly—Rafe had said that Sam and a house detective would be there. If he had said so, it would be the truth.

But she walked to the door carefully. "Sam?"

"No, no, Señorita Hill. It is the maid. *Por favor,* I must come in."

Tara frowned. It was definitely a woman's voice. And most probably the maid. But she had to be sure.

She bit her lower lip, then hurried to the door connecting her room to Rafe's. She unbolted the door on her side and tried to open it, only to pause, baffled, to realize that it was now locked from the other side. She couldn't slip into his room to peek out into the hallway to see who stood at her door.

Where was Sam?

She went back to the door. "I don't need any maid service right now," she said.

There was a pause outside, then a whisper reached her, a whisper that she recognized.

"Tara, please! It's me. Jimmy Saunders."

"Jimmy!" she exclaimed. Could she be wrong? No, no, she recognized his voice! The moment he had begun to speak, she had known that it was him.

"Tara, I can't stay out here in the hallway!"

She fumbled with the lock, then threw open the door. For a moment, terror struck her. She might have made a mistake. He was in a hotel uniform, and his hair looked darker than before; he was standing next to a beautiful Venezuelan woman, with a room service table between them.

And he was sporting a rich, full handlebar mustache.

"Jimmy?"

She backed away. But he started laughing good-naturedly even as he stepped into the room with the nervous-looking woman.

"It's me! It's me!" He ripped off the mustache—crying out a little at the sudden pain, then grimacing and stretching out his arms. With a glad little gasp she hugged him. He returned the hug and softly closed the door behind him.

"What are you doing? Where have you been?" Tara demanded. Then she lightly batted him on the shoulder. "Now that I can see that you're alive and well, I could strangle you! No one believed me! Why didn't you contact the authorities? Why didn't you—what the hell was going on that night?"

"Shh!" he warned her. Then he smiled and pulled the pretty woman forward. "This is Tanya. After the fracas was over, I apparently managed to pull myself to her doorstep. Tara, I nearly died. I never would have intentionally deserted you. But I didn't know who I was—and Tanya was frightened. She knew that something had gone wrong with the authorities and that I had been involved. She nursed me herself." He gave the woman a warm smile with so much tenderness in it that Tara felt a new wave of anguish sweep through her.

"Tanya, Tara. Tara, Tanya. I would have died without her," he said very softly.

Tanya, who didn't seem to understand what had been said, did understand the love in his voice. She blushed and offered Tara a shy smile.

Tara smiled wistfully at them both, then gave herself a little shake. "Jimmy, what are you doing here now? Like this? Why didn't you just call me? Why—"

"Sit down. And keep your voice down. The walls around here may well have ears," he told her.

She looked skeptical, but sat obediently. Jimmy paced before her while he spoke. "I started a new life here, Tara." He laughed. "I learned to blow glass! But that's beside the point. About three weeks ago, I saw in the newspapers that Galliard was doing another showing in Caracas. There was a picture of you on the front page. When I saw it, I suddenly remembered everything."

"So why didn't you call someone, Jimmy? Why—?"

He smiled patiently. "I'm going to go back further in time," he explained ruefully. "My family is into gems. Shipping and gems. That led us into antiquities. You know, financing expeditions for various museums, that type of thing. Anyway, I had gone to Mexico as a guest of the government to work at a Mayan site. We dug up some fabulous things!"

"The mask!" Tara interrupted.

"Precisely. Anyway, a number of things were stolen one night. They disappeared quite cleanly. We assumed they would take a nice circuitous trip through South America before appearing in some private collection somewhere in the world. But we did have a bit of a clue— the authorities had been investigating Tine Elliott. I had followed him here, and snooping around, I found his little cache up in the mountains. I took the mask as proof of what he'd been up to. I planned to go to the authorities, but then I met you, and from what I had learned of the man, I was afraid for you. I waited, and then you called me, and, well, you know the rest. Except that I came here like this today because I don't want Tine Elliott to know that I've found you again, or that you've found me. I know he's back, Tara. He wants two things: you and the mask."

"I don't believe this," she murmured. "Why wait for two years to try to—"

"Tara, that mask is made of gold, diamonds, rubies, emeralds and sapphires. Millions of dollars' worth, even on the black market."

She shook her head. "But he *had* money!"

"Not enough, apparently," Jimmy said. "Tara, he has to be caught this time—before he hurts anyone else. That's why I had to lie low. For your safety, and for Tanya's."

She stared at him, still incredulous. She was so glad to see him alive that she wanted to kiss and hug him again—except that she didn't want Tanya to get the wrong impression.

She started suddenly. He didn't know! He didn't know about Rafe! And despite her bitterness, she acknowledged Rafe's right to know as quickly as possible that his brother was alive.

She smiled at Jimmy. "We may have a clue. Your brother is at the police station right now, trying to identify a man who attacked me yesterday. He must be associated with Tine."

"What? Rafe is here?"

The gladness on his face and the pleasure in his voice touched her heart. He also sounded relieved—as if he had infinite faith that big brother could handle anything—and a little amazed.

"Yes," Tara murmured. "He's here. Or, rather, he's at the police station."

"You know each other?" Jimmy demanded.

Tara's mouth twisted in a wry smile. "You didn't read enough newspapers. We were supposedly engaged."

"Supposedly?"

"Long story. Anyway, that's over. Now that you've appeared!"

Jimmy was frowning. "You were attacked? I can't believe that Rafe would leave you alone after something like that."

"I'm not alone. Sam is out in the hallway. And a detective."

Jimmy shook his head. He and Tanya glanced at each other; then he shook his head at Tara again. "No one is out there."

"But I'm sure they are! Sam—"

Jimmy laughed with little humor. "Tara! I grew up with old Sam. Trust me. I'd know if he was out there!"

"Maybe—"

"Let's not worry about the maybes," Jimmy said worriedly. "Let's get to the police station as quickly as possible. Tanya—" He paused, and switched to Spanish to talk to the beautiful Venezuelan. She nodded; Jimmy explained the exchange to Tara.

"She's going to call the police. They'll send a car for us, I'm sure."

"The phone is right over here—" Tara broke off. As soon as she had said the word "phone," the thing starting ringing as if on cue.

"Maybe that's Rafe right now," she murmured.

Smiling a little too eagerly, she pounced on the receiver, speaking into it breathlessly. "Hello?"

"Hello, Tara. Have you missed me?"

It wasn't Rafe. Her heart seemed to skip a beat, then slam against her chest.

"Don't hang up, Tara. Speak to me, love. I promise you'll be very sorry if you don't."

Seconds ticked by in which she couldn't talk. She could just hear him breathing on the other end, and she knew that he was laughing.

"What do you want, Tine?"

She stressed his name, looking anxiously toward Jimmy, raising a hand when he would have rushed over.

"A couple of things, sweetie. I want the mask. And I want you. For the time being, at least. I watched you yesterday. Nice. Old George put on a real good show."

She sat down on the bed, afraid that she would fall. He had been able to watch her, all that time.

"They're going to arrest you, Tine. And put you in jail for years and years. You could even be charged with murder, Tine. Your blond friend was killed, remember?"

"She wasn't murdered; she just got in the way of a bullet. Her destiny, it would seem," he said pleasantly. "But nobody's going to get me, Tara. Know why? Because you're going to leave there. Right now. You're going to go down to the lobby, and you'll see a man who you're going to greet like a long-lost friend."

"You're crazy! I'm going to hang up and call the police immediately."

"No, you're not. You're going to bring Saunders and his pretty little girlfriend and come downstairs."

She couldn't restrain her gasp. How could he possibly know that Jimmy was here?

She heard him chuckle. Anger swept through her, along with the fear. "You're still out of your mind, Tine. Why the hell would I do a thing like that?"

"Why indeed?" he mocked her. "I'll tell you why. I just couldn't seem to reach you, Tara. Tyler was there, every damned place you were. But he's gone now. What did you do, have a blowout with him, too, sweets? All the better. I still have this little yen, you know? I always was the possessive sort."

"The criminal sort, you mean. You should be shot, Tine. But that's not my concern. I'll never come to you."

"I think you will. You see, Tara, you were nicely, safely guarded. Forewarned, after those fools messed up yesterday. I had to rethink my plans."

"What are you talking about?"

"An old friend of mine. A certain lovely little redhead. She's sitting here with me right now. So pretty, so young. And if you don't do exactly what I say, I'm afraid that I'll have to kill her. Ashley will die, and it will be all your fault, darling."

Tara sank all the way to the floor, the blood draining from her face. Jimmy came rushing toward her, ready to grasp the phone. Life came back to her even as desperate tears rushed to her eyes. She shook her head vehemently, holding the receiver tightly.

"Got you on that one, didn't I, love?" Tine inquired lightly.

"I don't believe that you have Ashley!" she cried.

"Oh, but I do. It was easy. She stepped into the hallway all alone. She was at the door, Tara, just about to open it. And we simply put this little cloth over her face and she was as docile as a lamb. The annoyance was getting rid of the old man. And the detective. Quietly, of course. You want to talk to her?"

Tara didn't answer, because Ashley was already on the phone, her voice definitely scared, but her words full of bravado.

"Tara, don't you dare do a thing he says! Go to the police right away! He—"

Tara closed her eyes, because Ashley broke off with a small scream, and Tine got back on the phone.

"Don't call the police, Tara. If I see so much as a hint of the police, I'll shoot her. Maybe I'll take out both her kneecaps first. I can't tell you how bad that hurts, baby. Nothing, no tricks. You and Saunders and his little tramp do exactly as I say. Go downstairs now. Come to me, baby. I've been waiting for you."

Jimmy tried to snatch the phone again. Tara covered the mouthpiece, shaking her head, tears in her eyes.

"He has Ashley. He says he'll kill her if we don't come right now. I know that he has her; I heard her. I heard her...scream."

Despite her protests, Jimmy wrenched the phone from her. "Elliott, you idiot. My brother is here, you know. He'll tear up half the country to find her!"

Tara didn't hear Tine's answer, but she could tell when the phone went dead in Jimmy's hand, because he stared at it for a minute and then hung up.

"What?" she whispered.

"He, uh, he, he expects to get in contact with Rafe. I imagine he wants to make a trade. Us for the mask."

"But Rafe doesn't have the mask."

"But I do. I had it when I stumbled into Tanya's doorway, and it's still there. Hidden."

Tanya said something to Jimmy. Tara came to her feet. "How did he see everything? What has he done with Sam? And Ashley!"

"We'd better go," Jimmy said.

"There has to be something we can do. Something that won't jeopardize Ashley's life."

"I think there is. Where's your purse? I can leave a note in it for Rafe. Unobtrusive, in case Tine sends someone in here to check after we're gone, but it's a place I'm willing to bet Rafe will think to look."

"Couldn't we call—"

"I wouldn't trust that phone. Hurry, get me a paper and a pen."

"But what are you going to say?"

"I've got a pretty good idea of where we're going. You forget—I stole the mask from him."

Tara gave Jimmy her handbag, paper and a pen. He scribbled a note and placed it inside the purse. Tanya remained quietly at his side. She must be frightened, Tara thought. But the other woman remained silent and poised. Tara decided that she was going to do the same. She couldn't do anything less. Of all people, Ashley didn't deserve to be in this mess.

"All right, let's go," Jimmy said.

He didn't bother replacing his mustache, and the three of them went down in the elevator together in silence. When they reached the lobby, Tara prayed wildly that a score of policemen would jump out from behind the counter and produce a handcuffed Tine.

It didn't happen. Some tourists walked by, chattering in French. A group of Americans went past, boisterously discussing the delicious meal they'd had for lunch.

Then a tall man with broad shoulders and a Latin accent suddenly threw his arms out toward Tara.

"There you are! Come, give your old amigo a hug!"

Tara gritted her teeth as the man embraced her. He reached past her, smiling as he shook hands with Jimmy and Tanya.

"Now. Out front," he ordered under his breath.

They stepped outside. A black limousine swept into the circular drive. The man who had met them tipped the doorman and hugged Tara's shoulders again—then shoved her into the back. She stumbled, because he was pushing Jimmy and Tanya in almost on top of her.

Instinctively, she grabbed for something to hold. A hand came out, steadying her, becoming a vise around her wrist as she sat down, horrified, next to Tine.

For a moment she could only stare at him. He hadn't changed a bit. He was still trim, sandy-haired, with blue eyes, as handsome as only the all-American boy next door could be, the high school football team quarterback, tanned, broad-shouldered, appealing.

Except that now she knew. Knew that his smile hid a wealth of cruelty. That the glitter in those blue eyes was the glitter of avarice.

He smiled at her, a smile that grew broader and harder as she tried to wrench her hand away.

"I've missed you, Tara."

She didn't respond; she only returned his gaze coldly while icy trickles of fear skated down her spine.

"Leave her alone, Elliott," Jimmy said.

Tine chuckled. "Just what will you do, big man?"

"I have the mask—she doesn't."

"That's right. But Tara and I have a few old scores to settle."

"Where's Ashley?" she demanded.

"You'll see her soon. Just sit tight, sweetheart. We've got a little drive ahead of us." His fingers curled around hers. Suddenly he stretched her arm out, catching sight of Rafe's magnificent diamond—the ring she still couldn't remove.

All traces of his smile disappeared. "You were going to marry him?"

"I *am* going to marry him," Tara lied smoothly.

"Take it off."

"It doesn't come off."

He smiled again. "I'll see that it comes off," he promised her. "One way or another."

Tara lowered her lashes, fighting the temptation to scream with fear and rake her nails across his face. She had to be calm; there was Ashley to remember.

She stared at Jimmy and Tanya, who sat silently, hand in hand.

The limo's windows were darkly tinted. She had no idea of where they were going, except that they were beginning to climb high into the mountains, and it seemed that the afternoon sun was waning. It would soon be dark.

"Relax, sweetheart," Tine said softly, slipping an arm around her shoulders. "You really haven't got anything to worry about—not for a while yet."

But she did. He was right next to her. Very fit, a strong man, agile and powerful. She had learned that once the hard way. It seemed that every nerve in her body cried out. She couldn't bear being next to him.

She had no choice.

She closed her eyes, clenched her teeth tightly and prayed for the ride to end—no matter what that end brought.

"Another ten minutes or so and we'll be home," Tine said, as if he were addressing a group of old friends. "Home, Tara. Nice, cozy home. Luxurious, intimate."

She still refused to react, and he laughed, a grating sound that was entirely horrible.

Rafe returned to the hotel in disgust—not one of the men in the lineup had even remotely resembled the man who had tried to abduct Tara the day before.

The only good thing about the trip had been that he had been able to spend some time with Lieutenant Costello, the one man who had given him a serious hearing when he had attempted to find Jimmy two years before. Of course, by the time that Rafe had realized Jimmy was missing, it had been long after the night on the mountain. The lieutenant had been stunned to hear that the man had actually existed; he'd admitted that they'd suspected Tara Hill of inventing him in a wild bid to exonerate herself. Costello was a good man; Rafe definitely felt more comfortable knowing that the police now believed wholeheartedly that Tine Elliott was alive and well and in their country. Costello assured him that it might take time, but they would find him.

He knew something was wrong as soon as he reached the hallway. He didn't think the detective would have left—and he knew damn well that Sam would never have voluntarily deserted his post.

He hurried into his room. It was empty; nothing seemed amiss. He rushed to the connecting door, ready to break it down if she didn't answer him.

He didn't have to break the door down. It was locked only on his side. And he hadn't locked it.

He burst through. Tara was gone, and there was no sign of Ashley. The room was neat and clean—no sign of a scuffle, at least.

Trying to remain rational and calm, he started toward the phone to call the police, but he never reached it. The phone was ringing in his own room, and he raced back to answer it.

His hello was anxiously hopeful.

"Rafael Tyler?"

"Who is this?"

"Just listen carefully. I have a number of people you care about here. Your brother. And—"

"My brother!" Jimmy. Jimmy was alive. Rafe had always believed that, but...

Where the hell had he been? Why hadn't he called, written, let those who loved him know that he was all right? Why in God's name—

A chuckle interrupted his thoughts.

"Yes, I have him. Your brother. Excuse me—stepbrother. Yes, *I have him.* It was the strangest thing! I've been pulling my hair out for the last two years looking for that boy myself. Seems I did hit him last time. Good hit, right in the head. Erased his memory. He's been wandering around down here with a native girl all this time—and then Tara shows up and triggers something in the boy's memory. It all worked out real well. So now I have him—and his Venezuelan girlfriend. I also have a redheaded model and, oh, a lady who we both know and love. The illustrious Tara Hill. Nice rock you gave her, Tyler. And I have a paranoid detective, and an old man."

"Elliott!" Rafe breathed between his teeth.

"How perceptive, Mr. Tyler."

"If you touch her, Elliott, you're a dead man," Rafe said quietly.

"Well, that rather remains to be seen, doesn't it? I want the mask, Tyler."

"I don't have the damn mask, and you know it."

"True. But you're going to get it for me. You and your brother."

"You can have it. But I not only want Tara back here—entirely safe and sound—but the others, too. I want them released, and then the mask is yours."

"Now, now, you know it's not that simple. First things first. I'll meet you at the glass factory—way out in the open. At midnight. I'll have your little brother with me. He'll tell you where the mask is and how to get it. And he'll be careful, because he knows I'll shoot his girlfriend if he lies. And you'll behave, too, I'm certain, because there's an entire memory lane that I could travel down with Tara—before I shoot her. Now, if you're even five minutes late, I'll start proving my point by shooting the old-timer. Got it all? Oh, no police. If I see anyone with you, anyone remotely near you on that mountain, I'll begin by breaking his kneecaps."

"I'll be there at midnight. Alone."

"See that you are. You know, I'm smiling at your girlfriend right now, Tyler. Ah, memories! She's something, isn't she? Just like a centerfold, huh?"

Rafe almost snapped the phone wire; it took all his willpower not to reply.

"How nice, a silent pair. Don't mess up, Tyler, huh?"

The phone went dead. Rafe started to click it to call the police, then wondered if Tine Elliott had enough power behind him to have the wires tapped.

He sat down, shaking. He tried to fight back the rising sensation of panic. He reminded himself that his brother was alive, though he'd never believed in his heart that Jimmy could be dead. And it made sense: injury, amnesia. Jimmy would have never let them go crazy with fear if he had been able to do anything about it. He had been hurt, but he was alive. Rafe should be grateful for that, at least.

But he couldn't be grateful. He felt too much panic. Tine Elliott had Tara. Tara. All that he could see in his mind's eye were pictures of her. The beautiful soft silver fox fur clutched to her throat. Her eyes on his when they had met over the marble tiger. Tara...that night in her apartment. Half asleep, her guard down, the attraction calling to them both.

Tara...the softness of her lips. The beauty of her passion. Her love pouring around and over him, and becoming more a part of him than his flesh or his blood or even his mind. He couldn't stand the fear, the horror, knowing what Tine Elliott had done to her, knowing that Tine Elliott had her again.

You can't panic! You can't sit here like a helpless idiot! he screamed silently.

Something inside him came to the fore, something sharp that reminded him that he'd never been helpless in any situation before—he'd always looked to action. But then, he'd never been in love before, not like this. This time another person was the essence of his soul, and the danger was all directed toward her.

Think! Act! By God, of all the times in his life, this was when he most needed to be effective!

Rafe forced himself to breathe deeply. He clenched and unclenched his fists. He looked at his watch. Eight o'clock, and it was almost completely dark outside.

Four hours. Four hours in which Tine Elliott could be doing anything to anyone.

Not to anyone. Tara.

He inhaled, exhaled, and gripped his fingers to stop them from trembling. How many people did Elliott have working for him? Probably not more than five or six—it would be too dangerous for him to have any larger a group.

Rafe knew he was probably being watched. But he hadn't been told not to leave his room. He'd have to risk it.

But he didn't have a damn thing to go on.

He walked back into Tara and Ashley's room, blindly groping for some kind of clue. The beds weren't perfectly made, he thought. And it seemed that the makeup and perfume bottles on the dresser were a little out of order, considering the kind of organization both girls were accustomed to, being quick-change artists.

Someone had been here. Either to take them...or check the room out after they had gone.

He sat down on the bed. If anyone had left him anything, it was surely gone.

He stood up, pacing the room, reminding himself that he had never been a defeatist. He paced and prowled, looking at the carpeting, stripping the beds, searching through the drawers. There was nothing.

But then he paused, opening the top drawer again. Tara's leather handbag was there. He pulled it out and dumped the contents on the table.

He almost raked the entire mess on the floor with disgust, then paused. Among the lipstick, compact, wallet, address book, pencils, pens, stamps and other paraphernalia was an old shopping list. He studied it, tossed it aside, and noticed another slip. It looked like the floor plan for a runway.

Except that it wasn't. It was some kind of a map. And it had been written by Jimmy and meant for him. At the bottom the words "Tanya's walk" were written.

His blood seemed to race and make him dizzy for a minute. He sat down on the bed and studied the map more closely. He began to make out the mountain by the glass factory. The forests, the main road, the dirt paths. Shacks and houses.

His fingers started to tremble again. Jimmy had been here. Tine Elliott had bided his time well. Jimmy had come to Tara; Elliott had snared them both together. But Jimmy was alive, and apparently he remembered something, someplace.

Rafe rushed out of the room. He had no illusions. Tine meant to get his hands on him, too, and probably dispose of the lot of them together. That way there would be no one except for an overburdened police department left to hound him.

No, he had no illusions. That was why he had to reach Elliott before Elliott could reach him. And he couldn't charge in like a fool; he had to have help. With luck, Elliott would count on his feelings, on his sense of panic. Elliott would be pretty damn sure that Rafe would do exactly what he had promised, that he wouldn't go to the police, that he would be where he'd said at midnight.

Midnight would be too late.

CHAPTER 14

They stopped once along the way. Tine got out of the car, but when Tara and Jimmy would have burst into conversation, they halted, because the man who had met them in the lobby took Tine's place—smiling and pointing a pistol at Jimmy's face.

Tine returned, pleasantly informing her that he'd made an important call. She knew that he wanted her to cry and plead and question him, so she didn't. He had contacted Rafe, she knew. She didn't need to ask, and she was sure that he wouldn't tell her anything until he felt like it, so she was determined not give him the pleasure of her anguish.

But with him next to her, Tara's only help was a complete retreat into herself. She had to think about something else. Of course, that was nearly as painful, because she thought about Rafe. The funny thing was that she'd felt that she had been betrayed by him just as she had been by Tine.

And now she knew. There were no comparisons between the two men. Rafe had lied to her—by omission. But he would never have hurt her. And he had lied only because he'd loved his brother.

And she'd never known fear with Rafe. Not the kind of horrible fear that was engulfing her now. He'd tried to talk to her.

She lowered her head, wishing bitterly that she'd given Rafe a chance. She'd been afraid to believe him. Afraid because she loved him so much. And right now she wanted nothing more in the world than to be back with him. To give him the chance to tell her that though their love might have begun in deception, the magic between them had been stronger than anything else, and if they let it, it could be with them forever.

But oh, God, did he really love her?

What did it matter now? She was certain that whatever else he had in mind, Tine did not intend to let her go.

By the time they came to a halt, Tara was numb—it was her only defense. She didn't know where they were, only that they had left the sophistication of the city behind, and the poor ramshackle cliff dwellings that crowded the mountains were far behind, too. They had climbed deep into the upper countryside, where there were few roads and few houses, and where the bracken and trees were the only life to be found. Rocks and treacherous ledges abounded here, and the darkness had fallen swiftly tonight, like evil wings.

"Here we are, love," Tine said. "Home. Please, come in."

He didn't help her out of the back; he jerked her out. Jimmy started to protest.

"Should have left that mask alone, kid," Tine said, then added, "along with the lovely Miss Hill. Let's keep moving, huh?"

Tara was glad to move, except that she didn't know where to go. She could barely make out the dusky path before her. As soon as they had gotten out of the car, it had been driven away. She realized with a sinking sensation that it appeared that there was nothing up here, nothing at all.

No one would find them.

"You remember the way, Saunders, don't you?" Tine asked pleasantly. "Back to the great scene of your crime."

"Where are Ashley and the others?" Tara demanded.

"Straight ahead, love. We'll have a nice little reunion with them, and then we'll have a nice little reunion alone. Sound cozy?"

She didn't answer. He prodded the small of her back, and she started walking along a narrow pathway through the trees.

She spun around to face him. "You can let Ashley go now. What good is she going to do you? And Tanya. Why on earth—"

"Tara, shut up. Go."

She turned around and started walking again. Jimmy was behind Tine. Tanya silently followed him.

The man with the pistol was behind Tanya.

Tara wouldn't have known that they had arrived if the hut hadn't been pointed out to her. It was made of wood and tin and seemed to blend right into the cliff that harbored it. As they approached, the door burst outward. There she saw the man who had nearly abducted her. He spoke to Tine in Spanish; Tine answered him.

"Go on, love. You want to see Ashley, huh?"

Tara went in, stepping past her assailant with distaste. She entered some kind of a crude living room with an ugly-looking fifties couch and a few chairs and a table.

She didn't see Ashley or Sam, or the unknown detective. She looked at Tine, and he indicated that she should go down a hallway.

She did; there was another man standing in a doorway. Tara ignored the massive weapon slung over his shoulder and raced past him.

Ashley was there. Ashley and Sam and a young, strapping Venezuelan man. The detective, she assumed. Sam and the detective were sitting on a cot; Ashley was pacing.

"Ashley!"

The door slammed and was bolted behind the newcomers; Tara was barely aware of it. She was dizzy with relief that Ashley seemed to be unharmed.

Tara rushed to her. The two of them clasped their arms about each other. Tara felt Ashley quiver, and felt her self-loathing grow stronger, having dragged others into this. "Oh, Ashley!" she said, then turned. "Oh, Sam..."

But Sam, straight and proud, was standing with a wonderful grin on his face despite the circumstances. He had seen Jimmy, and they were in each other's arms, a barrage of questions and answers going back and forth between them. Then the detective starting talking in Spanish, and Tanya entered the conversation, but Tara finally got Sam's attention so she could make sure he was all right.

"Meaning no disrespect, Miss Hill. I may be mature, but I'm not useless. Those scoundrels knocked us out unawares, and that was all there was to it."

She was glad that so far Sam seemed okay, just indignant that she had worried that he was too old to handle the situation. And he was indignant that they had been removed from the hotel in laundry baskets, along with a ton of dirty sheets.

"I'm so sorry," Tara murmured.

"Would you quit that!" Jimmy insisted, a protective arm around Tanya, as usual. "Tara, I started this whole thing. No, I didn't. Elliott started it all."

"Can't we just give him the stinking mask?" Ashley asked.

"That's the plan, I assume," Jimmy murmured, trying to sound cheerful. But his eyes met Tara's, and she knew that he was wondering, just as she was, how ruthless Tine was. Was he capable of killing them all?

She'd come to know too much about him to hope for much in their favor now.

"What do you think our chances are for escape?" she asked Sam.

"The man right outside the door is carrying a submachine gun. He could—" Sam cleared his throat. "It's a dangerous weapon."

"He could wipe us all out in thirty seconds," Ashley said bluntly.

"Then—"

The door reopened. The man from the lobby looked in. He pointed at Tara. "You, come on."

"She will not!" Ashley protested.

He ignored Ashley and grasped Tara's arm. Sam leaped to his feet; the submachine gun was whirled toward him.

"Sam, sit down. I'm sure I'll be right back. Don't forget, I knew Tine well once," Tara said, trying to sound assured. Yes, she knew Tine, and she was terrified! But she couldn't let it show; someone would wind up dead.

"Tara, don't—" Jimmy began.

"I'll be fine."

She wouldn't be, but she had to convince them. Oh, God. Now more than ever, thoughts of Rafe were crowding in on her, and her knees began to wobble as she was led back along the hallway. She thought of when she had looked up, that first time at the museum. Seeing the tiger, seeing Rafe. Feeling from that very first moment the sense of utter excitement. Wondering what it would be like...

And then knowing what it was like to be held by him. Loved by him. Touched...

She thought that if Tine were to touch her now, she would just as soon die. She'd known real tenderness, real care. Passion, beauty.

She swallowed sharply; surely Rafe figured somewhere in this. Tine would be coercing him as he had coerced her. He wanted both the Tylers, because he wanted the mask. He wanted them both stopped from hounding him. It had become an obsession. Tine was obsessive. He had never loved her, but had simply been obsessed.

She was scared that he would touch her. Scared that he would get Rafe. Rafe would do anything to prevent harm from befalling the rest of them. God, she wanted him. She wanted to be in his arms. She wanted...

Don't think! she warned herself. Don't think that Tine could trick him, could get him here—could shoot him. Kill him. In cold blood.

Deal with it moment by moment! she pleaded with herself. And she tried to convince herself that Rafe was no fool, that someone would miss them very soon, that maybe the police were combing the mountain at this very minute. Maybe she could even reason with Tine, convince him that he could never get away with it this time, that he would be found, that he would—

"Tara. I've waited a long, long time for today."

She stopped walking because he was standing there. At the end of the hallway, waiting for her. She didn't say anything; she was too wary of his next move.

"Let's go, Tara."

"Where?"

"A walk in the moonlight."

"I won't go."

"The hell you won't."

A second later she screamed, because he strode straight toward her, grim-faced, wrenched her arm behind her back and prodded her forward. Stay calm! she told herself desperately, and then she wondered, what good would it do?

He opened the door and pushed her out into the night. All she could see was darkness, though he seemed to know where he was going. The night had grown cool; she could see her breath in the dark. Under her feet, the ground grew rockier. Suddenly he yanked her back. She started to scream again, but he cut her off sharply.

"The ledge, you idiot. Another step and you'll be over it."

She saw it then, the point where the cliff ended. Below the city lights twinkled. So tiny, so far away.

"Sit down, Tara."

There was a tree with a clear space beneath it. Tara sat. He stood behind her and lit a cigarette.

"Tine," she murmured, when the silence became unendurable, "this is idiotic. You should have disappeared into the South American rain forest. You have to be crazy. If the authorities get hold of you this time—"

"I want that mask."

"Why?"

"Why?" He laughed shortly. "Simple. Money. I know the right channels. I could spend the rest of my life in outrageous prosperity with that thing."

"But you made good money!" Tara cried out.

"With Galliard, you mean?" he asked, amused. She felt the skin at her nape prickle. He had stooped down behind her. She could feel his breath touching her skin, and she tried not to shiver. The longer she could talk...

"I could have made a fortune with you, love. I would have known how to package you just right. But you didn't want me. And now you think you're going to marry Rafael Tyler. Hah! That's a laugh. I'm the one who dragged you out of the refuse, out of the gutter. And you betrayed me, you little bitch."

"You didn't pull me out of the gutter, Tine—you tried to drag me down into it. I knew some poor, poor people, Tine, but not one of them would have stooped as low as you—for anything. They were all rich in something called pride."

"I'm impressed, Tara. But it's a pity you feel that way. I might have taken you with me. 'Cause it'll all be over tonight, you know. I'll meet lover boy at midnight, he and boy wonder will get the mask—and take a tragic fall down the mountain."

"You wouldn't!" Tara almost choked on the words. "Tine, don't be foolish! So far, no one can get you for murder—"

"Hey, it's easier to get away with murder than a few other crimes I could mention," he said lightly. "I think that's about enough talk. It never was a high point with me. I missed you. That's the truth, you know. There's always been something special about you—"

"Don't be absurd. There's something special to you about anything in skirts," she said harshly, inching away.

She stopped when his fingers wound into her hair and jerked roughly.

"No, you aren't the only one, but you *are* special. I felt it when I watched you on that runway the other day. I had a hard time doing things slow and right, you know."

He tightened his hold on her hair as tears stung her eyes. He was laughing at her helplessness. She felt sick, almost overwhelmed by the panic that was sweeping through her.

"Come here, Tara!"

She was so close to the cliff—but she didn't care. Blind instinct made her wild and furious. He wrenched her around by the shoulders; she brought her hands to his face and raked furiously, bringing a sharp cry of pain to his lips.

"You stupid little bitch—" he began.

And he released her for just one second.

The second had been enough. She was on her feet, still wild, unaware that she had nowhere to go. She tried to retrace her steps. Tried to race away from the dangerous cliffs so she could find a way down the mountain.

There was someone on the path before her. Coming toward her. She halted, then gasped and started racing forward again, relief singing through her. It was George Galliard.

Tara cast herself straight into his arms. "George! How did you get here? Oh, thank God! Are the police here? Tine is right behind me. George—"

He held her stiffly, looking over her shoulder. She turned, gasping and crowding closer to him. Tine was almost on her, wrath and cruelty on his features; along with the blood-red gashes she had torn across his face.

"George...?" The name escaped her in a gasp. Tine kept coming closer. George's grip tightened—then he pushed her toward Tine. She stumbled; he caught her in a grip so venomous that she cried out.

"George?"

"Sorry, love," Tine said softly, with an edge of malice. "You hadn't guessed? How do you think dear George got his start? No one would buy his damn fashions. I never worked for him; he always worked for *me*. Gems, gold, artifacts, in and out so easily, because who would think to check up on a world-famous designer? He arranged this nice trip back very carefully, right after he talked to you and discovered that you were running a little low. He had a hell of a time squeaking by the authorities last time."

"Idiot!" George accused Tine suddenly. "Neither of us will get out of it this time! What the hell did you have to take half the town hostage for?"

"I only did what was necessary. Quit sniveling like an old woman. Go back to town. I hope you weren't foolish enough to be followed!"

Tara's knees suddenly gave out with shock. George! What had looked like salvation had been a merciless trick. She couldn't believe she had run to him for help and he had handed her right back to Tine.

"Get up!" Tine yelled at her. "George, get out of here! I've been waiting for the return of my love so patiently!"

He turned, dragging her with him. She screamed; she kicked; she fought. And she knew he wouldn't loosen his hold for a minute. Not this time.

* * *

Rafe took five different cabs, stopping at five different places and coming out on five different streets before taking the final cab to Costello's office. He chafed at the time it took, but knew that he had to take the precaution. He burst in on the lieutenant so wildly that in retrospect, it was a wonder that the man had listened. But he did, and it was probably another miracle that he studied the ridiculous map with Rafe, stroked his chin and agreed that they could probably find the location.

"I'll call in one of my men—Juan Ortega. He's from the mountain, a farmer. But if it is not the place, Rafael, then—"

"It has to be the place," Rafe said hoarsely. "Jimmy is alive, and he wouldn't have done this without being certain."

They sat down and went through the particulars. The only way to get up there without being seen would be to take the back roads. That would take time. And they'd have to count on surprise. Neither knew if Tine Elliott was ruthless enough to start shooting or not. Since the woman had died last time, Costello didn't think that an effort at negotiation would be worthwhile.

Four of them would go: Ortega, who knew the mountain so well; a sharpshooter; Costello; and Rafe.

It was nearly ten o'clock when they set off.

They followed the city lights, then turned into the mountains. They could only go halfway by the main road. Soon they were climbing, and Rafe stared out the window at the mountain. Purple and haunted and shadowed, wild and primitive, and anything could be hidden there.

They reached a point where they could no longer take the car. They would have a long walk, he was warned, and they'd have to study the situation when they reached their objective—a hostage situation was always tricky.

Ortega did know the mountain. He walked easily; Rafe and Costello were panting.

"Here, this path," Ortega said. "If the map is accurate."

They walked until Rafe's muscles ached, though not as badly as his heart. Time was his enemy. And it was passing so swiftly. All he could see was the forest. Tree after tree, branch after branch. Eternal darkness.

Ortega stopped short. Rafe saw the lights seeping through the trees. Costello gestured, and the four of them scattered, circling the hut, which seemed to blend into a crevice of the rock and the forest.

It was the sharpshooter who found the right window. He beckoned silently to the lieutenant. Costello went around the front; Ortega went with him. Rafe and the sharpshooter stared at each other and counted off the seconds.

Then Rafe crashed through the window. The sharpshooter followed, covering them both with a burst of fire directed at the door. Rafe found Ashley first and pulled her to the floor, shouting that the others should duck.

It was really ridiculously easy. The sharpshooter shouted to the armed man guarding the hostages that he would be a fool to die for the criminal *norteamericano*.

He gave up without firing a shot. By then, Ortega and Costello were coming in through the front, herding two more men ahead of them. To Rafe's amazement, one of them was George Galliard.

He couldn't dwell on that for the moment, though; he saw his brother and clasped him tightly in an embrace.

But then he even pushed Jimmy from him. "Where's Tara?"

"Out—out somewhere with Elliott."

"Wait!" Costello ordered Rafe. But it was too late—Rafe was already out the door, running into the night.

He paused a short distance from the hut, looking left, right and forward. The mountain was so dark. It seemed to have an evil pulse. No, the pulse was his heartbeat. It was the panic, the fear, the desperation bubbling up within him.

And then he heard it—a scream. Tara. Sick with dread, but galvanized, Rafe started running. He veered, he slid, he crashed into the trees. She screamed again; the sound was nearer.

He saw her, and his heart caught. She was so close to the edge. Struggling. And there was Elliott. A big man, his blond hair gleaming in the night. He was laughing as she screamed. Bending over her, saying something, taunting her, touching her...

Something burst inside Rafe's brain. He thought he could rip Elliott into a hundred thousand pieces, do it savagely, do it horribly. He didn't feel quite human. Power rippled through him and he didn't remember taking the last few steps; he was just there, driving his fingers into Elliott's hair, wrenching for all he was worth, tearing the man away from her.

Elliott came up swinging. Rafe ducked, something warning him that his adversary was tough. He pitched himself into the air, bringing his full weight down on Elliott. They wrestled, spinning in the dust, against the rock. Rafe felt it all. Elliott aimed a well-delivered blow at Rafe's jaw. For a moment, the night spun—stars bursting inside his head instead of against the sky. He saw the man's fist rise again; he saw the hate in the powder blue eyes, and he twisted just in time.

He saw Tara there, standing too close to the edge. "Move!" he shrieked to her. "Tara, damn you, move!"

He saw her indecision; he saw her anguish. She was trying to figure out a way to help him.

He catapulted, putting Elliott beneath him, slamming his fist against his jaw. He took a pause. "Get out of here so I don't have to worry about you, too!"

Elliott swung and caught Rafe's jaw again. "Go!" Rafe shouted.

Tara ran.

"Tyler!" Elliott raged. "If I go, you're going."

"Then let's do it, damn it!" Where the hell was Costello?

They started to twist again, and Rafe got in another blow. They broke and stood, coming closer and closer to the ledge. They used their feet; they used their hands. Rafe slammed a good right hook under Tine Elliott's jaw. Elliott let out a grunt and went down, but the impetus took Rafe with him—over the ledge.

So this is it, Rafe thought fleetingly.

But to his amazement he hit another shelf just a short way down. He looked over a few feet, dragging himself up, leaning against a rock.

He gasped for breath and dragged in the mountain air. Elliott was a foot away, out like a light.

"Rafael!"

Costello was above him at last. He saw Rafe and Tine, and he grinned. "You need some help?"

Rafe laughed. It felt good to laugh. "Yeah, yeah. I could use some help. Take the carcass away!"

Ortega and the lieutenant came down to collect Tine Elliott's unconscious form.

Rafe waved away Ortega's hand when he would have helped him. "I need to catch my breath. I'll be up in a minute."

Costello didn't really think when he passed Tara on the mountain path. There was terror in her eyes, fear, anxiety—she looked like a beautiful gazelle caught in bright lights, elegant, still, ready to bolt like lightning.

"My God, where's Rafe?"

"Down—down on the ledge."

She bolted.

Costello realized that he hadn't told her that the man was fine. He shrugged. She would see for herself.

Tara just ran, her heart racing. Only the moon and stars illuminated her way; nothing but raw emotion guided her. There was no time to think that he was a man who had betrayed her, too. She was terrified, more so than she had been through any of it. The fear for Ashley, the terror when Tine had dragged her out. None of that meant anything now, nothing in the past, nothing in the future. She only knew that if Rafe was injured or—oh, God! no, she couldn't even think the word—she would not be able to bear it. She had to hurry. If she could just touch him, she could stop his pain. It was madness, but it drove her relentlessly through the trees, over the bracken, branches ripping at her clothing, stones and roots tripping her. Nothing stopped her.

She found him just below the ledge. Scrambling precariously down to him, she clutched a decaying root and paused, her heart seeming to rise to her throat and catch there, no longer beating.

He was dead. Blood trickled from his mouth. His eyes were closed, and he was hunched back against the rock, as still and pale as the stone.

"Rafe!" Tara shouted in desperation. Frantically she scrambled the last few feet to reach him, kneeling at his side, touching his forehead, taking his hands.

"Rafe, Rafe, please, I love you so much. I've got to get help. Hang on. I'll be back. I've got to get them down here. Don't—don't—you have to be all right. You have to be. I love you. I love you—"

She started to rise. The hands she was holding moved; fingers curled around hers.

She didn't see his eyes opening to slits, still covered by the dark shadows of his lashes.

If she had, she would have realized that never before had he appeared so like a tiger.

Eyes glowing amber and gold, muscles corded, ready to pounce. He felt the greatest burst of triumph—and happiness—in his life.

"I love you." He was careful to keep his words a whisper.

"I love you. Please, I'll get help—"

"No!" he croaked, exerting more pressure against her hands when she would have risen.

"Rafe, you're hurt!"

Guilt touched him. He opened his eyes a little more and saw the terrible anguish on her beautiful features, in her moon-silver eyes. The guilt was painful, but there was the rest of their lives to consider, and he couldn't lose her now.

"Tara...you have to listen. Before God, I love you. I started falling in love with you the moment that I met you. The first night. And each time I saw you, I fell further under your spell. I thought at first that I was a fool, that you had bewitched Jimmy the same way, had led him into disaster. And then it didn't matter. I'd have died a fool if that had been the case, because I love you so much. Tara—"

"Oh, Rafe! It doesn't matter. Shh! You musn't talk. I'll get help. You need care—"

"No, no, Tara. Tell me you believe me. Tell me that—if I make it— you'll marry me."

"Rafe, you need—"

"I need your promise, Tara. Swear that you'll marry me...."

"Yes, yes, oh, yes! Now let me get help—"

He wasn't about to let her go. The tiger pounced.

He sprang up, sweeping her into his arms, kissing her lips quickly, pressing her against his chest and letting out a hoarse cry.

"Rafe..."

She accepted his hug at first, returned it with fervor and delight, but then, she realized that he was solid and warm and moving—and completely healthy.

"Rafe!"

Tara slammed her palm against his shoulder, pushing him away, her cheeks crimson. "You're not hurt at all!"

"I do beg your pardon. Elliott had a very nasty punch, and I've got a mile-long cut inside my mouth."

"Oh! You made me think—"

"Oh, yourself! Did you want me broken and bleeding?"

"No! No! Of course not! It's just..."

Her voice trailed away, because he was grinning, with relief, with a smug happiness that caught hold of her just as his energy could, just as the need to be with him had infected her from the very beginning. She was dizzy with relief, ready to throttle him—and then so incredibly happy that everything could have come out all right when it had begun so bleakly and horribly.

"You're terrible!" she accused him. "That was the most devious thing I've ever seen in my life!"

He brought her down to the ledge, kissing her swiftly again, staring into her eyes, hovering above her.

"Would you believe me if I swore never to be devious again?"

"No."

"Have a heart. You're supposed to trust your husband."

"Husband!"

"You just promised to marry me."

"You tricked me!"

He smiled down at her ruefully, his knuckles tenderly grazing her cheek.

"I had to have your promise. I might never have had the opportunity again, Tara. I had to make you forgive me." His smile left. He was suddenly, painfully serious. "Tara, when I knew that he had you, I almost went mad. And when I saw him with you, I think I did lose my mind. There were things I didn't say to you, but I swear, I never said I loved you when I didn't mean it with all my heart. I wanted to kill Tine. I felt like an animal. I wanted to kill him because he was endangering you."

She reached up and touched his hair, studying his eyes with tears forming in her eyes because she loved him so much and because she knew, with all her being, that he loved her just as deeply and that it was a good love, honest and real, and that it could and should last forever.

"Oh, Rafe." She smiled. "I do love you. And I'm glad you didn't kill him."

"In the end, I suppose, I'm not an animal. Just a man."

"Just a man," Tara repeated the words, a whimsical smile touching her lips. "Just *the* man who means everything in the world to me."

Slowly, he started to lower himself to her again. To touch her lips with the reverence that the night and the moon and the mountain demanded. He was just able to touch her mouth and taste the sweet salt of tears and the hunger and the warmth, when their moment alone on the ledge in the darkness came to an end.

"Tara! Rafe! Where are you?"

It was Ashley—anxious, concerned.

Rafe lifted a brow to Tara. "We're here, Ashley. Coming!"

"Are you all right?"

Tara answered her, curling her arms around Rafe's neck, meeting his eyes with a promise deeper than words, her eyes softening to a misted silver.

"We're fine, Ashley. We've never been better."

Rafe rose and helped Tara to her feet, and his arms were around her all the way up the cliff, as if he would never let her stumble again.

CHAPTER 15

The mask was really unique. It was up high in a protective glass case, and there was a plaque beneath it, giving a few brief particulars: that it was Mayan; that it was ceremonial; that among its stones were forty-five diamonds, sixteen rubies, and nearly eighty small sapphires. It was on loan from a museum in Mexico City.

It was unique, probably beautiful in its way, but Tara shivered as she stared at the grinning golden face. It seemed to be an evil thing—and it had brought only evil. She didn't think she was superstitious, but she'd be glad when the mask was returned.

She left the Mayan display and hurried down the corridor, knowing exactly where she was going. And when she reached the room she wanted, she paused happily, staring.

This sculpture really was magnificent.

It was in the Roman section of the museum, with a plaque under it: Anonymous, A.D. 100, Black Marble.

Tara was still entranced by it.

Her life-size tiger, standing, watching. He was all power, all grace. There was nothing she wanted to study so much as the tiger.

Her back was to the doorway when she became aware that she was no longer alone. Someone had joined her in the tiger's room. Watching the tiger? Or watching her?

She looked up. In the glass case around a majestic granite centurion, she could see the reflection of a man. He seemed as tall as the centurion in the display case, seemed to tower in the dooorway, blocking her way. He stood there, as striking and haunting as the ancient works of art on display.

She grinned and reached out as he came around to her. There was a simple gold band on her hand now, one that nicely complemented the diamond she had still never managed to take off her finger.

"Hi," he said, slipping his arms around her to pull her against his chest so that they both stared at the sculpture. His chin nestled in her hair. "I thought you wanted to see the mask."

"I did. I hate it."

"It's only a mask," he murmured softly.

"Encased in glass," she agreed, adding, "just like Tine and George are caged behind bars. I still can't believe that George was involved."

"George kept Tine's business going once he couldn't flit back and forth between the States and South America himself. One of us should have figured it out before."

She didn't answer. He knew that she was thinking of the years she had spent with such ruthless people, never suspecting. She shivered beneath the silver fox fur of her coat, and he hugged her more tightly.

"It's all over now. And there were a few good things that came out of it. Jimmy would have never met Tanya, and they're certainly happy. Ashley would have never started her own business—and Mary might never have run off to Italy with my ship's captain."

She turned around, meeting his dark eyes, smiling at last.

"Myrna thought I was a sleazy felon!" Tara laughed.

"No. A felon, but never sleazy. And you made her day when you told her you'd be pleased to death to have her take care of things. Jimmy and I in the same year, keeping her busy with weddings. And Sam was so proud to give you away." He laughed happily. "And I've never seen such a beautiful wedding party—Ashley, Mary, Cassandra! And, of course, the bride. In silver that matched your eyes..."

She felt the golden warmth of his eyes, alive, tender and, as ever, hungry...like the tiger.

She lowered her eyes, staring back at the marble beast.

"The first time I saw you," she murmured, "I was astonished by the similarities."

"Yes?"

She laughed. "Between you and this tiger. I told you."

"Oh, yes, the tiger." Smiling, he moved around, surveying the sculpture. He gazed at her wryly.

"I'm not sure I find that terribly complimentary."

Tara grinned, walking around to him, slipping her arm through his. "Oh, I thought you were gorgeous. Full of intrigue and sleek power and grace and...well, you were on the prowl. And you were damned well ready to pounce!"

He grimaced. "You promised to forgive me."

"Oh, I have. And I meant to give you a compliment. The tiger may be dangerous, but he's also totally fascinating. I was drawn to him. And I was drawn to you."

He caught her hands, eyed the room, and saw that they were alone and pulled her close to him. "*Was* drawn?" he whispered in the tone that always sent her senses reeling.

She gave him a slow, enchanting smile. "Am drawn."

"What time did you promise to meet Ashley for lunch?"

"One."

"It's only noon. We've got plenty of time."

"Time?" Tara said, startled.

"The apartment is close. Come on!"

"Rafe!" she protested, but she was laughing. He took her hand and they started toward the door. He paused, looking back at the tiger.

"Thanks, pal," he murmured softly, winking.

Tara was almost convinced that the sculpture winked back.

They left the museum, ran down the steps, and hailed a taxi on the street. Sam was somewhere in the museum, but Tara would have been horrified if Sam had driven them. Rafe wondered what difference it would have made—Sam was surely old enough to know what went on in a marriage, but Tara would have blushed and objected strongly to being obvious.

That was one of the things he loved about her. She had the unique beauty and sensual appeal of a siren, but she had somehow maintained the innocence of an angel.

It was the siren who entered the apartment with him, though. She walked straight through to the bedroom, heedlessly shedding her coat.

He followed her, tearing off his jacket.

Then she was barefoot, curled up on the bed, smiling, as she awaited him. The sun fell through the glass overhead, catching her hair, making it a gold finer than any created by the earth.

He came over to her, and she rose to her knees, making a sensual act out of undoing his buttons, moving her fingers slowly, following each touch with a kiss, with the softest, hottest flick of her tongue. When she reached his belt buckle a sound rumbled in his throat, in his chest, and he caught her hair at the nape, raising her head to his, kissing her as sensation flamed higher and higher within him. She played her fingers against his chest and rubbed her hands down his torso, then caught the waistband of his pants. She broke the kiss and laid her cheek against the coarse hair on his stomach; with far less grace than she, he swore softly and tugged at her sweater, pushing her on the bed in his haste.

She laughed as he kicked away the remainder of his clothing and fell atop her, hands busy on the waistband of her slacks, eyes golden on hers.

"I'll never forget the first time I saw you," he murmured. "I'd heard that you were beautiful. I'd read that you were extraordinary...but none of it meant anything until I saw you."

"Lust at first sight?"

"Hmm. Something like that. I wanted to strip you right there in the museum."

He paused for a moment, gazing down at her naked breasts, touching them reverently with the palm of his hand, catching his breath as she moaned softly, her nipples rising to taut rosy peaks before his fascinated gaze.

"Right there," he murmured softly. "I could have swept you off, into the Egyptian area maybe, into a temple, because you looked just like a goddess, and I felt..."

"Like?" Tara breathed, her lashes falling over her silver eyes glazed now with her growing ache.

"Like thunder. Like lightning. Like Zeus!—ready to take on any form to seduce the enticing maiden."

His hands slipped lower, sliding away her clothing, teasing her flesh mercilessly with the vibrant power of his own.

"I never accused you of being a god," she told him, smiling as he tossed her jeans away and moved over her, his shoulders gleaming in the sunlight. "Just a tiger."

He lowered himself, carefully holding his own weight, until his lips were just a whisper away from hers. "Grr..."

She laughed until his mouth touched hers. Then laughter became a moan.

Whispers grew to a melody of passion, but the song that rose between them was more.

It was tenderness, and it was love. Fantastic and real and binding. And without thought, Tara knew in her heart that it had all been worth it. The past, and the treacherous road that they had taken to the present. Without the trauma, she would never have known that a dream could live. That her fabulous tiger-man could be real, could offer the love she had dared not believe in.

Tenderness and laughter, passion and fervor. She would marvel forever that she could be his wife.

And he her husband.

A tiger still, fascinating, intriguing, sleek and powerful, and delightfully...

Well, never quite, but sometimes, exquisitely tame...

And then sometimes, exquisitely wild.

ANGEL OF MERCY

To Cherry Adair Tatum,
lots of love and many thanks.

CHAPTER 1

The car fishtailed and spun crazily. Brad compressed his lips in silence to bring the Chevy under control again. If he went off either side of the two-lane road, he would crash straight into swampland, into the endless "river of grass," a hot and humid, godforsaken hell on earth. He was heading west on Alligator Alley—a road that offered a weary traveler just about nothing at all except for the miles and miles of mud and muck and saw grass, the occasional cry of a bird and the silent, unblinking stares of an abundance of reptiles.

No phones here. No fast-food stands, no gas stations. Just miles and miles of nothing but the Florida Everglades.

Brad hated swamps.

Not that it mattered much now.

He straightened the car and quickly looked into the rearview mirror. Michaelson was still after him. Glancing ahead, Brad noted that steam was pouring from the old Chevy's front. Hell, he hadn't even managed to steal a decent automobile. And now here he was in the middle of nowhere, the object of a hot pursuit, cruising in an old rattletrap of a car that was about to die on him.

Sweat beaded along his brow. Without the car, what would he do? He hadn't seen a call box for miles and miles. There was only the narrow, two-lane road, stretching through this eternity of swamp. He wouldn't stand a chance on foot. He'd be a sitting duck. They'd shoot him down in a matter of seconds.

Something popped and whizzed in the engine and a cloud of steam billowed out, obscuring Brad's view of the road. He squinted; there seemed to be some kind of a dirt road up ahead, to the left heading southward. Another glance in the rearview mirror told him that Michaelson was almost on him. He had to take the chance.

With a sudden, vicious swing, Brad veered to the left. The wheels bucked as the car bolted and groaned. It was a road—of sorts. Saw grass slapped against the body and windows as the car plunged along. Brad could hear the eternal drone of the insects, even above the groan of the Chevy's overheated motor.

The car pitched into mud. Brad wrenched hard against the steering wheel. In growing desperation he tried to floor the gas pedal, hoping to bounce out of the mire. The wheels spun; the Chevy remained stuck in the mire.

Brad slammed out of the car. Black mud oozed over his leather shoes and knit socks, soaking his trousers up to his calves.

He paused, listening.

He could hear the motor of the approaching car—Michaelson's car. Following.

There was a sharp retort in the air. Gunfire. A bullet whizzed by Brad's ear. The sharp retort sounded again. Another bullet. Closer. *Whish.* Nearly nicking his ear, making a sick, plopping sound as it embedded itself in the swamp.

Brad turned and ran. His gun was back at the site of the drop-off, along with Taggart's body. Damn, he couldn't even go down fighting. There were three of them with Magnums and sawed-off shotguns, and there was him, without even a nail file.

What a bloody stupid way to go down. Running, unarmed, in an infested, insect-laden, swarming, sullen, putrid swamp.

The mud sucked at his feet with every step he took. He hadn't gone twenty paces before he had lost both shoes. Running was agony. There was nowhere to run to, anyway. Nothing but saw grass and rattlers, coral snakes and gators, water moccasins and mosquitoes...and swamp. Every time he put his foot down, he wondered what he would land on next.

Another bullet zinged by, close to his face. He felt the air rush against his chin. He was dimly aware that night was coming. The song of the insects was growing louder; the horizon had turned red, bloodred. Turning around to look behind him, he could see nothing but grass, tall grass, like needles, raking against his hands, raking against his cheeks. Saw grass. River of grass...that was what the Indians called this place, this Everglades. And it was. An endless river of grass, for as far as the eye could see.

Another bullet whined and whizzed by in a deadly, speeding whisper. Brad inhaled sharply and felt a stab of pain. His lungs were bursting, his hands were cut and bleeding, but he kept on running, always running. Suddenly he sank, plunging into a canal. Kicking and thrashing, he came up, sputtered and staggered onto higher land. He turned, resting his hands on his kneecaps, struggling for breath. All he could see was the grass. Were they still following him?

"Think we hit him?"

He heard the faint voice. Probably Suarez—he was the bloodthirsty one.

Someone snickered. "Does it matter? If we did not get him, Old Tom Gator will."

There was a spate of raucous laughter, then Michaelson, who never laughed, never even twisted his lip in the facsimile of a smile, spoke quietly.

"Keep still. Listen. See if we cannot lodge a bullet in his brain. I do not like leaving fate to Old Tom Gator."

Brad groaned inwardly and straightened, inhaling again for all he was worth to run once more.

The landscape had turned red, the setting sun casting a crimson pall over the flat swamp waters and the few trees straggled out upon the distant hammocks. Red...it was the color that seemed to fill his lungs as he gasped against the humid air, struggling to breathe. It was the color of the saw grass, the color of the single egret that perched in a distant tree, balanced upon one leg.

Rat-a-tat. Bullets flew by him again.

Then he felt a pain, sharp and piercing, stinging his temple. Instinctively, he reached up to touch his head, then stared at his fingers.

Red. It was the color of the night. It was the color of blood—his blood, seeping over his fingers.

He had to keep going. The hum of the insects seemed louder as he staggered along. He could hear no whispers from behind him, no laughter, no words. He gazed up at the sky and saw that the sun was falling. A coolness was descending. The breeze picked up.

Chills shot through him.

Red would not be the color of night. It would be black here—pitch-black. Florida Power and Light did not call upon the snakes and the reptiles and the birds and the wild orchids. Night would descend, and with it would come a blackness like ebony, sleek and impenetrable.

In truth, the horizon was still streaked with pinks and golds and burning reds. Yet Brad could no longer see them. His mind was sinking into the ebony darkness, just as his body was slipping into the oozing muck. All sounds around him were fading to a soft, lilting drone.

He was losing consciousness. He couldn't allow himself that luxury; he knew that. If he fell here, he would not survive the night. He would drown in the mire, become easy prey for the predators of the swamp, provide endless fuel for the bloodsuckers.

He could not fall.

But he couldn't go any farther. Besides, there was nowhere to go. Staggering, he paused. Everything blurred before his eyes.

He heard a humming sound. More bugs. Hell, he'd never seen or heard so many damned insects in his life. They were coming after him now; a herd of them, flying, floating together, in mass.

They were almost upon him. The noise suddenly cut off. Brad pitched forward, certain that he was crashing straight into the horde of insects.

But he fell against something hard. And he was dimly aware that something soft touched him.

Then the red landscape was completely enswamped by the ebony darkness.

* * *

Wendy screamed at first sight of the man. For several frozen seconds, after she had squinted against the mirage and cut the motor on her airboat, she simply stared at him.

He resembled the creature from the Black Lagoon. He was an apparition, a giant pile of black mud, rising before her.

She was accustomed to alligators and snakes and any number of slimy beings, but gigantic mud creatures were not indigenous to the Florida Everglades.

It didn't take her long to realize the figure was that of a man. A tall one, nicely built. Heavily built, she decided, grunting as she tried to drag him onto the airboat. Once she had him there, she paused again, panting for breath, trying to discern the place and extent of his injury. She checked his pulse first. Fortunately, he was still alive.

She slipped a hand into the water of the canal and tried to clean away some of the mud from his face. Against his temple she found the wound— a small gouge, still bleeding. What had he done? Tripped and fallen against something? She shook her head, and a rueful, somewhat contemptuous smile curved her lips. City slicker. It was written all over the man. Beneath the mud she could see a fashionably cut three-piece suit, silk tie and cotton shirt. No shoes at all—probably lost in the muck somewhere. She sighed, shaking her head again. When would these people learn? A swamp was a place to be respected. It was not welcoming to the unwary. And now, what to do with him?

She sat back on her heels, lost in the dilemma. He wasn't seriously injured, so he probably didn't need to be in a hospital. She had no idea where he had come from, so she couldn't really return him anywhere.

She couldn't leave the fool lying in the swamp. It would be tantamount to murder.

Wendy sighed. Maybe he should be in a hospital, but even so, she'd have to take him home first and call Fort Lauderdale for an ambulance or conveyance of some sort. Since her car was up in the garage, she couldn't take him too far herself.

"Well, sir, would you like to come home for dinner?" she murmured to her prone form, then she laughed with dry amusement. It was the first time she had ever asked a man to dinner. Well, except for Leif, and that had been different. They had never exactly asked each other to do anything; tacit consent had always seemed to rule between them.

Putting aside memories of Leif, Wendy settled the mud creature onto the boat, then started the motor and headed into the swampland. She turned on the lights; it was growing dark, and night fell quickly in the swamp.

Two miles inland, she came upon a high hammock and switched off the motor. She docked the boat, then stared at the huddled form again, trying to determine once more what to do. She was beginning to worry because he didn't show signs of coming to. Concussion? Maybe. She needed to clean him up, then she could give his condition a more professional assessment.

After a moment of hesitation, she decided to leave him while she went inside for a stretcher. He was simply too big for her to move without one.

Her house was little more than a cabin, but it was self-sufficient, and she had made it home. A generator provided electricity, and though she bought most of her drinking water, she had a purification system, too. The house itself was a square frame structure with two bedrooms, a living room and a big, eat-in kitchen. Her furniture was Early American, and her windows were dressed in earth-toned gingham drapes. It was possible to sit in the house and imagine that next-door neighbors could be found twenty yards away instead of twenty miles.

Wendy hurried through to the second bedroom and dug beneath the bed for the canvas stretcher. She had no problem carrying the stretcher out to the airboat; it was not so easy getting the man onto it. He was not only tall and very well muscled, he was unconscious, and therefore deadweight. Grunting and panting and working up a sweat, she at last managed to pull him onto the canvas.

His clothing was going to have to go before she brought him in. Not all of it, but she could strip him down to his briefs. Although Wendy lived in the swamp, she tried to keep mud out of her house. She wondered briefly what would happen if he regained consciousness while she was stripping him of his clothing, then shrugged. If he came to, he could damn well help her, and he'd better do so pleasantly. He could have been dead by then without her.

His socks peeled off easily. His suit coat proved to be a problem. She could not lift his shoulders high enough to pull the jacket away.

Wearing thin, Wendy sat back panting. Realizing that his wardrobe was ruined, she decided to cut his clothes away.

Wendy scampered back into the house in search of scissors. In the kitchen, she decided to bring out a bucket of soapy water and a wash-cloth. Once she had determined a plan, she set about it with a certain energy and will. Although she was handling a complete stranger, it was a little bit late to be reticent about the situation.

She hurried back outside and began cutting away his clothing with a vengeance. She rid him of his jacket, vest, tie and shirt and gently washed away all the muck and mud on his face and his shoulders. She sat back then, studying him and experiencing a shaft of acute discomfort as she did so.

She had thought his complexion was darker; it had only been an illusion created by the swamp muck clinging to his sandy-colored skin. His hair was a tawny color, the type that lightened in sunlight and grew darker in winter. He had a nice-looking face, a ruggedly handsome, masculine face. His nose was long and straight, his brow was high, and his well-defined cheekbones rose above a hard, square jaw. Even in repose, he had a determined look. She wondered how old he was, then guessed that he was between thirty and forty.

He'd been heavy and difficult to lift because he was composed of muscle, sinewed and taut. He was bronzed, as if he spent time in the sun, and he was hard, as if he spent time working with his body. Yes, it was a nice body.

Wendy recoiled quickly from touching him. She gave herself a furious shake, refusing to believe that she could be thinking this way about a stranger's body.

She searched his jacket for a wallet but found nothing except a piece of spearmint gum. When she tried to reach into his trousers' pockets, she found them glued together by dried muck. Determined, she stood, loosened his belt and tried to slip his trousers off. At first she couldn't budge them. Then they suddenly came free and she fell back, landing on her own hind end with the breath knocked out of her and more than his trousers in her hands.

His briefs had come free, too. The man was now stark naked on the canvas stretcher.

Wendy blushed profusely, then froze in a panic as the man stirred and let out a soft groan.

She hadn't been wrong to try to help him, to clean him or cut away his clothing. But she hadn't intended to go this far. What if he awoke now? What was he going to think? How could she ever explain this?

"Damn!" she swore to herself. She rose quickly, rubbing her derriere and thinking that she needed to procure a sheet before the stranger woke up. She tried to run past the man without looking at him, but something wayward within her soul tugged at her, tempting her to take a peek.

He really was a nice example of the human male.

Muscled, trim and lean, with a broad chest tapering to a slim waist and hips and long, muscular legs. His chest was furred in a mat of tawny, red-flecked hair, which became a thin line at his waist and broadened into another thick mat that nested his sexuality. Despite her usual restraint, she felt her heart plummet and hammer, and for the briefest moment she couldn't help thinking that he was, indeed, built very well. She'd been alone for such a long time...

Slightly horrified at her wandering thoughts, Wendy gave herself a shake. It hadn't been that long, and staring at an absolute stranger in such a way seemed so wanton and disrespectful. Strange, but she hadn't even thought about sex in the longest time, and now, just the sight of a man's body had made her mind start playing tricks.

Hot, fiery tears burned her eyelids and she realized she hadn't even had a good cry for a long, long time. But there was no time for that now. She needed to get a grip on herself, get inside the house and get the man a sheet.

"What the hell...?"

Too late. He was awake. The man blinked and struggled to raise himself. His gaze raked over his naked body, then he looked up, and his eyes caught hers. His eyes were tawny, just like his hair. They were neither brown nor green, nor even hazel, but a shade that combined all the colors and became tawny gold.

Tawny eyes, misted in confusion, anger, wariness—a wariness so acute that it frightened her. She took a step back, swallowing, not sure whether to be embarrassed or scared, suddenly wishing that she had left him stuck in the mud.

"Who the hell are you?"

His voice was raspy and deep and not in the least reassuring. The sound of it added another layer to the myriad emotions playing havoc in Wendy's heart. It inspired a certain fear inside of her; it also incited a definite anger.

"Wendy Hawk. Who the hell are you?"

"What?" The wary look shone in his eyes again.

"Who the hell are you?" she repeated irritably. He continued to stare at her, so she nervously went on. "I live here. You fell face forward into my airboat. I've been trying to help you."

Amusement flickered across his face, leaving a smile in its wake. And when he smiled, he was very attractive. "You were helping me—by taking my clothes off?"

She sighed, blushing furiously despite herself. "I didn't mean to—"

"They all just fell off?" he inquired politely.

"No, of course not. You were wearing half of the Everglades. I can't help it if your clothes were so tight that everything came off with one—oh, never mind. I was about to get you a sheet and drag you inside, but apparently you can—" She broke off, gasping as he hopped to his feet. It was one thing to stare at him while he was lying on the ground and unconscious; it was quite another now that he was towering over her, striding toward her with little self-consciousness. "You can walk," she murmured. "Would you stop, please? Haven't you a shred of decency? I'll get you a sheet—"

"I'm sorry," he said pleasantly. That easy grin was still in place and Wendy suddenly realized that his smile was duel-edged. He wasn't sorry one bit. "Frankly, I assumed you'd already had a good eyeful of everything."

"Wait!" she commanded, racing back into the house, spilling half of the things out of the linen closet in her haste to bring him a sheet. He accepted it and wrapped it around his waist.

"It is rather strange, waking up stark naked in the middle of a swamp," he said. His voice was still very deep, the kind of male voice that swept into the system, penetrating. Wendy trembled slightly. Perhaps it was just the night breeze, coming to dispel the dead heat of the day.

"I'm sorry. I was trying to help you."

"I noticed." He laughed, pulling the sheet tighter around his body. "Really. I was just wondering how you would have felt if it had been the other way around."

"Pardon?"

"Well, if I had been trying to help you, and you were the one who had woken up without a stitch of clothing."

"This is ridiculous," Wendy said, wondering if she should have left him in the mud. "There is no comparison. I'd never be in your foolish position. This is swampland. You were wandering around near quicksand pools! If I were you, I would just be grateful for my life."

"Oh, I am grateful. Very grateful," he said softly. He indicated the door behind her. "Were you really going to invite me in?"

Wendy hesitated, uncertain then. She hadn't felt threatened when she'd first dragged him home. Now he seemed dangerous. He might have been out of his element in the swamp, but this man was no fool. He was sleekly muscled and toned as if he were accustomed to taking on physical challenges. And there was an air of tension about him, as if, even when he smiled, he were wary and alert, ever watchful of his surroundings.

"Hey," he reminded her, as if he had read her mind. "I didn't touch *your* clothing. You were the one undressing me down to the buff."

Wendy groped behind her for the doorknob. She opened the door and went in, waiting for him to follow. When he didn't, she paused and looked back.

He'd been examining his clothing. He stared at her with reproach, holding up the bedraggled pieces of his shirt. "I would have stripped on command, if I'd known it meant that much to you," he said.

"I was worried about your life!" she snapped.

He nodded, hitching up his sheet to follow her. "Thanks."

As he came through the doorway he looked around, taking in the cool comfort of the air conditioning and the squeaky-clean butcher-block passthrough to the kitchen. He didn't seem to miss much. His gaze swept the hooked rug and the rocker, the deep, comfortable sofa and the cherry-wood coffee table. When at last he looked back at her, Wendy was glad to see the wary confusion in his eyes once again. His question was very polite.

"Where are we?"

"The Everglades," she replied sweetly.

"But—where?"

"East of Naples, northwest of Miami, almost dead-set west of Fort Lauderdale."

A tawny brow arced high. "We're in the middle of the swamp. And you *live* out here?"

"Yes, I do." Wendy smiled pleasantly again, glad to feel that she had the advantage once more. She walked around him to the kitchen. Although she wasn't sure if she wanted a glass of wine, she needed one. And producing vintage wine suddenly seemed like the right thing to do. It would only baffle him more.

She took a bottle of '72 Riesling from the refrigerator and fumbled in a drawer for the corkscrew. Suddenly, she heard his voice behind her.

"Please, let me."

She was startled enough to oblige, letting the corkscrew slip into his hands while she backed against the counter. A tingling warmth swept through her as he brushed by. His chest was still bare and smelled of the soap she had used upon him.

"You still haven't told me your name."

"Bill. Bill Smith."

He was lying. She wondered why. Only criminals lied about their names. He couldn't be a criminal.

Why not? asked a little voice in her head.

The man could very well be a criminal. She had found him facedown in the swamp.

"What were you doing in the swamp?"

The cork popped out into his hand. He lifted the bottle to her and she nervously turned around, searching for glasses. They clinked together when she handed them to him. When he took them, they didn't make a sound. He poured the wine and raised his glass to hers.

"Cheers. I was lost. A fool, just like you said. I'm afraid that I don't know much about this area at all."

Wendy was determined to pry some truth from him. She lifted her glass politely but did not let her eyes waver from his. "A swamp is a strange place to suddenly lose oneself."

"My car broke down." He lifted the bottle and studied the label. When he looked at her again, his voice was soft. "I am grateful to you for helping me. Thank you."

Wendy nodded, unsure of herself. "You should take care of the gash on your forehead."

"Gash?" He frowned and touched his temple. "Oh, right."

"You probably need some stitches."

"No, I'm sure it will be all right. I'm pretty tough."

"I can at least clean it out for you," she offered.

"I'd appreciate that." He touched the wound again, then ran his fingers through his hair. "I'm still pretty muddy."

"Well, you can take a shower for yourself now."

"Is there one? May I?"

"Down the hallway, second door on your left. Please, Mr. Smith, go right ahead."

"Thanks." He handed her his half-consumed glass of wine and strode down the hallway. Wendy heard the door close.

She gnawed on her lower lip for a moment then walked down the hallway, heading for her bedroom. After a moment's hesitation she knelt down and pulled out the bottom drawer of her dresser. She dug around for several seconds and came up with a T-shirt, jeans and a pair of briefs. This man was only a little bit taller than Leif, and they had similar builds.

Back in the hallway, she could hear that the shower was still running.

She tapped on the door. "I've left some clothes for you out here. I think they'll fit."

Wendy returned to the kitchen and thoughtfully sipped her wine again. Was she crazy to be helping him? No, of course not. She had known that she couldn't just let him die in the wilderness.

And yet she was wary, concerned by the effect he'd already had on her. Reluctant to think about it, she opened the refrigerator, idly picked out some vegetables and began to slice them. By the time he came out of the shower, clean and dressed with his hair still wet and slicked back, she had added diced chicken to the vegetables and was stir-frying the lot of it in a huge skillet.

He leaned across the counter. "Smells delicious."

"Thank you."

"Does it mean that I'm invited to dinner?"

"You have no choice. I don't think I can get you out of here today."

"Why not?"

"My car is in for repairs, and the garage closed at five. All I have is the airboat. Well, actually, I could take you back to the road and you could hitchhike—"

"I'd much prefer the dinner invitation," he said hastily.

By way of response, Wendy dished the vegetables and meat onto a platter and handed it to him. "Mr. Smith, if you'd set that on the table...?"

"Certainly."

Wendy took brown rice from the stove, emptied it into a bowl and joined him at the kitchen table, which she'd already set for two. He pulled out her chair, then retrieved both their wineglasses and the bottle before sitting down across from her. He smiled at her, and her heart gave a little thud again—she did like that smile.

"Thanks. For everything."

Wendy nodded, almost afraid to speak.

"Whose clothing?"

She swallowed tautly. "My husband's."

"Oh." His eyes narrowed warily. He was silent for a moment then gestured toward the table. "We're eating without him?"

"He's dead."

"Oh. I'm sorry."

Wendy nodded again. Strangers couldn't really be sorry. They couldn't really care. Especially this one. He was more relieved than anything else, she was certain of it.

"You live here alone?"

It was the question she'd dreaded. She was a prime target. And the more she saw of him, the more she became certain that he wasn't as innocent as he wanted to appear.

But her instinct told her she could trust him, that he would never hurt her. It was a foolish thought, a false sense of security, she told herself. Still, it was there, and she couldn't shake it.

"Yes, I live here alone."

"Wendy," he murmured. "Wendy Hawk." He leaned forward and reached out. Before she could think to protest, he'd curled a strand of her hair around his finger. "A five-foot-two, blue-eyed blonde named Wendy Hawk who looks like an angel and lives in this sultry pit of hell. Am I dreaming, or did I die and make it to heaven?"

"I'm almost five-four, my eyes are gray, and not even the most avid nature lover would ever compare this place to heaven."

Wendy gently tugged her hair from his grasp. Unable to stay at the table any longer, she picked up her wineglass and backed away, feeling as if a tempest were brewing within her.

"We need to do something about that gash," she murmured.

"You haven't eaten."

"I was just keeping you company. I had dinner with a friend before I found you." It was almost the truth. She had been coming from Eric's and she had eaten lunch with him earlier. "Please, go ahead, though."

She smiled a little weakly and turned away, sipping her wine as she moved into the living room. She turned on the television and ambled back to the sofa, vaguely noticing that the news was on while reproaching herself for abandoning a guest at the table.

He wasn't really a guest. She didn't know anything about him. When he had finished eating, she would do what she could for the gash in his forehead, then return him to the road.

The word *Everglades* suddenly caught her attention, and Wendy stared at the television with interest. She frowned, trying to catch up on the story; she had come in on the middle of it.

A violent confrontation had erupted over the illegal transport of drugs. The FBI had been involved; also the Drug Enforcement Agency and the local authorities. An agent had been killed, and the drug runners were still at large. A man's photograph flashed on the screen, then Wendy's vision was suddenly blocked.

Bill Smith stood directly in front of the picture. Without turning around, he flicked off the television.

Wendy straightened, glaring at him. "I was watching that."

He stared at her intently for a moment. His chilling look made her shudder, and she wondered again if she hadn't been a fool, bringing him into her home.

Then she realized that she wasn't trembling with fear, but with a strange warmth. He was wearing Leif's clothes. He was Leif's size, she knew that, and in the darkness, in the heat of passion, he might be very much like Leif.

No. He wasn't like her husband at all.

He was arresting and appealing all in his own right, and he was stirring up long-buried desires and emotions within her, feelings she was afraid to face.

And yet he was in her house. It was going to be a long night.

"The television," she reminded him. "I was watching the news program."

"I'm sorry. I needed your help."

"For what?"

"This gash. Would you mind? Have you got some peroxide or something?"

"Sure." Wendy went into the hall, pausing to flick on the television again. The news was already over, and a game show had begun.

Wendy hurried to the bathroom for the peroxide and Mercurochrome. When she opened the medicine chest, she flinched, surprised to see his reflection in the mirror. He was standing right behind her, his eyes intense as he watched her. "Where do you want me?" he asked.

She shrugged. "You might as well sit right here."

He did. Wendy poured peroxide on a cotton ball and gingerly sponged it over his temple. Although he didn't move, she winced at the sight of the wound. Whatever he had struck had caused a deep gash. She knew it had to be painful for him.

After she had finished with the peroxide, she hesitated.

"What's wrong?" he asked.

"This stuff is going to hurt."

He nodded. "That's okay. Do your damage, please."

Blushing, she took the medicine bottle from him. Although she dabbed at his head repeatedly, he remained stoically silent. She bit her lip, dabbing carefully. "I can't imagine what you hit," she murmured. "It's almost as if the flesh were spooned out...."

"Strange, isn't it?" he murmured. He took the second cotton swab from her, tossed it into the trash can and smiled again. "I feel better already."

"I'm glad."

"Can I make you some coffee?"

She shook her head. "No. But I will have tea."

Wendy followed him into the kitchen, where he filled the coffeepot and she filled the kettle. The man had a nice manner about him. He was able to be helpful and yet not seem intrusive. She was acutely aware of him, of every move he made. She was aware of too much. His smooth jaw...he had shaved that morning, she was certain. His scent...a musky odor that mingled with the clean smell of the soap. His eyes...tawny and alert.

She was so accustomed to being alone that the mere presence of another human being heightened her awareness. Wasn't he just a normal man? A lost city slicker?

No, this man was special. This man was arresting and alluring.

"What do you do?" she asked him as they waited for the water to boil and the coffee to perk.

"Do?" he said blankly.

"Yes. For a living."

"I'm in—pharmaceuticals."

"Salesman?"

"Er—yes."

"You were heading toward Naples?"

"Yes. Yes, I was."

"Do you live in Fort Lauderdale?"

"Well, actually, I live in New York. I was just—transferred down here."

The water boiled. Wendy turned off the burner and poured the water into the teapot. When she felt him watching her, a warm sensation surged through her blood. So this was it, she thought. This was the way it felt, that spark of attraction. She wasn't sure if it was right or wrong, or if it was painful or pleasant. He was a pharmaceuticals salesman from New York whose name was Bill Smith. He'd literally stumbled into her life, and she was feeling alive for the first time in years.

She spun around. He was studying her, his eyes warm, sparkling with a strange tenderness. He shook his head, smiling. "How did you get here? Do you really live here all the time? What do you do for a living?"

"Once upon a time, I was a nurse. Then I met Leif. He was an environmental scientist. This was his home. I came out here to be with him."

"And you've stayed?"

"It's home. I love it."

"How the hell can you love the swamp?"

"There's much more here than swamp, Mr. Smith."

He cleared his throat. "Someone who has seen me in less than briefs is still calling me Mr. Smith?"

She flushed but kept her chin high. "This is a beautiful place, Bill. You haven't looked. If you spent time here, you'd see the magic, and you'd understand."

He didn't believe her, not for a minute. He hated this place: the quicksand, the reptiles, the stinking insects. And yet, there had already been magic in the night. The fact that he was alive was a miracle in itself. He had awakened to see her standing above him, blond and petite and beautiful, an angel of mercy, protecting him from the darkness.

Now it was time for another miracle: getting his man, and getting out of here alive. He sobered quickly, hoping that Michaelson and his men had really given up. He needed to see a newscast, without Wendy around.

Wendy. He even liked the name. It suggested the clean coolness of a breeze, the exciting rush of a storm. A fitting name for this tempestuous angel.

Whoa. He couldn't let his mind wander. He had to find out what else had happened that day. He didn't think that Michaelson could have followed him here, into the thick of the marshy wilderness. Michaelson wasn't any good at navigating the swamps. But still, he'd have to be careful—very careful.

If he could just keep her away from the newscasts, he would be in a good position.

He reached out and touched her cheek. It was as soft as silk, golden tan against the nearly white halo of her hair. "Are you going to let me stay here?" he asked her softly.

"Once I picked you up, there really wasn't much choice," she told him. She cleared her throat. "There's—there's a spare bedroom next to the bath."

"Maybe in the morning you'll show me why you live here," he said. "Good night."

Wendy watched as he retreated into the dark bedroom, his words an echoing whisper that stirred and rustled in her heart.

CHAPTER 2

When he slept, he dreamed of her.

It was probably natural. His last conscious thought was of her, of those beautiful, silver-blue eyes, sparkling with determination when she'd sent him off to the guest room. She'd stared at him with a blunt honesty and self-assurance that he had found admirable. She wasn't a coy woman; she wouldn't play games. She lived here alone, she was damned vulnerable—and he knew it. But hers was a calculated risk. If she hadn't assessed him quickly and decided that he wasn't a trustworthy character, he wouldn't be here. She would have invited him back into the airboat and right now he would be standing on the roadside with a bandaged forehead and an upturned thumb.

And of course, she was perfectly safe with him.

But that didn't stop him from dreaming.

Sweet dreams.

She was an acre of heaven in a godforsaken wasteland, a diamond among pebbles, a bolt of silk among bales of burlap. He didn't know what it was about this woman that had seeped inside him so deeply, so quickly, but she had penetrated his world.

Even her voice was music—a smooth, lyrical melody, accented with tenderness, infused with laughter. In his dreams she walked to him, and he watched her, fascinated anew by the easy sway of her soft blond hair, hypnotized by the sparkling beauty of her eyes. He smiled and he reached for her, imagining how her supple body would feel in his arms. She moved in a night mist, a dusky fog that reminded him he was dreaming.

For now, a dream would suffice. She would be perfect, with a slim waist and smooth breasts that just filled his hands, firm breasts with dark rose nipples. Her hips were rounded, too, slightly flared beneath his hands. They didn't know each other very well, but they knew the really important things about each other, things that couldn't really be said but could only be sensed in another person. He wanted her, and he wanted her just this way—in tacit understanding, in sweet, ardent, mutual yearning.

She moved closer, and he exhaled. His entire body tensed and he reached out to touch her. He felt the bed sink as she curled her long, supple legs beneath her and sat there, staring at him. He could almost feel the warmth of her breath against his face.

Suddenly the subconscious realms of dream gave way to reality.

He wasn't imagining the weight at the foot of his bed.

Slowly, still struggling against the enticing darkness of sleep, Brad opened his eyes.

For the longest time he lay still, awake but perfectly still—and absolutely amazed.

There was a creature at the foot of his bed. It wasn't Wendy; it wasn't a woman at all. And it was certainly not the stuff of dreams.

It was some kind of cat. An enormous, fierce-looking cat.

At first, Brad thought of a tiger, but he knew that tigers weren't indigenous to this swamp. The creature had tawny gold fur and menacing yellow eyes. It stared at him for a moment, then curled back its lip and let out a bloodcurdling noise.

His blood seemed to congeal, but he remained perfectly still, staring at the hundred-pound monster. Great! He'd eluded Michaelson and escaped the perilous reptiles of the Everglades, only to become catnip for some giant feline.

"Bill?"

He heard Wendy's voice just as light flooded the room.

"Wendy, no! Get out—and shut the door!" he warned her. Standing in the doorway, with her hair a soft, golden cloud about her fragile features, she even resembled an angel. Her eyes shimmered with concern.

He wasn't about to let her become cat food.

Brad sprang up on his knees, ready to meet the teeth of the animal, ready to grab for its throat. He'd never come across anything quite like this in his training, but what the hell, a man couldn't live forever. If he could get to the cat before the cat got to her...

"Baby!" Wendy chastised, striding into the room.

"Wendy! I said—"

"I'm sorry, Mr. Smith." She marched in, heading straight for the animal at the foot of his bed. "Baby has her own little door in the back of the house. She comes and goes as she pleases. Guess I forgot to warn you about her."

Crouched by the pillow and clad only in the borrowed briefs, Brad arched a brow. Wendy sat down by the cat, scratching the animal's ears, flushing ruefully as she glanced Brad's way. "I am sorry. Did she frighten you?"

"Uh, no, not at all," Brad lied blandly. "Baby, huh?"

"She's a Florida panther. An endangered breed."

And she should be! Brad thought, but he didn't think that Wendy would appreciate the sentiment. Slowly he slid back under the sheets and pulled them up to his waist.

"Baby, huh?"

"Well, she was just a cub when I found her. Someone had made an illegal game hunt of her mother, leaving her an orphan. We kind of called her 'the baby,' and the name just seemed to stick. She's really very affectionate and very, very sweet."

"I'm sure," Brad agreed.

Baby let out another sound that was something between a roar and a purr, and Wendy flashed Brad another of the smiles that seemed to cascade into his libido—and his heart.

"Honest. She's gentle, I swear it."

Tentatively, Brad stretched out a hand to pat the cat on the head. "Nice kitty."

Baby licked her chops. Brad decided that Baby's teeth could have belonged to a saber-toothed tiger.

But she didn't nip at him. She merely stretched out on her back, thrusting all four paws up in the air.

Wendy laughed. "She likes to have her stomach scratched." Brad watched her slim fingers move over the silky pelt and he longed to tell her that he liked to have his stomach scratched, too. The very thought of it made a certain heat suffuse his veins. He wondered if his thoughts were revealed in his eyes. With one glimpse, Wendy blushed and pulled at the cat, hauling her down from the bed.

"Sorry," she murmured. "Come on, Baby. We should let our company sleep awhile longer."

When the door closed softly behind her, Brad exhaled, realizing just how damned tense he had been, and just how knotted and hot he still felt. His fingers were curled into fists, and the sheet didn't provide much cover for his body. Maybe she had noticed more than the message in his eyes.

Groaning softly, Brad tossed away the covers and rose. A soft stream of pink was filtering into the guest room through the soft cream-colored curtains. Brad walked over to the window and pulled them open.

The early-morning air seemed to be colored by the sunrise in shades of glittering gold and fairy-tale pink. From the window he could see that they were on a rise of higher ground, that trees and flowers and a little fenced-in garden surrounded this side of the house. The sun reflected off a pool of water beyond the trees, though, and Brad imagined that they were probably on a hammock that stretched out perhaps an acre before giving way to the canals and muck and saw grass of the swamp.

The view from the window was pleasant, though. Wild orchids grew in profusion over the cluster of trees, in shades of lilac, yellow and pink. Closer to the house, there was a garden of roses and a bougainvillea. The flowers provided an aura of silence...and a curious sense of peace.

Brad gave himself a mental shake. The last thing that surrounded him, he reminded himself bitterly, was any semblance of peace. He had to get dressed and get moving and decide what the hell he should be doing.

With that thought in mind, he quickly donned his borrowed clothing and stepped out of the bedroom.

A glance down the hallway told him that Wendy was already in the kitchen. She was wearing denim shorts and a tank top, socks and a pair of sneakers. Her blond hair was pulled back into a simple ponytail that fanned over her shoulder as she poured water into the coffee machine.

Brad smiled at her as he ducked into the bathroom. "You could have gone back to sleep!" she called.

He stuck his head out and grinned. "Naw, I'm awake now."

He washed his face studiously and used the toothbrush she had given him. Then he stared at his features. The gash in his head was ugly, but he could arrange his hair to fall over it. He probably should have had a few stitches, but he wasn't going to die from the lack of them. With a shrug, he splashed water over his face again. He had to know what was going on. He probably needed to act, but he didn't know what he should be doing. He really needed to talk to the boss. Hopefully, Wendy would take him to civilization, where he could make a phone call and find out what the hell was happening.

A little hammer seemed to slam against his heart.

Well, then, that would be it. His blond angel of mercy would drop him off, and that would be all. So much for dreams. So much for sweet images of her coming to him in the night, smiling, reaching out to touch him...

So much for dreams of reaching out and cradling the fullness of her breast in the palm of his hand, of tasting her lips.

"Damn!" he muttered out loud, shaking his head, dousing his face again in the water. He had to break this spell, get away from this woman.

But he still needed her help.

He turned off the water and combed his hair back with his fingers, carefully pulling a lock over the ugly reminder of the gash.

Outside the kitchen, the aroma of cooking bacon filled the air, and the scent was making him ravenous.

Baby was nowhere to be seen and Wendy was poised by the counter, looking out to the living room. Brad saw that the television was on, tuned into one of the popular, national news shows. National news...

Was he safe? he wondered. He hoped so.

She turned away from the television to greet him. "Hi. Sorry you were woken up."

He shook his head. "I'm not a late sleeper anyway."

She smiled at him, and again, he liked her lack of guile. "Want some coffee?" she asked.

"I'd love it. I'll help myself."

As he stepped into the kitchen, she brushed past him, going to the stove while he headed for the coffeepot. There was a beautiful scent about—something clean and fresh and light. He was tempted to grab her, sweep her into his arms, bury his face in the perfume of her hair.

But if he did so, he thought, grinning, he would probably end up wearing his coffee rather than drinking it. He poured himself a cup, then contented himself with leaning against the counter to watch her. He studied the golden hair that played over her sun-browned shoulders, the natural sway of her hips, the easy grace that seemed to rule her every motion.

Sensing his thorough observation, she turned to face him. "How do you like your eggs?"

He grinned. "I always feel lucky if I get them cooked," he told her.

She grimaced. "Scrambled, over easy, sunny-side up?"

"However you have yours," he said firmly.

With a shrug, she cracked an egg into a frying pan. He was having his eggs sunny-side up.

"As soon as we've eaten, I'll take you to the garage. There's a phone there. No use rushing, though. The phone is inside, and the garage doesn't open until nine."

"I'm not in any hurry," he said softly.

Wendy not only heard his voice, she felt the timbre of it. He hadn't really said anything, yet his words seemed to wash over her in a gentle, beguiling caress.

Nudging an egg with the spatula, she wondered why he had such an effect on her. She couldn't forget that he was lying about his name. And men just didn't lie about their names without a reason.

But here initial instincts had been right. She had trusted him in her house, and he had proven that he deserved that trust.

Face it, Wendy! she taunted herself. You don't know a damn thing about him, good or bad. The real truth is that you're attracted to him, and though you're incapable of going about a simple sexual relationship, you just want to hold on to him and think about the possibilities....

She swallowed, trying to ignore her unhappy thoughts. The eggs were done. She strained them with the spatula and slipped them onto plates. Her guest was right beside her, ready to take them from her.

Glancing his way, she couldn't help but admire the planes and angles of his face. He was handsome, but a far cry from pretty. The texture of his skin was masculine, as were the muscled structure of his sinewed form and the calluses that lined his strong palms. Idly she wished that she could have him unconscious again. Now she would be fascinated just to explore him from head to toe.

To touch him.

He set their plates down on the table a little too sharply. Wendy frowned, aware that the television had drawn his attention.

And then she heard it.

The newscasters were still reading the national news, but it seemed that her small part of the world had gained national attention. Wendy forgot her guest for a moment, trying to concentrate on the words of the announcer.

She and Brad both rushed toward the television set at the same time.

"Stop!" Wendy ordered.

For a moment, he paused and glared at her. Wendy could feel his eyes boring into hers.

Danger emanated from him, hot, desperate danger, sweeping around her, encompassing her.

Yesterday, there had been a shoot-out. "A violent exchange of gunfire," according to the Fort Lauderdale police. A federal agent had been killed, and law-enforcement officials were still looking for the gang of men involved, a gang of drug traffickers, arms dealers and murderers.

"You don't want to hear this."

He tore his gaze from Wendy's and strode toward the television. She began to protest, but when her mouth opened, a horrified gasp escaped instead as Brad's picture suddenly flashed upon the screen.

There were five men in the picture. One tall, blond man, three medium, darker men and Wendy's guest—Mr. "Alias" Bill Smith.

"Son of a bitch!" he swore. Too late, he turned off the television.

Wendy stared at him, her gaze wide and brilliant—and condemning.

"Wendy..." He lifted a hand to her imploringly. He wished he hadn't lied to her. The whole ordeal was going to be difficult to explain. Even worse, the look of betrayal in her eyes was going to be impossible to soothe. Those shimmering, beautiful, silver-blue eyes of hers, gem hard with hatred and reproach.

And fear.

He raked a hand through his hair, wondering how to explain. "Wendy—"

She spun around, ready to escape. He couldn't let her do that. He couldn't let her leave him stranded here, and he didn't dare let her risk a panicked run back to civilization.

God only knew who she might run into.

"Wendy, please wait!"

But Wendy had already begun to flee. She was at the door, tearing it open.

Freedom, she thought. Another second and she would be free. All she had to do was fly out the door and reach the airboat. She didn't need much of a head start. The swamp would slow down the unwary man, the one who was unprepared.

She threw open the door.

It was abruptly slammed shut before she could begin to get out. Acting on reflex, she swung around to face Bill Smith—or whoever he was! Now his handsome features bore a chilling countenance. She was frightened. This man was an impostor, a liar. The way he had slammed the door had proven his speed, strength and agility. He would be a powerful adversary.

"Wendy—"

She ducked beneath his arm and raced down the hall to her bedroom. Perhaps she could escape through a window....

All the while she could feel him behind her, following close. Gasping, she flew through the door to her bedroom, slammed it shut, locked it and leaned against it, panting.

Her heart caught in her throat as she felt him try the knob. "Wendy! You have to listen to me—"

"Stinking bastard—liar!" she retorted...her eyes surveyed the room. If she was lucky, the screwdriver would still be by her dresser, where she had left it after trying to fix a brass handle that had come loose.

"Wendy, I admit that I lied to you, but you have to give me a chance to explain."

The screwdriver was there, right on the carpet. If she could pull out a screen, she could escape through one of the large windows above her bed. She just had to keep him talking for the time it would take her to do so.

"So go on! Explain!" she snapped. Carefully, silently, she moved away from the door. She picked up the screwdriver and approached the window. "Explain!" she shouted back at him as she jumped up on the bed and set to work.

"Wendy, I'm not a bad guy. Honest." She heard his voice, coaxing, sincere, from the other side of the door.

Yeah, sure.

He'd fooled her once already. He must be thinking that she was the most naive creature this side of the Mason-Dixon line.

The first screw fell away in her hand. Holding her breath, she started on another. Her fingers shook. Oh, God. The FBI and the DEA were after him. An agent had been killed. This was serious business; her houseguest was a member of a drug mob.

"I should have told you the truth from the beginning. I was trying to protect you, and at first I didn't know whether I could trust you or not. I lied about my name to protect you. I was afraid of what the media would be saying. You've got to understand. The boss can't give out the real information because he assumes that I'm still with Michaelson and his group. But they found me out when they caught Jim. Jim is the one who was killed."

What the hell was he rambling on about? Wendy wondered. The third screw gave way in her hand and the screen came careening down. She caught it as it crashed against the wall. It was harder going now. She had to hold the screen and unscrew at the same time. Concentrate! she berated herself.

She probably deserved this. If she wasn't so frightened, so close to tears, she would laugh at herself. Maybe she shouldn't have stayed here, holed up alone in the Everglades. Maybe she had spent too much time mourning the past and licking her wounds. Because right out of the blue she had picked up a stranger, admired his face and form—lusted after him, Wendy girl, admit the truth! she chastised herself in silent reproach—trusted him and made a complete fool of herself. If she'd stayed a little nearer civilization, she might have been smart enough to smell a rat beneath her very nose.

The fourth screw finally gave way. He was still talking, but she had been too breathless to hear him. She set the screen down carefully, then silently hiked her rear up on the sill. With a groan the glass pane eased open, allowing her to slip through the window and fall onto the soft grass below.

"Wendy, do you understand?" Brad pleaded softly. There was no answer. Too late, with sudden, definite clarity, intuition warned him that no one was listening.

He slammed a muscled shoulder against her door. The flimsy lock gave way instantly and he stepped into her room. There was only a screen leaning against the wall and curtains that billowed in the gentle breeze from the open window.

Bolting across the room, he leaped onto the bed and propelled his body out the window. He fell to the grass and rolled.

On the path below, Wendy was running as fleetingly as a young doe, trying to reach the airboat.

"Wendy!" He tore after her, catching her just as she neared the water.

Caught by the arm, she flailed and kicked like a trapped animal. Her small, clenched fist caught him in the shoulder. Then she delivered a blow to his right eye, a punch that hurt like hell.

Now he was probably going to have a shiner to go with the cut in his temple.

Then she landed a hefty kick. He could only be grateful that she had aimed for his shin.

"Wendy—"

She wasn't listening. He was pleading; she was swearing. Brad ducked low, sweeping her over his shoulder. He ignored the hands that pounded against his back and the nails that scratched him through his borrowed shirt. Striding quickly, he entered the house by way of the front door. He had to calm this woman down.

He didn't stop in the living room, but proceeded to her bedroom at the end of the hallway, where the door with its broken lock hung open. He barged into the room and unceremoniously dropped her on top of the bed. Her fists were still flying and her hair tumbled over her shoulders in a golden cloud.

"Damn you, I'm not trying to hurt you!" Brad cried.

"And how am I supposed to believe that's not just another lie?"

"Wendy!"

There seemed to be only one way to calm her. He crawled over her, straddling, pulling her arms high over her head and securing her wrists. Her hair fell in front of her face; she tried to blow it away, growing silent at last but continuing to stare at him with a look that could definitely kill.

"You liar!" she shouted.

"I lied about my name. I'm sorry. It's Brad. Brad McKenna."

She lay still for a minute. Her body relaxed slightly, but the suspicion never left her eyes. They seethed up at him with simmering skepticism.

His heart ached for her, for the feelings of betrayal she was suffering. He still liked her, so damned much. And he was still so entranced by this silver-eyed angel. Her breasts rose and fell with agitation, and he could feel her warm body caught between his own thighs.

"Honest. Give me a chance to start over. Mrs. Wendy Hawk, meet Brad McKenna. Oh, Mr. McKenna, so nice to meet you. The pleasure, Mrs. Hawk, is completely mi—ine! Hey!"

She wasn't amused, not in the least. She bolted against him in a powerful surge that almost sent him flying, despite all his well-trained reflexes.

"Wendy!" He laughed. "Please, give me a break!"

"I gave you a break! I plucked you out of the mud and I brought you here and I fed you—"

"And bathed me," he supplied.

Her eyes narrowed and she barely skipped a beat. "Fed you and clothed you and gave you a roof over your head! I should have left you for a reptile feast!"

Brad inhaled and exhaled slowly. Deep inside, he was in anguish. What the hell difference did it make? he asked himself bleakly. So, she hated him. So what? She was going to take him to a phone, and she would never see him again anyway.

There had never been anything for him here at all. An undeniable attraction wasn't always worth pursuing. He didn't indulge where he couldn't turn his back and walk away with a clear and easy conscience.

It would be difficult to walk away from this silver-eyed sylph. But it would be devastating to know he'd caused her pain. And right now, she was hurting because of him. She had to understand. He didn't want her hating him.

"Wendy, please." He eased his hold on her arm. "I know I don't deserve your trust, but I really need it. I need it badly."

She didn't say anything; she didn't fight him. She stared at him defiantly. And for a moment, her mind wandered. She saw the familiar comforter on her bed and the walnut, antique dresser sets she and Leif had stripped and repolished themselves. She saw the daylight streaming through the cream curtains, and she felt the man above her.

Once she had lain like this, and laughed. And the man above her had been no threat. He had been her husband, and she had loved him. And now a stranger straddled her as Leif once had, asking her to trust him. It seemed a sacrilege.

Yet even with that thought, she realized that the panicked beat of her heart had slowed. Despite herself, despite everything she had seen on the news, she wanted to believe him. He couldn't be lying to her, not here.

And he couldn't be such an awful criminal. He could have already killed her if he'd wanted to. He could have strangled her easily, and there were plenty of sharp knives in the kitchen. There was even a double-barreled shotgun hanging on the wall.

She twisted her face aside, not wanting to look into the tawny gold eyes that pleaded so eloquently with hers. More than his words, more than the tenor of his voice, his eyes swayed her. His gaze poured into her, like a liquid warmth, promising honor and truth and even security, when there should have been none.

She swallowed and spoke softly. She couldn't have him touching her. She didn't want to feel the power in his thighs as they locked around her, and she didn't want to feel the warm whisper of his breath. She didn't want his hands so gently but thoroughly locking her own.

"If you don't want to hurt me, then let me go."

He hesitated, then unwound his fingers from her wrists and moved away.

Quickly, Wendy edged away from him, absently rubbing her wrists while she stared at him. He idly sat at the end of the bed and met her gaze.

"Brad McKenna?" she said doubtfully.

He nodded gravely. "I'm with the DEA, I swear it. My partner—the man who was killed—and I were working undercover. We had infiltrated one of the roughest gangs running cocaine, marijuana and hashish out of South America. This area's a target zone for us—especially since the drug traffic has increased. It's hard to stop—there are just miles and miles of coastline and an endless supply of pilots willing to risk their lives for the monetary rewards of bringing in one big supply. Anyway, Michaelson—the head honcho in this little group—caught on to us. He meant to perform a quick execution, but we'd gotten some word in about our location. We'd assumed that he was planning an exchange with the buyers. It all came down too fast." He hesitated, locking his jaw and swallowing painfully. "Jim was killed. I was next in line, but I stole a Chevy and took off down the Alley. The engine died on me, and Michaelson and his boys almost finished me off. But you found me instead."

She stared at him. "Pharmaceuticals?"

"What?"

"You told me that you were a salesman. Pharmaceuticals."

He shrugged. "I'm telling you the truth now, I swear it." He wanted so badly to reach out and touch her. He wanted to assure her.

He wondered if that look of contempt would ever leave her eyes. "Wendy, for God's sake, I'm telling you the truth now. Please, can't you believe me?" He reached out to stroke her cheek, but she twisted away.

"If you're telling the truth," she demanded, "why were you in that picture with the smugglers?"

He sighed. "I told you, I was working undercover. They can't reveal my identity at the office until they know for sure that my cover has already been blown." He paused. "Michaelson is wanted for first-degree murder as well as drug smuggling. If he gets a chance, he'll kill me."

Her arms were locked around her legs defensively, and she observed him warily from narrowed, long-lashed eyes.

"Wendy! You've got to believe me!"

"Why?"

"Because," he told her quietly, "I still need your help. I have to have your help."

She kept watching him in silence. He held his breath, then expelled it slowly. "Well?"

"I don't have much choice, do I?"

He lowered his head, smiling. "Thank you," he murmured. He reached out to stroke her cheek with his knuckles.

"But don't—don't even think of touching me again!" she said vehemently. Slipping away from him, she rose from the bed and strode, slowly and regally, from the room.

CHAPTER 3

"**A**re you coming?" Wendy demanded coldly. She was waiting for Brad in front of the house.

Brad closed the front door, eyeing her suspiciously. Where was that drat cat, Baby? He had forgotten about the animal when he had chased her outside. Baby was probably more useful against unwanted prowlers than a pair of well-trained attack dogs.

"I'm not sure that I trust you, Mrs. Hawk."

"You're not sure that you trust me?" she demanded indignantly. He didn't answer her. "Well of all the nerve!"

"Where's the panther?"

"Baby?"

"Your deadly kitty cat."

"How on earth should I know," she replied sweetly. "Any cat is difficult to find, and as you might notice, Baby has a big backyard!"

Brad issued an oath at her sarcasm. Forgetting that he had promised not to touch her, he grabbed her wrist and pulled her close. Her body was warm and soft against his. He felt the taunting fullness of her breasts against his chest, the smooth silkiness of her golden tanned skin. When he inhaled, her fragrance was clean and sweet, more haunting than any tormented dream.

Afraid that she could sense his heated reaction, he wanted to drop her wrist and push her away. And he wondered what she was thinking, for she didn't fight, she simply cast her head back and scowled at him with that unique silver magic in her eyes.

Brad gritted his teeth. "What I want to know, Mrs. Hawk, is if that cat of yours is slinking around somewhere, poised to attack."

She hesitated just a minute. "No."

"Are you sure?"

"What do you want—a sworn statement?"

"Yes!"

"Dammit, I'm the one who deserves one of those!" she protested.

"I asked you to trust me."

"But you don't trust me!"

He wanted to kiss her. He wanted to know if the heat that raged in her eyes would warm her mouth and fuse their lips together. The temptation was ungodly. His fingers trembled with the desire to snake into her hair, his body shook with the very force of his longing. Maybe it was the wild, primitive appeal of the ground he stood on. Maybe it was the defiant challenge in her beautiful eyes. He had never wanted a woman more. And he had never wanted one so passionately, so suddenly. He closed his eyes, praying that God would get him out of the swamp and grant him some sanity.

Then he released her. "I'm sorry, Mrs. Hawk. You're right. I am asking a lot of you. Forgive me. Shall we go?"

For a moment she stared at him in silence, then she turned with squared shoulders and started for the airboat.

Brad followed her onto the vehicle, releasing the secure rope she kept tied around a tree. As she started up the motor, Brad let the sights and sounds of the swamp fill his senses. The day was bright now, and growing hotter. He could hear the drone of insects again. A light breeze caused the distant saw grasses to bend beneath it, and the vista did, indeed, appear to be a green sea, with ripple after ripple of wave listing through it. He heard a ruffling sound and turned to see a long-legged, awkward-looking crane soar to beauty and elegance as it took flight from the ground and entered the arena of the powder-blue sky.

Wendy seemed to be deep in thought, staring straight ahead. He smiled; she seemed so small and fragile on the airboat, like an angel driving a two-ton semi.

What kind of a love had kept her here, in the deserted marshes, all alone? Could anyone, man or woman, be so self-sufficient that he or she needed nothing but the earth and sky to survive? The land, the air—and memories?

He quickly realized that she knew this land well. Having been unconscious, he hadn't seen where he had come from last night. He could determine their direction from the sun, but he'd be damned if he understood how anyone could navigate a swamp with no distinguishing landmarks. Or were there subtle, natural landmarks, evident only to those who sought them? A clump of trees that bowed at an angle there, old trees that had surely survived countless storms. A wide vista of the grass, to the right, and to the left, a sudden profusion of color where a hammock rose from the swamp to provide a home for scores of wild orchids and tall, blue-toned herons.

Birds burst out of the foliage before them—the airboat's motor was loud. He didn't know how fast they were going—maybe thirty-five miles an hour, tops—but still the breeze became a wind that whipped by them, fierce, challenging, invigorating. Brad closed his eyes, savoring the feel of the wind on his face while the sun beat down on his back. The scent of the swamp that had repulsed him yesterday now seemed rich, redolent.

When Wendy slowed the airboat, he thought they were idling near another hammock of high land. On closer inspection, he could see that strands of high grass hid the planks of a series of small, weather-beaten docks. Wendy tossed him the rope, and he secured the airboat.

Wisps of blond hair had escaped Wendy's neat ponytail. They played about the soft contours of her face as she squinted toward the small building.

"Thank you," he said quietly.

Her hands were on her hips as she continued to survey him. "The phone is inside the office," she said simply.

They crossed a groomed lawn—regular grass that had actually known the touch of a lawn mower—and just ahead of them Brad could see a bright, whitewashed rectangle of a building that sported a few gas pumps outside.

As they approached, an old man in overalls stepped out to meet them, staring curiously at Brad. He wiped grease from his bronzed and wizened hands, and his flesh wrinkled around a pair of light green eyes as he narrowed them upon the newcomer.

"Hi, Mac." Brad didn't realize that he was holding his breath, worrying, until she spoke. "Mac, this is a friend of mine. Brad McKenna. Brad, Mac Gleason." Mac arched a brow but reached forward to shake Brad's hand.

Brad reciprocated the gesture. "Hi, Mac."

The old man nodded, but kept staring at Brad. "You own that old Chevy that's all torn up near the Alley?"

"Uh—no, I don't own it," Brad said. That much was true. Some irate owner was probably making a claim with his or her insurance agent over the car right now.

"Brad needs to use the phone," Wendy said. "How's my car doing?"

"Car's all ready to go when you are, Wendy. Local call, son?"

"I—uh—I don't know. Fort Lauderdale." He started to fumble in his pockets, then he realized that they weren't his pockets and that he didn't have any money anyway.

"I didn't ask you for money, boy," Mac said indignantly. "I just asked you where you was calling. You want Lauderdale, you dial a one first, ya hear?"

Brad nodded. "Thanks. I appreciate it."

"Up in the office. Take your time."

Brad turned and headed for the office. He wanted to look back, but he didn't. He wondered if Wendy was whispering to the old man, sharing her suspicions that he was a murderer and a drug smuggler. Maybe the old man had a shotgun handy. Or maybe Brad would be greeted by a pair of pit bulls when he opened the office door. Here in the swamp, people were isolated, a breed apart, and they often had their own way of dealing with things.

Don't, Wendy, please don't. Don't betray me, he silently pleaded.

The office was cool and air-conditioned inside. There was a desk with a blotter and an old swivel chair to the right of the door. Against the wall stood a Pepsi machine, another machine that dispensed chips and candy, and a large glass globe full of ice water. Brad poured himself a paper cup of the cold water, drank it down and peered out the window.

Wendy was laughing at something the old man had said. Her hands were on her hips, her head was tossed back. When she glanced up at the shop and saw him, her laughter faded.

Brad walked over to the desk and dialed the emergency number. Gary Henshaw answered first. Brad smiled, filling with warmth as he heard Gary scream out in relief that he was alive. "Where the hell are you, buddy? No, never mind, let me get the boss."

Two seconds later Brad was talking to L. Davis Purdy, the man in charge of their operations in south Florida—the Boss, as he was known with respect and affection by his men. Purdy was no pencil pusher. He'd worked the streets for years and had gradually risen through the ranks of the agency. There were few tricks he didn't know. Michaelson was one of the toughest nuts Purdy had ever tried to crack.

"You're alive," Purdy said. The words sounded matter-of-fact, even a little cold.

"Yeah." Brad leaned back in the chair.

"Thank God." Purdy meant it. "Jim is dead."

Brad closed his eyes. "I know. Michaelson got wind that we were both DEA."

"We figured that much out." Purdy hesitated a moment. "Your town house was firebombed last night."

"What?" Brad sat up. His home here was gone? His collection of rare forty-fives, his stereo equipment, his lumpy old recliner, his college football jersey...little things that meant a lifetime. They were all gone.

But he was still alive, he thought soberly. Jim wasn't so fortunate.

"We're going to have to get you in under protective custody. Brad, you're the only one who can put Michaelson away now. He wants you dead, and usually Michaelson gets what he wants."

"Doesn't sound good at all," Brad said gruffly.

"You know the ropes. You're lucky to be alive now. Where the hell are you that he hasn't gotten wind of you? I'm trying to bring him in, but you know the man, and you know the system. He's as slippery as an eel, and his kind of money can buy all kinds of favors."

"I'm in the swamp."

"The swamp? You're out in the Glades?"

"Yes. I don't really know exactly where. That's probably why he hasn't found me." Brad hesitated, sitting forward. "Come to think of it, at the moment, this is a fine place to be." He started at a sudden sound.

He was slipping, he realized, slipping badly, letting down his guard.

Wendy Hawk entered the office. She sat at the edge of the desk and stared at him expectantly.

"Purdy, will you talk to someone for me?" Brad said. "That picture that came out over the news last night almost did me in."

"We sent that out before your home was hit," Purdy explained. "Who do you want me to talk to?"

"A concerned civilian who kept me alive last night," Brad said dryly, watching Wendy as he spoke. "Now she's afraid she was aiding a hardened criminal. Say something, will you?"

"She?" Purdy murmured.

Brad gritted his teeth. In the background he could hear Gary repeating the word, then embroidering upon it. *"She?* Leave it to Brad. Even in the damn swamps he can find himself a woman."

"Tell Gary to put a lid on it," Brad said with annoyance. "I'm putting on Mrs. Hawk."

He thrust the receiver to Wendy. Curiously, she took it. "Hello?"

"Hello, Mrs. Hawk? My name is Purdy, ma'am, and I'm with the DEA. I understand that you helped one of my men last night, and I'm exceedingly grateful. Brad tells me that you saw the news. I'm sorry about that. We had to take all precautions."

Wendy was silent. Brad, listening in as best he could, realized then that there was still no definite proof of his innocence. He could have called anyone, and the voice on the other end of the phone could be spinning lies as easily as he had.

He groaned softly, slumping back in the chair. Well, she'd believe him when they sent out a car for him.

No. Abruptly, he sat back up. No, the agency couldn't send anyone near here. That would put Wendy in danger. She was safe here in her swamp, because no one would think to come here.

Unless they followed someone in, someone coming for him.

He jerked the phone out of her hands.

"Boss—"

"We'll get a couple of cars out there with our best—"

"No! No, listen to me. I'm going to get out of here by myself."

"Brad—" He could almost imagine Purdy frowning. His brow would be furrowed, and his sharp blue eyes would be squinting.

"Really, Purdy, this plan is safer. I'm calling from a gas station with an old man, and I've been staying at Mrs. Hawk's home. And, Boss, I mean, I am deep in the marshes. There's no way that Michaelson can stumble on me here. It's just impossible. This place is a watery jungle. You need a map to go from tree to tree. If I get myself out, then Michaelson won't think to go after anyone who might have helped me. I'll start wending my way out this morning."

Wendy watched him, her eyes widening. She didn't know how or why she believed in this man, she just did. For all she knew, he could have phoned the Florida State Penitentiary; the man giving her the assurances could have been working on a chain gang.

But she trusted him. She was relying on instinct again.

Her heart was beating just a little too fast; her breath was coming just a bit too quickly.

Perhaps she should simply wash her hands of the man, then and there. She owed him nothing.

But before she even knew what she meant to do, she leaned forward and gently caught Brad's hand. "Maybe you should stay here."

"What?" Startled, he stared at her.

She hesitated, wet her lips, then elaborated. "Some guy is looking for you, right? This Michaelson character. Maybe you're as safe as you can possibly be right here."

"Wendy," Brad said softly, staring into the soft mystery of her silver eyes. "This guy is tracking me down to kill me. I am the only one who can testify against him."

She nodded. "I know. But you just said that he can't possibly find you here."

What was the matter with her? she wondered desperately. She didn't want him here! This man made her feel dazed and irrational. But she wasn't afraid of him. Even when he had held her, when he had pinned her beneath him, she hadn't been afraid. She had been aware—painfully aware—of his build, of his warmth, of his strength. She was captivated by the man, and it had been okay because he was leaving, but now...

Now she was sitting here, suggesting that he stay.

Why?

Her heart seemed to skip a beat, slamming mercilessly against her chest. It was foolish, it was all so foolish. But suddenly all that she could remember was the sight of blood, all the blood that had once spilled over Leif's chest. She could hear her own scream, echoing against the corridors of her heart.

Her memories ruled her now. She couldn't let the same thing happen to Brad. The swamp was her refuge; she knew it well, backward and forward, and it was a good hiding place. The Indians had discovered it years ago, but few men had charted it since. The Everglades could shield a man. The swamp was a tough and rugged mistress, but when her secrets were learned and respected, she could embrace and protect a man, an ideal—an entire people.

Conflicting emotions flickered across his face. He set his jaw in a hardened twist. "Wendy, I can't just hide here with you. Running is my forte—my job."

"No one has a job that says he has to get killed foolishly!" Wendy snapped. "Do you think you'll make it out of this wilderness in one piece? Don't be a fool. The law doesn't want heroics. The law needs you alive—"

"But I can look after myself—"

"I imagine that might be true in the big city," Wendy interrupted coolly. "Were you trained to elude a gang of murderers in the Everglades?" She crossed her arms over her chest.

"Brad! Brad!" Purdy was calling him, in an aggravated voice.

Still watching Wendy's eyes, Brad spoke into the receiver again. "I'm here—"

No matter what happened, Brad was due for some painful inactivity. Suppose he did make it out of the swamp? He would have to hide out in a safe house. He'd be locked up with a group of agents guarding him day and night. Brad would be in seclusion until they managed to catch Michaelson.

He groaned, holding the phone away.

Wendy snatched it from him. "Mr. Purdy, can you prove to me that Brad is innocent?"

"I can release the details to the news media," Purdy told her. He cleared his throat impatiently. "Will you please ask Mr. McKenna to remember that he works for me—and put him back on the line. He's going to be on a forced hiatus for even longer than he thinks if he doesn't stick with me this time."

Wendy smiled. Brad noticed that she had the smallest little dimple in the center of her chin. He took the phone back from her. "I've got an idea, Boss. It will keep me safe, and her safe, too. I'm going to lie low right here."

"What?" Purdy was screeching.

Brad moved the receiver away from his ear while Purdy went on and on about the lack of control in the situation. Brad was miles from civilization; there was no help nearby.

"That's right," Brad said quietly. "I am miles from anywhere. No one knows where the hideout is, and no one can squeal. Boss, think about it."

Purdy changed his tactics. "You're going to stay out in the swamp for a good week or more?"

Brad laughed. "Can't you boys do any better than that? Come on—I'll supply the proof. All you home militia have to do is rope in the target!"

Purdy swore. But then he paused. Brad knew Purdy. The Boss was always willing to throw "standard procedure" out the window if another solution seemed to be better.

"All right, McKenna. Now you listen to me for a minute, and listen good. You might be right. Michaelson is a smuggler and a killer, but he sure isn't any Daniel Boone. Sitting tight could be your best move. But remember, he'll have men on both ends of the Alley, and I'm willing to bet he gets some air coverage of the swamp, too. I want you to check in if you see anything, and I don't want you making a single move without my approval. Got it?"

Brad's muscles tightened. He hated the swamp. What the hell was he doing?

He inhaled. He was trying to live the dream. He wanted to go back to the house and lie in the bed, and so help him, he wanted to make love to the woman. He wanted to touch and taste her flesh, to explore the breasts that were so firm and full in his dream. He wanted to see her mercury eyes above him as passion filled them. He wanted to kiss her, to drown in her...

Purdy was still talking, but Brad couldn't hear him anymore. He stared up at Wendy, and he wondered if his own features had gone as ashen as hers. What was she thinking now? Was she regretting her impetuous offer? It was a mistake. He didn't know how to sit still; he hated to sit still. What the hell was he going to do in the swamp for all those hours?

Except to lust after his silver-eyed angel of mercy.

He swore softly and rubbed his temple. "Hey, Boss—"

"Not a move, Brad, unless you talk to me. They've run a trace on the phone number, so we've got your coordinates. I'm going to get my men out there to nail Michaelson. You do your bit—stay alive, huh?"

There was a dull buzz. Purdy had hung up on him.

He didn't put the receiver down right away. He swallowed, staring at Wendy. She was still so damned white. At last, Brad exhaled, slamming the receiver down. "You look as if you had just invited the Indians in for a scalping. I can see that you still don't believe in me. Maybe you should have kept your mouth shut."

She hopped off the desk and her hands rode her hips. "Ingrate!"

"Finished with the phone, son?" Mac, the old-timer grease monkey interrupted them.

Brad shook his head, and a slow smile came to his lips. Mac was perfect for the place. His hair and beard were clean but shaggy, his manner abrupt but well-meaning. It was evident that Mac was Brad's friend as long as Wendy vouched for him. And it was equally evident that the old man would defend her come hell or high water. "Yes, I'm finished all right," Brad said.

Mac nodded serenely. "Wendy, you want to take your car now? Or did you just come to use the phone? Is he going to drive the car while you take the airboat?"

"Uh—we just needed to use the phone."

Mac nodded. "Maybe someone will get a chance to drop it off later." He walked over to the old percolator on the counter and poured himself some coffee, not taking his eyes from Brad. "Coffee?"

"Yeah, thanks."

Mac poured him a cup. The brew was hot and strong. Brad had just taken a sip out of a stoneware mug when Mac said casually, "You got anything to do with those men running around in the big black sedan?"

He nearly spit coffee all over the floor. Instead, he swallowed and glanced from Wendy to Mac.

Mac smiled, enjoying Brad's reaction. "Yep, those boys were here wanting some gas last night. Can't rightly say I liked the looks of them, myself. They asked about the Chevy, and for some dark reason, I told 'em I'd never seen the thing. They were really looking for a man—a buddy of theirs they said they'd lost in the swamp. I told them that most things that get lost in the swamp stay lost. Why, I reckon, too, that if they come back, I ought to tell them that it's true—if they're still looking for a man, they oughta count on the fact that he's lost, deep in the darkness of the Glades, huh?"

Brad reached out and shook Mac's hand. "Thanks," he said gruffly. "Thanks. It's—it's really important. I don't know how I can prove it to you, but I'm really a decent man. And those guys are looking to stir up trouble."

"A man don't need things proved to him," Mac said. "And there's all kinds of good guys and bad guys in this world. Instinct, boy, that's what counts."

He nodded to the two of them and walked outside. When the door closed, Wendy glanced briefly at Brad, then hurried out after Mac. Through the dusty window, Brad watched Wendy give the old man a fierce hug and a kiss on his weathered cheek.

They were old friends, good friends. Brad felt a sudden stab of envy. The old man knew Wendy Hawk well. He knew the details of her life.

He probably had shared her past, had listened to her dreams of the future. And Brad didn't really know her at all. He knew only that he wanted her, that she intrigued him, haunted him.

Perhaps he ought to be hiding out from her instead of from Michaelson. Michaelson wanted his life. Wendy Hawk would steal his heart and his soul.

He followed her out. She waved goodbye to Mac, then climbed onto the airboat. For a moment the breeze rustled by, and they sized one another up silently. Then she walked past him and released the tie line.

The engine came to life; its powerful roar filled the air. Birds squawked and flew before them.

Wendy stared straight ahead.

Brad sighed and settled down on the boat. They were going home, to her home, together. The die had been cast. He watched as the sun danced along the golden highlights of her hair. Light, light, ethereal gold. As he studied the bronze of her shoulders and the feminine line of her body, he remembered holding her.

How long were they destined to be together? he wondered bleakly.

Maybe time didn't matter. They both knew it already. There was something between them now, simmering and steaming, wild and explosive.

They were heading home; fate had thrown them together. He suddenly knew that he would have her, would touch her, would love her, just as surely as he knew that the sun would set in the west. Despite their individual dreams and fears, their shared destiny was inevitable.

She turned to tell him something, to point out some landmark, but when her eyes met his, her words seemed to freeze in her throat.

Their eyes remained locked together, silver melding with gold, and surely creating some ancient alchemist's magical treasure. Or perhaps it wasn't magic at all. Perhaps it was a simple pattern of nature and life, as basic and raw as the need of a man for a woman.

When she found the strength to turn away from him, neither of them cared that some vague thought was forgotten. Among soul mates the pretense of words was unnecessary.

CHAPTER 4

The house seemed smaller. Brad didn't know how, but the house had shrunk, closing in around them.

Wendy threw out the breakfast that they hadn't eaten and started cleaning up the kitchen. He would have offered to help her, but he was certain that she didn't want his assistance now. The kitchen had gotten smaller, too.

Brad turned on the television. It was nearly noon. He tried different stations until he found one of the major networks. A soap opera seemed to be in the midst of its final, anguished, tear-jerking scene of the day. Brad hunched down and waited. He swallowed, realizing that he was watching the soap Jim used to watch. His partner had never known quite how and when he had gotten hooked, but he had. And whenever things were slow, whenever Jim and Brad were stuck on surveillance, sitting for hours and hours, drinking coffee and waiting for something to happen, Jim would dramatically recount all the latest episodes. Of course, he had missed the soap's broadcast most of the time, but he videotaped the show religiously.

Jim wouldn't be watching any more soaps.

They hadn't worked together long. Not even a month. Brad's old partner, Dennis Holmes, had left the DEA when he'd married the college sweetheart who had waited for him for ten long years. He was teaching in Boston now. Funny, Brad thought, he and Dennis and Jim had all agreed on one thing—their line of work and marriage just didn't mix.

But Jim would never have a chance to marry. The thought cut Brad to the quick. Jim had been shot down in the prime of his life. Damn Michaelson! He would pay for Jim's life. Like a cowboy in the Old West, Brad would give his eyeteeth for a walk down a long and dusty path, and the simple chance to best the man. But this wasn't the Old West. He couldn't meet Michaelson that way. The law needed Brad alive to testify. Then the judicial court system could determine Michaelson's fate. Brad knew the rules. But for once, he'd relish the opportunity to take justice into his own hands.

Brad started, aware that the images on the screen in front of him had changed. The soap opera was over; the news had come on. He tensed, then relaxed as the personable blonde went on in grave tones about the Michaelson smuggling case.

First Jim's picture was flashed onto the screen. Brad smiled even as a bitter sadness pierced his heart. The picture had been taken at a Labor Day picnic. Jim was wearing an old football jersey. His hair was all mussed up and he was smiling unabashedly for the camera. He looked so young—far too young to be dead.

The pretty blond newscaster announced that his body would be returned to his hometown in Delaware for burial.

Then Brad's picture flashed on the television screen. The photo had been taken the same day. He was wearing a football jersey, too, and cradling a football in his arm.

In his other arm, he cradled a buxom redhead.

Where the hell had Purdy come up with these pictures? What would have been wrong with a simple ID photo showing him in a blue suit and tie, a stoic, mug-shot expression and combed hair?

Leave it to Purdy.

In this snapshot, he looked like one of the good old boys. You could almost see the beer cans in the background. His hair was tousled and his eyes reflected the sultry laughter in the pretty girl's gaze.

Funny, but he couldn't even remember the redhead's name.

The reporter explained that Brad and Jim had been working undercover and that the previous incorrect information about Brad McKenna had been released to protect the agent's cover. However, it was no longer necessary. Brad had been found out. According to the newscast, Brad was missing, and authorities feared that he was dead. But Purdy had been true to his word to exonerate him—at least he was presumed dead as an agent rather than presumed dead as a drug smuggler.

The picture left the screen. The blonde came back on to state that the police and other government agencies were searching for Michaelson.

Brad realized that Wendy was behind him. He heard her exhale in relief. He was aware that she had been believing in him on instinct alone. Still hunkered down on the balls of his feet before the television, he looked up at her. Now, at least, her instinct had been somewhat vindicated.

"See, I am legit," Brad told her with a mild note of reproach.

Her gaze flicked down at him.

"Now I don't know what to think," she murmured. "They can say anything they want on the news, and we're obliged to accept the information." She smiled sweetly, and went back into the kitchen.

He rose slowly and turned the television off, suddenly feeling very awkward. What the hell was he going to do here—except try like hell to keep his hands off her?

"Hungry?"

The question came from the kitchen. He almost answered it with a sexual innuendo, yes, hungry like you'll never know, hungry for you. Instead, he forced himself to smile casually. "Yeah. Sure. We never did get to breakfast."

An accomplished cook, Wendy didn't seem to mind being in a kitchen. She flashed him a quick smile and reached into the refrigerator. Brad assumed that she was reaching for the makings of sandwiches or the like. She brought out an opaque white container and handed it to him. He frowned, then opened it up. A bunch of broken shrimp stared up at him sightlessly.

"What—"

Wendy smiled, turning away. "Let's go catch lunch." She opened the closet near the refrigerator and pulled out two fishing reels. "It's our bait."

Brad looked blankly from the fishing gear to his hostess. He grinned slowly. Thank God, they were going to get out of the incredible shrinking house. Fishing. It sounded great. "All right. In the airboat?"

She shook her head. "There's a little canoe around back. We'll try for some catfish. I've got a great Cajun recipe. You like spicy food?"

They were staring at each other again. Wendy flushed, walked past him and started digging beneath the counter. "I've a cooler in here somewhere," she muttered.

"I'll get the ice," Brad offered quickly.

In another ten minutes, they were ready. The cooler was filled with beer, ice, a block of cheese and a stick of pepperoni. Wendy had decided that they might get hungry while waiting for the meal to come along. Besides, when the meal did come along, it would more likely be closer to dinnertime than lunch.

The canoe was out back. When they walked around, Brad saw that the road was just barely discernible behind a patch of tall saw grass growing on the opposite side of the canal.

"How do you get to your car?" he asked her, puzzled.

"I take the canoe."

"You have to take your canoe to get to your car?"

Wendy laughed. "Yes. It isn't that difficult. And I don't drive that often. Most places I want to go around here are easier to reach by airboat."

"What a way to live," Brad murmured.

Wendy paused, cocking her head as she watched him with a musing smile. "It's really not so bad, city slicker. Everything that I could want or need is very close."

She stepped past him, carrying the fishing rods over to the canoe. Brad stared across the water to the saw grass and the road, trying to memorize the area and achieve a sense of direction.

Suddenly, Wendy screamed. By reflex, Brad spun, reaching to his waist for his Magnum. Then he remembered that it wasn't there, that it was lost. Without it, he felt naked. And Wendy was screaming...

He ran to her, ready to protect her with his bare hands. But even as he neared her, she was sitting back, laughing.

"Wendy, what happened? What the—"

"Baby!" she sputtered.

The great panther rose from the floor of the canoe, growled, then stretched against Wendy like any of her smaller feline cousins, seeking affection. Wendy scratched her ears, then shoved her away. "Baby, get out of here! You scared me to death."

The cat crawled out of the canoe. When she shimmied past Brad, he petted the panther's sleek coat. His heart was still pounding crazily.

Still laughing, Wendy looked up at Brad. He was not amused. On the contrary, he appeared a little gray and cold, and the contours of his face were hard-set.

"Is that shotgun the only weapon you've got?" he asked her brusquely.

She hesitated.

"Is it?"

Wendy shook her head. "I've got a police model Smith & Wesson .38 in one of the dresser drawers."

"When we get back, I want it," he told her. He lowered himself into the canoe beside her, shoving off in a fluid motion. For several moments, they drifted in silence. Wendy stared at Brad from beneath the shelter of her lashes, and she wished studiously that she had never told him the truth. She hated guns, hated them with a passion. She wished that Baby had not startled her so, and she wished that she hadn't screamed.

And she nervously wished that she had never, never suggested that she bring Brad McKenna back home. It was awkward already, and she had a feeling that it was only going to get worse. He didn't seem to understand that she had brought him back here just because her house was so damned isolated. No one could find him here; there was no danger here. He didn't need a gun.

The sun beat down on them. For miles the only sound seemed to be the dip of Brad's paddle against the water. Wendy realized he knew something about canoeing. His strokes were slow, steady and even. He'd rolled up the sleeves of the shirt, and with each of his movements she could see the muscle play of his arms beneath the bronze flesh. Deep in concentration, his face was handsome, but harsh.

It had been different in laughter, she decided. In the photo they had shown on the news, he had seemed young, and easygoing. He had appeared happy and relaxed. And...

Ready, able and willing, she finished dryly. Who had the redhead been? The sudden thought chilled her.

"Brad?"

"Yeah?" He had been paddling strenuously, becoming accustomed to the land around him, the river of grass, the calls of cranes and loons and herons. He was growing acquainted with the stillness of the swamp, punctuated by the occasional, startling cries of the birds.

"We've gone plenty far," she said. He set the paddle inside the boat. They were drifting idly. Balancing herself from years of experience, Wendy reached forward and grabbed her pole. She checked her weight and hook and secured some bait from the white bucket. All the while she could feel him watching her, silently, broodingly, watching her every movement.

"Live shrimp are much better bait," she murmured. "But these will do, I'm sure." With a skillful arm, she cast her line.

Brad took his time setting up his fishing rod. After his line hit the water, he reached into the cooler for a beer. "Ready for one?" he asked.

Wendy shrugged. "Yes, I guess so."

He popped open the can before handing it to her. She hadn't realized it was quite so hot out until she sipped the icy cold beer. It tasted good, but it hit her stomach with a churning swirl. She remembered then that they hadn't eaten anything.

She glanced across the canoe at Brad, who was staring at the water, pole in one hand, beer in the other. He wore Leif's jeans and denim shirt well, she thought. She would never forget how she had found him, not a full day ago, struggling through the swamp. A lot had passed between them since then.

Nor could she forget the way he had caught and held her this morning. She realized that her emotions were alternating between gloom because he had interrupted her peaceful life, and elation, because he excited her so. He was making her feel again. He was making her blood whistle and sing. Maybe it was wrong since he was such a stranger, but she didn't know whether she wanted to fight it or not. In one way, she felt the gravest sense of security around him. Brad McKenna would never take anything from a woman that she didn't intend to give—wholeheartedly.

But then she met his gaze and her mind grew wary, her heart raced in fear. He'd been thinking about her—physically, sexually—and that scared her. She could almost read his precise thoughts, and awareness of those desires caused her to tremble and burn deep, deep inside.

"Brad." She was startled by the huskiness of her own voice, dismayed by the sensual undertone of it. But she had a question that had to be answered.

"You're—" This was ridiculous. She had to moisten her lips to keep talking, and the breathless quality would not leave her voice. She shook her head, then she smiled in a rueful confession, because he was staring at her again, seeing into her, penetrating her thoughts. "You're not married, are you?"

He looked at her for a long moment, then shook his head. "No."

"Who was the redhead?"

Again he paused. A dry, pained smile crossed his features, and he winced. "Honest? I don't remember. I think her name was Chrissy."

"Oh."

He set his beer on the seat beside him and wedged his pole beneath a thigh. Reaching forward, he caught her face between his palms.

She couldn't move, and she couldn't breathe. She could feel his callused touch against her flesh, and it warmed her from head to toe, just as the sound of his voice seemed to feather inside of her, touching her everywhere.

"I'm not married, Wendy. And I'm never going to be. Do you understand?"

She wanted to jerk back. Hurt and confusion raged in her heart, and still she couldn't move. The sensations that warred against her flesh would not leave her, and she sat dead still. A mocking, chilling smile curled her lips. "Well, now, McKenna, I do remember asking you if you were married. But I do not remember going so far as to ask you if you wanted to change your status."

She was glad to see that he flushed slightly. "Wendy, it's just that you have been married."

"That's right," she drawled softly. "Have been, past tense. And I don't intend to marry again, Mr. McKenna."

Suddenly the atmosphere between them was tense and explosive, and hotter than the midday sun that beat down mercilessly upon them. He still touched her, held her with his hands. Their knees brushed, their breath mingled.

"Why is that, Wendy? Was the experience too good—or too bad?"

"Too good, McKenna. It could never, never be matched."

Silence swept and swirled around them, as stifling as the shimmering heat.

"Well, remember that, huh?" Brad murmured. "I wouldn't want you forgetting it in the future."

"I doubt if there's a chance of that."

"Really?" His lips moved closer to hers. "You'd better be careful. Very careful. I wouldn't want you to care too much." He moved his thumb, drawing it in a slow, sinuous line over her lower lip.

"And maybe you had better be careful, too, McKenna. I wouldn't want you to care too much. I wouldn't want you to get hurt."

"Watch out for your heart, Wendy." And then his lips touched hers.

Bold and brash and commanding, the sensual, intimate contact was still as gentle, as tender as a brush with morning dew. His touch was sure and steady. Wendy wondered if making love came naturally to him. The ultimate effect was devastating. Wendy didn't think about the words that they had exchanged, nor did she think about what he did for a living, nor did it even occur to her that she had known this man for less than twenty-four hours.

All she could think about was his kiss. All that she could feel was the sweet, subtle, sensual pressure of his lips against hers, his mouth, artfully claiming her own. The tip of his tongue explored her mouth, plundering the richness of it, filling it. She savored his lips and the smooth surface of his teeth, and every little nuance of passionate movement.

His kiss evoked feelings deep inside of her, where he did not touch her. She felt warmth invade her like showering rays of the sun. Passion curled and undulated in the center of her being, steaming through her limbs, sweeping into her breasts and hips and thighs. This was desire, liquid and sweet. She longed to drop everything and throw her arms around his neck. She yearned to press her body against him and feel the length of them touch and duel, as did their mouths.

Just in time, she remembered his words of warning. And she remembered that when she loved, she loved very deeply. Even if she sometimes felt desperate to reach out again for a pale facsimile, a pretense, of what she had known, this was not the time or the place.

And this cocky, overconfident city slicker probably wasn't even the right man.

His lips parted from hers. She opened her eyes and stared into the sharp, questing depths of his. Their breath still mingled. And, she noted with some satisfaction, his breath seemed to come faster than her own. Did the thunder of his heart outweigh the tremor of her own?

He arched a brow. She smiled as sweetly as she could. "Well, McKenna," she said softly, seductively, "I think my heart is safe. Quite safe."

He was quick, she noted, but not quite quick enough to hide his surprise at her words. His hands fell from her cheeks and he sat back, watching her. "Oh, yeah?"

"Yeah."

Then he laughed, and she found herself laughing, too.

"I must be slipping," he teased.

"Happens to the best of us," she agreed consolingly.

He picked up his beer and took a swallow, still watching her. Wendy kept her eyes evenly set with his, though she couldn't control the small, wicked grin that continued to ghost her lips.

He leaned forward once again. "I'll have to try harder next time."

"You're really going to have to be careful," Wendy warned him, her eyes growing innocently large. "If you have to try so very hard, you might find yourself tripping and falling on your own effort. Could be dangerous."

"I'm a big boy, Mrs. Hawk. I do know how to take care of myself."

Wendy smiled flatly. "And I'm a big girl. Far better able to take care of myself in the present circumstances, I think."

"Next time, Wendy," he warned with a devil's grin.

He had passed the first forbidden door; he had touched her. Now he flexed his fingers to stop the tense tremors that had claimed them.

"Is there going to be a next time?" There was nothing coy to the words, nothing demure. It was a blunt, direct question, voiced with an open, amused interest. She was still smiling, and the smile lighted up her eyes to a silver-blue so bright and alluring that Brad felt himself begin to tremble all over again. His muscles were hot and tight—everything was hot and tight—and he found himself grateful that denim jeans could hide a multitude of sins.

"You bet," he promised her pleasantly through gritted teeth.

Just then, his pole dipped in the water and dug into his buttocks where he sat upon it.

"You've got something!" Wendy cried delightedly.

He had something, all right, Brad decided.

He wasn't a bad fisherman. Although these rods were a bit different, he'd grown up near Lake Erie and had done his share of fishing.

He gave the fighting fish a little space, then reeled it back. Once more, he gave the fish a little line to play itself out, then he reeled in. Meanwhile, Wendy reached for a net.

"Do we need that?" he asked her.

"You get stuck by a catfish, and it hurts like hell," she warned him. "We don't have to have it, but it would be kind of foolish to need medical care now for something stupid." She offered him a rueful grin. "I got stuck once and needed ten stitches."

He smiled. "By all means, haul out that net. I'll play macho some other time."

"Oh. Like 'next time'?" Wendy taunted, but then she bowed her head quickly, wondering what on earth was goading her.

Finally, Brad caught the line, and Wendy thrust the net out over the water. He deposited his squirming catch in the net, letting out a pleased holler. It was a hefty catfish, which would definitely rate as a dinner fish. They could even invite company over and have plenty to spare.

"A pretty damned good fish, huh?" he demanded triumphantly.

Wendy nodded serenely. "Yeah. Pretty damned good," she acknowledged. But she couldn't resist adding, "For a city slicker."

Brad conceded the point. He sat back, watching supremely as Wendy put on a glove, then carefully freed the hook and line from the fish's mouth. He enjoyed watching her. She still seemed like an angel with those silver-mist eyes and all that near-platinum hair and her slim, fragile form. But she was capable, lithe and quietly self-assured.

But like hell his touch hadn't affected her!

She tossed the fish into a bucket in the rear of the canoe.

He reached into the cooler and offered her a new beer. "You deserve it," he assured her solemnly.

"What a sport."

"Yeah, I'm a sport. I'm going to do all the paddling back, just like I did all the paddling here. And, my dear lady, you will recall, I am the one who caught the fish."

"The first fish," Wendy said.

But she never did catch anything. When the second beer made her dizzy, she decided it was time to cut up some of the cheese.

To her chagrin, Brad caught another fish, a second catfish, bigger than the first. To console her, he assured her that he had gone fishing many times before.

Sunset was coming when they headed back. The canoe streaked through the water in silence, and Brad found himself mesmerized by the beautiful surroundings once again. Gold and pink highlights fell upon the soft white of a crane, giving the bird the hues of a rainbow. The water reflected the glow of the dying light, and the waves of grass dipped to the soft, cooler breeze of the coming night.

As Wendy sat facing him, she did not see the alligator when Brad first sighted the creature. It was so still, he thought that it was a log at first.

And then he realized that it was a giant reptile.

An enormous, grotesque creature. About twelve or thirteen feet long, with a snout full of evil teeth that seemed to be a third of the length of the body.

It was ugly, incredibly ugly, Brad thought. His body tensed as he stared at the prehistoric creature.

But he wasn't going to give her another chance to call him a city slicker. He had to start getting accustomed to the creatures that roamed here. He'd been ready to battle the big cat with his bare hands, only to discover that the panther was a beloved pet named Baby.

What did she call the alligator? he wondered dryly. Junior, maybe? Spot? Rover?

He swallowed and tried to relax. When they drifted by the alligator, Brad was going to be casual—even if it killed him.

He slid the canoe up on the embankment, shoving his paddle into the muck to bring the canoe up high and secure. He started to rise, but Wendy caught his hand.

"Wait!" she said tensely.

"Wait for what?" he drawled laconically. "Oh—the gator? I saw it already."

"You saw it!" Her eyes flew to his, rounded. She grabbed his hand and pulled him back down to the seat. "Then sit still and let him go first, you idiot!"

"What?"

Wendy stood, carefully. There was a small fallen branch nearby. She picked it up and threw it hard at the alligator. The monster with the evil yellow eyes just stared at her. She tossed another one. It plunked the alligator right on the head, and the animal slunk back into the water and glided away. A moment later, it disappeared into the darkness.

Brad stared at Wendy. "You mean it isn't a pet?"

She shook her head, frowning at him as if he had lost his mind. "Who in God's name would want one of those monsters for a pet? That thing was about twelve feet long. He could have consumed both of us in one gulp. They're dangerous. I mean, you're all right if you avoid them. But I'd sure as hell never want to befriend one. They're vicious in the water if they're hungry, and bear in mind, they can move about forty miles an hour on land, too."

She smiled and rose, grabbing the pail with their fresh catch of the day. Brad remained in the canoe, watching the fluid, languid sway of her buttocks as she strode toward the house.

He smiled. Okay, so only that TV cop kept an alligator for a pet. Panthers were surely more popular. He'd learn. Surely, he'd learn.

Brad rose, collecting their gear. He'd seen a hose outside. He found it again and rinsed off the fishing gear. Then he brought the gear back into the house.

Wendy had been a quick worker, too. The catfish were already headless and well on their way to becoming fillets. She smiled up at him, then finished her task, dropping the fillets into a bowl of marinade when she was done.

"I'm going to hop in the shower. Turn on the television, have some wine, make yourself at home. I'll be right out."

He leaned against the refrigerator, popping open another beer. "Want company?"

"No, thanks."

Brad shook his head sadly. "Couldn't handle it, huh?"

She paused, rising to the taunt. "I think that time will tell, city slicker, just who can handle what around here."

He lifted his beer can to her in a toast. Wendy saw that his lashes fell lazily over his eyes, and that beneath, he surveyed her in a long and leisurely fashion.

She'd seen Baby look at birds in much the same way.

But the look warmed her, causing a hot flush to rise and tint her cheeks. Maybe he was right. Maybe she was out of her league. Maybe she couldn't handle anything that was happening to her at all. He'd given her every chance to retreat. He'd warned her that she couldn't be anything more than a friend. She didn't want to end up like the redhead in the photo; he'd remember the color of her hair, but he wouldn't remember her name.

Wendy spun around. "I'll be out shortly," she murmured.

Brad stared after her, wondering what had caused the change in her.

In the bathroom, Wendy stood beneath a warm spray and trembled with the chill that had seized her.

Perhaps she didn't want him remembering her name. She just wanted him to touch her, because she had been so lonely, and because it would feel so good to be touched again. But darkness and anonymity held a certain appeal.

The water cascaded around her. The sound cocooned her.

She wondered how he would feel if he really knew the truth. Yes, she wanted him. The chemistry was right; the attraction was strong. They had both felt it. And there had been more. They'd had the chance to know that they both delivered in certain values in life, maybe in a certain sense of honor. They didn't know much about each other, but they knew the important things.

And so maybe it would be all right.

Except that he just wasn't the kind of man to stand in for another. Wendy was quite certain that if Brad McKenna even guessed that she wanted him only in darkness, as a substitute for another man, his smile would fade and his sensual suggestions would fall silent.

There was just something about him... Even if he intended to have a woman only once, he'd want her to know damned clearly just who she was with.

Wendy bit her lip. Yes, there was just something about him. And that unusual quality was drawing her closer and closer to the edge.

She jumped suddenly, hearing the bathroom door open quietly, then close.

"Brad?" she whispered. "Brad!"

There was no answer. The sound of the water cascading over her naked form and onto the tile was all that filled the room.

CHAPTER 5

"**B**rad!" Panic rose high in her voice.

"Shush!"

There was a heated whisper at last. Wendy didn't have much time to worry about the fact that the man had interrupted her shower. She pulled the curtain against her body and looked out. Brad wasn't even glancing her way; he was standing at the small window over the commode, looking out into the right side of the yard.

"What is it?" Wendy whispered. He stood at the window, tense and silent as a wraith. "Brad, what is it!" she insisted softly.

At last she had his attention. He stared at her pensively, then strode toward her. He didn't touch her but came close, so that their eyes met amid the steam that poured around them.

"There's someone out there."

"If you heard something," Wendy said with a relieved smile, "I'm sure it's just Baby."

"No, no it's not."

"Really, Brad, I understand your circumstances, but we are tucked so far into the swampland. I'm sure you're just imagining—"

"I don't imagine," he said, cutting her off bluntly.

Wendy tightened her hold on the shower curtain and swallowed uneasily. He was, after all, still a stranger. He'd entered her shower without the decent grace of a quiet tap against the door. And right now he was so solidly implacable and assured that it was like talking to a rock.

He had changed. He was a bundle of tension. She could see it in his eyes, in his stance, in the constriction of his muscles.

And it was frightening.

"Can you shoot?" he asked her tensely.

"Come on now, Brad—"

"I asked you if you can shoot!"

"Yes."

"Stay inside, but load that shotgun of yours and be prepared to defend yourself. Do you hear me? Stay here, and if something should go wrong, have the shotgun in your hand."

He spun around and left her. The bathroom door closed quietly in his wake.

Wendy turned off the water and hopped out of the tub, longing to call him back. There wasn't any danger out there—there just couldn't be! She had to catch him.

But she couldn't go running after him stark naked. She dried off with a lick and a promise and stumbled into her clothes. She came charging out, then paused. There was nothing out there, but maybe, just maybe, she should load the shotgun.

She raced to get it down from the wall, then she panicked when she couldn't find the shells for the gun in the box in the closet. Pushing things around, she finally found a second box. She loaded both barrels and started down the hall. Brad, she knew, was already outside somewhere. But where? There seemed to be an eerie silence about the place.

But then that silence was shattered. "There you are, you son of a bitch!" a male voice grunted out.

"I've got you now!" a second man swore.

"Oh, no!" Wendy breathed, recognizing both male voices and realizing what must have happened. She ran down the hall to the front door and threw it open. "Stop!" she screamed. "Stop!"

She was ignored, so she raised the shotgun, and barely aiming, she squeezed the trigger. The kickback of the shotgun nearly sent her sprawling as the explosive sound filled the night—to be followed by complete, stark silence.

* * *

Brad didn't know how he knew that someone was outside, he just knew. He hadn't really heard anything, just the whisper of the breeze, the rustle of foliage, all natural things.

And yet he had felt it, sensed it.

They were being watched. Someone was watching them, watching them carefully, in stealth and silence.

That surprised Brad. Michaelson was the type to come striding right in. If he had made it to a place like this, he could quickly ascertain that he was far more powerful in terms of manpower and ammunition. And he didn't make it a habit to tease, taunt or torture—he assessed things quickly, and just as quickly he relieved himself of excess baggage.

No, this didn't feel like Michaelson.

But then, who the hell else could it be?

Dusk had fallen when he finally slipped out the front door. He locked it behind him, intending to buy Wendy a little more time to get prepared just in case the trouble turned out to be serious.

Shadows fell all around him, and the lights from inside the house made them all the worse. Brad flattened himself against the wall, straining to see against the darkness. He could hear the sounds of the night, the chirps of crickets, the occasional grunt of a frog, the wind, slight and rustling in the trees, in the long grasses that bowed low before it. Nothing seemed out of the ordinary.

But someone, he knew, was near.

Brad began to move around the house. He probably should have taken the shotgun himself, but then he didn't know where she kept the ammunition, and he had wanted the element of surprise to be on his side.

Puzzled, Brad realized that although he was still certain that someone was on the hammock with them, he didn't know how he had gotten there. The airboat was still secured where they had left it that morning, and when he came around the house, he saw that the canoe, too, was exactly where they had left it. There were no other boats of any kind on the land, nor out in the nearby water.

He heard something, and he froze. He didn't know what it was, or where it had come from, but he had heard something. He came around the corner, squinting, flexed and ready, poised on the balls of his feet. He kept moving, certain that his quarry was just ahead of him. At last he reached the front of the house again.

Suddenly, he felt a whoosh of motion. He looked up just as a heavy weight fell on him from atop the roof. Falling and tumbling beneath his attacker, Brad swore at him, and the man instantly responded.

"I've got you now!" the man returned.

And he did, Brad thought. The man was straddled over him, and he was agile and powerful. His hold was nearly merciless. Brad strained with all his might, shifting his weight, throwing his attacker.

But the man was fast—damned fast. He spun around in the darkness, a fist flying. It caught Brad cleanly in the jaw.

He responded, slamming into the man's stomach. It was like shoving against steel.

A blow struck his shoulder; Brad responded by ducking his head and butting into the stranger, a move that brought them both careening and rolling and bitterly wrestling on the ground again. Poised over his attacker for a brief moment, Brad stared down and gasped in surprise.

The guy had green eyes, but his hair was pitch-black and long against his neck. A headband kept it from falling into his eyes. He was wearing jeans and a denim shirt, but his features were strikingly bold.

Just as another blow reached his chin, Brad swore and slugged back. No, it wasn't Michaelson. It sure as hell wasn't Michaelson. He was being attacked by an Indian.

"Son of a bitch—" Brad began, but then he was thrown, and he had to gasp for air to strain against the new hold on him.

"Stop!"

Vaguely, Brad heard Wendy's voice. "Stop!" It didn't really mean any-thing—not to him, not to the tight-lipped man above him. Somehow they had gotten too involved in their exchange of blows. The fight had become too serious.

They were evenly matched, yet each man was determined to win.

But then it sounded as if the whole earth had exploded around them, and simultaneously, they fell back, startled.

Brad twisted around, staring in stunned surprise at Wendy. She was sitting on the ground, with the shotgun resting in her lap.

"Stop it!" she insisted, gasping for breath. "Both of you, do you hear me, stop!"

Panting, Brad stared over at the man who had attacked him.

The Indian was stretched out on the ground, pushing up on an elbow—and panting from exertion.

Brad stared back at Wendy. "Who the hell is this?"

"Who the hell am I?" the man retorted, his voice sounding much like a growl emanating from the back of his throat. "Who the hell is this guy?" he demanded of Wendy.

Brad pushed himself to his feet, staring at Wendy, and then at the Indian, who wasn't about to accept Brad's vantage point. He stood, too, placing his hands on his hips. The hostility between them still seemed to crackle in the air.

"Wendy! Who is this?" the Indian demanded.

Leaning against the shotgun, Wendy came to her feet. She hurried over to position herself between the two men. They barely seemed to notice that she was there. Their eyes were locked and she could feel the hatred that radiated from the two of them, spilling over to her. What was it with these two? Men! Let's Punch Each Other Out First seemed to be their motto.

"Brad McKenna, this is Eric Hawk. Eric, this is Brad McKenna."

"So who is Brad McKenna?" Eric said flatly, maintaining his wary glare at Brad.

"Eric! He's a friend of mine."

Brad spun on Wendy. "*Hawk?* I thought you said that your husband was dead."

Wendy saw Eric's jaw clamping even more tightly and the line of his mouth drawing into a grim scowl. "Leif is dead. Eric is my brother-in-law."

Brad kept staring at the other man, wondering why the hell it was taking him so long to assimilate it all. "He's an Indian. You were married to an Indian?"

"Well, Wendy, this is one bright boy you've got here," Eric drawled sarcastically.

"What's it to you?" Brad returned.

Fists were going to start flying again, Wendy thought in dismay. She placed a hand on each of the masculine chests, as if she could push the men apart.

"I mean it, stop it! Or both of you can get the hell off my property right now!"

They both gave her a wounded look.

She breathed a little more easily. For another long moment she waited, watching them both warily. They still stared at one another with open hostility, but at least they were silent.

"Shall we go in? Are the two of you capable of behaving decently to one another?"

Brad shrugged and inclined his head accusingly toward Eric. "He was the one stalking around the house as if he were out on a scalping party."

"Brad!" Wendy snapped.

"What was I supposed to think?" Eric asked her innocently.

"Well, Eric, you could have knocked," Wendy insisted.

Eric wasn't going to accept the blame any more than Brad intended to. "I saw Muscle Man here slinking around the windows. I was afraid for you, Wendy."

"Okay, okay!" She turned away from the two men and started toward the house. "You want to beat each other up? Fine—go to it. Tear each other apart. Just don't come here for ice packs when you're done!" She swung around and retrieved the shotgun, mumbling to herself. "Honest to God, but they deserve one another!"

Wendy stormed back into the house. Brad surveyed the man he'd been wrestling. They were almost exactly the same height, and had similar builds. A real even match. He could feel his left eye puffing up; the other man had a trickle of blood coming from his lip down his chin.

"Leif and Eric?" he heard himself query.

For a moment, the other man was silent. Then he cast his head back and laughed, and Brad felt a smile creasing his own features. "Well, I don't know who you are yet, and I'm still damned curious. Wendy seems willing enough to defend you, so I guess you're all right, but it doesn't seem that she's told you very much about herself."

Brad shrugged. "No. I guess she hasn't," he admitted. "You are an Indian, right?"

Eric grinned. "Seminole through and through."

"Leif and Eric?"

"Mom is Norwegian."

"Of course." Brad lifted his shoulders. "Norse Seminoles. Why the hell not." Suddenly it was as if the hostility had disappeared, dissipated into the evening sky. He liked the man with the sharp features, strange green eyes and rueful smile. And he felt the same respect in return. "Want to go in?"

"Yeah, I guess we should."

Eric led the way. Another little tremor seized Brad as he realized that Wendy's brother-in-law was very comfortable in her home. Eric hopped up on the counter, smiling at Wendy as she soaked pieces of fish fillet in batter before dropping them into a skillet.

Wendy kept her lips pursed in disapproval. "Are you staying for dinner?" she asked.

Eric cast a glance Brad's way. "Am I welcome?"

"We've plenty of fish," Wendy said.

Brad kept silent. He'd been worried about being alone with Wendy, but now that their privacy had been taken away, he wanted it back.

Eric watched Brad, and his grin deepened. "Well, Wendy, you know how I just love your Cajun catfish."

Wendy nodded, her eyes on her task. "Eric, would you fix yourself and Brad a drink?"

"Sure." He slid off the counter and turned to Brad. "Name your poison."

"Jack Black on the rocks, if it's available."

"You got it. Wendy? A glass of wine?"

Wendy dropped a fillet into the sizzling oil, then looked over at her brother-in-law. "Tonight? Nooo...I think I'll have bourbon, too, please."

"Your wish is my command, Wendy. You know that." He looked at her so innocently.

At this point in her life, Eric was probably her closest friend. When Leif died, Eric had mourned beside her. No one could understand her grief more than Eric, because the two of them had suffered a loss together. For the longest time, they had been each other's only salvation.

It had all happened two years ago, but she knew that seeing her with another man like this had to open old wounds for him. But then again, Eric had always encouraged her to get back out in the world again.

That had been before he had actually found a strange man in her house.

Eric handed her a Jack Black on the rocks. She sipped it quickly, savoring the sweet, burning sensation.

Brad lifted his glass to hers. "Cheers."

She nodded and started to take another sip.

Oh, what the heck! she thought. Wendy cast back her head and swallowed the entire contents of the glass. Dinner threatened to be a long and nerve-racking affair.

In the end, it really wasn't so bad. Brad remained silent at the beginning, adding a bit to Wendy's uneasiness. But Eric talked about the family and Wendy was grateful that he kept to easy topics. After a few minutes, he even included Brad in the conversation. She told Eric that Brad had caught the fish and that she hadn't been able to hook anything. Then the two men entered into an enthusiastic discussion on fishing.

However, things were bound to get sticky. They did so when dinner was over, when Wendy started to rinse the plates and load the dishwasher.

Both men went to make coffee. This time, Eric deferred to Brad, but they were both scrutinizing each other suspiciously. Sensing the tension, Wendy decided to serve some brandy and Tia Maria along with their coffee. Just as she gripped the brandy bottle, Eric asked Brad what he did for a living.

The bottle slipped from her fingers and fell to the floor. The glass bottle shattered, and the sticky liquid flew everywhere.

Both men stared at her. Wendy smiled weakly. "Slippery fingers, I suppose." She knelt to start mopping up the spill.

"Let me help you," Brad said, hunching down before her. She cut her finger on a piece of glass and absently sucked upon the wound as she stared at him in a growing panic.

"Wendy—" Brad frowned at the state of her finger.

"Did you cut yourself?" Eric demanded, concerned.

"No, I—"

"Yes, she did," Brad said. He helped her to her feet, sticking her hand under the running water at the sink. It wasn't serious, but Brad started muttering about antiseptic and Eric said he'd get some peroxide and Band-Aids.

"Brad," Wendy murmured. His arm was around her as he held her hand beneath the faucet. She smiled slightly, admiring the planes of his face, noticing the concern he showed. She was surrounded by the heat of him, and the subtle male scent that suddenly seemed to tease her mercilessly.

"Hmm?" He was still concerned about her cut.

"What do I tell Eric?"

He looked into her eyes, understanding her question. "Do you trust him?"

"Of course. I'd trust him with my life."

"That's all that matters," Brad said softly. Then he shrugged. "Tell him. Tell him the truth."

He finished speaking just as Eric returned to the kitchen. "Just peroxide—it won't hurt," Eric told Wendy, taking her hand. Brad backed away while Eric cleaned and bandaged her cut with a tender care that probably outweighed the seriousness of the situation. Brad bent down and picked up the rest of the broken bottle, soaking up the spilled brandy with paper towels.

When Brad finished rinsing his hands, Eric confronted him again. "Well? Did you decide whether to tell me what you're whispering about or not? Wendy, I hope you didn't cut your finger just for my benefit."

"No!" she gasped quickly.

"DEA," Brad told Eric.

Without flinching, Eric kept his eyes on Brad, then nodded. They all stood in silence for a moment. "I thought you had to be with some branch of law enforcement," he murmured.

"Yeah?"

"Well, you were ready for me, and I'm pretty good at stealth. It's that 'Tonto' blood in me, you know."

Brad laughed and clapped Eric on the back.

Wendy decided that they were both crazy. She turned around and started to pour coffee.

"You're involved in that Michaelson deal that went bad?"

"Yes."

"And you're hiding out here?"

Wendy had been dropping shots of Tia Maria into the coffee. Now she tightened her trembling fingers and set the bottle down. She didn't need any more alcohol on the floor.

"Yes," Brad said at last.

Noticing Wendy's hesitation, Eric grabbed the Tia Maria bottle and added another shot to each of the coffee cups. He took a sip of his coffee, then muttered, "That's dangerous for Wendy. She shouldn't be so involved in this sordid business."

"Eric—" Wendy tried to interrupt him.

"Where did you meet? How did you meet?" Eric probed.

"Eric!" Wendy protested again. She loved her brother-in-law. And it had been nice to have him care for her, to be protective. It had been nice to know that he had been close, that there was still someone out there who loved her enough to risk life and limb for her. But he was prying into dangerous territory.

"It's all right, Wendy," Brad said. "Michaelson chased me out on Alligator Alley. My car blew a gasket or something after I'd taken a side road. One of his bullets nicked me in the forehead—Wendy found me facedown in the mud."

Eric nodded slowly.

"Couldn't we have coffee in the living room?" Wendy murmured. When they both ignored her, she decided to ignore them. She took her coffee cup into the living room and considered turning the television on. Tonight, some soothing music might be a better bet. She turned on the system that Leif had so painstakingly set up and slipped in a Beatles disc. As music filled the room, Wendy sat on the couch and closed her eyes, warming her hands with her cup.

Despite the music she could still hear them talking in the kitchen, their words growing louder.

"Excuse me!" she called. "This is my house, you know. I am the hostess, you are the guests. Want to come on out here and behave?"

They both appeared, slowly. Although they apparently hadn't been able to restrain their anger in the kitchen, now they had nothing to say.

Brad wandered over to the far side of the room, studying the titles of the books that lined the shelves. With a grimace, Eric sat down beside her on the couch.

At length, he sighed. "Wendy, it's dangerous—"

"He's right. I think I should go," Brad interrupted.

"Dammit!" Wendy exploded. She slammed her cup onto the butcher-block side table and flew to her feet, spinning around to face Eric, then Brad, then Eric again.

"Eric, if you really love me, trust me enough to know that I'm not a fool. And no one knows better than you do how deeply hidden we are here!" She turned back to Brad. "If I didn't feel that I could safely help you, I'd never have asked you here. I'm a grown woman, capable of making my own decisions. Don't try to run my life—behind my back!"

Brad picked up the TV guide and began to idly leaf through it. He cleared his throat. "Wendy—"

"It wasn't behind your back," Eric said.

She glared at them both. "Oh, hell!" she groaned, falling back onto the couch in mock defeat.

"This is great," Brad said, suddenly changing the subject. "Do you get cable out here?"

She smiled slowly. "Yes, I have cable TV."

"Ten o'clock, *No Way Out* is on! I've been trying to see that movie for over a year."

Wendy got up and turned off the Beatles disc. "Go ahead, turn on the television."

Eric rose. "Got any microwave popcorn, Wendy?"

"In the top cabinet over the stove."

Brad turned on the television; Eric went into the kitchen and found the popcorn. By ten-fifteen they were huddled together on the couch with Wendy in the middle, crunching away on popcorn.

It was strange, Wendy thought. Very strange.

But then, she thought that it was nice, too. It was as if they had all known each other for ages. Considering their precipitous introduction, Brad and Eric seemed to be getting along very well.

When the movie ended, Wendy yawned. Brad stood and stretched, picking up the popcorn bowl.

Slightly uneasy, Eric stared at Brad.

Wendy lowered her head. Although Eric knew that Brad was staying here, she sensed her brother-in-law's reluctance to depart, leaving this stranger behind. "Do you have to work tomorrow?" she asked him.

"Yeah, I do."

"Do you need me?"

He shook his head. "No. It's probably better if you just lie low. I'll drop by again in a few days."

"How did you get here?" Brad asked Eric, baffled.

Eric laughed and winked at Wendy. "You've got to show him where the stones are."

"The what?"

Wendy grinned. "There's a place in the canal where Leif set boulders into the water. The depth there is only about a foot—in the dry season, you can see them. Eric drove here—his car is right behind the saw grass."

"I see." With good grace, Brad grinned. The two men shook hands. Wendy felt that Brad sensed Eric's discomfort. "Well, I'm going to call it a day. Wendy, Eric, thank you both."

"Take care," Eric warned him softly. Brad nodded, strode into the guest room and closed the door.

"I'll walk you out?" Wendy said to her brother-in-law.

He set an arm around her shoulder and ruffled her hair. "Sure."

Outside in the darkness, Eric said, "I like him, Wendy. I mean, not that it matters. You're a mature woman, and you have the right to make your own decisions. But I have to admit, I like him."

Her lips trembled when she tried to smile. "Eric, nothing has hap—"

"Wendy, don't encourage me to act like a surrogate parent. I know you've needed to get out. Hell, *I've* been out. I've been out a lot," he said bitterly.

Yes, he had, Wendy thought, but she didn't voice her agreement. They'd had their different ways of coping with the pain after the horrible night when her husband and his wife had been killed together. For Wendy, it had been a complete withdrawal. For Eric, it had been a near fall into a world of reckless delusion.

But they had both survived, she thought.

"Good night, Wendy. I'll tell the folks hi—"

"I'll be in to see everyone soon." She paused. "Think I can bring Brad to the folks?"

"Yes, I think you can."

She smiled at Eric. The breeze picked up his sleek raven hair and moved it in the darkness, and for a moment, her heart caught in her throat as he reminded her of Leif. He kissed her on the forehead, and then he disappeared in the night.

Wendy went back into the house, locking the door behind her. When she reached the guest-room door, she knocked lightly.

"Yes?" Brad responded after a moment.

Wendy pushed the door open. Brad was still in jeans, but he had taken off his shirt. The room was dark, but light seeped in from the hallway. It gleamed bronze upon his bare shoulders while his features remained hidden in shadows.

"I wanted to thank you," she said.

She could sense his confusion. "For what?"

"Eric is a good friend."

"I noticed. You're close."

"Yes, we are, but not like that. I mean, we could never be involved. He's really like a brother in the truest sense. Since I haven't dated since Leif died, you see, and—not that we're dating or anything—but I think it was just hard for Eric to leave with you and me here alone. And, well, the way you made a point of coming in here, I..." As her voice trailed away, she stood there, wishing to God she didn't feel quite so foolish.

"Or anything?" he queried softly.

"What?"

"We're not dating, or anything?" he repeated, and she noticed a rueful smile on his face. "Come on, Wendy, we're doing *something* together, aren't we?"

She smiled, glad that he had a way of making her feel comfortable.

"Hey. Come over here," he said softly.

Slowly, she began to walk toward him.

She paused when she reached him. The light was still shielding his eyes, while it played over the rippled muscles of his bronze shoulders. There was a rich spattering of tawny hair covering his chest. She wanted to touch it.

She did.

She laid her palm flat against his chest.

And that was when he kissed her. Threading his fingers through her hair, he lowered his head over hers. For the longest time his breath seemed to tease her lips. Tentatively, she gazed into his eyes, soft gold and fascinated as they searched her. Then his lips touched hers, very gently. Her fingers curled into his chest as she felt the force of his mouth upon hers broaden, sweeping her away. His tongue bathed her mouth in a sweet, warm invasion.

Even with her eyes closed, she saw the man, knew the man. She felt his hands, and his kiss.

A delicious weakness overcame her. It would be so easy. So easy to give way to the liquid in her knees and fall. He would catch her, she knew. He would catch her and sweep her away to bed, where she could surrender to the darkness of night.

His lips parted slowly from hers, hovering above her. She felt the golden probe of his gaze again.

"Wendy..." he murmured.

They were spellbound, locked in a magical moment. She used her free hand to smooth the tendril of hair that had fallen over his forehead.

He inhaled, and then exhaled, shakily. With stony resolve, he lifted her hands and kissed her palms. "Go to bed, Wendy," he told her.

She lowered her eyes, nodding. Neither of them was ready. "Good night."

She started walking to the door.

"Wendy!"

In an instant he was beside her again, and she rushed into his arms. This time he kissed her with passion and fire, and then his hands slipped deftly beneath her oversized shirt, finding her bare breasts beneath it. As his palms caressed her nipples a jagged sob escaped her lips beneath the sweet and savage force of his kiss.

And then, just as she had imagined, he swept her off her feet, heading with purpose for the bed that loomed huge and enticing in the shadows of the night.

CHAPTER 6

With grave tenderness, he eased her down upon the bed. She could feel the urgent hunger in the heated length of his body as he lay down beside her. His kiss continued to sear her, and his touch lingered upon her. His hands were everywhere, holding her face, stroking her shoulder, caressing her bare back. He was staging an onslaught against her senses, and she wanted desperately to hold on to each feeling, to each nuance of emotion and reaction. He was awakening sensations she had forgotten, feelings she had forsaken when Leif died.

His passionate assault was like the sudden surge of the tide; swept into that tide, she found that thought was difficult. She explored his chest with her fingertips, marveling at the warmth of his flesh, the tension in his muscles. She loved the coarse feeling of the short, whorling hairs that teased her fingertips, and most of all, she loved the evocative feel of his body over hers, so much of him eclipsing so much of her.

She seemed to drown in his kiss, for it was never ending, although it evolved. Fiercely, he claimed her lips...then pulled away to press his mouth against the pulse in her throat, or the hollow of her collarbone. The inner circle of his palm fell gently against her breast, and his fingers closed slowly around the full weight of it, exploring and caressing sensitive areas.

Minutes passed...or aeons. She breathed in the enticing male scent of his bare flesh, and she arched to meet his kiss. It was easy to respond, far easier than she had expected, for she had not known that she was starved. The darkness quietly shielded her from any sense of reality, even as the full bulge growing against his denim jeans warned her that she was plunging, falling downward into a tempest from which she could not rise. She was falling into the forbidden realm, a realm of pleasure, where loneliness was masked, and thirst was sated.

But then, abruptly, without a word, he pulled away from her. The only sound was the belabored rush of his breath. She knew from the heat of his flesh and the hardened feel of his body that he had not lost his desire for her. But it was over. Whatever it had been, he had ended it.

In the dim light his eyes seemed to gleam like a great cat's, sizzling and gold. He rested upon an elbow and stared curiously down at her. Wendy bit her inner lip, wondering what had driven him away.

"What's wrong?" she asked, her words a whisper.

He drew the tip of his thumb over her cheek, staring pensively at her face. He shook his head. "This—I shouldn't be doing this."

"But I came to you!"

They remained still. The only movement was that of his thumb, the callused pad stroking her flesh. She could read no emotion in his eyes; she had no idea what he was thinking or feeling.

Suddenly, her emotions crumbled, stung by the rejection. She had laid herself on the line. She hadn't been dreaming of the past; no ghosts had drifted between them. She had offered herself—and he had refused her. He'd dealt the supreme blow to her confidence.

"Oh, dear God!" she muttered. Humiliated, she shoved against him. Apparently, he hadn't expected her to touch him, at least not so vehemently. She pushed him so hard that he rolled right onto the floor.

"Wendy! Dammit, wait, listen—"

Brad's kneecap hurt where he'd slammed it onto the floor. His head had bumped against the bed frame and, all in all, he felt like an idiot.

It seemed that a guy just couldn't win. He had known he was bound for trouble, wanting her as he did. But he'd expected her to be angry with him for taking advantage of her, not for trying desperately, with a restraint that went above and beyond, to respect her. "Wendy!" Muttering to himself and wincing in pain, Brad scrambled back to his feet.

Wendy was desperately fighting the urge to burst into tears—not a little rivulet of damp tears, but a thunderous storm of wet, sloppy tears. She tore into her own room, but there was no way to lock the door against him—he had broken the lock that morning.

Wendy slammed the door anyway.

It didn't do any good. "Wendy!" Brad knocked on the door. When she didn't answer, he opened it and waited in the doorway, still breathless. She sat at the foot of her bed, her back to him, fiercely cradling her pillow. Soft light spilled in from the hall, falling over her, striking her hair with a golden glow.

"Wendy! I want to talk to you."

"I don't want to talk to you."

"Wendy, please, listen to me." He stood behind her and rested his hands on her shoulders, surprised to discover how much she was trembling.

She tried to shrug him away, but he sat down behind her. "I'd really appreciate it if you didn't touch me," she said stiffly.

He let go of her shoulders but remained behind her. "We've got to talk," he said hoarsely. "Wendy, if you would just turn around and talk to me—"

She spun around then, putting distance between them. She jerked the band out of her hair and golden locks tumbled down to her shoulders. She shook them out in absent vehemence, staring at him with shimmering silver eyes that reflected light like diamonds. "What? Talk. Say whatever it is and then go away."

He sighed. "Wendy, you're not making this easy."

"Well, I hope you'll forgive me. It isn't very easy from my side, either. I'm not good at this to begin with. I've been out of practice for some time."

"Wendy, that's just the point."

She inhaled, holding back a sob. He reached out to touch her cheek again, and he felt the warm, liquid tears there. "Wendy..."

"Stop it! For the love of God, will you stop it?"

He pulled her into his arms. She fought him, tensing and straining against him. He couldn't let her go, so he held her until she stopped fighting him, until she collapsed against his chest and let him wrap his arms around her.

"Brad, please," she murmured against his chest. She could taste the sweet salt of his flesh when she spoke; she could feel the beat of his heart, strong beneath her cheek.

He smoothed back her hair, somewhat awed by its color in the night. Angel's hair. So soft, so silky, so beautifully blond. "Wendy, I want you so badly, don't you see?"

She stiffened again. "No, quite frankly, I don't."

In the darkness, he smiled. "Wendy, it's just too quick. I want you, but I want it to be right. I don't want you to wake up in the morning and be sorry. I don't want to be a substitute for your husband, and I don't want you to regret what you did in the darkness. I want you to want me."

She kept silent for a moment, warmed by his embrace, feeling ridiculously secure, since she knew he offered her no real security. On the contrary, he offered her danger, in many different guises. "I did want you," she said at last.

"Did you? Did you really?" He kissed her forehead. Then, very gently, he kissed her lips again and smiled at her. "You're a very special lady, Wendy. And we are going to make love. Here I've been racking my head all day trying to figure out how not to drag you into bed. And to top it off, you wander into my bedroom when I've been a damned saint and shut myself up for the night. I'll never be able to leave you without knowing what we have to share. But I care too much now, Wendy. I care too much about you to not take it slowly. That's what we really want, what we both deserve. A night of passion with no regrets in the morning." He finished off his words with another kiss, a slow, languid kiss.

She felt as if her heart still beat a hundred miles an hour, as if her blood still raced through her system painfully. She pushed away from him, groaning softly as she twisted her head. "Brad, if you have any feelings for me, please! Leave me alone now."

"No."

Incensed, she tried to break free from his hold. He caught her arms and held her close. With one deft, sure movement, he pulled her back onto the bed. His shoulders and head rested against a plump pillow, and her head was tucked against his chest, her hair splayed in a lustrous array upon it.

He longed to touch that hair. He longed to do much, much more. But he was afraid to release her. He kept his arm around her, aware of the tension in her, aware that she could easily bolt.

"Wendy," he murmured, "want to know my middle name?"

"What?" He could see her bewildered frown, but he also felt some of the tension ease out of her. Daring to ease his powerful hold, he stroked the golden hair that spilled over his flesh, haunting his senses.

"Michael. Brad Michael McKenna. I'm a Scorpio."

She started to laugh, twisting around to sit in his arms. "Brad, this is my bedroom, not a singles bar."

"All right, well, that makes things a little more intimate. What was your maiden name?"

She frowned again, then a slow smile curved her lips. "Harper. Wendy Anne Harper."

"And how old are you, Wendy Anne?"

"That's damned nosy, isn't it?"

He shrugged. "You can't be that old."

"Thirty-one," she told him. "And you?"

"Thirty-five, next November. When is your birthday?"

"February fourteenth."

"Valentine's Day baby, hmm? Do you like sushi?"

"I hate it."

"Well, I love it, but I suppose that's a minor detail. You live in the Everglades, but you hate sushi?"

She laughed. "What does that have to do with it?"

"You're surrounded by fish."

"That doesn't mean that I have to eat the things raw."

She settled down, nestling her head against his chest again. Her breath fanned against him, just as her hair tantalized his naked flesh like a feather tauntingly stroking skin. He inhaled deeply, breathing in her perfume, the scent of her shampoo and the sweet female scent of her body.

She was gentle against him, soft and relaxed. She brought her hand against her mouth, stifling a yawn. He kept stroking her hair. "What's my name, Wendy?"

"What?"

"My name? What's my name?"

"What is this game? Brad. Brad McKenna. At least, I think it's your real name."

Her eyes—shimmering, liquid silver—rose to his. A painful desire jolted through him again. Gritting his teeth, he tried to ignore the clamoring demands of his masculinity.

"Yeah, it's my real name. But it isn't my whole name."

She twisted her jaw slightly, half smiling, half frowning. "Brad Michael McKenna."

He nodded, pleased. "That's right, Ms. Wendy Anne Harper Hawk, who hates sushi and lives with the gators and creatures and became thirty-one last February fourteenth. Oh—and who likes the Beatles and keeps a wonderfully neat, hospitable home." He touched her chin, drawing her eyes closer to his. "Wendy, it is nice to get to know you."

She smiled. He touched her lips with his fingers, and she eased her head down against his chest again.

He didn't remember saying anything else—nor did he think that she did. They fell asleep that way and woke up beside one another, in her bed, but fully dressed.

Awakened by a stream of early-morning sunshine, Brad mused that it was a damned unusual way for him to start the day.

But then, Wendy was a damned unusual woman. Unique.

Special.

He leaned over, kissed her forehead and rose. She looked like a sleeping angel, with a serene expression on her beautiful features and wisps of blond hair clouding around her. He kissed her again, then quietly closed the door.

An hour later, when Wendy awoke, she could smell the enticing aroma of sizzling bacon. She didn't rise right away, but remained in bed, pondering the night.

She didn't know what to think. She liked Brad more than ever; she admired him. There was a streak of honor in his character, a quality that was rare and unusual, and she appreciated it. But, then again, the hell with honor. It could have been so easy—a pair of consenting adults indulging in a quick affair inspired by circumstance.

But no. The man who cared nothing about marriage just had to get to know her first.

Who would have ever imagined...he was a lot like Leif in that sense. Leif had always had his particular sense of ethics, and nothing could ever sway him. Bright and every bit as striking a man as Eric, Leif could have traveled anywhere and accomplished anything, but his heart was pledged to his tribe and his land. Despite rich opportunities elsewhere, this had been his home.

And Leif had moved slowly with her. He would have never forced her into anything. He had just let her fall in love with him first, and then with the curious, subtle beauty of the swamp.

Yes, there was something about them that was alike, she thought, no matter how strange. Her dark, patient husband with his love of the landscape, and this tawny-haired, cosmopolitan drug agent with his total disdain for muck and mud.

A tap on the door roused her from her thoughts. Brad stood in the doorway, freshly shaved and showered, and looking as young and cheerful as a college student.

"Breakfast is almost on. You've got time for a shower if you want."

Wendy nodded. "Thanks." He returned to the kitchen, and she stole into the bathroom for a long, hot shower.

The scent of shaving cream was still fresh in the bathroom. He had wiped down the tile in the shower and cleaned the mirror and the sink. And yet, a hint of his presence lingered there. Absurdly, Wendy felt like crying again.

It was reassuring, this lingering reminder of a man in the bathroom. A second damp towel, a second mug on the counter...

A second body in bed at night.

She stepped impatiently beneath the hot spray of the shower.

Damn Brad McKenna! Things should have been left to take their course. They would have enjoyed a swift, fleeting affair of mutual passion—and nothing more. She didn't want to wonder what it would be like to live with the man longer.

By the time she came out of the shower, her mood had brewed into a volatile tempest.

Brad awaited her in the kitchen amid the aromas of coffee, fried bacon and tomato-and-pepper omelets. Two places were set at the counter. He'd done a nice job of arranging things, with place mats, napkins and even a wild orchid nestled between the plates as a peace offering.

But Wendy just didn't feel very peaceful that morning. Brad seemed too at ease, too proud of himself.

"Mrs. Hawk?" With a flourish, he pulled back one of the rattan counter stools for her. Wendy sat, watching him as she carefully unfolded her napkin. He slid into the chair beside her.

"Made yourself right at home, I see," she said sweetly, eyeing him over her juice glass as she took a sip.

He stiffened. "I guess I did. Sorry. You've led me to believe that I was welcome to anything here—anything at all."

Wendy didn't know what was simmering inside of her. She was being completely unreasonable, and she knew it. He had done her the courtesy of creating a nice breakfast. She should have thanked him. Somehow, she couldn't do it.

"I must have given you the wrong impression. I'm so sorry. I really didn't mean to."

He watched her, his jaw hard and set. "You didn't mean to give me the impression that I could fix breakfast—or that I could sleep with you? What is the point that we're making here?"

She set her juice glass down carefully, staring at her plate instead of him. Forcing her voice to remain pleasant and calm, she explained, "You're a guest here, McKenna, nothing more."

"I'm a guest here because you invited me. And I can leave. No problem."

"You really are one rude bastard, you know that? I should have left you in the muck."

"Oh, yeah! Let's bring that up again." He bolted out of the chair and stood before her. Wendy swallowed. There was a pulse ticking away at his throat, and she sensed the pulse of his heart beneath Leif's old Miami Dolphins T-shirt. She closed her eyes, trying to remember Leif in that shirt. She couldn't.

When she opened her eyes and looked up, Brad still had his jaw set in that way of his that clearly spoke of anger and hostility. His eyes were gleaming, gold as a cat's. Bracing one hand behind her on the stool and one against the counter, he leaned close to her, warm and near and threatening.

She felt his breath against her flesh, sensed the rapid pulse of his anger. "Want to leave me in the swamp, Wendy? We can go right back out there if you want. This wasn't my idea, remember? You offered. Were you that desperate to have a man in the house?"

"Oh!" She spun on the chair, ready to slap him, but he was too quick. He caught her wrist and glared down at her. Using all her strength, she wrenched free from him and slid off the stool. Ignoring him, she sped through the house to her bedroom. She found her purse and headed back down the hallway, frantic to reach the door.

"Where the hell are you going?" he called after her. When she didn't stop, he chased her, finally catching her arm and swinging her back to face him.

"I'm going out."

"Out where, damn you?"

She freed her arm again and backed away from him. "I'm going into work."

"Work?"

"Yes, work! People do work."

"Who do you work for?"

She didn't want to answer him for various reasons: sheer perversity, perhaps, or the bubbling black cauldron of her temper, or the raw wound of hurt and rejection. "I work for Eric!"

"You work for Eric—where? Doing what?" he demanded suspiciously.

Wendy hesitated, feeling her anger sizzle and whirl inside of her again. It was the most awful feeling. She was being so unreasonable, but now she was trying to salvage something of her pride by leaving.

"I'm not one of your suspects, Mr. G-Man," she retorted, but he took another step toward her, grabbing her arms, wrenching her against him.

"I'm not a G-Man. Now tell me, *where* do you work for Eric, and *what* do you do for him?"

"My God, what does it matter to you?" She pulled back her wrist, but he wouldn't release her. At that moment she realized just how strong he was. He could be powerful and ruthless when he chose.

"I asked you a question," he hissed. "Why didn't you tell me that you worked? Why didn't you go to work yesterday?"

Wendy sighed, making a great show of exaggerated impatience. "I work for Eric, but I only go in a day or two a week. He spends some time working with the tribal council, but he also sold a book last year on Andrew Jackson's campaign against the Seminoles. This year he's doing one on the relationship between the Seminole Indians and the Miccosukees. I'm his research assistant."

"What?"

"There are two tribes down here, McKenna. Not just Seminoles. The Miccosukees have some tribal land south of here, fronting the Trail. But I'm sure you didn't know or care. This whole place is just an infested pile of wet mud to you, isn't it? Muck and savages, huh?"

Her cutting remark caused his lip to tighten. He pulled her even closer. "That's another thing. Why didn't you tell me that you had been married to an Indian?"

"What?" Wendy said blankly. Something inside of her ticked and then exploded. "Because I don't owe you any explanation! I didn't tell you that he was Norse, either. Did that matter? Does any of it matter?"

"Yes, it matters! Had I known the details, I wouldn't have gotten into a fight with your brother-in-law. I wouldn't have been frightened half out of my wits, thinking I'd enticed a criminal to your home!"

"Bigot!" Wendy snapped, trying to wrench away with all of her strength. It did her no good.

He gritted his teeth and held her even closer. "No, Wendy, I'm not a bigot, and you damn well know it. I may be ignorant about a few things that you surely know backward and forward, but that doesn't imply any lack of respect for a people. Honest to God, Wendy, I think that you do know that. Now would you mind telling me what this morning's fiasco is about?"

"I've got to go. Get your hands off me."

"Not until we straighten this out. Okay, you're mad. You're furious at me over something. You did invite me here. And I have a hard time believing that this whole temper tantrum thing is over the fact that I made breakfast! So what can it be? Oh, I know. I disappointed you last night. You thought you'd invited some stud in, and you didn't get quite what you really wanted."

"Damn you, McKenna, let go of me!" Wendy warned him. Her temper began to cool as she realized that his had risen. His eyes sparkled with a menacing sizzle, and every muscle of his body seemed to have tightened.

Wendy tossed back her head, narrowing her eyes. "I want to leave the house, all right? You're a guest. I asked you to stay. Foolish me, I thought that you might consider your life to be a valuable quantity. Now—let me go!"

He didn't let her go.

Instead his mouth bore down on hers with a startling and savage determination. His lips encompassed hers, his teeth grated against hers until she surrendered with a little whimper. His tongue plunged into the depths and crevices of her mouth so intimately that she shuddered, feeling as if her very soul had been invaded. Blind rage turned the world black to her, but then that blackness dissipated. His fingers threaded through her hair, forcing her against him.

But, despite herself, she melded to him. Despite herself, she felt her heart race, beating raggedly. Despite herself, she inhaled the scent of him, marveled at the sweet tension of his body, surrendered to the fierce and yearning power of the man.

His ankle twisted around hers; suddenly she was off her feet, swept to the floor. He lowered his weight over her. He stared at her for a moment, then his fingers plunged into the wings of her hair, and he held her still while his mouth ravaged hers again. His body was hard against her. Rigid and hard.

Hot tears played behind her eyes. She wanted him, but she didn't want the commitment. She was afraid to get to know him, afraid that she'd enjoy the smell of shaving cream in the bathroom, or tremble at the sight of a wild orchid beside her plate. She was deathly afraid of loving him...

Wendy twisted away, breaking the kiss. "Brad! Brad, damn you, this isn't right, this isn't..." Her voice trailed off painfully.

He went dead still. For endless moments, she felt only the soft, heated whisper of his breath against her throat. Then he moved. He hunched to the balls of his feet and then stood. He offered her a hand, and when she didn't take it, he reached for her, pulling her up to stand in front of him.

Wendy couldn't face him. She lowered her head, wishing that he would free her fingers. Suddenly, he dropped them.

He crossed his arms over his chest and stared at her until she felt compelled to face him, eye to eye. "This isn't what?" he demanded bluntly.

She shook her head. "I—"

"It isn't what you wanted, right?"

"Brad, please! Can't you just leave me alone to be humiliated in peace!"

He stared at her and shook his head slowly. The tension began to ease away from him, and a rueful smile worked its way into the line of his mouth. "No. You shouldn't be humiliated. Come here, Wendy." He reached for her, gently easing her into his arms. Tenderly, he kissed her nose and lips.

"Did I ever thank you?"

"What?"

"Did I ever really thank you? You did save my life."

"It was nothing," Wendy murmured raggedly. Her hand fell against his chest and she stared up at the gentle smile on his lips. "Still, I think I should go to work today. You are very welcome to make yourself at home. I just have to get out for a while."

He stared into her eyes and nodded. "I understand," he said softly, and she thought that he did. He grinned ruefully. "Think that the food is still edible?"

"This is the second breakfast we'll have to trash, I'm afraid," she murmured. "Well, maybe it's still edible, but I don't think that I can eat."

He nodded. "Well, worse things can happen than breakfast trashing."

"Yes."

"Wendy, seriously, where are you going?"

"Not far from here. Eric has a house on a plot of land that he owns."

"On the main road?"

She frowned, wondering at the question. "Well, the land itself fronts the main road. But the house is far back."

He stared at her, then sighed. "I should come with you."

"Not today!" she whispered.

"Wendy, Wendy!" He pulled her close, moving his fingers through her hair in a fervent massage. Then he held her away, searching out her eyes again. "Wendy, I really shouldn't be here. I'm afraid for you, Wendy. And I'll be afraid for you until this is over."

She smiled, touched by the timbre of his voice. "Brad, no one knows who I am. If your Michaelson character happened to be looking for you, he wouldn't know me. I've never seen him, he's never seen me. And I won't be passing any public places on the way. I go near the small family village where Eric and Leif's grandparents still live, but that's all. I'll be very safe."

He stared at her a moment longer, then exhaled slowly and nodded. "All right."

"I need you to move away from the door," she told him.

He nodded again, but it took him a minute to move. Then, when he did, he pulled her into his arms.

"Wendy," he murmured seriously.

"What?"

He gently smoothed back a wild strand of hair. "We are going to make love."

"Are we?" she queried, raising her eyebrows.

"Yes." He opened the door for her and grinned. "And don't worry. I'll be sure to let you know exactly when."

"Pompous ass!" she muttered to herself, hurrying to the airboat.

She didn't realize he was behind her until he caught up with her. He was laughing as his hands descended upon her shoulder. She swung around to face him.

"I heard that."

Wendy Shrugged. "Well, it's true. You are decidedly too sure of yourself."

"Shouldn't I be?" he demanded innocently.

"You'll tell me when," Wendy mimicked. "I just might change my mind about this whole thing, you know."

He shook his head. There was a grave expression on his face. "You won't."

She set her hands on her hips, cocking her head at an angle as she returned his scrutiny. "Ah, yes! You think I'll fall apart and fly into your arms by darkness again."

He shook his head, that slow smile lifting his lips. "No. It will be broad daylight, lots of light—or not at all."

"Oh, really?"

"Really." He started to return to the house. At the door, he paused and called back to her in a sensual drawl. "Don't worry about it. As I said, I'll make sure to tell you when." He grinned and closed the door.

Not sure whether to laugh or refute him, Wendy merely turned away and continued down to the airboat.

CHAPTER 7

Wendy stared down at the page she was reading and shook her head in annoyance. A history book lay open before her, and the information in it was inaccurate. She flipped back to the front of the book, looking for the copyright date. When she realized that the book had been written before World War II, she was able to take some of the misinformation more philosophically. The U.S. government hadn't recognized the two different and distinct tribes living in the Everglades back then—why would a white schoolteacher-turned-author know any better?

She set the book on the table and scratched out a note to Eric. A glance at the cypress clock on her brother-in-law's handsomely paneled study wall indicated that it was well past six. She should be heading back.

Just the thought of going home made her palms begin to sweat and her stomach churn. It was her house! she reminded herself. She had every right to go home.

She straightened all of her materials on the desk, turned off the computer, covered it—and sank back into the chair. She gnawed idly on her thumbnail. It was her house. Yes, the rights were hers. But she didn't have a right to act the way she had been acting. She had invited Brad to stay.

She'd actually invited him to a whole lot more. He was right about one thing: she needed to decide exactly what she was willing to offer.

The front door opened and closed. For a moment, Wendy sat up in panic, thinking that she'd been an absolute fool not to lock the door. But then, peeking down the long hallway that led to the front of the house, she saw that Eric was coming in.

"Wendy!" he called, spotting her from the end of the hall. She waved to him, smiling. He wore jeans and a colorful Seminole shirt, woven in various shades of red. The color contrasted with the warm bronze of his face and the startling shade of his eyes.

You need someone, too, brother-in-law, Wendy thought suddenly. He was a special man, so striking in appearance, so proud and ethical, so warm and generous to those he trusted.

Like Jennifer, his wife.

"Let me get something cool to drink," he called to her, "and I'll be right with you."

She heard the refrigerator door open, then seconds later, he appeared carrying a Sol for himself and a wine cooler for her. She smiled, thanking him. Eric knew her. Beer for fishing, wine with company dinner, ice tea or water if she was thirsty. Diet soda if she was determined on a diet, but her diets would seldom last long because she loved the taste of real sugar. She had known her brother-in-law for a decade. All those years bred real friendship, real closeness.

And Brad, who would go away very soon, wanted to know her birthday and her middle name. He should have been a dream, she thought. An imaginary lover, tan and sandy and agile and beautifully formed. A midnight visitor who would dissipate with the morning light of dawn.

"What are you doing here? I thought that you weren't going to come over while you were hosting the DEA." Eric studied her with frank curiosity.

Wendy shrugged, but she couldn't keep her eyes level with Eric's. "I—uh—I don't know. I guess I needed a little breathing space."

He took a long sip of his beer, set his booted feet comfortably upon the edge of his desk and leaned back. He surveyed her from beneath half-closed, jet lashes, then closed his eyes completely and smiled. "Sparks are flying too hot and wild for you to handle, huh?"

Wendy stared at him until he opened his eyes again. She wanted to tell him to mind his own business, but she shrugged instead. "No. I just needed some space."

"Get out of the kitchen if you can't take the heat," Eric quoted gravely.

"Eric," Wendy moaned.

He sat up, letting his feet fall to the floor. Reaching over, he tilted her chin upward. "There's something there, Wendy-bird," he teased her lightly. "I could feel it all night long. Palpable, thick." He released her, rose and stretched with the grace of a cat. His back was to her when he said, "So did you run over here because you did go to bed, or because you didn't?"

"Eric—"

"Well?"

He turned to look at her, and she felt the depth of his concern for her. She smiled. "Because I didn't. Eric, I don't know what to think. I don't know what I feel. I mean, he's going to go away again, right? He's just here for a few days. Until they catch this Michaelson character, or until something else breaks. I like him a lot, Eric—"

"So do I, for whatever that's worth."

"I hate what he does for a living. And he doesn't intend to get married—"

"Well, if you haven't made it into bed yet, why are you worrying about marriage?"

"I'm not! I don't want to get married again."

"So?"

She shook her head, then blurted out, "So then why doesn't it just happen? Why do we have to go through twenty questions?"

Eric stared at her for a long time. At last he spoke very softly. "Because he does care, Wendy. Because he didn't meet you on a bar stool, because he thinks highly of you."

"But he said—"

"Trust me, Wendy." As he sighed, a skeptical glaze clouded the lime color of his eyes. Wendy could almost see time rolling away in the shadows of his eyes. "Trust me," he repeated hoarsely. "When a man just wants solace, none of it means anything to him. Not the day or time or date, the color of the woman's eyes or her hair. Hell, her name doesn't even matter." He sensed her staring at him. He was remembering his own wild pursuits, just after Jennifer had died. Ultimately, he'd found little peace in physical satisfaction. "He cares about you, Wendy, and I'm damned glad. I know this sounds sexist, but hell, I'm an Indian, and we always had our trouble keeping up with the times. If he weren't a decent man, I'd probably be over there trying to throw him off your property. Maybe you won't ever marry him. Maybe you'll never even fall in love, but—"

"You don't understand, Eric. I don't want to get married again. And I don't want to fall in love—especially not with a DEA agent!"

He ignored her. As if she hadn't even spoken, he continued, "But what you will have, Wendy, will be good, and it will be caring."

"You might want to try that yourself," she retorted.

He slid back into his chair and took another long swallow of his beer. "Wendy, I don't want—"

He broke off, aware that he was about to repeat her words. He laughed and shrugged. "So how did work go? Did you get anything done?"

"Yeah. I found a couple of books that you can refer to for total misinformation."

"There's a lot of that, but thanks. It's just as important to know where the bad stuff is as the good." He grinned at her. "I was over at the Miccosukee center today. Things are going full speed ahead. They're planning even more on their reservation lands. Billy was telling me that it's hard to hone in on the Seminole bingo, so they're going to try and battle the Hyatt instead."

Wendy grinned. She'd also heard the Miccosukee leader speak about his ideas, and she liked the plans as much as she liked the young man making them. It was true, the Seminoles had managed their money well. The tribe did well with bingo, and with cigarette sales. The Miccosukees were looking into those enterprises, but they were also interested in catching business from the new linkup with Interstate 75.

"So you were fooling around all day, huh?" she said.

"Yes, and no." He leaned his head back and stared at the ceiling. "We were talking the same old route. Money, education, housing. I never know quite where I stand myself. I like my house. I like owning this land. Then again, I enjoyed going to school. The years I spent in the service were traumatic—bloody and—yet, they were somehow important. Now I stand here on a crossroad. I don't want to lose the value of our customs or traditions. But I don't want to see the children of the tribe growing up without every benefit of white America. Where is the right place to be, Wendy? What is the right stand?"

She stood up and gave him a hug. "I really love you alot, Eric, you know that?"

He laughed. "I didn't mean to give a soapbox lecture."

"And you didn't. You're super, and I'm going home."

"I love you, too, Wendy." He looked into her eyes for a moment, then told her, "I think you should know, everyone seems to be commenting on all the activity going on. Along Alligator Alley, along the Trail."

"What activity?"

"Well, knowing what I know, I assume that some of the men driving around and hovering around the airboat rides and villages work for the government. There have also been a lot—I mean a lot—of cops around, and you know that the police stations are really good about letting our own forces handle our own problems." The Seminoles had a police force of their own, just as the Miccosukees did. Eric had always said that Florida was a fair state when it came to respecting the tribal laws of the Indians. The city and county police from Miami and Fort Lauderdale and the other communities seldom interfered with the Indian forces.

"Well," Wendy murmured, "I guess that it is reasonable for the government to have men trying to keep an eye out for Brad—and for Michaelson."

Eric nodded, watching her. "There's something else, Wendy."

"Yes?"

"Some of our men seem to think that something big is going to happen. They say there have been seaplane drops in the swamp, down toward the Trail."

Wendy shrugged impatiently. "Twenty miles south! Eric, think about it! Think about the size of the swamp! You have to know what you're doing to find things out there!"

"That's true. But we don't know if these are just petty crooks, smuggling in a kilo of pot—or hired assassins, hunting for Brad."

"I'm not worried."

"You should be. At least tell Brad what I've told you. I don't believe that they can just walk in and find Brad, either. Only you and I know that he's there."

"And old Mac up at the gas station."

Eric shrugged. "Mac never says a word to strangers. Never. So your secret is safe. But I'm afraid that they might stumble upon you by accident."

"They'd be idiots to molest me."

"Wendy, they're criminals." He sighed, exasperated. "You of all people should know the danger of innocence!"

Duly chastised, she lowered her head. "I'll tell Brad," she promised.

"Just warn him, that's all. He has the right to know what's going on, the right to protect you both." He laughed suddenly. "Don't worry. I'm sure you won't have to give him up—yet."

"Very amusing, Eric," she retorted, but when she saw his grin, she smiled, too. "Want to walk me out?"

"Sure." Arm in arm, they followed the lawn to where it began to level and fall toward the canal.

"Want me to come home with you?" he teased her.

Yes! Wendy thought, but she had to fight her own battles. "I'm all right."

"You're better than all right, Wendy-bird. You're perfect."

She kissed his cheek. "Flattery is great stuff. I'll see you soon."

Distractedly, Wendy waved and started for home. The wind rushed around her and lifted her hair, gently calming her spirit.

Maybe Brad was right. He knew what she wanted, but he wouldn't give it to her, because he wanted her to have something better. And maybe someday, if she ever lay upon a psychiatrist's couch and poured out her life's story, she would be glad of it. Yes, I had a very bad time learning to step out again after my husband died. For two years I could do nothing. But then I met a man, and though he passed briefly through my life, it was something precious, and something very special.

As Wendy neared home, she made a few resolutions. She was not going to act childish as she had today. She liked Brad, and she was going to enjoy him. The teasing was fun, and it was fun to get to know him.

Of course, she'd be damned if she'd ever take another step toward him. If he really wanted her—whenever he decided to let her know when!—he'd better plan on coming to get her.

Humming softly as she cut off the motor, she wondered if he might have discovered something to cook for dinner. She walked across the lawn to the house with a jaunty step.

It wasn't until she reached the door that she began to sense something was amiss. Emptiness and silence abounded through the house. Carefully, she opened the door.

Nothing was disturbed—nothing at all. The house was neat and tidy. Rushing down the hallway, she discovered that Brad had straightened the beds. She flushed slightly, realizing that he had found the laundry hamper and the washer and dryer behind the slotted doors in the hall. He had washed the clothes that he had been borrowing—and her things. There was ample evidence of the chores he had done.

Only the man himself was missing.

Wendy let out a soft cry of fear, spun around and went tearing back out of the house. In dread she searched the yard, praying that she would not find a bloodied body. Pain glazed her heart. It was impossible. They couldn't have found him. Not here. She lived too deep in the swamp.

She kept telling herself that as she ran back into the house and found the shotgun.

Wendy loathed weapons, but she wasn't foolish. Brad was out there—perhaps in the custody of murderers. She cocked the gun and slung it over her shoulder. Fighting back the tears that stung her eyes, she set out to find him.

Nothing, absolutely nothing, should have surprised Brad about Wendy Hawk's house anymore. He had been accosted in bed by a wild panther and attacked from the roof by a green-eyed Seminole. He'd learned that the Florida panther did belong, but that only madmen kept alligators.

And yet, when he came into the living room to discover the very tall, withered old man, standing dead center in the room, Brad still didn't know what to think. There was no mistaking the fact that this man was an Indian. Half of his hair was white, the other half was blacker than midnight, long and straight. His face was near brown and weathered from constant exposure to the sun, and his features were solid and strong. His eyes were as black as onyx.

Brad thought of all the things he had learned in school. This man had the simple pride and dignity of a Chief Joseph. He had the unfaltering stare of a Cochise or a Sitting Bull.

Or an Osceola, Brad thought. This man was surely a Seminole.

I'm definitely slipping, Brad thought. He hadn't heard a single sound.

But the old man didn't seem to expect violence from him. In fact, he seemed to know that he would find him there.

"Hello," Brad said.

The Indian nodded. Brad fumed uncomfortably as he realized that he was being scrutinized, from head to toe. What if the old fellow didn't speak English? Brad raised a friendly hand, palm outward in friendship. "Hello," he repeated.

"I am old, not deaf," the Indian told him.

Brad felt like a fool. "Sorry. You didn't answer me."

"I hadn't decided what to answer."

"I didn't think it was that difficult a question."

"Where is your respect for your elders?"

"I meant no disrespect, truly," Brad returned evenly. He paused, "Uh, sir, who are you, please?"

A smile revealed a million wrinkles in the old man's face. "Hawk. Willie Hawk." He was dressed in faded dungarees, boots and a beribboned Seminole shirt. He stepped forward, offering Brad a hand.

"Mr. Hawk, my pleasure. My name is—"

"Yes, I know. You are McKenna. I have heard."

Brad frowned. He had heard? Hadn't he stressed the importance of his anonymity to Wendy? Had she told this man about him today? Or hadn't Eric realized that he was betraying Brad to give him away. Maybe Eric hadn't understood—

No. Eric was too bright not to understand the situation.

Willie Hawk seemed to have read the quick wanderings of his mind. His smile deepened and his face seemed to crinkle even more. "They have not betrayed you. Not Wendy, not Eric."

"Surely—"

Willie Hawk dismissed Brad with a wave of his gnarled hand. "You have judged them well. They have not betrayed you. I know the swamp, son. I know what happens here. I can listen to the earth. Even the alligator speaks to me."

Just what he needed, Brad decided—an Indian, and senile to boot.

Willie Hawk lowered his eyes, and Brad realized that the old man had read his mind again. "So Wendy has gone to work, and you are here alone?"

Brad nodded. "Yes, sir. Can I get you anything? This is your grandson's house. You are probably at home here."

"My grandson is dead. It is Wendy's house," Willie said, and Brad could not fathom with what emotion he spoke. If there was pain, it was well hidden. If there was love, that, too, was well hidden.

"Well, then—"

"You are alone here. There must be very little to do. The inactivity must weigh heavily upon a man who is accustomed to movement."

Brad laughed. "Yes, I guess it does get bad. The laundry is all done, and Wendy is too neat a lady to leave much else to do."

There was something intriguing about the old man's face. It suggested an ancient, enigmatic wisdom. The onyx eyes never seemed to leave his own or to cease their slow and careful assessment. He turned around suddenly. "Come with me."

"What?"

Willie paused. "Are you deaf, young man?"

"No, it's just that—"

"The Indian wars ended many, many moons ago, you know."

The old man was a bit of a dramatist, Brad decided. He saw the twinkle in Willie's eyes, and this time, the Indian laughed with him.

"What the hell," Brad said. "I'll live dangerously. But give me a minute, please. I want to leave Wendy a note. Under the circumstances, I don't want her to worry."

Willie nodded. "Yes, write a message. Tell her that you are with me, and she will not worry."

Brad scribbled out a note. He started to attach it to the refrigerator, then worried that she might get scared outside if she called him and he didn't answer. He followed Willie out the door, thinking that he'd stick his note in the mailbox. Then he realized that there was no mailbox. "How does she get her bills?" he wondered out loud.

"P.O. box," Willie advised him sagely.

"Of course," Brad murmured. He tried to shove the note beneath the door. It seemed to stick, more or less.

Willie had come by canoe. He pointed the handmade vessel out to Brad, and they started toward it. Brad offered to paddle, but Willie would have none of it.

"Sit still," he advised Brad. "There are not many times in life when you may enjoy the journey with no effort, with your eyes and ears and heart open."

"Right," Brad said. "Thank you, sir." He still worried that he should be doing the work, but knew that Willie would not appreciate his worry.

Just as they rounded out to slice westward along the canal, Brad noticed a black figure lurking around the house. On closer inspection, he relaxed. It was only Baby, prowling around the house.

"I wonder if I was supposed to have fed her something," he murmured aloud.

"She came by the village this morning. My wife gave her a chicken. Baby is fine."

Brad nodded. But Baby, he saw, wanted something. The cat was crawling up on her hindquarters to let out her savage meow. Baby wanted to go in.

Brad couldn't imagine a bag of Tender Vittles big enough for such a cat anyway. He was glad that she'd eaten elsewhere.

The canoe moved through the swamp.

Brad dismissed all thoughts of Baby, not realizing that the panther had clipped his note with one long toenail, and that, when she finally walked away, she shredded his note as she went.

Three hours later, Brad discovered himself sitting at the base of a tall pine. His hands were loosely tied behind his back, and he was smiling as a group of wild Indians danced and war-whooped around him.

As a kid he'd played cowboys and Indians. Sometimes he'd been an Indian, and sometimes he'd been a cowboy.

To the best of his knowledge, there hadn't been any cowboys in the swamps, but that was okay. He had met Marna Hawk Panther and Anthony Panther—and all the little Panthers. He had met Mary Hawk, whom Willie referred to as his raven woman because of the ink-dark tresses that still adorned her head, despite the fact that she had turned eighty on her last birthday.

Mike, Dorinda, David and Jennifer—the four little Panthers—suddenly ceased their war whoops. They raced over to hug their father, who gave them each a hug and a pat on the back. He whispered something to the children, and they all ran back to thank Brad for playing with them. Dorinda blushed and came close, giving a kiss on the cheek. "You're very, very nice, Mr. McKenna. I'm going to tell Aunt Wendy that, too."

He smiled. She was a very pretty little girl with her great-grandfather's onyx eyes, Mary Hawk's raven hair and her mother's lovely, golden skin. Brad nodded to her gravely. "Thank you," he told her. She blushed again, then ran off to join her siblings.

Tony Panther sat down beside Brad, leaning against the tree. He was a young man, dressed in a business suit that seemed somewhat ludicrous in the clearing of thatched-roof chickees. The clearing itself seemed to Brad to be a moment out of time.

Of course, there were cars nearby. Tony's Dodge was just beyond the tree. He was an accountant, who worked for the tribe. He drove in and out of Fort Lauderdale daily.

"That was nice, letting the kids play that way," Tony told Brad. "We didn't get to win very often in real life, you know."

Brad laughed, idly running the rope that had held him so loosely captive through his fingers. "I enjoyed them." He ran his fingers through his hair. "I remember playing cowboys and Indians when I was young. At the time, it was a total fantasy—pow-wows and peace pipes and scalpings."

"I'm just proud to still be here. It meant our Hawk ancestor was willing to fight and brave the swamps, rather than be sent west. But don't worry—we haven't scalped anyone in ages." Tony looked at him a long moment. "Did you really enjoy the afternoon?"

Brad mused over the question. He had. Mary had told him how the tribe had once raised pumpkins to survive. She had made him taste the old staple of their people, koontie bread, made from the koontie root. He had helped repair a chickee, and—since it was alligator season, he had also tasted the smoked meat of the creature. Tony, he had learned, was a Miccosukee, and from him, he had learned quite a bit about the two tribes who had coexisted in the Florida swampland. They shared their green corn dance and other festivals.

Then, sitting there against the tree, Brad felt the peace of the area sweep through him. The sun was setting beautifully. Out on the water, a great blue heron rose and swept into the sky. The entire horizon reflected the golden sunset.

Brad turned and nodded to Tony. "Yeah. I've enjoyed it very much."

"I wonder why Wendy hasn't shown up yet," Tony murmured, then he shrugged, seeing the worry that sprang into Brad's eyes. "She might know what Grandfather is up to. He came over to kidnap you on purpose, you know. Just to rile Wendy."

Brad laughed. "Did he really?"

He nodded. "I hope you don't find this too strange, but we are Wendy's family. Wendy and Leif met in college, when they were just kids. They married before they graduated. Her mother had died when she was a child, and her dad passed away right after they were married. She has been with us for a long time. We love her as if she were our blood."

"I'm glad," Brad said. Although he shouldn't be prying into her life, Tony Panther was willing to give him answers, so he decided to ask a few more questions. "What happened to Leif Hawk?"

Tony appeared startled. "She's never told you?"

Brad shook his head.

Tony stared off in the distance. "He was killed. In cold blood. Eric's wife was killed with him."

"What?" Brad demanded huskily.

He didn't get an answer. From the water, there was a sudden commotion. He looked up to find that Wendy had come at last.

She seemed to fly out of the airboat. She didn't seem to see anything or anyone—until her eyes lighted on him. Her eyes were huge and sparkling and silver and—quite suddenly—sizzling with fury.

She was running toward him with all the lean energy of a pouncing tiger. Warily, Brad stood up. A moment later she catapulted herself against him, half screaming and half sobbing in fury. "You son of a bitch! You stinking—cop!"

"Wendy!" She took a swing at him and he ducked. She flew around in a circle with the force of her blow, and he caught her, pinning her arms to her sides.

"Hi, Wendy," Tony said lightly.

She ignored him, and her fierce glare bored into Brad. "You inconsiderate, careless weasel! You scared me half to death!"

"Wendy! Wendy Hawk!" She tensed and swallowed, apparently aware that Grandfather was approaching the scene. "Wendy, you calm down."

Far from calm, she struggled against Brad's hold and managed to turn. "Grandfather! You wily fox! How could you do this to me! I was so frightened."

"Wendy!" Brad swung her back around again. "I left you a note—"

"Liar!"

"Wendy!" Grandfather said sharply. Immediately, her anger softened, and Brad realized how much she loved and respected the old man. Still staring at Brad with a look that could kill, Wendy exhaled slowly.

"Wendy, he did leave the note. You do not call a man a liar unless you know it is truth to do so. And to deny a friend, that is even worse. He is a man of his word. You must have known that, or else you would not have him at your house."

Wendy nodded, trembling in Brad's arms. "I even remembered the shotgun."

She had been truly frightened for him. Her concern was reassuring, though he hadn't meant to scare her. "Wendy, honestly. I left a note."

"I was scared to death." She tried to retain some of her anger, while regaining her dignity. Her words were still a whisper, and he longed to touch her, to kiss away her worry right then and there.

"I'm sorry, Wendy."

"Come on, Brad. Wendy, please? We're tucking the kids into bed, and they'll be heartbroken if they don't get to see you."

Wendy forced herself to tear her eyes from Brad and smile at Tony. "Of course, Tony. I'm dying to give them all great big hugs."

Brad lagged behind for a moment, wondering about the story Tony had been telling him. He needed to hear the end of it. Leif Hawk and Eric's wife had been killed—in cold blood.

The very thought of it was tragic. Wendy and Eric had shared a great deal, an ocean of sorrow, and Brad couldn't help the tug of pure sympathy that tore at his heart.

A young man, and a young woman, cruelly taken from life. What the hell had happened, and who did he ask?

"Brad, are you coming?"

They were waiting for him. "Yes, yes, I'm coming. Thanks."

As Brad caught up with them, the gold remnants of twilight left the sky and night fell, a blanket of darkness.

CHAPTER 8

It was late when they returned to Wendy's house. They'd spent the evening huddled around the cooking fire. By its eerie light, Willie Hawk had woven tales of the past, of a people forced to run away from a white government that had betrayed the Seminoles at every turn. Brad thought it appropriate that the name Seminole meant "runaway." He'd spent most of his career running from dealers and mobsters.

His head was fuzzy from folklore and brew. Brad wasn't sure what he had been drinking all night. Tony called it a "black" drink and assured him it wouldn't do anything to him that Jack Black wouldn't. But it was potent stuff—very powerful.

In the darkness of the clearing, a blackness alleviated only by the camp fire, he could almost see a mist around old Willie. And in that mist he could see the past: warriors, feathered and oiled, shaking knives and rifles in the air, clad in the colorful garb they had borrowed from the Spanish and adapted to their own use. He could see a million fires. He could hear a cry on the wind. He was entranced.

The night was black, but the wind felt refreshing against his face as they drove back to Wendy's place. Brad reveled in the quiet of the swamp when the motor died. They were sounds that he was coming to recognize and understand.

When they stepped back into Wendy's house, he felt comfortable, as if he were home. Wendy wandered into the kitchen, and Brad went to the stereo and began to browse through her collection of tapes and discs and albums. "Okay if I turn on the stereo?"

"Whatever you want," she called back.

Whatever he wanted.

Brad found an old album by the Temptations. He carefully set the needle on the vinyl record, then collapsed upon the couch. She had an impressive music system, with dynamite speakers. He closed his eyes as the music filled the room and soothed his spirit.

When he opened his eyes, Wendy was leaning against the counter, smiling at him tolerantly. He grinned at her, then rose slowly.

Whatever he wanted. That was what she had said. He wanted to hold her in his arms.

She was a vision of loveliness. Her hair fell free about her face, and her silver eyes sparkled. She was wearing jeans and a tailored shirt. Her shirt collar angled around her smooth throat in a manner that Brad found enticing.

Her smile was the killer. Her smile revealed her essence, the sweet, elusive quality that drew him to her, that excited him, that elicited the tenderness and the yearning.

He lifted a hand to her. His head was spinning, either from the Indian drink or the devastating effect of her beauty. "Want to dance?"

"Dance?"

"Move around on the floor. Step to the music. Dance."

He caught hold of her hands. There was silver laughter in her eyes as he drew her to him, enfolding her into his arms. The Temptations were singing about "sunshine on a cloudy day" as he held her close.

"See? Dance?"

"In the living room?" She laughed.

"Anywhere."

He released her slightly, swinging her out, then back into his arms. She was still laughing as he sang off-key to the music.

"This is a classic album," he told her, pulling her close. "You've good taste in music."

"Thanks."

The music faded, then another song began. He moved with the soft, slow tempo, grateful for the lovely woman in his arms. His left hand caressed the small of her back. He could feel her flesh beneath the cotton shirt. The softness of her breasts brushing against him caused a definite reaction inside him.

The music...it seemed to be a part of them. It was so very easy to move with Wendy in his arms. But suddenly he realized that he wasn't moving at all. He was merely staring down into her eyes, her beautiful eyes, with their startling silver color and their dark, sweeping lashes. She had to know what he was feeling, everything that he was feeling.

She smiled very slowly. The little vixen, he thought.

Did she know that his pulse was pounding hopelessly out of control? Surely she could feel that he was taut and tense and that his muscles were constricted with desire. She was so close, he could feel her softness. He could feel the fullness of her breasts, the pebble hardness of her nipples through their clothing. He could feel the trembling that swept her, the supple length of her thighs, the angle of her hip, the soft and almost indiscernible swell of her femininity.

She just had to feel the evidence of his desire, straining against his borrowed jeans. She just had to...

She did. He knew by the soft, silver clouds that filled her eyes. By her slightly parted lips, by the ragged whisper of her breath.

She moistened her lips with the tip of her tongue, and they somehow became even more tempting. Glossy and sleek and still tempting. Lowering his head while the Temptations serenaded them, he kissed her.

The feeling was riveting. Their mouths fused in a passionate union, hot and electric. For a moment, they broke apart, then he held her face, searched out her eyes and kissed her again. Gently, his palms kneaded the soft flesh of her back until he reached her buttocks. Lifting her against him, he fitted her to his form while her arms clung tightly to his neck and their mouths continued to meet, exploring, melding.

She broke away, gasping for breath. He stared at her with the rage of his passion naked in his eyes.

Had she ever felt like this? she wondered. So excited that it hurt? So sensually alive and aware that his kiss seemed to reach into her body and soul, warming her through and through.

She had been married to a man she loved, and theirs had been a passionate relationship. Maybe this desire was heightened by the loss of her only love. Maybe it was due to her loneliness.

And maybe it was just Brad, the man himself.

But she had never, never felt like this. Desperate to have more of him, she longed to latch her arms around his neck again and savor the sizzling heat that flared between them. She'd waited too long. She wanted to feel her flesh naked against his.

"Brad," she whispered against his mouth.

He paused, staring down at her.

"Brad, is this 'when'? I mean, you said you'd let me know when, so if this isn't it..." Her voice trailed away and her body grew heated and flushed. She didn't know if she was shamed by the bluntness of her query, or merely so hot with desire that fever was spreading through her limbs.

"Yes," he told her huskily. "This is 'when.' That is, if you're willing. You said I could have whatever I wanted. I want you, Wendy. God, do I want you. Now. Here. If—you're willing."

This time there was tenderness as well as fire in his gaze. She was willing, and he knew it. He didn't wait for her answer, but drew her into his embrace again, desperately moving his hands to mold her body to his. "Dear God, yes, this is when!" he murmured.

He kissed her throat and teased her earlobe. The brush of his lips grew more heated, more sensual, as he searched out the buttons of her tailored shirt. In seconds, he had cast the shirt aside. Deftly, he removed her bra.

His callused hands cupped the firm fullness of her breasts. At his touch, the pink, tawny nipples immediately hardened. Lowering his moist lips to her, he laved his tongue around a nipple, then sucked it hard into his mouth.

Wendy let out a little cry, arching against him. The staggering sensation swept like swift white lightning from her breast to her pelvis. The yearning pain between her legs intensified, so that she could barely stand. His hands splayed across her back, holding her up.

But she could not bear it. She tugged wildly upon his hair, whispering his name. Somehow she was borne to the floor. As she lay there, her heart thundering, he cast his shirt aside in such a fervent hurry that several buttons were torn away. His breathing was torn and ragged as he knelt by her side.

She couldn't stand to wait any longer. His chest was naked with its planes of muscle and tawny hair, and she had to know the feel of that nakedness against her own breasts. Whispering her wild desires, she reached for him, brushing her naked body against his. His muscles were rock hard. His hair titillated her throat and breasts, already so sensitized to his touch.

He was whispering to her, giving her hoarse little commands. His desires were burning like a flash fire, out of control. All the little things that he'd wanted to do, all the nuances of slow seduction, all were swept away amid a sudden tempest of need.

He had tried. God knew, he had tried.

Now, he couldn't wait any longer.

He pressed her to the floor and pulled off her boots and socks and jeans. Only then did he pause for the slightest moment to relish the sight of her. The spill of golden hair about her shoulders and the rise of her breasts made him wild with desire. His eyes lowered to take in the arch of her hips and the golden nest at the juncture of her thighs, visible beneath the lacy string bikinis she wore.

He looked from her supple form to her face. Her eyes were still silver, and her lips remained parted, wet and moist. And so inviting.

He let out a groan, a guttural cry of appreciation and raw need.

Burying his face against the soft, smooth eroticism of her belly, he let his tongue trail over her flesh, and then he kissed it.

"Brad!" She arched and writhed beneath him. His fingers slipped off her panties and curled over the apex of her thighs. She was hot and sweet and damp.

"Please!" She tugged at his hair. Desperation filled him again. They wanted the same thing. "Please, please," she whispered, tossing her head. Her hands gripped his jeans, tugging at them.

A roar rose in his head. Almost blindly, he brushed his fingers against that web of gold. Desire shot through him, as hot as molten steel. The roar in his head thundered, and the pulse inside of him throbbed to a frenzied pace.

He stripped off his shoes and jeans, then stared down at her again.

He towered above her, naked and very male. His thighs were well-formed columns over his long legs. His shoulders and chest were bronze, his masculinity was shockingly brazen, yet enticing.

Wendy closed her eyes, dazed at the sight of him, stunned at the intensity of the passions that swirled inside her.

Although her eyes remained closed, she could feel his hot flesh against hers as he lowered himself over her. He had become naked, removing her husband's clothing.

Leif. She had loved him. Didn't she owe him more?

"Wendy!"

Brad spoke her name so harshly that she opened her eyes wide, startled and guilty. His gold and amber gaze, penetrated her, inciting a new panic. Could he read her mind? she wondered. If he knew what she was thinking, he would go away.

He didn't go away.

He wedged himself between her knees, stroking the sensitive skin along her inner thighs. She gasped as a wave of searing desire raged through her. She closed her eyes.

"Wendy!"

She gazed at him again. There was no tenderness about him now, but neither was there cruelty. "Lift your legs around me, Wendy. Meet my eyes. Wendy, look at me."

She moistened her lips. She couldn't have begun to disobey him.

"Now look at us, Wendy. Watch where we come together. Watch how we make love."

She cried out as her entire being seemed to rock to a new, blinding pulse. In that languid moment of ecstasy, he plunged himself within her, driving deep, deep, until he filled her, until he was completely sheathed. He stayed there for a moment, keeping his eyes fiercely locked with hers.

Then he moved.

"Watch, Wendy..."

She watched until the excitement spiraled in her so deeply that she cried out again, reaching for him. She felt him inside of her, stroking her. She cast back her head, and he trailed kisses along her throat. He tucked his hands beneath her buttocks, bringing her ever more flush. Again his lips trailed over her breasts, leaving a lingering euphoria wherever they passed.

He brought himself to the edge of her, and she writhed madly to catch him. Then he would plunge again, deep, deeper. The ache inside of her was swelling, the anguish building until she passed through the wild storm, and sunshine seemed to burst upon her. Beautiful sunshine, in golden droplets, seeping into her, sating her, filling her.

He whispered her name, he demanded that she draw her legs higher. She could scarcely obey, and yet she did, and it all began again. His movement inside of her. His touch, guiding her. His kiss, wildfire burning her flesh, raking her nipples.

Fire flared once again. Wendy gasped, caught in the whirl of a second thrill, shuddering as she felt Brad's traumatic release, rich and hot. She lay gasping, her eyes closed, savoring what had happened. She felt the weight of his body, heavy over her now, and yet she loved it. She loved the warm, rich scent of him, she loved the slick feel of his naked flesh. She loved the way that they lay, entwined.

"Wendy, look at me again."

Wendy glanced up and smiled lazily. When she reached up to touch his cheek, he caught her hand.

They both became aware that the needle on the stereo was sweeping over empty space, making a strange sound. All the lights in the house were still blazing.

Wendy stared up at Brad and her smile faded. The hardness was still there about him. She couldn't understand it. She was still feeling aftertremors, feeling so close to him, and yet he seemed so distant from her.

She had been open and honest with him. She had wanted him; she had gladly given herself to him, trusting in him. And now, even as she lay there, naked and still filled by him, fear began to sweep into her. "Brad?" Her voice trembled slightly as she questioned him.

But then he smiled. Opening her palm, he pressed a kiss against it and lay back down beside her.

"I don't understand—" Wendy began.

"I just wanted to hear you say it. My name."

She inhaled, closing her eyes. She could have told him that she had known from the beginning that he would be no substitute for another man. Brad McKenna was in a class all his own.

"We were both afraid, a little, weren't we?" she asked.

He lifted his weight from her and stretched, resting on one elbow. His gaze remained on her, intense.

"Yeah. Afraid of Leif Hawk entering in here."

She couldn't quite meet his eyes. And when hers shifted, he abruptly straddled her, catching her cheeks between his palms. Intimacy seemed rampant between them again. She felt his thighs, his nakedness, keenly. She stared up at him, then her gaze fell away.

"You loved him very much," Brad said.

"Yes." She opened her eyes and met his at last, anger suddenly burning in her own. "But I made love with you, and you know it. So get off me, you oaf."

He caught her face in a tender hold. "That's why I made you watch me. Watch *us*. I wanted to be sure you were making love to me—not the ghost of another man." Now his kiss was slow, leisurely, yet thorough.

He rose then, a man completely at ease with his nakedness, naturally graceful in his movement. He picked up the stereo needle and set it back to the beginning of the album. Once again the room filled with music. Wendy watched him for a moment, then started to reach for her panties.

"No, don't," he told her, noticing her movement. A smile played across his features. "Please, don't."

She hesitated. He knelt down behind her, slipping his arms around her and locking his hands beneath her breasts. "It's nice just to hold you," he whispered, resting his chin upon her shoulder.

She let her head fall back against his shoulder. "It's nice to be held," she said.

Nuzzling her neck, he added, "And we have to make love again. Tonight. Maybe a few times, maybe several times."

Wendy twisted, trying to see his face. "For a slow starter, you do get quickly into gear once the motor is running."

"Slow starter?"

"I've been willing for some time now," she teased.

"Wendy, we haven't known each other for 'some time.'"

She leaned back again, slipping her slender fingers over his rougher, callused ones. "I knew that I wanted you."

It took him a minute to answer. "Last night you wanted a body in bed. Tonight, you wanted *me*. There's a difference."

She didn't reply; maybe it was true.

He hummed to the music. "We used to have sock hops back when I was a kid. Everybody used to go. This was what we played. I never did learn to disco. Did you?"

Wendy shook her head. "No."

"Want a glass of wine?"

"That sounds good. I'll get it." She didn't know if she could be as easy as Brad about walking around her house naked with all the lights on. Of course, no one would be near, and they couldn't possibly see in if they were.

She was just out of practice.

But it wasn't bad, not really. Although she keenly felt Brad's eyes on her while she moved, it was a nice feeling. She poured two glasses of white wine and brought out a platter of cheese, salmon and crackers, too. Brad was waiting for her, leaning against the bottom of the couch. She set the tray between them.

"Salmon. Perfect. I was starving."

He picked up a piece of the pink fillet with his fingers and popped in into his mouth. Wendy started to cut cheese for the crackers, but was interrupted when she realized that Brad was dangling a piece of salmon in front of her mouth. She licked it from his fingers, her tongue sensually bathing his fingertips. He flashed her a crooked smile. Blushing, she turned back to the cheese again.

"Oh, Wendy," he murmured. His eyes studied her intently. She had never imagined she could feel such a rush of warmth, just from the way a man looked at her.

When she handed him a cracker with cheese, her fingers were trembling.

He slipped an arm around her while they ate and sipped wine. Although their conversation was casual, Brad never passed the opportunity to add a few sexual innuendos. Every time he sipped his wine or nibbled on a morsel of food, he somehow intimated how the mouth could be used effectively on flesh. He promised to demonstrate.

"Brad!" Wendy protested at last. She was laughing, amazed at what words and looks could imply. But then again, he was touching her, too. His arm was around her shoulder and his hand dangled idly over her breast, his fingertips teasing her nipple. His whisper fell against her hair, her throat, her ear.

"What?" he asked innocently.

"You're making me crazy!"

His gaze was lazy, his tone sultry. His tawny lashes lay half-closed as he looked at her. "Why? I'm not going anywhere, you're not going anywhere." He paused for a moment, suddenly becoming serious. "I didn't mean to be so selfish. I just—I just couldn't wait anymore."

"Selfish?" Wendy echoed blankly.

He kissed her forehead. "Yes."

"But you weren't—"

"I intend to make up for it."

"Brad—"

"Cracker?" He slipped one in her mouth.

Wendy chewed it, watching him gravely. "Brad, I know that you're not married. But what you said about Leif...well, you were right. It wouldn't be fair to anyone if I tried to find a substitute for him. And maybe I did want to do that at first. But you'd never stand for that." For a moment her voice trailed. "I know you don't have a wife, but I really don't want to be a stand-in, either. Your lover, just because of this 'convenient situation.'"

He lifted her chin and kissed her lips lightly. "There's no one special in my life, Wendy. Honestly. Just you." He didn't release her but kept studying her eyes. "Wendy, what happened? To your husband—to Eric's wife?"

Wendy inhaled sharply. She wanted to wrench away from him and crawl into the darkness. His words brought the past rushing in on her and despite the healing effect of time, the wounds of the past still hurt.

"They were killed."

"I know that. How did it happen?"

She shrugged. "We—we were having a party at Eric's. It was his and Jennifer's third wedding anniversary. Jennifer was partial to a certain burgundy, so as a surprise, Eric and I had ordered some from a friend who owns a liquor store."

She paused, swallowing. She hated remembering that night. Hated it. The last time she had seen her husband and her sister-in-law, they had both been laughing. The four of them had been so close, she and Jennifer, Leif and Eric.

She told Brad about how stunning Jennifer had looked in her white dress. Her honeyed skin had posed a striking contrast, as had her waist-length, jet black hair. She'd been so happy, and so in love. Leif had also been clad in white, a white dinner jacket. The shirt he wore beneath it had almost matched the unusual shade of his eyes.

At the last minute, the friend who owned the liquor store in Fort Lauderdale had been detained at the shop. Wendy had been cooking, since she had ordered Jennifer not to do a thing for the party. Eric had been trying to help Wendy with the outside grill.

And so Leif and Jennifer had gone together to pick up her present. Jen had been so pleased with the gift, the picture of giddy innocence in white. The two of them had left, arm in arm.

"They walked right into an armed holdup," Wendy explained. "The owner of the store was already dead. When one of the robbers slapped Jennifer to the ground and aimed the gun her way, Leif sprang upon him. He strangled the assailant with his bare hands, trying to buy Jennifer some time. But there were four robbers, and Leif was unarmed. As she turned to flee, Jennifer was caught."

Later the police told Wendy that the first shot had killed Leif instantly, piercing his heart.

They'd shot Jennifer three times. She had suffered slowly, bleeding to death.

I shouldn't have asked, Brad thought. He shouldn't have done this to her. And yet the story went on as Wendy continued in a strange monotone.

She and Eric had had to visit the morgue to identify the bodies—the hollow shells of Jennifer and Leif.

"And all I could remember was the blood. So much blood, staining the beautiful innocence of their white clothing. So very, very much blood." Wendy swallowed down her wine in a gulp.

Brad saw that her eyes were wide and unseeing. He understood why she had hidden herself here in the swamp for so long. And this certainly explained the closeness between Wendy and Eric.

But she had reached out, leaving the past behind. She had wanted him.

And now, he saw, they'd lost that special warmth. Wendy was shivering now, reaching for her clothes, ashamed of the way that she sat with him. She set her glass down. "I'm going to take a shower." She stood up. Brad reached for her, trying to catch her fingers.

"Wendy, wait—"

"Damn you, Brad! Leave me alone!" She ran down the hallway.

He sat back, brooding in defeat. He couldn't let her retreat to the past she had begun to leave behind.

Brad picked up the remnants of their meal and brought them to the kitchen. Deep in thought, he stared down the long hallway. Despite her denials, he knew that Wendy was trapped in the past, haunted by the memory of her husband. He couldn't let her wallow in that misery.

The shower was still spraying loudly when Brad strode into the bathroom and ripped open the shower curtain. With a bar of soap in her hand and her hair plastered over her face, Wendy turned to him. "Brad, damn you, leave me alone! Don't you understand—"

She gasped as he stepped into the shower. The water hit his hair and his back but he seemed not to feel it as he stared down at her.

"Brad, get out of here!"

"No, I don't think so, Wendy." Her skin was wet and slick and fragrant with the clean scent of soap. The shower water slid over them as he slipped his arms around her waist.

She twisted away from him. Tears stung her silver eyes. "You made me remember! Can't you understand—"

"I'm sorry. Yes, I made you remember the past. But now I'm going to help you forget." He planted a kiss on her neck. "Come on, Wendy. Let's wipe the slate clean."

Her eyes narrowed in amazement and fury. "Well, now, McKenna," she spat out, "you can damn well guarantee that I'll be thinking of him."

"Oh, no, Wendy," Brad assured her with confidence. "I can damn well guarantee that you won't."

Holding her squirming form in his arms, he kissed her with his mouth and his teeth and his tongue. He clung to her naked, dripping body with his left hand, while using his right to explore and caress her. He followed the pattern of her spine, kneading her buttocks. Tracing the curve of her hips, he found the soft apex of her legs and gently explored the feminine flesh there, seeking and finding the soft button of greatest pleasure.

Overcome by sensation, she went limp against him.

Then her body tautened. Her lips parted willingly to his, her tongue met and mated with his. Rising up on her toes, she buried her head against his shoulder. He leaned to whisper against her ear. "Everywhere I touch you, I will love you."

The water was hot as it pelted their skin. With the drive of the water against his back, Brad tasted her lips again. Then he cast her into a sea of trembling as he slowly, determinedly, kissed her breasts, taking his sweet time, his sweet pleasure. Bracing herself against his shoulder, she whispered his name, and then moaned in ecstasy.

As he lowered himself against her, she could feel the texture of his wet body against hers. Beneath the cascade of the shower, he knelt, gripped her buttocks firmly and buried himself against her.

Fire swept through her loins as she trembled fiercely and fought to hold on to his shoulders. The sensations were so overpowering that she could barely think. All she could do was feel and arch and undulate and burn.

"Brad!" She tore at his hair. He knew no mercy. "Please, really, I'm collapsing."

Her words had no impact. Breathlessly, barely able to form a coherent sentence, she continued. "Please! I'll fall against the tile. I'll die of a concussion."

Finally her words reached him. He rose, wet and gloriously handsome. He did turn off the water.

But that was the only concession he gave the shower, or their drenched state. He swept her off her feet, dripping and naked, and carried her into the bedroom.

When she was safely nestled upon the bed, he continued his assault. She tossed her head and cried out his name. And he reminded her that she could not fall, for she already lay before him.

In seconds she soared to a volatile climax, and then he climbed atop her, parting her thighs to slide inside her. Exhausted and spent, she whispered that she could not go any further.

But he proved that she could. He touched her, inside and outside, and she felt the heat kindle inside of her again. He was the match to set her aflame. She ached again, she wanted again.

And she burst with the sweetness of it, once again.

She fell asleep in his arms, exhausted.

Brad lay awake for a long while, stroking her hair. Listening to the velvety sounds of the night, he felt the peace of the swamp surround him.

CHAPTER 9

Brad woke late. The sun was high in the sky when he opened his eyes. But then, it had been very late when they'd gone to sleep. Wendy was still sleeping.

She was curled halfway upon his chest, her hair a teasing cloud fanned over his shoulders. He carefully shifted her head to the pillow, then he watched her as she lay there. Her skin was as smooth as honey and cream against the sheets, and he was tempted to touch her all over again. She looked somewhat like an angel, he thought, a tender smile curving his lips. It was the color of her hair, he knew, and the classic lines of her face that reminded him of a heavenly spirit. And also, perhaps, her inner purity, her essence, that had warned him that Wendy was someone special, someone unique. A woman not to be taken lightly.

A woman to whom a man could lose his heart.

Warmth invaded his system again. No angel last night, he mused, but a siren, a tempest, stirring him up, beguiling him. Of course, he had wanted her. He had wanted her from the start. They'd been destined to come together. But it was wrong. He didn't belong here. He would have to leave, return to his own life in a world miles away from this marshy refuge. He swallowed fiercely, remembering his partner who now lay dead. Wendy did not belong in his life. He did not belong in hers.

She opened her eyes slowly, her dark lashes blinking over soft silver-and-gray eyes. At first she studied him with a misted confusion, then she smiled with a soft, almost shy welcome.

She yawned and shifted, and the dusky crest of her nipple became visible to him. He groaned inwardly. It was his fault. She had just wanted to be held; she had wanted a figure in the darkness, a man to hold. He had insisted on knowing her. He had wanted her to know him, to make love with him, and not with some forgotten dream.

Yes, he had wanted to know her. He had wanted it to be slow and careful, a union that mattered. But now the mere sight of her smile sent him plummeting into a downward swirl that gripped his loins and his heart in a painful vise. He should be running for his sanity.

Yet he could not leave her. He didn't know how much time they had in this strange Eden, but while it lasted, they were entwined, and he could not give that up.

She reached out and stroked his cheek, running her fingers slowly down his torso. She paused at his waist, drawing circles idly with her fingers, then her hand curved seductively and plunged lower as her fingers locked around him. She edged toward him. The tip of her tongue played over his chest.

Spasms of desire stabbed him like a white-hot lead. He leaned over and kissed her.

This was no angel, he thought as he lifted her above him. Her hair fell in golden sheets over her rosy breasts. She was as beautiful as an angel, but she moved with an ancient, earthy wisdom. And she gave herself to him, completely.

"Wendy..."

He pulled her down. Hers was the kiss of a total temptress, a seductress who made love with her body, her soul and her heart. Soon, Brad forgot that there was a world beyond them. All that mattered was the steaming crest they rode, in a writhing glory of kisses and whispers and slick, entangled limbs.

When it was over, she smiled at him. So sweetly. An angel again. She curled up just like a kitten and fell asleep against his chest.

Later, Wendy reflected that it was one of the best days of her life. She'd never known what it was like to have so much fun doing so very little.

She was more of a sleeper than Brad. She woke again to the scent of sausage. He was lingering in the doorway, naked, a tray of food in his hands, a wild orchid held in his teeth. When she laughed, he nearly dropped the tray. Instead, he deposited it on the floor to leap on top of her, mercilessly tickling her and demanding that she show more respect.

She laughed all through the meal.

When breakfast was over Brad turned on the news, but there was nothing reported about the case. Then an old-time mystery came on, and they watched the show, lazily entwined. An hour or so later, Wendy decided she wanted a shower. Brad decided to shower with her, and they made love once again, with Brad promising Wendy that he could do so in the shower without killing her or causing a serious concussion. She laughed until she cried out with the ecstasy of it, until she was breathless and spent, until his gold-and-amber eyes locked with hers and the world went still.

They sat in the living room and pored through her music collection. He told her grimly that his home had been destroyed, and Wendy was painfully reminded that Brad was a stranger here, that he belonged elsewhere. She told him that he was welcome to begin a new collection with some of her old albums. He shook his head with a rueful smile, then reached out and stroked her golden hair. He whispered that she was incredible, and then he kissed her and made love to her again.

Wendy prepared stuffed Cornish game hens for dinner, and despite the fact that Brad kept pulling her out to the living room to dance to some old treasure that he had found, she managed to put the meal together rather well. Baby made an appearance at the door soon after. After consuming a hefty slab of raw beef, the panther settled down at the foot of the couch.

Later on, Brad led Baby back outside. He didn't want that much company tonight.

When Wendy locked up for the night, Brad was waiting for her in the darkened hallway. He kissed her there, lifted her into his arms and carried her off to bed. They made love again, before drifting into a deep and peaceful sleep.

The next morning, when Wendy awoke, Brad was no longer with her. Worriedly, she jumped out of bed, wrapped the sheets around herself and hurried down the hallway. Finding the house empty, she opened the front door and breathed a sigh of relief. He was there. Baby had come prowling home. Brad was petting the panther's head as he stared out over the swampland, watching as morning burst upon it.

The sun was radiant, glittering in diamonds upon the water. The sound of silence was awesome, until some distant gator let out a grunt—very much like that of a pig, Wendy had always thought—and a mockingbird let out a screeching call.

He was wearing a pair of Leif's faded jeans, along with a Seminole cotton shirt, richly colored in deep blues and crimsons. Mary Hawk had made it for her grandson, as a Christmas present one year. Wendy bit her lower lip, remembering how tenderly Leif had thanked his grandmother. Leif had always shown Willie and Mary deep devotion and respect. That was one of the things that had always made her love her life here, despite the fact that her in-laws were so near. The members of the Hawk family cared for one another. They knew an ancient courtesy and a tender wisdom.

But Brad shared some of those qualities. She had been in a flying fury the other night when she had found him—she had been so worried by then. And it had taken her a while to realize that Willie—that sly old fox!—had been determined to find Brad, introduce himself in his unique way and make his own assessment.

And it seemed that Willie had judged Brad well. Brad had been a natural in Willie's small village. Willie was an old man who liked the old way of life, and many of the younger people, too, were now trying to maintain tribal traditions. Brad hadn't made judgments. He had fitted right in.

A sledgehammer suddenly seemed to slam against her heart as she watched him. She truly admired Brad McKenna. It was difficult to believe that it had not quite been a week since she had met him. And yet it was all too easy to remember that first night, to remember removing his muddy clothing and thinking with inner tremors that he was really beautifully built, powerfully male. She had admired him then; there was no denying the way she'd been drawn to him. Perhaps her loneliness had contributed to the attraction. But since then she had discovered so much more to respect, so very much to like.

And he was going to leave. He'd warned her not to care too deeply; he'd warned her that he would never marry.

And she had assured him, and herself, that it didn't matter.

But it did, now. It mattered so much.

It was easy to live with him, easy to adjust to the extra damp towel in the bathroom, his coffee cup in the sink. It was easy to share things with him—meals and laughter and conversation—and most of all, it was easy to sleep beside him, held tight in his arms.

Don't fall in love...

I'm not in love, Wendy assured herself. As an independent woman, she had opted for this. When he walked away, she'd hold her head high.

And it would be all for the best, wouldn't it? she demanded silently to herself. If she had ever thought that he could stay, she had been living in a fantasy.

Suddenly she found it difficult to breathe. Horrid images flooded her mind as she remembered the violence that had made her a widow. Leif had stumbled upon that violence. Brad made a living at it.

If she and Brad were to fall helplessly in love, it would still be a dead-end relationship. She wouldn't be able to bear it. Every morning when he left for work, her palms would sweat and then she'd begin to tremble...

Brad turned around suddenly, as if he sensed her thoughts. She wanted to raise a hand in cheery greeting; she wanted to smile. She couldn't. Something in his somber gaze warned her that he had been having similar thoughts. Those thoughts were causing harsh lines to become ingrained upon his features. In silence, she merely held the sheet closer to her as a soft breeze whispered against her flesh. Then she returned to the house.

When she had showered and dressed, Brad was in the kitchen. He had made coffee, scrambled eggs and toast. Solemnly, he sipped his coffee.

"Thank you, that looks delicious," Wendy said. She slid onto a stool and tried to take a bite of the eggs. Unfortunately they stuck in her throat. She set her fork down and swallowed some orange juice.

"I need to go back to the gas station and make a phone call," he said.

She put her fork down. "I'll take you in. I need my car anyway. I want to drive into the city and buy some groceries and things." She stood and picked up her plate to take into the kitchen. She couldn't even pretend to eat.

Brad leaned across the table and caught her wrist. She paused, looking down at him. "Wendy, I don't think I should stay any longer."

She forced herself to shrug, pulling at her wrist. "Whatever you think."

"Wendy—"

"Brad, do whatever you think is best."

He stood in annoyance, taking the plate from her hands and setting it on the counter. His eyes burned a passionate gold, and his face was strained and tense. "Don't. Don't do that to you, or to me."

"Don't do what?" she demanded, trying to retain the coolness of her first words. She wanted to remain aloof and above it all.

"Don't pretend that it doesn't matter!" He was nearly shouting.

She couldn't quite meet his gaze, but she managed to speak with extreme impatience. "Pretend what, McKenna? You're the one who made the big deal out of this. 'Let's get to know one another.' You're the one—"

"Wendy, I care about you, you little idiot. You just weren't made for one-night stands—"

"Why not, if I so chose? Damn you, I made a decision." Both their tempers were rising. Although Wendy was trying to hide her emotions, they spilled from her. Anger seemed the only way to combat them. She so desperately wanted to hold on to her pretense of sophisticated distance. But sarcasm entered her voice, a sharp, sharp edge that rang out like a call of battle.

"I made a decision, Brad!" she repeated. "That first night. Yeah, it's been a while. I took one look and decided, an attractive guy. Just what I need—a little uncomplicated sex. When you warned me not to care too much, it seemed so perfect. A mature, adult relationship...a consenting man, a consenting woman—"

"Wendy, stop it! We both know—"

"We don't know anything! What is your problem? If you want to leave— leave! There's nothing keeping you here! You are the last person I want as a permanent fixture in my life. My God, you kill people for a living—"

"That's not true!"

"Your partner was just killed, for God's sake!"

"Yes! And planes crash, and trucks kill people crossing the road."

"But you ask for it!"

"Wendy, other than target practice, I think I've actually fired my gun three times in almost ten years."

She backed away from him, her hands on her hips. "Why are you trying to convince me—"

"You're making it sound like I'm some kind of contract killer!" Two steps brought him back to her. He gripped her shoulders, staring furiously down at her. "I try to keep crack off the streets, Wendy, that's what I do. I try to keep drugs from high-school kids. And I try even harder to keep them out of the grade schools. Ever see a twenty-year-old dead on a cocaine mix? Or a kid in junior high with needle tracks on his arm? It doesn't do any good to arrest that poor kid—you can only pray that he kicks the habit. You have to get guys like Michaelson. The guys who orchestrate the big deals—and make big bucks on the drugs."

The heat that emanated between them seemed to crackle like dry lightning. "Fine, Brad. You go after the Michaelsons in the world, and quit worrying about me! I've gotten what I wanted from you—"

"What?"

His tone was so sharp that she paused for the fraction of a moment. She was trembling, rocked by fury and fear. The truth had descended upon her like a falling weight. She was falling in love; she *had* fallen in love. But she could never use that to hold on to Brad.

"I said, I've gotten what I wanted—"

"Sex?"

"That's right."

He stared at her incredulously. "Just sex?" His temper was roiling and boiling, but it didn't change the way he felt about her. He still wanted her. He had desired her when she laughed, and when she stared at him with tender, sultry eyes. And now, despite the way she lifted her chin and scowled at him with cool, complete disdain, he still wanted her.

Her cool facade was a hoax. He could swear that it was all a lie. Brad wanted to rant and rave; she could evoke such extreme reactions in him! But he didn't. Even while a hot, soaring pulse took hold of him, he forced himself to smile lazily. He wanted so much from her, and he was desperately afraid that this fantasy would end. Couldn't he touch her soul? Couldn't he reach her heart? He had to find out.

"Just sex, huh? Is that it, Wendy? You took one look at me and decided that I'd do for a fling?"

Something in his tone warned her. "Brad—"

Fiercely, he pulled her into his arms. His kiss was sweet and savage; his hands moved in torment.

Although she wanted to lash out at him, she was losing the desire to fight. His lips nearly bruised hers; his tongue ravaged her mouth. His body was white-hot, fevered. The anger, the tempest, the sudden blinding need exploded from him and filled her. A surge of urgent longing seized her, spiraling into her loins. She knew she should twist away from his kiss, but she could not. Instead, she pressed more closely to him. And with the desperate, lingering assault of each kiss, the idea of protest faded from her mind. Instinctively, her fingers curled into his hair. They played over his neck and raked his back. She felt his hands beneath her shirt, freeing her breasts from her bra, stroking them.

He unsnapped her jeans, then slid his fingers beneath the waistband, searching for her most sensitive area. She wrenched his shirt from his pants, touching his bare back, moaning softly.

Somehow, together, they lowered themselves to the floor. For a moment she was a tangle of clothing, and then she was naked. She prayed that he would come to her swiftly, that he would assuage the yearning, the desperate longing.

He did not. With a feverish pitch, Brad made love to her more thoroughly than he ever had before. She whispered to him, pleading and crying out...begging him. But still he explored her, finding new erogenous zones, leaving no sweet inch of bare and vulnerable flesh unaware of his touch, of his kiss.

When he came to her at last, it was instantly explosive, but he did not let it lie at that. He moved while she lay limp, until he roused her again. Then her cry mingled upon the air with his, as they soared above the earth.

Their descent was slow and leisurely. Time had no meaning for Wendy when she was locked in Brad's warm embrace.

"Wendy, I know it's—"

He broke off, and they both jumped at the sound of a tapping against the door.

"Dammit!" Brad swore, casting her a quick, angry glance as he moved to the window. "I am slipping to hell since I've met you!"

"Wendy? Brad? Anyone home?"

Although Brad relaxed at the sound of Eric's voice, Wendy was overcome by a sudden panic. She knew that Eric liked Brad. But still, a terrible feeling of guilt swept over her, dark and poignant. Like a high-school girl caught necking in the car, she scrambled for her clothing.

Brad watched as she stumbled quickly into her clothes. She was such an enigma to him, this sultry, silver-eyed angel. After all, she had claimed that she wanted sex only. She had hurt him with her callous words. But what else could she have said to him? *I understand, please do go, we are getting too involved. Yes, you're right, please do get out of my life before I fall irrevocably in love with you.*

"Would you please get dressed!" Wendy whispered hoarsely.

He looked at her as if he were weighing her words for a moment, then he shook his head and pulled on his jeans. Wendy had barely tucked her blouse into her jeans before he smiled with sarcastic sweetness and strode over to open the door. His shirt hung open, and his feet were bare.

"Hi, Eric," he said, opening the door.

Eric hesitated in the doorway, looking from Brad to Wendy. Eric's emotions were always almost impossible to read. Wendy unwittingly put a hand to her hair, trying to smooth back the wild disarray. Eric glanced at Brad. "Bad timing. I'm sorry."

"Don't be ridiculous—" Wendy began.

"The timing is just fine," Brad interrupted her. "In fact, it's good to see you. We were heading off to the garage to use the phone in a few minutes. Come on in."

Sensing the tension, Eric offered Wendy a curious frown. She smiled at him as innocently as she could. "Want some coffee, Eric? Ice tea, a beer?"

"I'll have some coffee, thanks."

Eric noticed their breakfast plates, barely touched.

Wendy was relieved that he made no comment, but accepted a cup of coffee and turned to Brad. "Willie enjoyed taking off with you, you know. He did give Wendy quite a scare, but he enjoyed having you so much that it was worth it, I think."

Brad told Eric that he had enjoyed meeting his family. When the two men moved into the living room Wendy exhaled, relieved. She picked up the breakfast plates and mournfully realized that they seemed to have a serious problem with breakfast. No matter who made it for whom, the meal had a tendency of winding up in the garbage.

What are we going to do? she wondered in a fleeting panic. Then she realized that she had no choice. Their future was in Brad's hands. Whenever he left, it was over.

A glance over the counter told her that the men were still engrossed in a discussion. Retreating to the bathroom, she brushed out her hair and splashed cool water over her face. As she stared at the reflection of her own wide, silver-gray eyes, she was certain that they wore a telltale glaze, the glow of a woman in love.

"Wendy!"

Brad's voice came to her like a roar. She was sure Baby had never sounded more menacing. The sound of it irritated her, and she gritted her teeth.

When she squared her shoulders and strode out to the living room, her hands on her hips and her brows arched in an irate query, she discovered that Eric was staring at her the same way Brad was—as if she were a child.

"What?" she snapped. They exchanged glances with one another.

"Eric said that he gave you a message for me. About strangers in the swamp—possibly here to hunt me down."

She hesitated, feeling mortified that she could have forgotten such an important warning. But first, she had come home to find him missing. Then they had spent the evening in the village with Willie and Mary and the family, and then when they had come back...

She shook her head. "I—I forgot."

"You what?" Brad said, his eyes narrowing.

"Wendy, it was important," Eric said mildly.

"I'm sorry."

"Sorry!" Brad looked as if he were about to go through the roof. He spun around, hands on his hips, his head lowered, as he fought to control his temper.

But she didn't think that he was so angry about the omission. Even a minor problem would test the limits of his temper right now. Because nothing had been settled between them, nothing at all.

He turned around again, looking at Eric. "You think they've got seaplanes coming in to the swamp? Near here?"

Eric nodded.

Brad shook his head. "That's why we were here, trying to infiltrate his organization. We knew he was securing his stuff out of Colombia, but we could never get a fix on the checkpoints. I knew that he was up to something out here. We were trying to trap him...that's when I wound up out here." He glanced Wendy's way. His eyes were dark, unreadable. His gaze lingered upon her, then he returned his attention to Eric. "But I don't understand how our agents haven't caught him if he's still operating here."

Eric interrupted him with a soft laugh. "Brad, you're not considering the size of the swamp. The grasslands go on forever. There are endless miles of marshes, deep canals and high, dry hammocks with pine trees. There are also lakes, large lakes, with plenty of room for a small seaplane bearing millions of dollars worth of white gold to land."

"So Michaelson's got a drop spot near here," Brad said, calculating. "I've got to find it." Tension constricted his muscles as he studied Eric appraisingly.

"Oh, no!" Wendy swore suddenly. "McKenna, you royal son of a bitch! You haven't the sense to hide out from a man who has one purpose in life besides the pursuit of money—killing you! And if you think that you're going to take my brother-in-law—"

"Wendy!" Eric stopped her furiously.

"No!" Tears stung her eyes. "You idiots! Eric, it would kill your grandfather if something were to happen to you! And, Brad, damn you,

I know your boss didn't hire you to act stupid! To foolishly get yourself killed—"

"Wendy, stop it!" Eric insisted. He reached for her, but she twisted away. "Wendy, I prowled the jungles of Asia. If I'd been killed, Grandfather would have understood."

"We're not going anywhere or doing anything," Brad murmured. He paused. "But I told you this morning, Wendy. I don't think that this is safe for you anymore."

She didn't believe them. She was convinced that Eric intended to take Brad deep into the swamps, deep into all the villages to meet with his friends, Seminoles, Miccosukees and the whites who made their homes out there. Michaelson was hunting him, and Wendy realized that Brad was growing tired of it. He was ready to hunt Michaelson instead.

"Well, maybe leaving here is the best thing for you," Wendy said softly. Then she went back to her bedroom and snatched her purse and the airboat keys that sat on her dresser.

Brad was in the hallway when she emerged. He still looked angry, but not as angry as she was becoming.

"Get out of my way."

"Wendy, you have to understand. We have to talk."

"Talk? No, I don't think so. I don't want to talk, Brad. I want to get out of here. I want to go talk to some store clerks and salespeople—maybe a bartender or two. Someone who doesn't make a living at violence!"

"Wendy, I told you—"

"Yeah, yeah, yeah, you never draw your gun. I found you with a bullet hole in your forehead. That's what it was, right, Brad? A bullet hole. And you're ready to leave, right?" Tears were as hot as molten lead behind her eyelids, and she was afraid that she would shortly grow hysterical and throw her arms around his legs and tell him that she couldn't bear it, she couldn't let him go anywhere, she couldn't let him go away and get himself killed. She was in love with him.

But she was the fool; she was the one losing control. Brad could handle this. He had warned her that he couldn't love her. He had warned that he had to leave.

"Wendy—"

"No!" She shoved past him. "Eric will take you to the gas station. I'm sure that he and Mac will see that you make your phone call—and that you're able to get wherever you want to go."

The tears were about to spill over. Blindly, she spun around. "Good-bye, Brad."

Not wanting to break down in front of him, Wendy ran out of the house to her airboat. Eric would understand, she thought. Eric would see that Brad got wherever he wanted to go.

She doubled over, listening to the drone of the motor, barely seeing the grasses that dipped and swayed as she passed them, barely aware of the wind that dried her tears.

He had been safe. He had been safe at her house—surely, no one would have found him there. But he couldn't stay put, he just didn't have the patience to keep hiding out.

He was gone. He was out of her life. She had claimed that she had gotten all that she wanted, and he was gone now.

No, he wasn't gone—not when she could close her eyes and feel him with her still. The subtle scent of him lingered against her skin. She could imagine his touch in each lilting breeze. She could remember his laughter, his tenderness, his raging passions.

She would never forget his golden eyes and his soft words. There had been so very much between them.

But no amount of passion could deny the disparity between their chosen lives. He wasn't a killer. She knew that. She understood his job. And she understood that he could have no room for her in his life, while she couldn't bear to live with a man in his profession.

She scarcely knew him, she tried to tell herself.

But it didn't matter. Imagining a future without him now seemed as cold and austere as an arctic plain.

CHAPTER 10

L. Davis Purdy had been silent on his end of the phone for so long that Brad began to think that they had been disconnected. When he answered at last, he chose his words carefully.

"What do you know?" he asked Brad.

"What do I know—for fact? Very little. Except that I have a—a friend—" He paused, looking out the window. Eric Hawk was leaning against the building, listening to old Mac go on while he waited for Brad to finish the call. Eric wore a low-brimmed hat, jeans, a denim shirt and cowboy boots. His jet hair fell over the collar of the shirt, but even with the brim of the hat covering his eyes, there was an air of quiet confidence about the man. Yeah, Brad decided. If Eric Hawk had said that something was going on, then it was going on. Hawk would make a good partner. More so than many men Brad had worked with, he felt as if he could trust the Indian with his life.

He cleared his throat and continued. "I have a friend who knows this place like the back of his hand. He says that the deal is going down in the swamp, and I believe him. Michaelson is out here. He's waiting for the next drop, and it's going to happen here. I'm sure he's still looking for me, too, but money means more to him than revenge."

Brad vaguely heard Purdy warn him to investigate, but not to make any moves without checking in. Somberly reminding Brad of his partner's death, Purdy admonished him to be careful. Brad clenched his teeth in anguish, reliving that moment. But then as Purdy's voice went on about procedure, Brad's mind wandered.

He had meant to leave today, to go back to the city, to do it by the book, live under constant guard until they could do something about Michaelson. He'd meant to leave Wendy, to get out of her life. To leave her safe and alone. To leave her, before...

Before they fell in love.

She had told him to go ahead and leave. When she'd stormed out of the house, she hadn't even looked back. She wouldn't expect him to be there. Maybe he shouldn't be there, maybe he should stay with Eric. But he wasn't leaving. Purdy had agreed that Brad was better off staying in the swamp—especially since his agents were getting closer to Michaelson.

Brad had to talk to Wendy; he had to see her again. They couldn't just leave things the way they had.

He realized that Purdy had finished his lecture, and that he was hanging up. Just in time, Brad made the proper response. Promising to stay in touch, he hung up the phone.

He left the office and came upon Mac and Eric still involved in conversation. "Can't tell me these guys are all here for gator season," Mac insisted. He spat on the ground. "No sirree, I know the hunters when they come. I know the office boys who dress up in khaki and shoot up beer cans and sit around in their skivvies, and I know when I see a horde of people comin' through here that don't belong. They just don't look right. They look like they're still wearing suits, no matter how they try to dress like hunters."

Brad winced. He was sure that half the guys who looked so ridiculous in khaki or denim were either FBI or his own associates from the DEA office. But all the telltale signs were evident. The swamp was crawling with men—bad guys and good guys. Brad hoped to God he would know the difference when he came across someone.

"Well, if anyone asks, remember—you've never seen this man," Eric instructed Mac.

The old man grinned at Brad. "I've seen the news, Eric. I know when to keep quiet."

"Thanks a lot, Mac."

"Nothing to thank me for." He looked at Eric again. "You going to be out on the swamp today?"

"Yeah, I thought maybe we should check out a few of the canals."

"You want me to fill up the cooler?"

Eric laughed. "Sure. Fill her up with some cool brews, and some mullet, if you've got any. And throw in some snacks—cheese balls, corn chips—whatever you've got handy."

Mac loaded the airboat with supplies from his limited stock of grocery items. When they stepped back into the airboat, Eric suggested that Brad pilot the vehicle. Within a few minutes, Brad had more or less mastered the craft, and he loved it. Eric grinned tolerantly as Brad let out a whoop and raced pell-mell across the open water.

When Eric warned him that they were coming into a narrower channel, Brad cut the speed and Eric took over.

They spent the morning traversing a myriad of hammocks. They came upon a few isolated Indian villages and a few deserted shacks that weekend hunters had built but didn't really own because the state had taken over the land. Although they didn't run into any hunters, they did discover one shack that had been recently inhabited by someone who smoked expensive cigars and drank high-grade brandy.

Setting an empty bottle back on the rough table, Eric arched a brow. "Michaelson?"

Brad nodded slowly. "Maybe. Though I can't see Michaelson coming this deep into the swamp. He's a city boy all the way. He likes his conveniences—brushes his teeth with mineral water. But it might be a couple of his boys, copying his habits."

"We'll wait it out a while, see if they come back," Eric said.

They waited on the airboat, hidden behind a pine hammock a few yards from the rustic cabin. Eric broke out the beer and a bag of potato chips. After casting fishing lines into the water, they both leaned back.

Brad took a long look at Eric. "Thanks. I realize I'm taking up a lot of your time."

Eric shrugged. "I don't live a nine-to-five life. I use my time when and where I think it's important."

It was hot and humid as a summer day in Hades. Brad swallowed down half a can of beer, then shook his head. "Still, I appreciate what you're doing."

"Sure thing."

As the strange silence of the swamp surrounded them, Brad realized that it wasn't silent at all. He could hear the buzz of insects, the chirp of birds and the rustling sound of the breeze. When he heard a grunting noise, he knew it was the sound of a distant gator.

"She's right, you know," he said.

"Wendy?" Eric grinned.

"Yeah. I have no right dragging you into this."

Eric swore. "Look, I'm here because I want to be, all right? This is my land those bastards are screwing up. My territory. I'll deal with Wendy."

Brad nodded, enthralled by the sight of a long-legged crane that stepped delicately over a patch of marshland. He finished his beer, and Eric tossed him another.

Brad nodded at Eric. "Wendy told me what happened. To her husband—and your wife. I'm sorry."

Eric's muscles tightened as he swallowed. "Thanks. It was a long time ago. I guess we've dealt with it differently, Wendy and I. I spent months alone, then I went wild. Eventually, I settled down, finding peace in this land, getting support from my family. Wendy has just stayed home—alone." He hesitated. "I wanted to find those guys myself. I wanted to bring them out here and kill them my way." He looked across the water. "I did find the one guy in the end. I managed to turn him over to the cops. Then I knew that I could go on. Wendy, well, Wendy never had the same satisfaction, but she goes on. I think you've been good for her. Damned good for her." He shrugged, managing to smile again. "So, I may have a bit of an argument on my hands. But, come to think of it, you're going to have more to explain to Wendy than I will."

Brad looked back at Eric. "I—I don't know if I should even go back there."

Eric appeared amused. "She doesn't bite. Or does she? Whoops, wait a minute, none of my business."

"You sure about that?" Brad grinned.

"About what?"

"It being none of your business."

"All right. It is my business. But only in the sense that I care about her happiness."

"So what do you think I should do?"

Eric shrugged. "What do you want to do?"

"You heard her this morning," Brad said huskily. "I don't think that she wants me around."

"I'm willing to bet that she'll open that door for you if you go back to her."

"She thinks I'm a killer."

"She knows you aren't a killer. She's scared, and in defense she's lashing out with accusations. She has a right to be scared. She's been hurt before. She's had her heart and soul severed. Tolerate her."

Brad laughed. It was so much more than a matter of tolerating a nervous streak! "I don't know, I have no promises for her."

"No one really has promises these days. I think you owe each other more of your time. While you've got it, you owe it to one another."

"Maybe."

Eric grinned suddenly. "Grandfather has a great saying for any dilemma. He says that life is a river, and we chart out that river with our hearts, our minds and our souls. When it matters most, he says, the heart should be the guide. The mind is made of logic, the soul is saddled with pride. Only the heart has no logic, and only the heart can bypass pride. You're welcome to come back home with me tonight. Or else I'll take you back to Wendy's. You decide. Just let me know."

"Yeah, I will," Brad answered, though it was only a pretense that he needed to make a decision. They both knew where Brad was going for the night.

"Hey!" Eric cried suddenly.

"What?" Brad set down his beer can.

"I've got a bite on my line!"

"Oh," Brad said in relief. Then he laughed. "Oh."

Eric looked up at him, realizing that Brad had thought someone was near them, stalking them. He grimaced. "Sorry." Then his line plunged, and he rose to battle it out with the fish. But it was too late. The fish had cleverly slipped off the hook.

"You made me lose him," Eric complained.

"I made you lose him?" Brad protested.

Amid an easy chorus of laughter Brad took out two new cans of beer, and they settled down to wait again.

Dusk came, illuminating the canals in shades of gold and red and mauve. The white cranes on the water seemed to be bathed in pink. Then darkness fell, nearly complete.

"I don't think that anyone is coming back here today," Eric said.

Brad shook his head. He could barely see Eric in the darkness, but his eyes were starting to adjust to it. "They've got something going here, though, I'm sure. Maybe every third day or so. How the hell did they ever find this place?"

"Airboat. There are shacks all over the Glades. Somebody found it to be a convenient spot. Maybe they're gone for good, maybe they'll come back. We can check it out again tomorrow."

Brad nodded. "Thanks."

"Quit that, will you?" Eric charged him. "I told you—this is my territory your man Michaelson is messing with." Eric started the boat motor, and they began to sluice through the canals, the headlight on the airboat their only illumination except for the stars above. There was barely a sliver of a moon that night.

Although he still hadn't said anything to Eric, Brad realized that they were heading for Wendy's house.

But as they came upon Wendy's, Eric quickly cut the motor. The house was too empty; it was too dark.

"We'll go around to the marshy side where there's more saw grass to hide us," Eric whispered.

As Eric secured the airboat, Brad stepped off into deep muck that pulled at his borrowed shoes. He hurried through the marsh until he reached dry land. Eric joined him shortly, moving more easily in his high boots.

"She isn't here!" Brad said tensely.

"Well, maybe—"

"It doesn't take that long to go shopping!" Brad insisted. Fear clawed at his throat and ravaged his gut. What if Wendy's cabin wasn't hidden deep enough in the swamp? If someone had been biding time in an old wooden shack, couldn't they have also discovered Wendy's handsome home with all the modern conveniences?

He tried to swallow down his fear for her; he tried to think professionally and rationally.

"I'm sure," Eric said very quietly, "that she just hasn't come home yet. She might have gone out to the village. And she might have visited some friends in town. There are any number of things that she could be doing."

Sure, Brad thought. Any number of things. All he knew was that she wasn't nearby, where he could touch her and see her and know that she was safe. "Let's check it out," he said softly.

By instinct, they nodded at one another and stealthily crept around the house in opposite directions, Brad going left, and Eric moving to the right.

Although Brad's instincts told him that there was no one there, he couldn't control the pounding of his heart, the naked fear that Michaelson might have snatched Wendy.

At last he reached the back of the house. He sensed movement, then heard a birdcall. Despite his tension, he smiled. It was Eric. It was a damned good birdcall; a week ago he would have thought that it was real. One week in the swamp had sharpened his senses.

He stepped out around the back. Eric joined him.

"Nothing?" Brad asked him.

Eric shook his head. "Nothing. I don't think anyone has been here since we left earlier today. But come on, we'll check the house."

"Think we really ought to break in?"

"No." Eric grinned. "I have a key."

When they surveyed the house, Brad quickly saw that nothing had been touched since they had left that morning. He expelled a long sigh and sank onto the sofa.

"What if Michaelson grabbed her?" he said out loud. "What if he somehow figured out that she was sheltering me, and he grabbed her out in the swamp?"

"Come on, Brad, she's a big girl. She was upset. Probably wanted to talk to Grandfather, or maybe a friend, as I said." He grinned. "Ordinarily, she would have talked to me, but hell, it looks like I've joined the enemy. That meant she had to find someone else. She's all right. I'm sure of it."

Was he so sure? Brad wondered. Despite his words, Eric was pacing, too.

Then they both froze.

There had been no sound of a motor, no sudden flash of headlights.

But someone was outside now, moving around the house in secrecy and stealth.

They looked at one another and rose quickly. Silently, they headed for the front door. Brad opened it cautiously, then both men paused to look out. There was nothing there. The lawn was covered in a soft glow of light from the house, but the edge of the yard was surrounded by shadow. The high pines to the right seemed like a dark forest where a million demons could dwell—a million Michaelsons.

Eric motioned to Brad, who nodded. They started to retrace their earlier steps, silently circling the house.

When Brad came around the back, he saw the form, dark and huddled low, trying to look in one of the windows. Quickly, silently, Brad began his approach. The figure started to turn, to rise, but he was already upon it.

With impetus in his last step, Brad hurtled himself against the form. A low growl issued from his lips. Then he heard a whoosh of air and a soft scream.

He was on the ground, straddled atop her, before he realized that the figure in the darkness was Wendy. With her wrists pinned to the ground, she looked so frightened and helpless.

"Wendy!"

"Brad!" Her eyes opened wide, and then narrowed. "Brad! You slimy son of a bitch—"

"Well, what a nice reunion!" Eric interrupted brightly. He was leaning comfortably against the wall.

Wendy cast him an evil glare, then turned her furious stare upon Brad once again. "What the hell—"

"Where were you?" he demanded hotly.

"What?" she returned.

"Where were you? Where the hell were you?"

"That isn't any of your—"

"You scared me to death!" Brad shouted.

"*I* scared *you*! You muscle-bound Kong—you attacked me! You're sitting on me. You—" She paused. "Eric! Tell him to get off me."

Eric smiled as he hunkered down on his toes near her head, chewing on a blade of grass. "I'll bet if you just ask him real nice, he'll get up on his own."

The grate of her teeth was audible.

"Dammit, Wendy, where did you go?" Brad insisted.

She exhaled. "This is ridiculous!" Despite her anger, there was a glaze to her eyes, as if she had been crying. Dimly, through the maze of fear and relief and anger, Brad wondered if she had been crying because of him.

Then he wondered what the hell he was doing here, making the situation worse. But wasn't this better? If someone had stumbled onto his trail, they would find Wendy—whether they found him or not. Now she was better off with him than without him. Now they would both be better off not to take any chances at all.

"Wendy!" Nervous energy racked his body. She meant so damned much to him.

"You..." Her teeth grated again as she struggled against his hold. Her eyes grew brighter, as if she were on the verge of tears.

"Not that my whereabouts are any of your business!" she hissed, twisting her head to stare at Eric. "Or yours!"

"I'm just an innocent bystander."

"Could you go stand somewhere else?"

Eric laughed, but he didn't move. Wendy stared from one man to the other—Eric, who seemed to be having the time of his life, and Brad, who still seemed deathly pale in the darkness.

"I went to the damned store!" she spat out.

"All day?" Eric queried politely.

"Where's the airboat?" Brad demanded.

"I have my car!" Wendy snapped. "The boat's across the water. I went into the garage, I talked to Mac. I got my car. I drove into Fort Lauderdale. I went to the drugstore, and I went to the grocery store. You want to know what aisles I perused? I bought a can of Pepsi from a vending machine. I stopped for a copy of the newspaper."

"That still doesn't take all day! Dammit, Wendy, you scared me half to death."

"Well, dammit, Brad, you did the same to me! How the hell do you think it felt to know that someone was in the house?"

"You knew that Eric has a key."

"But neither Eric's car nor his airboat were visible. Why the hell am I explaining this to you?" Wendy exploded. She swallowed, wondering whether to laugh or cry or keep screaming. She was shaking, trembling inside and out because he had come back, because he was still with her.

Grandfather had told her that he would be there. He had smiled and told her to be patient. He had told her to go home and wait, to trust in her heart.

Although she had told Brad to go away, she had prayed that he wouldn't. She had bought groceries for two. In the drugstore she had tried not to indulge in fantasy, but she had bought extra shaving cream and toothpaste and soap...

For two.

Which had been foolish. Eventually, he had to go away.

Eventually, but please, God! Wendy silently prayed, not now. Let us have some time. I need that second damp towel in the bathroom just a little longer.

"You're explaining it to me because you worried me to death!" Brad yelled back at her.

"You're not even supposed to be here!" she reminded him.

Eric cleared his throat. "Maybe we should hassle over the finer points inside." He cleared his throat again. "Brad, er, I think you're about to cut off her circulation at the wrists."

Brad instantly released Wendy's wrists. Then he took her right hand in his own and began to rub it. "Did I hurt you?"

"No," she replied. "Just move, will you please?"

Slowly, he came to his feet, then reached a hand down to her. She took it, eyeing him warily as she stood.

"Did you leave packages in the car?" Eric asked.

She nodded, then smiled sweetly. "Except for the bag that I was carrying. I dropped it in the bushes there when the G-man jumped me."

"Oh, well, no harm done," Eric said, shaking out the tattered brown grocery bag and collecting the canned goods and cereal boxes that had fallen out.

Brad and Wendy were still staring at one another heatedly. Eric shoved the bag into Brad's arms. "Why don't you take this into the house," he suggested. "I'll go for the rest."

"Yeah, thanks," Wendy said. Brad was still staring at her. Rumpled and handsome, his tawny hair was all askew. She brushed by him and headed for the front.

He set the bag down on the kitchen floor. By then, Eric had returned with two more sacks. "On the counter, Wendy?"

"Yes, thank you."

Brad stood by the counter. "Wendy, where were you?"

"I wasn't out making a million-dollar coke deal, if that's what you're asking," she said flippantly.

"Oh, jeez," Eric groaned.

Brad grabbed her arm. "Wendy, I'm asking you a civil question! I want a civil answer!"

"Civil!"

"Wendy—"

"I told you, I went to the stinking store! Then I came back and I went out to see my family. I went to the village. I had dinner with Willie and

Mary and the kids. That's it, that's all! And it's none of your business, anyway! You told me that you were leaving!"

He swung around on his heel. Wendy glared at Eric, who merely shrugged and followed Brad outside.

Brad was on the lawn, still tense and angry—but deflated. He looked at Eric. "Where the hell is her car?" he demanded.

Eric laughed. "Come on. I'll show you."

He led Brad to what looked like dark water, but there were stones beneath the water, which was barely an inch deep. It seemed that they walked across water, but of course they didn't. There was even a trail hacked through the tall grass on the other side, and there, high on a dry clearing near the end of a dirt road, was Wendy's small station wagon.

Together, the men collected the rest of the groceries, then returned to the house.

Wendy was putting things away, slamming every door she touched.

Eric set the last of the grocery bags down. "Want some help, Wendy?"

"No," she said curtly.

"Suit yourself. You want a beer, Brad?"

"Sure," Brad said.

Eric sauntered casually past Wendy and reached into the refrigerator, helping himself to two cans of beer. He tossed one over to Brad.

Wendy stood at the sink, separating a pack of steaks into individual freezer bags. She sniffed. "The two of you already smell like a brewery."

"What?" Eric protested. "I'm crushed."

Wendy swung around to face him. "All right, where the hell have the two of *you* been all day?"

"Fishing."

"Fishing." She paused in her efforts and stared at him. "Fishing. All day. *All* day?"

"Fishing. Shooting the breeze. Swilling beer. You know. Having a good old time."

Wendy turned back to her steaks. "Liar," she said softly.

"Ask Brad. I had a catfish on the line that you wouldn't believe. He made me lose it. City slicker."

She looked up at Eric. He smiled blandly. "You going to let him stay on here?" he asked her bluntly.

"What?" She flushed.

"Well, I'm going home. I was wondering if I should take him with me?" Brad's eyes opened wide in amazement. "Eric, I can sink my own ship!"

"Stop it!" Wendy snapped. "Brad can stay."

"Stop shouting. I just asked a question," Eric said defensively.

Brad swallowed a sip of beer. Wendy was alive and well, and they were together. Heat filled him at the idea that their time together wasn't over yet.

"Good night." On his way out of the kitchen, Eric offered Brad a wink. "Just watch out! She's dangerous."

Wendy swung around. "Watch out? *He* tackled *me* out there, and I'm supposed to be the dangerous one."

"I think I can handle her," Brad said.

Wendy glared at him. A curious golden light was in his eyes as they swept over her. It made her feel warm. No, it made her feel hot, as if she would melt to the ground. Just seeing him there, tall, ruffled sandy hair, bronze and sinewed, made her remember the morning. She remembered what it felt like to run her fingers over his shoulders, over his back. She remembered watching the play of his muscles as he held her, remembered seeing the taut flicker of passion in his face as he gazed down at her...

"Yes," he said softly, "I think that I can handle her."

"Maybe," Eric said. "Maybe not. You know, friend, she could be trying to trap you."

"What?" Wendy and Brad said simultaneously. They both stared at Eric, who maintained his facade of a friendly calm.

"Trap you, Brad. She's always wanted a baby. Did you know that? Did she ever tell you? She was trying to get pregnant before Leif died. Maybe she's using you. Maybe she intends to trap you into marriage.

"And on the other hand, don't you think you're misleading her? You're not the kind of guy to settle down. You've got important work. A hell of a job. And heck, any damn day of your life could be your last. Do you use that as a ploy to take advantage of lonely women?"

"Eric!" Wendy snapped in disbelief and horror. No. Eric was her friend, he loved her. Why would he ever say such things? "Eric!" Her voice was small but strong, and it was laced with anguish. "Get out of my house! Get out! How could you—just get out!"

She was as white as chalk.

Eric nodded. "I was just leaving."

He walked out the front door. She heard it close. In absolute dismay, she let her eyes meet Brad's at last.

He was staring at her, staring at her hard. He started walking toward her. "Wendy..."

"No!" Knowing that she was going to burst into tears, Wendy turned to run down the hallway. She just couldn't stand any more, not today.

Brad caught her by the shoulders, then swung her around into his arms.

"No!" She struggled against his hold.

"Use me, Wendy, if you would," he whispered softly. Then his lips caught hold of hers, hot and searing, and she gasped at the power of his hands moving over her. He was lifting her, lifting her high into his arms, she couldn't help but respond to the feverish heat of his body.

CHAPTER 11

It was so good to touch her, so good to kiss her, to hold her soft and pliant in his arms. Her lips fused to his, seemingly as hungry as his own. He could have held her all night, drinking in a kiss such as this...

At first he ignored the sound that came to him from the swamp outside.

But then it came again, that sound in the darkness of night, and it penetrated Brad's mind. It was a birdcall, soft but clear, cutting through the night, cutting through Brad's desire and causing a prickle of danger to streak along his spine.

Brad slowly lowered Wendy until her feet touched the floor. Her arms were still around his neck, but her eyes met his. She, too, had sensed the danger.

"Eric?" he asked.

She nodded. "Yes, it's Eric."

"You said you had a pistol. What about ammunition?"

She nodded and quietly slipped away from him. He stayed in the hallway, listening. Concentrating, he tried to clear away all other sounds. Then he heard the footsteps outside.

He knew that Eric was out there...somewhere. But Eric had called to him, warned him, because someone else was out there, too.

Wendy returned with a Smith & Wesson .38. He took the weapon from her and cocked it. "Stay here," he whispered. "I want you to find a sheltered corner and stay low. Hold on to the shotgun. All right?"

At last she nodded. He turned away from her and hurried down the hall to the front door. The lights were on in the kitchen and the living room.

He turned them off and went to the window, where he stared out across the lawn. Nothing moved. He went to the front door and slipped out.

Perched on his haunches by the corner of the house, Brad hesitated, then sprang around. His weapon was aimed straight ahead, at the ready. There was no one there.

He moved silently along the side of the house. The night was dark, so damned dark.

The birdcall sounded again. Someday, Brad decided, he was going to have to ask Eric what kind of bird it was supposed to be. An owl?

It didn't matter now. What was important was that he knew that Eric was moving almost opposite him, on the other side of the house. Within a few minutes, they'd both be at the rear, and their prey would be caught between them then.

Their prey...

He knew that someone else was there. He could feel it, smell it, sense it. All he had to do was turn the corner.

At the edge of the wall, Brad paused, his heart thudding against his chest. He held the gun steady with both hands, and then he sprang smoothly around, prepared to shoot.

A man was there, in back of the house. He hadn't heard or sensed Brad or Eric yet—he was busy at work on Wendy's bedroom window.

"Hold it right there. Get your hands up—up high, clear in the air!" Brad demanded.

The man dropped low. Brad saw a glint of the pale moonlight gleaming upon something in the man's hands. He had a gun, too, and he was getting ready to shoot.

Brad shot first. Carefully, very carefully, he squeezed the trigger. The gun went flying and the man screamed, clutching his hand.

Eric flew around the corner, stooping silently to retrieve the thrown gun even as the fallen intruder tried to reach for it. Brad came forward, keeping the .38 aimed at the man.

"Three fifty-seven Magnum," Eric observed. "He meant to plug a few holes in you for keeps."

"Yeah," Brad said softly. "Michaelson's men do play for keeps."

"Cripes! I'm bleeding to death down here! You're supposed to be the cop, McKenna. You'd better get me to a hospital quick, or I'll be screaming my head off about police brutality."

Brad squatted down by the man, seeing a swarthy, pockmarked face. He'd thought he recognized the voice.

"I'm not a cop. I'm worse than that, Suarez, and you know it. I'm DEA. A fed. And you know what? We've been losing some good guys to scum like you lately. We don't take the same heat as the poor local cops. I don't care if you rot away of gangrene, Suarez."

"You know him?" Eric asked.

Brad nodded, careful to keep the gun aimed at the slender but dangerous man on the ground. "Tommy Suarez. He's so high up with Michaelson that he rarely has to take on the dirty jobs these days. We think that he killed a lot of people to get to his position. He used to give me my 'order'—where to pick up cash, where to drive, that kind of stuff." He hesitated. "This bastard killed my partner." He pulled back the trigger so that it clicked.

In a timeless moment he gritted his teeth, realizing he had to stop. He was emotionally involved here. But this guy had been the triggerman who killed his partner. Suarez had also been working away at the window to a bedroom where Wendy might have been sleeping.

Sleeping, all alone. If Brad had left, Wendy would have been there—alone, innocent, vulnerable. And God alone knew what Suarez might have done with her to extract information about Brad—or just for the hell of it, because she was a beautiful woman.

He aimed the gun straight at Suarez's temple.

"Hey!" Suarez whined. "You can't do that! You're—"

"Who else is hanging around here, Suarez?" Brad demanded.

"No one," he said sullenly. "Hey, my hand is bleeding. You've busted it all to hell, you ass—"

"Hey!" Eric grinned. His teeth were a bright white slash against his bronze skin in the pale moonlight. "My turn, Brad. I'm not with the government. I don't have a scruple in the world, dealing with this swine. You hear that, Suarez? I'm not a cop, and I'm not an agent. I'm an Indian.

And you know what, buddy? I've had enough of you guys slipping that rotten crack to our teens. They're not starting out with a real fair deal to begin with. You know how many overdoses we've had out here in the last year? Since your friend Michaelson decided to make a septic tank out of our swamp?"

Suarez licked his dry lips. Eric held him by the lapels of his shirt. His eyes darted nervously from Brad to Eric and back to Brad again. "Tell him to let me go. Tell Mr. Rain Dance there to get his hands off me!"

Eric's laugh was harsh and bitter. "Rain Dance, Sitting Bull, yeah, you got the message, Suarez!" Brad hadn't known that Eric carried a knife until he saw the flash of the steel blade pressed against Suarez's throat. "Mr. McKenna asked you a question."

"Please!" Suarez whined. He seemed afraid to even swallow. "Please, tell him to get the knife away. He's going to kill me."

Brad nodded to Eric. Eric sheathed the knife beneath the edge of his boot. "Hell," he moaned. "And I thought I was going to get to see if a rat could live after it had been scalped."

"Who knows you're here? How did you find this place?" Brad asked. Suarez remained silent, his eyes wide with panic. Brad swore softly. "So help me, Suarez, start talking or I'll just turn my back and let Rain Dance experiment on you."

Suarez kept stalling, until Eric brandished the shiny blade of his knife once more. Ultimately, Suarez believed the threat. He started talking. No one knew where he was; he'd come out on his own. He'd been holed up in a hunter's shack, but some hillbillies in an airboat had been hanging around all day, guzzling beers and trying to catch fish. He hadn't dared go in anywhere close, so he'd done a little exploring on his own.

"Come on, Suarez, you weren't out here alone."

"Charlie Jenkins is supposed to be with me. He had to take a ride this morning. I'm alone, I swear it."

"Okay, okay. You and Jenkins have been hanging out in a shack in the Everglades." That rang more true. Charlie Jenkins had grown up in southern Georgia, in the Okefenokee swamp. He would know how to get around down here.

"Why are you guys staked out here?"

"We're looking for you," Suarez said.

"There's more," Brad told him.

"Yeah, all right, yeah. Michaelson has been using the Everglades. You knew that—hell, half the law enforcement in the state knows that." He sneered, revealing tobacco-stained teeth. "Everyone knows that. But Michaelson is slick, real slick. He can't be caught. Just like the water moccasin, he slinks away when he doesn't want to be found."

"When is the next shipment coming in?" Brad demanded.

"I don't know—"

Quick as lightning, Eric pulled his knife out and pressed it against the man's throat. The blade glinted even in the dim moonlight. "I swear it! I swear it!" Suarez screamed, looking apprehensively at the blade so near his jugular vein. "Charlie Jenkins is supposed to know, when he comes back."

Convinced that Suarez was telling the truth, Brad nodded to Eric. Eric backed off, silent as the night.

"I've got to take him in," Brad said.

"You mean we don't get to kill him?" Eric sighed deeply in mock disappointment.

When Suarez shivered, Brad was barely able to suppress a grin. "Not this time, Tonto. Sorry."

Eric grinned. Suarez started blubbering again. "I swear, I'd tell you anything. I don't know nothing else, honest."

"Let's go tell Wendy—" Eric began, but just then an explosion rent the darkness of the night.

"Hands up, everyone. All the way up."

Apparently, Wendy had waited long enough. She had silently crept around the house, but the kick of the shotgun had announced her arrival and sent her stumbling backward. Fortunately she hadn't lost her grip on the weapon; she still held it cocked and aimed.

"Wendy!" Brad snapped. "Dammit, I told you to stay in the house!"

"I told you she had definite problems," Eric warned.

"I was worried when you didn't come back."

"But I told you to stay inside—"

"Like a sitting duck. You might have needed me."

"Well, we didn't! Everything is well in hand." Or it had been, Brad thought. Now he was trembling again. Maybe it was a damned good thing that he had come here. Suarez had just been exploring in the night. He would have stumbled upon Wendy, and she would have been completely unaware. He would have attacked her in the night, and she could have screamed forever, and no one would have heard her....

Wendy. His angel. She held the shotgun with poise and regal grace. Her hair gleamed in the dim moonlight with a splendor all its own. She seemed so small and slender, and yet so feminine. It was strange how something like denim work jeans could hug a woman's figure, making her appear so sexy. And it was strange, too, how a simple cotton shirt could hang so evocatively upon a body.

Suarez inhaled sharply. Brad looked down at the man. He was watching Wendy with a sizzle in his eyes.

"Wendy, get back into the house, now!" Brad ordered.

"I am not your personal lackey!" she protested. "Damn you—"

"Break it up, break it up," Eric interrupted. "We've got to deal with this guy. Brad, his hand is shot up badly."

"You shot him?" Wendy accused Brad.

"Well, excuse the hell out of me!" Brad returned. "I shot him before he could shoot me, do you mind?"

When she rushed over to examine Suarez, Brad stopped her. "It's not a pretty sight."

She stared at him, then pushed his hand away. "I told you, I was a nurse. Trust me, I've seen worse."

She hunched down on the balls of her feet and examined the man's hand. Suarez stared at her in that same way that made Brad so uncomfortable, and yet he blessed her in Spanish and in English and told her that she was an angel of mercy.

She scowled at Brad. "This wound is serious. He needs to be in a hospital. You shouldn't have kept him here so long."

"So long!"

"I heard that shot a long time ago," Wendy said.

He wanted to grab her and shake her. She didn't realize that this sleaze might have friends, nor did she even seem to realize that he meant to break in through her window and...

"Don't pull a Florence Nightingale act on me. This man meant to come through that window, and rape you. And hell, he might have even killed you."

"C'mon, break it up for the moment, huh?" Eric suggested lightly. "Wendy, this guy isn't exactly Mr. Rogers, you know, dropping in on the neighborhood. Let's get him in—"

"I'll take him—alone," Brad said. He didn't want Wendy along, and he wanted Eric to stay with her.

"That's well and fine, but I'm not sure you can find your way around at night," Eric reminded him.

That was true, Brad thought dismally. Although he'd become familiar with the swamp, he couldn't safely navigate at night.

"What about the car?" he asked Eric.

Eric shrugged. "You still shouldn't be venturing out alone. Why don't you call your boss. I'll turn this thug over to the tribal police. From there he can be transferred over to your people."

Brad nodded. Eric's plan made sense.

Wendy turned around. "I'm going to get some bandages."

"I don't want her left alone," Brad said to Eric.

"Want me to take him in?"

Brad shook his head. "I'll have to call Purdy and see what he wants to do with this scum."

"That's some *chica*," Suarez said nastily.

"Shut up." Brad kicked him, then turned away. "I don't want her left alone, Eric."

"Then we'll all go. I'll drive. Wendy can ride up front with me, and you can ride in the back with our friend here."

Brad thought about it for a minute. He didn't want Wendy anywhere within reach of Suarez, but Eric's plan seemed like the best solution. Brad didn't want her left alone, either. He definitely didn't want her alone.

Jenkins was coming back somewhere along the line—according to Suarez—and Brad wasn't going to take any chances.

"All right," he told Eric.

Wendy returned with a bottle of antiseptic and white gauze bandages. A true professional, she knelt down by Suarez. In a no-nonsense tone, she warned him that it was going to sting like hell, then she poured the contents of the bottle over his hand. He screamed in pain, trying to clutch his hand away, but Wendy didn't let him. Deftly, she wrapped the injured hand in clean gauze. She handed him a little white pill and told him to swallow it. "Percodan. It will help the pain."

"Let's get him a suite at the Biltmore," Brad murmured sarcastically.

"Brad, you did put the man in pain," Wendy said.

"Yeah. And he meant to put me six feet under."

"Are you two going to take him into town?" Wendy asked, smoothing back a loose strand of her hair.

"No, *we three* are going to take him," Brad said.

Her eyes widened. "I don't want to go."

"You're going."

"The hell—"

"You're going." His teeth were grating and his muscles were tightening. It had been such a damned explosive evening that he was ready to throw her over his shoulder and carry her into the car. Of all the damned times for the woman to be so stubborn!

"Okay, okay!" Eric stepped between them. "Wendy, give the guy a break, will you? He's worried about you. Brad, I'm glad that you're in law enforcement and not the diplomatic corp. Now, for God's sake, let's get this show on the road!"

"I'm all for that, Rain Dance," Suarez agreed. The Percodan was working fast, Brad thought. The guy's eyes were already glazing over. Suarez almost looked agreeable.

"Rain Dance?" Wendy's eyes widened. Brad almost smiled. He could see her fury growing. She'd fight anytime for someone she loved, and she loved her brother-in-law. "Why, you slime mold!" She hissed to Suarez.

Her love was so fierce, so loyal. *I want you to love me with that fury, that passion,* Brad thought. *But like a lover.*

Eric groaned. "Wendy, I've got it in control, okay? Can we please go?"

"Let's do it. Suarez, up," Brad said.

Brad was holding the gun, so Eric gave the man a hand. He struggled to his feet. Brad stared at Wendy fiercely.

She returned his stare, then her rich lashes fell over her cheeks. "I'll be just a moment," she said, hurrying back into the house. When she returned, she was still carrying the shotgun. Brad was sure that she had more shells for it, too, probably packed away in her brown leather purse.

Suarez was convinced that they were trying to drown him when they told him to walk over the stones. Then, when Eric showed him how it was done, Suarez was convinced that Eric was an Indian god.

"What the hell did you give him?" Brad demanded of Wendy.

"I told you—Percodan!" She proceeded over the stones herself. "See? I swear, you'll barely get your feet wet."

Suarez followed her at last. He looked back longingly at the canoe, drawn up on the shore, that had brought him to the house in the woods. "I shouldn't have come here. I should have shot those hillbillies in the airboat and drank up their beer."

"Nothing like hindsight, is there, Suarez?" Brad said, prodding his prisoner with the barrel of the gun. "Let's move."

At last, Suarez gingerly walked over the stones. When they reached the car, Brad helped Wendy into the front seat, then pressed Suarez into the back. Eric asked Wendy for the keys, and she tossed them to him.

The car was eerily silent as they started out. Eric flicked on the car radio. A latino tune came on, and Suarez decided to sing along.

Brad was getting a horrible headache. He tried to watch the terrain as Eric drove, but the headlights of the small car didn't alight upon any recognizable landmarks.

By car, it was a long trip. Brad understood Wendy's affection for her airboat. It took less than forty-five minutes to reach Mac's garage by way of the airboat. Now time seemed to drag horribly. They drove for more than an hour before they pulled up beside the garage.

"We're going to have to wake up Mac," Wendy said. Eric turned the car off, and she hopped out.

"I have to go," Suarez said.

Eric and Brad exchanged looks of annoyance. Eric came out of the driver's seat and opened the door. Brad followed Suarez out, keeping the gun trained on him at all times. He knew these people too well to trust even a simple call of nature.

Between them, they led Suarez over to a clump of bushes. Brad looked toward the station and saw that the office door was opening. Wendy had managed to rouse Mac from his bed in the back room of the office.

He handed the gun to Eric. "Don't trust him."

"He won't pull anything," Eric said, "if he values his life."

Hurrying toward the station, Brad smiled, shaking his head slightly. Suarez was thoroughly convinced that Eric was probably worse than the entire Indian contingent at the battle of the Little Bighorn.

"Come on in, Mr. McKenna. Come in and make whatever calls you want," Mac said, opening the glass door.

"Thanks, Mac," Brad said.

"Wendy, you want some tea or something?"

"Sure, I'd love some tea," Wendy murmured. It would give her something to do while Brad started dialing numbers.

Brad phoned Purdy, who agreed that it was a good idea to bring in the tribal police. His people would meet them at the entrance to the swamp and extradite Suarez. Purdy planned to interrogate Suarez as soon as he had received medical attention.

Brad glanced over at Wendy. "I—I can't come in now."

Purdy was quick, Brad gave him that. He hadn't gotten where he was by being stupid.

"You don't want to talk? You're worried about your friend? The girl you're staying with?"

"Yes. Exactly."

"Fine. Hand Suarez over to the tribal police and go back with her. Call me tomorrow at noon. Maybe it's time to get some backup out there."

"Yeah. I think it might be."

"But play it smooth, huh? You've got a nice trap sitting out there. Maybe we can bag something else."

"Carefully."

"Carefully, beyond a doubt. We won't let the woman get hurt, Brad."

"Thanks." He dared another glance at Wendy. She was talking to Mac, but he was sure that she had heard everything he had said. He was glad that he had kept it simple, glad that Purdy was perceptive.

He hung up. Purdy was going to contact the tribal police.

"Everything taken care of?" Mac asked.

"Yes, thanks. Thanks a lot," Brad told the old man.

Mac smiled. "Tea?"

"No, thanks just the same." He shook Mac's hand. He wondered if there was any way that he could repay the old guy, if there was anything that Mac wanted. In many ways, Mac had helped keep Brad—and Wendy safe.

When Brad left the office, Wendy started to follow him.

"Stay inside with Mac," he told her.

"Don't you—"

"Please! Stay with Mac."

Wendy looked into his eyes, so fiercely gold, so powerful. Her rebellious nature balked at the order, but she swallowed her pride and went back inside to wait with Mac. It had been such a rough day! She'd been trying so hard to pretend that her life was entirely normal.

But life wasn't normal anymore. Brad had entered into her world, and she had fallen in love with him. She had cried as she'd strolled down the aisle in the grocery store, and despite herself, she'd bought enough food for two. She'd burst into tears in the drugstore, and again, she'd bought supplies for two.

And at first she hadn't been able to go home to her empty house. She'd gone to see the family, because she had needed them so badly. She'd needed Grandfather's wisdom, and Grandmother's support. Willie had held her when she cried, and she'd known with an even greater strength than ever before just how much they loved her. Leif was dead, but the Hawks still loved her. They were such good people. Blood was a strong tie to them, but love was even stronger. She was Willie's granddaughter, blood or no, for he claimed her as so. He knew that she had loved Leif.

And he knew that she loved Brad now.

"He is a good man," Grandfather had told her.

"He is gone."

"Go home. Wait for him. He will come back."

"What if he doesn't?"

"Then you will cry, but life will go on. And you will be richer for the time that you have shared."

And now, looking out the window at Brad, she didn't know whether to laugh or cry. He had returned to her house, he had returned to her arms. But danger had come between them.

She was a fool. Brad McKenna lived with danger—it was an occupational hazard.

And yet she loved him anyway.

A while later, Wendy saw the flash of headlights. When the car parked outside, she recognized the emblem of the tribal police. After a very brief conversation with Brad and Eric, the tribal police took Suarez away.

Then Brad opened the door and stretched out a hand to her. "Wendy, it's time to go back home."

Back home. Yes, it was time to return to her home—with him.

Eric drove again. Wendy sat in front with him; Brad sat silently in the back. The only sound was the music from the radio, though Eric switched the station a dozen times.

At last, they were home. Still in silence, they parked and locked the car, then traveled over the stones to reach the house.

"You need to give Brad a decent pair of boots," Eric commented. "He's soaking his shoes on those things."

"They're your brother's shoes," Brad said.

"Yeah, well, my brother had boots, too. And he can't use any of them now. Boots are a necessity in swampland. Leif's old leather pair were strong enough to break the grasp of a rattler or a cottonmouth."

Ahead of the two men, Wendy was unlocking the door. "Leif's boots are in the closet. Take them."

It had been a long, long night, and it was nearly three in the morning. Too tense to be tired, Brad glanced at Eric, wondering when they were going to tell Wendy what they had decided while waiting for the tribal police.

Wendy went in and set her purse on the counter. She looked at the two men invading her life, her brother-in-law and the lover she was so afraid of losing.

"Do you two want anything?" They were staring at her so expectantly, like two big dogs.

"Yes!" Brad said, suddenly realizing that he hadn't eaten a decent meal all day.

"Yes, please!" Eric echoed.

She opened the refrigerator. "Like what?"

Brad requested two of the steaks she had just brought home. Eric agreed with that, and he also wanted broccoli in cheese sauce. Brad thought a salad would be great. Eric said they should add some microwave baked potatoes to the menu, too.

So at 3:00 a.m., they started cooking.

The conversation remained casual and polite. Wendy kept her distance from Brad, who seemed careful to do the same.

When they had eaten and cleaned up the dishes, Eric still remained. Wendy looked at him curiously.

Brad cleared his throat at last. "Uh, Eric is taking the first watch."

"First watch!" Wendy looked from Brad to Eric and back to Brad again.

"First watch, Wendy." Eric reached over and squeezed her fingers. "I'm going to stay awake, while Brad sleeps. Then we'll switch. It's safer that way."

"I see." Wendy set her dish towel on the counter and turned away from them both. "Well, then, good night."

She walked down the hallway. Maybe she was just so tired that she felt like a zombie. Maybe she was so desperately in love she was losing her spirit. She showered and dressed for bed in a long cotton gown. She was so overtired that she was afraid she would throw some ridiculous, childish fit if she encountered either of the men, so she hurried into her bedroom and closed the door.

Sleep eluded her. She heard someone go into the shower—Brad, she assumed. The water roared on, then there was silence.

A few moments later she heard a soft knock at her door.

Brad leaned in, his hair still damp and glistening from the shower. "Good night," he told Wendy softly, then closed the door.

"Good night," she called after him.

She sank back against the pillows for a moment, then threw back the covers and raced to the door. She opened it and saw Brad standing in the threshold. Her heart skittering away, Wendy ran to him. She leaped off the floor, hurtling herself into his arms, locking her legs around him.

He held her to him, kissing her hungrily. Holding her so, he walked straight to her bed. Together they fell backward onto the billowing sheets.

Wendy broke from his kiss. "The door. We're not alone."

Brad got up and closed the door. When he reached for her again in the darkness, she was naked.

And she was waiting for him.

Forgetting the turmoil of the day, he buried his heart, his soul and his body into her never-ending sweetness.

CHAPTER 12

Brad was beside her, sound asleep, when Wendy woke, late in the morning. She assumed that he had spelled Eric, staying awake for the second part of the night, and that he'd come to bed after that, to sleep for the first time.

She showered and dressed. Eric wasn't in the living room when she came out. Looking out the window, she saw that he was sitting on the lawn, sipping a mug of coffee. Apparently, he had just fed Baby; the big cat was curled up next to him just as sweetly as a Persian kitten.

She watched Eric for a moment, remembering what he had said before all the commotion had begun last night. He'd made some lousy accusations! She went into the kitchen, poured a glass of ice water and went outside.

She couldn't sneak up on him; she knew that. When he looked up and flashed her a smile of greeting, she smiled back. She came up behind him, then squatted down to pat Baby.

"Sleep well?" he asked her innocently.

"Fine," Wendy said sweetly. Then she poured the water directly over his head.

He sputtered, swearing and jumping to his feet. "What the hell was that for?" he demanded in outrage.

"You know damned well what that was for! Your wonderful little performance last night!"

Annoyed by the whole thing, Baby stretched and walked away in search of peace and quiet. Dripping, Eric stared at Wendy, then started to laugh.

"Well, apparently it didn't do any harm."

"Eric! How could you say those terrible things about me? You're supposed to be on my side!"

"Wendy, Wendy..." He opened his arms to give her a big hug.

Wendy quickly realized that he only wanted to drench her, too. "Eric!" She eluded him, but sat down on the lawn a safe distance from him. He sat down beside her. The sun was high in the sky; he would dry quickly.

"I *am* on your side," he told her.

"Then what was that all about? Brad's going to leave. We all know that."

"Do we?" Eric arched a brow to her and she flushed. "Oh, yeah, that's right. You don't want anything to do with a fed agent, do you?"

"Eric—"

"Well, whatever I said, it didn't seem to do any harm to either of you. Seemed to me that things went well enough."

"Eric—"

"You know, Wendy, your life is your business. And Brad's life is his business. Your decisions have to be your own."

"Then—"

"I just wanted to make sure that you were both playing with a full deck, that's all."

Wendy groaned. "You're making me crazy!"

He grinned, glancing over his shoulder. "Well, morning has broken. Here comes the fed. Excuse me. I think I'll make more coffee."

Wendy twisted slightly. Brad was coming out the front door, shirtless, shoeless and clad only in a pair of jeans. His hair was still tousled, and though she could see that he had shaven, he still looked somewhat bleary-eyed and disoriented. He was carrying a coffee cup. Eric, heading back into the house, paused. The two men exchanged a few words, then Brad joined Wendy outside. He cradled his coffee cup in his hand and smiled at her. "Good morning."

"Good morning."

They didn't say anything else for several long moments. He took a sip of the steaming coffee and stared out over the terrain. Baby reappeared and curled up beside Wendy.

Brad slipped an arm around her. She watched his profile, setting a hand lightly on his knee.

"None of that was true, you know."

He looked her way again, a small smile playing against his lips.

"What Eric said."

He paused. "You didn't want a baby?"

She looked down at the ground. "Well, yes, I did. That was true, but the rest—was absurd. I would never try to trap you."

He set his coffee cup down and threaded his fingers gently through her hair, kissing her tenderly. "Would you want to trap me?" he asked softly.

She shook her head. "No one should ever be forced into anything. I wouldn't, I just wouldn't, and I hope you believe that." She spoke flatly, trying to escape his hold. He laughed and pulled her tightly against him. His hand lay beneath her breast, and they could both feel the pulse of her heart.

"I know that you would never force anyone to do anything. Sometimes it's difficult to get even an opinion from you."

"What do you mean by that?"

"You don't want to admit how you feel."

Wendy scratched Baby's ears and looked out over the water. "I let you know how I feel," she said softly. "You know that I care." She turned and stared searchingly into his eyes. "You know that I'm afraid of your work. You're afraid of what it can do to two lives—you've warned me not to care too deeply. Nothing has changed. This—" She hesitated. "This will end. But I want you here with me, for as long as possible. I'll never regret this time. I—"

She wanted to be open and honest. But she couldn't tell him that she had fallen in love with him. She knew that he cared about her, but love was another story altogether. And because she loved him, she would let him go. What she had said was true. She was afraid of losing him...but he had set his priorities long ago.

His fingers curled tensely around hers. "What were you going to say?"

She shook her head, looking down at Baby again. Fortunately, she was spared when the door opened loudly.

Eric had come out. "Hey, Brad, aren't you supposed to call in at noon? We've just got time to make it in to the garage."

Brad was still studying Wendy. "Yeah," he said with a soft sigh. "I guess we'd better go."

Before he could slip into the house for a shirt and shoes, Wendy caught his hand. "Brad?"

"What?"

"I take it that you and Eric were the 'hillbillies' sitting out there fishing and watching that shack that Suarez was talking about last night?"

He hesitated. "Yes."

"Is that what you're planning to do today?"

"Wendy, it's my job. Charlie Jenkins will probably come back to the shack. He's my link to Michaelson." He ruffled her hair, then reached down to take her hands. "Come on."

"Come on?" She raised her eyes to his.

He exhaled again in a soft sigh. "Wendy, I can't leave you here alone."

"It's broad daylight. I know how to use a shotgun. And Baby is with me. People don't argue with her."

"Baby is a big cat, but Michaelson moves around with big guns. He's been known to carry M-16s. I want you to come with us."

She opened her mouth to protest.

"Please!" Brad said before she could say anything more.

"All right." Wearily, she rose with him. The sun cast a golden sheen along the ripples of his shoulders. She didn't want to argue with him, and she didn't want to dread the future. She wanted to run her fingers and her tongue over that sleek bronze flesh and feel him come alive to her touch.

She couldn't do that. Not now—not ever.

She was losing him. She felt it. Some force beyond their control was tightening its grasp around them, surrounding them like a writhing python. They had discovered something, and now they were losing it, before they could ever hold it tightly and give it a name.

"Brad?"

He paused.

Placing her palms against his chest, she rose onto her toes. She kissed his lips softly, then slid to her feet against him.

"What was that for?"

"I just needed it," she told him.

He gave her a quick hug. "I needed it, too. I needed it, too."

They headed for the house together. As Brad went into the bedroom to dress, Wendy called to him that he really should be wearing boots.

"Where are they?"

"In the closet."

Five minutes later, he still hadn't found the boots. Wendy came into the bedroom and began searching through the cluttered closet. When she glanced up at Brad, he was sifting through the collection of Leif's clothing that still hung in the closet.

He shook his head, looking down at her. "Wendy, you've got to get rid of these things, really."

She nodded, finally locating the box with the boots in them. "You should be glad that I kept this stuff," she said, handing him the boots. "I don't think that my jeans would have fit you."

He smiled at her, leaned down and brushed her cheek with his knuckles. "Very cute, smarty-pants. But seriously, I hope you don't plan on stripping every stranger who crash-lands on your doorstep."

"What an interesting possibility to explore," she said sweetly.

He pulled her to her feet and kissed her. She let out a surprised cry as his palm circled around her rump. "Not amusing, Wendy," he told her. "Now, behave."

"I was behaving!"

He sat at the foot of the bed and pulled on the boots. They were a little tight, but the rugged leather would provide necessary protection in the swamp. Brad gazed at her curiously. "Want to suggest a shirt?"

She turned around without a flicker of emotion and pulled out a red plaid. It still hurt, she thought. Even discovering that she was in love again could not completely release the past. She'd never been able to get rid of Leif's things; it had seemed so cold, so final. She couldn't throw away Leif's clothes any more than she could throw away his memory.

But Brad was right, she knew. She shouldn't throw things away, she should give them away to someone who needed them. That would be the best way to remember her husband.

Brad took the shirt from her and slipped it over his shoulders. "Thank you." She nodded while he buttoned up and slipped the shirttails into his jeans.

She lowered her eyes, trying to ignore the tight knot of fear in her throat. It was as if a noose were tightening around them. Something was going to happen. She was going to lose Brad—she could feel it in her blood. Then her life would be empty again, and it would be just as if this had never happened between them. No, Grandfather had told her that she would be richer for it.

She hoped that she could feel that way when he was actually gone.

Impetuously, she went up on her toes, and she kissed him again, tasting him, inhaling him. She did want to hang on to him, she didn't want to let him return to his real world.

It was wrong.

She broke away, turning around, reaching for the door. "You've got to call your boss, remember?"

"Yeah, I remember."

Half an hour later, they were back at the garage.

Brad went inside to call Purdy. Eric lingered beside the gas pumps, talking to Mac. Wendy hovered near the airboat, afraid that she wouldn't make much of a conversationalist that day.

The air was hot and sticky. Listening to the endless drone of a horde of mosquitoes, she absently lifted her hair from the back of her neck. She could see Brad through the glass enclosure. He looked so serious, almost like a stranger. She bit her lower lip. He was serious—very serious about his work. Unlike the man she loved, this Brad frightened her. He meant business.

She turned away, clenching and unclenching her fingers as she idly walked along the canal. She was so nervous that she didn't realize how far she had wandered. Nor did she notice the car that crept along the road, or the canoe that moved silently behind her, coming closer and closer.

She was so involved with her thoughts that she didn't begin to sense danger until it was almost upon her. And then, it was too late.

Behind her, a shadow loomed against the sun. Absently noticing the darkness, Wendy turned, frowning.

Two men stood before her. The first was tall and lean, with watery blue eyes and steel-gray hair. The second man was younger. He was huskily built, brawny. His eyes were brown, but they had the same chill glaze of ruthlessness.

Every nerve tensed as she sensed danger, cold, sharp, lethal. She opened her mouth to scream, but she was never able to issue a useful sound.

The brown-eyed man caught her by the neck and stuffed a cloth into her mouth. She thought she would choke to death, but she couldn't even cough properly, he held his hand so tightly against her. Desperate, she tried to lash out, but the smell of the cloth, sickeningly sweet, assailed her. She started to grow dizzy. The sun, the man, the sky, the world...everything swirled before her.

Dimly, she realized how foolish she had been. She had followed the canal around a curve. Eric wasn't really so far away, but he was talking to Mac beyond the rise of the grass. He couldn't see her, and she couldn't scream, so he couldn't hear her.

Her world was dimming so rapidly. She tried to struggle. She tried to free herself from that restricting hand, but it was like a steel band. The man's fingers bit into her flesh as he held her tighter and tighter. Barely, just barely, she managed to free her right arm and drag her curving fingers against his cheek.

He swore softly as her nails caught his face, drawing blood. He secured her hand again and hissed out a warning to her.

But he didn't lift the soaked rag from her face. The sticky sweetness created a buzz around her. Wendy never felt the cuff he gave her across the cheek. By the time he struck her, she was already falling. The world was spinning to blackness.

She was unconscious when he hoisted her into his arms and silently turned to follow the other man through the tall grasses to the waiting airboat.

Brad thoughtfully hung up the phone. It was basically over—if not the case, then at least his strange idyll out here. He was going to spend the day prowling through the swamp keeping an eye out for Jenkins or Michaelson. By tonight, he'd have a number of reinforcements out here: a few men to keep an eye on the shack, and more men to spread out, to wait for the drop that was scheduled. They didn't have Michaelson yet, but he wouldn't be looking for the man alone anymore. The noose was being tightened— and all they had to do was hope that they didn't scare their quarry away.

Purdy was determined to see Michaelson locked up. He was banking on Brad's eyewitness testimony against the man. And if they played it right, they could catch him red-handed with the drugs coming in from South America. The big machinery was moving. Brad realized that he was just a small part of it now, and he didn't know whether to feel relieved or deeply bereft.

Things wouldn't be the same. He wouldn't have a chance to be alone with Wendy again. Not as a pair of castaways in a strange paradise, isolated from the world. Today he would have to accept Eric's help, and he didn't want Wendy along with them. It was too dangerous. He had never known that Suarez had been watching him and Eric in the airboat the other day. Even if Suarez hadn't been able to come close enough to recognize him, he had seen Brad and Eric. To Brad, that was unnerving. He decided that Wendy should spend the day in the village with Willie and Mary. She should be safe with the family. Brad was certain that Willie knew how to protect his loved ones.

It was almost over. The realization hurt so much that he could hardly stand it. Hell, he'd known he had no right touching a woman like Wendy. They'd both said that they could take what came. They had both claimed to be adult, mature—willing to accept an affair for the time that they had together.

She had warned him not to care too deeply, just as he had warned her. And now here they were, at the end of it all....

And he felt like doubling over with pain, it hurt so damned much. Pain chewed at the walls of his stomach—and his heart.

She cared for him. He knew that. But he also knew that she didn't want a life with a man who lived in danger. She definitely didn't want a life with him. So that was that. There was a real world, and he had to return to it. He had a job, and he'd always known that it wasn't a job that was conducive to...

Marriage.

He wanted to marry her. He wanted her beside him when he woke up in the morning. She was a radiant angel, and he knew that she would be every bit as beautiful to him in fifty years. He wanted her all to himself for a while, and then he wanted to have that baby with her that she had once wanted and could surely want again.

But he had no right. His job was a necessary one, and he was good at it. He had no right to want her to suffer for him.

Maybe he owed them both the honesty of the depths of his feelings. She had told him this morning that nothing had changed in their life-styles. But the feelings between them had grown. She might have denied them a future with her words, but her kiss had said otherwise.

When he saw Eric smiling at him through the glass, Brad realized that he had been standing at the door for several long minutes.

This was idiotic. The idyll might be over, but Michaelson was still out there. And he had to be caught.

Swallowing hard, Brad impatiently turned to leave the office. Eric excused himself to Mac and came over to Brad, looking at him expectantly.

"There'll be some backup here tonight. We're still going to lie low, because we want to catch Michaelson with the goods. I want to keep my eyes open for Charlie Jenkins today—then I need to meet some men here tonight. They're sending a few to keep an eye on the shack, and—" He paused. "And a few to keep an eye on Wendy's place. Purdy agreed that we've put her into the path of danger. She needs some solid protection until this is really over." Brad didn't have to admit that he was too emotionally involved to be effective himself. Though he and Eric were a good pair, they'd be better off with some objective help around. "Would you mind taking a ride back out by the shack?"

Eric shook his head. "Not at all. What about Wendy? I take it you don't want her home alone, and I don't think she should be along with us."

"I thought we'd take her to Willie's." He grimaced. "She's not going to like it, but..." His voice trailed away and he shrugged. "We might as well get going."

Eric nodded, turning to look toward the canal. Suddenly, a frown compressed his features in hard lines. "I don't see her."

Brad's entire body seemed to constrict as he stared across the gas pumps toward the road. A car whooshed by, moving fast. He turned toward the canal. He had just seen her. He had been looking out the window while he had been talking to Purdy, and he had seen her standing there. Her hair had been loose on her shoulders, catching the sunshine. Her hands had been jammed into her pockets, her boot heels dug impatiently into the ground as she waited. She had been there, just moments ago.

He and Eric started to run at the same time. They reached the canal and the high grass together, sloshing their way into the water. His heart in his throat, Brad prayed that he would not find her. There'd be a bullet in her heart if Michaelson had found her. She'd be facedown in the swamp if she'd met with a cottonmouth or a diamondback. No, no, Wendy was too smart and too savvy to panic at a snakebite. She would have called for help. She would have known what she was doing. It had to have been Michaelson....

They didn't find her in the water. Brad tried to breathe, he told himself that he had to breathe. As Eric stared at him with his curious lime-green eyes, Brad noticed that behind the stonelike mask of the bronzed warrior, Eric was fighting a raw, clawing fear himself.

"Look at the road."

Brad did so. He saw where her boots had been dragged against the earth; he saw the scuffle of footprints.

"Michaelson," he swore in anguish.

"I don't think that he's killed her," Eric said tonelessly.

Brad shook his head, trying to clear it. "No, he wants her for something. Or else he would have—he would have killed her, quiet and quick, right here." He stared at Eric for a moment, then plunged through the shallow rim of grass and muck to the airboat. He looked about hastily, until he saw what he wanted. A stone held a note to the flooring by the motor. Brad tried to read the words, blinked furiously and made sense of the letters at last. He nodded at Eric.

"He's taken her to the shack."

"And he wants you to come?"

Brad nodded. "Both of us. Precisely—'bring the Indian along.' No one else, or he'll slit her throat."

"Why me?" Eric murmured.

Brad thought he understood. "I just got word that his plane came in—crashed in the swamp. Purdy thinks that it's out there buried in the muck somewhere, and Charlie Jenkins, the boy from the Okefenokee in Georgia, just isn't good enough in this maze. I'll wager that Michaelson wants you to find his stuff."

"And you?"

"He wants to kill me. I'm just a case of revenge."

Eric frowned. "And Wendy?"

"He'll keep her alive long enough to make you do what he wants." He paused, breathing deeply. "Hell, who knows. He—he might want more." He swore softly again.

Eric lowered his head, his fingers winding into impotent fists at his sides.

Brad realized that he was praying when he needed to be thinking—or maybe he needed to be doing both things. He braced himself and got a grip on his emotions.

"I'm calling Purdy back. He should know that Michaelson has Wendy. Maybe there's something he can do to help. Then we've got to get out to the shack. Is there any way to come around on that cabin from a different direction?"

"Go call. Let me try to see the terrain in my mind."

Brad hurried in to call Purdy. The boss was going to put his machinery into action sooner.

After he'd hung up, Brad gritted his teeth and explained the situation to Mac. Then he hurried down to the airboat to join Eric. The plan was risky, but it was their only chance. Otherwise, they were surely dead.

This way they had a chance. The odds were bad. Very bad.

But then, they were the only odds they had.

Brad leaped onto the airboat. Eric was already starting up the motor.

"I think we can approach from the back," he said. "I'll cut the motor and we'll paddle around the rear of the hammock. We'll have to wade through muck, and there might be quicksand. But we can come up around the back of the shack."

Brad closed his eyes and breathed a prayer of thanks. The odds were beginning to look a little bit better.

"Let's try it," he said. Eric nodded. They were tense and silent then as they wound their way back into the primitive depths of the swamp.

Wendy woke with a foul taste in her mouth, a taste similar to the sickening smell that had brought her to unconsciousness. She had a horrible headache and the world was still spinning so rapidly that she didn't know if she was sitting, standing or lying flat. Her arms ached, but not as badly as her head. For several long minutes, she was aware only of pain.

She opened her eyes and closed them again. She fought a wave of nausea and swallowed hard. Then she tried to open her eyes again.

She was able to focus this time. Above her were the boards of a bare and rotting roof. She was lying flat. Her arms hurt because her wrists were tied tightly together with rough rope. Her flesh was chapping and her shoulders were being wrenched by the miserable position.

"He's taking his sweet time."

At the sound of the voice, Wendy closed her eyes again. As heavy footsteps moved by her head, she slit her eyes open, feigning unconsciousness.

It was the man with the brutal hold, walking by her. The man with the brown eyes who had nabbed her and shoved the chloroform over her face.

"He'll come, Jenkins. Trust me. He'll come."

Another voice, very soft and somehow more menacing for it, answered. Wendy tried to let her head fall naturally to the side so that she could see the man.

It was the gray-haired man with the ice eyes. She didn't need to be told that this was Michaelson. Sitting at a crude table in the center of the small shack, he seemed entirely out of place. She could see that his shoes were expensive leather loafers. His suit looked to be fashionable linen. In the midst of the swamp, he was wearing a tie. He had spoken calmly, but he obviously didn't feel comfortable here.

"He'll come, yeah, but what about the Indian? What's the connection there?"

A third man spoke, a man with a definite accent. Wendy tried to survey the small cabin. She didn't dare open her eyes fully, and even the slightest movement was painful and difficult. It was the typical cabin of the weekend hunter, hastily built by non-professional labor. There were two windows, a bunk in one corner of the room, and a table in the center. A dark man, cradling some type of huge firearm, sat on one of the windowsills, dangling his legs. The brown-eyed man, Jenkins, kept pacing by Wendy's head. At least he was better dressed for the occasion, wearing military khakis. A rifle was slung over his shoulder.

She clenched her teeth, afraid that she was going to start shivering. These men meant to kill her, to kill them all. For a moment the horror of it was so great that a wave of icy fear washed over her, paralyzing her. She nearly screamed in sheer panic.

She fought it, clenching her teeth more tightly. She was a victim, just as Leif had been. But Leif had fought to the bitter end, and, dear God, she would fight, too. They were trying to trap Brad, but she was sure that he would realize that. And they were talking about Eric, too....

"We need the Indian," Jenkins said.

Michaelson let out a snort of derision. "Yes, we need the Indian. Because you have proved yourself worthless!"

Jenkins lunged over the table and slammed his fist against it. "You fool! Don't you understand! I'm good at tracking, damned good. You wouldn't have the girl if it wasn't for me. I'm the one who followed Suarez's trail to her house. I'm the one who knew about the girl, about McKenna's involvement with her—and even the damned Indian you want so badly now. But listen to me, and listen good. This mire out here is deadly, can't you comprehend that? Your plane went down in the middle of an area that's infested with snakes, and riddled with quicksand pits. Only a man who really knows this swamp can salvage the damned thing."

Michaelson rose, his face rigid. He continued to speak softly. "Don't ever address me in that tone of voice, Jenkins. Ever." He strode over to the window and looked out. "If the Indian doesn't come, we'll have to rely on the girl." Wendy felt his gaze fall her way. "She lives out here. She'll know what she is doing."

The dark-haired man with the accent let out a snickering sound. "I'm sure she knows what she is doing. I'm sure she does it very well."

"Shut up, Pedro," Michaelson said. "Keep your mind on business and off the girl. When the plane is found, you can have her. Hell, you can have her any way you want her. But not until then, do you understand?"

"*Sí!*" Pedro agreed sullenly.

Wendy felt the bile rise in her stomach again. She swallowed, fighting off another rise of panic.

"Hey!" Jenkins said suddenly. The sound of his footsteps seemed to slam against Wendy's head, and then she did scream because he wrenched at her shoulders, dragging her up. "She's awake. The little bitch is awake. She's been listening to us."

He jerked her to a sitting position and she nearly screamed again from the pain in her arms. Her eyes flew open, meeting his stare with a gaze of silvery fury. He laughed, watching her. "Pedro must be right. I'll bet she's a lot of fun."

"Leave her alone," Michaelson said. "There's work to do."

"Hell, we've got to sit here and wait..." Jenkins said. He smiled. His face was so close to Wendy's that she could feel the foulness of his breath.

She spat at him and he howled in outrage, slapping her.

"I told you, leave the girl alone!" Michaelson's voice rose at last. He indicated the window. "You think that McKenna is a fool? I don't. I don't want him attacking us while you lie there with your pants down, you fool! Now, get away from her."

Jenkins shoved Wendy back down to the floor and wiped the spittle from his face. "Later, baby. I'll make it good. I promise."

"What's that?" the Latin man said suddenly.

Michaelson and Jenkins both moved toward the window.

Wendy heard a birdcall—soft and low, but clear and beautiful, slicing cleanly through the air.

"It's McKenna!" Jenkins said, startled. "It's McKenna, walking straight toward us."

Wendy tried to rise. She sat up, wincing against the hold of the rope on her wrists. Her heart began to leap and slam—and sink. What was he doing? Tears stung her eyes. He was coming for her! Well, of course he would. It was his job. Even if he had barely known her, he would have come for her. It was what he did for a living.

But he shouldn't have. Not that way. He shouldn't have just come to give up his life for hers. Didn't he know…?

"He's alone," Jenkins said harshly. "He took the damned airboat and came out here alone. We don't need him! We need the damned Indian."

Michaelson looked pensively at Wendy.

"We've still got the girl."

She forced herself to stare straight at him, trying to look calm. She had to stop panicking.

Brad was no fool. Nor was he alone. She had to proceed carefully.

Michaelson turned back to the window.

"When he comes close enough, shoot him," he told Jenkins.

"No!" Wendy screamed.

"Shoot him in the kneecap. Make it painful, make it slow. Make him see what happens to spies in my camp."

"No!" Wendy staggered to her feet. "No! So help me, you touch him, and I'll never help you find a thing. Your dope can rot out there with your pilot—"

"I can make her docile," Pedro interrupted. He glanced out the window, then sauntered toward Wendy and picked up a handful of her hair. "I can make her scream and cry and take you any damned place you want to go, boss."

Wendy jerked her head back, staring at the man defiantly. "Can you? You'll have to kill me first, and you won't get anywhere at all if I'm dead, too, will you?"

"Get away from the girl!" Michaelson ordered. "Leave her the hell alone until I say! Jenkins, you, too, ass!" Jenkins had turned to watch the Latin man. Michaelson scowled at them both, then turned to look out the window again. "Where is he?"

"What?" Jenkins demanded.

Michaelson seemed to explode. "He isn't there any more! McKenna has disappeared. Where the hell is he? I can't see him anymore!"

"He has to be out there!" Jenkins insisted.

"Yes, he's out there," Michaelson said. "He's out there, but it's a trick! It's some kind of a trick!"

There was silence as they all stared out the window. Then Michaelson cursed them all. Swerving around, he pulled an automatic from his breast pocket. Long strides brought him to Wendy.

He wrenched her in front of him, shoving the smooth steel of the gun against her cheek. "Let's go, sweetheart. I want McKenna dead almost as much as those jerks want you alive. The same kind of pleasure, you know, the same kind of high."

She tasted the steel. A small cry of pain escaped her as he prodded her with the gun. He threw open the door and pushed her out into the sunlight.

"McKenna! Show yourself." The nose of the gun pressed against Wendy's jaw. "Show yourself. Or else your girlfriend loses her face. You've got ten seconds. I'm counting. Do you hear me, McKenna? I'm counting."

Wendy winced, afraid to swallow. She heard the gun cock. She felt it, icy cold and hard against her skin. She closed her eyes, afraid to imagine the explosion of the flesh.

"I'm counting, McKenna. I'm counting!" Michaelson repeated in fury. "You've got until ten. One, McKenna. Two. Three, McKenna. Four. Five. Six..."

CHAPTER 13

"Stop!"

The metallic nose of the gun relaxed against Wendy's face at the cry. But it wasn't Brad who appeared this time; it was Eric.

He eased out from the tangle of foliage on the hammock and started walking toward them with long strides.

"I want McKenna, boy!" Michaelson called out. "You and your little girlfriend here can give us a few directions, and then go on your way. But I want McKenna. I have a score to settle with him."

Wendy thought that she would lose her mind with fear. Michaelson was still holding a gun on her, Eric could be shot and killed any second, and Brad had disappeared somewhere.

"McKenna took off on me, the stinking coward." Eric spit into the grass. "He's hiding here somewhere. Give me a chance—I can catch him."

Wendy winced as Michaelson raised the nose of the gun to her temple. "You'd better not be bluffing, boy."

"He's got to be back here. Help me. We'll get him."

Wendy sensed Michaelson's hesitation. Then he lowered the gun and aimed it against her spine. "Walk, girl. Walk straight toward your Indian friend." He turned back to the house. "Jenkins! Pedro! Come on—now!"

He pushed Wendy forward. She started walking. As she moved ahead the grass was growing thicker and the ground was beginning to give way. The shack stood on the high part of the hammock. This was treacherous ground below. Her boots sank in the mud.

As she came closer and closer to Eric, she stared into his eyes. Green and steady, they gave nothing away.

Where the hell was Brad? she wondered.

Michaelson was wondering the same thing. "This better not be a trap, Injun boy. If you make one false move, she's dead. I'll kill her slow. I'll crack her spine and shatter her tailbone."

Wendy shivered. She could still feel the cold steel barrel of the gun.

"No trap, I swear it," Eric reassured. "That slime just lit out of here. He was willing to let Wendy get killed in his place. If I find him, I want him. I know how to make people die slowly, too."

Michaelson grunted. Wendy stared at Eric, praying for courage.

The muck was growing deeper. Leif had taught her to avoid terrain like this. Too easily, the muck became quicksand. They shouldn't be walking here. Any step could be a false step.

"Come on, Wendy!" Eric called to her. "We've got to find that bastard! He split and ran out on us!"

"Eric...?"

She looked at him, begging for an answer. Ignoring her fear, he led her farther away.

Michaelson shoved her in the back with the gun. "You heard him! Move. I want that G-man dead."

"Move, Wendy!" Eric persisted. She kept coming.

Then she realized that there were no sounds coming from behind them. Michaelson had ordered Jenkins and Pedro to come along behind him. They hadn't done so.

Michaelson muttered something. As Wendy felt the suck and pull against her boots, she remembered that Michaelson was wearing fancy leather loafers.

Struggling to lift her foot, she took another step. She stumbled, barely recovering before falling forward. She tried to pull her foot up again, but the suction was too strong. She sank deeper.

Michaelson crashed into her and his gun slipped from his fingers. Beneath them, the ground gurgled. Wendy looked down, watching as Michaelson's weapon was swallowed into the muck.

He began to swear again. Even as the words came out of his mouth, the muck rose around them.

It wasn't rising, Wendy thought hysterically. They were sinking together.

"Bastard!" Michaelson screamed out. Wendy realized that he was screaming at Eric, who continued to stare at him.

The ground held on to them, tightly. Wendy realized that she'd sunk up to her thighs in the grasping muck. A scream rose in her throat.

Just as she cried out, a terrible sound of agony exploded on the air. Michaelson twisted. Wendy realized that the bellow came from behind them, from the cabin.

Michaelson wrapped his arms around her tightly. "She goes down with me! Bastards! She goes down with me!"

Wendy cried out in pain and panic. His arms were choking her. He was bearing her down, down deeper and deeper into the relentless hold of the earth. He no longer held the gun, but he held her. And there was no escape.

She cast back her head and screamed.

Inside the cabin, Brad heard Wendy's scream.

So far, things had gone like clockwork, smooth as ice. He and Eric had carefully pondered the plan, and though it hadn't been foolproof, it had been the best they could do.

But it had gone well. He had managed to walk straight toward the cabin, then disappear flat against a side wall. If Michaelson, Jenkins or Pedro had looked around, he would have been finished before he had ever begun.

But they hadn't.

And Michaelson's temper had snapped, just as Brad had gambled that it would. Michaelson had dragged Wendy out. Then it had been hard to concentrate. Brad had reminded himself that their lives depended on his action during the next few minutes. Pressed flat against the cabin, he told himself that he was trained for this, that he needed to be cool and calculating.

It was probably the hardest thing he would ever do.

Watching Michaelson slam the gun against Wendy's cheek, he'd turned and darted around the building, entering the cabin the very way that Michaelson had just exited it.

Pedro and Jenkins had been standing at the window, staring out.

Jenkins hadn't realized that Brad was in the cabin until he'd already knocked Pedro out with the rifle butt.

Jenkins was good with terrain, but he was too heavy to be a good fighter. He couldn't move quickly enough. Brad grimly took him with a knee jab to his gut and a swing of the rifle butt against his chin.

Pedro would be out for a long, long time. Although Brad was pretty sure that Jenkins had a broken jaw, he used his belt to tie up the man's arms. Jenkins was dangerous, more dangerous when he was wounded. Just like an animal. Hell, they were animals.

Brad was just finishing with Jenkins when he heard Wendy's scream.

His heart soaring to his throat, he burst out of the cabin and raced around the side.

He could see Eric running. He was a burst of speed, racing toward the quicksand pool.

And Brad saw why.

Wendy had played it like a trouper. Eric had worried that she would sense the quicksand and panic. But she had played the stoic and kept walking. Michaelson had become disarmed, which was even better than they had hoped. They had figured they would have to bargain for the gun.

But now they were going to have to bargain for Wendy's life.

Michaelson had her in as tight a grasp as the sucking earth. He was moving frantically, and with each movement, the two of them were sinking deeper.

"Let her go!" Brad hardly recognized his own voice, nor could he feel his feet against the ground. "Let her go!" he screamed again. He needed to be logical; he needed to talk, to tell Michaelson to calm down, to stay still. "Let her go!" he thundered out the command again.

Eric had already reached the black pool. He laid his body flat, reaching for Wendy's hands.

Brad thrashed into the mud. Instantly, he felt the pull of the muck, slithering over him, grabbing on to him. It was like an evil, living creature.

He ignored it. Wendy was before him, but Michaelson's arms were around her neck. The muck was up to her breasts.

"Brad!" she whispered his name. She was white as ash, filthy and trembling. Michaelson's hands were around her throat, bearing down on her. And still her eyes were beautifully silver. She was slipping away from the world, and still, her eyes were telling Brad that she loved him.

He let out a yell, a sound that he'd never heard before. It was a cry of the wild, as harsh and merciless as the land.

He caught on to Michaelson's hands, wrenching them from their choking hold on Wendy.

Michaelson wasn't beat. "Bastard!" he hissed at Brad. "Fed bastard, you'll go down with me."

Brad got off one good punch. Michaelson staggered in the muck, trying to aim back at him. Brad turned to shove Wendy toward Eric. She was slipping farther and farther. The pool of black mud was rising to her chin. "Give me your hand!" he called to her, reaching into the endless blackness. His fingers curled around hers. He screamed out a curse and a prayer. With a horrible sound, the muck relinquished Wendy's hand.

Eric reached her; Brad was afraid that he would not be able to hold her, that the muck would be too slick and slippery.

Eric's fingers were a vise around Wendy's wrists. He had her.

Just in time. With peripheral vision, Brad saw Michaelson locking his fists to pound them down on him. He leaned to the side and Michaelson's blow just grazed him. Brad was sinking deeper, he realized. The muck really did seem to be alive. Like a breathing, black demon, it swarmed over his body, caressing his flesh with a sure promise of death.

"You're going with me, cop," Michaelson said. He started to laugh. Brad decided that the man was insane, but then, anyone who had ice in his veins instead of blood, the way Michaelson did, could not be completely sane.

"I'm not a cop," Brad said. "I'm DEA." Unfortunately, Brad realized, it was a moot point under these circumstances.

"Brad!" Wendy screamed his name. Twisting around, he could see that Eric had pulled her free. She was covered in the black muck, but she was free.

And he was nearly up to his throat.

"Brad! Take my hand!" Wendy cried. Those beautiful silver eyes of hers were on him. Her hair was covered in muck, but her eyes were pure.

"No, Wendy—"

"Take her hand!" Eric yelled. Brad realized the grip that Eric had around Wendy's legs. His heart pounded. *No,* he thought. *Wendy, go. Wendy, you're safe. Run out of here, I dragged you into this.*

"Brad!" she screeched.

"Dammit! I know what I'm doing!" Eric said.

Brad realized that he was suddenly exhausted. He could barely lift his arms. It required a supreme effort to move.

"Brad!"

Her cry gave him strength. He reached out, and her fingers curled around him. He could feel the tremendous effort that she and Eric put forth. He closed his eyes. He was the rope in a tug-of-war. The earth wanted him.

Then it began to give. Staring at Wendy's mud-covered fingers on his arms, he realized slowly that they were overcoming the pull of the muck. He was easing out of it.

There was a long, mournful sound. The muck seemed to cry out.

Then it bubbled and gurgled, and suddenly, he was free.

He landed on top of Wendy and Eric. Although they were all covered in mud, they began to laugh.

"Bastard! You lousy bas—"

Michaelson never finished the last word. His head disappeared with a sickening whoosh of suction.

It was almost me, Brad thought. It had almost been Wendy.

"Oh, God!" Wendy whispered.

He kissed her. She tasted like mud. When he released her, she was still laughing.

Then his spine tingled with awareness. A strange shadow had fallen over them.

Wendy's eyes widened as she felt the sudden constriction in Brad's muscles. She looked up and saw a stranger staring down at the three of them. Tall and lean with silver hair, he was a striking man. His eyes were blue, and they looked as if they could be hard. But there was warmth in them now—warmth and amusement.

"Purdy!" Brad said, astonished. "Sir!"

L. Davis Purdy stared down at the three of them, his hands on his hips. "McKenna, I run my ass ragged, I drag that distinguished older gentleman—" he paused, backing away slightly. Wendy saw that Willie was just behind him "—around the swamp, and what do I find? You—mud wrestling with his granddaughter."

"McKenna, you do get the hard assignments." A younger man stood at Purdy's side. He was shorter than Purdy, but lean and rip-cord hard. He had red hair and freckles, and he grinned at Brad and winked at Wendy.

"Gary," Brad said.

"What is this?" Eric demanded.

"Eric, Wendy—meet Mr. L. Davis Purdy. And Gary Henshaw."

Wendy automatically reached out a hand, then realized that she was covered in mud and still lying on the ground.

Purdy laughed, clutched her hand and helped her to her feet. "Mrs. Hawk, it's a pleasure to meet you. And Eric." Eric jumped to his feet by his own power then. Wendy offered Purdy a wavery smile, then she turned and ran to Willie, who hugged her fiercely.

"How did you get here?" Brad began, then he gazed at Willie, and the old Indian nodded to him gravely.

"Your friend from the garage, Mac, got us out to Mrs. Hawk's home, where we found the senior Mr. Hawk. He brought us out here." Purdy's pleasant smile faded for a moment. He inclined his head toward the quicksand pool. "Michaelson?"

Brad nodded to his boss.

"Maybe it's just as well," Purdy murmured. Then a smile curved the corners of his mouth. "You are a mess."

"Yeah? Well, where were you when we were becoming a mess?"

Gary laughed. "We checked out the shack. It looks like Pedro is waking up, but I don't think he's going anywhere."

"Oh?" Brad said.

"There was this great big cat standing over him. I was ready to shoot the thing, but Mr. Hawk assured me that the panther was a trusted and loyal pet."

"Baby!" Brad said.

"Honestly." Purdy looked at Gary and shook his head. "Leave the boy alone in the woods for a week, and he goes right to hell. Mud wrestling. And he thinks a hundred-and-fifty-pound panther is a pussycat. Hell. What's this man coming to?"

Brad glanced at Eric, and both men laughed. Purdy started walking back toward the shack. "We've got a few things to pick up at the shack. McKenna, you need a bath. Let's get moving here, shall we?"

He wasn't going to get any time alone with Wendy, Brad saw that quickly. From that moment on, they weren't even together.

Purdy ordered Gary to stay with the Hawks and help them in any way possible. He wanted Wendy and Eric to come back with them for statements, but he intended to let them go home first to bathe and change.

He wanted Brad to come with him immediately. It seemed there would be an informal interrogation with Charlie Jenkins and Pedro.

Before they parted, Brad noticed Wendy watching him. He saw the silver light in her eyes, glistening like tears, a shadow of sadness.

His heart plummeted and hammered. She considered it over, he realized. Right then and there, it was over.

He wanted to scream out her name, to push everyone aside and race to her. If he could hold her tightly enough, he could tell her that they were stronger than life's obstacles, that they could make it together.

He never had the chance to say a word. She stared at him a final second, and then she turned away.

"Brad, let's go," Purdy admonished him impatiently.

From then on, the day became a blur of rapid-fire activity. Purdy conducted questioning in the shack. Neither Pedro nor Jenkins put up much of a fight. Purdy wanted to know about the plane, and they were willing to answer questions, not that they could provide much help. Michaelson knew that the small cargo plane carrying his shipment had crashed somewhere in the vast swampland almost two days ago. They assumed the pilot was dead—there'd been no radio contact. Jenkins drew pictures on the ground, showing them where he thought the plane was. Then he begged for a doctor to set his jaw.

Purdy nodded to one of his men, a medic. The young man came over to Jenkins, gave him a pain pill and wrapped his jaw tightly. "There will be a chopper out here soon to rush you down to Jackson," Purdy assured Jenkins.

Purdy had barely spoken before the helicopter could be heard hovering above them. Since it couldn't land in the swamp, Jenkins was sent up first in a basket rigging, then Pedro followed. Brad stood on the ground and watched them go, rising into the sky. They would both heal. They would probably get stiff prison terms. Along with whatever else the D.A.'s office charged them with, kidnapping was sure to be a part of the prosecution.

Purdy set up a task force to search the swamp for the plane. He radioed in for air assistance, then he surveyed Brad from head to toe. Taking in the drying muck, he smiled.

"Well, it's over for you, McKenna."

Over, God, he hated that word. It couldn't be over. Even if she had turned away from him, it couldn't be over.

"Let's go back in," Purdy said. "I told you, you need a bath. Badly."

"Sir, I've come to know something about this place. I might be helpful in searching for the downed plane."

"Brad! It's over. You've done your job. And I need you back at the office to file reports and give your statements to the D.A. Let's move."

Brad exhaled and started walking. "I don't even have a lousy home to go to for a bath! My clothes are gone...my record collection is gone. I'm just damned grateful that I didn't have a German shepherd!"

Purdy slapped him on the back. "I rented an apartment for you—right on the water. The boys and I put together for a few outfits, and if I'm not mistaken, your insurance check is on the kitchen counter. But I need those statements and paperwork from you this week, so come on."

There wasn't anything wrong with the apartment Purdy had rented for him. And Purdy and Gary and some of the others had gone out and bought him some things, so he was able to take a shower and dress in a clean suit. There was even some stoneware in the cabinets, a few groceries and a kettle, so he was able to brew himself some instant coffee before heading into the office to start the endless paperwork.

There was nothing wrong with any of it. He had to admit that the apartment was even nicer than the one that Michaelson had blasted. The guys knew his taste fairly well, so the clothes were fine.

But the apartment seemed empty—empty as hell.

It wasn't his apartment that was lacking, it was his life.

He sat back on the sofa and closed his eyes. What would he be doing now, he wondered, if he had come back to his life exactly as it had been?

He'd have played one of his discs while he showered and dressed, for one. And what else? Well, he'd have gone back into the office, and when he was done, he'd have gone out with the guys to celebrate the fact that the job was done. It was over. They'd have gone to a nightclub on the beach for a few drinks.

And there might have been a woman. Someone career-minded, pretty, flashy. Someone out to have a good time, with no strings. They'd have liked each other, sure. They'd have had a good time. They might have made breakfast in the morning. They might even have remembered each other's names.

But Brad wasn't going out that night—not even for a few beers with the guys. He was going to file his paperwork, and he was going to try to see Wendy.

Unfortunately, his plan was thwarted. When Brad reached his office, he discovered that Wendy was being questioned by the district attorney. When he reached the D.A.'s office, he found out that Wendy had already gone.

Amazed, Brad asked Gary, "That's it? She's gone?"

"Oh, well, they may need to call her in again before the trial. The attorneys will want to talk to her again, I'm sure—"

"No, no. I mean, she left? Just like that? Did she—" He hesitated, his pride tripping him up. "Did she leave me a message?"

Gary shook his head. Brad stared at him a long moment.

When Brad was interviewed by the D.A., he answered every question in a tired monotone. When he was done, he headed back to his office, initiated the extensive paperwork, and later returned to his empty apartment.

He drank a beer, then drank another beer. He picked up the phone, and then he remembered that Wendy didn't have a phone.

She hadn't left him a message. She hadn't even said goodbye. Hell, they were worth more than that.

He had another beer. And another. Around 3:00 a.m. he finally fell asleep whispering her name. He didn't know if it was a curse or an anguished plea.

There was one nice thing about living alone, Wendy thought: privacy.

For two days, she'd been able to mope around the house. She'd been able to indulge in ridiculous crying sprees and talk out loud, cursing Brad and railing against him. She'd spent long, pensive hours staring at the blank television screen, reminding herself that she did not want him anyway.

She couldn't live with his job, and she knew that it would be wrong to ask him to change it. Even if she did, he would eventually resent her for it. It just couldn't work.

And the wretched man hadn't even come to see her when she had spent all those miserable hours with the D.A.! She'd answered a million questions then they'd somberly reminded her how much they would need her testimony to put away Jenkins and Pedro. The district attorney had seemed concerned over her volatile emotional state. She couldn't explain that her unbidden tears had nothing to do with the case—but with the DEA investigator. Fortunately, Eric had accompanied her. He had assured them all that Wendy was far stronger than she appeared.

And so she waited. For the first few days, she waited. She was convinced that he would come to her. She dreamed that she would wake up to find him there, standing in the doorway, dressed in old jeans. He would walk across the room, bend down to her and take her in his arms. In her dreams, their clothing would miraculously disappear, and she would feel the hot fire of his flesh next to hers.

But then she would wake up—alone. Or else it would be worse—Baby would be sprawled out on the bed, and she would growl and hiss in annoyance when Wendy threw her out.

Wendy returned to work at Eric's, but she couldn't concentrate on her work. She didn't know that she was absolutely worthless until Eric came in one afternoon, pulled the book she was reading out of her hand and turned it right side up.

Eric sat across from her, folding his fingers in contemplative fashion, studying her for several moments. "Why don't you go in to Lauderdale and see him?" he suggested at last.

She shook her head. "If he wanted to see me, he would come here."

"That seems logical to you. What if he's thinking the same thing? That you'd come see him if you wanted to?"

"I was there and he wasn't!"

"He probably had a million things to do, Wendy. Be reasonable. I'll tell you what. I've got a dinner date with some old friends on Las Olas next Friday night. I'll drop you by Brad's, and if you're unhappy there, you can just come and join me."

"No."

"Why not?"

"It's not right. I mean, what for, anyway? He likes his life the way that it is. I can't really be a part of it."

He grinned at her and leaned forward, taking her hands. "Wendy, people change. They fall in love, and their priorities change."

"Who says he's in love?" she whispered.

Eric shrugged. "I do. As Willie says, life is a river. To live it, you must follow your heart."

"I'll let you know," she told him softly.

By the time Friday rolled around, she had summoned up some courage. She had spent the day in a tub of bubble bath, washed her hair, given herself a manicure and a pedicure and laid out a silk cocktail dress.

At four in the afternoon, she was practically whitewashed. But her hair was still soaking wet and she was pacing around in a worn, floor-length terry robe, trying not to chew her nails while she thought it over.

She was confused about her purpose. What was she going to say? Can we hop into bed one more time, Brad, for old time's sake? Hi, Brad, I was in the neighborhood, so I just stopped over?

What if he had a woman there?

Her courage was beginning to fade when she heard the sound of a motor. She was surprised to see that it was Eric. They weren't due to leave for the evening until about seven, and he was supposed to be driving over. She opened the front door and saw her brother-in-law walking toward her with a packet of mail. "I picked this up at the post office," he said, handing her the mail. "And I just wanted to check on tonight. We still on?"

"I don't know, Eric—" Wendy began.

"I'll be back in a couple of hours." He waved to her and hurried away. She thought about calling him back to tell him that it was definitely off.

She didn't. Maybe she would just go to dinner with Eric and his friends. It might be good to get out.

Wandering into the bathroom, she examined her pale face and wet hair and decided that for a woman who had spent the entire day trying to look and smell delicious, she'd failed miserably.

Then she wandered back into the kitchen, idly leafing through the mail. She found the usual assortment of bills and junk mail, then her heart began to pound when she saw that one of the letters addressed to her was from Brad's office.

The bills fell to the floor as she ripped open the official-looking letter.

After she had opened it, she read it over and over. Then she felt as if she were a kettle, that heat was rising inside of her and she was fast approaching a boiling point.

It was a thank-you from the department. An official thank-you for her part in accommodating the agent.

It was meant from the heart, she was sure. But it was all so formal, so final.

"There are definite advantages to living alone!" she screamed in fury, throwing the letter down and stamping on it. Still, she didn't feel any better.

"That son of a bitch!" she swore, pacing up and down the hallway. She stormed into her bedroom, threw herself on her bed and slammed her fist against her pillow.

Then she realized, very slowly, that she wasn't alone. She swung around.

He was there, just as he had been in her dreams. Well, he was dressed in a blue business suit, but he was standing in the doorway, staring at her.

He looked good—damned good. He was handsome in navy. His white shirt was tailored and crisp, and he even had good taste in ties. His hair was combed back. His eyes appeared a little more haggard, his face a bit leaner.

But he was standing in front of her.

Automatically, her fingers moved to her wet hair. She'd planned this out so well! She'd meant to come to him in complete control, svelte and sophisticated, armed and armored against any vulnerability.

But he had come to her when she looked about as sophisticated as Tinkerbell. Her temper soared again. Wendy sprang to her knees, and then to her feet.

"You bastard!" she hissed.

"I—uh—I did knock. You didn't hear me."

"I didn't hear you?" She began to advance on him. "I let you in, I turn my home, my life, inside out. I get kidnapped by dope dealers. And do I get anything from you? Like maybe, goodbye, Wendy, thanks, it's been sweet? No!" She slammed both her fists against his chest. "No! I get a thank-you from the department for accommodating you!"

"Wendy—"

"I hate you! I absolutely despise you. You're a ruthless ingrate!" She took a swing at him. He ducked and caught her arms, imprisoning her against his body.

"Wendy—"

She struggled against him in a frenzy. "You weren't even there! I came into that office and I was a wonderful, model citizen, and you weren't even there!"

"Wendy—"

"You can go and rot in hell, Brad McKenna!"

He scooped her off the floor. Automatically, she looped her arms around his neck and stared into his eyes.

He started walking toward the bed. "I tried to see you," Brad said.

Her heart seemed aflame, her flesh seemed aflame. He was touching her, holding her again. He was walking straight toward the bed.

He laid her down. Gently tugging on the cord to her robe, he watched as it fell open. He caught his breath at the naked length of her. She saw the pulse start up against the bronze flesh at his throat. He laid his face against her and kissed her belly. She slipped her fingers into his hair.

"I was coming to see you tonight. I had it all planned out. I was going to wear silk. I was going to be beautiful."

"You are beautiful," he whispered huskily against her flesh. "Beautiful."

"You are a horrible, inconsiderate bastard, and I hate you," Wendy breathed. She could feel his lips, just grazing her skin.

He straightened and looked into her eyes. "Will you marry me, Wendy?"

Her eyes widened. "What?"

He loosened his tie. "I've thought about it. I know the way that you feel, but I think that we can come to some compromises. Life means much more to me now. I never knew how much it could mean until I found out what it was like to share. I love you, Wendy. I can't change what I am, my convictions, or the way that I feel, but I love you. I think that you love me, too. I've sat home these weeks staring at empty walls. I wanted you so badly. I thought that maybe you could forgive me for what I was. I thought that you would call me—"

"You didn't call me!" Wendy protested.

"You don't have a phone," Brad reminded her. "That's one thing that we're going to fix."

"What?" she said carefully. "We're going to live—here?"

"Well, it will take me at least an hour to get to work in the morning. But I figured that when I was working in Manhattan, my commute on the trains took me an hour, too. I'll still be with the DEA, but I'm through with the fieldwork. I want to come home at night—to come home here, to spend every night with you. We'll live here. With a phone."

"With a phone," Wendy repeated.

Brad's tie fell to the floor. His jacket, vest and shirt followed, but Wendy was still just staring at him, dumbfounded.

When he kicked off his shoes and trousers, she trembled and shuddered, alive with anticipation from head to toe. He stretched out over her and took her lips, kissing her slowly, savoring her lower lip, playing with her tongue. His left hand caressed the fullness of her curves, dallying over her breasts and between her legs. She was breathless when he pulled away from her, seeking her eyes. "Well?" he whispered.

"What?" Her mind wandered. What was he talking about? She returned his kiss so ardently and touched him with such fervor. He couldn't begin to think that she would deny him—not at this point.

Slow down, she warned herself. She smiled sweetly, trying to ignore the spiraling need inside of her. She drew her fingers down his chest and tightened them evocatively about the aroused shaft of his desire.

"Well? What's the verdict?" He kissed her lips, nuzzling his clean-shaven cheek against her throat. Then he met her eyes again. "Will you marry me?"

"Yes! Yes, I will!"

"Good." Brad smiled complacently. Then he lowered his weight upon her and thrust deeply inside of her. Deeper, and deeper, and then he held still. "I missed you so much," he whispered. "I can't leave you again. I really can't."

Wendy wound her arms around him. "I love you." She swallowed, savoring the feel of him. "I love you, and I don't think that I could ever let you go again."

Brad murmured something else, but she couldn't decipher his words. As he began to stroke her, hard and fast, the words just didn't matter anymore....

* * *

They were still lying there, drowsy and half-asleep—having made love several times to make up for lost time—when Wendy heard the motor of the airboat.

"Oh, dear!" She tried to leap up; some weight stopped her. Baby! The cat had come in when they had drifted off and made herself very comfortable, despite the two humans in the bed. "Baby, get off!"

"Out!" Brad commanded. Baby growled at him. He gave her a shove. "Off, I said!"

Baby obeyed. Wendy laughed, struggling back into her robe. "That's Eric," she told Brad. He arched a curious brow, lacing his fingers behind his head and stretching out comfortably. "Hey!" She shoved him. "You get up, too!"

He laughed and stepped into his trousers. "He's going to know exactly what we've been doing," Wendy wailed.

Brad laughed. "And what did he think he was bringing you into the city to do?"

"To go respectably out to dinner!" Wendy lied indignantly. Brad just laughed and walked into the living room. By the time Wendy belted her robe, she could hear the two men talking to one another. Guiltily straightening her tousled hair, she joined them. Brad swept her into the circle of his arm.

"He says that he'd be honored to be an usher at our wedding. He's sure that Willie will be delighted to give you away, and that maybe he'll break down and get a phone when we do, too."

Wendy burst out laughing. Eric laughed and kissed her.

"I told you, Wendy," he whispered, "we are all fated to follow our hearts." He gave her a squeeze. "Hey, have you got any champagne in here?"

Wendy did. It was warm, but they plopped a few ice cubes into it, and Eric toasted them.

Two months later, in the Church of the Little Flower, Willie did give her away. She wore a dress of soft gray, which highlighted the silver in her eyes.

Later, Brad told her that she was the most beautiful bride he had ever seen.

"Really?" she asked him. He had just been telling her how much he loved her gown, but that didn't seem to stop him from being overly anxious to remove it.

"Really."

"I'm so glad we were married."

"So am I," Brad said absently. There were a million little tiny hooks on the gown, and she wasn't helping him one bit.

"'Cause I think we're going to have a beautiful little newcomer," Wendy said demurely.

"That's nice," Brad murmured, annoyed by the maze of hooks on the damned dress.

Suddenly his fingers went still as he turned her toward him. "What?"

"Well, it could be a tawny-haired little visitor with golden eyes." Her voice trembled suddenly. "Do you mind?"

"Do I mind?" He could barely whisper. "I—I—no!"

He couldn't seem to find the proper words to tell her that he loved her, and that he was thrilled and awed by the prospect of a child—their child.

So he leaned over and kissed her, and showed her instead.

BORROWED ANGEL

CHAPTER 1

"There's nothing a woman needs.... Nothing...but the primitive earth...and her Tyler jewels. Nothing, nothing at all...."

Stretched atop a fake boulder in the midst of wild orchids and lush foliage, the woman whispered the words softly and sensually for the camera. She was leaning on an elbow, her knees slightly bent, her mane of red hair curling over her shoulders. She wore a strapless tiger-striped bikini. Her lipstick was a fiery orange-red, and her green eye shadow brought out the highlights in her eyes. She wasn't just beautiful; she was as erotic and sensual and arrestingly pagan as any man could imagine. Perhaps it was the abundance of her fire-colored hair. Perhaps it was her eyes, or the curve of her body, or maybe just the pulse of life that seemed to exude from her—seething, simmering, exciting. And dangerous, perhaps, but so vital that the sight of her, the sound of her whisper, seemed to dip into the very heart of every man's fantasy and every woman's dream of what she should be.

Around her throat she wore an emerald pendant. Emeralds dangled from her earlobes, and she wore one emerald ring and one emerald bracelet. Against the light tan of her flesh, the jewelry was striking. The emeralds matched her eyes. Eric Hawk was convinced that no woman could wear them more beguilingly.

He shifted suddenly, feeling uncomfortable. She was seducing him. She was making his heart beat too quickly, his breath come too hard, too fast. His muscles felt tightly wired. She seemed to be calling to every part of his body.

"Good!" someone called to the model.

She sighed, about to move from her perch. "Wait! Let's go again!" the director of the commercial shouted.

The redhead gritted her teeth and glared at the man. She quickly covered the emotion, though, and waved to the young couple standing behind him.

She settled back down on the boulder. "There's nothing a woman needs.... Nothing...but the primitive earth and her Tyler jewels. Nothing...nothing at all...."

She seemed to purr. Fascinating sensuality gleamed from her eyes. She was feline and graceful and striking.

Watching her, Eric Hawk had little notion that he was striking also. He was a tall man, nearly six-three. His hair was not just dark but the blue-black color of a raven's wing. He wore his hair layered and slightly long. It fell over the edge of his collar and sometimes tumbled over his forehead and into his eyes. From the ancestors who had given him the color of his hair, he had inherited an arresting face. His cheekbones were high and and broad, his chin decidedly square, his nose long, and his eyes large and set wide apart. His brows matched his hair, and he was highly bronzed from constant exposure to the sun. Eric was an integral part of the wild and savage land where the company had come to film. He could move in absolute silence over the grasses and swamp and hummock alike, and he did so not with conscious thought, but by nature. He was as lean and sleek as the endangered panther that wandered the land; he could strike as swiftly as the snake.

From a different set of ancestors he had acquired one of his most striking features—his eyes. They were not the emerald shade of the model's, but they, too, were green. And bright, penetrating, startling against the dark bronze color of his face. People looked his way and were caught by those eyes.

"One more time."

"All right, all right!" the beautiful redhead called out. "One more time." She paused, looking up at the sky.

The sun was leaving them. It was only early afternoon, but clouds were rolling in. Eric looked at the sky, too. There was a big storm brewing over Cuba and South Florida was on hurricane watch. The storm had barely gathered hurricane force during the last weather report Eric had seen, but he knew that storms picked up strength over the open water. Besides, here in the swamp, even a minor storm could be serious and even deadly. These people needed to finish—and get out.

He turned around and walked over to the handsome young couple who stood some distance from the director.

Rafe Tyler, tall and with a commanding presence, flashed him a friendly smile. "Mr. Hawk." He extended a hand. "Nice to see you. We didn't hear you'd come."

His wife, Tara, a beautiful blonde with wide blue eyes, an enchanting smile and belly swollen with child, spoke softly. "Thank you for coming! And thank you again for the use of the property. I think it's wonderful."

"The ad was Tara's conception," Rafe explained.

Eric nodded, smiling at the couple. He had been startled by his liking the Tylers. Eric had read somewhere that Rafe was one of the hundred richest men in the world. He hadn't expected a lot from the man, but curious about Rafe's proposition, Eric had agreed to see him. He had been impressed with the man's energy, but Eric had explained that he didn't feel right about letting his land be used for a commercial and receiving a fee. Rafe had convinced him with a deal—Eric wouldn't be paid; instead Rafe would make a large contribution toward building a vocational school for which Eric had been working long and hard. In the end, the contribution had doubled, because Rafe had liked the children and seen the need.

"Mrs. Tyler—" Eric began.

"Tara, please."

"Tara, I think that it was a wonderful idea."

"Thank you, Mr. Hawk."

"Eric," he said grinning.

She laughed easily. "Eric. Anyway, I'm very pleased. We thank you sincerely."

"Thank you," Eric said. He looked at the sky again. "I was just thinking that you should wrap up here soon. I could be wrong, but I think that the storm is coming this way."

"We'll leave soon," Tara promised him. "I just want to say goodbye to Ashley."

Rafe handed Eric a card. "If you're ever in New York, or if I can ever do anything for you, please don't hesitate to call."

Tara touched his hand. "Please do come see us!" she urged.

He nodded. "Sure. I'll come sometime," he told her. "I'm going to go and see that my family is all battened down. Don't take too long, now. A storm here is nothing to take a chance with."

Rafe's arm tightened protectively around his wife. "I promise you that we'll be out quickly."

Eric nodded to them, smiled again and headed for his airboat. His sister-in-law Wendy's house wasn't far, just right across the canal, and he wondered if he shouldn't go back and bring the Tylers to Wendy's. Then he shrugged, deciding that he should check on his own family first and return to see if the Tylers had made it out. With that plan in mind, Eric hastened on his way.

On her rock, Ashley Dane repeated her lines again. For the fifth "one more time."

She knew that Harrison Mosby, the director, was giving her a hard time on purpose. He was talented, young, handsome—and up-and-coming. She couldn't stand him, and she was tired of the way he treated her, touching her, taunting her with off-color remarks. She had almost protested to Tara and Rafe about his being there, but she knew that Rafe thought Harrison was a good director. Rafe didn't know him as a man. Ashley had decided to endure.

"That's great, Ashley!" Tara called to her, smiling happily from behind the cameraman. Ashley grimaced. Tara would have said that she had done great even if she had looked and sounded like the Incredible Hulk. Tara had talked her into the assignment.

"Thanks."

"Ashley, super!" Rafe proclaimed. He was the owner of the illustrious Tyler Jewels and Tara's husband and Ashley's good friend. "Let's get
one more, though, okay? We don't want to have to come all the way back
here to film again." He looked at Harrison. "Just one more, Harrison. We
have to get out of here. The storm is going to break."

"The storm?" Harrison asked.

"The storm," Rafe said firmly. Harrison shook his blond head, but he
didn't dare argue.

"Is one more okay, Ashley?" Tara questioned worriedly.

"Sure!" Ashley agreed. She looked Tara straight in the eye and shivered. Tara laughed.

"Come on, Ashley, it's not that bad!"

"You come over here and stare at this giant, man-eating reptile for a
while!" Ashley said indignantly, indicating the live creature leashed not
twenty-five feet away from her.

The reptile wasn't all that big by alligator standards, Ashley had been
assured. The gator's name was Henry and he was only four feet long, but
two feet of that seemed to be his mouth alone. Besides Henry, who had
been hired and whose trainer would be well paid, there might be dozens
of other creatures just hanging around for whatever—and whoever!

Ashley and Tara had come to the Florida Everglades years ago when
they had both modeled for the world-famous Galliard. A cloud of scandal and danger had hung over Tara's life at that time. It had been solved
in Caracas only two years ago when she had met Rafe and they had discovered that the danger had been caused not only by an ex-flame, but by
Galliard himself. Wealthy, charming Rafe had fallen in love with Tara,
and she and Ashley had gone into fashion design for themselves.

When Ashley had first heard the setting for the commercial that
would kick off the massive new ad campaign for Tyler Jewels, she had
protested. "I don't think that it's right for me. I just don't care for things
that crawl."

"Oh, Ashley!" Tara had laughed. "Rafe will be there and I'll be there,

and nothing will crawl over you, I promise. This is a big deal for us. We're
putting months of planning into it!"

"There are snakes and alligators and who knows what else out there
in the Florida Everglades."

"But we'll be fine!"

"You do it! You're a model."

"I can't do it!"

"Why not?"

"We're going to have a baby!"

Ashley had stopped protesting then, because she had been so happy
for Tara. Tara explained that they were planning the shoot earlier than
Rafe really wanted just so she could be there.

Still, Ashley had never liked the idea of coming out to the swamp. She
simply didn't like things that buzzed and flew and crawled and slithered.
Not insects, not snakes and certainly not the disgusting alligators that
opened their mouths that were filled with endless rows of teeth and made
noises that sounded remarkably like the grunts of pigs.

"Harrison," Ashley said impatiently, wondering what he was waiting for.

"Makeup!" Harrison shouted. "Come on, people, get with it! She has
a sheen like a neon light on her face. Let's move, people, let's move."

Mitchell Newman, the makeup artist, quickly approached Ashley
and powdered her face. Grace Neeley, his assistant, rushed up behind
him to redo Ashley's hair. Ashley closed her eyes and waited patiently.
She gave Mitchell an encouraging smile; Harrison had been on his case
all day, too.

To her horror, Ashley blew her lines on the next take.

"Ashley, how could you!" Harrison groaned.

"What's the matter with the first takes?" she demanded.

"Take five!" Harrison snapped.

Gritting her teeth, Ashley jumped off the rock. She'd been afraid to
leap to the ground in her bare feet, but she had been watching Tara, and
thought that her friend looked very tired.

She smiled at Norm Dillon, Gene Hack and Tory Robinson, the three cameramen. Susie Weylon, the representative from Tyler Jewels, looked as if she were about to have apoplexy. "Ashley! The jewels!"

"I'm walking ten feet to see Tara, that's it!" Ashley promised.

Susie stood back, looking disgruntled. "Be careful!" she warned.

"Of course!" Ashley said. She watched where she was walking and hurried to Tara and Rafe. Rafe smiled and kissed her on the cheek. "Perfect, Ashley."

"Thanks." She grinned, then laughed. "I feel ridiculous. As long as I've been a model, this is absolutely the least that I have ever had on. I wouldn't do this for just anyone, you know. I feel as if I'm half naked."

"You are half naked. And you're a sweetie," Tara said. She grinned broadly. "But honestly, you look great. Doesn't she, Rafe?"

"Now, am I damned if I do and damned if I don't answer that?" Rafe asked her, his eyes ablaze with tenderness.

"You're to answer honestly."

"You look great half naked, Ashley. And you, darling, look stunning pregnant."

Tara laughed delightedly. "I look like a house, but I don't mind it a bit." The wind lifted her blond locks.

Ashley looked up at the sky. The storm was supposedly going in another direction, but now Ashley felt nervous. "Rafe, take her out of here."

"We'll wait for you," he said, glancing at his watch with a shrug. "It shouldn't be much longer."

"No, please."

"Ashley," Tara said, "I know how you feel about Harrison—"

"I can handle Harrison. I'll get a ride with Grace. I'll be fine, I promise. Please, Tara, you're making me so very nervous. I don't like you out here with this storm."

"Okay, okay. We'll leave right now, and we'll see you back at the hotel."

"Okay! Now go!"

She kissed them both quickly. Rafe cast Harrison a warning look. He seemed about to say something, then seeing Ashley's imploring eyes, clamped his mouth shut. "All right. Take care. And you're perfect."

Ashley watched them head through the dense foliage. It was difficult to believe that a major road lay just beyond. Well, not a major road. Alligator Alley was growing—or so Ashley had been told—but it seemed to her that there were still endless stretches of absolutely nothing but saw grass and swamp and canals and the occasional crane or egret standing one-legged in the water.

Ashley shivered and stepped back, looking up at the trees. There were snakes here, which could drop from the branches. She rather liked her boulder, come to think of it. Nothing was really close to her when she was on top of it. The mosquitoes didn't even bother her.

"Ashley, let's go," Harrison called to her.

"I'm ready when you are."

"Norm, get some extra shots of that gator," Harrison commanded the cameraman. Norm nodded in silence. Ashley climbed back up on her rock. Harrison called for hair and makeup and she was primped and powdered again.

Ashley gritted her teeth. She wouldn't be here if it weren't for her friendship with Tara and Rafe. She had started to grow weary with modeling when she was still with Galliard. Then, she and Tara had gone into fashion design. They did well. Ashley made enough money to support herself comfortably, and that was all that she needed. Rafe was paying her an absurd amount for this assignment, but she hadn't done it for the money. She had done it for him and Tara—because it had been Tara's concept and because the jewelry was Rafe's.

She sighed. Not much longer. She could survive it.

One more time...

She said the lines without a hitch. She offered, very sweetly, to do it again. Harrison smiled at her. She hated his smiles; they were purely lascivious. "Right, sweetie, you do it one more time. For me, especially, hmm?"

He wouldn't have dared sound that way had Rafe stayed, Ashley thought. But she didn't want Rafe fighting her battles. She could handle herself. She had lived in New York City alone for years, and she knew how to handle the Harrison Mosbys of the world. She had met enough of them.

"Let's just do this and go home, huh?" she said sweetly. She looked up. The sky was growing black. There was going to be a storm—one heck of a storm.

"Ready? Let's go. Roll 'em," Harrison said.

Finally the last take was in. Ashley sighed and watched idly as the cameramen packed their gear. She hesitated to ask Grace for a ride, seeing that Grace was still busy. She started when Harrison touched her back.

"I want to talk to you, Ashley."

The first time that she had met him, she had thought he was handsome, talented and witty. She had gone out with him once. He had drunk too much at dinner and bragged about himself all through it. He had forced his way into her apartment, and he had nearly forced himself on her. But she hadn't been afraid to scream like a banshee and he had left her, swearing that she would never work in a commercial again. She had laughed at the threat; she hated commercials. It hadn't been so long ago.

"I don't want to talk to you, Harrison."

"Come on."

"No!"

He grabbed hold of her wrist, dragging her from the rock. Norm looked up. Ashley saw confusion and worry cross his features. He didn't know what do do. He needed to keep working, and he didn't want Harrison Mosby blackballing him back in New York City. On the other hand, Norm was a gentleman, married to a lovely woman, the father of three beautiful daughters. He couldn't watch ill come to Ashley without taking some step. He would try to help her—and wind up jobless himself.

"He'll be sorry if he interferes," Harrison muttered.

Ashley smiled at Norm and waved, assuring him that she was all right. She could handle Harrison herself. He was just an obnoxious braggart. Harrison wrenched her wrist again, pulling her barefoot into the swamp.

"I hope a rattler gets you, Harrison," she said sweetly.

"The coral snakes are the deadly ones, I hear," he replied. He glanced back at her and smiled, showing gleaming white teeth. "They're small snakes and bite between the fingers—or the toes of barefoot people."

"I think that the snake might well worry about chomping into you," she said pleasantly. She was starting to tremble. She should have let Norm help her, and let Rafe help Norm.

They were moving deeper into the savage swamp. Trees and roots grew thicker, with vines tangled in the branches. Muck and mud were beginning to show in potholes. An occasional wild orchid dangled from the treetops. The earth seemed dangerously silent as the sky turned black overhead.

Harrison stopped very suddenly and Ashley crashed into his back. He swung around, taking her into his arms, bringing his lips down hard upon hers. She struggled against him and found he was surprisingly strong for his lean appearance. His hands might have belonged to an octopus; they were everywhere. He was tugging at her bikini top, and she was afraid that she was going to lose it at any second.

She managed to jerk her head aside. "Harrison, stop it!"

"Quit playing hard to get. I saw you looking at me when you were whispering. I saw your eyes. You want it, Ashley, and I'm going to see that you get it."

"You're sick."

"I can't stand it any more. I can't leave you again."

"Let me go, and I mean it."

He just wasn't listening. His arms held her tighter, bringing her flat against his health-spa toned chest. She gritted her teeth and looked up. "Let me go."

"Feel it, Ashley. Feel the storm in the air, feel the storm inside me. Feel the pagan earth beneath our feet. We were meant to be. We were meant to be—right now."

"We've been through this before! Now let me go!"

He didn't let her go. He tried to drag her down.

Ashley was growing desperate. She kicked him as hard as she could.

He groaned. His hold on her slackened, and she shoved him with all her might. He staggered, bending over, still moaning. Then suddenly he reached into his pocket and pulled out a pocketknife. He flicked it open and pointed the blade at her.

"Don't be a fool!" Ashley gasped, feeling stunned. Don't panic, she warned herself. She'd been in tough situations before. She'd been kidnapped and held at gunpoint once, when Tine Elliott had used her as a bargaining point to get his hands on Tara and Rafe. She hadn't panicked then and had come out of it okay.

"Harrison, if you stop this right now, I won't say anything, and nothing bad will happen. If you come near me one more time, I will accuse you of battery and rape. Do you understand me?"

"Get over here, Ashley." He was straightening up, his teeth clenched against the pain.

She felt the hair rise at her nape and goose pimples appear on her arms. "Harrison—"

"I can do things for you that you wouldn't begin to believe."

"Harrison—"

He took a step toward her. She didn't give a damn about being barefoot. She spun around fast.

But not fast enough. He caught her arm, wrenching her around. He forced her back against a tree, placing the blade on her throat, then lowering it to the valley between her breasts. He made a quick movement, slashing the bikini top. It fell to the ground. She kept staring at him, hating him. "I will prosecute you to the full extent of the law, Harrison Mosby."

"You do what you think you can. Not a man alive who saw you on that rock would call another guilty on a sexual charge."

"Rafe Tyler—"

"To hell with Rafe Tyler. Toss his name up to me again and you'll really be sorry."

He pressed the cool blade against her left breast and smiled. "Now, come on, Ashley, cool down. I know that you liked me when we met. I've thought of no one else since. You're a tigress, honey."

"Let me go."

"Not on your life."

"Someone will come looking for us soon."

He shook his head. "No, they won't. I told Gracie that you and I were going to dinner. No one will come, and no one will wait. And honey, if you want to get away from the snakes and other creepy things, you'll just have to lean on me."

"You're the creepiest living thing in this swamp, Harrison, and I'd walk the entire distance out of here on my own."

He was going to touch her, and she didn't think that she could bear it. She couldn't believe that she had sent Rafe and Tara away, and that this was happening to her. She had managed to survive in New York, and thus she had gained a false confidence. But now she was in a swamp with a treacherous storm brewing overhead.

"Ashley..."

His free hand closed over her bare midriff and inched toward her breast. There was a knife against her flesh, but she lost all sense of reason. She brought her hands up against his chest, shoving him and screaming.

He fell backward, flat upon his rear.

He stared at her with pure, murderous rage. Ashley didn't take long to think about it. She turned to run as fast as she could. Thunder cracked in the air and the clouds roiled dark and threatening.

"Ashley!" Harrison screamed.

She needed to get back to the clearing, to the crew. She had to reach them before they left her here with a storm and Harrison Mosby.

Suddenly the rain was falling. It didn't begin gently, with a soft pattering. It poured with a driving, blinding force.

Ashley tried to trace her footsteps back to the clearing. She pushed past trees and when something brushed against her, she shrieked, certain that a snake had found her.

She must have taken a wrong turn; she couldn't find the clearing.

She heard a loud sound. A loud snorting sound. Her heart thundered in a sudden panic. She knew the sound. It was the sound Henry had made.

There were alligators nearby.

She paused, fighting for reason. She pushed the wet hair from her face and blinked against the onslaught of rain. Blackness had descended. She could barely make out the trees before her.

"Help me!" she screamed.

Had the makeup and camera crews managed to pack up so quickly?

No. She could see people up ahead in the darkness. She heard a heavy splashing sound.

"Help me!"

She staggered forward. She wrapped her arms around her naked breasts and fell against a tree. She saw that there were three people in rain slickers standing near one of the deep canals. She couldn't tell if they were men or women.

She opened her mouth to call out again, but no sound came out.

One of the figures reached for another, dragged it to its chest, and produced a huge knife. She could see the blade through the darkness and the rain. But she couldn't see faces—their backs were to her. She just saw the slicker-clad forms and the blade.

One figure drew the blade against the other's throat. The body collapsed, just like a deflated blow-up doll. And the murderer very calmly tossed the body into the water of the canal.

A scream tore from her.

Suddenly the two remaining figures turned her way and stared straight at her.

The cold of the rain sliced through to Ashley's bones. Then thoughts rushed in her mind. She had just witnessed a murder. She could recognize none of the persons, but they could see her standing there, bedraggled and dressed only in the tiger-striped bikini bottoms and her Tyler jewels. She was nearly naked and dripping with emeralds. They would know her....

One of them took a step toward her.

She roused from her shock and spun around. Gasping for breath, she turned to run again. The rain was beating on her so mercilessly.

She hated the swamp. And now she was racing through it, in a blind panic. She couldn't find her way. Her feet were sinking deeper and deeper into the mud, and the foliage seemed to reach out and grab her, trying to trap her. Sobs tore from her throat. She was growing hysterical.

She had to calm down. She had to think and reason, find the clearing, then the road leading away from the snakes and the alligators and the storm—and murderers who stalked their victims in the mud.

She fell against a tree, bowing her head against the rain, gasping for breath. She heard a snap behind her and pushed away from the tree. She started to run.

She suddenly found a trail beneath a row of pines. She tore down it, slipping, falling, rolling through the mud. She rose and ran again, keeping her eyes straight ahead.

But then she slipped again, crying out as she fell into the mud. She came up on her knees.

Then she saw the boots.

Someone was standing before her—someone wearing black, knee-high boots.

She allowed her gaze to rise to the thighs encased in tight denim, to the lean hips and a drenched colorful cotton shirt stretched across a broad chest. She looked up higher and brought her hand to her mouth, holding back a scream.

His hair was as dark as the night that had come with the storm. His features were hard, his jaw was set, but his mouth was full and sensual. He was a striking, powerful-looking man.

A man with piercing light eyes that stared down at her, offering no mercy. She stared back at him. She couldn't help but do so for his eyes held hers—and fascinated and haunted her. He was the most potentially dangerous man she had ever seen.

A murderer?

He reached down to her.

"No," she whispered. "Please!"

The rain fell on her, running over the curves of her bare breasts and down the line of her spine. The mud was rinsed off, and all that remained was a beauty. Like a supplicant, she remained kneeling before the tall dark man towering over her.

"No, please," she gasped.

Strong, dark arms closed around her bare flesh, lifting her from the mud. She wanted to scream, but her scream froze in her throat when she met his eyes. They were like the sea, startlingly alive during a tempest.

She started to struggle and realized she hadn't the strength.

"Stop!" he warned her.

She went still, aware that she could never break the steely band of his arms. She looked into his eyes, aware of their color, feeling the world swim around her.

"Don't...don't hurt me," she whispered.

"Hurt you? My God, woman, I'm trying to bring you in from the rain," he said irritably.

It was too much. Her eyes closed. The blackness of the storm consumed her, and she saw no more.

CHAPTER 2

Ashley felt as if she had come out of a thick fog only to be cast into a field whipped by wind and rain. She was running again, running for her life, down paths with tangled vines and roots. She tripped and fell and ran again. It didn't matter which path she chose; she always stumbled upon the same thing. Three figures, silent in the storm. And one figure produced a knife that flashed and glittered, and plunged it into the heart of another.

She ran....

But she couldn't escape the vision.

Then she jerked up, a scream forming on her lips. She held it back just in time, realizing that she had awakened. There were no roots, no tangled vines around her, only muted shadows and darkness. The swamp was not real; she was dry, warm and wrapped in a cocoon of softness. Only the wind and rain were real, sounding as if all the demons of hell had been let loose.

The murderers were not real, not anymore....

Ashley shuddered violently, then looked down. The softness she sat on was a queen-size bed covered with a luxurious deep-blue comforter and crisp white sheets. She was wearing a man's tailored shirt and underneath that...

Nothing, she discovered. Her sodden bikini bottoms were gone. The Tyler emerald pendant lay cold in the valley of her breasts, and she still wore the ring. But the bracelet and earrings were gone.

She turned, and in the dim light of the room, she saw the missing jewels. They flashed from a bedside table.

She swung her feet over the side of the bed and stood, glad to see that the tailored shirt fell well down her thighs. She looked around the room. There was a tall pine armoire and a handsome matching dresser with a brush, after-shave and other toiletries on it. Masculine toiletries.

Ashley drew in a sharp breath, remembering the man who had accosted her in the swamp. Accosted? No. He had helped her, hadn't he? He had brought her here, out of the swamp, out of the rain. A peculiar warmth snaked along her spine. This was his room, whoever he was.

She started to shiver. She'd never seen anyone like him, not with such ebony hair and striking green eyes. She'd never seen features like his— hard, proud, rigid, ruggedly masculine. They were also cold, betraying no emotion.

Were they the features of a killer?

"Oh," she murmured, shivering again. Where was he? Her tongue went dry. She had to get out of there, back to the city.

What light there was in the room filtered in through a partially opened door. There was another door, partially opened, too. Ashley tiptoed to the first doorway and saw that it led out to a hall—and to the rest of the house, Ashley imagined. He would probably be out that way. Perhaps the second door led to a back exit?

She tiptoed toward it, pushed it open, and discovered a modern bathroom. It was so dark that she could see little, but she could make out a huge whirlpool tub in front of a glass window. Some sort of shutters had been pulled down over the window outside. She moved closer, trying to see if there was any opening. She bumped her head on a towel rack and swore softly. This was not a way out.

Her heart started to hammer hard as she wondered anew about the figures in the swamp. She tried to assure herself that the man who had picked her up could not be one of them. Why carry her here? It would have been easier to murder her on the spot. Slit her throat clean through—

"Stop that!" she whispered to herself. She needed to slip out of the room, find a phone and call a cab. Or she could call the police. Maybe she could sneak by him. Maybe he wasn't even here. Maybe—

Stop with the maybes! she chastised herself firmly. She turned around, on her tiptoes again, and came out of the bathroom. She started across the room for the other door, then stopped, a scream in her throat.

He was there—leaning against the doorframe, arms crossed over his chest, watching her. He had been there for some time, she decided. She hadn't heard him at all.

She tried to swallow her scream, but it came out anyway—as a little squeak.

In the dim light, she thought that she saw him smile. He was dry now, too, in jeans and a long-sleeved denim shirt. His dark hair fell in layers that just brushed over his collar.

"How—how long have I been out?" Ashley asked.

"A while."

"Where...am I?"

"My house. Were you looking for something special?" he inquired politely. His eyes didn't leave hers. They didn't flicker over the length of her once. She had the feeling that he didn't need to look at her—he already had. And he hadn't been very impressed with what he had seen.

"A—a phone," she said.

"In the bathroom?"

"Er, lots of people have phones in their bathrooms," she said defensively.

He shrugged. Dark lashes fell over his flashing eyes. "Not in these parts, they don't, Miss...?"

"Dane. Ashley Dane." She gave him her name hurriedly, then she quickly fell silent. What if he was the murderer? What if he just wanted her name so that he could go out and kill all of her friends, too?

That was insane! she told herself. She was letting her imagination run rampant, and if she wasn't careful, her imagination would be her downfall now.

"It doesn't matter," he said softly. "The phones are out."

"Out?" she repeated. She could be locked in with a murderer, and she couldn't even call for help.

"Out," he said, watching her curiously. His face was enigmatic. He was perfectly polite; his voice was low-key. She sensed that he didn't think very highly of her. "There's a storm out there, Miss Dane. A bad one. You shouldn't have been running around in it. Phones, electricity—everything goes off at a time like this."

With that he turned around and left her, walking down the hall. For several seconds she just stood there, frightened and confused. She shouldn't have been running around! Well, she hadn't been running around on purpose, what did he think? He hadn't even asked her what had happened! Could she have told him? He might very well be the murderer.

No. She determined that he couldn't be since he hadn't killed her, and he'd had ample opportunity. She ran after him, passing a few more doors along the hallway and then coming to a large room with stone walls, a fireplace, comfortable earth-colored sofas and carved wood side tables. A counter separated the huge living and dining area from the kitchen. Ashley knew that he had walked into the kitchen but she paused anyway, looking around.

Candles covered the tables and the counter, giving off a warm glow. She could hear the vicious cry of the wind and the slash of the rain. But here inside, she was safe. And the room, for all its size, was an inviting place. It was curiously decorated, however. There were western landscapes on the wall, and two striking sculptures made of etched buffalo skulls and feathers flanked the doorway. Little straw dolls adorned some of the tables, and a Navajo rug covered much of the hardwood floor. She turned around and nearly jumped, having discovered that he was leaning casually against the counter, and was watching her with his eerie silence once again.

She gasped, looking from the hard contours of his face to the decoration of the room. "You're an Indian!" she said, and then she wanted to bite her tongue because the words had sounded so bad when she hadn't meant them that way at all.

He didn't move, not really, but everything about him tightened—his jaw, especially—and his eyes seemed to take on an especially cold glitter. "Yes. How very observant you are, Miss Dane."

If he hadn't meant to kill her before, he probably wanted to do so now. She wanted to say something more, to explain, but he was already turning away from her with that disdain he had previously shown her. Undeserved disdain, she thought, and her temper soared. She was at his mercy, even if he wasn't the murderer, but she wasn't about to sit still for his attitude problems.

She strode to the kitchen and reached for his shoulder, spinning him around. She was glad to see the frown that furrowed his brow and the sharp narrowing of his eyes. She smiled sweetly. "You've a chip on your shoulder a mile wide, Mr.—sir. You've no need to take it out on me."

He picked up her hand from where it lay on his shoulder. Ashley knew he meant to drop it, but he didn't. His fingers curled over hers as he stared at her. She looked up into his eyes and a startling whisper of heat seemed to settle over her. She felt it first in her fingertips, felt it sweep through her limbs, then streak like laps of fire down the length of her spine. She should have pulled away from him. But she didn't.

There was very little space between them, and she felt that she really saw him for the first time. His skin was so bronzed it was nearly copper, and her own tan seemed pale next to his. His scent was clean and both rich and subtle, and so overwhelmingly masculine that she was aware of him as a man as she had never been aware of any other man before. She was fascinated by the square contour of his chin, the arch of his brows, and his eyes, so vividly green against his bronze skin. She was even aware of his breathing, faster now, like her own. She was aware of his heart-beat, aware of her own pulsing faster and faster with the sound of the wind and the rain, as if the earth itself had found a rhythm within her. Color mounted onto her cheeks.

They were alone. This man had carried her here. He had stripped away her sodden bikini bottom and he had dressed her in the shirt. He was a stranger who knew her intimately. He was a man who frightened and compelled her. She had felt his arms around her, and she had no doubt of his strength of muscle or strength of will. He confused her; he made her hot and breathless. She didn't know him at all!

Suddenly she jerked her fingers free, as if she had been burned. She pulled away, turning her back to him, staring over the candlelit counter. "I'm sorry. I'd just like to leave if I could, please."

"Leave?"

"Leave. If I can't call for a cab, I've some friends—"

"Phone for a cab!" he repeated incredulously. Ashley spun around indignantly. He was laughing at her, his perfect teeth flashing white in the candlelight. "Don't you understand yet? There's a killer—"

"A killer!"

"A killer storm out there, Miss Dane. Most of the people out here have moved into shelters. The phones are already out; the electricity is gone. The swamp is swollen, the canals are swollen, and I assure you, not even the gators are moving. There is no way out of here right now. No way at all."

"But—"

"Lady, this has become a full-fledged hurricane. Cara, that's her name, if you're interested."

"Cara," Ashley murmured. She couldn't stay here. Not with this man. Not after what she had seen. She needed to get to the police. She needed to get away from him. "But—"

"Can't you understand? There is a storm—"

"But it wasn't that bad when we came out."

"What it was before doesn't matter. If you'd had the sense to leave instead of running around—"

"Running around!" Ashley protested furiously.

He was reaching into his dark refrigerator, but he paused, turning to look her way with a brow arched in question.

"I was not running around in your stinking swamp!" she hissed.

He shrugged, pulled out a can of beer and hesitated. "Want one?" It almost sounded as if he begrudged her a drink! Ashley gritted her teeth and didn't answer him. She was starving; she was thirsty. She was miserable.

Damn him. Let him begrudge her to his heart's content!

She walked over to him and icily took the beer from his hand. "Thank you. Thank you so much for your charming warmth and hospitality. I'd like to thank you personally, but since you haven't bothered to introduce yourself, I can't quite do that."

He watched her. She thought that the hint of a smile tugged at his lips, but he didn't move, and he didn't speak right away. Then he reached for a second beer and popped the flip top. "It's Eric," he said.

"Eric?" She should have shut up while she was ahead, but his attitude had gotten to her. "Eric? It isn't Running Brave or Silver Arrow or—"

"Hawk," he interrupted her very softly. "Eric Hawk." He said it with tremendous menace.

Ashley went still, inhaling deeply. She walked back to the living room and sank down on the sofa. Her tailored shirt rose and she tugged the tails down. She swallowed several mouthfuls of the beer; her head started to swim instantly. She hadn't eaten for hours. She didn't even know if it was day or night. It had been such a long day. First she had been attacked by Harrison, then she witnessed the murder in the swamp. Then she had run into this brick wall of a man, and now she was stuck with him.

And he might be the murderer! He might be the very man she had been running from!

He was behind her again, she realized. She hadn't heard him move, she hadn't heard him come, but she knew that he was there. She swung around, her hair flying around her face and shoulders. She swept it back from her forehead, leaped nervously to her feet and stared at him. "What? What is it?"

He grinned at her. "Do you like your burgers rare or well-done, Miss Dane?"

"What?" she asked blankly.

"I have the sterno going for dinner. Hamburger it is, though, I'm afraid. How do you like yours?"

"Oh. Rare. Please."

He nodded and walked away. Ashley watched him go back into the kitchen. She hesitated a minute, then followed him. She didn't speak to him. She didn't offer to help, and he didn't ask for her assistance. She pulled up one of the bar stools and sat at the counter. The smell of the ground beef searing in a frying pan was irresistible.

"What time is it?" she asked him.

He shrugged. "Around midnight."

"Midnight!"

"Yes, around midnight," he repeated.

"Then—then I was really out a long time."

"Yes. I tried to find your friends, but they were gone. Some people do have the sense to get out of the rain."

Not all of them! Ashley almost said. But she couldn't mention the murder to him. Not when she still didn't know whether he was the murderer or not.

"My friends," she murmured. "So you knew about the shoot?" she asked him.

His gaze lifted from the frying pan to meet hers. "Yes. It was my land you were on."

"Oh." Absently she rubbed her earlobe.

"Your earrings are in the bedroom," he said sharply.

"I know."

"I thought you were imagining me a jewel thief."

"You do have a chip on your shoulder."

"Actually I haven't. I like everything that I am."

"Do you? I haven't known that many people who take pride in being hostile and rude."

He stiffened, and Ashley smiled sweetly. "I said rare, if you don't mind?"

He flicked the burgers out of the frying pan and onto a plate. His eyes were hidden in the shadows, so she couldn't tell if her remarks had angered him or not. She saw the bowl of salad greens on the counter, and he served that along with the hamburgers. Ashley kept her eyes lowered and thanked him.

"What were you doing running around in the swamp?" he asked her. "What were you running from?"

She glanced up. His eyes were so sharp, so piercing. She was tempted to reach out and touch him. She wanted to run her fingers over his cheeks and his jaw.

Except she was certain he didn't want to be touched. And she still didn't know anything about him. He had been in the swamp, too. He was probing her carefully. Maybe he just wanted to know what she had seen.

She answered with wide eyes and innocence. "You allowed Rafe to film on your property. You know what I was doing there—a commercial."

To emphasize her words she reached into the V of her shirt and pulled out the emerald pendant. His eyes fell upon where it lay in the valley of her breasts.

He impatiently waved a hand in the air. "You know what I mean."

"Why should I? You're treating me like a featherbrain."

He hesitated, then bit into his hamburger and chewed. He was leaning over the counter. Too close to her, Ashley thought. Why was it that she became unnerved whenever he was near? He was rude and hostile.

He was also unlike any other man she had ever met. She liked his low voice. She even liked the way he moved in silence. She had liked the feel of his arms, muscles rippling, as he had picked her up in the swamp. He was tall and lean, but he was like steel. Yet he was warm to touch....

He was staring at her intently again. She swiftly reminded herself that killers were often very regular-looking people, even attractive.

"What were you doing in the swamp?" he repeated.

She sighed. "The director is not a friend of mine. He insisted on having a conversation. I didn't like the way the conversation was going. I ran."

His eyes flicked over her. She knew that he was remembering how she had looked when she had crashed into him. There was a certain amusement tinging his words when he spoke. "Maybe he didn't mean to...frighten you. Maybe he just got a little carried away himself. Maybe he believed that you needed 'nothing, nothing at all but the primitive earth and your Tyler jewels.'"

Ashley gasped and leaped to her feet. He had been there for the shoot, she realized. And he was assuming that because of it, Harrison had had a masculine right to attack her.

She tried to control her temper. But she had always thought—with remorse—that the saying about redheads having bad tempers was true. She just couldn't take the taunting remark.

She shoved her plate toward him with a vengeance. The china slammed into his and sent it sliding off the counter, right into his lap. Then it fell on the floor and broke.

Guilt struck her. She hadn't meant to cover him with his dinner. The plate had simply moved with great speed and violence.

He was looking down at the chopped beef and lettuce leaf that fell on his knees. Then his eyes came up to hers. Her throat went dry and her knees threatened to give. She fought for the return of some courage.

"I'm sorry. It's just that you have no right at all to make assumptions about me. You've been incredibly rude and hostile, and I don't deserve any of it!"

"I just said—"

"I know what you said! And I know what you've been thinking every step of the way!" Her temper was back.

She spun around, not sure of what she intended to do, but anxious to be away from him. She strode toward the living room, but she hadn't taken two steps before he was behind her and whipping her around by the shoulders to face him.

"*I'm* rude! You come crashing out of the bushes screaming for help and pass out in my arms. I bring you in out of the storm, dry you and dress you, feed you and offer you a safe harbor, and you call me rude!"

"Yes!" she flared, staring at him. "Yes! You just acted like...you acted like—oh, never mind! You wouldn't understand. You couldn't begin to understand. You don't have to offer me 'harbor'! I didn't come here to disturb you on purpose. And I have no desire to be here whatsoever!"

"You're acting like a featherbrain!" he told her furiously. "Don't you hear the wind and the rain?"

She could hear them raging and roaring. But she suddenly felt that the tempest outside was no greater than the one within her. She couldn't begin to understand the feelings that played havoc with her heart. One second she was shivering, wondering what manner of man he might be. The next second she was feeling warm, wondering what he would look like without his shirt, and what it would be like if he took her into his arms. She trembled, thinking that he would kiss a woman with fire and demand, that he would be fierce and tender, and that his touch would consume all thought and all reason.

She tried to jerk free from him. She could not. His powerful hands were fast upon her.

"I'm sorry," she said stiffly. "I really am. I just know that you don't want me here, and I'm trying to tell you that it isn't my fault at all."

He sighed deeply. "I know that it's not your fault. But there's nothing to be done about it, Miss Dane. Not now, not for quite some time."

Her teeth were chattering. "I'll stay away from you, all right? I'll just keep out of your way."

"Perhaps that would be best."

"Fine."

His hands dropped away from her, and he walked back toward the kitchen. Once he had turned, her courage came flooding back in a vehement stream. "Arrogant, redskinned bastard!" she muttered beneath her breath.

He heard her.

He turned around very slowly and stared at her with a burning gaze. "Come here, Miss Dane. If you would be so kind."

She shook her head.

He arched a brow and spoke softly. "If you don't, you just might regret it all of your life."

Her pride somewhat salvaged her courage.

"Oh?" she said. "And just what will you do if I don't?" It was an outright challenge. She never should have issued it, not unless she was ready for the next battle, and she certainly wasn't.

His smiled deepened, his eyes narrowed. "Why, I'll scalp you, Miss Dane."

He took a step toward her. Panic surged through her, and she turned to run for the bedroom.

She realized that he was right behind her, running silently. Her pace quickened. She thought only of reaching the safety of his bedroom and slamming the door.

But the hallway was too short and he was too fast. She was just reaching the room, breathless and almost triumphant, when she was suddenly lifted off her feet. She landed flat on the floor with him on top of her. Her shirt rose high on her thighs and his denim jeans were rough against her bare flesh. She writhed and struck at him to free herself, but he caught her hands and leaned down close to her face.

"Get off me!" she charged.

His jaw twisted. "What the hell is the matter with you? I just wanted you to help me pick up the pieces!"

"What?" she gasped.

"I said—"

"But you came after me, as if you were assaulting me!"

He laughed suddenly. "The assault and battery was on my dishes. Did anyone ever tell you that you have a dangerous temper, Miss Dane?"

"You provoke it," she said quietly.

He started to smile, and she suddenly felt the anger and the fear within her drain away. His fingers were still wound around her wrists. He was straddling her, but he didn't hurt her—he held his own weight. She wished that they were still arguing. She was suddenly and keenly aware of her near nudity and his touch. She felt the heat and power of his thighs, and she felt the magic of his eyes.

Then he wasn't holding her at all anymore. His fingers threaded through her hair. He spread the thick, rich tresses out, his eyes a green fire of fascination as he watched his own handiwork. Ashley caught her breath, watching him in turn. She should protest but she couldn't. She was completely mesmerized by his hands upon her. She lay completely still, and again the desire to touch in return came to her. She wanted to stroke the hard and handsome planes of his face, to touch his ebony hair and feel the coarse strands against her fingers.

He moved his hand away suddenly, as if her hair really were fire and it had burned him. He straightened, and Ashley quickly pulled down the tails of the shirt.

He started down the hallway in silence.

She bit her lower lip in consternation, then got to her feet and followed him.

When she walked into the kitchen he was busy with a broom and a dustpan, picking up the mess.

"I'll do it," she said. "I caused it."

"It's already done."

"But I don't want to make you mad again. I, uh, I really don't want to lose my scalp."

He paused. He actually seemed to smile, his lashes falling over his eyes. Then he looked at her, and his smile deepened. "Miss Dane, that mass of red hair is glorious where it is. I wouldn't dream of denuding you of it." His gaze ran over her, from head to toe, lingering along the way.

Then he continued with his task. Ashley held still, startled by the compliment. She finally stepped forward and bent down to pick up the large pieces of plate. "Where's the garbage?" she asked him.

"In the closet."

She opened the closet door, found the trash can and pulled it out. He swept up the small pieces and dropped them into it. He turned away, walking toward the counter, and smothered the sterno.

Ashley stood still, watching him. Then she nearly panicked. Her breath caught in her throat; her heart beat like wildfire.

He turned toward her with a huge butcher knife. The razor-sharp blade glittered and shone in the candlelight. He took a step toward her.

He would never reach her. Her heart was beating so frantically that she thought she would simply drop dead, and he wouldn't have to kill her.

He took another step. Her scream rattled in her throat; it refused to burst from her lips.

"Could you hand me the dish detergent, please?"

"Wh-wh-what?" she gasped.

"The dish detergent." He tossed the knife into the sink and walked past her to the closet door. "I'll let this stuff soak in cold water," he murmured, picking up a plastic bottle of pink dish soap.

She was going to fall to the floor. She felt so relieved and so weak.

He set the soap on the counter and reached for her shoulders, holding her carefully. Concern narrowed his eyes.

"Are you all right?"

"I'm—" She paused, moistening her lips. "I'm fine. Just fine. Honestly."

"You look as if you've seen a ghost."

"No." She shook her head. "No ghost."

Her fear faded. His presence and his nearness were overwhelming. His hands fell from her shoulders, but he stayed there before her. They were very close again. He brushed her cheek with his knuckles. He reached out and picked up the emerald pendant that lay between her breasts. His fingers brushed her flesh, and sparks of fire and life seemed to leap in her. He studied the stone, and then his eyes rose to hers. "No insult intended, Miss Dane. You do wear emeralds—and the primitive earth—very, very well." His smile took away any edge to the words. He laid the stone against her, and again she felt the brush of his fingers, and a hunger, unlike anything she had ever known, swept mercilessly through her.

"I'm going to shower," he said huskily, turning away from her and picking up a candle.

"But you haven't any electricity. It'll be freezing," she murmured.

"I know," he replied pleasantly enough. "Excuse me. I don't wear hamburger meat and salad that well."

He disappeared down the hall. She realized that he was going to the room where she had awakened. It was his room. It was his shower.

She wandered into the living room and sat and realized that her teeth were chattering. She didn't know anything about him.

She wanted him.

She had never felt this way, so swiftly and so completely.

Ashley hugged her knees to her chest. For the life that she had led, she was innocent in many ways. She had always imagined that she would fall deeply in love, that she would marry, that she would have children. But she had always been careful, not stupid. She enjoyed the company of men, and she dated. But she hadn't become involved. She had been close to Tara, and she had seen the horror of her friend's involvement with Tine. Then she had been stunned to realize that her trusted employer would have gladly killed them all to better himself. Men were not proving to be very trustworthy, not in her world. If it hadn't been for Harrison Mosby, she wouldn't be here now.

She smiled. There was Rafe. She had liked him from the beginning, but she had known that Rafe had been for Tara and Tara had been for Rafe. They were both her very dear friends.

And it was thanks to them that she was stuck here in this storm with

Eric Hawk.

She groaned and paced the floor. She had never been more miserable. She kept telling herself that Eric couldn't be a murderer—but she had seen a murder, hadn't she? Or had she gone absolutely insane out there?

Ashley suddenly stood dead still.

The rain had stopped. The wind had stopped.

It was over! she thought. The storm was over!

Ashley inhaled, thinking that she owed Eric some thanks and an explanation. But perhaps she owed herself more. She was in a situation that she couldn't control. She was terrified, and she was excited beyond belief. It was a dangerous brew, an explosive combination.

She wanted him.

She needed desperately to be away.

She didn't even have any clothing! she reminded herself.

That didn't matter. Surely he had a car or some other vehicle outside. She would borrow it. She would send him reimbursement later. And a thank-you note for carrying her out of the swamp.

But first she had to escape from him.

She started for the door and then remembered the earrings and bracelet. Rafe and Tara wouldn't blame her if they never got the jewels back. Rafe always cared for people more than he did for things, even if those things were priceless emeralds. But she was responsible for them. It would take her only two seconds to go back to the room and retrieve them.

Ashley ran along the hallway and entered the room. She could hear the shower going strong. She hurried over to the side table and picked up the bracelet, slipping it over her wrist. She put on the earrings, then paused.

There was a framed picture on the side table. She picked it up. Straining her eyes in the poor light, she saw there were four people in the picture, including a beautiful, petite blond woman who smiled broadly. She seemed to be in Eric's arms. Then Ashley realized that it wasn't Eric but a man who looked just like him. A brother or a cousin—they had to be related to look so much alike.

The other man in the picture was Eric. He was with a beautiful and exotic woman, with hair so dark it seemed to be a cobalt hue, so sleek that it was a satin blanket hanging over her shoulders. Her eyes were black too, and her features were striking. She was a full-blooded Indian, Ashley thought, and looked stunning with the pride in her eyes and a gentle, knowing curve to her smile. She was slim and elegant, full of laughter and full of love.

Ashley set the picture down suddenly as if it were hot. She felt she had intruded upon something. It wasn't the woman's smile that had gotten to her; it was Eric's.

He looked so different in the picture. No cynicism shadowed his eyes. He smiled with ease, with warmth, with an abundance of love, as the woman did.

Who was the woman? Ashley wondered. And why did the picture make her feel like crying? It was none of her concern.

She turned and fled from the room. It couldn't be any of her affair. She hated the swamp and the shoot was done. If the storm was truly over, she could fly home. At the moment, New York City, as crowded, dusty, dirty and crime-laden as it might be, seemed a haven of safety.

When she returned to the living room she glanced around for a set of keys but didn't see any. If he had a car, she reasoned, he probably left his keys in it. Who would come out here to steal a car?

The front door, however, was locked. There were two dead bolts on it, and both had been locked. She opened them and stepped outside, carefully closing the door behind her.

Everything was so deathly still.

She looked around, amazed at the destruction.

If Eric had a lawn or a car, she couldn't see it. Nor could she tell if there were canals nearby, or where there might be trees and where there might be saw grass. The whole panorama before her was green. Palm fronds and branches lay over everything and were ankle-deep on the porch where she stood several steps off the ground.

She wasn't going anywhere, she thought bleakly. Nowhere at all.

Suddenly she felt the breeze pick up. Her hair rose and curled around her face. She looked out at the horizon. A bolt of lightning suddenly zigzagged in a long and furious streak across the sky.

It was like a signal to the tempest. The wind rose in a shrill cry; the cold rain came back in an instant, beating upon her. Amazed, Ashley whirled around to go back into the house.

She didn't make it. The wind caught her at the midriff and pulled her down like icy hands. She screamed as she fell on top of the leaves and fronds at the base of the steps. She tried to rise, but the wind was too strong. It swept her around again, pulling her farther and farther from the house. She saw a tree and clung to it. The wind roared as if it had life, as if it had a murderous streak. Like an evil demon, it sought to tear her away from the tree and throw her out into the tempest.

She could scarcely hang on. Her fingers were frozen and almost numb. They would lose their grip any second, she thought. She couldn't hold on any longer.

She cast back her head and started to scream.

"Fool!"

Suddenly warmth surrounded her. Something hard and determined pressed against her back, and then strong arms were around her. She tried to turn, but she couldn't fight the force of the wind, or of the man.

"Come on!" His voice rose in command over the fury of the storm. "When I say move, move!"

She nodded, blinded by her sopping hair. His fingers curled over hers and he tugged her. "Now!"

She tried hard to follow him. But when she turned, her foot caught in a root, and she stumbled, falling with a scream. He caught her and lifted her into his arms. He braced himself and fought against the wind, step by step, heading back toward the house. They reached the porch. He staggered, then staggered up. He opened the door quickly, dropped her on the floor and caught the door before it could disappear into the grasping fingers of the wind. He slid both bolts. Then he fell down to the floor beside her, gasping for breath, soaked to the bone.

They both lay on their backs, panting. Only then did Ashley realize that he was wearing nothing but a big white towel wrapped around his hips. The wind had nearly managed to strip it away.

He turned to her. She saw the whole slick breadth of his chest, hairless and coppery and sinewed with muscle. She saw the furious set of his jaw and the cold green sizzle in his eyes. He reached out for her throat, and if she'd had the least bit of energy left she would have screamed.

"No!" she murmured. He meant to kill her, she was certain.

His fingers just lay against her flesh. "You *are* the worst featherbrain I have ever met in my entire life!" he thundered. His fingers crawled over her shoulder and he shook her with a vengeance. "Make a move toward that door again and I will scalp you! I'll skin you alive!"

He released her and stood with agility. He nearly lost the towel but it didn't disturb him. He wrenched it into place, then turned back to her, ready to yell again.

His words died on his lips.

Ashley realized that once again she was barely clad. Her shirt was soaked and torn open, revealing her breasts, and it had risen up to her hips.

She was clad in practically nothing at all....

Except for her Tyler jewels and the primitive earth.

CHAPTER 3

"I'll say one thing for you," Eric muttered darkly.

"What's that?" she murmured nervously, trying to pull down the tails of the sodden shirt.

His eyes fell upon her. "You're a beautiful featherbrain. Come on, let me help you." He reached down to her. She hesitated, then accepted his hand.

"I am not a featherbrain," she told him. "I have a college degree. I worked hard for it, too." What difference did it make? she wondered. She had tried to leave; she had failed. She was stuck in here with a man who might well be a killer.

"You could have fooled me. That was one of the most idiotic stunts I've ever seen."

"The storm had stopped."

"That was the eye! It hasn't stopped at all."

"Well, I know that now," she retorted.

He left her standing there, went down the hallway and returned with a handful of towels. He tossed her one, watching her with unabashed curiosity.

"Why?" he demanded.

"Why what?"

"Why would you be so desperate to get out of here that you would run barefoot and half naked right back into the storm?"

"I thought that the storm was over!" Ashley insisted, toweling her hair. He was walking around her in his soaked towel, heedless of the water that dripped to the floor. He circled her, like an inquisitor.

"But you were still willing to take off—barefoot—into the swamp," he said sharply.

Like a featherbrain, she thought resentfully. She didn't know if she wanted to hit him or run. She wasn't sure at all if the greatest danger lay in the storm—or in the man. "No," she said flatly. "I was planning—"

"Oh, wonderful!" he interrupted her, throwing his hands up in the air. "You wanted to steal my car."

Ashley looked at him, inhaling deeply for courage. Custer, she was certain, had not faced such a menace at the battle of Little Bighorn. This man was furious with her; he was like a keg of dynamite with a slow fuse. He crossed his arms over his chest. She inhaled again.

"I didn't mean to steal your car."

"Excuse me. You were going to take my car."

"I told you—"

"No, you haven't told me anything at all, have you?"

Her own temper soared and snapped, and no desperate reminder that he might be a murderer could do anything to control it. She exploded with a sound of fury, throwing her towel down on the ground and setting her hands on her hips. "I have to get out of here! Don't you understand that? You stop acting like a damned DA and leave me alone! Do you understand?"

"Do I understand." His black brows shot up in astonishment. "Listen, lady, I dragged you out of the swamp—twice. Now I want a few explanations."

He was walking toward her, and she found herself backing away, heading toward the kitchen. She turned suddenly and fled. When she reached the kitchen, she realized that he was behind her. She felt in the cold soapy water for the knife he had tossed there and faced him, braced against the sink, the knife raised high.

He had stopped short before her. He watched the knife not with fear, but with respect. He stared at her as if convinced that she was not a featherbrain but a complete maniac.

"What do you think you're doing?" he asked her calmly.

"Just stay away from me!" she insisted.

"You should never, never pull out a weapon unless you intend to use it," he warned her.

"Don't push me," she advised him.

"Put it down and tell me what the hell is going on."

"I—I can't."

He smiled and leaned back against the counter, watching her. "The storm could go on for another day. It could sit right on top of us and go on for two days, even three. The roads will be impassable for at least a week, I imagine. Even the canals will be clogged and swollen and dangerous. Can you hold that knife on me that long?"

No, of course she couldn't, and it had been foolish to dive for it, but he had scared her so thoroughly. She bit her lower lip, trying not to panic, trying to convince herself once again that he couldn't be the murderer.

She thought about it too long. One second he was as still as the calm of the storm, then the next second he was in motion, reaching for her wrist with the speed of lightning. She screamed as he caught hold of her, snapping her hand so that the knife went flying down to the floor where it clattered and glittered. She was pulled hard against him and her eyes widened and she gasped with shock—he had lost his towel in the maneuvering.

If he noticed, he gave his own state of undress no heed.

"Talk to me," he told her.

"I can't."

"You'd best!"

His breath warmed her cheek, and the heat and vibrant strength of the length of his body seemed to touch her with flames. She was terrified; she could barely stand, and she was painfully aware of every inch of him. His fingers were iron around her wrists. She even felt the pulse of his heart and had to wonder just where his beat began and her own ended. And most of all she felt his eyes on her.

"Talk to me! Now!" he insisted. She fell to her knees—and gasped. She found herself facing the very masculinity of him. Quickly he was down with her, still insistent. "Talk to me!"

She looked up at him. "Don't—don't kill me!" she whispered. And she was horrified by the other thoughts racing through her mind—that she wanted him to touch her.

"Don't kill you?" he asked incredulously.

"Please."

"Don't be absurd." A confused and rueful smile touched his lips. "I'm upset, but I'm not mad enough to kill. I was kidding, you know. I'm almost positive that the Seminoles haven't scalped a single soul since the last decade. And we were never known for skinning women alive. We were always much bigger on keeping our female prisoners captive than we were on murdering them."

She hadn't expected the light, easy tone from him, not after his fury.

Nor had she expected the soaring sensation of relief that filled her. It came to her so swiftly and completely that she lowered her head, and to her horror and absolute disgrace, she started to cry.

"Hey!" He took her into his arms, holding her so that she cried on his shoulder.

She was all too willing to bury her head against his neck, and he let her remain there for some time as she sobbed. Then she started to sniffle. He disengaged himself and without any awkwardness at all managed to rise smoothly, wrap his towel around him, then pull her to her feet.

Ashley, her pride shattered, wiped the tears from her cheeks. He helped her, finding a napkin to dab away the last of them. She caught his hand and the napkin. "I'm all right. Thanks."

He nodded. He didn't believe her. "Ready to talk yet?"

"I...never thought that you were going to scalp me or skin me alive," she told him.

"Well, that's a relief."

"I thought that you were going to stab me."

"Oh. Well, that's better, I suppose. Murder without tribal torture?"

His tone wasn't so light this time. She shook her head desperately. "I saw...I saw a murder."

He frowned and turned away from her. "Maybe we need a little stiff drink here," he murmured. He reached under the counter and came up with a bottle of Jack Daniel's Black. He drew two glasses from the cupboard, poured, and handed a glass to Ashley. She managed to smile. "Have you got any ginger ale?"

"Probably. And I'll bet I still have ice."

He fixed her drink, then sipped his own straight. He leaned against the counter, watching her. "Hang on," he told her. He set his drink down and walked off. A moment later he was back with a floor-length velour robe. He offered it to her. She started to slip it over her shoulders but he cleared his throat with a little smile. "You're soaked underneath, and that won't help. I hate to state the obvious, but I've already seen what there is to see, so you can ditch the shirt here. I'll even turn around like a perfect gentleman. We haven't been known for too much plunder or rape lately, either."

Ashley blushed furiously but he had already offered her his back. She knew that he meant what he had said and in that moment, she realized that she could trust him. She stripped away her shirt and wrapped the warm velour robe around her. It dragged on the floor and carried a pleasant scent—his soap or his after-shave, she wondered. She felt wonderfully comfortable and secure in it.

He turned around. He was still slightly amused, and it was the way she liked him best. She loved the gleam in his eyes and the very slight curl of his lip.

Except that it wasn't an amusing situation at all.

"I really did. I saw someone murdered."

"Who?" He picked up his drink and handed her the bourbon and ginger ale, then steered her toward the living room. He sat her down on the sofa and took a seat beside her.

"I don't know who," she told him earnestly.

"Then—"

"Honest to God, I'm not hysterical, and I'm telling the truth. I saw three people—"

"You don't know who any of them were?"

She shook her head. "They were in yellow slickers."

"How did you come about seeing them?"

She hesitated.

"Come on," he urged her. "Explain. Why weren't you with the Tylers?"

"Tara's baby. One more shot was needed, but Rafe and I didn't think Tara should stay any longer—"

"They're good friends of yours?"

"The best," Ashley said solemnly. "Why?"

He shook his head. "No reason." But there had been a reason, Ashley thought. "Come on. Tell me the rest," he said.

"There's very little to tell. I already told you about Harrison, and you already gave me your reaction."

He shrugged. "I said I understood how he might have gotten carried away. I'm not sure how many emeralds that ad will sell, but men across the country will be racing for cold showers."

"I wonder if that's an insult or a compliment, Mr. Hawk," Ashley said sweetly.

"It's a statement of fact, and that's all," he told her. "You were talking about a murder."

"Tara and Rafe left because of the storm and the baby. I stayed behind for the last take. Then Harrison said that he wanted to talk to me."

"So you just blithely went along."

"I didn't want to cause a scene. I had other friends there who might have tried to help me and Harrison could have hurt them."

"Hurt them. How?"

"In New York, when they wanted to work again."

"The almighty dollar, huh?"

"No. Survival, Mr. Hawk."

"You must really scrimp and save to survive."

"Cameramen do not make fortunes."

"Finish the story."

"I'm really trying. It's just that you really are capable of being one nasty—"

"Injun?"

"Mr. Hawk, I don't care if you're a spaceman!" Ashley straightened, putting all the distance she could between them. He could anger her so easily and so quickly. She didn't understand it. He came close, and then it was as if he wanted a wall between them, as if he purposely built barriers. "You've problems, sir."

"No, I don't," he murmured, his dark lashes covering his eyes, his head lowered as if he spoke to himself. "Except with...you."

He looked up quickly, as if he hadn't said the words. "All right, I'm sorry. What happened next?"

"Harrison got carried away in the bushes. I got away from him and started running. Then I saw them. There were three of them, all in slickers. Two of them were arguing with the one in the middle, I think. Anyway, the man to the left drew out a knife and stabbed the man in the middle. Then he threw him right into a canal."

"Then?"

She frowned, then shivered. "Then they looked at me."

"Who were they?"

"I—I don't know. The rain was coming down so hard. The victim's back was always to me, and I couldn't begin to see the killer's features. I ran. I ran and ran—and I ran into you."

"Why did it take you this long to tell me this?"

"Because..."

"Because I might have been one of them?"

"I have no way of knowing."

"Um."

Ashley swallowed some of her drink, deep in thought. She reached out suddenly to touch his arm, her face full of hope. "If I couldn't see them, then they couldn't see me, right?"

He hesitated. "If they were there, and you saw three figures, you can be sure that they saw you."

"How?"

"Unless they were completely blind, they would have seen a woman dressed only in a bikini bottom and those emeralds sparkling all over the place."

"Oh," she murmured, lowering her eyes. Then she stared at him sharply. "You said 'if'!" she accused him.

He shrugged. "Yeah. I said, 'if.'"

"You don't believe me!"

"There's a very bad storm out there, you know."

"So what?"

"So how can you be absolutely sure of what you saw?"

"Because I'm not blind! I'm telling you the truth, the absolute truth."

"I'm sorry, it just doesn't make sense. That's my property you were running around on. Most people would have been wary of the storm, and if they didn't have to be out in it, they wouldn't have been. Maybe—"

"There are no maybes," Ashley said stiffly. She grated her teeth. He didn't believe her, and that was that. She was a featherbrain to him. One who saw things.

"In the morning, things might look different."

"They aren't going to look any different, but you're not going to believe me no matter what I say." Ashley finished her drink and set the glass on the table. He was still watching her, still clad in his towel, still with the same dignity. "You've no right to judge me, you know."

"I'm not judging you. I just—"

"You've been judging me since you brought me here. No, you were judging me when you watched us shooting the commercial. I can wear a bikini and I happened to be modeling Rafe's emeralds, and so I'm a featherbrain."

"You're a featherbrain because you have a tendency to act like an idiot," he corrected her warily.

"I didn't know about the eye of the storm."

"You didn't know that this whole place could be dangerous, storm or no storm."

Ashley shook her head, and stared at him, her eyes as brilliant as the emeralds she wore. "No. None of that is true. You judged me from the very beginning. You assumed that I was a stupid, chattering fool because I was a model. And you assumed that I would be a prejudiced against you for being an Indian."

"I—"

"You did, deny what you like. Well, you're wrong. I come from New York City, and every kind of people live in New York. The United Nations meets there, you know."

"Does it really?" he inquired politely, settling back. "They haven't invited the tribe in yet, you see."

She smiled sweetly. "You, Mr. Hawk, are the bigot."

"The hell I—"

She didn't know what she was doing, but she reached across and caught his chin in her palm, squeezing his jaw. "Yes, Mr. Hawk, you, not I, are the prejudiced one. I didn't make a single judgment on you. Not a one—"

"Except that I might be a murderer," he said, freeing his jaw from her grasp. He held her hands tightly.

Ashley tossed back her hair. "That wasn't personal. You just happened to be in the swamp. While you—"

"Yes, do go on."

His eyes glittered, his tone was dangerous, and his fingers were warm and strong on hers. She didn't care. She lifted her chin. "You almost came right out and said that I deserved whatever I got from Harrison—because of a commercial! And, of course, I must be stupid. And I must be careless of others and crude because I have money, too. So before you ever got to know me, Mr. Hawk, you had me branded. I was a foolish, stupid, callous, rich girl. Right?"

He was smiling. There was a certain cynicism there, but still it was nice, and a warmth spread throughout her. She felt as if she had reached him—reached in and touched just a little bit of him.

"I made only one assumption," he told her.

"And what was that?"

Outside the wind raged and the rain poured down. But at that moment, she knew only the power of his eyes as he stared at her for a long time. Then he released her fingers and touched her cheek, and she didn't draw away. He smoothed back a tendril of flame-colored hair. "I just assumed that you were every bit as sexy and beautiful and sensual as the woman who was perched on that rock and totally destroyed my equilibrium."

Ashley smiled slowly. "Is that a compliment?" she whispered.

"The highest."

She thought that he was going to kiss her. That he would pull her against him, cradle her in his arms and kiss her.

And if he had, she wouldn't have protested. She wouldn't have been able to do so. She had studied the fullness of his mouth time and time again now, and she knew that his kiss would be instant wildfire.

And so little lay between them. If he kissed her, more could follow. She had ached too many times to stroke his shoulders. She had been fascinated by the ripple of his muscles, by his hard, lean belly, by the copper glow of his skin, so dark against her own. If he kissed her, more would follow, and she wouldn't protest. It wouldn't matter that she had spent all the adult years of her life taking the gravest care in every relationship, in learning to distrust, to search out the heart. None of that would matter, because it would be him. That she barely knew him wouldn't matter. She wanted him. She ached for him.

He did kiss her—but not as she had expected. He didn't draw her near. He sought out her eyes, then he leaned forward, and his lips just brushed hers.

Instant wildfire. The briefest caress, his lingering nearness, ignited deep yearnings within her. His fingers grazed her cheek and touched her jaw. They slipped around her neck, and he drew her close. His tongue traced the outline of her lips, then probed deeply into her mouth, and she was enveloped by the sweetness of the sensation. There was no hesitation about him. His fingers slid beneath the collar of the robe and over her shoulder, curling over the bare flesh of her breast, exploring the shape and weight and contour. His palm scorched her nipple, and she choked a cry of ecstasy.

He drew away abruptly. His touch ceased, his lips left hers. Startled, and suddenly ashamed, Ashley closed her eyes and leaned back.

She had known that he thought little enough of her already. She should never have allowed this.

Eric stood and looked down at the woman on the couch. A fierce shudder suddenly went through him. He'd never seen anyone more beautiful in his life, but it was more with Ashley Dane. He'd never seen anyone more sensual. The sound of her voice was in his head, in his soul and body.

Maybe it was her hair. As red as fire, long, thick, a fascinating and feminine cape about her shoulders and face. Maybe it was her eyes, so darkly lashed, so emerald. Her skin was fair and slightly tanned. She had no freckles, just a smooth, perfect complexion. All of her was smooth and perfect. Her breasts were full and firm, the flare of her hips was as evocative as the rounded firmness of her derriere. And her lips...

They were moist from his kiss. From the contact that had left him shattered and barely in control—and hating himself and hating her even more.

His wife had been dead for a long time now. Almost four years. And it wasn't as if there hadn't been other women since.

But he had never seen their faces. Never.

Certainly not as he saw Ashley Dane's. She drew out every primitive ache and longing inside him. She touched his senses and his soul. She was like a perfect angel cast down from the heavens.

Not an angel. A tormenting little witch. One covered in emeralds and dripping with wealth and savvy and he sure didn't need to be touching her. She needed to be back in New York City. She didn't belong here in the swamp. She didn't know the swamp, its people or wildlife, and she could never appreciate its beauty.

He shouldn't touch her. He would get burned.

"My room is yours," he told her curtly. "You may as well get some sleep. I'll be in the guest room if you need me, but I really can't see why you would."

He turned around and left her. He didn't see her eyes open wide with shock and hurt. He didn't see anything at all as he walked blindly into his office, slammed the door and cast himself down on the couch.

He didn't see....

But he still felt her. He stretched out his fingers, closed them and stretched them out again. And still, he felt her. He felt her breast, heavy in his hand, felt the pebble-hard peak of her nipple, the very softness of the silky skin surrounding it. He felt her cheek, her face, the slope of her shoulders, and whether he opened his eyes or closed them, memory taunted him.

She had been so cold when he had carried her here. He had tried to warm her. After he had assured himself that she breathed and that her heart beat, he had cleaned away the mud and stripped off the soaking bikini bottom. He hadn't meant to pause, but he had. She had looked very beautiful and perfect, and she had somehow seemed as pure and sweet as well.

Angelic...

An angel, yes, perfect and pure, and so enticing that the whisper of her breath haunted his soul mercilessly. She had lain upon his bed, and all of her had been more glorious than anything created on earth.

God had created that beauty, he had thought.

Maybe, just maybe, he had hoped that she would be vain and callous and shallow.

It might have been guilt. Because he really had thought that she was more beautiful than any other woman he had ever seen, including his wife. Maybe he had determined to dislike her from the very first.

He rolled over, groaning. She made him think, and he hated to think. He hated to remember love.

Eric lay there in the darkness and breathed softly for a long time. Then he rose and went out to the living room. He picked up a candle and carried it with him into the kitchen. He dug beneath the counter until he found the Jack Black. He reached for a glass, shrugged, then just swallowed a whole fiery gulp straight from the bottle.

It felt good going down. It warmed the part of him that had grown cold.

It eased the parts of him that had knotted with lust and desire and yearning.

He turned around at last and carried the bottle into his office. He closed the door, tightened the towel around his hips and lay back on the sofa. He stared into the darkness and frowned.

Her story couldn't be true. She believed it herself, but it just couldn't have happened. No one would have been out in the swamp in the storm.

Not an Indian, not a white man.

He sighed. It didn't matter; there was nothing he could do. It would still be some time before the downed wires were fixed, before the roads were cleared.

When the rains stopped, he would see what he could find.

In the meantime, it seemed to make some good sense to drink himself to sleep.

All through the night, the wind howled.

Ashley lay awake for a long while, listening. Sometimes it seemed that the wind and the rain would destroy the house, but the building always stood firm. Ashley reflected that Eric Hawk would not be here if his house hadn't been built strongly to weather the elements. Just as he would weather them himself.

She twisted, wishing that she could sleep, wishing that she had never allowed him to kiss her. She wasn't accustomed to feeling so miserable. Nor was she accustomed to being the one doing the wanting. She'd been hurt one time, but she had weathered it well. She knew how to take care of herself. Perhaps her life was easy now because Tara was her best friend and the shadow of Rafe's power fell her way. Life was charmed, but only to a certain extent. She was still independent, and she still had the Harrison Mosby types to deal with, and she still had attitudes like Eric Hawk's to deal with.

She gave up trying to sleep while listening to the fury of the wind. Swinging her feet over the side of the bed, she stood and walked back to the little table. She picked up the picture again and wondered about the woman with the long black hair. Who was she? His wife, his friend, his lover? All of the above?

The woman meant something to him. A chill passed over Ashley's heart, and she was suddenly convinced that the woman was dead. If not, she would be here in this room, not Ashley.

Curious, she picked up a candle and walked over to the armoire. She hesitated, then opened the pine door and looked in.

It was as she had expected. The closet was filled with a woman's clothes. Ashley gently touched the shirts, blouses and skirts. There was an array of styles. Denim jeans and T-shirts, attractive dresses and a beautiful sequined evening gown.

The colorful clothing of the Seminole nation was there, too. Beautiful beaded blouses and skirts, with bands of red and yellow and black—striking and typical.

In the rear of the armoire, Ashley found a gown in a clear wrapping. It was a wedding gown, an antique one, more cream than white from age. It combined the elegance of European fashion with Indian beadwork. It was one of the loveliest things Ashley had ever seen.

"What do you think you're doing?"

She almost dropped the candle as she spun around, so startled that she cried out softly.

He was there again, standing in the doorway, his hands on his hips.

He was wearing a pair of jeans now, but his feet and chest were still bare. She couldn't see his face, but she knew that it was filled with fury.

He strode into the room with such purpose that she cried out again, jumping out of his way. He didn't come near her, though. He slammed the armoire door shut.

"You've no rights here!" he lashed out suddenly.

Ashley sniffed the scent of Jack Black in the air. She backed away from him, wishing that she had never met him. "I didn't mean any harm."

"You're a snoop!"

"I wasn't snooping!"

"What were you doing?" he demanded.

"Looking! Just looking."

"What—"

"All right! I was trying to figure out why you act like such a complete bastard!"

"Why, you...!" he muttered. Then he added with a bitter growl, "You had no right to look in there."

"You have no right in here!"

"It's my room."

"I'm a guest," she declared.

"An uninvited guest."

"A guest, nevertheless. And you're drunk."

She still couldn't see his face. The candle was shaking in her hand, the shadows in the room were spinning crazily, and all the while, she could hear the wind increasing again. The storm was raging with an even greater force.

He was watching her tensely. "Didn't you know? That's a big problem out here. We have a lot of alcoholism."

"You're not an alcoholic," Ashley retorted. "You're just trying to ruffle me. You like to disturb and upset me, and I'm not at all sure what I did to you to deserve it." She was trembling, and she didn't know why. He hadn't even touched her. He stood his distance, but she was so acutely aware of him there that it hurt. She wanted him to leave.

And she wanted him to stay. She wanted to demand to know just what hold he had over her, and she wanted to tell him that she was sick of his temper and his attitude and that she didn't want anything to do with him. He was right—this was the swamp, and he was part of the wilderness, and she hated the wilderness.

"What you did to me?" he repeated. She thought that he smiled. She thought that there was a flash of green fire within his eyes. "What didn't *you* do to me?" he said.

"What?"

Suddenly the candle was snatched out of her hands. The holder rattled as he set it upon the table, and the soft glow fell upon him. His dark hair fell over his forehead. The hard planes of his face were filled with a fascinating tension and his lips were curled into a sardonic, haunting smile.

Then she saw his face no more.

He snuffed out the flame with his thumb and forefinger.

He reached for her, pulling her against him in the darkness. His voice was husky, his body seemed to be an inferno. "Come here, Miss Dane, Miss Ashley Dane. I'll show you exactly what you've done to me."

CHAPTER 4

His arms went around her. She felt his lips come down hard on her own, felt the moist heat of his tongue as it seared past the barrier of her teeth to delve deep within her mouth, bringing into her the very soul of his passion and longing.

The darkness was a sweet deliverance, allowing her to yield to her own desires, to give to him in that first kiss all that he demanded. Liquid heat invaded her and she trembled. It was only the strength of his arms and the power in his lean body that kept her from falling.

The wind was with them once more. It lived inside her—wild, tempestuous, heedless of the night. She felt its pulse and its strength. She cried with the wind's abandon. She didn't understand him, she didn't understand the night, but she was glad and reckless.

She could no more deny what burned within her than she could deny that the wind did swirl and rage. They were both its captives perhaps.

His lips broke away and his eyes met hers, and she realized that the darkness was not so complete that she couldn't see something of the man. She saw the blaze in his eyes, and she realized that there was fury in them, that he didn't want to want her.

But she saw, too, the anguish and the hunger. She opened her mouth, wanting to protest. She never spoke, for his lips closed upon hers again, and it wasn't the anger she felt at all, but the force of a need beyond time and place.

She was in his arms, lifted high, then brought down on the bed where she had lain before, only now she was so much more aware. The sheets were fresh and cool...or else her body was hot. Her mouth had gone dry and her limbs felt weightless as she lay there waiting.

She heard the hiss of his jeans zipper, and she tried desperately to tell herself that now was the time to stop before it was too late. He barely liked her; no, he despised her, but he would leave now if she asked him to.

He didn't despise her. He waged war with some past devil, she thought, and it was because of her tonight that he had been waging his war with a bottle of Jack Black. She needed to reason.

He stood over her.

She wanted nothing of reason, not tonight. In the dim light she could see him—whipcord lean, coppery dark skin as smooth and sleek as metal. Muscle rippled in his shoulders, across his chest and his belly. Not a single hair marred the golden expanse of his chest, while below, at his groin, there was a thick ebony profusion of it, a nest for his maleness, pulsing now, aroused, raw and exciting. She felt her breath catch, and she looked at his eyes. But shadow covered him now, and she couldn't see his face.

There was still time to protest....

His hands fell on the robe's sash and she couldn't speak. Her lips were slightly parted, they went dry and she had to wet them with her tongue. She remained still, watching his long fingers as they untied her simple knot and moved aside the velour. He stared at her, then drew her against him, and she felt the raging fever of his body. She tried to hold him, but he was pulling off the robe with impatience. Then she was down again and he was straddling her. He was as magnificent naked as man could be. She knew that he watched the emeralds she still wore sizzle their green fire against her bare flesh.

A deep, harsh cry escaped him. It seemed to come from the very earth and was older and deeper than time. She knew at that moment that she would never deny him. She didn't understand him, but she could feel him and all of the things inside him.

She kept her eyes on his as he reached out and brushed his palm over her nipple. He enveloped her breast, then his fingers closed upon the peak.

She caught her breath again, seeking not to cry out with the sensation. His left hand came upon her, too, and he covered both breasts and touched each hardened peak until she couldn't bear it any longer and a cry broke from her lips. Then he bent his head toward her. He caught the pendant between his teeth and tossed it aside. His tongue drew a burning path in the deep valley there and where his hands had lingered. Moisture formed around her breasts. His hand caressed their fullness, his lips and teeth and tongue closed around the buttoned peak, nipping, suckling. Ashley dug her fingers into his hair. Whispers tore from her, words that had no meaning.

Small, sweet fires broke loose inside her. Flames that teased and tormented and raced like the wind. Deep within, the flame took root. She arched against him, gasping. She felt the pulsing length of his maleness against her bare belly, and that made the fires race more fiercely. They reached the juncture of her thighs, the very core of her desire. She gasped softly. His hands roamed free, curving over her breasts, her hips. She, too, made an eager exploration. Sensation soared like lightning from her fingers as she stroked his flesh, marveling at the smoothness of his shoulders, the ripple of muscles on his chest and the strength of his back. He swept his lips over her midriff and down below, taunting her belly. His hands, large, fascinating, exciting, moved up and down the length of her thighs, then swiftly parted them.

His eyes were upon hers, but she couldn't meet them as he rose over her again. Her lips went dry once more and she felt that she ceased to breathe. He stroked the downy red triangle between her legs.

She felt his fingers deep inside her, exploring, demanding.... Her eyes flew to his and she saw the fascination within them. Her lashes fell to shield her own secrets as a moan of sheer ecstasy burst from her. She tried to rise but he fell against her, holding her to his leisure and his exquisite play. His lips found hers. Then the fiery thrust of his body replaced his taunting touch. She shuddered and cried out again, stunned by the sheer impetus of him and quivering with sensation.

The wind had ceased, or so it seemed. The world had ceased to revolve. There was only one thing of which she was aware, and that was the power of this man, joined with her in their intimate lock.

He held still, holding her lips to his, stroking her breasts, grazing her throat with the tip of his tongue.

And then he moved.

The wind began to whip again beyond the harbor of their bed, and then within it. The rain came down, slashing with fury against the walls. Ashley didn't stroke his back or run her fingers through the hair that had so fascinated her. She clung to him. Each thrust touched her with a little lap of fire. She trembled in his arms, and husky gasps escaped her, until the gasps became cries, and she didn't recognize the sounds as coming from her. She didn't realize that she arched and writhed and twisted, finding him more necessary than the air she breathed. Without him, she thought, she would die. The flames burned brighter between her legs. Then they rose high, burst and cascaded down all around her. She'd never thought that such sweet ecstasy really existed, that the body could reach such heights. She held him and felt him still. Eric groaned, going tense and rigid. Then he shuddered and fell beside her, groaning softly again. He pulled her against him, his fingers playing gently with her hair. They heard the wind again, and they were silent together. The silence stretched on.

Ashley closed her eyes and bit her lip. Her body grew cold, and she longed to cover herself, but she didn't dare move. There was so much to be said, and yet she couldn't say anything at all. She opened her mouth, but words wouldn't come, and so she kept still, all the while feeling colder.

How, she wondered, could anything so beautiful have become so horribly awkward?

The seconds ticked on. The wind continued to moan and howl. She tried to turn. Her hair was caught beneath him.

"Eric?" she murmured tentatively.

He didn't respond. Ashley carefully tugged her hair. She pushed up on an elbow, searching out his features.

His eyes were closed. He hadn't noticed that she had moved. She took the opportunity to study the man she barely knew, the man with whom she had just made love so intimately. She should be ashamed of herself, she thought. But she wasn't. Through all of her life she had been careful and distant, but something about Eric Hawk had enticed her beyond reason, and because of that, it had to be all right. Maybe she had known that making love wasn't necessarily like this; her previous experience had certainly left her untouched. Maybe that was why she had waited, and why everything now seemed like a touch of heaven.

She was tempted to reach out and touch him, but she didn't. She just looked at the way his black hair fell over his forehead, and she gazed at the high, broad planes of his cheekbones and the long, straight line of his nose. She liked his mouth—in repose, when he smiled, when he laughed, even when he was angry.

And she was fascinated by his body. She loved the sleek feel of his flesh, the hardness of him, the ripple of his muscle beneath her fingertips. She loved the leanness of his hip and the sinewed length of his legs, and she loved the very part of him that made him so intensely male, so demanding, so combustible. She probably shouldn't be studying him so....

She glanced back to his eyes, and she saw in the dim light that they were open, that they glittered upon her. "Anything different?" he asked her with a long drawl.

She stiffened. He was going to ruin something that had been special and precious to her. She wouldn't let him. "Different from what?" she demanded.

"From the men you're accustomed to," he said huskily.

"What men am I accustomed to?"

"White men," he said flatly.

Ashley tossed her hair back and sat up, throwing her feet over the side of the bed. She spoke with her back to him. "Yes. You're incredibly insensitive and rude. Are those special traits?"

She started to rise. She gasped, startled, when his fingers caught her hair. He released her as quickly as she cried out, but she was already down on the bed once more and he was leaning over her. She expected some awful flare-up of his temper but that wasn't what she received at all. He studied her with his eyes and stroked her cheek.

"I'm sorry. I didn't mean to hurt you."

"Physically?" she asked softly. "Or with the barb of your words?"

"I didn't mean to hurt you," he repeated. "It's just that—"

She stared at him in the dim light, wishing that she could see more. But she knew that what she wanted to see lay inside of him, and no light would help her see that. Only he could allow her the vision she wanted, but he wasn't about to.

"Just what?" she whispered.

"You're different." The words were tender. "You're very different from what I'm accustomed to, and I'm not doing well, am I?"

He didn't wait for an answer; he didn't want an answer. He lay down, turning his back to her. Ashley listened to the wind and to the steady beat of the rain. The tempest was dying again. And she was colder than ever.

"Eric?" she murmured. She rose and looked at him, then sank back down, not sure whether to be furious or perplexed.

He was very definitely sleeping.

Ashley shoved him, grabbing the covers. She plumped up her pillow and in the darkness she wondered how on earth she had begun her day that she had wound up here tonight. She should get up and leave him and go elsewhere.

But she didn't seem to be able to do so. She hadn't the energy. She hadn't the will.

Then he moved. His hand landed on her stomach, then his fingers curled around her midriff and he pulled her against him. The soft rush of his breath moved over the top of her head, ruffling her hair. She lay still, feeling how his fingers fell just beneath her heart.

He slept on, and she gritted her teeth, innately aware that it was the woman in the picture he held so warmly and so gently. She definitely should move.

But he sighed then, deeply. His fingers moved gently upon her, and he drew her even closer.

"Eric," she whispered. Tears filled her eyes. She didn't want to be here. She was being used, she thought. She, Ashley Dane, who could turn any man down sweetly, coolly, determinedly, with great sophistication, whatever the occasion demanded. This man had used her—and used her still. She had to get away from him. It hurt.

But she didn't move. Something told her that maybe it was good for them both, and so she stayed. For a long time she remained awake, looking up at the darkness, seeing patterns on the ceiling. She refused to give up the taste of heaven. He couldn't hurt her, not unless she let him.

She shivered suddenly, listening to the rain. A man had been killed out there today. Or a woman. Eric hadn't believed her, but she knew what she had seen.

And the murderer had seen her, perhaps recognized her. She hadn't thought about it all. She had forgotten the events in the swamp when she had been in Eric's arms.

Then she knew why she didn't move away. She felt safe with him. Even if he had stripped away the rapture and the fantasy, she still felt safe.

The rain beat on. Ashley prayed that it would stop. Then, with tears scalding her lashes, she prayed that she would be able to go home, to escape the swamp and the fear and the man by the next day.

Especially the man. His effect on her was more disturbing than everything else.

Eventually light from outside began to seep in through the shutters into the room. Only then did Ashley sleep. It was morning. And with it would come freedom.

Eric awoke with a splitting headache. He knew that he opened his eyes in his own bed. His mouth tasted like turpentine; it was dry and sticky and awful, all at the same time. He thought that the wind was still swirling, then he realized that it was only in his head. Even the rain, it seemed, had stopped.

He tried to move—and groaned. He hated himself for the way he felt. He'd been no more than twenty the last time he had imbibed so freely. No, that wasn't true. After the shooting he had drunk himself clear into oblivion on a few occasions. But he had lived in a haze then, in the midst of a nightmare. Thanks to his family, and especially Wendy, he had survived. He'd learned to care again—about his writing, about his heritage.

There had been very bad months when he'd lived in total reckless abandon, not caring if he died. But that had been over three years ago now. He knew that he mattered, that the things he had done mattered.

But last night...

He stiffened and realized that he was not alone in his bed. He turned around and found that she was still beside him. She slept sweetly, silently.

Her breath escaped from slightly parted lips. She lay with the covers just below her breasts, the curve of her body revealed beneath the white sheet. Her hair fanned out in a burst of flaming color. It curled over her breasts and framed the perfect shape of her face. Redheads were supposed to have freckles, he thought, but she had none. She did have green eyes. Enormous green eyes, dazzling green eyes. They were closed now, but he would never forget their brilliance. He would never forget anything about her.

Damn, he wanted to forget....

But he never would.

From the moment he had first seen her, first heard the whisper of her voice, he had felt the overwhelming draw. He had trembled to touch her, and right or wrong, that touching had been inevitable. Now he was tempted to draw away the sheet, to reach out and feel the warmth of her breast, to savor the lushness of its feminine fullness. His body grew hot and tight, and he quickly looked away from her, wincing, willing his body to forget her.

Never.

What the hell was she doing in his life! he wondered furiously. He didn't want her. She was a contradiction in every move and word. Her sensuality was bedazzling; her honesty was a slap in the face. She had played no games with him; she had walked into his arms as sweetly as an angel....

An angel from New York City, he reminded himself. A woman in business with one of the richest men in the world. A woman who had traveled the world, who could have anything at all. A woman entertained by him, he well imagined.

Never to be his. Not really.

His fingers clenched and unclenched. He didn't want her to be his. He had known once what it was like to love and hope and dream with a woman who loved him, who lived for the times they spent together, who dreamed with him of a better world and a better time in which to raise their children. He could never have her back again. With her gentle laughter and quick smile and earth-warm loving, she was gone. She would never come again.

Ashley Dane. Even the name sounded big city. Like a high-fashion model. Like someone with lots and lots of money, dripping in jewels...

Dripping in emeralds. They sparkled now in the daylight. Green fire lay against her hair where it dangled from her ears. It shone from her wrist, from her fingers. It dazzled there against the rise of her breast, next to the rose-colored peak.

He didn't want to touch, but his fingers were already moving. He touched the cold stone, then the warmth of her body. Fire seemed to singe him, sizzling down the length of him. He wanted her more than he had ever wanted her before. Now he knew that she could be an angel, breathing life into him, crying out with surprise and pleasure, arching to his touch, writhing beneath the rhythm of his hips. Now he knew how her breasts could swell in his hands, how his touch could bring her hot and moist and make her want him in return....

He drew his hand away from her, gritting his teeth, swallowing hard, as if he could swallow down the rise in his anatomy. Damn her for stumbling half naked into his life, for tearing him to pieces with this desire. If he thought that he could wake her rudely and have his fill of her, he might have done it. But something warned him that that wouldn't be the end of it.

That would only make him want her more.

She was a sultry temptress and an angel all in one. Peaceful and pure in sleep, sensual in movement. And whenever her eyes looked at him, it was with a shimmering, dazzling light to vie with the sun.

A borrowed angel, at best, he reminded himself sourly. And he had already borrowed her. A shower was in order. He was not a slave to his wants and desires, and he would walk away without touching her again.

Cursing and furious with her and with himself, he got up.

He showered in the icy water for a long time, then dressed in jeans and a polo shirt. Coming back into the bedroom, he saw that she still slept. She had not moved. He tensed and his body went hot again. Swearing soundly beneath his breath, he turned around and strode out of the room.

He had to get rid of her.

He hurried to the front door and flung it open. The wind and rain had stopped. The sky, though, was gray. The destruction before him was complete. Each plant in his yard had been ripped from the ground and tossed everywhere.

He walked outside carefully. Storms could toss up some mean snakes, too. He stepped over the debris and looked out to the road and the canal. He couldn't even see the road, and the water had risen very high. If he was lucky, maybe he could make it as far as Wendy's house in a day or two.

No one was going anywhere that day.

He muttered an expletive and stomped back to the house. He had always loved the solitude he found there. Today, though, he despised it. Solitude was only good when he was alone. This wasn't solitude anymore.

He made coffee, almost cracking the pot as he set it over the sterno burner. He closed his eyes and started to breathe slowly. It's what his grandfather would have told him to do. Close your eyes and remember that for all men, there was a greater purpose. Peace did not come from without; it came from within.

He opened his eyes. At the moment he was convinced that his grandfather was full of rot. He had no peace inside himself whatsoever.

With a sigh, he poured himself a cup of coffee. The storm had moved on. Maybe it would return—hurricanes had been known to double back on places where they had already done destruction—but right now he desperately wanted some daylight.

He went to his office, opened the shutters and looked out the window. He had always loved it here. He loved the tall grasses and the cranes and egrets and great herons. He loved the sunsets that stretched on for eternity. The Everglades wasn't for everyone. It was a wild and lonely beauty. It was his heritage, and the swamp had shielded his people when nothing else could. Though peace had failed, though war had failed, the swamp had endured. The Indian had never been removed from the Everglades, and he still had his tenacious hold here on the land. In the nation of greatest plenty on earth where political refugees flocked, the Seminole still fought to be an ordinary citizen. Eric believed in the future. Change came slowly, but he believed it came. Wendy had taught them all that men and women were all alike. His white mother had fallen in love with his Indian father and they had combined their dreams of happiness. It was a good world, a good fight, and he loved it.

It was all that he had.

He sat down with his coffee, smoothed back his hair and picked up some of the research notes that Wendy had left him last week. His eyes strayed to the mantel and the pictures there. Wendy and Leif, hugging and laughing, in the airboat. Wendy and Leif, Eric and Elizabeth, together. Then there was the newest picture—Wendy and Brad and Josh. Brad the proud father, Josh a beautiful baby, and Wendy looking beautiful because she was always beautiful, inside and out. Eric smiled slowly, and his eyes touched upon Josh's face. He knew that he was as much an uncle to Brad's son as he would have been to his own brother's. Love was always the tie that bound men, not blood.

"May I have some coffee?"

The soft words startled him so badly that he rattled his cup against his desk.

She was dressed in his robe again. She'd been in the shower. Every trace of makeup had been washed away and her face was even more beautiful without it. Her hair was wet and slicked back and her ears were stripped of the emeralds.

Her eyes, though, still dazzled. Just like jewels.

Eric stretched out a hand, grudgingly indicating that she should take the swivel chair in front of his desk. "Yeah. Yeah, I'll get you some," he told her.

She sat, folding her hands in her lap. He walked into the kitchen and poured her coffee, then realized he hadn't asked her how she liked it.

Black, he decided. If she wanted sugar and dry creamer, she could come back for them herself.

He walked back to his office with the coffee and handed it to her. She nodded without looking up at him, her fingers closing around the cup. Long, elegant fingers. Her nails were glossed with a fiery orange-red color that complemented her hair.

He remembered those nails, never hurting as they raked over his flesh, bring him alive. He remembered those elegant fingers stroking his shoulders, clinging to him....

"There's sugar in the kitchen," he said curtly, walking behind his desk. "Help yourself."

She didn't move. Her gaze rose to meet his at last. "The wind has stopped. Can I get out of here today?"

He shook his head. "No."

"Why not?"

"There's just no way. The roads are flooded. Power lines are down."

"Oh."

She stood and started to wander toward the open window. The V on the robe dipped low. It wasn't her fault. It was just that the garment had been made for a man, not a woman. She was tall, so it didn't hang ridiculously, but watching her move was still the most disturbing thing that he had ever seen.

"It's beautiful out there," she murmured.

"What?" he snapped. Sitting behind his desk, he swirled around. She had her hand on her throat and was staring out at the endless sea of grass. She didn't look his way, and he wondered at her words.

"I rather thought you hated the swamp."

She flashed him a quick smile. "Oh, I do. But seeing it from here, it's beautiful."

"Beautiful and deadly," he corrected. Just like you, angel, he thought, then he almost laughed aloud at himself. She wasn't deadly; it was his soul she was consuming alive. He started to stand but sat back down quickly because she was walking by him to the bookshelves. He loved to read and he had everything—research books by the scores, classics, ancient masterpieces and contemporary spy thrillers. She honed in on his research material, running her finger over the spine of a book entitled *Seminole.*

"It means runaway, right?" she asked.

He shrugged. "That's the general consensus."

"But you're not the only Indians down here. The Miccosukee live in the same area, too, right?"

His eyes narrowed sharply and Ashley was pleased. She knew something about the area, and a lot more than he would suspect about North American Indians.

"Yes," he replied.

Smiling very sweetly, Ashley continued, "Two separate and distinct tribes, although they weren't recognized as such by the American government until fairly recently. Two different languages, although both peoples practice some of the same feasts and rituals, such as the Green Corn Dance."

"How do you—" he began, but broke off quickly with a shrug. "What did you do? Go and watch the alligator wrestling? Take a stroll through the village?"

She ignored his question. "Why do you hate me so much?" she asked suddenly. "Someone in your family was obviously white. Hawk—that's your father's name, I assume. So your mother, maybe?"

"She was Norwegian," Eric admitted with irritation in his voice.

Her eyes widened tauntingly. "Well, that's certainly white," she muttered.

He didn't reply. His hands folded in his lap, and he stared at her. His life was none of her concern.

Ashley turned back to the books, wishing she could quit feeling like crying. He was acting as if nothing at all had happened between them. Well, two could play that game. She could play it very well.

She faced him. "When do you think that I'll be able to get out of here?"

He shrugged. "Tomorrow, the next day. It may take a whole week for the rescue people to get out here."

"A week!"

"Don't worry. As soon as the water in the canals is down a little, I'll get you over to Wendy's."

"Wendy's?"

"My sister-in-law's. I think you'll be happier there. Brad can take you into town as soon as possible."

"Your...brother?" Ashley said.

"My brother is dead. Brad is Wendy's husband. He's with the Drug Enforcement Agency in Fort Lauderdale."

She nodded and sat down. Silence fell between them. Ashley lifted her hands, then let them fall back to her lap. "Well, thank you."

He stood abruptly then, almost knocking over his coffee. "Wait a minute," he told her curtly.

He walked out of the room. Ashley leaned her head back. She was still exhausted even though she had awakened so late. She felt as if blood and life were drained from her.

He reappeared carrying a pair of jeans cutoffs and a short-sleeved tailored blouse. "Here. Try these."

The clothing fell on her lap. She looked up at him. "Your wife's?" Ashley asked.

He shook his head. "Wendy's. She's much shorter than you are, but I thought that they might do."

Ashley nodded slowly. "Fine. Thank you." He wasn't about to let her touch anything that had belonged to the woman with the raven hair and warm smile.

"Maybe you could read," he told her.

He wanted her out of his office. She smiled. "Sure." She walked over to the bookcase and purposely picked out *Seminole*. "Maybe I can find out what gave you your warm and witty personality."

Eric didn't respond. He watched her as she walked out of the room with the clothing and the book.

Ashley went into the bedroom and changed. The shorts were very short, but they fit. The blouse was a little better. She decided they were better than worrying about losing the robe at any minute.

Worrying...

How on earth was she going to endure the day? It was terrible just being near him. It was awkward and painful. She hadn't expected anything from him, not flowers, not avowals, not commitment, but neither had she expected the ice, the absolute coldness, his acting as if he really did hate her.

There was a knock on the door. Ashley hesitated, but he didn't wait. He pushed the door open and stepped through but kept his hand on the knob.

"I just—I just wanted to say that I was sorry."

"Oh?" she said. "About what?" Being rude. He knew that he had been rude.

"About last night."

Ashley gritted her teeth. "Last night? Just how do you mean that you're sorry, Mr. Hawk?"

"Too much Jack Black—"

"I see," Ashley broke in coldly.

"No, you don't!" he countered. "I'm trying—"

"I don't think that you've really tried to do anything in years!" she told him.

"Oh, really?" He paused, his jaw twisted, his fingers tightening on the doorknob. His eyes narrowed as he stared at her, his muscles constricting. "Just what do you know?"

"Enough," Ashley said defensively.

"You don't know anything."

"I know enough not to deny what I've done, or felt!" she cried.

He took a step toward her and she didn't know why but she panicked. She backed away to the bed, picked up a pillow and held it before her like a shield. He kept coming toward her. "You don't seem to know anything!" she told him. "Not about honesty or courtesy."

"I don't?" He was closer. But smiling, she realized. She smiled, too, as he snatched the pillow from her. She grabbed the second pillow.

"You don't remember how to laugh or how to have fun. Or how to apologize or—Wait!"

He was almost on top of her and not listening at all. She thrust the pillow against his chest to stop him, but he deflected her move with his own pillow and she staggered down to the bed. "Wait!" she cried, "you're not listening—"

She struck again.

He staggered back, his hair tumbling over his forehead and his eyes. He stopped in his tracks, staring at her. And then he started to laugh.

"Eric..."

Disheveled, striking, sexy, he leaped down beside her, still laughing. He caught both of their pillows and cast them aside, sweeping her into his arms. She shrieked in protest, trying to regain her pillow as a barrier against him, but she couldn't begin to counter the strength in his arms.

Her hands went still upon his upper arms and suddenly she was breathless. For a long moment, they just stared at each other. Her wet hair was in wild disarray and fell over his fingers. Her eyes were alive with laughter.

"I'm not half as bad as you say I am," he told her.

"No?" she asked, moistening her lips.

"I really am sorry," he said softly.

"Do me a favor?" she whispered.

"What?"

"Don't be. Sorry, I mean. I wasn't."

He shrugged. "All right. If it was nothing—"

"I didn't say that it was nothing. It was everything. Think what you like, I can't change you. But I don't do things like that. Ever. It meant everything."

When his smile faded, the laughter left her eyes. He pulled away from her. "Don't say that."

"Damn you, will you stop that! How can you so horribly ruin something that was decent and wonderful." He stared at her blankly. Ashley knew that he saw her as the sophisticate, the big-city girl with tons of experience. She knew then that he was just the opposite, that he might have been in love once, but that nothing had been special to him since. "Don't you—" she began, then broke off with a sigh. "Never mind. Just move, please!"

But he didn't move. He was staring down at her as if he hadn't even heard her. He smoothed a tangle of hair from her face, his green eyes intense and brilliant. Then he leaned back and gave himself a shake. "What?" she murmured.

He seemed to regretfully push away from her and stand. He took a step but then turned back. He reached out a hand to her, and a rueful smile touched his lips. "Once more, Miss Ashley Dane, I'm truly sorry that I'm such a rude bore. Try to forgive me?"

She hesitated.

His smile deepened. "Honest. I'm sorry—About being rude, crude and abrasive. And have it your way—I'm not sorry at all about last night. I enjoyed every second. Every touch, taste, scent and move."

That wasn't exactly what she had wanted. His words brought a deep flush to her cheeks, and more. They brought back memories. Of his hands, of his lips...

She lowered her head and accepted his outstretched hand quickly. He helped her up.

"Want more?" he asked softly.

"What?" she murmured, looking up and meeting his eyes in confusion.

"I could go on," he told her blandly. "About last night. About everything that I liked about last night. In detail."

"No! No, that's all right."

"All right," he said agreeably, then laughed at her perplexity. The sound was easy and good, and she was glad of it. His fingers curled warmly around hers, and she was glad of the touch, too. Their eyes met, and his gaze was warm.

But maybe that wasn't so good. Her breath quickened and her heart took flight, and she was left wishing desperately once again that she could leave him then. Right that very second.

There were murderers out in the swamp. Even if he didn't believe her, a murder had taken place. There might be extreme danger for her. But she could hardly think of it now that she was with him.

Because it wasn't her life that was in peril then, she knew; it was her heart.

CHAPTER 5

Warily, Ashley followed Eric into the kitchen. He went to the refrigerator and felt around inside. He seemed satisfied. "Still cold," he told her.

"Without the electricity?"

"I've got synthetic ice blocks in there," he said. "They're great. Well, what will you have?"

"What are my choices?"

"Oh, koonti bread, alligator tail. What's your preference?"

She didn't know if he was teasing her. With her nose imperiously high, she took a stool by the counter. "I've had alligator tail, Mr. Hawk."

"Have you?" He turned around with a wry smile. A little shiver shot along her spine. She wished he wasn't quite so attractive, not that he was attractive in any nice, civilized way. He called upon something primitive inside of her with the curve of his lip and the sure, casual sway of his walk. The way he stood now, black hair falling over his forehead, that smile in place, somehow suggested energy and passion and something wonderful and vital that was just barely leashed.

"Yes," she said with dignity and arrogance. Then she smiled, too. "They serve it at Disney World."

"Disney World!"

"In the Grand Floridian, at the restaurant out on the lake. They serve it as a steak, and they make the most wonderful bread spread out of it, too."

"Oh, do they?" His brow was arched high; he was still smiling.

"Yes."

"Damn. Then it will have to be koonti bread," he told her. "Or do they serve that at Disney World?"

Ashley laughed. "Who knows? Maybe they do, but I haven't tried it. What is koonti?"

"A root. We survived on it for years and years, and women like my grandmother still grind it the old-fashioned way and make bread from it. I think she's convinced that if I eat enough of it, I'll come to a good end after all."

"Oh? Are you heading toward a bad end?"

"A terrible one," he assured her. "Iced tea?"

"Umm. Love some."

He went back to the refrigerator for a pitcher and poured them each a glass of tea.

Ashley watched him. "Seriously, do you often eat alligator meat?"

"Only after the season."

"The season?"

He nodded. "Once, they were endangered. They've made a remarkable comeback, so now there's a yearly alligator season, and so many hunters are given licenses." He smiled. "That's when you really have to watch out in the swamp. Reporters follow the hunters and it's as if a pack of wild animals had been let loose!"

"You don't mean that," Ashley said with a laugh.

"I do. Have you ever met a newsman hungry for a good story?"

"Yes, as a matter of fact, I have," Ashley said. Media people had come after Tara like vultures at times. "Okay, so they can be bad. But not as bad as an alligator, I'm willing to bet."

He shrugged. "Alligators aren't my favorite creatures, but they're fascinating. As old as the dinosaurs, as simple in their being. There have been some horrible incidents with them lately. 'Nuisance' alligators, that's what they're called. Gators that get into canals and make it to the residential sections, things like that. There was a little girl killed just a few years ago. A beautiful, blond girl. An alligator took her right down. I hated the creatures like crazy when I read that. But I've seen the hunters out here, too. They kill the alligators using everything, and it can get quite gruesome. I doubt, though, that the alligator meat at Disney came from hunters. There are alligator farms all over the northern part of the state now. People breed them for their hides and their meat.''

"And yours?''

"Brad bagged him. He'd taken to playing around too close to the house.''

Ashley shivered violently. Eric grinned gently. "That's why you shouldn't just go running out of here,'' he said softly, then added, "but don't worry. They're usually very wary of humans and since they've been hunted again, they've grown shy.'' He returned to the refrigerator and rummaged around. "I've got it!'' he cried.

"What?''

"Ham and cheese?''

Ashley started to laugh, and she was amazed because it was so easy. "Perfect. Want me to help?''

"No, I think that I can handle ham and cheese. Mustard or mayonnaise?''

"I like surprises,'' Ashley told him.

He smiled and turned to the task. A few minutes later, he tentatively set a plate before Ashley. "You're not going to throw it today, are you?''

"Not unless you're absolutely obnoxious,'' she told him sweetly.

"Maybe we'd better eat fast.''

"Can't control that nasty streak, eh?'' she teased. But then she wished that she hadn't spoken because something dark clouded his eyes. She thought that it was truth, that there was something in his behavior toward her that he couldn't quite control. She looked quickly at her plate. "Hmm. Looks wonderful.''

"Thank God. I was worried. Not a drop of caviar or paté in the house.''

She glanced up at him. "For your information, Mr. Hawk, peanut butter is one of my very favorites. I can't bear to eat anything at all that's green or greenish or mushy brown, such as paté. I never, never liked fish eggs.''

"Excuse me,'' he told her lightly.

"I will try,'' she promised.

He chewed a bit of his sandwich, watching her. "I like you that way,'' he told her.

"What way?''

"Without the makeup."

Ashley shrugged, wondering if he meant it. She wished that he wouldn't look at her so. It made her feel as if her flesh came alive. She became achingly aware of herself all over. She let her lashes fall over her eyes. "Thanks."

"So tell me about New York."

She glanced at him again. He had about downed his sandwich and she was still picking at hers. "What's to tell? Have you ever been there?"

He nodded. "Interesting jungle."

She laughed. "Yes, it is."

"Do you live alone?" It was a pointedly personal question. Of course, Ashley thought quickly, they'd already been as personal as it was possible to be. But then he had been the one to start building the walls.

He had also been the one to call the truce.

"I live alone. I have an apartment on Columbus Avenue, not far from the Museum of Natural History."

"And what do you do when you're not wearing a bikini in the Everglades?"

"What do you do when you're not rescuing women in bikinis in the Everglades?"

"Bikini bottoms," he reminded her.

He wanted to draw a reaction. She wasn't going to let him. "Bikini bottoms," she agreed sweetly.

"I asked first."

"But you should humor the weaker sex."

He offered her a very slow, amused and strikingly sensual smile. His words had a soft drawl when he spoke. "I'm not at all sure that there's anything weaker about you, Miss Dane."

"All right. I design clothing. With Tara Tyler. We both worked for a man name Galliard for years—"

"Galliard?" He frowned. Ashley was certain that he must have read something about it in the papers. Galliard had been a very well-known designer. When he had been arrested in Venezuela for murder, the news media had played up the story.

"Of course, Galliard," he said. "I remember reading something about it in the papers. I looked it all up again when Rafe Tyler reached me about using the property." His eyes were very sharp upon her. Wary even. "It must not have been a very good time for you," he said.

"Well, I don't think that I was ever more frightened in my life. Tara had been involved with a man named Tine Elliott. By accident she met Rafe's brother who was working for the authorities. Tine was trying to steal priceless artifacts, and Tara got involved in a shoot-out. They tried to accuse her of murder. Later, when we all came to Venezuela together, Tine kidnapped me to get to Tara." She shivered violently.

She saw his hand move on the counter, as if he would reach out to her. But he did not. Ashley frowned. "But I wasn't alone, you see. Rafe's brother was there, and Sam, an old friend and employee. And then finally Rafe and the authorities arrived, and everything was all right. But I'd never been so scared in my life, and never was again until..." Her voice trailed away. She flashed him a furious glance. "Until I saw that murder take place in the swamp."

He had been chewing. He stopped. "All right. So maybe I didn't believe you," he admitted.

"Do you believe me now?"

"I don't know. I believe that you think that you saw something take place."

"That isn't the same thing at all. I'm not given to hallucinations, and I'm not the delicate type to fly off the handle at anything."

"You've said that you hate the swamp. The rain was coming down in torrents, and you were frightened of everything already. Maybe you did—just this once—hallucinate a tiny bit."

"I did not!" Angry, Ashley stood. "I can't wait to get out of here!"

He stiffened like a poker, straight and hard, and something as cold as ice fell over his eyes. He stood, too. "Well, we'll get you out of here just as fast as we can, Miss Dane," he promised her. He came around the counter. "Excuse me, will you? I've got work to do."

He walked away down the hall. Ashley followed his departure, wishing her temper wasn't quite so explosive.

He opened the door to his office and disappeared into the room. The door closed with a slam. Ashley even heard the lock bolt home.

"So go sulk!" she whispered after him. But, she thought, he wasn't sulking. He was angry with her. And she would never change his mind about her.

"And why should I care?" she muttered. He was just a temperamental stranger who had dragged her out of the swamp. She couldn't wait to leave. She wanted to be with buildings, not saw grass. Her type of jungle was concrete, not this overwhelming swamp and muck and canal and wilderness. It was best if they kept their distance.

"Stay in there!" she told the empty hallway softly. "You just go ahead and stay in there!"

She felt like throwing a dish again, but that seemed to be what he expected of her. Instead she inhaled and exhaled slowly, picked up the few dishes and determined to wash them.

Despite the storm, his water was still running, and it seemed clean and fine. Ashley decided that he must have his own well on the property. She was glad of it. She not only washed the dishes but also scrubbed the sink and the counter, not that they were particularly dirty. Eric Hawk seemed to be neat and organized.

When she was done she sat in the living room for a moment, studying the buffalo skulls with their feathers and etching. They were wonderful art pieces, she decided, and she'd love to have them herself.

Then she noted that it was growing dark again. She rose and looked around the kitchen and dug through the drawers until she found candles. She walked around the living room picking up the holders and digging out the previous night's candles, then setting the new ones into them.

Eric still had not appeared.

With the candles lit, it seemed that night came on completely. Ashley had no idea of the time; she wasn't wearing a watch. The clock over Eric's mantel said that it was one, and she knew that that wasn't true. Her stomach was growling, though, so she dug through his refrigerator. When she opened the meat drawer, she found that his meat was neatly wrapped in white butcher paper and clearly labeled. She stared at the markings, annoyed that her fingers moved over the handwriting. She even liked his script. His letters were big and bold, well formed and slanted, and somehow, they endeared him to her even more.

She glanced down the hallway and her lip tightened. "Damn him!" she muttered. She almost shoved the package of meat back into the refrigerator and slammed the door. She held on instead and read the wrapper. A slow smile curved her lips. It was alligator tail.

Newly determined, she lit the sterno and found a covered frying pan. She dug around in his cupboards for seasonings.

A half hour later the kitchen smelled deliciously of garlic, butter, cayenne and black pepper. She'd cooked the meat along with some green peppers and onions and potatoes, and whether it was a recipe or not, it even looked really good, too.

She found a bottle of German Riesling, poured a glass and added a few of the remaining ice cubes. After preparing herself a plate, she sat down to eat. She tasted her creation and decided that it was really darn good. But Eric Hawk still hadn't appeared.

She sipped her wine and took her time. He still didn't come. Finally she gave up. She washed her plate and set out one for him. She poured herself a second glass of wine and went to knock on his door. He didn't answer. She didn't care. "There's dinner in the kitchen if you want. If you don't want, make sure you go blow out the sterno. I just put your stuff back on to warm."

She quickly went down the hall, balancing her wine and a candle.

In his room, she set down her candle and wine, plumped up the pillows and lay down, finding the book she had chosen earlier from his study. She opened the pages and looked at the door. She still hadn't heard a thing.

She wouldn't be able to concentrate, she thought. But she opened the book to a page past the introduction and started to read. Without realizing it, she quickly became absorbed.

The first chapter was on the advance of the Seminoles, an offshoot of the Georgia Creeks, into Florida during the beginning and middle of the eighteenth century. The next chapter focused on the First Seminole War, and Ashley found herself more engrossed. The narrative spoke about Andrew Jackson's dead-set determination to eliminate the Indians, and it spoke, too, of the Indians' desperate struggle to survive. Their way of life had already changed. The "chickee," the thatched-roof house on stilts, had not always been their home. They had built houses of logs at one time, but these were burned time and time again, and so they adopted the cool shelter of the chickee.

The stilts protected them from creatures of the night, from the Florida alligator, from the snakes, from any other hungry creature. But nothing had protected them from man. Nothing but the swamp itself.

The telling was wonderful. It was not fraught with detail, and yet everything was there. Her heart was torn for a people trying desperately to survive, but there was an explanation about Jackson's hatred—he had lost kin to an Indian attack. If there was a message or a moral in the book, it was not that the white man was to be entirely mistrusted or abhorred, or even hated for the endless treachery practiced upon the Indians. Savagery created more savagery, and to this day, the United States and her native sons and daughters were working on coming to terms.

A slight sound finally caught her attention. She looked up. Eric Hawk had made his appearance at last. He was standing in the doorway, leaning there actually, watching her. She thought that he had probably been there some time. She didn't know why she was so certain, but she was.

"You shouldn't sneak up on people that way," she told him.

"I didn't sneak up on you. You just weren't paying attention."

"I was reading. Can I help you?" she asked sweetly.

A slow smile came to his lips. "I just came to say thanks."

"Oh?"

"That...that whatever it was, was delicious."

"Oh, the alligator tail."

"Umm. I enjoyed it thoroughly."

"Good."

He came into the room. She was looking right at him, and he was staring right at her, and she still had the sense of being stalked. He moved with such utter silence, with such smooth confidence. He was completely dressed, but she discovered herself imagining him naked again. He was so beautifully built, offering everything in a woman's fantasy, even when the woman didn't even know that she'd had fantasies.

His green eyes flashed when he came to the foot of the bed. He rested an elbow on the bed and grinned up at her. "Like the reading material?"

She flushed, then forgot his eyes with a rush of enthusiasm. "Yes! I love it. It's the most marvelous book. It's all history, it's factual, but it reads like a novel. It made me feel as if I knew them all—the Seminoles, the whites, all of them. I love it." She cast him a semisweet smile. "I'm going to finish it right now, even if I read all night, because of course I know you would never dream of lending it to me, and I want to get in every single word of it."

She thought that her sarcasm would irritate him. It didn't. "You're just saying that," he told her.

"I'm not."

"You are. To appease me."

Ashley sat up straight, tossing her brilliant red mane over her shoulder. "First off," she informed him, pointing a finger straight at his nose, "I wouldn't dream of appeasing you. Secondly, why on earth should I appease you by liking a book? Just because it's about the Seminole Nation?"

"Because I wrote it."

"What?" Ashley gasped, looking into his eyes. They still danced with humor, but there was a seriousness there, too. He was telling her the truth.

She looked at the book again. The title was in huge print. The author's name, down at the very bottom, was much smaller. But it was there, sure enough. Eric Hawk.

Startled, she stared at him again. "You did write it."

"Yes," he said softly. Then he crawled forward, very much like a circling cat, pulled the volume out of her hand, and let it drop to the floor. She stared after it.

"Why—?" she began.

"Because," he interrupted her. He was beside her then, sitting cross-legged and facing her. Close. "You don't have to finish it now. And you don't have to borrow it. It's yours. Take it with you when you go."

"You don't have to—"

"Yeah, I do," he said. He reached out and stroked her cheek softly. That rough and tender touch evoked a whole new tempest of longing within her. His eyes continued to hold hers. His fingers moved, his knuckles brushing the length of her neck, then grazing down over her breast. He touched her lightly, and she realized that she ached to be held by him, ached to be bare and to feel his hands hot and demanding, upon her. But still she didn't move. She met his eyes because the things that couldn't be said out loud were spoken there. He had to want her without the bitterness, without the dreams of a past. And then she realized that he did. He still might not like her, and perhaps he even still judged her, but his wanting was for her. And at that moment, that was enough for her.

She cried out softly and threw her arms around him and he captured her within his own embrace. Their lips met and simmering passions exploded. He delved deeper and deeper into her mouth with his tongue, searching and hungry, as if he demanded the soul of her. Their lips parted and met again, and she sought the liquid thrust of his tongue with her own. Then she broke away from him, panting, yearning.

"I should stay away from you," he whispered.

"Why?" she demanded.

He sat back again, touching the ring on her finger. "Because you're like a Tyler emerald. Beautiful to look at...and far beyond bounds."

"I'm not a stone!" Ashley protested. "I'm not a thing, or an object, or an ice-cold piece of rock. I—"

"No, no, you're not rock!" he agreed heatedly, lacing his fingers through her hair, then catching hold of the buttons on her blouse. They opened easily beneath his practiced fingers and he held her bare breasts in his hands. Rising up on his knees and bringing her with him, he kissed her again. His lips trailed from her mouth to her earlobe. His thumbs found the peaks of her breasts and rubbed them, creating twin streaks of fire that shot through the length of her to the very center of her longing. His lips hovered above her again. "And you're not cold. There's nothing about you that's cold in the least. And there is everything, everything that's beautiful."

"Oh," she whispered softly, and her lips came against his throat as she held him tight. She thought of his bare chest, how the ripple of muscle fascinated and drew her, and she tugged on his buttons. She was not as deft and tore off a button.

She pulled away in horror, gasping out an apology, amazed that she could have wanted anyone with so great an abandon that she would have ripped clothing. She opened her mouth to speak, but she was quickly back in his arms. "It's the best button I've ever lost!" he assured her, laughing. But the laughter was tempered by fire. It was throaty and husky, and entered inside her just like his touch, making her hunger, making her yearn.

He pulled away from her for a second to strip away his own shirt. He crushed her back against him and just held her there. Together they knelt on the bed, and his passion took flight again. His hands scorched endless trails over her back, bringing them together hip to hip. Ashley bent her head, nipping his shoulders, trailing her tongue over the smoothness of his flesh. Her fingertips brushed and kneaded him, and her lips and teeth and tongue followed. She tentatively set her teeth over the hard brown knot of his nipple, moving her tongue around it. She grazed her fingers low over his belly and felt him shudder, heard his ardent groan.

He caught her hair and held her face away, searching out her eyes. "You are like an emerald. Sparkling, dazzling green fire. Hard to touch, hard to hold, tempting beyond all measure. God, what you do to me...."

He kissed her again. While their lips met he found her hand and brought it against him. She almost recoiled, startled by the fierce pulse of his arousal. Then everything about him came to her in a rush. She felt the tempest of his breath, so ragged, and she felt the ferocious thunder of his heart, the burning constriction of his body. His palms, calloused and hard and masculine, were demanding, yet so tender as they closed over the fullness of her breasts.

Suddenly he broke away from her lips with a cry that rocked the length of her, saturating her with a liquid shimmer of deep desire. He cradled her breast with his hand and took the hardened peak into his mouth, to lave it with his tongue, tease it with his teeth, to suckle it. She couldn't believe his touch on her upper body affected her whole length, and she tugged on his hair, hardly aware that what she begged him for was mercy. He released her at last, but only to caress and suckle and tease her other breast until she could kneel no more, until she fell against him, desperate for more of him, yet not at all sure that she could endure more of his fierce lovemaking.

She was not about to be denied. He laid her down upon the pillow and shed his jeans. Breathing hard, she watched him and tried to rise when he came to her. He wouldn't allow her to do so. He kissed her lips and then trailed his tongue down her body, between her breasts, over her ribs. He paused, twisting her, to kiss the length of her spine. She tried again to reach for him, to bring herself against him, but he held her still.

He found the snap on the cutoff jeans she wore and began to tug them down her hips. He put his lips on her waistline and belly, and when the cutoffs were finally off, he parted her thighs. The tip of his tongue teased her thighs until it came between them. Then he delved into her with leisure and determination, finding the tiny button that coursed out its hunger and ecstasy and need to all of her—to her blood, her limbs, her heart...

The world blackened around her. Life before this night faded, and all she knew was the sweet blinding urgency, and then the shattering, volatile storm of rapture that broke and cascaded throughout her. She screamed, shaking and trembling, and barely knew that she had done so. Blackness did come. She died, she came back to life, and then discovered the tension in his face and the sheer masculine pleasure and triumph in his eyes as he crawled over her. Embarrassment racked her and she stared at him in dismay, trying to lower her eyes as if she could hide. He laughed— deep, rich, throaty—and found her lips and kissed her hard. Slowly he laid the length of his body over hers. She felt his sex, huge and pulsing and unappeased, against her thighs, and then she felt his movement and she forgot to be embarrassed. She melted to his touch. He sank into her, slowly and completely, while looking into her eyes once again. When he was fully inside her, she felt a touch, as if it were deep down inside her womb, and it awoke every hunger within her again. She opened her mouth, but no sound came. She wetted her dry lips, and his came down upon them again and he locked his arms around her.

All hell broke loose within him.

She felt as if she rode a tempest, rode the wind, rode the wild splendor of the earth itself, and it was wonderful. He was fury itself, liquid motion. When she thought that she could take no more, he held himself away from her and moved slowly...until she became the tempest, arching against him, setting her own rhythm. Then he ceased to tease and caught hold of her desperate flight, smoothing it into a sensual, sweet rhythm once more. It went on and on until she reached the final peak and clasped it tightly. She closed her eyes, and the stars exploded before her. Emerald stars, dozens of them, dazzling in the darkness all around her, settling her down, within the damp enclosure of his arms.

They lay there in silence for a long while. The candle flickered against the walls, and its glow grew smaller and smaller. Ashley closed her eyes. She must have halfway dozed, for she didn't so much awaken but rather became aware of him again. His fingers moved up and down her back, along her spine. Then his hands slid over her buttocks and caught hold of her hips and pulled her taut against him. He slipped inside her. Her breath came hot against his earlobe, and his whisper encouraged her to take flight along with him again.

When it was over they didn't break apart. His arm remained around her and her back lay flush against his chest. He stroked her arm softly and she didn't sleep. She heard his whisper.

"You're addictive," he told her.

"Am I?" she whispered.

"Um. Like caviar. I like caviar. I like it a lot."

She laughed softly. "First I was like an emerald. Now I've been reduced to fish eggs."

He chuckled and pulled her around to face him. She buried her head against his chest, loving the smoothness of his flesh, the tautness of the muscles there. She suddenly wished that there was no world other than their own, that the storm had taken away all roads forever, and that she could stay just where she was for eternity.

With a man who barely liked her, she reminded herself. But that was hard to believe at the moment. His long fingers moved tenderly through her hair, and she couldn't accept the fact that he hadn't come to care for her if only a little bit. She blessed the storm that had brought them together.

"It's almost daylight," he said.

"Is it?"

"Umm. I should have taken the shutters up yesterday. There was no reason to leave them down." She felt him grimace. "They're automatic. A touch of a button and they slide up."

"Umm," she murmured, content to be where she was.

"Did you sleep at all?" he asked her.

"Very well, except someone woke me up."

"Sorry."

"Please, don't be. It's quite all right."

"Good, because I'm really not sorry, not in the least." He was silent for a moment, then he sighed. "I'll be able to get you out of here either today or tomorrow, I'm sure."

Ashley didn't say anything. Her heart seemed to slam painfully against her chest. She couldn't believe that she really didn't want to go. Going meant returning to everything that she loved. The Met and the theaters and the massive buildings and Central Park in autumn. Macy's chocolate chip cookies. Her and Tara's cozy offices by Rockefeller Plaza. Ice skating...

Staying meant this man, the strength and security of his arms.

Except, of course, that he didn't want her to stay. He wanted her out. He liked his privacy and his quiet world. She was an intruder, even if she could cook and be entertaining in bed.

She pulled away from him, biting her lower lip as she stared up at the ceiling. She felt him prop up an elbow to watch her, but she didn't look his way.

"What's wrong?" he asked her.

"Nothing," she said, shaking her head.

"You're anxious to leave, I take it."

"That's not what I was thinking. Not at all."

"Then what?"

"Then what?" she repeated, and hesitated. Then she rolled over to look at him. The candlelight was not quite gone. "I was just thinking how strange things are, the way that they happen."

"Meaning?"

"This. The storm. Everything that happened. Being here. No matter what, I'll never regret it." She didn't like the way that he was looking at her. She wondered what she had said wrong.

"You'll never regret *it*? *It* what? You, me, the two of us? Making love? What are you talking about?"

"Do you have to get so particular!" Ashley exploded. "I—I meant us. I meant you. Everything I've learned from you and about you. I love the book about the Seminoles. I love what it says about you as a man. And I'm talking about us, too. Making love, or having sex, whichever the hell it is with you!"

"Oh," he said coolly. "I passed muster then, I take it?"

"Stop it!" she lashed out. It was ridiculous. She was going to start crying any second. No, she would not. Never in front of him. "It was wonderful. You were wonderful—"

"Well, I'm so glad!" he muttered, shooting up from the bed with fury. He reached for his jeans, and stepped into them as he continued to speak with a controlled wrath. "Wonderful, huh? Maybe I should be really grateful for the description. Maybe I'll have a whole flock of little socialites down here to try out the goods, huh? What is it with you? Try out an Indian, ye old noble savage, then fly down to Tijuana and try out a Mexican?"

Furious, Ashley stared at him, speechless for a moment. Then she jumped up, screamed something completely savage and came tearing around the end of the bed. She did so with a vigor and vehemence that made him wary but she didn't pelt him. She stopped just a foot before him. "You bastard! You stupid, egotistical, self-centered, neurotic, lousy bastard! Noble savage! There isn't a single thing noble about you, savage or otherwise!" She slapped him across the face as hard as she could.

Then she nearly cringed. Anger unlike anything she had ever seen leaped into his eyes. They glittered like knives. She prayed that he wouldn't strike back. She was frightened and was sure that she would scream and cry and...and either run or beg for mercy. No! She couldn't, she couldn't.

But if he took one step toward her, she probably would.

He did not. He didn't touch her, and he didn't say a word. He stepped around her and left the room. She didn't hear his footsteps as he strode down the hall. She did hear the front door open and slam with a terrible vengeance.

Ashley sank on the bed. She could still feel her palm stinging from the slap. He was gone, and she allowed hot tears to well in her eyes.

Thank God she would be out of here soon.

Swiftly, almost desperately, she raced into the bathroom. There wasn't much light, or hot water, but she didn't care. She jerked on the shower and stood beneath the water, which felt no colder than her heart. She picked up the soap and scrubbed herself furiously, not so much to remove any traces of their lovemaking, but because it seemed that if she tried hard enough, she could scrub him out of her mind and from under her skin.

When she was finished and shivering, her teeth chattering, she toweled herself dry with great fury. She was still seething. No, she wasn't seething—she was miserable. If it were in her power, she would stomp out the front door alone and find whatever help she could.

If she wasn't able to leave soon, she would do just that. She would run out again, reckless and heedless, just to get away from him.

She came back into the bedroom and started to straighten the sheets and the bed with a vengeance. Then she paused.

There was someone or something behind her. She didn't know how she knew, whether she had heard something or just sensed something. But it was there, in the doorway.

Eric, she thought. He had come back. He was either going to say something curt or cruel, or he was going to break down and apologize. Grudgingly she admitted that he was capable of a very good apology. Maybe he thought that she was the one who should be apologizing. She had actually struck him, and he had leashed his temper fairly well. She didn't owe him an apology, not after the awful things that he had said.

No, he had come back to tell her that he was sorry. Well, she wasn't forgiving him. Not this time.

But he wouldn't say anything. He would stay there in perfect unnerving silence until she turned around and acknowledged him.

She dropped the pillow she had been holding and spun to face him, crossing her arms over her chest. "Don't ask me to be sorry, Hawk, because I'm not—"

Her eyes widened with horror. It wasn't Eric standing in the doorway. It wasn't even a man.

It was a cat. A huge cat. A huge, tawny cougar—a mountain lion. It looked at Ashley, then it opened its mouth and gave an awful screech, displaying enormous curved teeth.

She moistened her lips, opened her mouth and stood perfectly still. Don't move, stare the creature down! she thought. But it wasn't courage holding her still—she was simply paralyzed with fear.

Then the huge cat moved. A lot like Eric. Step by step, massive paw after massive paw, the cat began to move. Big eyes, seemingly rimmed in black, surveyed her.

As if she were prey.

The cat stepped toward her. And then began to run for the bed, leaping toward it.

At last Ashley's scream tore from her throat.

She screamed and screamed again.

Because the giant cat was coming straight for her.

CHAPTER 6

"**A**shley!"

Eric burst into the room. For a second he stood in the doorway, searching out the danger. Then he made a flying leap, landed on the big cat and wrestled with it on the bed. Ashley, terrified and backed against the wall, closed her eyes. The big cat growled in fury. Eric yelled something, but she didn't understand his words. She remained flat against the wall, trembling.

Then she realized that the cat and man were off the bed and moving into the hallway. Eric slammed the bedroom door behind him, and after a while she heard the front door slam, too. She staggered over to the bed and sat down. She realized that he might get hurt. The great cat could scratch him or bite him or mangle his limbs. And there would be no way to reach help.

"Eric!" She leaped up and hurried to the door, flinging it open. He was already standing there. She threw herself into his arms with a tremendous burst of happiness and relief. "Oh, you're all right! I was so afraid of what that awful cougar—"

"Panther. It's a Florida panther. On the endangered species list," he said.

"Who cares!" she gasped. Her cheek lay against his shirt, her arms wound tightly around his waist. His hands fell on her shoulders slowly, then he pulled her close. "You could have been hurt! Oh, Eric, I was so desperate, and you came so quickly when I screamed, and you might have been torn to bits. Just torn to bits."

"Ashley, I was never in any danger—"

"Eric, thank you. Really."

"Ashley, honestly—" Eric broke off, mesmerized by the liquid green eyes that stared up into his. It was on the tip of his tongue to tell her the truth—that the cat's name was Baby, and that Baby was a pet. Wendy's, Brad's and his. Like any cat, Baby was independent. She was a bright creature, too, affectionate and very loving. She could be trusted with his cousins' little children. She was also a good ally. He and Brad had worked with Baby, and she could be commanded to attack, to run and leap on the enemy and hold him down. She could also be told to get away.

She hadn't threatened Ashley. Baby had just been curious. She wasn't accustomed to finding strangers in Eric's house.

He meant to say all of that to Ashley. He meant to explain. It was just that harsh words rose between them so easily. His fault, he thought. He didn't want to want her, but he did. He didn't want to care that she was a dazzling angel cast down from the heaven of the north, and that she would return to her glittering high palaces in no time at all. She was just a touch of green fire that lit up the dark swamp. Or maybe his soul, he didn't know. She was a red-haired angel, a borrowed angel.

He should really tell her the truth. He should explain....

It was just that she was shivering so violently in his arms. And she had that look in her eyes, as if she forgave him for all things. Then there was the feel of her skin as he held her, and the soft scent of soap emanating from her body mixed with everything so feminine and magical about her. Her hair fell against him, soft as a silken web, radiant as a blaze.

Words died on his lips. He had just left her. He had to be with her again. He lowered his mouth to hers and kissed her. Then he kissed away the dampness on her cheeks. His lips fell on her throat where it was arched to him. Her breasts were crushed against him and despite the clothing lying between them he could feel the hardness of her nipples and the fullness of her breasts. He groaned because he was lost.

He swept her up into his arms and brought her to the bed. He couldn't get enough of the touch of her, or of the beauty of her eyes. She was only borrowed, he reminded himself time and time again, but that made it harder for him, because he had to touch her more thoroughly to remember her. He had to lose himself within her completely, because the chance might not come again.

He groaned, and his arms came around her fiercely, and his mouth, teeth and tongue raked her endlessly. Nothing had ever touched him as she did; nothing had ever made him forget the pain.

In her arms, there was only the sheer fascination with every part of her—the satin feel of her flesh, the velvet texture of her hair sweeping over his shoulders and chest, teasing the length of him as she moved. She nuzzled his breast, nipped his flesh and moved down over him. There was the molten warmth of her mouth upon him, the stroke of her fingers. There was the feel of her knotting him into explosive ecstasy, making him soar over the world.

He allowed her to lead until he could take no more. He shuddered and cried out at her caress, and then he seized her and swept into her fiercely, hungrily. He thought that he branded something of himself upon her, and still he realized that her arms took more. Her soft and tender touch and her whispers took something of him. In her arms he was healed.

He was whole. His anger seeped from him just like his seed. She took from him gently, and when he lay back, soaked and shuddering and spent, he knew that his world had changed, and that she had changed it.

He let the air cool his body and curled his fingers around hers. "I have a confession to make," he told her.

"Oh? What's that?" she asked warily.

He turned around, propping up on an elbow, looking down into the emerald sea of her eyes. He wished that the moment could go on forever. Her hair was a spill of fire all around her. She was damp and beautiful and so natural at his side. She was naked, except for the emerald ring and pendant. Her lips were curled into a rueful, curious smile.

He touched her lower lip with his thumb. "She's a pet," he said.

She frowned, and her gaze fell on him, narrowed with suspicion. "She...?"

He laughed. "No, there's no pleasure palace in the basement. I don't even have a basement. She, the cat. Her name is Baby. Wendy picked her up as a kitten, her mother was dead. She spends her time prowling around between the two houses and the village for handouts. She wouldn't have hurt you, not in a thousand years."

"She's a...pet?" Ashley repeated.

"Yes," he said, then hesitated. "Are you angry?"

"Hmm. I should be," she muttered, her lashes falling low over her eyes. But she stared at him with the familiar fire in her gaze. "I should be furious. You kissed me, and all—" she paused, then indicated the bed with a sweep of her hand "—all this, under false pretenses!"

"Well—"

"I should—" she interrupted "—slug you. Right in the jaw."

"But you already did that," he reminded her, and with a broad smile he crawled over her, straddling her hips and catching her wrists. He bent low over her. "You already did that."

"And I'm not sorry. You deserved it."

"Oh, yeah?"

"Yeah."

"Well, I didn't take kindly to it," he warned her. He loved holding her and feeling the length of her. And he loved the way her chin tilted up in defiance. He knew that she wasn't afraid of him in the least, and if she had been afraid, she'd still have fought. Their fingers were wound together and he felt the thrust of her breasts against him. His lips very nearly touched hers as he spoke. "I let you get away with that once, but not again."

"You let me get away with it because you knew you deserved it," she said sweetly.

"You're impertinent, did you know that?"

She shrugged. She seemed about to retort, but those words died. Instead she whispered, "You're the most fascinating person I've ever met. And I'm sorry if that offends you, but it's the truth."

He held still, then kissed the tip of her nose and her lips. He carefully rolled his weight away from her. He stood and looked toward the east, and a small part of him urged him toward the window. He found the switch for the shutters and pressed the button, and with no more sound than a slight jingle, the shutters began to roll into their casings. The day appeared before him, beautiful, with the sun bathing the landscape. It was a wilderness out there, complete, alien and harsh to those who did not know it.

She was a borrowed angel, he thought. Brought by the storm. Borrowed angels sprouted big silver wings, and then they flew *away*. Maybe it had been all right to touch her, even to lose himself within her, and maybe she had done more for him than anyone else. But the storm was over. Their time was over.

He turned around and came back beside her. He knew that she had been watching him and wondering at his thoughts, but she hadn't spoken. He touched her hair and kissed her. "And you're the most beautiful woman I've ever seen. On screen, in a picture, in the flesh, ever."

He left her again, going to his dresser to dig out some clothing. He turned around to tell her that he was heading for the shower, but his words faded away.

Her back was to him. She was propped up on an elbow. The sheet just fell over her hips, her hair cascaded from her shoulders to the bed, and the long line of her back was visible down to the rise of her buttocks. She was framed by the rays of the sun beating down upon the hummocks and trees and the river of grass. She looked so beautiful. He wished that he could hold that moment forever, too.

Except, he reminded himself, that things were hidden from him. He couldn't see her eyes. And he was certain that they stared out on the forbidding swampland with fear and loathing.

"I'll be in the shower," he said softly. She didn't acknowledge him; he wondered if she had even heard him. He walked into the bathroom and pushed the button for the shutters there, too. They rolled up, showing what lay behind the tub. There was a redwood privacy fence surrounding the windows, and within the fence grew philodendrons, vines, creepers and a few wild orchids. Soaking in the tub was almost like lying in a pool in the wilderness.

He needed to go out and kick the generator, he told himself. He could use some hot water right now.

He grabbed a towel and walked through the bedroom. Ashley seemed to be sleeping so he moved silently. Outside he unlocked the wooden shed and went in. He wished that the generator worked as easily as the shutters. He had to rev the engine again and again before he could get the generator to kick into action. Finally it began to hum. Eric looked around. The day was almost deathly still. It wasn't hot, though. The storm seemed to have swept away a lot of the late summer heat.

Where else could a man stand in nothing but a towel and fight with his generator? he asked himself. There was nothing around him. The road wasn't really far at all, and the canal by his property led north to the Big Cypress, or south toward the Tamiami trail. There were other homes like his. Not many, but there were some. And there were still the small villages, like the one where his grandfather chose to live. Grandfather preferred the company of his old friends. Eric understood. If there was one thing he cherished most about his family it was that they all sought to understand one another and to give each other room.

The generator was humming away. He looked at his airboat at the back of the shed and thought that it was time to take it out, too. If Baby had made it to his house, then there was surely a way to reach Wendy's by now.

A sharp pain suddenly ripped through his midsection and he almost bent over. He didn't want to let Ashley go.

All the more reason to get her away just as quickly as he could.

He gazed out over the expanse of his property and a little trickle of unease touched his spine. Maybe it was more important than he was imagining it to be to get her to Wendy's place right away.

He had thought that she was hysterical when she had told him about the murder. And even when he had convinced himself that she wasn't the hysterical type, he still thought that the storm had frightened her so badly that she had imagined things.

But why should she have? The swamp had long been a place where grievous sins could be hidden. Men had been lured to murder here time and time again. What better place to hide a body than this endless river of grass where little was seen by any eye?

Maybe she had seen something. And if she had, Brad would be the best one to deal with it.

Eric picked his way through the fallen shrubbery back toward the house. He should never have come out barefoot, he told himself. Storms threw up snakes. There had been a time when Indians very rarely died from snakebite, a time long before antisnakebite kits and antidotes. They lived with the snakes, they were bitten, and they gained immunity. From the rattlers, anyway. The coral snakes could be deadly, though, their venom was so powerful. To this day, any Indian child living in or near the Everglades knew a coral snake very well by sight and avoided it.

And anyone with half a brain wouldn't be walking over the fallen vegetation without shoes!

Cursing to himself, he went inside the house, still haunted by a feeling of unease. He locked the front door carefully, then came into his study. He opened his closet, took down his shotgun and loaded both barrels. He set the gun back on the high shelf. Then he went to his desk and dug in the bottom drawer for the ammunition box, assuring himself that he had plenty of bullets. He set the box back in the drawer and headed for his bedroom.

Ashley was still sleeping. He went into the bathroom and turned on the hot water. He had to let it run a while. When he noted the steam rising, he switched on the whirlpool jets and crawled in. It felt good. He'd taken so many cold showers lately that the hot bath was wonderful. He closed his eyes and leaned back.

He jolted up almost immediately, aware that the door had opened. It was Ashley.

"Hi there, fellow—" she started to tease, but then she saw the steam rising and the foliage outside the window. "Oh, how lovely! And hot water!"

"Want to join me?" He raised his eyebrows devilishly. She laughed, wound up her hair, then sank into the tub. She closed her eyes, sinking lower. Her toes met with his calves, and she smiled, allowing her feet to be bold and brazen. He caught her toes. He kneaded her feet and drew her closer, stroking the length of her calves. She smiled, but then her eyes shot open and she gripped the side of the tub, stiffening.

"Heat! Hot water! Then you've got electricity!"

"Yes."

"Then the phone must work!"

Something inside him seemed to die a little bit. He hadn't expected her to be so desperately eager to leave. His jaw clenched tightly. He shook his head. "The phone lines are still down. I've got a generator." He sat directly in front of one of the jets. The water shot against his lower back. It eased his tension, but he found new constrictions forming within him. He caught hold of her ankles and pulled her against him. She paid little heed.

"Oh," she said disappointedly. Her lashes fell, then they flew open again. "A generator! Then we could have had electricity this whole time!"

"If I had wanted to go out in the midst of the storm," he said dryly, "I suppose we could have."

"But yesterday—"

"I can live without it for a day or two."

"But—"

"Sorry. I didn't realize that electricity meant so much to you."

She shook her head impatiently. "It isn't that! It's—"

He didn't let her finish. He found her mouth and kissed her almost savagely. Maybe she wouldn't realize the awful tension inside him. Maybe she would think that the tempest was simply the swirling water, the steaming heat.

It wasn't. It lay within him. He just wanted to taste all of her one more time.

She tried to pull away from him once, then no more words escaped her. He made love to her with a fierce and vehement passion that was all encompassing and completely overwhelming. When it was over, she was as exhilarated and exhausted as she had never been before. She lay against his wet chest in the water and Eric idly stroked her hair. "I'm taking you out of here this afternoon," he told her.

Ashley stiffened, wondering at the coldness in his words when there had been such incredible heat in his arms. She opened her mouth to speak, but Eric went ramrod tight against her, his fingers winding like wire around her arms. He pushed her forward slightly to stand and grab a towel.

"What is it?" she asked.

"Nothing. Nothing," he told her. But there had been something. He wrapped the towel around his waist and pulled her out of the tub. He put a towel around her shoulders and took her into the bedroom. He pushed her down into a corner by the bed. "Stay there."

"But—"

"Stay there!" he commanded in a sharp whisper.

Not daring to take any more time, Eric hurried along the hallway to his office. When he was about to enter he ducked down low.

Someone in black was passing by his window.

Eric crawled to his desk and dug out the .38 Special. Then he stood, back against the wall, thinking. He'd heard someone come. There were a dozen good reasons why he shouldn't have expected anything other than a friend.

And yet he had known that this was no friend.

The figure was gone.

He hurried back into the hallway and looked down it. Walking silently, he came to the bedroom door and peered in. Ashley was there, in the corner, where he had left her.

He smiled at her.

Then suddenly, the day came alive. The window shattered into a thousand pieces, bursting in upon them like tiny diamonds. A bullet whizzed by and struck the wall.

Ashley screamed, covering her head. Eric screamed to her, "Down! Stay down!" He turned toward the window in a split second, aiming his gun quickly. He fired, then ducked as he saw the nose of a gun come around the corner of the window. A bullet soared past him. He fired in the direction of the shot. He heard a thumping on the porch and then a thrashing in the grass. He leaped for the broken window and used the butt of his gun to clear away the shards of glass, so he could jump out. He landed on the porch and searched the area. There were drops of blood leading into the brush. He followed the trail, but even as he rushed along, he heard the sound of a motor. Out in the canal, a boat was leaving. He would never catch up on foot.

Swearing, he turned back. He realized that he had cut his foot, and hobbled on through the grass. Then he sped up. He didn't want Ashley alone, not for a minute.

He leaped over the window ledge, intending to hurry to her where she sat in the corner. She pitched herself into his arms instead.

"I told you to stay still!" he yelled at her, catching her arms and shaking her.

"You shouldn't have gone after him!" she countered, meeting his gaze boldly. But she was trembling. He relented slightly, pulling her against the thunder of his heart.

"What in the hell is going on here?" he muttered.

"I told you. I saw a murder," she murmured softly, her voice quivering.

He pushed her away from him, slamming the button to lower the shutters again. They crunched over the broken glass but closed with resolve.

"Ashley, it's all right. It's over," he said.

"It isn't over. It's just beginning," she said dully. She slammed her fists against him. "You shouldn't have gone out there! You might have been killed!"

"Stop it. I know how to take care of myself, especially out here."

She sank down on the bed, believing him. Still clad in the towel, he paced the room. She noticed that his foot was bleeding and she pointed to it. "Your—your foot."

"What?" He glanced down. "Oh, yeah." He smiled. "Want to get me a Band-Aid?"

She hurried into the bathroom and searched through the medicine chest until she found the Band-Aids. Then she paused, feeling as if the big picture window that had delighted her so was now a giant eye. She stared at it uneasily, then realized that Eric was behind her, holding her shoulders. "It's all right, Ashley. He's definitely gone—for now, anyway." He released her and pushed the button to lower the shutters. "It's safe, see?"

She nodded. She did feel safe with him, but she began to tremble again. He might have gotten himself killed out there, and if he had, it would have been all her fault.

"I'm sorry that I involved you in this."

"You didn't involve me in anything," he told her harshly.

"But I did."

"Listen, I still don't know what I believe," he said sharply. "You saw a murder. Maybe. But tell me, how did the murderer follow you here? How did he—or she—find you here?"

"I—I don't know."

"So maybe you're not at fault at all. Maybe it's someone after me."

Ashley didn't believe it for a minute. But then again, how could the murderer have found Eric's house? She started to shiver. "Maybe he followed us here when you picked me up."

"No. Unless he's an incredible tracker. Unless he knows this area. Listen, I don't know what's going on."

"Who would be coming after you?"

"Who knows?"

Ashley turned away from him worriedly. She almost screamed when he touched her shoulders to turn her around.

"Ashley—"

"I'm still afraid that I've put you at terrible risk."

He hesitated a second. Then a smile curved his lips and he touched her chin and gave a wonderful Bogart imitation. "If you have, you've been worth the risks, kid. Here's looking at you."

She smiled, but then her smile faded. "What are we going to do?"

He shrugged. "We could stay here. With the shutters down, the house is like Fort Knox. I'd have the advantages..." His voice trailed away, and he shook his head. "No, because if I don't show up at Wendy's, she or Brad will come here, and they could be taken unaware. We should move. Get dressed," he told Ashley. "Get something from the armoire. Jeans, socks, boots and a long-sleeved shirt. There might be a lot of mosquitoes out."

Her eyes held his and she nodded, as if in a daze. He gave her a little shove out to the bedroom and picked up the clothes he had already chosen for himself off the bathroom floor. When he came back into the bedroom, he paused.

She was in jeans, just as he had suggested. And in a soft pink long-sleeved and tailored shirt with mother-of-pearl buttons. He hadn't seen the outfit worn in a long time. Not in over four years. He hurt for a second. And for another second, he wanted her to look horrible in it. Her hair should have clashed with the pink. Elizabeth's hair—black as ebony, straight, lush—had been beautiful over that pink.

But he couldn't remember his wife's face at that moment, not as he was looking at Ashley there. Her eyes emerald bright, she was pale but resolved, calm and almost stoic, awaiting his next words.

He glanced to the side table. The emerald earrings and bracelet were still there. He snatched them up and shoved them into his pocket.

Was someone after the Tyler jewels? Or were they after Ashley?

Or had someone come to settle an old score with him? He just didn't have the answers.

"Come on," he told her, reaching for her hand.

"Where are we going?"

"To Wendy's. I told you before, Brad is with the DEA. Maybe he'll have some idea what's going on."

"But what—what if someone's out there?" Ashley asked.

Eric shook his head. "Whoever it was is gone now, and it's going to be almost impossible to reach us if we're moving in the swamp. Here, take this."

He thrust the gun at her. He was afraid that she would jump back or refuse to take it, but she closed her fingers over the handle. "It's loaded."

"You just saw it fired," he said.

She nodded.

"Do you know how to shoot?" he asked her.

She nodded. "Yes. Not well, but I've been at a range a few times."

"That'll do," Eric told her. He gripped her free hand and drew her along the hallway with him. He paused in his office for the shotgun and to close the shutters. Ashley winced. He glanced at her with a frown.

"I'm afraid I've got longer feet than...than your wife," she said softly.

He didn't reply but took her out the front door.

"Eric?" Ashley asked him quietly.

"What?"

"How did your wife die?"

She searched his features. No anger touched his eyes or tightened his face, but he didn't answer her, either.

"It's too long a story for now," he told her. "I want to get moving."

"But what if someone *is* out here?" she demanded.

"No one's here."

"But how—"

"I would know," he assured her. Looking at him, Ashley fell silent. She knew that he was telling her the truth.

He led her around the back to the large shed. He went in but left her standing outside. She heard the loud hum of the generator and saw him walk toward a large airboat.

Ashley determined to keep silent. It was hard. She was terrified.

Almost as frightened as she had been when she had watched the one figure plunge a knife into the chest of the other. What was happening? How had she been traced to Eric's? How could anyone find her here? They had seen her...and they had seen Eric, too. They had seen him sweep her up and take her away, and they had only waited for the storm to abate before coming for her.

She heard a startling clang. Eric had opened the back doors and pulled out a ramp, and the airboat was clattering its way down the ramp to the grass. He reached for her hand. She frowned. "Don't we need a canal?"

"That is the canal," he told her.

"Oh!"

Despite the danger, he smiled. And she smiled, too.

She was glad of the boots she wore, even if they were too small, because she sank ankle deep into muck as he led her to the airboat. She saw that he was right, that they were on a canal. But it was swollen with grass, and it was very hard to tell what was supposed to be water and what was supposed to be land.

"Have a seat," he murmured to her. "And keep that gun ready. Just in case we need it."

He turned to start the motor, but then he paused, looking toward the land. Ashley started to shiver, not knowing what he heard. Then she heard it, too. A certain rustling through the grass.

"Eric?" she whispered.

"It's all right," he told her.

"All right?"

"It's just Baby."

Ashley swallowed hard as she saw the big cat come bounding out after them. Neither muck nor grass nor water seemed to bother Baby. She headed toward the airboat full speed. Ashley felt her heart rise to her throat. The cat suddenly leaped off the ground, landing almost on top of Ashley.

She fought hard not to panic as she stared into the panther's huge tawny eyes. Baby stared at her, then shoved its silky soft head against her shoulder.

Ashley almost screamed. She gritted her teeth and looked up at Eric. "Nice kitty. Nice, nice kitty."

Eric grinned. "She likes you."

"Wow."

He laughed, then started the motor. He must have kept it in good repair, for it burst to life almost immediately.

Baby sat down at Ashley's feet.

Eric crawled up to the seat and took the wheel, steering the craft over the canal. Ashley leaned back, feeling the wind on her face. They went faster for a moment, but then Eric slowed down. Ashley looked around in dismay, feeling as if she had dropped off the face of the earth. She had never seen anything so forlorn. It seemed that destruction was everywhere. Branches and whole trees were in the water. The airboat could glide over the long grass easily enough, but she had a feeling that the endless tangle of fallen branches and shrubs was harder to negotiate.

She looked up to find him studying her. She tried to smile, but he didn't smile in return and only continued to watch her.

"How do you know where you're going?" she shouted against the roar of the motor.

"It's just like New York when you get used to it!" he said.

"How!"

"Well, we're on Fifth Avenue now. But we'll have to start taking the little side streets soon!"

She laughed and looked down at the cat. Tentatively she placed a hand on the panther's head. Baby closed her eyes, delighted as Ashley stroked her ears. A pet, huh? She'd heard of the "love me love my dog" type, but this...

This was more, she realized suddenly. To love Eric, a woman would need to love his world. It wasn't that he wouldn't accept another, it was just that he would always need to come back here. It wasn't simply the swamp, or his family, or even his people, it was the whole way of life. It was the choices he lived with, the solitude and the independence. Even if he said that he would give it up, he most probably could not. He wasn't a crusader, but he was a link between the old world and the new, between progress and heritage. He would never let one go for the other; he was always open to both.

She rested her chin on her hands and closed her eyes, and she wasn't afraid. No one could reach her as she was soaring across the swamp. She didn't need to be afraid.

It wasn't circumstance, though. It was Eric. No matter what he chose to do, she would feel safe with him. She would believe in him.

She swallowed hard and wondered what had happened to her in the past few days. She couldn't help but think what it would be like to stay. She found it hard to remember New York City, harder still to remember that her goals had centered on her business, and even harder still to think of dressing up in silk for drinks at the Plaza.

She'd always loved the city. It had its own magic, its own dangers, its own pulse and personality. But she didn't want to return. Instead she wanted to pretend that a bullet had never shattered her dream world and that she could go back into Eric's bedroom and lie with him....

With her Tyler jewels and his primitive earth.

The wind blew hard on her face again and she set the gun down to wind her hair into a knot. Baby settled her head on Ashley's lap. Then Eric lowered their speed once more. Ashley looked around her. A thick mass of wild orchids clogged the way before them. The water was strewn with logs. Then she realized that one of the logs came equipped with eyes. Beady, dark alligator eyes. They stared at her and she shivered as the alligator's nose moved into the water. Farther along the embankment she noticed a second alligator. Its mouth was wide open. The endless rows of teeth were fully visible, along with the creature's tongue and throat.

It waited, Ashley realized. It waited dead still for its dinner to come along and walk right in.

She sensed he was looking at her again. Ashley looked up and grimaced. "Cute!"

He didn't reply, but his dark lashes fell over his eyes, and she thought that he hadn't been too disappointed in her response to the creatures. She hadn't gone completely with instinct. She hadn't screamed hysterically and begged him to get her far away.

She shivered, then set Baby's head on the deck. She stood, coming close to Eric. "They're horrible-looking things," she told him.

After a moment, he placed an arm around her shoulders. "But as you might have noticed, Miss Dane, the deadliest creature in any jungle is still man."

"I noticed," she said softly.

He pointed ahead. "There, up there. See the hummock?"

She didn't, at first. Then she did see the large island and the spot of color just beyond the trees. A house. A home. Life in the midst of wilderness.

"Your sister-in-law's?" she asked.

"Yes!"

Ashley tried to smooth back her hair, but the wind wouldn't allow her a pretense of tidiness. Even as they came around the last bend and Eric cut the motor completely, the breeze tossed around tendrils of her hair. The airboat slowly came toward something like a dock, heavily laden with bracken and brush, as everything else was. She could see the house then. It was neat and storybook perfect, and a lot like Eric's. The front door burst open and a small blond woman came running out. A tall, broad-shouldered and dark-haired man followed her more slowly, a grin on his face.

"Eric!" the woman called. He leaped from the airboat to the mucky shore, and she hugged him fiercely. "You're all right? Any damage? I thought that you were going to try to come back. But then everything picked up so suddenly, didn't it? I was anxious—"

"Wendy!" the man interrupted her softly. "He's not alone."

Eric turned around, reaching out a hand to help Ashley to the shore. "Ashley, Brad and Wendy McKenna. Brad, Wendy, this is Ashley Dane."

"But we know that already!" Wendy said, her voice soft and musical and touched with a pleasant laughter. "We've been waiting for you."

Shaking hands with the woman, Ashley frowned. "You've been waiting for me?"

She nodded, looking over her head at Eric. "Your friends are here. Didn't Eric tell you?"

Ashley looked back at Eric and smiled sweetly. He shrugged. "I didn't know if they were still here or not. You were going to try to get them into town, Brad."

"I couldn't get them into town. It was too late and too much was happening."

"What are you talking about?" Ashley asked.

Then the door slammed open again and she heard her own name called. "Ashley! Thank God you're all right!"

Tara came running out and threw her arms around Ashley. They almost fell. Ashley hugged Tara in return and realized that there was something very different about her friend.

"The baby!" she cried in alarm, stepping back.

"The baby is inside and just fine," Brad said. "And Wendy, don't you think that you should get your patient back inside?"

"Yes, we should all get inside," Eric said.

Ashley saw that Brad cast him a quick glance, and she knew that Eric had managed to convey a sense of their danger with those few words.

"We should all get inside," Brad agreed. He lifted a hand, indicating that the women should precede him. Anxious to see Tara's baby and Rafe, Ashley started walking. But then she paused.

She looked back at Eric. He stood some distance from her, but he was watching her.

She shivered suddenly, because his glance was cold. And he seemed very distant.

His lashes fell, and he shrugged at her questioning gaze. What had been between them was over, she thought desperately. He had delivered her here, and that was that to him.

"Shall we go in?" he persisted.

She turned around blindly to follow Tara, praying that she wouldn't cry, then determined that she would never do so.

CHAPTER 7

There were several moments of confusion after they entered the house, and Ashley didn't realize that Eric and Brad had not followed them in. Rafe was there, sitting on a sofa with a bright-eyed toddler on his lap, and watching the tiny infant who slept in a crib created from a bureau drawer. He stood quickly, throwing the little boy onto his hip. "Ashley, thank God!" He gave her a fierce hug, with the little boy pressed between them looking on in wide-eyed wonder.

Wendy rescued her son, saying, "This is Josh. Josh, this is Miss Dane. Get your sticky fingers out of her hair."

Ashley laughed and untangled her hair from the beautiful little boy's fingers. He couldn't have been two years old; his coloring was his mother's, his handsome features were his father's. He would grow up to be a heartbreaker, she thought. "You can pull my hair whenever you like, Josh," she told him. "And you can call me Ashley."

He gave her an enchanting grin. "'lee!"

Wendy smiled, shrugging ruefully as Josh reached out again for the bright hair. "It's the color, I think. Oh, that sounds so rude! But it's just beautiful—"

"Please, it *is* red!" Ashley laughed, bending down to study the baby clad in a long sack gown. "A girl or a boy?" she asked. The infant had a head full of dark hair. Rafe's hair, certainly not Tara's.

"Amy," Rafe told her proudly.

"Amy! Oh, she's just beautiful, too. But how? When? Shouldn't you be in a hospital, isn't—"

"Ashley, everything went beautifully!" Tara swept her arms around Ashley's shoulders and sank to the couch with her. "Wendy used to be a nurse. She was wonderful, I'll never be able to thank her enough." She flashed a grateful smile to Wendy, who flushed and shrugged.

"It was nothing, really."

"It was everything," Rafe said softly. The McKennas had a friend for life, Ashley thought.

"Wendy doesn't think that Amy is really premature. She thinks that I miscalculated, which is possible, I suppose. The sonogram readings always were a bit off."

"And I'm glad!" Wendy admitted. "We would have had to take some drastic measure to reach a hospital if the baby had needed an incubator. But—" she paused, grinning again "—by the meat scale in the kitchen, Amy Elizabeth Tyler was born at a good eight pounds, one ounce."

"Ready for the world," Rafe commented. "Although her mother deserves a good talking to."

"Rafe, I promise I'll never, never do anything like it again."

"You're right. When we have another child, I'll lock you up in a tower for the last two months."

Wendy laughed. "You're not supposed to talk about another child when your wife isn't even a week past her introduction to labor pains, Rafe Tyler. Ashley, how about a glass of wine?"

Ashley glanced at the door. Eric and Brad were still outside. Eric must be telling Brad about the shots, and surely about the murder she had witnessed. She should feel relieved. The police would have to be notified. She was aware that the DEA and the regular homicide department were not the same thing, but she was also aware that drugs poured into south Florida from South America, and so the murder might be in Brad's jurisdiction after all. They would all believe her now. Eric's house had been shot up.

"Ashley?" Wendy said.

"Yes, I'd love some wine. Let me help."

"No. You sit and watch the baby. I think that Tara was more worried about you than she was about her labor pains. I told her that you'd be okay since we sent Eric back to make sure that everyone had gotten out."

She gave Ashley a dazzling smile, and Ashley smiled in return. "Brad can help me." Then Wendy frowned. "Where is he? Out with Eric still? What can they be doing?"

Ashley looked at the baby. Amy was so tiny and perfect, and she slept so peacefully. Tara was radiant and everything seemed to have come out so very well.

Thanks to Eric.

Wendy, holding a bottle of white wine in one hand and balancing Josh on her hip with the other, looked at Ashley worriedly.

"I'll call in Eric and Brad—" Rafe began but broke off when Ashley jumped to her feet.

"Eric is telling Brad...what happened."

"And what happened?" Rafe asked, frowning.

"We...were shot at. In his house. And I think it's because I saw a murder."

"A murder?" Rafe echoed.

Wendy was very still. Tara stiffened. For several seconds, they looked at one another, and then at Ashley. Rafe walked over to her and took her gently by the shoulders. "A murder? Where? When? What are you talking about? There was the storm—"

"Rafe!" Ashley loved her best friend's husband, but at the moment she didn't like the tone of his voice. "I'm telling you the truth and you know that I don't imagine things."

"But, Ashley—" Tara began.

"All right, tell us about it," Rafe said. "Wendy, let me help you with the wine. I'll have a scotch myself, if it's handy."

"Of course," Wendy murmured politely.

"Come on, Ashley, talk," Rafe reminded her gently.

She shook her head suddenly. "I shouldn't have come here! Tara is here with the baby, and Wendy has her little boy, and I shouldn't have— I shouldn't have taken any chances!"

"Tara and Amy are going to be fine," Rafe assured her.

"Ashley, will you tell us the story, please!" Wendy said, and she smiled with serene assurance. "Trust me. We can deal with it."

Ashley hesitated just a second, then started to tell her story. After she described everything that had happened, they all stared at her.

"Ashley, are you sure about what you saw?" Rafe demanded.

"Absolutely."

"But still—"

"Rafe, we were shot at today in Eric's house. He'll tell you that that's the truth."

Wendy moistened her lips and started to hand out the drinks. She smiled at Tara. "We do believe you. But it's going to be all right. You're safe here now. We're all with you."

"And in danger," Ashley added.

Rafe sat her down, taking her hands. "Brad is with the DEA and you've known me a long time, I can handle whatever comes up." He brushed her chin lightly with his knuckles.

"Ashley, whatever you're into, we're with you, and you know that!" Tara announced.

Wendy pressed a glass of white wine into Ashley's fingers. "You needn't worry about us. No one could have followed Eric here, not in an airboat. You can see for miles and miles."

"If he goes home," Ashley murmured miserably, "he'll still be in danger."

Wendy watched her with a curious smile, then shrugged. "He made it through three years in Vietnam and helped Brad and me once when we were involved with one of the most cold-blooded killers in history. And no one—no one—knows the swamp like he does. Trust me. Eric will be fine." She clinked her wineglass with Ashley's. "Cheers. Come on now, Ashley. Dinner is almost ready, and we'll get to the bottom of this. I promise."

Outside, Eric was telling Brad what he knew, from the time that he had found Ashley running through the swamp up to the shots that had been fired into his bedroom.

They sat together on the high slope of lawn leading to the house. Baby had crawled between, as she often did. Eric and Brad had been good friends since Wendy had first met Brad. Then Brad had been the one lost in the swamp, the victim of an undercover operation that had burst wide open.

It had been strange at first, seeing Brad in his brother's house with Wendy, his brother's wife. And despite the fact that Brad had brought danger down upon them all, he had liked Brad. He had probably tormented Wendy and Brad by trying to make them see that they could live without one another, but that it wouldn't really be living.

And he had become involved in the drug case that had brought Brad into the swamp. If he and Brad had not trusted each other instinctively and instantly, Wendy might have been lost to them all.

As it had happened, Eric had found himself the best man at Wendy's wedding, and his grandfather had given her away, just like a true daughter. And Brad McKenna had become his best friend.

"I didn't believe her at first," Eric told Brad as he chewed on a blade of grass. "I thought that she was hysterical. I mean, she came out of that swamp half naked, screaming wildly. And she hates the swamp. She hates it more than you did. I thought that maybe she'd seen a snake or a gator or something and gone a little berserk."

Brad shook his head worriedly. "But then you were shot at—in the house?"

"Yep. We sat out the storm. I even let a day go by after the storm before rolling up the shutters." He looked at Brad sharply. Brad's tawny eyes were clouded.

"There was a murder out here," he said slowly.

"What?" Eric demanded, half rising. "How do you know?"

"Billy Powell with the tribal police airboated his way here this morning. He had a few messages for me from the office, and he warned us about the body."

"The body?"

Brad nodded gravely. "They found a man in a yellow rain slicker in one of the canals. He had been stabbed to death."

"Then she was telling the truth," Eric said. "Obviously she was telling the truth. First the shots, and now the body. Those prove the whole thing."

"And that's why you brought her here?"

Eric shrugged, then grinned. "Where else would I bring my problems?" he asked.

Brad surveyed him for a long moment. "She's a very beautiful woman. Probably the most exotic I've ever seen."

"Careful," Eric warned. "You're married to my sister-in-law, remember?"

Brad laughed. "Sure, I remember. I was just commenting on your behalf. Just in case you hadn't noticed."

"I'll bet he has noticed," a voice said cheerfully behind them. Eric swung around. Wendy had come out. She fluffed her shoulder-length hair and slid down into her husband's arm. Looking at Eric, she said, "I think he's noticed, don't you, Brad?"

"Wendy-bird, you're trouble," Eric warned her, using the nickname he had given her when they had been very young.

It didn't bother her in the least. She stuck out her tongue at him and smiled up at Brad. "Uh-oh." Her eyes widened as she watched Eric's narrow, but her smile deepened. "I think he has even noticed that she isn't an ordinary woman in any shape or form. Look at him, Brad. He looks as if he wants to scalp me."

"She needs a good one on the rump, Brad," Eric said.

"Hey, I sympathize, but what can I tell you?" Brad replied.

"Brat," Eric commented.

"Hey, watch it, Tonto!" Wendy protested.

Brad looked at his wife sharply. Wendy was one of the few people who could get away with such things with Eric Hawk. And she was pushing it now. "Children, children! We've got a problem here."

"She told us all. I think that she's concerned about Rafe and Tara's baby more than anything else." Wendy smiled demurely. "I told her that we weren't the type to panic, that we'd weathered a few of our own storms. And I don't think that Rafe Tyler is the type to panic and run half-cocked, either, do you? Let's go in and have dinner."

"Dinner?" Eric murmured.

"Yes, it's a meal one eats at night," Wendy said sweetly.

"I think maybe I ought to head out. Talk to the police, see the family—"

"Dinner, I think is what Wendy suggested," Brad said flatly. Then he smiled, his eyes on Eric. "Runaway. That's what Seminole means, right? You're the one who taught me. You aren't thinking about trying to run away from a redhead, are you?"

Eric scowled fiercely. "I don't run from anything, and you know it."

Brad grinned. "This is fun. I never thought to see you behaving so strangely. It must have been one heckuva storm."

"You know that it was a bad storm. You weathered it here."

"No, no. I'm talking about the one that took place inside your house."

"I told you about shots being fired and that Ashley saw a murder take place and—"

"And I'm talking about your love life. Hmm, this is going to be fun. Remember how he tortured us as first, Wendy? He didn't want to leave you alone with me."

"For good reason," Eric retorted.

"Then he kept telling us all the reasons we shouldn't be together."

"So that you would see how stupid you were being," Eric told him with exasperation.

"This is going to be fun," Brad repeated to Wendy.

"It isn't going to be anything," Eric said softly. "The emerald lady is going to fly away. Back to New York, away from danger. And that's that."

"What did happen during that storm?" Wendy whispered softly to Brad.

"Shots were fired—" Eric began.

"But this is far more important in the long run," Wendy insisted, her silver eyes huge and taunting.

"There won't be any long run if this doesn't get settled," Eric said, standing. He stared at the swamp, pointedly ending the conversation.

"Let's have dinner," Brad said. "No one's going to bother anyone with Baby prowling around out here. And I haven't taken down many of the shutters. We'll be safe inside. I don't think that anyone could have followed you here anyway, not without your seeing them. You didn't see anything, did you?"

Eric shook his head slowly. No one had followed him here, he knew. He relaxed. "Dinner," he agreed, and they went in together.

Rafe was in the living room, and he was quick to demand to know

Eric's version of everything that had happened. Then he thanked Eric for keeping Ashley safe.

"I don't need to be thanked," Eric told him.

"None of us would have made it without you," Rafe said. Eric noticed that Ashley, talking to Wendy across the room as she sipped a glass of wine, had looked up. His eyes met hers, and he quickly turned away with a shrug. He shouldn't have come here, except that he'd had to. But then he should have dropped Ashley off and run. Runaway. Just like Brad had said.

He turned back to Rafe, who was sipping a beer. "I'm just glad that Wendy knows her stuff."

Tara appeared and kissed Eric's cheek, demanding he come to see the baby. Amy was in the guest bedroom now, in her little drawer, and sound asleep again. Something about the infant and her mother's sublime happiness touched him and he smiled, daring to caress the tiny cheek. "She's...beautiful," he told Tara.

Tara shivered. "And alive, and healthy, and so am I! We're so very grateful." She laughed softly. "Well, we might have survived without you. Rafe is resourceful, but he wasn't counting on my miscalculations. He didn't want me to be out there, but I had been so insistent, and well...never mind. I'm awfully glad that you found us and brought us here." A shadow passed over her eyes and she shivered. "And then there's Ashley. She's like a sister, and if she'd been left alone there with a murderer...I don't even dare think about it."

"I didn't do anything. She stumbled into me."

Searching out his eyes, Tara smiled suddenly. "Don't ever kid yourself, Mr. Hawk. Ashley is tough. She's made it through a number of very rough spots before, and she's never lacked courage."

"She did very well," he heard himself say.

"She's been shot at before."

"I heard about the trouble in Venezuela."

Tara blushed. "Yes. I guess it made a lot of the newspapers."

"I'm glad everything came out so well."

"Yes, so am I." She tucked a tiny blanket around her baby. "Thank goodness your sister-in-law has supplies for a baby!" She looked up at him. "The police have promised to get us a chopper tomorrow. I have to go to a hospital with the baby. I've never felt better in my entire life, but Wendy insists that I should go and Rafe agrees. I almost hate to leave, but I'll be glad to get Ashley away, after what has happened."

She was smiling and speaking so sweetly, so softly. He felt as if she had cast scalding oil over him and sliced him from midsection to groin. Ashley would be going away with them. Back where she belonged. She hadn't told him.

It didn't matter that she hadn't had much of a chance. It just suddenly hurt like all hell, and then he felt like a fool. He had known it all along. She was a beautiful gem cast down in the mud, and he had picked her up and cleaned her off—but now she was going back to her different world where she could shine in a black-velvet setting. He had been a fool to get involved.

Somehow, he just hadn't expected her to leave so quickly.

"I guess we'd better get on out," Tara whispered, taking his arm. She led him back to the living and dining room combination. "I did want to say thank you. You did so very much for us."

"I didn't do a thing. Wendy did."

Wendy heard him. She laughed. "I know all about birthing babies!" she teased with wide eyes. Then she came over to them, dragging Ashley along with her. "Isn't she just darling? Oh, Eric, she's just beautiful. All that hair! Josh didn't have that much hair until he was almost six months old! Come, let's eat."

They sat at the dining table, and the longer the meal went on, the more Eric wished that he had departed right after bringing Ashley. It wasn't that Wendy couldn't cook—she could. She and Brad had a generator, so she had been able to make a big tray of lasagna with canned spinach and tons of garlic bread.

And conversation flowed easily. Brad had lived in New York for a while, and he and Rafe discussed streets and buildings, theater and music and ball games in the park. Tara got Eric's attention by telling him how her labor pains started about two minutes after he had left them at Wendy and Brad's door, and now they had called the hospital only to be warned that the roads were already impassable and that she was best off staying where she was.

Ashley smiled at Eric, but it wasn't a warm smile. "You never mentioned any of this."

"I thought that they were well on their way out of the swamp," he said, looking at her. He smiled crookedly and took a long sip of burgundy wine. "You never mentioned, Miss Dane, that you were flying out of here in a helicopter tomorrow."

"I didn't have a chance."

She was hurt, and he knew it. He hadn't touched her, he hadn't gone near her, he had barely acknowledged her existence, and she was sitting right next to him.

She didn't understand. They were back in the real world. The Tylers might be the nicest people in the world, but theirs was still a different world, and pretty soon, Ashley would realize that. Wendy's table was set with beautiful linen and china and crystal wine goblets, but the table still sat in the middle of the swamp.

And Ashley was still a glittering gem, accidentally dropped into that swamp. Somehow, being here with Wendy made the past cascade down on him with great ferocity. He didn't want to, but when he closed his eyes, he could see Wendy's face when they had gone to the mortuary together to identify Leif and Elizabeth. He could imagine his own face. He could see the blood spilled all over his wife's white dress and Leif's white dinner jacket. His brother had died defending Elizabeth, and he had sworn then that he would always defend Wendy. Wendy had Brad now, but she and Eric would also always have their link. Stronger than blood, maybe. He knew that Wendy wanted him to have a future, but tonight, all he could see was the past. He suddenly felt wrong. He'd had women before, but he'd never felt the way he did with Ashley. Never felt the guilt, as if he were giving more than he had the right to give, as if he were taking more than he had the right to demand.

"So, Eric, how did the two of you manage during all those days of wind and rain and havoc?" Brad asked.

Eric glanced down the table. Brad had a mischievous and very self-satisfied look about his eyes.

"Fine," Eric said flatly.

"No television, no movies, no music! What on earth did you do to keep occupied?" Wendy questioned innocently.

"I can imagine what he wanted to be doing," Brad said not so innocently.

Eric heard a choking sound. It was Ashley. Brad patted her on the back, handing her a glass of water. "Sorry, Ashley. Are you all right?"

"I'm fine!" Ashley gasped.

"That was a guilty choke if I ever heard one," Tara said, then smiled sweetly.

"Still choking," Brad said, shaking his head. "I hope that she's all right."

"I doubt if she is," Wendy said sweetly. She looked at the Tylers with wide, innocent eyes. "He's such a son of a gun, my brother-in-law."

"Nasty as all hell," Brad agreed pleasantly. Then he looked at Eric again. "How did you pass the time? Ashley, was he decent to you?"

"Brad!" There was an edge to Eric's warning.

Ashley still looked as if she were strangling. Beautiful, pale, stunned and very ill at ease. "Of course, he was decent."

"A perfect gentleman," Wendy drawled.

"Wendy!" Tara piped in sweetly. "I'm sure that he was good to her, much more than good."

"Tara!" Ashley snapped.

"What were you all expecting?" Rafe asked pleasantly. "The man is very ethical."

"Well, you just never know with Eric," Brad said. "We had a bit of trouble down here a few years ago on our doorstep and Eric had one of the culprits convinced that he was about to be skinned alive."

"Finding a naked, red-haired beauty in the swamp, who knows what he did!" Wendy said sweetly.

"I was not naked!" Ashley protested. She looked at Eric, and her eyes shone brightly against the porcelain beauty of her flesh.

He tried to smile but gritted his teeth instead and turned to his sister-in-law. "Wendy-bird, the great spirits might very well come out of the sky and get you for this," he warned.

"I'll take my chances," Wendy said with a laugh.

Eric stood, achingly aware of how he wanted to sweep Ashley into his arms, hold her against him and tell them all to go to hell and that he'd enjoyed every second of the storm. But the storm was over.

She wasn't admitting anything. Neither was he.

He decided he wasn't going to be very good company, not for the rest of that night.

He spoke, careful to keep smiling. "I've got to go."

"Go!" Wendy said.

"I want to check on Mary and Willie and the kids. I know that they went to Big Cypress, but I'm willing to bet that they're back at the village. I would have gone earlier except for...except for Ashley. But she's safe here with you."

Ashley was already standing. They all were. Eric reached into his pocket for the emeralds he had scooped off his side table. "Here, these are yours, right?"

Rafe glanced down at the gems and looked into Eric's eyes. "Thanks for returning them. But they aren't important. My wife is, Ashley is. If we don't get to see you again, thanks for everything you did for them. And if you come to New York, make sure you see us. Please. If there's anything you ever need..."

Eric nodded. "I do come to New York from time to time. Maybe I will see you. Tara, good luck with the baby." He faced Ashley at last. "And good luck to you, Ashley," he said simply.

He turned away quickly. He didn't want to see the widening of her emerald eyes when she looked up at him. He didn't want to think of her, and he didn't want to remember her. It was over.

He started to say goodbye to Wendy, then paused, frowning. He heard something.

Baby. She was screeching and growling, the way she did when some stranger came around. Then he heard a distant airboat motor.

"What is it?" Wendy asked him anxiously.

"Someone, something," he said.

Ashley felt a coldness settle over her. The three men were already moving. Eric pulled his .38 from his waistband and headed for the door. Brad reached in the hallway closet, took a gun and tossed one to Rafe.

They were all ready for danger, Ashley thought. It was chilling.

Wendy's hands fell on her shoulders. "Come on, get down," Wendy said softly.

Eric was already out the door. She heard him explode with an expletive.

Then he stuck his handsome face back inside. She would never forget the way he looked at that moment. His black hair fell straight against his collar and his eyes were nearly lime against the dark hue of his face. His full mouth was curved in a wry smile. He seemed invincible, and yet terribly human. Strong, masculine...almost reachable and capable of laughter again.

"It's okay, guys. We can all stand up again."

"Who is it?" Wendy demanded irritably.

"Seems we don't have to go to the police," he said. "The police have come to us." He turned around, looking back outside. "Baby, stop that and behave. It's just Billy Powell and Mica. They're the good guys, Baby. Are you ever going to learn?"

CHAPTER 8

"**H**ey, Billy!" Eric called out.

Billy swore, hopping ankle deep into the muck and wading to the house. He looked at Brad, Rafe and Eric standing in the doorway with guns, and with Wendy, Tara and Ashley behind. Billy was a man of medium height with coal dark hair and eyes, striking wide cheekbones and broad shoulders. Mica, an older, leaner man, followed him. There was a tag on their airboat proclaiming them tribal police. Billy was wearing a light brownish gray uniform with insignias on the shoulder. The older man was wearing uniform pants with a brightly colored Seminole shirt. He nodded to them in silence, letting Billy do the talking.

"What are you all expecting, the holdup of Fort Knox?"

Eric smiled and shook his head. "We heard you found a body."

"Yeah, I found a body." Baby was sniffing his hands. "Leave off, Baby, I haven't got anything for you," Billy said, then looked directly at Eric. "I just went by your place and saw all the broken glass. I figured your window was shot to hell. Mind telling me what's going on?"

Eric shrugged. "I was hoping that you could tell us. But about your body, well, we might know something." He pulled Ashley forward and introduced her to Officer Billy Powell, and Sergeant Mica Crane.

It seemed to Eric that Billy held Ashley's hand a long time and that it took him a long time to manage to speak again. "Hi, Miss Dane. It's real nice to meet you. Real, real nice."

"My pleasure, officer," Ashley said. Then she nodded to Mica. "Sergeant Crane."

"Mica. Just Mica," Wendy said, smiling at the older man. "It's short for Micanopy, which means chief. And he is a big chief, very important on the council."

"Mica." Billy released Ashley's hand. Mica took it. The old coot was flushing, Eric thought.

"Why don't you tell them what happened, Ashley?" Eric asked her.

"Let's bring them inside first, hmm?" Wendy said, and they all went in. Ashley found herself on the couch next to Billy with Eric behind her. Hesitating a bit, she explained about her walk with Harrison Mosby into the swamp.

Rafe exploded with anger. "Mosby was harassing you! Why didn't you tell me?"

"I thought I could take care of it myself, Rafe," Ashley said softly, her lashes lowering. "Anyway, then I was lost. I was just running blindly. Then I saw the three men—"

"Men?" Billy asked.

"Well, the three figures. You're right—I've no idea if they were men or women. I never saw faces clearly at all. I never saw the victim."

"But you know that they saw you?" Billy said.

She nodded, trying to explain. "They turned—the two living figures—and looked at me. And I ran again."

"Into Eric."

"Yes." She said the word so softly it was barely heard. "Yes, I ran into Eric."

"And today someone tried to kill you."

Ashley looked up. She felt Eric standing close to her.

"Someone shot my room," he replied for her.

"Your bedroom?" Billy asked.

There was a slight hesitation. "Yes," Eric said flatly. "It was one of the rooms where I had opened the shutters."

"What makes you think that they were aiming at Miss Dane when they shot into your bedroom window?"

"Because she was a guest in my house, sleeping in my room," Eric said smoothly. Then he snapped, "Hell, Billy, I don't know what's going on. Maybe someone was aiming for me. Who knows?"

"Yeah, who knows? Tomorrow morning, Miss Dane, we'll have you identify the body. We've got it in Mac's big freezer at the gas station. We still can't reach the city. Phone lines are down everywhere. Roads are flooded. Airboat and helicopter are the only way out, and we'll be airlifting him out tomorrow afternoon. If you don't mind, Miss Dane, I'll bring you to see the corpse and help me with a little paperwork before then."

"Of course I don't mind," Ashley said.

"You're staying here tonight?"

"Yes," Brad answered for her.

"And you, Eric?"

"I'm going out to check on the folks."

"Maybe you shouldn't—" Billy began.

"I can take care of myself, and you know it," Eric told him.

Billy looked at Eric for what seemed like a long time. Ashley longed to turn around and study Eric's face, but she didn't allow herself. She watched Billy's eyes instead, and he seemed to know that Eric could take care of himself.

"Well, one of us will stick around outside for the night," the officer remarked.

"That's good," Eric said.

"It's probably not necessary," Brad said.

Billy smiled. "No, it's not, G-man." He laughed. "But if I don't stay, you won't sleep, and with everything going on, you should probably have a decent night's rest."

Brad shrugged. "Suit yourself. I tell you what. I'll spell you."

"Sounds good."

"I'm moving on," Mica said. "Check on some other people."

"I'm going, too," Eric said.

"I'll need your statements, too, Eric." Billy told him.

"I'll walk you all to the door," Brad said.

Ashley watched Eric leave. He didn't turn to look behind; he walked cleanly away.

Outside Mica paused, looking intently at Eric. "John Jacobs is out," he said.

Eric inhaled sharply. "What do you mean, out?"

"Who the hell is John Jacobs?" Brad demanded.

Eric didn't answer; he couldn't. Jacobs had been one of the punks who had broken into the liquor store—and shot his brother and his wife.

He couldn't seem to find the words to explain, and he was glad that Mica was there, with his passive, lined face and onyx eyes telling nothing of emotion or pain. "Jacobs was in the gang that killed Elizabeth and Leif."

Brad's lips parted as if he were going to speak, but they closed. Then he blurted, "What the hell is he doing out?"

"Calm down, McKenna," Mica said. "It wasn't the state, and it wasn't the legal system. Well, all right, maybe he took a long, long walk down death row, but his appeal had been turned down and his death warrant had been signed. He escaped."

"How the—"

"He killed a guard. Switched clothing, and walked out clean as a whistle."

"I should have killed him," Eric said flatly.

"And you could have taken up residence at Raiford Penitentiary," Mica said flatly. "I just wanted you to know that he was out and that maybe those shots didn't have anything to do with your girlfriend. You keep your ear to the ground, huh, Eric Hawk?"

"Yeah. Thanks for the warning, Mica."

The tall old Indian walked down to the airboat, and Brad and Eric both watched in silence as he disappeared around the bend.

"Damn," Eric said. He felt ill. He couldn't believe that Jacobs was walking free again. Brad's hand clamped down hard on his shoulder.

"They'll get him back."

"Yeah," Eric said without much conviction.

"They will. You've got to have some faith."

"I do. I have faith in me," Eric muttered. He smiled, not wanting Brad to know how upset he was. Fires seemed to have been lit inside him. He ached; he hurt. He wanted to scream violently and tear someone to shreds. He swallowed the emotion and poked Brad lightly in the chest. "And you!" he accused Brad. "What were you doing in there?"

Brad laughed, relieved that the subject had changed, yet wondering if it really had. He kept grinning, leaning back against the closed door and folding his arms over his chest. "You deserved it, you know."

"Did I?"

"I'm surprised she didn't throw her lasagna on you."

"Yeah? Well, she's flying away tomorrow."

Brad shook his head. "Well, she isn't going to be able to leave with the Tylers. They're going out early. Ashley will have to stick around."

"She needs to get out fast. She could be in danger here."

"You're the one in danger now, Eric. Have you thought of that?"

Eric frowned. "You think that Jacobs—"

"I don't know about Jacobs. I don't know the man at all. I wasn't here then. But the person who pulled that trigger, whoever he was, knows where you live, not where Ashley is now."

Eric hesitated. "I really can take care of myself, and damned well. You know that."

"I know you're good. But I don't know a man alive who couldn't use a little help now and then."

Eric paused again. "Don't leave her alone anywhere, all right?"

"Hey! This one's your ball game, not mine!" Brad protested.

"Wait a minute. When you needed help—"

"You were around, yes. And I'll be around. I'll be wherever you want me. But it's your ball game. You want to keep her safe, you better plan on being around."

"I have to leave now. I have to see about the folks."

"She should be all right tonight. I'm here, Tyler's here, and now Billy's here, too. You can leave tonight. You need to leave tonight. Yeah, it'll be good for you. Purge your soul, my boy."

"McKenna—"

"Just remember that she's here."

"Don't worry. I won't forget."

Eric whistled for Baby. The big cat padded around the corner of the house. He was amazed that she came so quickly. Actually he was amazed that she had obeyed him at all. Training the panther had not always been a successful project.

He shrugged. "At least the cat listens."

Brad laughed and waved. "See you. Give the family our love."

Eric nodded and headed down to his airboat. He already felt as if here in knots. He was amazed to realize that it wasn't Jacobs he was thinking about. It wasn't even revenge.

It was Ashley. He felt empty and more alone than he had ever felt in his life. It was almost as if he had severed a hand and left it behind. It was insane, it was madness. They hadn't been together that long; he couldn't care that much. He wasn't in love with her.

But as he leaped aboard his airboat, he admitted that he was in something, even if it wasn't love. Love was something that grew. It came in little things—in smiles, in sharing a sunset, in sharing desires and dreams, and in building dreams. He couldn't love Ashley Dane.

Maybe it was fascination, maybe it was lust. He couldn't forget her. Not for a second. When he closed his eyes he saw her.

He didn't want to see her.

Jacobs was out.

He wouldn't come here, Eric thought. He would probably try to leave the country. There was nothing that Eric could do about it—finding Jacobs would be like finding a needle in a haystack. He could be almost anywhere in the world by now.

It gnawed at him.

But not as fiercely as the thought that he could no longer take Ashley into his arms and forget the whole world.

He could not forget her.

And as he motored away from her, he silently damned her a thousand times. He would bury himself that night in the swamp, where she didn't belong. And maybe he could forget her there.

Ashley sparkled.

She talked, she laughed, she insisted on helping in the kitchen, and she washed the dishes so swiftly that Wendy assured her that if modeling and designing ever failed, she had a sure shot as the McKenna housekeeper.

Tara, who knew her better, watched her in silence. Even Rafe—and Brad, who didn't know her at all—kept a wary eye on her. Every time she caught someone staring, that someone would smile, make no apology and keep staring.

She had to keep moving and talking and laughing. It was the only way she could stay sane. Eric's departure had been brutal, and she really wanted to hate him for it. She might have been okay if she could have just gone home, but she couldn't, not yet. She had to stay and talk to the police, and she had to go to the morgue and look at the body that had been found in the swamp. There hadn't been a single identifying mark on it, so Brad had been told. Maybe Ashley could help.

She didn't mind helping. She minded staying in the same section of the state as Eric. No, she minded being in the same part of the country.

She wanted to kick herself a thousand times. She'd known not to get involved, but she had done so anyway. Everything about Eric had fascinated her. Even while rinsing a plate to put into the dishwasher, she was barraged with memories—of his arms knotted with muscle, of his smooth and sleek chest a color between copper and bronze, of his eyes, of the tone of his voice, of his arms wrapped around her, of his body deep within her own...

"Wait a minute, Ashley!" Wendy pleaded. "I don't put the salad bowl in the dishwasher. Takes up too much room."

"Oh. Oh, sorry!" Ashley said quickly.

Wendy shook her head, perching on one of the bar stools. "It isn't every day that I have thousand-dollar-an-hour models to do my dishes!"

"I don't make a thousand dollars an hour," Ashley said, grinning. Wendy hadn't been offensive, though. There was nothing about her that could be offensive. She and Brad were charming. They had welcomed the whole slew of them to their home, and Ashley already felt as if she had known both all her life. They were warm and natural. "I don't even model any more," she said. "I design clothing with Tara. I only did this commercial because they both asked me to."

"That was nice of you then."

"Thanks."

Wendy was grinning and playing with a teacup. Ashley paused, salad bowl in hand, because Wendy was so nakedly and unabashedly curious about her.

"What have you been doing for the past few days?" she demanded.

Ashley almost dropped the bowl. She tried to smile and stammer some kind of answer, but then Wendy laughed apologetically and spoke. "I'm sorry. I really am. It's just that, well, Eric is my brother, in almost every sense of the word. I love him very much. I hope you'll forgive me, but I did have the most marvelous time torturing him." She smiled and shrugged. "He'd put me through a bit, if you can imagine. And it's so damned hard to reach through his reserve! I haven't seen him react to anyone the way that he reacts to you in...years," she said softly.

Ashley turned around, washed the salad bowl, then dried it carefully. "I don't think he reacted at all. He left."

"Umm. In a bit of a huff, too."

"I didn't see him 'huffing.'"

"And you never will see any of his emotions, especially a 'huff'!" Wendy said wisely. She looked past the dining room to the living area. Brad and Rafe were sitting with their heads low, deep in conversation. Billy had gone out for a walk around the property. Tara was in the guest room nursing the baby.

Wendy smiled sheepishly. "He isn't an insecure man, not at all. It's just that sometimes..." She shrugged and her voice went so low that Ashley had to set down the dishrag and come over to the counter to hear her. "Eric and his brother were a lot alike. Leif was like that. When he was really mad, he walked away. When he was upset, he walked away. Eric almost never raises his voice. I was thrilled to see him the way that he was today." Wendy nodded her head at Ashley, indicating the clothes that she was wearing. "I was startled to see you in Elizabeth's things."

"Well, that hardly means anything. He really couldn't allow me to run around with nothing."

"He might have tried tying you into a pair of his own jeans!" Wendy laughed. Then she sobered. "Does he mean anything to you, Ashley? I probably don't even have the right to ask this, but I like you, and as I said, I love Eric."

"I could, too," Ashley whispered before she realized what she was saying. Her face flooded with color. She moved away from the counter. "I...didn't mean that. I—"

"Didn't you?" Wendy asked. She sounded so sweet and so earnest that Ashley lowered her head.

"It can't work," she said softly.

"Why not?" It was a new voice asking the question. Tara had come out of the bedroom, looking sleepy and a little weak and pale, but somehow staunch as she smiled at Ashley.

Ashley lifted her hands to them both. "Because he doesn't want anything more to do with me."

Wendy looked at Tara. "I'm sure that he does want more to do with her."

"Right," Tara agreed. She surveyed Ashley from head to toe. "I mean, he couldn't just walk away, not from her, could he?"

"I don't think so. Where is he ever going to find that hair again?"

"Hey!" Ashley laughed. "Wait a minute, there's really nothing more to discuss here. He's gone. I'll see the police tomorrow, and then I'm going home."

"I'll take odds on that," contributed a male voice.

Startled, Ashley whirled around to see Brad. He had slipped an arm around his wife's waist and was resting his chin on her head. Rafe was there, too, holding Tara against him. "I'll say that he comes back here by twelve noon," Brad said.

"I don't know about twelve." Rafe said skeptically. "I'll say one on the nose."

"Oh, no!" Ashley moaned. "What is this! No wonder he ran out. I think that I would run, too, if I had half a chance!"

Brad came around the counter, helping himself to coffee from the pot.

He winked at his wife and smiled at Ashley. "I know where he is. I can take you there if you want to go."

"I do not want to go," Ashley said firmly. "And really, I do hate the swamp. I hate the stupid sounds those rotten alligators make. I hate the mud and the muck. I hate mosquitoes. I love concrete—honest, I do."

"Hmm," Brad murmured. But he was watching her very closely again.

"Keep an eye on her. She throws things," Rafe warned.

"I do not!" Ashley protested.

"Okay, enough!" Wendy decided. She was studying her husband curiously.

"Is something wrong?" she asked him.

He shook his head. "No, of course not, what could be wrong?"

"I don't know, I just feel like you're torturing this poor woman to keep quiet about something else."

"No," Brad said thoughtfully, and grinned. "I'm torturing her for the sheer pleasure of it."

"Okay, okay," Wendy groaned. "Let's leave her in peace, shall we? Come on, Ashley, I'll show you to the women's quarters. It's kind of a small place, do you mind?"

"Mind? Of course not, I'm just grateful to be here!" Ashley said. Brad and Wendy looked at each other and smiled. Wendy led her down the hallway into the back bedroom, touching her finger to her lip when they walked past the drawer-crib with the sleeping baby. Ashley paused and knelt to look at the tiny life. Amy was so small and so perfect, and her coloring was already beautiful. Ashley's throat and her heart constricted. She had always known in a vague sort of way that she wanted children, but she had never realized until this moment just how desperately she did.

The years were ticking by, she thought. She had just passed her thirtieth birthday. Not much time left.

Women were having children in their forties these days, she reminded herself.

Yes, but dangers increased with each year.

"It's a wonderful age," Wendy whispered from behind her. "They sleep almost all the time, and they never, never answer back."

Ashley smiled but didn't reply.

"Is something wrong?" Wendy asked softly.

Ashley stood away from the baby and smiled. "Yes. I'm getting old."

"Not that old. How old are you. Twenty-seven, twenty-eight?"

"Thirty."

"Well, I'm thirty-five, and I'm not old, so that makes you a spring chicken," Wendy assured her.

"Thirty-five?" Ashley asked, stretching across the bed.

Wendy, putting a pillow into a new case, nodded. "You just made me feel eighty."

"No!" Ashley laughed. "I was just thinking about your son."

"You've plenty of time ahead of you," Wendy said, just as if she read Ashley's thoughts. "Not—" she added teasingly "—that I would want to waste any of it."

"Meaning?"

"Nothing. I'd just like to see you stay around for a while, that's all."

Ashley shook her head slowly. "I have to get out of here. And quickly. I was scared to death in the swamp when I saw the murder. And then when we were shot at..." Her voice trailed away and she shivered.

"And that's not it at all," Wendy said pragmatically.

Ashley sat up, crossing her legs Indian fashion beneath her. "What— what did happen to his wife?"

Wendy paused a long moment and then she sat down. "She was killed. Shot to death."

"Oh, my God!" Ashley gasped.

"With Leif," Wendy added, running her fingers over the pillowcase. "Eric and Elizabeth were having a wedding anniversary party, and he had ordered a very special wine from a friend who owned a liquor store. He was supposed to deliver the wine, but the party was right near Christmas, so he was very busy that night with customers and couldn't come. I was fixing some things in the house because I had insisted that Elizabeth wasn't to lift a finger. Eric was fooling around getting the barbeque going, and so Leif and Elizabeth went together to pick up the wine. She was so excited. Eric was quiet, even with her. He wasn't the type to say

'I love you' all the time, but he showed it in little ways." Wendy shrugged. "She was really beautiful."

"I've seen her. I've seen her picture, I mean," Ashley said.

Wendy nodded, as if that said it all. "They were in white that night." She flashed Ashley a quick smile. "Don't get me wrong—I'm happy now. I love Brad with all my heart, but until the day I die, I won't forget that night."

"What happened?"

"There was a holdup at the liquor store and Leif and Elizabeth walked right into it. One of the men struck Elizabeth and Leif tried to fight him. They shot them both. Leif was killed instantly, one bullet to the heart. They shot Elizabeth four or five times. It was horrible, absolutely horrible. Friends on the tribal force came to the house for us, but I guess we both reacted very badly. It was terrible for Leif and Eric's grandparents, and the rest of the family, too, but I don't think that anyone could have understood how Eric and I felt, except Eric and me." Wendy fell silent then. She looked at Ashley. "Think you understand him any better?"

Ashley looked at Wendy. "I understand how very badly he must have been hurt. But..."

"But what?"

"I still don't understand his attitude toward me."

Wendy shrugged. "Fight him. He probably thinks you're a beautiful wildflower brought by the wind and soon to be swept away again. He's a hard man. There's only one thing sure about Eric."

"What's that?"

"If you want him, you're going to have to fight for him."

Ashley was determined to salvage a bit of her pride. "I'm not sure if I want him or not," she said flatly.

"There's more that you should know," Wendy told her gravely.

"What's that?" Ashley asked.

"He went after the men who murdered Leif and Elizabeth."

Something seemed to lodge in Ashley's throat. "And—and what happened?" she said.

"Eric caught one of them."

"He—he killed that man?" Ashley said. "In cold blood?"

"It wouldn't have been 'cold' blood," Wendy murmured. "No murder would have been more violently hot. But he didn't kill the man. He turned him over to the police. He's still on death row up in Raiford."

Ashley exhaled. Then she smiled slowly. "I'm glad."

"I was glad, too. Once he passed that obstacle, he made an effort at living again." Wendy walked toward the door. "I'm going to check on Josh before I turn his room over to the guys. Help yourself to a night-gown—they're in the third drawer over there. Cotton-shirts to lace and frills. Take whatever you like and please don't be shy. There are towels and washcloths in the bath. Do you need anything else?"

"No. Thank you very much," Ashley said, smiling at Wendy and liking her very much. "You've already given me much more than I expected."

Wendy smiled in return and left.

Ashley lay back and wondered how she could have possibly come to care for Eric Hawk so deeply and so desperately and so swiftly.

And then, like Rafe and Brad, she began to wonder if he would show up the next day.

When she fell asleep that night, it was with a prayer on her lips that he would.

Five miles away, in a distant hummock, Eric stood atop a chickee in his grandfather's village and stared at the moon. It was a full moon, ex-ceptionally big and beautiful and brilliant after the days of the storm.

Toward the center of the small village there was another chickee where a fire burned—the communal cooking fire. It was slowly dying to embers.

Eric heard night sounds. The occasional call of a crane or a heron, the whir of insects, the distant guttural grunt of a gator, all blending together in a strange and beautiful harmony.

Eric stood tall and straight and shirtless and let the night breeze wash over him and cool him. But it did little good.

He had come to forget her. Yet she was ever more present with him here.

He wanted to show her how the grass looked like a river in the moonlight. He wanted her to feel the air, and he wanted—he burned—to hold her beneath him, to make love to her in the moonlight.

She wouldn't need her Tyler jewels at all. And he would require nothing but the primitive earth and the sweeping beauty of her eyes.

She wasn't meant to be his.

One of the men who had killed Elizabeth was out, and Eric should be hating himself, because he was wishing that he could be with a woman other than his wife, instead of wondering if there was any way to catch the murderer.

There was not, he told himself, not tonight. But if God had any mercy, the murderer would be on death row again by tomorrow or the next day.

Ashley could be in danger.

Ashley would soon be gone.

But she wasn't gone yet, and she wouldn't be gone tomorrow. She was in the swamp, and she could be in danger.

He clenched and unclenched his fists at his sides. Not far away, his grandparents were surely sleeping. His whole family was probably asleep, happy to be back in the village where they spent their summers. Brad and Wendy even came there sometimes. In the Seminole nation, a man joined his wife's family, and so Brad had become part of the Hawks. They were as close as any full-blooded relations.

But Ashley...

He wasn't going to think about her.

Great. He was going to spend his night with a tame and half-trained panther curled up beside him when he could have brought Ashley with him here.

Ashley? Here?

No.

He wasn't going to think about Ashley.

He stared at the moon a moment longer and felt the air upon his bare flesh. It didn't help. It was a moon meant to be shared. He turned away, unrolled his sleeping mat and lay down on it. Baby crawled beside him.

"You're a poor excuse for company!" Eric charged the cat. He closed his eyes, then opened them again. He had no right to be worried about her. Brad and Tyler were with her. She was safe.

He sighed. He knew that he would head back to Wendy's first thing in the morning. Whatever happened, he was going to be with Ashley. Billy wanted to talk with him about the shooting, so he had to go back. He should go back to Ashley.

He would go back. Early. It wouldn't be for the police, though. It would be for Ashley.

He sighed deeply. It was going to be one hell of a night, lying there in a searing state of fury, longing to go back in time—to strangle John Jacobs with his bare hands.

Eric had done the right thing. The law had dealt with Jacobs fairly. There had to be law; it was important for all men, Eric knew. A half smile curved his lips. The Seminoles were one of the "Five Civilized Tribes."

Still he wished that he could get his hands on Jacobs again.

There was nothing that he could do. Except, of course, dream of Ashley.

He sat up, swearing. Baby growled, annoyed that he had turned. He settled back down to try to sleep again. He would not dream....

But dreams could not be denied.

And softly, slowly, hauntingly, Ashley came to him like an angel of the night and touched him with the gentle fingers of the breeze. In the darkness, she was there, an angel to sweep him into dreams.

CHAPTER 9

"**O**h, my God!" Ashley gasped, staring down at the bloated face of the body. They were in a garage belonging to a nice old man named Mac, and the body, covered by a white sheet, was on a shelf in his back freezer.

Tara and Rafe were in Fort Lauderdale. They had been taken out that morning by helicopter. Brad and Wendy were behind her, Billy was next to her.

And Eric was there, too. He was leaning casually against the doorway, watching, waiting. No one got to see whether he would come to the house or not because Wendy had insisted on airboating to the little village to leave Josh with Willie and Mary, Eric's grandparents. Wendy wasn't taking her young son to see a corpse.

They had reached the village by eleven. Eric had been up and dressed, and had come down to the airboat, ready to accompany them. Wendy had run up to the chickees with Josh alone, and they had all waited for her in silence.

Ashley had wondered if Eric didn't want her to meet any other members of his family. It seemed that way.

Eric's appearance had given Ashley little comfort. He was cool and distant, so carefully polite. She hated it. He was with her only because he had to be, she knew. Because the police officer was going to question him again about the shots fired at his house. It would have been better if he hadn't come at all.

He was there, though, leaning against the doorway. He was wearing sunglasses that completely hid his eyes, a leather headband and a Seminole shirt in shades of red and green. His jeans fit snugly, and he looked so much like a renegade.

As much as his manner had hurt her, Ashley was more concerned with the body in front of her. She was stunned.

Bile rose in her throat. She was going to be sick. She'd never seen a corpse before, except for her grandfather's, and his body had been touched up by the mortician. He'd worn his best pin-striped suit, and he had looked as if he were sleeping.

The flesh on this corpse had gone gray. The time in the water had caused a hideous swelling. She didn't even dare think of the other things about the corpse that were just not human anymore. She knew she would feel sicker and sicker.

Because she recognized the man. She had known him in life. "Oh, my God!" she repeated, and turned around. She had to get away from the horrible stench that wafted to her despite the icy cold of the freezer.

"Ashley!"

She felt Eric's hands on her shoulder. He had moved at last. His touch was firm as he guided her outside.

"Leave me alone!" she begged him. "Please!"

"Look, it's all right, it's all right," he tried to tell her.

It wasn't all right. She managed to tear away from him and reach a patch of saw grass, and then she was violently ill. She fell down flat on the earth, afraid that she would pass out.

Eric bent down over her and smoothed a damp handkerchief over her face. She couldn't see his eyes, just her own pathetic reflection in his glasses. "Let me help you up. Mac can get you some water."

He didn't give her time to answer, but brought her to her feet. By that time, Wendy and Brad and Billy were out with them. And Mac was coming her way with a paper cup full of water.

She drank it gratefully. Wendy took over for Eric, grabbing the handkerchief, smoothing back Ashley's hair. "Are you all right now?"

"I'm sorry—" Ashley began.

"My stomach almost went in there," Brad assured her, smiling. Then he cast a quick glance at Billy. "Ashley, you recognized the body."

"Yes. It was Harrison Mosby. He was the director of the commercial we were shooting. He was the one who—who—"

"Who lured you into the swamp?" Eric finished softly for her.

She looked his way, but she could still tell nothing of his feelings. Those damned glasses hid everything.

"Well, then," Billy murmured, "at least we know who this stiff is. Sorry, miss, if he was a friend—"

"He wasn't a friend," Ashley said quickly. "But I wouldn't have wished this on a—on a—"

"On a dog!" Wendy supplied.

"On a dog," Ashley said without warmth.

"Billy, can we take her out of here now? That was pretty awful for all of us, and having to see someone that she knew..." Eric said.

"Yeah, sure, sure," Billy replied. "Eric, Miss Dane, I just need you to sign your statements, and then you're free to go."

Seconds later, Ashley was done, having scrawled her signature where Billy wanted it. He thanked her, telling her that without her help they might have spent aeons identifying the man. Now, thanks to her, they did have something—if very little—to go on.

"What will you do? How will you try to solve this?" Ashley asked.

"Oh, we'll check around. If he was from New York, we'll get cooperation from their police department. The storm washed away anything that might resemble a clue, but eventually, the top-notch detectives will make it out here and see what they can come up with. We're not at a dead end, so please, don't worry. Eric, she's still awfully pale. Why don't you all get going?"

"Yeah, we'll do that," Eric said.

"You're not going back to your house?"

"Not today. I'm going back out to Willie's."

"We all have to go back out to Willie's. Josh is there with Mary," Wendy said.

"All right. Take care," Billy told them.

He waved as Brad led the way toward their airboat, one hand gently on his wife's back, and the other on Ashley's. Eric followed at a slight distance, with Baby at his heels.

He caught up with them at the airboat, taking Ashley's arm and turning her around to face him. "Are you all right?" he asked softly. "You're still as white as snow."

She nodded, deciding that maybe he was not completely heartless. He swore slightly then, and she appreciated the protective gesture until he muttered, "This was wrong. You just weren't cut out for stuff like this."

"No one is cut out for murder!" Ashley protested.

Eric waved a hand in the air. "I mean all of this. The swamp, the storm, the place, what has happened. All of it."

She lifted her chin slightly and smiled. "Don't kid yourself, Tonto. I'm tougher than I look."

She didn't wait for a reaction from him but tossed her hair over her shoulders, and walked onto the airboat behind Wendy. She turned around and called to the big cat. "Baby, here, Baby, come here!"

To Ashley's astonishment, the graceful feline decided to be on her side, and padded silently away from Eric to leap up beside her.

"Damned cat!" Brad laughed. "We've done a great job with her, huh, Eric?"

"Yeah," Eric muttered, hopping onto the airboat along with Brad. He sat behind Ashley. She felt his presence there with all her heart. It was as if just his being near made fire blaze down her back.

"You'll like Willie and Mary!" Wendy shouted to her above the roar of the motor.

"I'm sure I will!" she called back.

"And the kids!" Brad added. He laughed. "Just be prepared to be tied to the stake. They like to play cowboys and Indians."

"Do I get to be a cowboy or an Indian?"

"Maybe a cowgirl," Wendy said. "Or a prisoner. Or if you're real lucky, they'll let you be a healer."

Ashley smiled. Then she noticed that Eric was staring into the distance and that his countenance was as hard as rock. He wasn't into games, not that day.

Ashley let her hand rest on the panther's head. She closed her eyes and opened them. Wendy nudged her, pointing out a half dozen blue herons standing at the edge of the water among the grasses. The birds were elegant and beautiful and stared at them for their impertinence in coming through. The sound of the motor didn't frighten them. They glared with regal disdain.

"They're not afraid of the motor," Ashley said.

"They're accustomed to the sound," Wendy shouted back.

"They're brave!"

"Not when it comes to the natural enemy!" Brad shouted back. He grinned. "Watch a gator move in there, and you'll see all the flapping and flying you could imagine."

Grim, Ashley thought with a shiver. The swamp was beautiful and deadly in so many ways.

She looked at Eric. He had not moved and was still staring into the distance. To the future, she thought. And she was not part of that picture.

Brad cut the motor at last and the airboat came to rest against the embankment. There was a path leading to the circle of chickees where the Hawk family lived. Baby went racing off first, then Eric stepped off. He started to walk on, but stopped and turned back. He offered Ashley a polite smile. "Here, give me your hand. Careful," he said stiffly. "The muck gets deep here."

He helped her down and then he started up the path again. Ashley caught his hand, pulling him back. "Why don't you want me here?" she asked him.

He looked her up and down, as if he'd just met her for the first time. His gaze carried disdain. "Because you don't belong here; it's that simple."

"Why not? Why does Brad belong here? Why does Wendy belong here? Why don't I?"

"Well, for one, Wendy doesn't drip with emeralds."

It was a low blow. She wasn't wearing the emeralds anymore, not even the ring that belonged to her. Tara had packed them all up to take into the city.

"Unfair. I wasn't born wearing emeralds."

"This isn't your world, Ashley," he said softly. "It just isn't."

"Why—?"

"Because we don't like pretty little white girls who like to play games. This is real life. If you want to drop in to study tribal ways, go to the open villages and the tourist traps. You can walk around and gawk to your heart's content. You can see the way that it was, and drive away in an air-conditioned car. This isn't a place to just drop in and make judgments and act condescendingly and then turn around and fly back to your penthouse."

"I don't live in a penthouse," Ashley said, and suddenly she was mad. She stepped forward, heedless of Brad and Wendy who had discreetly gone around them. She poked a finger hard at his chest. "You're acting like a martyr. As if you have some special hold on the evils of life. So all right, one of my best friends is married to one of the richest men in the world. So what? If you tried for a million years, you couldn't begin to imagine the world where she came from. Awful, awful, white American poverty, Mr. Hawk. It does exist. She grew up with no electricity and no plumbing and not because she wanted to live in the wilderness. There was no beautiful clean wilderness to run to. So quit judging people right now!"

"You couldn't make a single night out here!" Eric told her.

She straightened. "Bet me."

"What?"

"Bet me. I can make it."

"You hate the swamp. You've said so yourself."

"Bet me," she challenged. It was true. She hated the swamp. But she'd see him eat his own words if it killed her. She was staying.

He threw up his arms. "You're on. But you're on your own. No help from me on anything."

"Then I should definitely manage," she said sweetly.

He smiled pleasantly, then went past her. Ashley turned to follow him. Almost instantly she stepped into a hole filled with muck that reached nearly as high as the boots she was wearing. Elizabeth's boots. She swore softly, then pulled her leg out. While she was trying to clean the boot on the grass, someone spoke softly to her. "It's kind of a mess right now with the storm and all, but at least there's no quicksand around."

"Quicksand!" Ashley said, startled. She turned around to stare at a handsome young man with onyx eyes and black hair in a contemporary cut. He had on worn jeans and a T-shirt advertising a rock group. He offered her his hand. "Anthony Panther. Tony. I'm Eric's brother-in-law."

"How do you do?" Ashley murmured, taking his hand.

"Come on. Meet the rest of the family. They're all dying to meet you."

"Oh?" Ashley said curiously.

"Eric mentioned you last night."

"Did he say a lot?"

Tony chuckled softly. "It's what he didn't say that has us all interested. Let me take your arm."

They passed by the first of the chickees, and Ashley was startled to see just how high it was above the ground and just how low the thatched roof sat over the dwelling. "Height to keep creatures out, the slant of the roof to protect against the elements," Tony said, watching her gaze.

She smiled. "Thanks."

"There they are!" someone cried, and they were surrounded by a group of children who had raced down the ladder of a large chickee.

"Whoa, kids. Wait!" Tony commanded.

Suddenly they went still, all six of them, in jeans and T-shirts, except for the oldest girl, who was wearing a denim skirt and a wild print blouse, and was adorned with all the jewelry customary of any teenage girl. She had her long black hair tied up in a French braid, and she was very petty, her smile showing a set of deep dimples.

She had green eyes, like Eric.

She smiled shyly at Ashley, fascinated.

"This is Elizabeth," Tony said, indicating the oldest girl. "And here we have Michael, David and Dorinda—mine and Marna's brood—and these two are Charlie and Jemina. They belong to Eric's cousin, Tom, and his wife, Sharon."

"How do you do?" Ashley said, and shook all of their hands, one by one. By then Tony's wife was approaching. She was a tall woman with her eldest daughter's dimples and Eric's magnificent green eyes. She offered Ashley a beautiful smile.

"Welcome, Miss Dane. We're delighted to have you here, and we're so sorry to hear about all the trouble. Wendy was telling me that you knew the dead man." Her voice was soft and musical.

"Yes."

Marna caught Ashley's hand and drew her along. "We won't let you think about it while you're here. Come on over and meet my grandparents. Mary is cooking. I hope you'll enjoy dinner."

"I'm sure that I will," Ashley told her. She was delightful, just like Tony. And not a thing like Eric.

Marna led her to the chickee's ladder, and Ashley quickly climbed the distance to the floor. Brad was there and helped her crawl inside. Wendy was there, too, with Josh in her arms. She smiled at Ashley. "We're in luck. Mary's catfish, koonti bread and wild turnips. I wasn't in the mood to cook and neither was Brad, and this far out, it's hard to call for pizza!"

"Ashley, this is Willie Hawk and Mary Hawk. Willie, Mary, Ashley Dane," Marna said.

The man took her hand first. Ashley was instantly fascinated. His face was wrinkled, yet somehow it was still beautiful. She imagined that as a young man, he must have been completely compelling and striking. And she imagined, too, that in the days of the war, such a face would have ignited terror within the heart of the enemy.

She murmured the right things as he looked her up and down with unabashed interest. Then he told her that she was welcome anytime as his guest. He drew his wife forward. Mary was small, and despite her age, she still had nearly ink-black hair. She smiled shyly and only said hello.

"She doesn't speak English very well," Wendy explained.

"Oh," Ashley said. She took the small woman's hand and squeezed it while smiling warmly. Mary smiled back, and she was instantly beautiful. She turned and said something to Willie.

A sudden noise came from the area of the far support pole. Ashley saw that Eric had been leaning there. He straightened and said something with anger.

His grandfather spoke back sharply. After a moment, Eric stepped over to his grandmother, kissed her cheek, then turned around to face everyone. "Excuse me for a bit, will you? I'll be back in time for dinner."

They were all silent as he crawled down the ladder. The children below called to him, laughing and clinging, as he walked away. He spoke softly to them, and they let him go. He strode toward the trees that grew high on the hummock.

Mary said something to her husband, then shrugged. After eyeing Ashley calculatingly, she smiled like the Cheshire cat.

Tony cleared his throat and asked Brad a question. Ashley turned to Wendy. "What was that all about? What did Mary say that got Eric all upset?"

Wendy grinned. "*Hoke-tee*. She called you Eric's woman."

"Oh," Ashley murmured, a dark flush creeping to her face. She lowered her eyes. Wendy, however, wasn't about to allow her any discomfort.

"You're safe here, you know. Whoever followed you to Eric's house couldn't possibly find this place. I myself have trouble at times. Are you worried still?"

Ashley looked around. "No, I'm not worried out here," she said softly. "Not at all. Honestly."

"Good. Because no one can find you here." Wendy tossed back her hair, changing the subject. "Have you tried koonti bread yet? It's from a root that grows in the swamp, and without it, the Seminoles—"

"And the Miccosukees," Tony interjected.

Wendy grinned. "Tony is a Miccosukee," she explained. "Anyway, none of the Indians would have survived without the koonti root."

Marna flashed her a beautiful smile. "And pumpkins. Years and years ago, we grew pumpkins. You won't find many in the swamp these days, though."

"Times change," Willie said. He sat down by Ashley, watching her curiously as he spoke. "That was one of the ways that the soldiers finally defeated many of the Seminoles. They found the villages and destroyed the food supplies. Many families moved west. There are many, many more Seminoles in Oklahoma today than there are in Florida."

"Out of the swampland," Ashley murmured.

"They were given a barren desert," Willie said dismissively. He shrugged. "I like my swamp. Do you like my swamp?"

She laughed. "Well, I guess I'm coming to like your swamp." She hesitated and glanced at the others. "I like the people in your swamp, Mr. Hawk. Very much."

He patted her hand. "That's good. People matter more than a place." He stood and walked over to his wife.

Marna caught her watching Willie, and smiled. "He's the greatest old man in the whole world. Beyond a doubt."

"He would have never surrendered," Brad said, laughing.

"Hey!" Tony protested. "The Miccosukees were the ones who never signed a treaty."

"Hmmf!" Marna retorted. "Those of us who stayed here didn't sign any treaties."

"Children, children," Willie said. He turned around, his eyes sparkling. "None of us were alive back then, so we didn't sign or not sign treaties!" He looked at Ashley. "And don't let them fool you. None of them live here full-time. Tony and Marna are here as often as they're not, but they have a nice house with a white picket fence. And Brad and Wendy—"

"Wait, wait, now," Brad dared to interrupt. "I surrendered the first time I came out here, bear that in mind."

They laughed and the conversation eased. Marna explained to Ashley that Miccosukees and Seminoles had been grouped together for years and years, though they weren't even from the same language-speaking groups. "Now, of course, we've melded a lot. We've been intermarrying for years and years. History is always fun."

Ashley smiled. "I know something about what went on. I read Eric's book. And—" she stopped.

"What?" Marna said.

"Don't tell Eric!"

They all looked at one another and shook their hands in conspiracy. Ashley grinned. "My brother is married to a Nez Percé. I've spent a fair amount of time with them out in Arizona, and Liz has a wonderful library, so I've done lots of reading."

Wendy burst into laughter and hugged her. "No, I'll never tell Eric!" she promised. "Never."

Ashley glanced at Marna. "I made a bet with him. He said that I wouldn't make it here one night. I said that I'd stay."

Marna's brows shot up. "Well, it isn't quite like camping in the Yosemite," she said. "I'll show you his chickee."

"No, I'm on my own."

"Ashley," Wendy warned, "maybe you don't want—"

"Wendy," Brad interrupted her. "Maybe it's the best place in the world for Ashley. You said it—nobody could possibly find her here."

"And we'll all be here," Marna said. "If she needs help, she can call on us." She stood. "Eric will be here, too. You know that. He may be rude at times, but he's never careless." She shook her head at Wendy. "That brother of mine! Ashley, come on, and I'll show you where you can sleep. Your place," she told Brad and Wendy.

"Fine," Wendy said.

Brad nodded. "Of course. Just don't let the kids tuck you in. They like to tie people up!"

"Thanks for the warning," Ashley said. She and Marna went down the ladder.

"You really will be all right," Marna assured her. "The storm has hurt us some, but..." She shrugged. "There's a clear pool through here. The water is good. Eric has a man out to check it once a month. We're in the wilds here, which has its advantages. Clean water is one. Even with the flooding, it's a beautiful area. I'll show you."

Marna pushed through the brush, and they came to a small pool surrounded by pine trees and wild orchids. It was one of the prettiest places Ashley had ever seen. "It's delightful," she told Marna.

"I'm glad that you think so. Come on, I'll show you the chickee."

She led Ashley to one of two chickees that were far away from the others. "Wendy and Brad's." She hesitated. "It was Leif's, you see." She pointed to the second chickee. "Eric's. If anything does go wrong, just scream like hell. I promise you that he'll be there in an instant. Go on, climb up."

Ashley did so. She had expected the chickee to be empty, but it was not. There were mats rolled up in a corner and a large hardy trunk by the far pole. "Anything here is Wendy's, and you're more than welcome to it. Wendy would insist. There's a pitcher and bowl in the trunk if you want to bring back some water from the pool. She has dishes in there, too, and clothing. Wendy is short, so I guess you'll need to keep Liz's jeans, but I'm sure there's a nice gown to sleep in. Want to take a bath down by the pool later?"

"Sure," Ashley agreed. Then she hesitated. Did she? Weren't there all kinds of slimy creatures in the pool?

Marna winked at her. "Come on. Let's get back for dinner."

Eric was there already eating when they returned. The Seminoles had a matriarchal society, but by custom, the men ate first and were served by the women. Wendy had helped Mary serve. When Ashley arrived, Mary served her next, then urged her into a seat beside Eric.

She didn't look at him, but she felt his eyes on her. He had stripped off his shirt and boots, and she was acutely aware of his chest. She was ashamed by the depth of her desire just to touch him. He didn't want her; he didn't even want her there accepting his grandparents' hospitality. But she couldn't forget the days that had come before yesterday, the days in which they had done nothing but touch. She suddenly gave her bowl a very fierce attention. She needed to get out and away as fast as she could. She was falling in love with him, and he was the one playing games.

"I showed your guest to her quarters," Marna told Eric sweetly.

His head shot up and he glanced at his sister. "What?"

"I showed her to her chickee," Marna repeated. "You did invite Ashley to stay, didn't you?"

He stared at Ashley. She felt the power of his eyes and she almost shivered. Then she longed to demand to know why he was casting something so wonderful to the wind.

"Yes," he said softly, studying her. "I did invite her to stay." He smiled. "So you think that you'll enjoy yourself?"

"Yes, I think that I will."

"Well, good." His eyes widened in mock menace. "Lots of creepy crawlies around here," he said pleasantly. "The mosquitoes will be out soon, too." He lowered his voice. "Remember, you're on your own."

"I remember," she whispered. "Do you mind if I'm sociable with your sister?"

"Not at all. But you curl up for the night alone."

"I'll try," she said. "But Baby is really beginning to prefer me, you know. She might come up, and I have to admit that I'm not at all sure about pushing a panther out of my bed."

"Funny," he assured her. He stood and kissed his grandmother's cheek, then excused himself to the others. "I'm going to wash up and turn in," he said apologetically. Brad and Wendy said good-night; the children kissed him. He started down the ladder.

"Excuse my grandson's rudeness," Willie said loudly. Ashley could hear that Eric's descent had ceased. He shook his head, making a *tsking* sound. "It must be the Viking in him."

"The Viking!" Brad laughed.

"Umm," Willie said. "And his mother was such a good woman, gentle and kind. I don't understand. But it is not the Seminole in him who is so rude. I want you to know that."

They all heard the soft expletive that left Eric's lips as he walked away from the chickee. "Cover your ears, chicks!" Marna warned her children.

"What's wrong?" David asked his father.

"Nothing, nothing. Uncle Eric is on the warpath again," Tony said serenely. He looked at Ashley. "You haven't even tasted the koonti bread yet. How is it?"

"Different," Ashley admitted. It wasn't a soft bread, and it had a nutty flavor. "Good!" she said. She wasn't going to worry about Eric, she determined. His family was charming, and she was going to have a good time with them all. "And the catfish is wonderful."

"Freshwater," Tony told her. "Freshwater catfish is always good. Stay away from the saltwater variety."

After a while, they finished dinner. Brad and Wendy said that they were going to take Josh home.

Ashley walked them down to the water with the others. It was hard to see them go. In the short time that she had known them, she felt as if they had become very good friends. She hugged them both, thanking them for everything. "Come back whenever you're ready," Wendy told her.

She smiled. "When they clear the roads, I'll have to get back. Tara is going to take time off with the baby, so I'll have to go into the office and see how things are going."

Wendy nodded. "It's important to you then, your work?"

"I like designing. I don't care about the office or administrative part very much, but after Galliard, Tara and I decided that we wanted to work for ourselves."

Wendy nodded. "Well, don't worry, we'll see that you get into the city when the time comes. And we'll be with you until you're safely away."

"Thanks," Ashley said, hugging Wendy again. Then the small blonde and her husband departed, waving to everyone.

"Well, this is it then!" Marna told her. "Come on. It will be sunset soon."

Marna led her back to the center of the village. She went up to her own place and came back with towels and clothing and her two girls at her heels. They stopped by Wendy's chickee and Ashley borrowed a long white cotton gown, a comb, brush and a bar of soap. They started down for the water. Elizabeth was entranced by Ashley and asked her dozens of questions about New York and modeling and all else. Ashley, equally entranced with the girl, combed out her hair and answered everything. "Would you like to live in New York?" she asked her.

"I'd like an apartment there," Elizabeth said. "But I'd want to be able to come home, too."

Marna had stripped and moved out into the pool with little Dorinda. "It's wonderful! Like a cool bath!" she cried delightedly.

Elizabeth took off her clothes and went dashing out to the pool. Ashley couldn't help but hesitate. The water looked black.

Marna laughed. "See the way that Elizabeth came? Run out that way, on the path, and you won't hit any muck at all."

"There's really nothing in there, is there?" Ashley asked. "A coral snake—"

"They don't like water; they like dry!" Marna assured her. "So do the rattlers. And we've yet to find a moccasin in here."

"Yet!" Ashley wailed.

"It's all right!" Elizabeth yelled.

Ashley stripped off her clothing and headed along the pine path. She closed her eyes, swallowed and dived in.

The water was cool. She didn't stand on muck, but on rock and sand. Still, she couldn't see below the surface very well, and she determined not to move very far. "It's all right!" Marna said, and swam away. Dorinda and Elizabeth followed, tried to make Ashley join in.

"Oh, what the hel—heck!" Ashley said at last, and squinting her eyes, she moved deeper into the water and swam with the others. Elizabeth splashed her, and she splashed the girl. It was fun.

She lost all awareness of time and place.

She even forgot Eric.

But he had not forgotten her. He had walked down to the pool and discovered the women. He was about to turn and walk away discreetly when he heard Ashley's laughter. Then he paused and came forward.

She was there, in the water, with his sister and nieces, as natural as Eve, and looking comfortable in the wilderness.

She played and splashed with the others, then climbed out and picked up a towel. He watched her standing there, still smiling, wet and slick and framed by the sunset. The dying light touched her hair with a spectacular radiance, and fell over her flesh, defining every beautiful curve and nuance of her body. She had never been more beautiful.

And he had never wanted her more.

With a soft groan he turned away and wandered back to the solitude he had ordered on himself. He indulged in his grandfather's potion, in the black drink, and he lay down, wishing it would release the tempest from his body.

It did not.

Ashley dressed in Wendy's long white cotton gown. She felt refreshed and clean. She went to Marna's chickee where Tony was reading to the boys by lamplight and brewing tea.

"Seminole tea?" Ashley asked him.

"Lipton's," Tony said with a grin. "I'm just a tea drinker at heart, what can I say."

Ashley laughed and sat down with them. She had a cup of black tea and brushed Elizabeth's hair again. Then she did Dorinda's. When it started to grow late, she yawned and said that she needed to get some sleep. Tony walked her back.

"There's always a fire burning in the center of the village. There's always light," he assured her at the bottom of her ladder.

"Thanks!" she told him.

"You're going to be all right?" he asked.

"Fine," she assured him.

He wished her a good-night and left her, and she wasn't at all sure that she would be all right. She had never felt so alone in her entire life. There might be a fire burning in the center of the village, but it didn't seem to reach her chickee.

There would be a lamp up there, she thought. Brad and Wendy would have something.

She crawled up, and suddenly the darkness seemed terribly menacing. She thought that the floor was alive with living creatures—snakes and spiders and cockroaches or palmetto bugs. She was afraid to walk.

"And I'm going to sleep here?" she asked out loud.

She hurried to the trunk, found a battery-powered lantern and switched it on, bathing the chickee in yellow light. She smiled to herself and breathed more easily. The place was swept clean. She was certain that everyone had seen to their property as soon as the storm was over. Surely she was in a far better place than a New York City delicatessen.

"I will survive this just fine!" she assured herself. She found a reed mat and unrolled it. Then she found a pillow in the trunk and laughed softly, glad that either Brad or Wendy still required a few comforts of the white world. She set the pillow down, found a blanket, curled up and tried to close her eyes.

She couldn't sleep with the light; it was too bright. She pulled the lantern close and turned it off. Then she lay back down.

It wasn't a hot night because of the wind that rushed past the chickee, bringing all kinds of sounds. Like a bird calling and crickets chirping. Like that peculiar stalking noise, as if something was moving through the trees by the pool.

She jerked up, reaching for the lamp. A scream rose in her throat. Someone, something, was moving up the ladder. She opened her mouth as a creature appeared in the doorway.

Her scream escaped—then broke off abruptly. She laughed and choked. "Baby!" she exclaimed. The panther had preferred her company to Eric's tonight.

"Bad cat, you scared me half to death!" she said. Baby snarled, them promptly curled up beside her. To her amazement Ashley found herself hugging the huge beast. "Well, you're safer than anything else around here!" she declared. Baby licked her arm; the cat's tongue was like sandpaper. "That's enough. We haven't decided that we're friends for life or anything!" Ashley announced, then turned out the light and lay down.

She had barely closed her eyes when tension streaked through her again. There was someone inside. He had come in silence, but she felt him now.

Her eyes flew open. There was a man towering over her, his skin completely bronze in the pale moonlight. Her scream died. She recognized him instantly. The muscle-rippled chest, the cock of his head, the way that he stood.

"Eric!" she gasped, shivering.

"Ashley!" His tone was harsh. "You screamed. Why the hell did you scream?"

She sat up, smiling ruefully. "I'm sorry. I thought I caught it before anyone heard me. I was just startled. Baby came up here."

"Oh." He looked at the cat for a long moment. "You're all right then," he said to Ashley.

She nodded. "I'm all right."

But still he hesitated. Then he reached down, urging the cat away from her. "Go, Baby, go sleep somewhere else!" Snarling from being disturbed, Baby waved her tail disdainfully and headed for the ladder.

Eric reached for Ashley, pulling her to her feet.

Ashley saw the pulse that beat furiously at the base of his throat. He held her against him, then caught the hem of her gown and stripped the garment from her body. She stood before him in the moonlight, naked and touched by the softest glow. His breath left him in deep and ragged sighs as he watched her in silence. Gently, he touched his lips to hers, then set his mouth on her shoulders, her collarbone and her breasts. Slowly he caressed the length of her, and where he touched her, she became molten. He moved his lips over her belly, trailing liquid passion across the bare flesh. Then he caught her buttocks in his hands and kissed at the juncture of her thighs, he sought every intimacy, stroking and teasing the very bud of her desire. She cried out softly and collapsed in his arms. He lowered her gently to the floor, shed his jeans and he was one with her.

There was magic in the night, Ashley thought, and in the power of the primitive earth. This was where she longed to be—with this man. His temper was fierce, his pride was ice, but he loved like fire, with all the fury and passion of life.

She strained and writhed and arched against him, and she whispered his name. The moon exploded with a soft and mystic glow, and she drifted down with it, to kiss the earth and lie upon it in naked splendor.

She drew his head against her. She felt his light kiss on her breast, and he held her close. Words hovered on her lips. I think that I love you, I think that I have been falling in love from the very moment that I first saw your face....

She didn't speak. He wouldn't want to hear her words; he would think that they were a lie. She couldn't say them.

Tomorrow he would probably be ice again. He would spurn her; he would forget tonight.

He didn't know how to believe in love anymore.

She had to let go completely; it was the only choice that she had. It was strange how very clear that seemed at that moment.

She would let go tomorrow. But tonight...

She held him close and savored his nearness. When his lips found hers again, she greeted them eagerly. She made love fiercely and savagely, knowing that she would take and hold dearly the memories of this moment between them and the moon and the breeze and the sky and the primitive earth.

CHAPTER 10

"Tell me something. Honestly. Have you ever seen a more beautiful sunset?" Eric asked her softly.

It was very early evening and they were down by the pool together, lying idly on the leaf-carpeted bank and watching the coming of night. Ashley shook her head. No, she had never seen a more beautiful sunset. Golden light fell on a profusion of wild orchids, branches swayed in the breeze, and far across the water a great blue heron stood on a single foot in a motionless vigil. She still considered the swamp deadly, but it touched her that a place so dangerous could also offer such peace and tranquillity. She was grateful to be here.

And grateful to be with Eric.

For two days now they had stayed in the village. Almost friends by day, parting by evening and coming together again by the moonlight. It was his grandparents' home, and they both respected Willie and Mary, but they were far away, and here, privacy was deeply respected, too. She was comfortable in her surroundings. Eric was discreet, as was his sister and Tony and the cousins and uncles and others she was coming to know.

The second night he had played with her fingers and told her that tribal law had nothing against consenting lovers. Warriors and maidens had often dallied before marriage. Adultery was the sin. Warriors and maidens alike could lose their ears or noses for that offense. Marriage was sacred and to be honored.

She liked that idea, but it left her wondering about his feelings for her. She wasn't his wife. He'd had a wife whom he had loved beyond all else.

But she didn't think about it long. She was there on borrowed time already. When the roads were cleared and the downed electrical wires repaired, she would leave.

Until then...

Tonight, they had the sunset.

She had awakened alone that morning. Instinct had drawn her to the pool, and that's where she found him. Like the great blue heron, he had stood silently, watching the sun rise. She had almost left him there with the peace he seemed to need and to have found. But though he stood away from her, with his back to her, he had heard her, and without turning, had called to her.

He had faced her at last, and a smile had touched his features. He was content. She had walked into his arms while the sun rose, drying the morning dew, warming them as they lowered to the ground together. The breeze had whispered soft encouragement, and she had learned in those moments that no man or woman needed more than the primitive earth, that everything else of value and beauty came from within. In his arms she hadn't feared any creature of the swamp, because she was with him.

She didn't think that there could be anything more beautiful than lying there together, watching the day awaken. They hadn't spoken; they had just been together, and it had been wonderful.

The rest of the day had been very full. Ashley had spent the time with Marna and Mary, learning what a koonti root was and just how hard it was to grind one to make bread. Her palms were blistered and every one of her nails was cracked and broken, and she didn't care in the least. She was just delighted that she had more or less survived the initiation.

Lying idle now on the bank, she thought of how Marna and Tony and the children were delightful, how Willie was both wise and funny; and she was almost sorry that somewhere else in the world was her apartment, her friends, associates and employees. She realized she didn't want to leave this place. Especially not when Eric was like this—his mood light, his eyes filled with laughter and a certain amount of pride in her, too. Maybe it was his pride in her that mattered the most. She wasn't sure. And even if she couldn't hold him forever, she would be able to cherish the memory of this time always.

She watched his face as he chewed on a blade of grass and gazed at the distant horizon. Then he glanced her way, and she couldn't begin to read his thoughts. He smiled, dropping the blade of grass, and planted a kiss on her lips.

"You've done real well, white squaw," he told her teasingly. He picked up her hand and gently rubbed his finger over a blister. "I had always thought that you wouldn't be able to bear a broken nail."

She pulled her hand away, looking with a certain superiority out over the water. "I've done exceptionally well for a featherbrained *hoke-tee*," she said sweetly, and he laughed. Then his laughter faded and he rose and walked some distance away from her. He leaned against a pine tree, still gazing out on the pool as the sun fell.

"I know I've been harsh with you," he said quietly. Then he faced her. "I meant to be. I meant to be cruel."

"Why?" Ashley asked him.

He smiled, turning back to the water. "Because It's a harsh and cruel world here."

Ashley shook her head, seeking the understanding that he was trying to give her now. "It's not a horrible world. Your grandparents prefer the wilderness. You live in a nice, comfortable house, and so do Brad and Wendy and the others. Actually you seem to do exceptionally well."

"I do well because my father did well. He was in the army during World War II and he learned a lot about the world. He met my mother during the liberation of Norway and brought her home. She loved being here, but she made him accept her life, too. My mother knew the importance of education, and my father remembered enough of the past. He said that most of America wasn't even aware that there was still a war being waged within the country. We might not have ever surrendered, but as Indians, we were never going to win a war against white America. If we wanted to win any battles, we were going to have to win as men, not Indians. Then, at the same time, we all know that heritage is desperately important." He shrugged. "Dad started buying land, as an individual. He sent us all to good schools. And he taught me that words were the weapons we had to use in this day and age, and that words were far more powerful than any ax." He paused, shrugging. "'More powerful than the sword.' But this isn't an ideal state. It's far from it. We do fight poverty, we do fight illiteracy, and it's my fight, I can't forget it."

"I understand—"

"No, Ashley, you don't," he said quietly. "Or maybe you do, but not completely." He walked back to her, smoothing his thumb over her cheek. "You really are so beautiful, wild and exciting with emerald eyes and flame hair." He sat down beside her, holding her hand. "Elizabeth—my Elizabeth, Marna named her oldest daughter for her—wasn't a Seminole."

"She was a Miccosukee."

"No." He shook his head. "She was a Cherokee, and her mother brought her family down to Miami when her father died. She was horrified when Elizabeth fell in love with me—because I was an Indian. I was part of the world that she had run from. No one had ever taught her to be proud, not where she came from. It was a harsher world then, people were very cruel. Indians weren't allowed to drink out of 'white' water fountains. It took her years and years to believe that she did have a heritage in which to take pride."

Ashley looked at him and shook her head. "But your mother was Norse, and you're so very close to Wendy and Brad, and by the tone of your book—"

"What?"

"There's no bitterness in you with Wendy, and your outlook in the book is optimistic and humorous, and there's so much hope there! Why is the...bitterness only with me?"

"Maybe because it just suddenly mattered so much with you, and I just wasn't expecting it, and I didn't want it."

She caught her breath at his admission. She was glad and reached up to him, placing her palm against his cheek. She knew with a certainty that she was in love with him, that she would be in love with him all of her life.

But it didn't really change things, she knew. She had to walk away. If he followed, then there was hope. But the final decision had to come from him.

Ashley looked down at her boot. "That's nice," she said quietly.

"That's nice?"

She looked at him and smiled. "Yes. It's much, much more than I expected from you."

He swore with a sudden fury, grasping her shoulders as if he would shake her. "You still don't understand. This isn't all that it appears to be. I don't spend all my time in my nice air-conditioned house, or with Brad and Wendy, or even with my grandparents and sisters. Sure, it's a nice, normal life in a way. We have parties, we go to movies, I have good friends in Broward and Dade. But there's a lot more to it. There're kids down here who we fight to keep alive, we've got prostitution, orphans, old people who need help—and bingo. Where would we be without our bingo and our cigarette sales? Don't you understand, Ashley? It isn't always pretty. We're noble, we're proud, but you'd swear that a lot of our people just forgot about those virtues, or no one in the twentieth century remembered to tell them that we're supposed to be noble and proud. We have a council, and I'm on that council, and I will always give the tribe my time and my effort."

"Eric—"

He seemed to realize just how tightly he was holding her arms, and he released her abruptly. "It's close to a normal life, Ashley. But don't you see—your life isn't normal. You're accustomed to snapping your fingers and a secretary arrives. Hail a cab, send out for Chinese or sushi. You're worried about the latest fashions from Paris while we're just trying to keep decent clothing on all of our kids. It's an uphill battle. It's my fight, not yours. You can't even begin to see it. Life is like the lay of the land, Ashley. Sometimes the rivers and the grass lie soft in the breeze, and all that you can see for miles and miles is peace and beauty. But always lurking, soundlessly like a jutting log, is the deadly gator or the slinking coral snake or the rattler. I love this place, Ashley. I would never, never leave it."

She jerked away from him, leaping to her feet. She'd meant it to be so very different, but he had the most awful effect on her temper. "Who ever asked you to leave it?" she demanded. "No one has asked anything—anything at all—from you! And no one will, Eric. If there's anything that you want, you'll have to come and get it."

"What are you talking about?" he demanded harshly.

"You can't be that cold, that stupid, or that wrapped up in your own little world! But you needn't worry about demands being made on your life. I'm leaving. Tony said that the roads would be cleared by tomorrow, and he and Marna have offered to take me into the city. I'm flying out on the first plane that I can get."

He stood stiffly for a long moment, then frowned suddenly. "You can't just leave like that," he said harshly.

"I can't? You spent the entire week trying to get rid of me. I'm going, and you stand there and tell me that I can't leave?"

"You're in danger," he said softly.

"I'm in danger in the swamp," she corrected him. "I won't be in danger in the city."

"It was your friend who was murdered."

"He was not my friend."

"Sorry," Eric responded offhandedly.

There was something about the way he said it that clawed its way up her spine, irritating her beyond belief. She screeched something totally incoherent and threw herself against him.

For once, she caught him completely by surprise. He cast up his arms to catch her, but she had come too hard upon him, and they both fell to the ground. Not even that curbed her temper. She slammed her hands hard against his chest. Startled, he coughed at the blow. Then a fire sizzled in his eyes, and he shouted. "Ashley, damn it, stop it!"

She didn't listen. She hit him until he caught her wrists, and with a loud grunt, flung her beneath him. Still, she was seething. He straddled her, holding her down, and she yelled for all that she was worth. "You are just too much! This is it! You should be scalped yourself. I'm—"

"Ashley, stop it."

"I will not stop it!" With a burst of energy, she freed one hand and took a swing at him. He ducked, but the motion sent them rolling down the bank. To her horror, they plunged right into the pool, where there was mud and muck and who knew what else. She sank first, and gasping and gurgling she kicked against the muck to come to the surface.

"Here, take my hand," Eric offered. He was already out, and standing on the bank. Ashley ignored his hand.

"I can get out myself!" she sputtered furiously. But one step sent her sliding down. Eric came to get her, sweeping her into his arms. She didn't appreciate the effort. She beat against his shoulders. "Put me down! I don't want your help; it isn't worth it! A damned rattler is a friendlier creature! Put me down, and so help me, I mean it!"

His teeth grated. She heard the sound and saw a vein bulge in his throat, along with the muscles that constricted in his neck and bunched and rippled in his arms. "You want down?"

"Yes!" she snapped.

"Fine!"

He released her. She crashed back into the mud. He turned on his heel and walked away. Ashley found her footing. It wasn't easy, but she managed to make it to the bank. Eric was already moving along the path to the little circle of chickees. Ashley tossed back her hair and started the same way. Suddenly she heard a giggle, then laughter. Elizabeth and Marna came out of the bushes.

Marna tried to compose her features. "Can I give you a towel, Ashley?"

"Yes, thank you!" Ashley took the towel with a nod, following with her eyes the trail Eric had taken. Elizabeth giggled again, and Ashley smiled slowly, aware that she was covered with mud and that swamp grass was trailing down from her hair. But her smile faded suddenly.

"Marna, I do need you to take me out of here in the morning, if you would, please."

Marna's grin faded, too. "Of course," she said sweetly. "We'll leave in the morning. We'll take the airboat up to Mac's garage. Our car is still there."

Ashley smiled her thanks, and Marna looked her over from head to toe. "Why don't you get rid of that muddy stuff, and I'll bring you some of my clothes? Take a bath in the clear water. You'll feel better, I promise."

Ashley shook her head slowly. "Nothing is going to make me feel better, but thanks, Marna."

Eric didn't show up in the communal kitchen chickee for dinner, or appear later. Ashley tried to enjoy herself, and she managed to laugh and talk with the others, and smile a lot, but she was wretched inside. She hadn't wanted it to end this way. Before she had dreams; she allowed herself illusions.

And now he wasn't allowing her any illusions.

She went to bed early, not disrobing, but lying down on her mat with her pillow in the beautiful and brightly colored Seminole shirt that Marna had given her. She stared into the darkness, with her lantern turned off. She could already make out sounds in the night. She heard a cricket, an owl, and from a distance—thankfully—she heard the piglike grunt of a gator. The air smelled nice. There was the scent of the campfire, mingled with the gentle fragrance of wild orchids. She closed her eyes, torn apart inside, yet still feeling the peace around her.

She heard him when he came. She heard his footsteps on the ladder.

She had expected him to come, and she knew in her heart that he was every bit as torn as she. But there was a difference. She had faith in him— and that was what he lacked. He had no faith in her.

She thought that if she had any pride and dignity, she would walk away from this relationship. She would sit up, wait for him to arrive, and tell him to leave her alone.

But she had one more night, and she wanted it.

She kept her eyes half closed and saw him come inside and walk toward her. He stopped suddenly, inhaling sharply, his body silhouetted in the moonlight. His fists clenched. Ashley wanted to move, to say something, to discover what on earth was wrong. But then she knew, because he whispered a name.

"Elizabeth..."

His wife's name. In the dim light he had seen her in the beautiful blouse, her hair spread beneath her, and he hadn't been able to tell that that hair was red, not black.

He knelt down beside her, and Ashley still couldn't bring herself to stir. He reached out and touched her hair with trembling hands, and some harsh sound like a sob escaped him. The illusion had not lasted long. He had quickly realized who she was, and that the moonlight had played an eerie trick on him.

She wanted to open her eyes fully, she wanted to tell him that if he would reach out, she would be there. She loved him, and nothing about life mattered at all, if only she could live it with him.

The words would not come to her lips.

"Ashley," he murmured. "Ashley."

He lay down beside her and threaded his fingers through her hair. She should have turned him away, but she could not. He buried his face against her throat. "I'm so sorry. I never meant to hurt you."

She touched him at last, reaching out to stroke his face. "I have a bad temper," she said.

He smiled. "I shouldn't be here."

"Just whisper my name again," she told him softly, and he did. He whispered it again and again, and she clung to him. He moved his lips against her throat, and his fingers worked over the tiny buttons on the blouse. Moments later they were entwined in each other's arms, their clothing shed. He made love that night with a raw, near-desperate passion, his arms tight around her, his every stroke and thrust fierce and sweetly explosive.

"How is it possible to want a woman so desperately, and know that it's all so terribly out of sync and without rhyme and reason," he whispered to her. He had risen above her again. His fingers touched and studied her face, and lingered over her hair. "You are an emerald to me, Ashley, can you see that? A beautiful, exquisite gem, but one that I can't afford, one that isn't within my reach. I love everything about you so much. I love your eyes and your hair, and I love every line and curve of your body. I love your breasts and your throat, and sometimes I can't imagine that you're real, and that I'm touching you. I love to make love to you."

She wanted to say something, but inside she was aching. He loved her eyes, her hair...but he did not love her. He couldn't love her, or so it seemed. Maybe he couldn't allow himself to love her.

She stared up at him, wishing that he would leave, because she felt like crying. But he didn't move. He seemed locked in that straddled position over her, all bronze and sleek with sweat, a rawhide band holding back his black hair. In the night his eyes were luminescent, like a cat's. He brought his knuckle against her cheek.

She turned her head aside, choking on a sob. Gently, he held her face so he could see her eyes.

"What is it? What's the matter?"

She shook her head.

"What?"

"I—I love you," she said softly. "I—I've fallen in love with you."

He stiffened instantly, going as taut as a drum. From his throat to the lean rippled muscles of his belly, he went cold and straight. "No, you don't love me," he said. He stood quickly, walking away from her, restless as a panther. Ashley closed her eyes and fell back in misery. Telling him hadn't helped her.

Only leaving would help her.

He strode back to her and glared down at her angrily. "You don't love me. You're going to leave here. You're going back to New York."

"Yes! Yes, I'm leaving!" she cried.

"This has been fun and games. Dick and Jane in the jungle. Fall in love for a lark, and fly away to your next adventure."

"Stop it!" she yelled at him. "Just stop it." She was on her knees, challenging him. "You're an idiot! I told you that I love you because it's the truth. I've had one affair in my entire life, and that's it, so tell me about the world. I've learned to survive, too, even if my world's a bit different. I'm sorry about Elizabeth, damned sorry. And I'm sorry that the world isn't fair—it never has been, it probably never will be. I don't mind that you fight the unfairness. I would be happy to fight it with you—"

"It isn't your battle—"

"It is anyone's battle! Anyone can want to see it change! You fool! I can survive the swamp, and I can love the beauty, and I can deal with anything that you can create to hold against me. What I can't combat is you! I can't fight your belief that you can't love again because of Elizabeth, and I can't fight your total lack of belief in me as a human being!"

"What?" he said, startled, his eyes narrowing.

"Me, Eric, me. I don't understand how you could want me the way that you do, and not care in the least about the woman who I am! Yes, I own a Tyler emerald, a damned good one! Rafe gave it to me, as a friend, and I accepted it from him, as a friend. But I don't need jewels to survive. I don't even need New York to survive. But I am leaving, I am going home. Just as fast as I can!" Tears streamed down her face and she let them fall unchecked. She rose, naked and unaware of the fire in her hair, cascading down all around her, unaware that she was exceptionally proud and beautiful and more so for the truth and humility of her words. "I don't need the city, but I do need to be loved. I need to believe, and to be believed in. I can't survive without...faith. I do love you."

"Ashley!" He called out her name with fury. "You—you can't! I don't believe you."

"No, Eric, you don't believe in yourself anymore. And you can't let Elizabeth go."

He exhaled slowly. He came toward her as if he wanted to touch her, but he didn't. Instead he turned away. His shoulders stiffened, and a horrible sound, like a sob, escaped him. He stood very still then, tired, weary, almost as if he were defeated. "No," he said. "No, I can't forget her right now. You're right, I just can't. Not while her killer is on the loose."

He didn't touch her again or linger longer. He found his jeans and put them on. She couldn't rise to stop him, she couldn't even move. He was silent in the night as he left her, climbing down the ladder into the darkness, never once looking her way.

She lay awake, listening to the night and the sound of her own breathing. She closed her eyes and clenched her teeth against more tears. And she prayed that he would come back to her. She wanted him so badly, even though he had denied her. She wished that she had never spoken, that she could just lie with him and hold him in the darkness.

Where was Baby, she wondered? Tears burned at the back of her eyelids, and she hoped that the big cat would come back. She could cry into Baby's tawny pelt, and she wouldn't feel so terribly alone.

Then she heard motion in the darkness once again. She pulled the sheet over her. Eric was coming back. There was a God, and he had listened to her prayers. Eric was coming back. She closed her eyes, silently saying a prayer of thanks.

Then she felt the cold steel against her throat.

Her eyes flew open and she would have screamed, except the steel pressed more tightly on her flesh. She could feel the razor sharpness of the blade. She was certain that a trickle of blood had already formed on her throat.

She stared into the face of an Indian, but not one she knew, and not a full-blooded Seminole, but a man of mixed race. His face was dark and harshly lined, and there was a ragged scar that cut across his forehead.

She hadn't the faintest idea who he was. Or why he would want to kill her.

He smiled as he looked down at her. He was between thirty and forty, she thought, and yet he might have been any age. His eyes were nearly as dark as his hair, cut short, almost a crew cut. He wore a plaid shirt and worn jeans, and his lips were full. His eyes were icy cold. She knew instinctively that slitting her throat would mean nothing to him. He had killed before, and he would kill again very easily.

"That's right, don't scream, Ashley. My name is Jacobs. John Jacobs. Does that name ring any bells with you? It doesn't matter. Your name is Ashley, right? That's what he was calling you."

She didn't respond and he drew the knife down her body, pulling the sheet from her breasts to prick the shadowed valley between them. A little point of blood appeared.

"Careful, Ashley, I like you. You've got all kinds of fire and temper, huh? And you seem to be a smart girl. Be nice, and I may let you live."

"What do you want?" she demanded. The words came out in a harsh whisper because she barely dared to breathe.

"Eric Hawk," he told her. "That's what I want. I want that bastard half-breed. I've been sitting on death row because of him, and he's going to be the one to pay this time."

The night swam before her. She was going to black out, or be sick. This was the man who had slain Wendy's husband. The man who had killed Elizabeth so heinously, leaving her white gown a spill of crimson blood....

"Get up," he told her.

She exhaled, unable to move because of the knife. She had thought he would rape her, and she had known she would have preferred death to being touched by a man with so much blood on his hands. He smiled, seeing in her eyes all of her fears. "We may get to it later, baby, but I want out of here before Eric returns."

"But I thought you wanted him," she said quickly.

His teeth grated. "I want him on neutral ground. Not here."

"You have no right to be here. Anyone here would kill you with his or her bare hands alive."

"Smart, lady, real smart. Now get up and get dressed, and let's go."

"Where?"

"Don't ask any more questions. I'll start to reckon that it might be easier to leave you dead and let him come after me in revenge. Just get dressed. Now. Quickly."

He kept the knife tight on her body, and she hadn't the courage to move. He made a sound like a growl, pressing the point of the knife against her breast. She found courage and stood. She fumbled for her shirt, then the jeans—and Elizabeth's boots. She almost screamed when she pulled them on, thinking that they belonged to a woman this man had killed.

He made a sniggering sound, and she hated the look in his eyes as he stared at her. "Funny, ain't it? Here I am making you get dressed at knife point. Should be the other way around, huh? Excepting that I don't usually have no trouble with the ladies. Naw, they like me well enough." He flashed her a quick smile. "Thanks to Hawk, though, I've had me a dry spell for a while. Up in Raiford. It's a mean place, Miss Ashley, that it is. You should see it when they do get to an execution. The bleeding liberal hearts are all on one side of the fence, screeching about God's right to take lives. Then there are the bloodthirsty vamps on the other side, chanting 'Fry 'em!' Yep, it's a hell of a place."

Ashley swallowed hard. "You murdered people. You were sentenced and condemned."

"I never wanted to shoot, Ashley. 'Specially not the girl. Damn, but she was a looker. I didn't hit her—it was Robbie Maynard did that. Then that half-breed Hawk—Leif Hawk, that is—steps in, trying to defend her. We had to shoot him, and then, well, she'd seen our faces. She had to die. It was real regretful, but..." He shrugged. "Only they knew who we were anyway. We had gloves on and all, but we peeled 'em off too soon. I had a record, so—" He paused again, looking her up and down in the dim light. "I could have gotten away with it. I was the one who knew the swamps, I knew where to run, and I knew where to hide. Except that Eric knew where to find me."

If he kept talking, Ashley thought, someone would come. Eric might, maybe to apologize to her. And if he did come back, what then?

"Let's go," Jacobs said.

"Where?"

"Down the ladder. Move."

She walked across the floor as slowly as she could. She wished desperately that she could think of something clever to do, or that she had the courage—or foolish bravado—to scream. She wished that she did belong in the swamp so she could plan some way to escape this man.

Where was Baby? The damned cat had run off when Ashley really needed her the most.

"I said move."

She started down the ladder, wondering if he was armed with only the knife. Maybe she could get ahead of him and run and start screaming.

"I've a nice-size Magnum in my waistband, and I can blow the whole of your head off with one bullet. So crawl down nice and quiet, huh?"

Ashley looked up—straight into the evil barrel of the gun. She no longer had to wonder just how well armed he was.

He smiled and followed her down the ladder. On the ground, he caught her arm. "This way!" he ordered.

He was leading her away from the pool and the village, toward the canal—into the absolute and horrible darkness of the swamp.

"Faster!" he said harshly.

She couldn't run any faster. Her heart was thundering and she could barely breathe. She tripped and cried out.

"Get up!" He jerked her arm.

She tried to get up, and touched something very soft. She looked down and a scream froze in her throat.

She knew where Baby was. The great cat lay silent and still beneath her.

"Oh, my God!" she whispered, and suddenly it all seemed more horrible than she could bear. He had killed that beautiful cat.

But then he had killed human beings, she reminded herself dully. What could the murder of the cat mean to such a man?

Tears stung her eyes as she stumbled to her feet. He started to drag her.

"You killed the cat. And you killed a man here, on the first day of the storm."

"Shut up and keep moving."

"You killed a man—"

"I didn't kill any man the first day of the storm. But if you don't shut up, I will kill you. I tried. I tried to reach the two of you at Eric's house after the storm. You got lucky then. Stay lucky, Ashley. Stay real lucky, and shut your mouth for now. Later, you can scream all you want. Yeah, honey, you can scream all you want."

CHAPTER 11

$\mathbf{E}$ric cursed himself. If he wasn't so wrapped up in the past, he might have the good sense to worry about the present.

He couldn't go back to Ashley. He didn't know how to explain to her that Jacobs was out and that there was no way for him to find peace—or to escape the past—until Jacobs was behind bars again.

Or dead.

He walked down to the pool. Baby wasn't around, he noticed, but then she was more mobile than any of them. She had probably gone on to Brad and Wendy's. Eric mused that not even Baby seemed to like him very much these days.

The cat had good sense, he thought, staring out across the water. He wished that he could stay the hell away from himself.

Ashley Dane was like a star, fallen from the heavens, and she hadn't been meant to remain here. Not in his life. When she saw that, he thought, his heart hardening anew, she would feel like a caged beast. This wouldn't be a wonderful wilderness and freedom for her, it would become a prison cell. Maybe she even believed the things that she said to him, and she did know how to touch deeply. But she also knew how to wound, and she knew how to hurt. He had let her come close. He had wanted her to come close. He had played with fire, and now he was burned.

Suddenly he stiffened. He didn't know quite what it was that alerted him, but he felt that something had changed. Instinct pulled him, and he walked back to the cluster of chickees. He stared at his own and saw nothing—no movement, just the natural quiet of the night.

But something wasn't right. He knew because he felt the night breeze all along his spine and on his nape—and the breeze seemed to whisper of evil.

He paused below his brother's chickee—Wendy and Brad's now—and heard nothing but silence there, too. He looked toward his grandparents' chickee, far into the center of their small village. Someone was moving about.

He didn't think twice about running back to his chickee, where he strapped his knife to his ankle and shoved his .38 into his waistband. He climbed down and hurried to the center of the village.

Below Willie's chickee, flat against one of the corner poles, was a figure.

Eric circled, coming up on the figure from the back. He crouched low and moved across the earth in dead silence.

Then the figure sensed him and swirled around. Eric crashed into the figure, bringing it down with him before it could fire or throw a weapon.

"Son of a gun!" came a mutter. "Eric!"

Just about to throw a hard punch to the jaw, Eric paused and blinked against the darkness, the voice registering slowly in his mind. "Tony!" he gasped. He muttered an expletive and they got to their feet together.

"You scared the hell out of me!" Tony said. "My heart's still beating faster than the storm!" He dusted off his shirt.

"What are you doing here?" Eric demanded of his brother-in-law.

"I was worried about Willie and Mary. I thought I heard something. I could have sworn someone was around here. I heard Baby crawling around, and then I couldn't find her. I just thought that something was up, and I was worried."

"Are they all right?" Eric asked quickly.

"Yeah. I checked on Willie and Mary; they're sound asleep."

The two men both started when they heard Willie clearing his throat above them. He came down the ladder. "I may be old, Anthony Panther, but I'm not dead. I'm not sleeping. I heard you moving. What's going on here?"

At a loss, Eric shook his head, but the feeling that sent both ice and fire all along his spine was growing worse. "I don't know, Grandfather. Something." He turned to Tony suddenly, desperately. "My sister. Marna—"

"Marna's fine. The kids are sleeping, and she's wide awake and sitting up with the shotgun. No one's going to bother her."

They all swung around then, looking to the canal far away. They could hear the sound of a motor, and a pale light was coming out of the darkness.

"Airboat," Tony commented unnecessarily.

They started for the water, but Eric paused suddenly, looking down. His heart caught hard in his throat, then seemed to slam against his chest. He dropped to his knees.

It was Baby. Dead, he thought.

He clutched the huge cat into his arms, pulling her onto his lap. Her heart was still beating, he realized. He pulled open her lids and stared at her pupils. She was barely breathing, but she had no visible injury.

Poisoned. She was such a beggar. Someone who had realized that the cat could be more trouble than a pair of pit bulls had managed to see that she could spread no alarm.

Eric picked her up, staggering to his feet. Carrying her on his shoulders, he followed his grandfather and Tony. He heard Wendy's voice and realized that Brad and his sister-in-law had come.

It was late for a visit. Very late.

"What is it? What's happened?" Eric demanded.

The motor was already cut; Wendy was standing on dry land, and Brad was leaping over to join her. "Oh, Eric," Wendy began, then stopped. She stared at Baby; her eyes widened with surprise, then went damp with the threat of tears. "Eric, you tell me, what's happened? Is she—is she dead?" Wendy rushed forward, lifting the cat's head, opening her eyes as Eric had done.

"Poison, I think," Eric said.

"But why?" Wendy demanded blankly. "Baby needs a vet, but we'll never make it to one on time. We'll try to induce vomiting. Marna must have something for the kids. And it could be the wrong thing to do, but we've got to do something. Let's get her up to the cooking chickee. And get Marna. And—"

"Wendy," Brad interrupted his wife softly. "If Baby has been poisoned, there's a reason, and we've got to find it. And you've got to tell Eric the message we're supposed to be bringing, remember."

"Here, I'll take Baby," Tony said, and he lifted the cat from Eric. "Wendy, get Josh from Brad. He's sleeping, isn't he? Good, I'll get him over to Marna. And now, Wendy, you come with me. Brad, you tell Eric whatever it is."

Brad nodded. "The phones are working. Rafe Tyler called. Two of his chief management officials confessed to charges of murder yesterday when confronted with evidence against them. They were in a conspiracy with Mosby to heist the emeralds in the storm. They were after Ashley. Harrison had been given some big bucks to lure her into the swamp where they could get their hands on her—and the emeralds." Brad paused, watching Eric. "The body should have been Ashley's. They killed Mosby for losing her, for screwing up the deal. They probably would have killed him when they were done anyway." He shrugged. "They weren't the brightest crooks. Rafe has a half-brother who works covert operations and he was able to trace a few telephone messages and get his hands on some written material that clinched it all. Anyway, it's over."

Looking at Brad, Eric slowly shook his head. "It can't be over. Something is happening here. Baby—" he broke off in horror. He hadn't actually seen Ashley. He had gone to the chickee, but he hadn't seen Ashley.

An expletive escaped him like an explosion and he turned around and started to race toward where Ashley was sleeping. He berated himself furiously as he ran, his heart thundering against his chest. He took the ladder two rungs at a time, and then his breath escaped him in a ragged gasp.

She was gone.

There was no sign of a struggle. Eric hurried over to the mat and fell to his knees. He remembered how he had left her. On her knees, her hair streaming behind her. Looking almost as she had when he had first seen her in the swamp, and she had fallen wet and bedraggled in her tiger-striped bikini bottom at his feet in the mud. But there had been nothing wet or bedraggled about her tonight. She had been stunning, proud, her bare breasts beautiful and high in the glow of the moon, her eyes an emerald fire, her hair a river of flame. Her voice and words had seared his heart, and he had longed with all of his being to believe.

That was all that she had wanted—his faith in her as a woman.

And he had left her.

He dared not think of it now. She was gone, and time was passing. Someone had come here, someone who knew what he was doing. Someone who could come quietly, who could watch and wait. Someone who knew the swamp....

He swallowed hard as bile formed in his stomach.

Jacobs.

He knew what it meant for blood to run cold then, for all of his limbs were constricted by ice. He breathed the cold, and he felt it around his heart. He stiffened and cast back his head, barely suppressing a savage scream. For in those moments, he could see it all again—walking with Wendy into the morgue, watching the attendant cast back the white sheet, then seeing Elizabeth's beautiful face, frozen in death, and the endless blood. The white dress that had been so beguiling against the copper of her skin was stained to crimson.

Jacobs was prowling the swamps with Ashley. He had taken her just as if he had dropped a calling card. Come on, get me, he was saying. It was a cat-and-mouse game. They were well matched. They both knew the swamp. They knew how to hide and move in silence.

Evenly matched! If Eric had had half his wits or his senses with him, Jacobs wouldn't have made it into the village. Eric would have heard him or sensed him before the damage had been done.

He stood quickly and came down the ladder. Brad was hurrying toward him. "She's...?"

"She's gone," Eric said quickly. "I'm going after her."

"I'm coming."

"You can't."

"Eric—"

"Brad, you don't understand. This is a private thing between Jacobs and me. If he sees you, he'll kill her."

"He won't see me," Brad said firmly.

"But if he does—"

"Eric, four eyes have to be better than two. And if Jacobs does manage to kill you, he'll kill Ashley anyway. The man has no conscience. He's already condemned to death. Let me come. I'll be quiet. I'll stay low."

"He's going deep into the swamp, I'm certain—"

"I know the swamp real well," Brad interrupted him softly. "I had the best teacher in the world—you. And you're forgetting something else."

"What's that?"

"He killed your wife and your brother. But he also killed Wendy's husband, and I won't be able to go home if I don't get into this with you."

"Wendy wouldn't want—"

"*I* want."

Eric hesitated a moment longer. Brad was a good man to have on his side, and maybe what he was saying was true. Maybe it was personal for Brad, too. "Let's go," Eric said.

They started down toward the canal, then paused, hearing footsteps behind them. They turned around and saw Willie. His huge dark eyes were haunted. "Jacobs?" he asked Eric.

Eric glanced at Brad, then nodded slowly to his grandfather. Willie exhaled slowly, swallowing and closing his eyes, and Eric knew that he was thinking about Leif and Elizabeth.

Willie opened his eyes. "Last time, son, I told you not to kill him. I was afraid that your heart and soul would fester with the hatred, and that you could live better knowing that you'd had the strength to trust in the law. And the law was fair—the law of our state condemned him. I'll tell you the same thing now. Don't kill with hatred."

"Grandfather—"

Willie lifted his hand. "But if he threatens your life, or Brad's, or if he hurts that pretty woman in any way, then I say, blow the monster's head off and be done with it. Just remember—do what is necessary, and that will sit well in your heart."

"All right, Grandfather. I'm taking the canoe."

Willie nodded, and Eric and Brad walked on. The old man called out, "Wendy will save the cat."

Eric's lips curved in acknowledgement. "Yes, she will."

"Tell Wendy where I am," Brad said.

"Wendy will know where you are," Willie answered.

Eric pushed the canoe out from the shore and into the water, and they saw Willie, standing calm and stoic upon the land.

As they moved away from the village, darkness settled down upon them.

"I'll get the lantern," Brad said.

"No, just the flashlight. We don't want to advertise our presence."

"It's black as Hades," Brad reminded him.

And it was. The moon went behind a cloud, and the canal water and the saw grass seemed to be one with the sky. "I just need a pinpoint of light," Eric said.

"How do you know—"

"He's leaving me a trail, Brad. He wants me to follow him." To prove his point, he stopped rowing as they passed beneath a branch, and showed Brad the broken twigs and the bracken. "He's leaving a trail as broad as daylight. He knows that I'll come."

Eric sank his paddle back into the water in rhythm with Brad. The canoe glided on through the water.

Ashley stared out into the night as Jacobs sent his canoe skimming through the water. She could see very little, not even see his face. Yet he was moving through the darkness, sure of his way.

A cloud shifted, and a small amount of moonlight shone down upon them. When they had first left the village, she had thought about braving the water to escape him. He must have read her mind, for as soon as they turned around the first hummock, he had ceased to paddle and had brought his knife against her throat, demanding her hands. Now they were tied before her with thin strips of rawhide, which chafed and tore her skin. She hadn't a prayer in the world.

He smiled at her, seeing her face in the moonlight. "You didn't want to go swimming anyway, not here and not at night. Look over there at that log—only it's not a log. Put a juicy morsel like you into the water, and that log will come alive faster than you can spit. They're mean, gators are. Did your boyfriend warn you about that? Even if you made dry land, that gator could come right after you, and fast."

She shivered although she didn't want to. He leaned close to her, and he had that awful look in his eyes again. He might like women—he had said that he liked her—but he liked killing more than anything else, she was certain about that.

"Eric and I are old friends," he said. He waited for her to respond. When she didn't, he kept talking. "Leif and I went to school together, did he tell you that? Man, those Hawks, they just excelled at everything. Everyone knew that they wouldn't be sitting around in any kind of poverty. When they were kids, all the adults talked about what the Hawks would bring to the council. They were the promise of our people. Kind of makes you a little bit sick, huh? They went off to college; they got to be football stars—and the nation don't give a damn about what color you are as long as you can carry a pigskin ball over a goal line! Then Eric went off to Vietnam, and he was a hero all over again. It wasn't that smooth for me. My old man was a no-account trash who had a night's fun with an Indian girl at a festival and then took off. Mom picked a last name out of the phone book—Jacobs. It has a good ring. It looked good the first time I was arrested. I never could get the right numbers in bingo, and so I just decided to take the pot without them. I wasn't loved by the tribe like the Hawks, so I went behind bars. Then I started up with Maynard and Fitz. They were in on a house razing deal. We got together real good when they found out just how well I knew the swamp—and just what could be hidden in it.

"You want to know something that was true? As much as I hated those Hawks, I didn't want to kill them on the night of the holdup. It was just that Leif Hawk wasn't going to let it be. And now—now there's Eric. And this is him and me. And he is going to die tonight."

Ashley laughed suddenly because she was so horribly nervous. "I think you might have missed your mark. We had a bit of an argument, remember? He'll probably stay away all night. And when he finds me gone in the morning, he'll think that I just left him. It's what he's been expecting me to do."

She felt a new chill seize her as Jacobs slowly shook his head. "No, I don't think so. He'll figure out that something is wrong right away."

"Why is that?"

"I killed the cat, remember?"

"Oh!" Feeling sick, she lowered her head. She swallowed and tried very hard to control her panic. She had been in rough spots before. Tine Elliott had kidnapped her at gunpoint to get to Tara. He had threatened her life, but she hadn't become a helpless victim. She had fought back— and help had come.

But this was different. This was the swamp. This was a darkness worse than anything.

Yet she didn't want Eric to try to rescue her. Because Jacobs meant to kill him. And then her.

"It's not much longer, Ashley," Jacobs told her.

She shook her head. "You're a fool. You escaped. You should have left the state, you should have sailed to the islands, you should have hidden—"

"It isn't easy for a half-breed Indian to blend with the rest of humanity, lady," he said dryly.

"Out west—"

"It doesn't matter. I'm going one way or the other. Florida is tough, if you haven't noticed. My death certificate has been signed. They'll get to me sooner or later. I didn't escape to live."

"Then—"

"I escaped for revenge. And I'm going to get it."

She lowered her head again and tried not to cry. There had to be some way out of this. Eric wasn't a fool, he wouldn't come alone.

"Ah, hope springs eternal in the human breast!" Jacobs laughed. "If he comes with a friend, count on it, the friend will die right along with him."

She tossed back her hair. "What if he comes with an entire S.W.A.T. team?"

Jacobs stopped paddling. He leaned forward. "S.W.A.T. teams are loud, even *if* one could get out here right now. You have to know the swamp, honey. But if he does come with a pack, well then..." His voice trailed off.

"Then what?"

He shrugged. "Then I kill you. Just like his wife. Four bullets to the chest. And he may not be dead himself, but life will be over for him. He'll know then that he's just hell on women, and that will be that."

He was going to kill her anyway, no matter what.

"We're almost there," he told her. "Just up ahead. That nice dry hummock there. See the little shack. For weekend hunters. White boys. They come out here and shoot up beer cans. Big men. They don't know the first thing about hunting." He hesitated. "But Eric does. That's why we're going to play real safe."

The canoe scraped the edge of the bank. In the darkness she could barely make out the tiny cabin and what was beyond it. There was water around them, and there seemed to be a bog of deep black muck and high saw grass to the left.

There was death in the darkness. Alligators were nearby, and deadly snakes. But Eric had been right when he had told her that there was still no creature as deadly as man.

"Get up careful—" Jacobs began.

But Ashley was already standing, causing the canoe to dip and sway. She had never been so scared in her life—and never been more blindly determined. She wasn't going to help him kill Eric. She'd rather take her chances with the swamp.

"I said—" Jacobs continued, but it was too late. The canoe capsized, and they both fell into the murky waters in the pitch-black of the night.

Eric suddenly stiffened where he sat in the front of the canoe. He raised his paddle and lifted his hand so Brad would do the same.

"What is it?" Brad barely mouthed the question.

"I don't know. Something," Eric said. He turned off the flashlight and sat very still.

They both heard it—a splash. Then, from somewhere not far ahead, a scream. It was high and long and shrill, filled with terror and pain. Ashley.

Eric's jaw constricted and his stomach went tight as a drum. He drove his paddle into the water and raced along the water.

Ashley screamed again.

This time, her cry was choked to a stop. Eric could hear the sounds of splashing water, of fighting in the long grasses not a hundred yards away.

He sank his paddle deeply into the mud, bringing the canoe to a halt. He turned to Brad. "Can you face him down? And I'll come around."

Brad hesitated. They'd worked together before, and they'd been a good team. Then, Eric had swaggered calmly out to do the luring. He had helped saved Wendy's life.

The waters here were deadly. Eric intended to plunge into the canal, Brad knew it. They could both figure what had happened. Ashley had tried to escape, and now she was struggling for her life.

"Go on," Brad said. "I can handle my part."

Eric nodded. "Thanks." Silently he stepped over the edge of the canoe and sank in the water.

"Hey," Brad said.

Eric surfaced, watching him.

"I was going to tell you to be careful, but you can be meaner than any gator I've ever come across when you've got the mind to be."

Eric smiled. He grasped Brad's hand for a moment, then plunged back in the water.

And he disappeared into the night.

"You stupid bitch! I should plug you right now, I should do away with you this very second!"

Ashley had barely dived into the blackness before he'd had his hands on her. His fingers gripped her hair, and he dragged her back to the surface. She came up gasping for air, then screaming for dear life.

Surrounded by the muck and the saw grasses, she kicked at him with fury and desperation, screaming again.

And he dragged her down deep in the water. Her lungs began to burn. She felt her head spinning and a blackness more complete than any other falling upon her. She nearly opened her mouth to inhale the water into her searing lungs when he jerked her up at last. This time, she kept quiet. She choked and coughed and didn't have the breath left to whisper, much less scream.

He jerked her against him hard, staring into her eyes. "Don't do it again. I don't have to kill you, you know. Plenty of people know my face. I die if I kill you, and I die if I don't. If I get Eric Hawk, I might feel generous. I might let you live. And then—" He paused, and Ashley wondered why.

Then she saw the snake.

It was slithering in and out of the grasses to their right. It was large. Desperately, she tried to remember what Eric had told her. Rattlers like hummocks. So did coral snakes. There were only four poisonous snakes down here, and one of them liked water.

The cottonmouth...

Neither of them was breathing. They both stared at the creature as it silently streamed through the water toward them. They both watched....

The snake ignored them. It continued moving. In another second, it disappeared.

"Nice place, the swamp. You like it here, Ashley?" Jacobs whispered to her at last.

She started to shiver. She couldn't help it. She desperately wanted to get out of the water.

Abruptly, Jacobs set his knife against her throat. "We're going to move now—" he began, but then stopped. He swung her around in front of him in the waist-high water. Ashley didn't understand. Then she saw the faint light and heard the dip of a paddle in the water.

"Playtime!" Jacobs whispered against her neck. "And I'm not quite prepared the way I wanted to be, thanks to you. Come on, now, move!"

He started dragging her to the shore. They didn't make it. A voice called out in the darkness.

"Jacobs!"

It wasn't Eric. It was Brad.

Jacobs swore furiously. "Get the hell out of here. You come any closer, and the girl is dead."

"How do I know that the girl isn't dead already."

Jacobs pressed his knife against her flesh. "Say something, sweetheart."

"I'm—I'm alive, Brad." She hesitated just briefly. "But don't come any closer. All he wants to do is kill us all and—" she broke off, screaming in pain as Jacobs knotted her hair viciously into his fist.

"You stay where you are because I want Eric Hawk. And I'll kill her if I don't see him out here alone in a matter of minutes. You got that."

There was silence out on the water. Ashley felt something move against her legs. She swallowed, terrified of the steel against her throat, wretchedly aware of the death that lurked in the water.

"I mean it!" Jacobs claimed. "You get that half-breed out here now— or she dies!"

She felt something sure and hard against her leg.

Suddenly the water beneath her exploded. She screamed as she was torn from Jacobs's grasp and sent flying farther out into the water. She sank low, then surfaced, thrashing and panicking. All around her, the water was still exploding, splashing wildly.

Then she realized why. No snake had touched her leg. It had been Eric. He had reached them from beneath the surface of the water and had wrenched her from Jacobs's grasp before the madman's knife could sink into her flesh.

And now he and Jacobs were engaged in deadly combat. She couldn't even tell who was who in the consuming darkness as the men fell and sank, then rose, gasping.

Ashley strained to see. Jacobs had Eric in a headlock and was pulling him down again. Eric locked his fingers on Jacobs's arms, dragging him forward. They sank together again. They rose, apart this time. Eric cast himself against Jacobs. They fell.

They moved closer and closer to the shore, fists flying. Jacobs caught Eric in the jaw, and he went down, splashing hard, his grunt of pain seeming to echo in the night.

Ashley screamed.

She heard the lap of the water and realized that Brad was coming up with the canoe. "Ashley, shut up!" he warned her.

"Brad, do something! He's going to kill him—"

"Ashley, just stay very still."

She stared at Brad in horror, then realized that something was slithering by her again. She stood very, very still, and tried not to hear the sickening crunches of the vicious fight taking place just yards away.

The snake was back. It was circling her and swimming around and around her.

"Dead still, Ashley. Do you understand me? Blink, if you do."

She blinked. She didn't move. The sounds of the fight faded behind her.

Eric burst from the surface a split second before Jacobs. It was the advantage he needed. He blinked once and saw Elizabeth, dead, in her pool of blood.

He slammed his fist into Jacobs's face with all the strength in his body. He heard bone crack, then Jacobs went down, his eyes closed.

Jacobs's jaw was broken, Eric thought impassively, but he wasn't dead. He should go back to Brad and get a gun and blow Jacobs's head away. He clenched his hands into fists at his sides.

He still believed in the law. He had bested Jacobs bare-handed and should hand this murderer back to the police. He would meet his fate in the electric chair, or rot forever on death row. He wouldn't escape again.

Something hot and horrible inside of Eric wanted to kill Jacobs in the worst way. He knew that he had killed in the war. But he had never murdered.

And he had to believe in the law. His father had taught him that law was the dividing line, and man's belief in it made him civilized, and separated him from the savage. It had nothing to do with color or creed or race; it was about right and wrong.

Jacobs was dung, and he might be better off dead. He probably would be dead soon.

But it wasn't for Eric to be judge and jury—or play God. He exhaled slowly and turned around. He needed to call Brad over so that they could tie Jacobs up. Once he awakened, he wouldn't hesitate to try to murder Eric again.

But when Eric turned, he forgot Jacobs.

He saw Ashley in the water. She was dead still, and Brad was talking to her very quietly, his Magnum aimed at the water. But he seemed to be having difficulty getting a fix on his target.

A snake. With antivenom, she could survive a bite. Except that they were deep in the swamp, and it could take a long time to get back to the village.

"Ashley!"

He hadn't meant to speak; her name escaped him.

Ashley heard her name called out with a horrible anguish, and she realized that it was Eric. He was alive. There was no more motion in the water, just the silent, deadly dance of the snake.

She felt movement near her. Eric was making his way toward the canoe. Brad was speaking to him very softly. "I can't get a fix on it."

"Give me the gun."

"Be still," Brad whispered.

"Ashley, dead still!" Eric warned her, just as Brad had done.

And the water exploded all around her as a shot was fired. She screamed when pieces of snake carcass and snake blood splattered her.

Then she was pulled up, by strong arms. She looked up and discovered deep green eyes, full of care and anguish and concern, staring into hers.

One of Eric's eyes was already sporting a bruise. Blood trailed from his nose and his jaw. She wanted to ask him what had happened to Jacobs, but when she opened her mouth, no sound came. She wanted to smile, too, because Brad was there, looking down at her with the same concern.

"Jacobs," she mouthed.

"He's worse than I am," Eric promised her.

Then her eyes widened suddenly, because she could see what they could not.

Jacobs might be worse than Eric, but he wasn't down. He was coming at them again, his knife poised high.

She screamed out the warning just in time. Eric ducked as Jacobs rose from the water. Eric turned around in the bottom of the canoe, Jacobs rose from the water. Eric turned around in the bottom of the canoe, ready to fling himself at the assailant.

But it wasn't necessary.

Another shot rang out in the darkness. Jacobs, stretching high with his lethal knife glinting evilly in the moonlight, suddenly opened his eyes and mouth wide. He looked down at the huge hole burning in his chest.

Then he pitched forward into the water.

Stunned, Eric, Brad and Ashley turned around.

Willie Hawk was balanced carefully on his knee in the canoe that now came toward them. He carried a shotgun, and the muzzle was still smoking. Wendy was behind him, rowing.

Willie nodded to them, then looked impassively down into the water. "Never kill in anger; it's bad for the heart. You can take a life only to save a life. And that's good for the heart. Come on, now. It's time to get back. Eric, you're going to need a hospital. Marna is at Wendy's—and Brad's house. The police will come soon enough."

He turned around and smiled at Wendy. "Let's go home."

They returned to the village with Jacobs's body.

Wendy insisted Eric had three broken ribs, maybe more, and made him lie down in the hut. She gave Ashley instructions on binding his chest. Eric protested, of course; he was a lousy patient. And there wasn't a moment for him and Ashley to have even a single moment alone together. Brad explained everything that had happened with Harrison Mosby, and she was sorry to hear that greed had brought about the downfall of so many. Then she was furious to hear that she would have been murdered herself.

She was also grateful to Eric. He had saved her from the jaws of death not once, but twice.

Eric didn't see it that way at all. Wincing as he lay on a mat on the floor of his grandfather's chickee, he caught her hand. "I'm so sorry. What a fool I was. I thought you were safer out here, when I was actually putting you in danger."

"You did save me, you idiot," she assured him. Her lips were suddenly chattering. She hadn't dried completely, but she didn't really care. "They would have killed me before the storm—if I hadn't found you."

He smiled and closed his eyes, and she was worried. She looked at Wendy and at Mary, who was surveying her grandson with grave concern. "Concussion, I think. That was one hell of a fight," Wendy murmured. "We can't let him sleep—" she began, but then they heard the arrival of the helicopter.

Eric was lifted in a stretcher, followed by Jacobs's body.

"Go with him," Wendy told Ashley.

She hesitated.

"There's room." Wendy sighed. "All right, I'll come, too. We'll both go, and Brad can come in the morning with clothes. Let's go."

Ashley wasn't sure if riding in the helicopter wasn't almost as bad as being in the black water with the snake. She closed her eyes, feeling the breeze, and she knew it didn't matter. That night she wanted to be near him.

It was almost dawn by the time Eric was admitted into the hospital. Wendy and Ashley took a cab to a nearby hotel, where they stayed the night.

Ashley barely knew that she had slept until she awoke to find herself still wearing muddy clothes.

"It's all right," Wendy said, laughing at Ashley's expression. "Brad came—the roads are fine—and he's left us stuff to wear. He's over at the hospital now."

"That's wonderful," Ashley said. She showered, and when she came out, Wendy was just finishing her makeup. "I'm ready whenever you are," she announced.

Ashley hesitated. "I'm not going with you, Wendy."

"What?"

Ashley hesitated again. "I don't know if you can understand this or not, but I need to go shopping. I'm—I'm going to fly back to New York tonight."

"But why—" Wendy began, then stopped speaking. She shook her head. "Never mind. It's none of my business. It's between you and Eric."

Ashley shook her head, too. Then impulsively, she kissed Wendy on the cheek and gave her a warm hug, which Wendy returned. "I'm in love with Eric, Wendy. I told him so. And there's nothing on earth that I wouldn't do for him. But he has to want me first. For what I am, not what he thinks I am. I'm going to see him before I leave. I'm just going shopping first."

"You have to do what you think is right," Wendy assured her.

Ashley called a cab and went down to the Bal Harbour shops where she looked for something that was ridiculously expensive. She took her time and bought a smart red suit with a tight skirt and a jacket that flared at the waist. She also bought a floppy, wide-brimmed hat, black heels, a black handbag and black gloves. She had her hair done in a chignon.

Then she took a taxi to the hospital.

Brad and Wendy were in Eric's room. One of Eric's eyes was horribly black. He was shirtless, his ribs were taped and a needle was stuck in his arm so fluid could drip into him from an intravenous tube.

Despite all that, her heart beat furiously and she could barely breathe. He was still the most striking, magnetic man she had ever seen. The dark slash of his hair against the sheets and the bronze color of his body all added up to the man she loved.

He had been talking animatedly, but when he saw Ashley, he stopped.

So did Brad and Wendy. They stared at her openmouthed. Ashley smiled sweetly, drawing off her gloves as she came in, a large box of chocolates in her hand.

"Ashley!" Brad gasped at last.

Wendy laughed then and tapped his jaw. "Shut your mouth, my love, before you drool. And come on, let's leave them alone together for a minute."

Ashley cast her a grateful glance. Brad winked, and he and his wife left. Ashley took the chair that Wendy had vacated. Eric just kept staring at her.

"You look great," he finally told her.

"Thank you." She crossed her legs elegantly. "It was nice to have a hot shower. But I shouldn't have said that, right? That means I'm not suited for the swamp."

Eric breathed slowly. "You're not suited for the swamp, Ashley. I'll never forget—"

"Forget what?"

"Your face when the snake was moving around you."

"Oh, I see. If I was suited for the swamp, I would jump up and down and say, 'Oh boy! A cottonmouth. What fun!'"

He flushed, then glared at her. His hand shot out and his fingers closed around her wrist with startling strength. She looked at his hands and remembered the way they felt on her and how they looked against her flesh. She swallowed. She had to go. She had known it for some time.

"They're going to release me tomorrow morning," he said somewhat irritably. "Talking about this will be a heck of a lot easier once I'm up and about."

"No, it won't. Because I'm leaving this afternoon."

"You're what?"

She snatched her hand away quickly. If he decided to hold on to her, there wouldn't be a prayer in the world for her to escape his strength.

She stood and looked down at him. "I've told you how I feel. And I made a fool out of myself."

"Ashley, wait a minute. You don't understand. I knew last night that Jacobs was out. I had no idea where he was, but Mica had told me that he had escaped. I couldn't begin to think of a future when—"

"No, you couldn't think of a future, but you could make love. Well, I want more than that. My cards are on the table, and they have been there, faceup, everything naked for you to see. You have to bury Elizabeth, Eric, once and for all. And you have to do more than that—you have to want me. If you do, you come talk to me. You know where I live."

With that, she turned around to leave.

"Ashley!"

She heard him jump out of the bed and swear because of the needle in his arm.

She stepped outside. Brad was there, smiling. "I'll handle Tonto for the moment," he said. Then he kissed her warmly on the cheek and went back into the room.

Wendy didn't say anything at all. She just gave Ashley a big hug.

Ashley started down the hall and ran into Willie Hawk. He was very handsome and dignified in a business suit and a cap with an egret feather.

"Goodbye, Willie. Thank you for everything," Ashley told him.

"You're leaving?" he asked.

She nodded, then said, "I have to."

He nodded, too. She didn't know why she kept speaking, but she did. "I'm in love with him. He doesn't love me. Not enough."

Willie smiled and patted her arm. "Do you know there are many roads? They wind around and around. And maybe there are many roads that lead home. It doesn't matter which one you take, just as long as you get there. Goodbye, Ashley. We'll miss you."

He kissed her cheek and hurried toward his grandson's room.

She left the hospital. And though tears clouded her eyes, she didn't look back.

There were many roads...

And many of them lead home.

She could only hope and pray that she had set upon a course that would bring her home.

CHAPTER 12

Four weeks later Ashley stood at her window and looked down at the human traffic in front of Rockefeller Plaza. She arched her back, trying to do away with the little cricks and pains caused by her hunching over her desk.

When she had first returned, she had wondered how she would ever settle down to work. She had believed that Eric would come. She had wanted to believe so desperately that he loved her enough to come for her. But days had passed, and then weeks, and still there was no sign of Eric Hawk. She began to give up hope.

Then she discovered that all that she cared about was her work. So she sat for hours and hours over sketches, and she drove the staff crazy demanding more and more fabric samples.

She was even driving Tara crazy by calling all the time before making decisions. Because of the baby, Tara wanted nothing to do with work.

"Fly back to Florida," she told Ashley irritably.

"No!"

"Then come over for dinner. Rafe's having a few old friends over to see the baby and—"

"No, I don't want to come to dinner. Thanks anyway." She hung up quickly. She didn't want Tara to do any matchmaking for her. She just wanted to be alone—with her work.

But it seemed that she had been working just too much. She looked out into the hallway and called her secretary. "Jennifer! Make me lunch reservations at the Plaza, will you, please?"

"Are you going alone?"

"Yes. And don't tell anyone where I am, please."

"Whatever you say, Ashley," Jennifer promised.

It wasn't lunchtime, but Ashley left the office anyway. She took a cab partway, then had the cabbie let her out. The air was just a little bit cool, and the leaves were beginning to turn. She loved the park in the fall.

As they did every so often in a most annoying way, tears burned against her eyelids. They had no fall in the swamps! she told herself. And it would be awful for Christmas. There was probably very little ice skating down there.

But her assurances rang hollow in her ears. She had made the mistake of falling in love with the right man. And autumn didn't matter at all, neither did the beautiful color of the leaves. Where she lived didn't matter at all. Who she lived with mattered tremendously.

At last she left the park behind and started across the street for the Plaza. She checked her coat and the maître d' gave her a secluded table in the corner. She ordered a glass of white wine, sipped it and leaned back in her chair. She closed her eyes.

Seconds later, she heard a stir around her, and curious, opened her eyes. People were looking around, staring and trying not to look as if they were staring, the way they did when a celebrity was present.

Ashley wondered who it might be. Several big stars were in town, appearing on Broadway or filming movies.

She caught a glimpse of a man's back. He was tall, broad shouldered and dressed in a very handsome tailored black suit. His hair was very dark and very straight, just over his collar.

He was the man who had turned all the heads, she realized. And he was seated right by her. Only an oak pillar separated them.

She sipped her wine again, forgetting the attention-grabbing stranger. She shouldn't have come, she decided. It wasn't restful at all.

She ordered lamb and began to sketch on her napkin. Suddenly she realized that the waiter was hovering by her table.

"Yes?"

"*Madame*." With a flourish he set a package wrapped in white tissue paper before her.

"What—" Ashley began.

"A present," he said with a broad grin, turning away.

"But who—" The waiter had already disappeared between the tables. Someone had tipped him well, she thought with annoyance.

Then her curiosity got the best of her and she started to open the package. The tissue fell apart, and the contents—a little ball of material—fell on her lap.

Amazed, she stared at the material, then picked it up.

Her breathing stopped. It was the tiger-striped bikini bottom she had been wearing when she ran into Eric Hawk in the swamp. She gasped.

Then she looked up.

Eric was standing in front of her.

He was the man in the black suit, she realized, and he wore it well. His shirt was white and startlingly attractive against the hue of his skin. His hair still fell, over his forehead.

But he was elegant, too—sleek, handsome, virile. He smiled slowly, his green eyes flashing, his full lips curving, as he reached for the chair opposite from her. "May I?"

She nodded. He sat.

"I thought maybe I should return those," he said, indicating the bikini.

She swallowed. Her teeth were chattering and her fingers froze. "It's, uh, very, very rude to surprise people in restaurants," she told him.

"Oh. Sorry. Well, I may need help in New York, you know." He lowered his head. "I'll try real hard to be civil."

She nodded. "Good."

He reached across the table and took her hand. "Forgive me?"

"What?"

"I couldn't believe that you could love me. And now, well, I'm still as scared as a high-school kid, but I just can't stand being without you. I had to come and tell you that. I love you, Ashley. Did you mean what you said, that you loved me?"

She nodded again, still not believing that he could be there.

His fingers moved over hers. "I'm not easy to live with, you know that already. I've a bad temper. But then, yours is horrible, so we're about even there. I had thought that maybe you could keep up your work. The mail service is incredible these days. I wouldn't want to take away anything that is you, and I think that you like to design. Do you?"

She nodded once more.

He reached into his pocket and produced a little jewel case. He popped it open. A beautiful diamond was inside. It was huge; it was a wonderful cut, and even if it had been just glass, it still would have brought tears to her eyes.

"Tara gave me the size," he told her.

"Tara!" she gasped.

He nodded, and a teasing light touched his eyes. "I'm pretty good at picking up a trail, but in a city of eight million people, I thought I should get a hold of her to find out where you might be. I tried to get you at work. You weren't there, but thankfully, Tara was—showing off the baby—and she assured me that this was a very good place to look for you. I'm glad that she knows your habits well." He cleared his throat. "Will you marry me, Ashley? I was trying to find a few good points to sell myself, and all I could remember was that I was pretty hard on you. Let's see. I don't snore. I take out the garbage. I'm a fair to middling cook. I like to make love. I'm fairly handy with the plumbing—and I love you.

I love you with all of my heart, and I believe in you. Ashley, say something, please."

She did. She shrieked so that every head turned, and she jumped up, knocking over everything on the table, and she kissed him.

He kissed her back, then he turned to the startled old couple beside him.

"She's just a little savage at times!" he said, shaking his head. He tossed some money on the table and lifted her into his arms. With the whole restaurant staring at them, he carried her out to the street.

"My coat!" she told him.

"I'll go back for it," he promised, his eyes locked on hers.

"I love you. I'll live with you anywhere," she told him. She touched his hair with her fingertips.

"I love you, too."

"People are watching us."

"So they are."

"Where are you taking me?"

"To your apartment. It's been a long four weeks!"

Seconds later she was deposited into a horse-drawn carriage, and Eric was giving the driver her address.

"Tara?" she asked.

"Tara," he agreed, holding her hand. "Now, I've figured it out. We can always spend a season here—"

"Fall," she said.

"Fall, it's my favorite. Oh! Until we have children. Then we'll have to settle down because of school. Fall until we have children, then the summer."

"Fine."

"And Christmas! Maybe we'll come for Christmas."

"Maybe. Now and then."

The carriage stopped in front of her building. Eric paid the driver, and holding hands, he and Ashley hurried past the doorman, who received a beautiful smile from her. Then they were in the ornate elevator heading up to the fifteenth floor. "Nice," Eric commented.

Ashley laughed. "You hate it."

"I love it. For fall."

The door opened. She hurried along the hallway to unlock her apartment, and he followed. She was suddenly nervous. She wanted him to like her place. It was furnished with antiques, the window opened to a view of Manhattan, and the tile and carpet were soft beige.

"Well, what do you think?"

But he wasn't looking at the apartment at all, he was looking at her. He walked across the room and swept her into his arms again. "It's beautiful. Where's the bedroom?"

She whispered the answer into his ear and he carried her to her bed with its comforter and satin sheets. "We can be married down in Florida. Tara and Rafe and the others can come."

"Umm," he murmured. He tugged off her shoes while she stared at the ceiling, floating on clouds. She felt his hands on her shirt.

"Oh, we have to be here for Amy's baptism next week. I'm a godparent."

"That's wonderful," Eric murmured. Her clothes seemed to be melting away from her, and he was up again, tossing pieces of his elegant suit all over the place.

"And I'm keeping my emerald ring. I'll be very happy to live with you in the swamp, but I am keeping my one Tyler emerald."

"Good for you! I'll try very hard not to be jealous of your one Tyler jewel," Eric assured her, and laughed. He stretched out on top of her, and his eyes filled with fire and mischief as he moved his hands along the length of her. Her breath caught and he frowned suddenly, looking down at her. "Is there something else you need?" he asked.

She loved the tone of his voice. He did love her, and he believed in her. He didn't question any longer that their worlds could be combined.

She offered him a dazzling smile and threw her arms around him. "There's nothing...nothing," she said softly, sensually, "that I need. Nothing but the primitive earth—and you."

He cast back his head and they laughed. Then he kissed her until they could laugh no more.

EPILOGUE

Three months later they were married. The wedding took place at sunset, and it was as if nature had made everything spectacular for the occasion.

Ashley told Eric that she didn't mind having the ceremony in the south if he didn't mind having a wedding with all the frills. He told her to go right ahead and plan it, and she did.

It was a big wedding. Ashley had two sisters-in-law and three very close friends, including Wendy, for bridesmaids; Tara, of course, was her maid of honor. Brad was Eric's best man, and by the time the wedding day arrived, Rafe had become a good friend, and so he was an usher. Tony Panther, an old army buddy and two friends from the council rounded out Eric's lineup. The wedding-guest list was huge, and as the time for the ceremony drew near, Eric realized that he hadn't even begun to meet Ashley's relatives. They had been arriving all day, up to the last minute.

He saw Ashley running into the church's nave. She laughed, seeing him, and he would have laughed in return, but she was so breathtaking a bride that his breath caught and he reached for her hands. "This is it," he whispered. She had chosen a soft cream color for her long gown. It was traditional in cut, almost a Renaissance style, and had a fabulous pearled train. She wore a tiara with a sweeping veil, and beneath it, her eyes were stunning. He was suddenly very humble, thinking that God had granted him this angel, not to be borrowed, but to be cherished forever.

"This is it," she repeated. "You're sure, right?"

"More sure than I have ever been in my whole life about anything." He forgot her dress and her veil and his own tuxedo and he drew her against him, kissing her deeply.

Someone cleared a throat loudly. "Ashley!" It was Tara. "He's not supposed to see you in the gown and Father O'Neill's saying that we must come into the chorus room and get ready!"

They separated, though their gazes remained on each other. They both smiled with tremendous happiness.

"For heaven's sake, Eric! You'll be married soon, and you can stare at each other all night!" She grabbed Ashley's hand and pulled her away. Eric, still smiling, turned around to walk outside for one more moment before taking his place by the altar.

He was startled to see a very pretty girl of about thirteen come racing up to the church. She paused, just as startled to see him.

Her hair was ebony and fell down her back in blue-black swirls. Her complexion was deeply tanned, her eyes a soft hazel. She was an Indian, and yet he didn't think that she was a Seminole or a Miccosukee. He was almost positive that she wasn't related to him. He didn't think that he had any long lost relatives.

"Hi! You're—you're him, right? Eric? Oh, thank goodness, if you're here, then I'm not late. I had to wait for the sitter for the baby. Mom said that he was just too young for the ceremony. It was tricky finding the right person to come to the hotel room. I'm talking too much, right? I'm sorry, I'm nervous!"

She paused, gasping for breath and just staring at Eric with a beautiful smile on her face.

He smiled himself. "You're not late," he told her. "And, yes, I'm Eric." He hesitated just a second. "Who are you?"

"Leah. Leah Dane. I'm Ashley's niece." She stuck out her hand, flushing again. "And you're almost my Uncle Eric. If that's all right, of course."

After a moment, he started laughing. Leah just stared at him, and he tried to sober quickly. "Leah Dane, I'm delighted to make your acquaintance. And I'll be quite delighted to be your uncle."

"Thanks," she said. "But what's so funny?"

"Your aunt," he assured her. He set his hand on her shoulders and turned her toward the church. "I think I should be getting down to the altar. There's Brad motioning to me. You'll meet him soon enough. By the way, what is your tribe?"

"Nez Percé," Leah said. She glanced at him slyly. "Aunt Ashley never told you, huh?"

"She never told me," he said solemnly. He smiled and pushed her ahead. "We'd better get on. We'll get a chance to talk more later. And maybe you can help me get one back on Aunt Ashley, huh?"

She flashed him a dazzling smile and walked into the church.

Brad called softly to Eric, and minutes later, Eric was standing by the altar. An organ, a harp and two guitars were playing, and the last of the attendants had walked down the aisles. Ashley came toward him at last. He saw the emerald fire in her eyes beneath the veil, and he saw her smile. Though night was falling, he felt as if the sun's radiant beams were shining down on him. He smiled, remembering Leah.

We are going to have beautiful, beautiful children, he thought. Then he took Ashley's hand in his hand, and turned around to face the priest. He vowed his love, and all of his life, to her.

* * * * *

New York Times Bestselling Author

LINDA HOWARD

Tears of the Renegade

Susan Blackstone married into a powerful Mississippi family; she
loved and then lost the Blackstones' favorite son. Even after her
husband's death, Susan held her own, running a business empire
and winning the support of her in-laws. But those bonds are tested
when black sheep Cord Blackstone returns for a long-overdue
showdown against the family who robbed him of his birthright.
Now, Susan must choose between her husband's memory and Cord,
a reckless interloper wreaking havoc with the town, the family and
her very soul.

"You can't just read one Linda Howard!"
—Catherine Coulter

Available January 2001 wherever paperbacks are sold!

A glorious tapestry of love and war,
where the fiercest battleground lies within the heart...

G O L D E N
PARADISE

A brilliant scholar, Lisaveta Lazaroff is both beautiful and
outspoken, an independent woman who refuses to play by
the rules that govern men and society. A bold attempt to ride
through the Turkish desert alone nearly ends her life, until she
is rescued by Prince Stefan Bariatinsky, a man whose passions
are as intense as the battles he wages. His only weakness lies
in a woman who challenges him for the one thing
he has never lost—his proud heart.

SUSAN JOHNSON

Available January 2001 wherever paperbacks are sold!

International Bestselling Author

DIANA PALMER

At eighteen, Amanda Carson left
west Texas, family scandal and a man
she was determined to forget. But the Whitehall
empire was vast, and when the powerful family wanted
something, they got it. Now they wanted Amanda—and her
advertising agency. Jace Whitehall, a man Amanda hated and
desired equally, was waiting to finish what began years ago.
Now they must confront searing truths about both their
families. And the very thing that drove Amanda from this
land might be the only thing able to keep her there.

THE Cowboy AND THE Lady

"Nobody tops Diana Palmer."
—Jayne Ann Krentz

Available February 2001 wherever paperbacks are sold!

Merline Lovelace

The Horse Soldier

A story of passion, adventure and new beginnings in a wild land

She came looking for her husband...

Determined to locate her missing husband, Julia Bonneaux makes a dangerous journey to the Wyoming Territory. But at Fort Laramie she comes face-to-face with Major Andrew Garrett: the dashing rogue she had secretly married seven years before...and the man she thought was dead all these years.

And found the man she loved.

Time has eased the pain of Andrew's months in a Confederate prison—but not the memory of Julia. When she asks for his help, Andrew is torn between duty and desire. With his career—and his heart—in jeopardy, he must choose between the misunderstandings of the past and the promise of a new beginning.

Merline Lovelace "writes with humor and passion..."
—*Publishers Weekly*

On sale January 2001 wherever paperbacks are sold!

CARLA
NEGGERS

Fun and a little hard work was all Tess Haviland had in mind when she purchased the run-down, nineteenth-century carriage house on Boston's North Shore. She never anticipated getting involved with the local residents, and never imagined what it would be like to own a house rumored to be haunted.

Then Tess discovers a skeleton in the dirt cellar—human remains that suddenly go missing. And she begins to ask questions about the history of her house…and the wealthy, charismatic man who planned to renovate it, until he disappeared a year before. Questions a desperate killer will do anything to silence before the truth exposes that someone got away with murder.

THE CARRIAGE HOUSE

"When it comes to romance, adventure and suspense, nobody delivers like Carla Neggers."
—Jayne Ann Krentz

On sale Febraury 2001
wherever paperbacks are sold!

MIRA®

MCN790_TR